TOO CLEVER BY HALF
An Inspector Alvarez novel

Art expert Justin Burnett was found with a revolver by his side and a note in a nearby typewriter. It seemed a clear case of suicide, and Inspector Alvarez accepted it as such. But then Phillipa Burnett claimed that although the gun was her brother's and he had been suffering from serious ill health, he was no fighter and would never have killed himself. His death had to be murder. Reluctantly, Alvarez began to investigate the life of a man who had become almost a recluse, and sure enough some curious inconsistencies emerged. When a second death, seemingly accidental, also revealed some irreconcilable facts, Alvarez was in no doubt that he was dealing with a murderer.

TOO CLEVER BY HALF

An Inspector Alvarez novel

Roderic Jeffries

A Lythway Book

CHIVERS PRESS
BATH

First published in Great Britain 1990
by
William Collins Sons & Co. Ltd
This Large Print edition published by
Chivers Press
by arrangement with
HarperCollins Publishers Ltd
and in the USA with
St Martin's Press Incorporated
1991

ISBN 0 7451 1418 0

British Library Cataloguing in Publication Data available

CHAPTER ONE

The sharp sunlight was reflected off the surface of the swimming pool to dance in waves across the ceiling; the sitting-room was oppressively hot and stuffy. Yeo-Eaton looked at the blank television screen and thought about the latest video he had been lent, in which, apparently, there were a couple of ripe scenes. He wondered if he'd be allowed to see them or whether Bronwen would fast-forward.

'I think not the Varleys,' she said.

He turned and briefly looked at her as she sat at the small, beautifully proportioned roll-top desk. Bronwen meant white-breasted, so it was ironic that she should have been christened thus since she regarded such specific anatomical references as disgusting.

'Well?' she said impatiently. 'Don't you agree?'

He jerked his thoughts back to immediate matters. 'Agree, dear?'

'It would help if you'd pay some attention when I speak to you.'

'Of course, dear. Sorry.' He needed a drink, but she believed very firmly that a gentleman did not drink before six-thirty in the evening. Alcohol and sex, she was fond of saying, were the Devil's advocates. He wondered why it was

1

that the Devil enjoyed all the good things in life.

'You agree that we do not invite the Varleys?'

'But I thought you got on with them quite well?'

She had thin lips and when she pursed them, they tended to disappear; her refined voice sharpened from exasperation. 'You know as well as I do that there are people to whom one is pleasant yet whom one doesn't wish to entertain in one's home.'

'He plays a good round of golf.'

'That ceased to be the mark of a gentleman the day they allowed professionals into the club house.'

'But the Varleys do a tremendous amount for the community. They even helped pay most of the fare back to the UK for that couple who hadn't enough money.'

'She sometimes drops her aitches.'

He visualized Hilda Varley. Generously built in all the right places, curly blonde hair topping a round face, and moist lips which promised what her brown eyes suggested. He doubted that she developed many headaches when it was time to go to bed . . .

From the hall came the sound of high-heeled shoes on the tiled floor and Victoria appeared in the doorway. 'I finish,' she said in her fractured English. 'I go.'

Bronwen inclined her head. He said: 'Good-

2

bye, see you tomorrow.'

'Adios, señor.' Victoria flashed him a smile.

He watched her disappear out of sight. She was at the stage, reached early by most Mallorquin women, when beauty had matured to the point where it was teetering towards overripeness. When Bronwen was not present to censor his thoughts, he sometimes fantasized and endowed her with a sharp passion for a retired colonel who had been a dashing subaltern before he'd married his colonel's daughter . . .

'Not the Varleys.' She crossed out the name on the list. She had inherited the desk from a great-aunt who had been Vicereine of India. He had once translated such rank as vice queen. She had expressed sharp displeasure at such stupidity. She used a lace-edged handkerchief to wipe the glow from her forehead (horses sweated, men perspired, ladies merely glowed). 'When on earth is the engineer coming to mend the air-conditioning? Didn't you tell him it was urgent?'

'I said we were nearly expiring from the heat. He promised to come as soon as possible, but apparently he's a tremendous amount of work in hand.'

'A mere excuse. I should have spoken to him.'

He didn't resent the inference, accepting that it was true. She spoke no Spanish, let alone

Mallorquin, yet she possessed the ability to get things done even on the island. A natural sergeant-major of an officer.

She returned her attention to the guest list. 'I suppose we do have to ask Phillipa, even though she never returns hospitality.'

'That's because she can't afford to.'

'Then she should not accept it.'

He knew that it was not Phillipa's poverty to which Bronwen objected, but the fact that she was a woman of marked character, ever ready to speak her mind. She was one of the few people whom Bronwen did not treat with condescension.

'So, with Gerald, that makes thirty-two people.'

He said, surprised: 'D'you mean Gerald Heal?'

'I wasn't aware that we knew any other Geralds.'

'No, we don't. But I thought . . . I rather imagined . . .'

'Do try not to bumble.'

'Yes, dear.'

She closed up the desk and automatically looked around the large, oblong room to make certain that everything was exactly in its place. Clean and tidy in person, clean and tidy in mind. Satisfied, she walked across to the settee and sat. 'Why are you surprised that I'm asking Gerald?'

4

'Well, it's not all that long ago that you called him distinctly NOCD.'

'He is of the vulgus, obviously, but one can hardly blame him for his unfortunate background.'

'But earlier you said that you wouldn't ask the Varleys because—'

'Godfrey, why do you always have to argue about everything?'

He knew that if he wished to avoid her sharp, bitchy displeasure for the rest of the evening, he should not pursue the matter, but a sudden sense of recklessness made him say: 'You won't ask the Varleys because they're brash, never mind how much good they do among the community, so surely even less should you be ready to ask Gerald, who can be a lot brasher and almost certainly has never done any good to anyone but himself.'

'You don't see the difference?'

'No, I'm afraid I don't.'

'Then it's hopeless trying to explain. There are times when it's quite impossible to talk sense with you.'

As he stared through a window at the pool, the lawn, the lantana hedge, and the mountains, he remembered a brief conversation he'd once heard between two of his subalterns. 'Have you asked him?'—'Not yet.'—'Why the hell not?'—'Because every time I've seen him, Charlotte Corday's been there.' He savoured the

5

memory, even though there'd been no certainty that he and Bronwen had been the two concerned.

'By the way,' she said, 'Ruth rang while you were down in the village collecting the paper.'

'How is she?'

'All right,' she answered.

Even after so many years, he could still be saddened by Bronwen's lack of maternal affection. Just as he could still be amazed by their daughter: first since her presence on earth had called for certain acts of a physical nature; secondly because she had so warm and caring a nature. Ironically, she'd undoubtedly have led a far happier life if her character had been slightly less warm and loving and far more like her mother's. She concerned herself too much with the inadequacies and misfortunes of others and as a result was usually suffering from badly bruised emotions. She had been married once and had later lived with a man—Bronwen had never learned about this—and both relationships had ended disastrously.

Bronwen said: 'I've told her to come a week earlier than she was planning.'

'Then that means she'll be out in just under a fortnight's time.' His pleasure was immediate.

'She wanted to bring some friend, but I said it would be much the best if she came on her own. One never knows how extraordinary her friends will turn out to be.' She paused, then continued: 'I'm quite breathless down here so I'm going up to our bedroom for a while. You did remember to switch on the air-conditioning earlier?'

'Yes, dear.'

As she stood, so did he. His manners were as old-fashioned as his sense of duty. He believed that a man should honour his wife until death relieved him of that burden.

As soon as he heard her climbing the stairs, he crossed to the tall, heavily inlaid cocktail cabinet and poured himself out a very strong whisky, then went through to the kitchen and picked out three ice cubes from the dispenser in the refrigerator. Back in the sitting-room, he sprawled out in a chair and drank, his pleasure all the sweeter because it was not yet quite six o'clock.

He thought how odd it was that Bronwen should have suggested Ruth came out to the island a week earlier, since normally she liked arrangements to be strictly adhered to. Another odd suggestion of hers had been to invite Gerald Heal to their forthcoming cocktail party and Gerald was being invited because, so local rumour had it, he was divorcing his wife. What a ridiculously impossible idea! Gerald Heal wouldn't look twice at a plain, often awkward woman; and in any case, Ruth would have no truck with him because wealth never blinded

7

her to a man's failings; only his inadequacies did that.

CHAPTER TWO

'Can't I move?' asked Alma.

'No,' Guy Selby replied.

'But I'm getting pins and needles and I'm sweating like a pig and dying of thirst.'

'Do pigs sweat?'

'I don't know, I don't care, and I'm damned well going to move.' She unfolded her right leg and rubbed the inside of her thigh. 'God, you need a contortionist.'

'Find one who'll keep still for more than two seconds at a time and I'll be happy. Provided she's a body like yours.'

'Your only interest is in my body?'

'Of course.'

'You're a swine.'

'Why not? You're sweating like a pig.'

She stood and stretched. 'I'm not only dying of thirst, I'm starving. Where shall we go for lunch?'

He pointed his brush at her. 'Are you reckoning to eat like that?' She was naked.

'Why not?'

'Mallorquins are conservative. They've only just got used to skinny sunbathing and skinny eating would really throw them.'

'Check with the waiters; you'd find them willing enough to be thrown ... How's the painting coming along?'

'Lousy.'

She threaded her way between the furniture and piles of books, magazines and general mess on the floor until she could study the canvas on the easel. After a while she said: 'I can never make out whether you denigrate your own work because you're over-modest or are fishing for compliments.'

'Think the worse.'

'You say you're not very good at the human figure and need to practise and practise, yet this is really great.'

'Before you let your enthusiasm overwhelm your critical faculties, you do realize that it's not finished yet, don't you?'

'Of course I do, you idiot ... You seem to have endowed me with some quality I can't identify. What is it?' She studied his face—rugged, expressing determination and some bloody-mindedness—and knew before he spoke that he was going to answer facetiously.

'Heat, hunger, thirst, and cramp.' He cleaned one brush in a pot, dried it on a square of linen. Six feet one tall and broad-shouldered, his chest bronzed by the sun, there was little of the stereotyped artist in his appearance.

'Be serious,' she begged.

'You're wondering if you remembered to take

the Pill and are beginning to panic.'

'You're bloody impossible! Why can't you sometimes admit to being sentimental and not always trying to hide your emotions behind cheap cynicism?'

He cleaned a second brush, then the palette—he was obsessively tidy in his painting, carelessly untidy in the rest of his life. 'Haven't you yet learned the most important fact in life? Whenever you get starry-eyed, you tread on a banana skin.'

'Life can't always have been that tough for you.'

'The consumer society is only fun for people with plenty of money to spend.'

'You can't tell me you'd really like to be a yuppie, for God's sake.'

'Wouldn't I? In my Porsche, driving back to my Docklands pad, my only worry which restaurant to take which girlfriend to? Wouldn't I sell my artistic soul for material wealth after I've spent a humiliating hour trying to interest a gallery owner and he's been yawning away because for him I'm just another slob who's stupid enough to think his daubs are the new van Goghs?'

She said earnestly: 'You must know that with your talent you have to be successful.'

'Cue for the heavenly choir.'

'Go to hell!'

'My lovely dryad, do you really believe that

10

ability always triumphs over indifference and ignorance?'

'Yes.'

'Then I salute you as the last remaining innocent on earth.'

'Can't you ever be optimistic about the future?'

'Right now, I'm very optimistic about the immediate future.'

'You've stopped thinking about painting. I'd better go and dress.'

'Scared? Are you so nervous because you're a virgin?'

'Gallup poll your own sex life, not mine.'

'But yours is so much more interesting.'

'Not for me, I'm hungry. So let's get ready and go out to eat.'

His tone changed. 'I'd rather eat here.' He began to pack tubes of paint into a metal box.

'On what? The fridge is about as bare as Old Mother Hubbard's cupboard.'

'So I'll nip out and buy a barra and some cheese.'

'We are going to Ca'n Toni for lunch.'

'I'd rather—'

'With gentlemanly grace—and I'll explain the term—you're going to agree to do what I want to do, for once.'

★ ★ ★

11

The triangular-shaped area to the south of the island was known as La Cuña and it was unusual in two respects—although its longest side was coastline, very few tourists visited it and there was not a single tourist hotel, bar, or restaurant. This absence of tourism was partially because the land was virtually featureless (being so poor it was covered in scrub), but far more importantly because there were no beaches, only cliffs, up to a hundred and fifty metres high, which plunged into the sea.

Of the two villages within La Cuña, Costanyi was the larger. Inevitably, there had been changes there within the past fifty years, since the ripples of prosperity reached everywhere, but compared to other parts of the island, here time had stood still. Ca'n Toni had no sign to mark it as a restaurant, the windows were small and allowed very little light inside, the wooden tables looked as if they must be almost as old as the building, even in summer much of the cooking was done on an open fire in one corner of the room, and the verbal menu offered few dishes.

The waiter—he had only one eye and two fingers on his left hand due to an accident in a quarry—told them the menu and then waited, his expression suggesting a total disinterest.

'I'm going to have shoulder of lamb,' Alma said. 'The same for you?'

12

Selby shook his head. 'I'll have frito Mallorquin.'

'But you've always said that you reckon the shoulder of lamb here is absolutely delicious.'

'I'm not hungry.'

'What you really mean is, you're too proud to eat what you'd like.'

'Goddamnit—'

'I know. I've been told before that I can't be taken anywhere because I never know when to keep my big mouth shut ... Guy, this is meant to be a treat for the two of us. Don't spoil it, please.'

He scowled, muttered something un-intelligible, then in easy, if ungrammatical Spanish, asked the waiter for two shoulders of lamb and vino corriente. The waiter, who never spoke unless obliged to do so, nodded, left.

She reached across the table and put her hand on Selby's. 'When one of your paintings becomes the star attraction at a Christie's sale, you can treat me to a meal at the Four Seasons.'

'Don't start working up an appetite for the next ninety-five years.'

'I expect to gorge myself at your expense before I'm twenty-five.' In all other respects self-confident to the point of cockiness, when it came to his work he suffered a seemingly endless succession of doubts and she presumed that these were responsible for his many black moods. 'You are going to become very, very

13

famous. People will fall over themselves to buy your paintings.'

'And break their necks before they sign the cheques.'

The waiter returned to place on the table two glass tumblers, an earthenware jug of wine, a small plate full of olives and a larger one on which were slices of pan Mallorquin.

Selby filled the glasses, passed one across. He made an effort to lighten his mood. 'All right, let's drink to the day the hammer drops on the first million-pound Selby.'

The wine, locally made, was harsh and earthy; the olives, locally grown and cured, were bitter. She had learned to enjoy both and as she dropped an olive stone into the wooden ashtray in the centre of the table, she said: 'Gerry was in a good mood at breakfast, so I talked about you.'

'That must have put him off his imported muesli.' Try as he did, he could not mask his sudden sense of resentment. 'Why the hell d'you do that?'

'To try to help you.'

'When I want helping, I'll ask.'

'Bad-temperedly ... He's in a position to do something for you, so why not find out if he will?'

'Kowtow to the mighty dollar, yen, or whatever currency he's in at the moment.'

She laughed.

'What's so funny?'

'The thought of you kowtowing.'

Reluctantly, he smiled. 'I ought to be good at it. I've spent enough time banging my head against brick walls.'

'You've actually laughed at yourself! Have another glass of wine and who knows what will happen.'

'I'll leave on all fours.'

'Kowtowing all the way ... I showed Gerry that painting you gave me. He says you're talented.'

'Then there's no further argument. Move over, Leonardo.'

'Sarcasm is not only the lowest form of wit, it also identifies a limited mind. Just because Gerry is stinking rich, it doesn't mean he's an artistic moron. In fact...'

'Well?'

She was silent for a while longer, then she said: 'He's a strange man—almost seems to be two people sometimes. He wants people's envy and often spends money merely to prove his wealth, yet there are times when he does something that only a person of real taste could do.'

'You mean he decides not to gild the cold water bath taps as well as the hot?'

'He recognizes beauty where others have failed to do so. Some years ago he was browsing around in an antique shop in Hastings which specialized in paintings and one of these, so dark from varnish and dirt that the subject was only just discernible, caught his attention. Nine hundred and ninety-nine people would have looked at it and decided it was worth only what the frame would fetch; he was the thousandth and he saw something which made him buy it. He had it cleaned and examined by an expert and it turned out to be by a reasonably well known Dutchman who lived part of his life in England at the time of Charles the First; some name like Myens.'

'Daniel Mytens?'

'That's right. Well, the whole point of all this is that he'd never heard of a painter by the name of Mytens and if you put a Mytens next to a van Dyck the chances are he couldn't identify which was which, but he saw in that dirty, indistinct painting something which told him that it was of a totally different quality from all the others. He couldn't begin to define how he knew, he just did. Something in him responds to quality. So when he says you're talented, you damned well are!'

'Who am I to argue any further? But so what?'

'So we are going to persuade him financially to back an exhibition of your work.'

Selby could not contain the excitement such a prospect engendered. 'You think he really might do that?'

'Provided the idea is presented attractively.'

'We tell him he'll be a noble, perhaps eventually ennobled, patron of the arts?'

She smiled briefly. 'Very much more to the point, that he'll make a profit.'

He finished the wine in his glass, refilled both their glasses to empty the jug. 'But hell, even if every painting were to sell, the profit he'd see wouldn't be any more than loose change to him.'

'It's not how much he stands to make that'll attract him, it'll be the fact that he'll make it riding on your back. If you can take advantage of someone, you've proved that you're the smarter.'

He sat back, glass in his right hand. 'You've a funny way of talking about your old man. D'you hate him?'

'D'you know, I've often wondered that.' She rested her elbows on the table, her chin on her hands, and stared into space. 'But the only answer I've ever come up with is, I just don't know. I certainly loathed him every time he chased after a fresh woman and made my mother's life such hell that in the end she left him; he's never seemed to give a damn about me or what I'm doing; and yet I come here to see him from time to time because in spite of everything I recognize a bond between us and I don't think there could be that if I really hated him.'

17

'There could if your subconscious demanded belief in such a bond because you couldn't face the truth that you do hate your own father.'

'Goddamn it!' She spoke angrily. 'You love digging the knife deep and making me uncertain of myself, don't you?'

'Maybe I'm trying to discover the real you.'

'Why?'

'To see if I'm painting the truth.'

'Has no one ever told you that sometimes a lie can be kinder than the truth?'

CHAPTER THREE

Phillipa came to a halt and used the handkerchief, tucked into the short sleeve of her dress, to mop the sweat from her forehead. It was extraordinarily hot for early May but, as she replied whenever asked about what weather to expect in Mallorca, the only certainty was uncertainty.

As she rested she stared at the view, which for her never staled. Llueso, centred around the hill on which it had first been built as a defence against the Moors, looked timeless except on the outskirts, where modern boxy blocks of flats had been built; the hermitage on Puig Antonia to the south, if no longer housing hermits because solitude and self-denial had ceased to attract, still reached up to heaven; the farmland was good, though not as rich as that around nearby Mestara, and crops were heavy; the bay, ringed by mountains, remained as beautiful as ever because from where she stood the development around it was hidden ... Development. The cancer of the island. Right then, she could hear a concrete mixer turning and a pneumatic rock-breaker at its even noisier work. Llueso council had imposed a total ban on all new building because even they had dimly realized that with each extra house or block of flats a little more of the peace and beauty was lost, but no one paid the slightest attention to their edict. She'd first come to the island so long ago that she could remember when beyond Palma the roads were dirt and hardly a foreigner was to be seen; when to reach the new Parelona Hotel, one had to travel to Parelona Bay by boat because there was only a mule track over the mountainous promontory; when the Mallorquins had been a kind, contented people whom one could trust in everything ... She shook her head. She was old. Had things really been as perfect as she now remembered them, or was she forgetting what she wished to forget? She could no longer be certain. People said that age brought compensations. She was damned if she'd discovered any.

She resumed her walk up the gently rising

road which eventually led into Festna Valley. On either side were metre-high stone walls which trapped and reflected the heat, and as the sweat rolled down her face and back she could feel her heart beat more quickly than was welcome. She should have forgone a second brandy after her meal.

She passed a house recently reformed, in front of which had been built a large swimming pool. Foreigners who rented houses in the summer now demanded pools and so dozens had recently been installed; every pool lost a lot of water through evaporation and this had to be replaced; the greatly increased consumption of water from that and other causes was lowering the water-table, with the consequence that in the height of summer the water of Llueso was turned off throughout the day, leaving the locals resentfully waterless because the tourists in the port must not go short, while in the port most of the wells were being contaminated with salt water ... Yet still the development continued.

The road became more level, making walking easier. The journey was too short to warrant her using her very old Seat 600 and normally she would not have made it until the evening had brought cooler conditions; but when she'd rung Justin, he had not answered the call and she was very worried that something had happened to him.

She came abreast of another gateway and in the field beyond, weeding between recently transplanted aubergines, was a woman dressed in a shapeless frock and a wide-brimmed straw hat. There was at least one aspect of island life which hadn't changed despite all the development, Phillipa thought; the women worked in the fields whilst the men talked in the bars. She called out: 'Antonia.'

Antonia, her face bronzed by the sun despite invariably wearing a hat, slowly straightened up. 'Good afternoon, señorita.'

'How's your leg now?' If asked, Phillipa always claimed to be a fluent Castilian and a reasonable Mallorquin speaker; in fact, her Castilian was heavily accented and frequently grammatically faulty and her Mallorquin raised smiles behind her back.

'It's healing very slowly, señorita. I saw the doctor yesterday afternoon and told him it was still hurting and he said that it must do after so deep a cut.'

'You should rest it more.'

'How, when there is work to do?'

'By telling García to do it instead of chatting to Ramón.' When she had first come to the island, the ordinary people had been poor and virtually illiterate and it had seemed reasonable to speak to them with an inquisitive, condescending authority. Antonia's generation still accepted this arrogance without any

21

resentment, but the younger people did not; Phillipa would have been deeply upset to learn how much ill-feeling she often caused. 'And tell García that just before lunch his beastly goat ate one of my special geraniums.'

'How terrible, señorita!'

'The seeds cost a thousand pesetas.' It was her contention that the only way in which to bring home to a Mallorquin the seriousness of any situation was to present it in financial terms. 'And I told him only yesterday that that fence would never keep a goat back for five minutes if it decided to try to get out.'

'But all the goats were hobbled.'

'Since when has hobbling kept a determined goat from wandering? You tell that husband of yours that he must put up a much stronger and higher fence. If his beastly animals eat any more of my special geraniums, I'll make him pay for new seeds.'

'He'll do that, never fear.'

Phillipa walked on. It was unlikely the fence would be strengthened. Either Antonia would forget to pass on the message, or García would agree to do it and minutes later forget what it was he had agreed. Mañana was as much about forgetfulness as deliberate evasion.

She reached the house that her brother, like her, rented on a life lease. It was considerably larger than hers and possessed over fifteen hundred square metres of land in which grew orange and lemon trees and one very large fig tree whose fruit was small and really only suitable for drying and feeding to animals. Justin Burnett was no gardener and the few rose-bushes were losing their fight against a host of weeds, but the bright red bougainvillæa seemed to thrive on neglect and one wall was aflame with the bracts.

She opened the front door, stepped into the entrada. 'Justin ... Justin, are you all right?' she shouted. She tried to recall the doctor's name and couldn't because of an increasing tension.

Then there was a shout from upstairs. 'What's the matter?'

'I telephoned and there was no answer.'

'For God's sake!'

She went into the sitting-room. Around the walls Justin had had shelves fixed and on these were the books which had been in their father's library; also present was their father's desk. To sit surrounded by such things was to be reminded of the library in their old home, an evocation that was both sweet and bitter; sweet because of the hours spent listening to him reading from the classics, bitter because it had been there that they'd first learned of their father's financial loss and the probable consequences of this ...

Justin, dressed in open-neck shirt and shorts, his sparse hair in disarray, came slowly down the stairs and into the sitting-room. 'For God's sake, what's brought you here in siesta-time?' he asked in his high-pitched, querulous voice.

'I've just told you. I phoned to see how you were and you didn't answer.' He was ageing very, very rapidly, she thought. His long face had always been thin, but now the skin was sinking to make it look skeletal; when he had arrived on the island, he had been able to conceal any baldness by growing his hair long, now that was impossible; once he'd walked with an upright carriage, now his shoulders were bowed. 'You had me really worried. Couldn't you see I would be?'

'Since I didn't know it was you phoning, how could I?'

'Who else would it have been at that time?'

He sat heavily in the second armchair.

'You might have—'

He interrupted her roughly. 'When my head was pounding like a bloody steam engine, I wasn't concerned who it was.'

Her resentment turned to fresh worry. 'Again? But it's only a couple of days since you last had a terrible headache.'

'D'you think I don't know that?'

'You must go back and see the specialist again . . .'

'He can't tell me anything I don't already know.'

'Don't you think . . .'

24

'For God's sake, stop bothering me.'

Her lips tightened, but she did not reply. She had been brought up in a family in which the men had had to be honoured and humoured and she still accepted that responsibility, even though she was by far the stronger character. When their father had lost his money through unwise investments, it had been she who had faced up to the consequences while Justin had desperately tried to insulate himself from reality; it had been she who had first gone out to work, braving a world for which their upbringing had not prepared them, while for months afterwards he had remained at home, too frightened and resentful to follow her example ... She spoke, trying to force him out of his present black mood. 'One of García's goats broke into my garden and ate one of those special geraniums.'

He might not have heard.

'I told him that the fence he'd put up wouldn't hold the goats, but he wouldn't listen.'

'They're all stupid.'

'Stubborn rather than stupid.' To others, even her brother, she always defended the Mallorquins and it was only to herself that she admitted that the truth was that they so often behaved stupidly because they were seemingly incapable of foreseeing trouble.

'Lydia called this morning,' he said.

25

'That was nice.'

'It wasn't. My head had started and she insisted on going on and on about that family of hers.'

'She's very proud of them.'

'Why can't she be very proud of them somewhere else? Why should I suffer just becuse Vernon's got an IQ in four figures?'

'His name's Redmund; Vernon's the Praters' son.'

'What's it matter what his name is?'

'He's expected to get a very good degree.'

'By cheating, no doubt.'

'Justin, I wish you'd go back and see the specialist again.'

'All he can say is, I should have the operation. I won't. D'you understand, I won't.'

'It might not be nearly as bad as you fear. D'you remember Tony? He came through the operation wonderfully well . . .'

'I don't give a damn if he enjoyed a resurrection. I'm not going to have it and that's that.'

She could not quite erase the word 'coward' from her mind. 'Would you like some coffee?'

'No.'

'I would, so if I make some, will you drink a cup?'

'You think coffee's going to clear my head?'

'It might make you feel a little better.'

'You can be incredibly stupid.'

26

She only just stopped herself from finally delivering a very tart rejoinder. She stood. 'I'll make enough so that if you change your mind there'll be a cupful for you.'

The kitchen was very much better equipped than hers and instead of a laboriously hand-operated coffee-grinder, he had an electric one that reduced beans to near powder in seconds. She opened a cupboard, to bring out the coffee-maker, and discovered that he'd bought himself an electric percolator. He'd always been of an extravagant nature ... Disloyalty, she told herself, was the eighth deadly sin. If he could afford to buy a new coffee-maker, why shouldn't he? It wasn't as if he didn't help her quite often financially ... Groundless resentment was the ninth deadly sin. She'd no right to wonder why he, the weakling, should have ended up with a substantial career pension, fully index-linked, while she, because of misfortunes quite beyond her control, had only a small, non-index-linked pension to supplement her state one...

The coffee made, she poured it into the silver coffee jug which had come from their mother's family, searched for the matching milk jug before she remembered that recently he had dropped and damaged it. Naturally, the son had inherited all the silver. But if the milk jug had been hers and it had been damaged, she would never have just put it into a drawer and forgotten it, not caring enough to find out if it could be mended locally.

CHAPTER FOUR

When Gerald Heal had bought the property, it had been called Son Temor; having little time for history and none for modesty, he had renamed it Ca'n Heal. It was a manor house, imposingly large, set at the head of a long, wide valley. Originally, all the valley had been owned, but now the holding was reduced to just over two hectares. Close to the range of outbuildings was a large well with an almost limitless capacity even in midsummer, so that there was far more water than was needed; the farmers who now owned the surrounding land had wanted Heal to sell them the surplus water, but he had refused. What was his, was his.

The square house, four floors high, was built around an inner courtyard. In this, he had had built a stone fountain and now no matter how stifling the heat, the courtyard was a place of musical coolness. The house had been unreformed, so he had engaged an architect from Madrid to modernize it. The architect had been a man of vision and taste, very generous with other people's money. When Heal had added up what the reformation had cost, he had

28

been shocked and ever afterwards referred to 'that swindler of an architect'. But since the work was of a quality rarely met on the island and there was extra envy to be gained from being so rich that one could be that handsomely cheated (he hadn't been; on the whole, Madrileño architects, unlike many local ones, were both conscientious and honest), his resentment wasn't as great as his words suggested.

He had filled the house with valuable possessions. Most had been bought on the open market but some, like the Mytens painting, he had acquired at a fraction of their true value because of his gift of being able to discern the beauty of genius. Those possessions bought in the open market were often so ostentatiously impressive as to be ugly, but all his 'finds' were truly beautiful. There was here a dichotomy of character almost impossible to understand until one knew and understood his past.

He had been born into bastardy and considerable hardship, if not quite poverty. That bastardy was an unfortunate condition was first truly brought home to him after two older boys had enjoyed themselves immensely, beating him up on the grounds that as a bastard he was a polluting influence. The tears he had shed had been tears of humiliation as much as of pain and this humiliation, which he never learned to forget, had been responsible for firing him with a burning ambition to prove himself a lot smarter and tougher than all those lucky enough to have been born with two parents and in some comfort.

He'd made his first million by his twenty-fifth birthday, nine years after starting full-time work in a builder's yard in Camberwell. By the time he was forty he was worth, on a conservative estimate, ten million. Unlike most other rich people, he saw money not as power, but as a means of buying admiration and envy and so he retired rather than continue to work at making still more money which he'd never have the time, or eventually the ability, to spend with profit to himself.

He'd naturally had no intention of allowing any government to tax him and then waste his money on half-baked social schemes, so he'd moved all his capital out of England and into a bank in Jersey and from there to a company in Switzerland which invested it through a company in Liechtenstein. His Liechtenstein company bought the house and he was their tenant. Since the Spanish government had made the mistake of introducing a modern system of taxation which caught anyone who lived in the country for more than five months and thirty days, he made certain it could not be proved that he did. He paid most bills on credit cards whose accounts were settled in the States in dollars and he drew cash through cashpoints since their records of withdrawals were not kept locally; no snooping Spaniard was ever going to find it easy to prove that he was liable to pay Spanish income tax. As a Rothschild had once said, a rich man didn't necessarily have to be a fool.

The company employed five servants, three in the house and two in the garden; the house was always spick and span, the garden a blaze of colour. He treated them fairly, but did not allow them the slightest familiarity, as did so many expatriates. All men weren't equal, not by many bank balances.

He was tall, well built, had broad shoulders and a slim waist; many women thought him handsome. He was quickwitted, intelligent, and possessed a humour which could match itself to his listeners. Introduced to three strangers at a cocktail party, within minutes they would be listening to him rather than to each other. Most people liked him on first acquaintance and it was only the confirmed snobs, or the very perspicacious, who saw in his moustache an accurate indication of character. One of his many women, locked out of his 'love' flat for no reason other than boredom with her, had labelled him a barrow-boy made good. It was difficult to think of an apter description.

Alma stepped from the vast entrance hall into the snuggery—the small sitting-room which he used when not entertaining and impressing, in which were television, video and hi-fi, naturally all of the highest quality. ''Evening, Gerry.' She treated him as a friend (or enemy), not a father, and he preferred this because sentiment made him uneasy.

He looked up. 'Your mother rang earlier and wants you to phone her back immediately.'

'Is something the matter?'

'If there is, it can't be serious because she didn't complain.'

She hated him for this open contempt. It had been his blatant infidelities which had finally brought about the separation. 'D'you mind if I phone her?'

'For God's sake, you don't have to ask.'

If she hadn't, she thought, he might well have complained. There was a phone in the snuggery, but this was a call she did not want overheard. She returned to the entrance hall and crossed to the library. The shelves were filled with leather-bound books and any man who'd read them all could count himself educated. She doubted he'd read any of them. She sat on the edge of the large partner's desk, lifted the receiver, and dialled 07. When the connection with International was made, she dialled 33 for France and then the number. As she waited, she nervously wondered what had happened to make her mother ring through and face having to speak to her husband.

'Who is it?'

Her mother's words sounded slightly slurred; it could be distortion or it could be drink. 'It's Alma. I'm sorry I was out when you rang. Gerry says you want a word?'

'I'm surprised the bastard remembered to tell you.'

She'd never been able to decide in her own mind whether her mother had believed the marriage could last, despite the difference in characters, or whether it had been a simple case of being dazzled by wealth. 'Is something wrong, Mother?'

'I've just had a letter from the bastard's solicitors. And d'you know what they've written . . .'

She listened patiently to a long and involved story, the gist of which she had guessed immediately. Her mother had run out of money, had written to her father's solicitors to ask for more, and had been refused. Her mother spent money with an abandon that was at times breathtaking; for her, financially there was no tomorrow. If she saw a dress that attracted her, she bought it no matter what the cost and even though the cupboards in her house were filled with clothes; another gold bracelet was a necessity for a well-dressed lady; one never ever drank vin ordinaire, only château-bottled wine . . .

'You have to tell him.'

'Tell him what?'

'Haven't you been listening to a word I've said? Tell the bastard that I must have my allowance increased. I can't go on like this while he's wallowing in luxury. When I think of what he should be giving me . . .'

Alma leaned across the desk and opened a silver-gilt cigarette box, brought out a cigarette, lit this with a gold Dunhill lighter. Drink always exacerbated her mother's bitterness, resentment, and envy.

'. . . so tell him he must agree to let me have more money.'

'I don't think that that would be a very good idea.'

'Why not?'

'You know how his mind works. Tackle him head on and he'll refuse. If you really think it's worth your while asking him, write him a letter and very quietly explain how the cost of everything keeps going up. And don't be definite unless you're absolutely certain you're right—you know how he checks up on things. At the end, just ask him to let you have a bigger allowance if he can afford to be generous—he won't want to appear to be unable to afford. Don't complain, don't moan, and be pleasant.'

'Pleasant to that bastard?'

'Yes, Mother, pleasant. That is, if you really want any hope of getting your allowance raised . . .'

'Why d'you keep saying "allowance"? It's

money he owes me.'

'I know how you feel about it, but remember what those solicitors in London said. The marriage has irretrievably broken down and if you both lived in the UK you'd have a legal right to a proper share of his assets that could be enforced. But neither of you lives at home and it's certain that Gerry's transferred all his assets overseas. In such circumstances, it's almost impossible to make certain your rights are enforced. In fact, if he decided to cut you off without another penny, in practical terms there's probably very little you could do about it. And if you annoy him too much, he will cut you off.'

'He's a bastard.'

'So you mentioned.'

'He doesn't care that I'm living in penury.'

'Mother, there are a hell of a lot of people who would like to live in your"penury". If you could cut back on some of your extravagances...'

'Extravagances! If I'm so depressed I buy myself a little something to try to cheer myself up, I suppose that's being hopelessly extravagant? Maybe even continuing to live is a hopeless extravagance...'

She flicked ash from the cigarette into the silver ashtray that was shaped as a dolphin. She was a go-between. Her mother vented her anger, and Gerry his resentful contempt, through her . . .

'All right, Mother, I'll see how things go and speak to him if the right moment turns up.' It was not a promise that she intended to keep. It was usually safe never to prophesy how Gerald would react, since he delighted in being contrary, but in this instance it was—he would do whatever was likely to hurt his wife the most.

She said goodbye, replaced the receiver, slid off the desk, stubbed out the cigarette and returned to the snuggery. On one of the small coffee tables there was now an ice bucket in which was an opened bottle. 'Champers or something else?' he asked.

'That'll do.'

He smiled. Since she was his daughter, he didn't mind her occasionally mocking his lifestyle. He lifted a tulip-shaped glass from the silver salver and filled it, passed it across.

The champagne was vintage Heidsieck Monopole and must have cost a fortune, she thought. Even the better Spanish cavas were far cheaper, but he never drank them; probably he'd read somewhere that a man with any pretensions to a palate would rather enjoy one glassful of champagne than suffer ten glassfuls of sparkling white.

'Well, is there a crisis in France?' he asked.

'She wanted a chat, that's all.'

'Something at which she's always been

proficient.'

'Among a great number of other things, as you'd have discovered if ever you'd taken the trouble to find out.'

He shrugged his shoulders. He understood Alma's desire to stick up for her mother, without ever accepting that it was justified. 'What kind of a day did you have?'

'Painful. I kept being threatened by cramp, starvation, and death by dehydration, but sympathy was there none. When he's working, Guy's a lesson in selfishness.'

'What kind of painting is it?'

'A full-length study.'

'Yes, but . . .' He refilled his glass. 'Decent?'

'It's certainly not pornographic.'

'Then you are dressed?'

'No, I'm not.'

'Why not?' he demanded sharply.

'Because the object of the exercise is for him to have practice in painting the human form, warts and all.'

'Why doesn't he hire a model?'

'Mallorquin women aren't into nude modelling.'

'I should bloody well think not.'

'Gerry, you're being delightfully Victorian.'

'Because I don't like the thought of my daughter appearing in the nude?'

'A painter sees his model as something to paint, not screw.' She was amused by the hypocrisy not only of her last statement, but also of the whole conversation; Guy's thoughts were often of a non-artistic nature and a moral attitude sat uneasily on her father's shoulders.

'I don't like the idea.'

'Will it make you any happier if I tell you that I won't indulge in a Bohemian life just for the hell of it.'

'I disapprove.'

'Why be a parent if one doesn't disapprove of one's offspring's activities? ... Gerry, the art critic on *La Vanguardia* saw two or three of Guy's paintings and said they showed tremendous talent.'

'For pleasing dirty old men?'

'He didn't see the Mallorquin Venus. He mentioned a very influential art gallery in Barcelona which is always on the lookout for new talent and he reckoned that the owner would probably give Guy an exhibition. That would really be something, because Barcelona has become a very important centre.'

'Presumably you're telling me this because you want something?'

'You don't think that that's being horribly cynical?'

'You tell me.'

She did not accept the challenge. 'I didn't realize this before, but art's rather like car racing.'

'Surely one of the more recherché comparisons?'

'Not really. If you want to succeed, you have to be known, but in order to be known, you have to succeed. The only short cut through that Catch 22 situation is to find a sponsor who'll make you financially attractive to a team manager. In the same way, if an artist wants to succeed . . .'

'Cutting things short, you're trying to say that Guy wants a sponsor.'

'Who'll put up a relatively small sum of money in the certainty of making a good profit.'

'The certainty being, no doubt, of the same order as that of a Derby favourite?'

'You don't quite understand. I've been checking and the way the galleries in Barcelona work is that either they stage an exhibition entirely at their own cost and take fifty per cent of all sales, or they charge a flat sum which covers all overheads plus, and take either a much lower or no percentage on sales. Obviously, if a painter probably won't make more than a couple of sales, it's in his best interests to work under the first scheme; if he's likely to do well, the second. But to be able to choose the latter, he has to put down a full payment in advance.'

'Which no artist can?'

'Very few, certainly.'

'Guy's not one of the very few.' It was a flat statement of fact, not a question.

'Unfortunately, no.'

'So he thinks I might play the sucker?'

'I've no idea. I naturally haven't discussed the idea with him.'

'Naturally?'

'He has to paddle his own canoe.'

He was perplexed. 'Then why are you telling me all this?'

'Because by my calculations, if Guy had an exhibition where he paid the flat sum and the gallery took either no or very little commission on each sale, the backer would make a handsome profit if half the paintings sold and would double his money if three-quarters did.'

'Where would all this profit come from?'

'In the agreement the backer would be given a percentage on all sales over and above repayment in full.'

'If it's so certain he'll sell well, why doesn't the gallery owner insist on a percentage rather than a flat sum?'

'Because every gallery owner can remember exhibitions which have failed dismally.'

'So now the story returns to earth!'

'Failed because the owner misjudged the value of the work. The history of art is full of people who've misjudged paintings becuse they didn't have that special something which says whether a painting really is, or is not, truly great. Let's face it, very few people have. But you're one of those very few. And you said that

Guy's work is really good. Which means that there has to be a strong chance it will sell well. So you could stand to make a handsome profit for doing nothing more than relying on your own judgement.'

He drained his glass, refilled it. 'Does he have enough paintings?'

'It would take some time to set up an exhibition and by then he would have, yes. Of course, he'd need a loan for framing, transport, catalogues, and the party on the opening night. Like you, he's a cynic and he reckons that an artist's reviews bear a direct relationship to the quality and quantity of the champagne he serves on his opening night.'

'Any additional loan would have to have the same priority of repayment as the main one.'

'Of course.'

He drank. After a while he said forcefully: 'I'm not subsidizing him to show a painting of you in the nude that grubby little men in raincoats leer at.'

She smiled. 'You really are sweet, Gerry!' She added, in a conspiratorial tone: 'If you'd put up the money, surely you'd be able to claim the right to tell him he mustn't exhibit that painting?'

CHAPTER FIVE

Bronwen's august, commanding, and pervasive presence did nothing to make the Yeo-Eatons' cocktail party any more pleasurable than were other people's. She would not let events take their natural course, but insisted on her guests mixing and not staying in tight little circles so that more often than not she forced together people who disliked each other; also, being a prude, she made a point of disturbing pleasure and she spoke sharply to two men who were trying to persuade two ladies to strip off to their underclothes for a swim in the pool, headed off a couple who had been making for the shadows which lay beyond the lantana hedge, and dragged her husband away from an interesting conversation with a forty-year-old divorcee...

Much to Phillipa's annoyance, the Brookers had been shepherded by Bronwen into talking to her.

'The rise in the cost of living, as measured by the price of a bottle of brandy ...' Brooker gave a neighing laugh. 'The most accurate index of inflation there is, I always say.' He turned to his wife, who had chosen a long dress and was worried because only two other women had done the same. 'That's what I always say, isn't it, dear?'

'Yes, dear.'

'Well, the price of a bottle of brandy has gone up by ... I'll bet you can't guess?'

'A hundredfold,' replied Phillipa shortly.

'No, no, not quite as bad as that! Although I must admit that it sometimes seems like it...'

'When I first came to the island, a bottle of reasonable brandy cost six pesetas.'

'Oh! Is that a fact? Then you must have been here a very long time ... Well, I was really thinking of the time we've been living here. Things really have shot up in the past three years.' He turned to his wife. 'Haven't they, dear?'

'Yes, dear,' Denise replied.

'The cost of living has shot up everywhere in the civilized world,' said Phillipa.

'But more here, dear lady, at this end of the island. Take the humble vegetable. A lettuce used to cost...'

'Dear man, I'm as capable of appreciating the rise in prices as you are.' The unaccustomed amount of champagne she had drunk had made her more aggressive than usual. 'I live on a small pension. In the old days I could afford to eat at a restaurant several times a week, now I'm lucky if it's once a fortnight and I have to be satisfied with the menu del dia.'

'Of course you know what the trouble is, don't you?'

'Do I?'

43

'They've all become so greedy.'

'And who exactly are "they"?'

'Why, the Mallorquins.'

'Then who's made them greedy? It's the foreigners who come and pay the maids six hundred an hour when they're not worth two hundred because none of them is trained to do anything but break crockery and electrical plugs.'

'But . . . but that's what they're asking in the port.'

'That's right,' said his wife, hoping Phillipa did not know that she paid her maid seven hundred an hour.

'They always ask for more than they expect to get because that's the Arab blood in them. And when they get paid what they ask, they know they're dealing with fools.'

Brooker, his drooping jowls and double chin increasing his resemblance to a turkeycock, said plaintively: 'If they won't come unless you pay them what they ask, there's no alternative.'

'There's an excellent alternative. It's called doing the work oneself.'

Rosa, a cousin of Victoria, who was helping with the service, approached them. Proud of her English, she said: 'You like more?' The lower half of the bottle of champagne was carefully swathed in a serviette to hide the label. The Yeo-Eatons did not wish to embarrass anyone by making it clear that they were serving a cheaper champagne than they normally drank since to do so would underline the truth that their palates were superior to those of most of their guests.

Phillipa held out her glass. 'How's your mother?' she asked in Spanish.

'Much better, thank you, señorita. She went to see a new doctor and he gave her some different pills and her stomach's happier.'

'That's good. And your sister?'

'She has a good job with the bank. Her novio finishes his milly next month and they are to marry in June.'

'Have they a house?'

'José's mother was left one by an aunt and she's given it to them to live in. I'm helping to decorate it.'

'I hope I'm to be invited to the wedding?'

'But of course, señorita. It's unthinkable that you shouldn't be.'

'And to the christening.'

Rosa giggled.

Brooker, who'd been becoming more and more impatient, said: 'I and the wife would like another little drink if that's not too much trouble.'

Rosa hadn't understood the words, but the nature of the request had been unmistakable. She refilled both glasses, which emptied the bottle, and left.

'I wish I could speak Spanish as well as you

do,' said Denise ingratiatingly.

'You never will until you try,' retorted Phillipa.

'But I do. My trouble is, I forget the words. And it's all so terribly difficult when things have different genders. I mean, how am I to know if a tree's masculine or feminine?'

Brooker laughed coarsely. 'That's obvious, isn't it? It's masculine . . . What I say is, what's the point in bothering. If they want something from you, they understand English soon enough. Make 'em speak English, that's what I say.'

'You don't surprise me,' said Phillipa. She turned and, careless about such rudeness, walked away. Back in Britain, the Brookers had been no more than prosperous, conventional, small-minded suburbanites, yet on the island they looked down on the Mallorquins with intolerant condescension; condescension that frequently turned to dislike when they were faced with the resentment their attitude bred.

She joined a small group of three, just beyond the steps down into the floodlit pool.

'Hullo, Phillipa,' said Heal. 'You're looking very chic.'

'And you're as big a liar as ever.' She had identified him as a cad at their first meeting, but in her long life had come to the conclusion that, provided one did not have to do business with

46

them, cads were more entertaining than the righteous.

'You know what they say, don't you? A lie a day keeps one rich and gay ... Gay in the old-fashioned sense, I hasten to add.' He was, as always, a shade too smartly dressed; yachting jacket, silk shirt, linen trousers, and white buckskin shoes.

McColl, in his late sixties, small but without the peppery character of many small men, said: 'It's a great pity "gay" has come to mean a homosexual. It used to have a connotation that's difficult to define now. For instance, how can you describe the kind of person we used to call a gay woman?'

'Bubbly?' suggested his wife, built on a generous scale and unworried by the fact.

Heal said: 'Talking about bubbly, let's see if we can get our glasses recharged.' He looked round, saw Victoria, smiled at her and she came across, a bottle in one hand, a plate in the other. She refilled their glasses, but they refused the tired, dispirited canapés.'

Conversation was general for a few moments, then McColl looked at his watch and said they ought to be moving because they had to go to another party that evening; his wife made a face, suggesting that had the choice been hers, she would have returned home. They said goodbye, left.

'So are you thinking of going back to England for a holiday?' Heal asked.

47

'My cousin's daughter has had a baby and I'd like to go to the christening,' replied Phillipa, 'but I can't afford to.'

He hastily turned the conversation away from money; naturally, being very rich, worried that she might be about to ask him to help her financially. 'Given the alternative of staying here or returning home in order to go goo-goo over a baby, I'd stay here.'

'Of course. You're demonstrably undomesticated, despite having an attractive daughter ... And incidentally, I haven't seen her this evening. Has she gone back home?'

'She's still with me, but she wasn't invited. I asked if she'd like me to speak to the Yeo-Eatons, who probably don't know she's staying with me, but she said she'd rather enjoy life.'

'Sensible gal.' She drained her glass.

'Phillipa, you know everyone worth knowing. Who's that who's just appeared?'

'Appeared where?'

'Under the covered patio. She's talking to our hostess.'

Phillipa squinted as she tried to focus her gaze more clearly. 'Irma, the Contessa Imbrolie. If that were my name, I'd change it; too close to imbroglio. In any case, Irma Imbrolie is tautologous.'

'What nationality is she?'

'Probably more English than you, since she

was born in some place like Wolverhampton. She married an Italian count, which is no difficult feat since in that country counts seem to be two a penny. Her husband died last year, from some sort of stomach trouble. Italians eat far too much pasta.'

'That's a very elegant dress she's wearing.'

'Is it?' She again concentrated her gaze. 'I suppose it is, if you like exaggeration. But in any case, next to Bronwen most dresses look like haute couture.' It wasn't until he chuckled that she realized she needed to control her tongue.

'D'you know her well?'

She spoke more carefully. 'I've met her a couple of times at parties, that's all.'

'She looks good fun.'

'That depends on what meaning you accord "good fun", doesn't it?' She made up her mind; nothing more to drink and so to bed. 'I must be moving.'

'Can I run you back in my car?'

'Thank you, but the walk will do me good.'

She left. As she passed the Contessa Imbrolie, she decided that Heal had been right; probably the dress had come from one of the major Italian or French fashion houses. Rumour had it that the Count had been a very wealthy man; wealthy, but not very sensible, since he'd married a woman so very much younger than himself.

Heal parked his Mercedes 500 alongside the white Ford Fiesta, left the garage and crossed to the west door of the house. When he entered he could hear the music, even though the snuggery was on the other side.

Alma used the remote control to turn down the volume of the CD player. 'How was Bronwen? Noble Roman nose held high?'

'She's not too bad if you don't take her seriously.' He sat in the nearest armchair. 'As a matter of fact, it was quite an enjoyable party.'

She cocked her head slightly to one side as she studied him. 'Praise like that must signify something. Was the booze good or did you meet a tasty dish?'

'You won't credit me with simply a pleasure at being alive?'

'Not unless you've found a way of turning that pleasure into profit.' She switched off the player, stood. 'You may be full of contentment, but I'm quite hungry. You said you wouldn't want a cooked meal after a cocktail party and I'm just as happy with a very light meal, so Carolina's just left out a salad, pâté, cheese, and a homemade spinach coca. How about a couple of eggs on top of a slice of coca?'

'Sounds good.'

'I'll go and do that. Shall we eat here, on our

laps—there's a programme on the local telly I want to watch which come on after the news?'

'In Spanish?'

'Of course. I'm managing to understand enough to get the gist of things.'

'You're a smart girl.'

'A compliment from you? You are in an extraordinarily good humour! Maybe it's the moment to remind you that there are only seven months to Christmas.' She laughed. 'Don't panic, I was only joking. Diamonds may be a girl's best friend, but they've never said very much to me.'

As she left, he settled back in the chair and stretched out his legs. Diamonds did a lot for the Contessa Imbrolie. The necklace had looked superb on her. That one piece must have cost more than all the jewellery the rest of the women had been wearing . . .

Marriage had its drawbacks—as he could testify—but there were times when it had something to offer. A couple were received more often and more willingly than a single man. A wife could run the house properly and be ever ready to be a gracious hostess. She stopped malicious suggestions from small-minded people who professed to see special significance in a man's liking for sartorial and personal smartness. Should she have a title, she'd open doors that would otherwise remain closed. And if in addition she owned a fortune in her own right, then she could not be marrying for money ... Yes, there were many good reasons to think of marrying again.

CHAPTER SIX

Dolores put a bowl of hot chocolate on the kitchen table. 'It's already past nine.'

Alvarez sat down on the stool. 'It's of no account. The superior chief went off to some conference in Madrid and isn't due back until midday.'

'But I thought you were complaining you'd so much work to do, you didn't know how you'd ever get even half of it done?'

'And I still don't know.' He broke off a piece of ensaimada, dunked it in the chocolate, ate.

'Well, you're not going to discover how all the time you sit here instead of hurrying off to the office, are you?'

'You don't understand.'

'That's just about right. And d'you know why I don't? It's because I'm a woman who has to do ten different jobs every hour and doesn't have the time to worry about how to do them.' She stared challengingly at him, but he merely dunked another piece of ensaimada. She sighed as she turned away and went over to the refrigerator. One could feed a mule oats, but one would never make butter out of its milk.

The phone rang, kept on ringing. 'Well,' she demanded, 'aren't you going to answer?'

'It might not be for me.'

'It might not be for me, but you seem to expect me to go.' Handsome head held high, she left.

He used a handkerchief to wipe the sweat from his forehead and neck. It was extraordinarily hot, even when one remembered that it was now mid-July. Heat sapped the strength from a man and left him good for nothing . . .

She returned to the kitchen. 'The call was for you! The sargento wants a word.'

'What's up?'

'Perhaps you'd like me to go back and find out if it's important enough for you to interrupt your meal?'

Morosely, he dunked a last piece of ensaimada. The sargento was, on the whole, a sensible man and therefore would not have rung this early in the morning had the matter not been urgent. Had the superior chief returned early from Madrid, rung the post and demanded to speak to the inspector? It was the kind of sneaky thing that an essentially sneaky man would do. As he finished the chocolate, he mentally composed several excuses for his absence from the office and tried to decide which was the safest.

He left the kitchen and walked through the dining-room-cum-living-room into the entrada, which was also the formal entertaining room and therefore used only on high days and holidays and kept so scrupulously clean by Dolores that any speck of dust in it felt lonely. He lifted the receiver. 'Yes?'

'You've finally managed to drag yourself out of bed, then!' said the sargento.

'I've been down at the port since eight, looking for a witness.'

'Only in your dreams, you lazy old sod ... Listen, Enrique. There's been a death in the Huerta. An Englishman by the name of ... Burnett.' He had considerable difficulty pronouncing the name. 'Seems to have blown his brains out with a revolver.'

'When?'

'How the hell should I know? You're the inspector, not me.'

'Then are you smart enough at least to have asked where it happened?'

'Ca Na Torrina. His sister, Señorita Burnett, phoned the post. She'd gone to his house because he hadn't answered the phone and she found him dead.'

At the conclusion of the conversation, Alvarez returned to the kitchen and sat. Dolores, who had been writing out a shopping list with some difficulty—her schooling had been very brief and she should have worn glasses—looked up. 'Is it serious?'

'No. An Englishman has shot himself.'

'Mother of God! You call that not serious?'

'If a man shoots himself, there can't be the kind of complications which upset a superior chief.' He spoke with grateful satisfaction.

He left the house ten minutes later. His new, blood-red Seat Ibiza was parked in front of the house and he stared at it with possessive admiration. Twenty years ago it would never have occurred to him that he could ever own a car; ten years ago, the limits of his ambitions had been a secondhand Seat 600; now, a magnificent new Ibiza was his. And since the age of miracles was therefore not past, why should he not eventually own the finca of his dreams with soil so rich that it grew tomatoes the size of pumpkins? He unlocked the driving door and smoothed out the seat cover before he sat.

The engine started immediately and he drove off. Eduardo was by the corner and he slowed down and waved; Eduardo acknowledged the wave, but nothing more. Too jealous to admit any admiration for the new car...

At the Lariax road he came to a halt at the Stop sign instead of going on regardless as he would have done in the 600. He began the drive along the narrow, twisting lane, bordered by stone walls, which passed through the centre of the Huerta de Llueso. Huerta meant market garden. Years ago, the land had grown all the fruit and vegetables that the villagers had needed. Now, both had to be imported because most of the properties were either owned by foreigners or let to them in the season and much of the land had been lost to swimming pools or to growing roses instead of radishes, plumbago instead of peppers, lawns instead of lettuces . . .

Ca Na Torrina was an old house without a garage or a drive, but on the opposite side of the road was a triangular-shaped piece of land, too small and awkward for profitable cultivation, and he parked the Ibiza there.

He stepped out of the car. Despite the many trees which surrounded him, part of the bay was distantly visible, as was Puig Antonia. Ignore the constant thudding of a pneumatic rock-breaker that was working nearby and listen only to the cicadas. Could anywhere in the world be fairer than this? The island had many names, but Fortunate Isle was the sweetest and perhaps the truest. Possibly the Garden of Eden had been here . . . He brought his thoughts down to earth and back to the present. On the far side of the road was a dead man who had killed himself; it had been no Eden for him.

He was half way across the lane when a man appeared around a corner and called to attract his attention. He stepped back into the shade of a holm oak and waited. His mother had said that the cicadas cried, 'Hurry. Hurry. Hurry.' But why they should have been so insistently frantic in a land of calm, he couldn't now remember.

The man, old, time-creased, dressed in a dirt-stained shirt and patched trousers, stepped off the road. He stared at Alvarez for several seconds, screwing up his eyes against the glare, then said: 'You're Dolores Ramez's cousin.'

'And you're García Goñi. D'you know anything about the English señor who's been shot?'

Goñi answered with scorn. 'Work the land, don't I? It was my old woman who heard the señorita scream, wasn't it, and who went to see what the trouble was and then called me.'

'The señorita is the dead man's sister?'

'So they say. Seems difficult to believe, them being so different.'

'How d'you mean?'

Goñi brushed his thick, calloused hand across his forehead as he considered the question and tried to find the words to express what he wanted to say; the sunlight picked out a deep scar on the right-hand side of his face, the stubble on his chin, and several pieces of chaff in his grey, curly hair. 'She'd always something to say,' he finally answered. 'Like with the goats a while back. I told her, they was hobbled and I'd put up a fence. Didn't do no good. She went on and on about what would happen if

57

they broke free ...' He stopped as a car rounded the corner a hundred metres above them and he watched this with the perpetual curiosity of a countryman until it had passed them and reached the corner below.

Alvarez moved forward and crossed the road and Goñi followed him into the overgrown garden and then continued speaking as if there'd been no interruption. '... and wouldn't listen to what I had to say. Knows everything, that one does.' There was more respect than resentment in his voice. 'One of the bloody goats had to break its hobbles and smash through the new fence and eat a geranium. You should have heard her! Said it was a very special geranium and the seed had cost a thousand pesetas and if my goats ate any more, I'd have to buy new seed. As if I'm such a bloody fool as to believe any flower seed could cost that sort of money.'

Alvarez watched a hoopoe fly in curves and dip out of sight behind some orange trees. 'And what of the brother?'

'Completely different. Never said anything. Didn't give orders like she does.'

'It was she who found him, wasn't it?'

'She'd come up to see him, like she often did. Shot himself. Bloody silly thing to do.'

'I imagine she was very upset?'

'She's a real tough 'un, but she was crying away just like a local.'

'She'll have been badly shocked. I don't suppose the señor's a pretty sight?'

'There's some blood on his head,' replied Goñi dismissively. During a long life, which had spanned action in the Civil War, he had seen far worse sights.

'Is the house open?'

'I don't know how she's left it, do I?'

'You weren't the last out?'

'How do I know?'

Alvarez's patience when dealing with the peasant mentality was almost inexhaustible. 'Anyway, as far as you can tell, it's not locked up?'

'That's right.'

'Then I'll see if I can get inside.'

'You'll not be wanting me anymore?'

'Not right now.'

'Then I'll get back to work.'

Alvarez had turned and crossed half way to the wooden front door when he remembered to ask: 'Where's the señorita live?'

Goñi, who had reached the road, stopped. 'What's that?'

Alvarez spoke much louder.

'Ca'n Pario, of course,' replied Goñi, contemptuous of such ignorance. He continued on his way, his movements ponderously deliberate after a lifetime of working the land.

The front door was shut, but not locked. Alvarez stepped into the entrada and from there

59

into the sitting-room. He was surprised by the rows of leather-bound books and wondered how any man could be clever enough to absorb such learning? Nothing else could have so clearly and immediately identified this as a house occupied by a foreigner.

He returned to the entrada and went from there into the sitting-room. Violent death always shocked him, not because the sight of injuries revolted him, although they did, but because it was so clear a statement that life was transitory. He approached the body.

Burnett had fallen sideways off a chair and lay slumped on the floor. The entrance wound was near enough in the centre of his forehead and looked surprisingly insignificant, since the flesh had largely closed, for a wound that had killed. Some blood had flowed on to the tiled floor and congealed. His face was white, his lips partially drawn back to reveal yellowing teeth. A metre away was a small, snub-nosed revolver which lay with muzzle pointing towards a butano fire in the corner of the room.

The dining-room table was circular, with a very thick top and a cumbersome central pillar; locally made, Alvarez thought. On it stood a three-parts-empty bottle of Bell's whisky, a used glass, and a typewriter. A sheet of paper had been wound into the typewriter and on this had been typed: 'I have to do this. But immortality can defeat death. *Si monumentum requiris, Paris, circumspice.'*

Alvarez scratched his right ear. The first sentence confirmed suicide, the second seemed to be meaningless since suicide seemed unlikely to make the Englishman immortal, and the third was so much Greek to him. He looked at the whisky. If the bottle had been full or near full to begin with, then perhaps there was the reason for the strange form of the suicide note.

He crossed to inspect the revolver. It had one of the shortest barrels he had ever seen and walnut chequered grips. Knowing that the grips could never record prints, he picked it up and then, using a handkerchief, broke it. There were five chambers and all were loaded; two of the bullets had been fired. He looked back at the body. There was only the one bullet wound visible. He put the revolver back on the floor, straightened up. A man could move after he had suffered a fatal wound that would normally be presumed to have occasioned instantaneous death and men who had been shot through the heart had been known to walk around before they collapsed and died. So had the señor suffered the mortal wound, yet after that involuntarily fired a second time before collapsing?

He carefully examined the floor and near the right-hand corner of the room found a lead bullet, so distorted that had he not known what he was looking for he might never have identified it. Close to the bullet were several chips of stone and some very fine powder and on the wall, not far from a framed photograph, there was a starred mark. Clearly, the bullet had pulverized the Mallorquin plaster and then crumpled against the stone underneath. A second, involuntary shot or—the thought occurred to him—a first one to make certain gun and ammunition were working? He picked up the bullet and dropped it into his right-hand trouser pocket, reminding himself as he did so that he ought at the first opportunity to find something more secure to put it into. Before turning away, he studied the photograph. It depicted a stone head, the top part of which had been cut off, that possessed a triangular nose but no other features. Modern art?

The telephone was in the entrada and he used it to speak to one of the local doctors, who carried out forensic work that did not require a specialist's knowledge, and to the mortician. Each said that he would be out immediately. Knowing that neither man would arrive for quite some time, Alvarez went out into the garden and moved a patio chair into the shade. Once seated, he closed his eyes, the better to appreciate the peace.

★   ★   ★

The doctor was a small, bustling man, an

amateur archaeologist who had for years been trying to interest his fellows in discovering and preserving the island's past. 'He died roughly between eight and twelve hours ago.'

'Can't you be a little more precise?' Alvarez asked.

'Not with the heat we've been suffering. In any case, you ought to know that at best it's always only a rough estimate.'

'Are there any other wounds?'

'Only bruising on his left shoulder which probably occurred when he fell off the chair.'

'It's all right to move the body now?'

'As far as I'm concerned. You said he lived here on his own, but his sister has a place nearby. Have you seen her?'

'Not yet. I thought it best to wait until I'd spoken to you.'

'It'll be a good idea to try to find out what sort of a state he was in over the last few days or weeks. I haven't had much experience in suicides, but I've never known one without a history of mental problems of some sort or another.'

'You're surely not saying you believe it might not be suicide?'

'Good God, no! Just suggesting you confirm things. The man was lucky, mark you, to hit himself in the brain, like that. It's all too easy to miss causing fatal damage and to end up alive but paralysed, a cabbage.'

One might be fit enough to run up Mount Everest, have just won the lottery, and be about to escort Miss Spain to dinner, thought Alvarez, but a quick chat with a doctor was enough to make one take to one's bed.

'Well, I've work for six so I'll be away.'

Alvarez said goodbye. He then spoke to the mortician who had arrived five minutes previously and gave orders for the body to be moved. That done, he checked the time. Did he speak to the señorita now or later? Later, he decided.

He locked up the house, crossed the lane to his car. He drove into the old square in the village, parked in a taxi rank, and went into the Club Lleuso for a coffee and brandy.

*   *   *

Alvarez dialled Palma. The lady with a plum voice said: 'This is Superior Chief Salas's office.'

'It's Inspector Alvarez. When the superior chief returns, will you tell him . . .'

'Señor Salas has returned from Madrid. I'll put you through.'

'Hang on, there's no need . . .' He was ignored. He cursed himself for not having phoned before merienda, when he would have managed to miss his superior.

'Yes, what is it?' said Salas curtly.

'Señor, I have to report that an Englishman, Señor Burnett, committed suicide either late last night or early this morning by shooting himself in the head.'

'You are sure that he's dead?'

'Of course I am ...'

'Don't you give me any "of course". When you report that a man is dead, I expect him to turn up very much alive within the week.'

'The doctor has examined his body.'

'Then provided he's considerably more competent than you, that should at least confirm that someone's dead. How d'you know he's Señor Burnett?'

'His sister identified him, as did a local farmer.'

'How d'you know it's suicide?'

'The evidence all supports that.'

'The evidence, or your interpretation of it?'

'There is a suicide note.'

There was a long pause. Finally, Salas said: 'Then it seems that for once I can accept a report of yours as accurate.'

CHAPTER SEVEN

Alvarez stared up at the ceiling of his bedroom. There were, he thought, in every day two moments which epitomized pleasure and pain;

65

when one closed one's eyes at the beginning of a siesta and when one opened them at the conclusion.

He sat upright and swivelled round on the bed until he could put his bare feet on the tiled floor. He looked at his watch. It was nearly five o'clock and he'd slept longer than he'd intended, but that surely meant that he'd needed the sleep even more than he'd realized?

He dressed in short-sleeved, open-neck shirt and cotton trousers, eased his feet into sandals. The window was wide open with the shutters shut, but even so the room was like an oven. Not the weather for rushing.

Downstairs, Isabel and Juan were watching television and Dolores was in the kitchen, beginning to prepare the supper. He slumped down on the stool. 'My God, it's so hot it's difficult to move!'

'Unless you're a woman who has to slave in a kitchen because her men can think only of their stomachs.'

These days, she was always complaining. Perhaps it was because of her age; there was a time of life when every woman became even more illogical than usual. Or perhaps it was the pernicious influence of all that nonsense about women needing their own identities. Jaime should long ago have taught her that it was a woman's privilege, not her penance, to look after her menfolk, but he was too scared of arousing her wrath . . .

'Well?' she demanded. 'You feel like telling me something?'

He hastily shook his head.

She turned back to the stove and stirred the diced onion, just beginning to hiss, in a saucepan. 'Aren't you working this afternoon?'

'Yes, of course. I've a lot to do.'

'Then why aren't you out, doing it?'

'I thought . . . I was hoping you would be very kind and make me some coffee before I leave.'

'Men! As polite as debtors when they want something!'

Twenty minutes later he drove to La Huerta and Ca'n Pario, which proved to be roughly half a kilometre down from Ca Na Torrina. He parked by the side of a large estanque set back from the lane, and walked up a rough dirt track to a small caseta, the kind of place in which the poorer peasants, farming on a share-cropping basis, had once lived.

He knocked on the front door of the single floor, drystone building, turned and looked out across the land. The garden was a profusion of plants and shrubs, at times inextricably mixed, many of which were in flower; the kind of garden of which he approved—that was, if land had to be wasted—since it was sufficiently haphazard in form to suit the setting. Beyond was a large field in which, under regularly spaced orange, lemon, and loquat trees, were being grown beans, tomatoes, sweet peppers, aubergines, melons, and late potatoes.

The door opened and he turned back. The moment he saw the señorita, he remembered her. Some nine months previously he had been investigating the theft of a bicycle and in the course of those investigations had questioned a boy. The señorita had appeared and told him, in no uncertain manner, that he was an idiot if he thought that the boy could have anything to do with a missing bike since he was the son of a friend of hers. Overwhelmed by the vehemence of her illogical argument, he had accepted the boy's innocence, gratified to find a foreigner who concerned herself so sympathetically (if aggressively) with the islanders. His sense of gratitude had in no way been diminished when, later, he'd discovered that the boy had in fact taken the bike. 'Señorita,' he said in English, 'I am Inspector Alvarez of the Cuerpo, General de Policia.'

She replied in Spanish. 'Please come in.'

To his initial surprise, she was not wearing black but a cotton frock in quite bright colours. But any suggestion that such lack of mourning denoted lack of suffering was negated by the expression on her heavily featured face. He stepped into the house, noticeably cool because of the thick walls. 'Señorita, I am very distressed by what has happened. Please believe

68

me that I would not be troubling you if it were not absolutely necessary.'

'It may be better to have someone to talk to,' she said wearily.

He wanted to ask if she did not have friends to whom she could turn in this time of grief, but knew that the question might well be resented. Foreigners, and especially the British, did not always wish to share their grief, unlike the Mallorquins.

The living-room had uneven stone walls which year after year had been painted white with cal so that now this was over a centimetre thick, and a sloping roof with exposed timber beams. Small initially, it had been made smaller by the bookshelves and free-standing bookcases filled with a few hardcover, but mainly softcover books. Set in front of the open fireplace were two well worn chairs; the seat of one had on it a pile of books and she picked these up. 'You can sit here, now. Books are my one luxury.' She put the books down on the floor, sat on the second chair. 'My parents taught us ...' She stopped, nibbled her upper lip above which there grew a vestigial moustache. 'They taught us to love books. I remember how, when every penny became important, I still would buy ... But you haven't come to hear an old woman rambling on about the past.'

'Señorita, I have come to try and understand

the tragedy and therefore I must learn as much as is possible.' If she talked at length, he thought, she might be able to ease a little of her sorrow.

'I imagine you drink?' she asked abruptly.

'Yes, señorita.'

'Would you be shocked if I offered you a drink this early in the evening?'

'Why should I be?'

'Of course you wouldn't. I'm not thinking straight. The Mallorquins are far too sensible ever to suffer the British hypocrisy of calling for the sun to be over the yardarm before drinks are served. You're a straightforward people and I'm sure that that's because until recently you've all been close to the things in life which really matter. Your tragedy is that in the past twenty years, you've been pitchforked into the consumer society and now the young think that a new car is more important than a new plough.'

He further warmed towards a foreigner who recognized that there could be merit in simplicity and stupidity in sophistication.

'I can offer you wine or coñac; which would you like?'

'Coñac, please, with perhaps a little ice?'

She stood, crossed to the doorway on the far side of the room and went through into the kitchen. Behind him was another doorway and that would give access to a single bedroom.

70

Either off the bedroom or the kitchen would be a bathroom—so small it probably could not hold a bath, only a shower. That was the extent of the caseta. There was another link here with his early life. He had been born in a place no larger than this and he, his brother and his sister, had slept in the same room as their parents. They had learned much at an early age . . .

She returned and handed him a tumbler which was half filled with brandy in which floated three ice cubes. As soon as she was seated, he said: 'You were beginning to tell me how your parents had taught you to like books, señorita.'

She stared into the past; a shaft of sunshine, coming through the single, high-up window, provided a sharp backcloth to her profile emphasizing both strength and stubborness. 'I was the elder and right from the beginning Mother used to read to me; later, of course, it was to both of us. She said that if one loved books one could be poor but travel the world, be a nobody who met the famous, be alone and yet surrounded by friends. I suppose I didn't understand the truth of that until Father lost all his money and we were left with little but books.' She drank. 'Justin could never gain as much pleasure from them as I did and I've always thought that that was because Father was old-fashioned enough to believe that

71

reading should always improve one's mind and therefore to read solely for pleasure was not only a waste of time, but also rather sinful. So while I was left to read what I wanted, be it Jane Austin or Margery Allingham—I was only a woman, so Father didn't bother about the state of my education—Justin was instructed in what was permissible and what was not. He loved Henty and Ballantyne, but had to conceal the fact that he even knew the names ... When he came here to live, he brought out Father's library, but I am certain he never opened any of the books. He felt he had to honour his father's memory by maintaining the library, yet at the same time could now prove his independence by not reading a book from it. Without ever realizing it, parents weave tight nets for their children, and the more certain the parents are that what they're doing is right, the more dangerous and damaging the nets become.' She drained her glass. 'I've always been grateful that I've never had the impossibly difficult task of bringing up a child.'

He wondered how truthful she was being. The old were adept a suborning wishes to results. Why hadn't she married? When young, she must have been good company, even if no beauty. Intelligent men were as attracted by character as by looks. Had there been a romance which had ended in tragedy? As his had, when Juana-María had been pinned against the wall by a drunken French driver . . .

'Father was old-fashioned over more than books. He believed that stern discipline put backbone into a boy. Mother tried to make him understand that Justin needed to be treated sympathetically, but he wouldn't listen. For him, Justin's habits and ways of thought marked him as "soft" and a "soft" man was a weak one. Of course, all this made Justin very resentful. In fact, when we learned Father had lost his money, Justin was frightened, naturally, but he was also . . . well, just a little glad, despite the bleak future, because it showed that Father was far from the perfect man he seemed—to Justin, at least—to set himself up as . . .' She stopped, was silent for a moment, then said as she stood: 'You'll have another?'

'Thank you.' He handed her his glass.

She went through to the kitchen, returned, handed him back his glass, sat. 'You have to remember that Justin had a very uncertain younger life. If one's had security and this is suddenly snatched away so that one has to learn how harsh the world can be, one's bound to be bewildered and resentful.'

Security had vanished for her as well, he thought, but she had overcome the loss, and, rather than being weakened by the experience, had been strengthened by it. 'Was he ever married?'

'Before my father died, more to get away

from home than any other reason. She was a pleasant creature but with a very limited and conventional mind. Always worrying about what other people thought.'

Which, surely, the señorita never did. 'Were they divorced?'

'No. She died after he retired.'

'Looked at broadly, would you say it was a successful marriage?'

'They were too far apart, emotionally and intellectually, for that. She couldn't take the slightest interest in his job and attacked him because his income was relatively low and wouldn't begin to understand that to him, far more important than money was the fact that he had a chance to prove himself a man of consequence.' There was pride in her voice as she continued: 'He'd always had a very strong interest in the arts and for quite a time he worked in eighteenth-century paintings. Then he made a complete switch—the only time he did anything so revolutionary—to the Greco-Roman periods. When he retired, he was curator of the Greek and Roman department of the Northern Museum and an acknowledged expert on some matters. Sotheby's sometimes consulted him. He wrote a book on Roman armour that one critic called definitive. Yet all his wife could do was complain that this book didn't sell tens of thousands of copies like the latest romantic mush did. She wanted to buy new curtains, because their neighbours had just hung new ones, and his book didn't make enough money for that.'

'Did he come to live here soon after she died?'

'It was quite a while later. You see, he was not a man who normally would ever take a risk unless it seemed he had to. After she died, he was obviously lonely and I wrote and suggested he came out here because most people are prepared to be so much more friendly; but he wouldn't.'

'He didn't have many friends?'

'The marriage had made certain of that. He liked intelligent people, she didn't, so while she was alive she made his friends unwelcome and naturally they stopped visiting. After she died, he didn't want to keep up with her friends and since he was no longer meeting people at work, there was no one left.'

'What changed his mind about coming here?'

'He had a very nasty car crash and was badly injured. I went home to help after he left hospital and when I saw how very depressed he'd become, I bullied him into selling up and moving out.'

'Did he enjoy living here?'

'At first, yes, he did. Because we're a small expatriate community, differences in backgrounds often don't seem to matter so much. He saw a lot of people, some of whom were of a similar intellectual background. But then the after-effects of the crash began to trouble him and he withdrew into himself and stopped seeing many of the people . . .' She sighed. 'To be honest, he let the problems overwhelm him rather than fight back.'

'What were these after-effects?'

'Mainly headaches of increasing frequency and intensity. A couple of months ago he returned to England and saw the specialist who'd operated on him, but that didn't help.'

'Señorita, when you so tragically discovered him, did you notice the gun on the floor?'

'Yes,' she answered harshly.

'Did you recognize it?'

'Father had owned it. When he died, Justin kept it and brought it out here. I said that this was ridiculous and to get rid of it, no one needed that kind of thing out here, but he wouldn't.'

A revolver, Alvarez thought, often offered a suggestion of strength to a man who knew himself to be weak. 'From all you've told me, señorita, your brother was neither a fit nor a happy man. Sadly, it cannot be too much of a surprise that he chose to kill himself.'

'Justin wasn't a fighter.' Her voice was strained. 'But our family was a religious one and he never lost his faith. He couldn't have committed suicide. He must have been murdered.'

76

CHAPTER EIGHT

They stood in the dining-room of Ca Na Torrina. The body had gone, but nothing else was missing. Alvarez hoped that she did not realize the significance of the stains on the tiled floor. 'Señorita, pain can be so severe that it alters a person's character, especially ... well, especially if that person is not of a very strong nature. Is it not possible that the headaches the señor had been suffering had become so frequent and so severe that he decided he must find a release from them, despite the abhorrence of suicide that his religious upbringing had instilled in him?'

'No,' she answered flatly. 'Perhaps you're forgetting that it's a Christian duty to suffer, if called upon to do so.'

Could one ever be quite certain about how another person under extreme pressure would behave? he wondered. 'There is a suicide note. Perhaps you did not notice it?'

'No, I didn't. I ... When I saw him ...'

'Señorita, there is absolutely no need to explain.' He crossed to the typewriter, unwound the sheet of paper, handed it to her. He waited until she'd read it, then said: 'That makes it clear that he intended to take his own life.'

'It does nothing of the sort. On the contrary, it makes it clear that he did not.'

'I don't understand.'

'Justin was always very precise with words and never wrote in a mandarin style; if he'd written a suicide note, it would have been precise and immediately understandable. This was written by someone who thought that, being an academic by nature, Justin would have written it in what the writer regarded as an academic style.'

'You don't think that under such severe mental confusion, he might not have acted as he normally would?'

'This was written by someone else. It doesn't even make sense.'

'Do you understand the last sentence?'

She looked down at the paper again. 'If I remember correctly, it's the epitaph inscribed on Sir Christopher Wren's tomb in St Paul's Cathedral. It means: If you seek his monument, look around you. But in the original, of course, there is no mention of Paris.'

'Did your brother visit Paris very often?'

'Never, as far as I know. His wife would never have allowed him to go to a city of sin. She thought in clichés, most of them completely outdated.'

'Then why should there be this mention of Paris?'

'For the simple reason that it's nonsense.

78

Traditionally, suicides are not of sound mind. So whoever typed out the bogus note tried to give the impression of a man of learning whose mind was unsound.'

He took the paper back from her, but instead of placing it on the typewriter, he folded it up and put it in his pocket.

'You don't believe me, do you?' she demanded.

'Señorita, I am certain that you are saying exactly what you believe to be true. But at such a time of great emotional stress...'

'I've been terribly shocked, but I'm not a hysterical female who can't face facts. Justin would never have committed suicide. Even if he had, he would have explained why sensibly, instead of writing nonsense in a ridiculous style. But if you won't accept what I've told you, answer this: why is there a bottle of whisky on the table?'

'Forgive me, but all you have told me suggests that your brother was not a man of natural courage and perhaps he needed to drink to try to find some.'

'He never drank whisky.'

'Are you certain?'

She answered sharply: 'Of course I am. He actively disliked it. He drank brandy, gin, and vodka, but never whisky. He only kept it in the house for guests.'

'Perhaps there was no brandy, gin, or vodka

available, nevertheless he had to have a drink?'

She walked over to the far end of the dining-room and to a large Mallorquin sideboard, extensively carved in a traditional pattern. She opened the right-hand door, motioned with her hand.

He moved forward until he could see inside. He counted three bottles of brandy, one opened, two of gin, one opened, and two of vodka, both unopened. He said, his voice troubled: 'Perhaps he did not realize, because of the state of his mind, that he had taken out a bottle of whisky rather than cogñac...'

'Fiddlesticks!'

'Señorita, if one approaches all the questions you've raised from a different viewpoint, then...'

'Approach them from this one. Who was it who'd been arguing so violently with him in the morning?'

'How do you know someone had?'

'I walked up here to see him and heard the argument going on. The other man was so heated, I was a little scared, but I didn't do anything because Justin always became so annoyed if he thought I was trying to ... well, to support him.'

The weak man, needing assistance but resenting any offer of it because not only did that underline his own weakness, it also identified the other person's awareness of it.

'Did you recognize the voice?'

'No.'

'Have you any idea what the argument was about?'

'None whatsoever. I didn't stay in case Justin saw me.'

'At what time was this?'

'Around eleven.'

He rubbed his chin, which reminded him that he'd forgotten to shave that morning. 'Did you return and see your brother later on?'

'No. I phoned to make certain he was all right.'

'And was he?'

'So he said.'

'Did you ask him what had been the trouble?'

'No. Don't you see, I didn't want to seem to be prying and he'd have brought up the subject if he'd wanted me to know.'

'Were you able to make any judgement on his state of mind? Was he very depressed?'

'He sounded more cheerful than for a long time.'

'Señorita, what I must do now is to think about what you've just told me and then make the further investigations which will be necessary.'

'Remember the most important thing of all. Because of his beliefs, he could not have committed suicide.'

'I will not forget . . . If I discover that you are

81

right, can you suggest what motive there might be for your brother's murder?'

'No.'

'He was not a rich man?'

'Far from it.'

'Has he recently been very friendly with a lady?'

'No. There really is nothing more I can tell you.'

'Then you will want to leave. It has been very kind of you to help.'

They left the sitting-room, crossed the entrance and went outside. The late sunshine highlighted the lines of sorrow in her face and he would have liked to comfort her, but found he lacked the words. In any case, he decided, she was of so independent a character that perhaps she would resent, rather than find comfort from, the solace of a foreign stranger.

When he returned to the dining-room, he stared at the bottle of whisky. How far did he accept her contention that no matter how desperate the turmoil in Burnett's mind, he would never have drunk whisky? ... Whisky was such a universally liked drink that nothing would seem more natural to a murderer trying to suggest suicide after a bout of heavy drinking than to put a bottle on the table, little knowing that the dead man was one of the few who disliked it ... He walked round the table and examined the wall, near the framed photograph of the blindly ugly stone head, where the bullet had struck. Nothing to say whether this had been fired to test that gun and ammunition were in working order, or a shot fired involuntarily during a struggle to gain possession of the revolver . . .

He shook his head. This had to be suicide and the señorita's wild assertions were those of a sister who could not, would not, accept that her brother had been as much a weakling at his death as during his life.

He left the house, locked the front door and pocketed the key. As he walked towards the small wooden gate, he heard a man singing, the song filled with the wailing intonations which dated it back to the time of the Moors. He turned away from the gate and pushed through the overgrown garden to the boundary fence. In the field beyond, Goñi was irrigating several rows of tomatoes.

He climbed over the fence and walked up between rows of beans and sweet peppers to where Goñi was working. 'Have you got a moment?'

Goñi might not have heard. He stared down at the rushing water in the main channel, fed from a large estanque in one corner of the field, mattock held ready; when one side channel was filled, he stopped that off with the plug of earth taken from the next one, which now rapidly began to fill.

'Were you working here yesterday morning?'

Goñi looked up very briefly, his weatherbeaten face expressing contempt. 'D'you think I was down in the port, boozing my legs silly?'

'You've other fields; you might have been in one of them.'

'Well, I weren't.' He diverted the water to a fresh channel.

'Then did you hear anything unusual?'

'What d'you mean?'

Alvarez accepted that Goñi wasn't necessarily being bloody-minded; like most peasants, his life was lived in literal terms and therefore he liked things to be spelled out exactly, leaving no room for ambiguity.

Goñi opened up the last channel which fed tomatoes, hurried back along the main channel to the estanque where he turned off the large gate valve, cutting the rush of water. He stood on a rock to peer into the estanque.

'How's the water holding out for you?'

'There ain't enough,' he answered automatically. The estanque was fed by the aqueduct that came down from spring in the Festna valley which, despite the growing shortage of water on the island, still flowed freely; but only a fool risked the gods' jeering wrath by boasting all was well.

Alvarez brought out a pack of cigarettes from his pocket. 'Smoke?'

'Giving something away! What are you after?'

'Information about yesterday morning.'

The sun dropped behind a mountain crest and abruptly they were in shadow; directly overhead, the sky became shaded with the mauve tinge that was seen only in midsummer; small birds began to sing, active once more now that the intense heat was easing. Alvarez struck a match and they lit their cigarettes. As frequently happened, the light breeze earlier had died right away and the air was so calm that the smoke rose vertically for quite a while before lazily beginning to shred.

Alvarez leaned against the side of the estanque. 'When did you have your merienda yesterday morning?'

'Same time as always.'

'Which is when?'

'When I want it.'

'Do you reckon you wanted it before eleven?'

Goñi thought, finally decided he could admit as much. 'Aye.'

'When you were back at work, did you hear anything unusual from that direction?' Alvarez jerked his thumb in the direction of Ca Na Torrina, hidden from them by the estanque.

Goñi hawked, spat. He smoked. Finally, he said: 'There was shouting. Is that what you're on about?'

'Who was shouting?'

'How should I know?'

'If it was the señor, you'd surely know?'

'Well, it wasn't.'

'Then who was it?'

'Ain't I just said? I don't know.'

'How many people were at it?'

'I only heard the one.'

'What kind of shouting was it?'

'Bloody loud.'

'D'you think it was an argument?'

'It wasn't someone being friendly, that's for sure.'

'This man was angry?'

'Sounded like he was bloody crazy.'

'What language was he shouting in?'

'Wasn't Mallorquin or Spanish.'

'English?'

After a while, Goñi said it might have been English.

'How long did the argument go on for?'

A shrug of the shoulders.

'Was it a long or a short time?'

'Time enough for me to go off and harness up the old mule and be back and him to be at it still.'

'Did you catch sight of whoever was doing the arguing?'

'Too busy working.'

'Is there anything about him you can tell me?'

'Only that he'd a bloody big red Mercedes that was in the sitjola.'

'The what?'

'The bit of land opposite the house that's not good for anything, of course.'

'Of course. How can you be certain it was his car?'

'Who else is going to park there?'

Alvarez drew on the cigarette a last time, dropped the butt to the ground and carefully ground it into the dust with the heel of his shoe. 'Did you see the señor after all this?'

'Saw him not long after the car drove off.'

'How did he seem?'

'Looked like . . .' Goñi scratched his head.

'Like he was really upset?'

'Like he was kind of . . . Well, something good had happened.'

It was difficult to decide what Goñi really meant. A man who had just had a very bitter row and who, within roughly thirteen hours, was going to commit suicide, was hardly likely to be in a laughing mood. No, the expression had been false or Goñi had falsely interpreted it. 'This Mercedes you saw in the sitjola—have you any idea who it belongs to?'

'Never seen it before.'

'You say it was big and red—anything more you can tell me about it?'

'Only that it had dark windows.'

How accurate was the marque identification? Goñi, like most men of his generation, had never owned or driven a car and it might be

87

supposed that he'd have very little interest in them and therefore would be unlikely to be able accurately to identify a make. But of all the consumer goods which had corrupted values, television and cars were the two which were the most popular and they had aroused the sharp interest of even the oldest and most reactionary of peasants.

Goñi looked up at the sky. 'I'd best be moving.'

'Just wait a second. Did you see the señorita yesterday morning?'

'Aye. When she had something to say about a wall at the end of her garden. By God, she's a tough 'un!' He spoke admiringly.

'Was this before you heard the row in Ca Na Torrina?'

'While it was going on. She walks up the road, listens for a moment, turns back.'

'I'd like to know who was around late last night, but I don't expect you were?'

'I was in bed and asleep, where anyone with any bloody sense was.' He stomped off, then came to a stop just before he reached a turn in the dirt track. 'Oi!'

'Yes?'

'I've just remembered. The Mercedes was on tourist plates.' He continued on his way.

If the bitter row had had anything to do with Burnett's death, it probably was that it had further depressed him and edged him that

88

much closer to committing suicide (the expression Goñi had noted might well, in fact, have been one of exhausted relief; the final decision had been made). But because the señorita was a woman of such determination, she was going to say that it had led up to her brother's death, almost certainly at the hands of the unknown man who had had that blazing row. Alvarez sighed. It seemed there was no longer any option left to him. Very soon, he was going to have to report to Salas.

CHAPTER NINE

Alvarez replaced the receiver, slumped back in the chair and stared at the top of his desk without seeing the jumble of papers, files, memoranda and letters that lay strewn all over it. He had spoken to an assistant at the Institute of Forensic Anatomy and asked him to check specifically whether the wound in Burnett's head had been self-inflicted and whether on his hand there were powder residues to prove he had fired a gun. He had also spoken to the fingerprint department and asked them to check the revolver for prints and had accepted, without voicing any resentment, the jeering comment that because of the shape of any revolver, it seldom recorded a print of consequence, and that one with a chequered handgrip was even less likely to do so. Soon, he would go back to Ca Na Torrina, put a fresh piece of paper in the typewriter, and type out the suicide note in order to confirm, by a comparison test, that the original had been typed on the machine on the dining-room table ... All work carried out because when he telephoned his superior chief and informed him of the latest development, Salas would, in his normal discourteous and aggressive manner, demand to know if the investigations were being carried out efficiently.

He looked up and through the opened window which, since the sun was not yet on it, he had left unshuttered. Before he rang Salas, it would undoubtedly be an idea to slip out to the club and have a coffee and a brandy; after all, any sensible bullfighter prayed long and earnestly before he went into the ring.

He stood, crossed to the door, then came to a sudden stop as he realized that he had not yet phoned Traffic and asked them to identify all red Mercedes on tourist plates. If he'd spoken to Salas before doing that...

★　　　★　　　★

Alvarez said: 'Señor, there can be no doubt. But when the señorita made this claim, I decided I had to undertake a full investigation.'

90

'In other words, unbelievably you've managed to complicate even a simple suicide!'

'Not I, the señorita. As you so rightly say, señor, it is a simple suicide. But the señorita is English...'

'This has nothing to do with nationalities; it has everything to do with your inability to deal with any matter in a sane and sensible manner. Had you been in charge of the case, we still wouldn't know who murdered Abel.'

'But when the señorita said...'

'Elderly foreign señoritas say and do the most ridiculous things; I expect my inspectors to recognize that fact. Which, of course, is a mistake since it is necessary to remember that among my inspectors is one who is incapable of distinguishing between what is and what is not ridiculous.'

'Do you wish me to close the case?'

'How in the devil can you do that when you've allowed her to make this ridiculous allegation?'

'Where the señorita's concerned, it's more a case of what she...'

'I doubt it's even crossed your mind to ask for a test for powder residues?'

'I have arranged that.'

'What about the gun?'

'That is with the prints department.'

'And the typewritten suicide note?'

'That, together with a comparison note typed

on the machine in question, is being forwarded to the laboratory.'

'And the car?'

'Traffic have been asked to prepare a list of all red Mercedes on tourist plates.'

'The bottle of whisky and glass?'

Alvarez silently swore. How could he have forgotten them?

Salas allowed the silence to continue for some time, then said: 'Even allowing for so many unfortunate occurrences in the past, I am still surprised that you could fail to see the need to have both bottle and glass tested for prints.'

'Señor, I was intending...'

'Your convoluted road to hell must be luxuriously paved with good intentions ... Should there be prints on either, these will need to be compared with the dead man's prints.'

'Naturally, I will see...'

'And should there be some which are not the dead man's, perhaps it will be best if you get in touch with me so that I can try to explain the full significance of this.'

'I do understand...'

'An assumption I would prefer never to make.'

*　　*　　*

Alvarez parked in the sitjola for the second time that morning, crossed the road, unlocked the front door of Ca Na Torrina and went inside. There was a flash of movement on the right-hand wall of the entrada as a gecko made a lunge for, and caught, a small moth. Then it 'froze', no doubt hoping that it would be ignored by the intruder.

He went through to the dining-room and packed the bottle of whisky and glass in cardboard containers, using bubbled plastic to make certain that they were held tightly in place. Burnett's prints would be on both, he assured himself as he left. Stress could alter a person's behaviour out of all recognition; it might easily have left Burnett quite unaware of what he was drinking.

He followed a large Volvo shooting-brake down the narrow, twisting lane, then drew off into the parking space in front of the estanque by Ca'n Pario. As he opened the gate and stepped through, it occurred to him that the difference between this garden and that of Ca Na Torrina was not a bad indication of the difference between the characters of sister and brother.

Phillipa, wearing a shapeless hat with a wide, floppy brim, a brightly coloured frock, and flip-flops, was sitting in the shade of a tree. She had been reading and as he approached she carefully inserted a leather marker, closed the book.

'Señorita, I hope I do not disturb you?'

'I'm always glad of company. Do sit down.'
She waited until he was seated, then said: 'As a
matter of fact, I was going to telephone you. I
want to know when I can go ahead and arrange
the funeral.'

He said, very sympathetically: 'Señorita, I am
very much afraid that for the moment it is
impossible to answer you. Certain inquiries
have to be concluded.'

'You mean, there has to be a post-mortem?'

He might have known that she would want to
face the facts. 'Yes, señorita.'

'Then you now believe that Justin did not
commit suicide?'

'The post-mortem is required because of the
nature of his death, whatever the possible
cause.'

She fidgeted with the cover of the paperback.
'The cause is, he was murdered.'

'The facts have yet to be established and I
have asked for certain tests to be conducted.
Nothing more can be said until the results of
these are known.'

'You sound as if you still think it was
suicide?'

'I'm afraid I do.'

'That is quite impossible.'

He decided it was no good arguing. She
would remain convinced that her brother's
death had not been suicide because she was so
loath to face the truth of his ultimate weakness

94

until it finally became impossible not to do so.

'I presume you're here because there's something more you want to know?'

'Yes, señorita.'

'Well, before I tell you anything, I need a drink and I don't suppose you'll refuse one. Will you have coñac?'

'Thank you very much.'

He watched her stand, go into the house. Indomitable was the word which occurred to him. Naturally still deeply shocked, yet determined not to show such 'weakness'. The famed stiff upper lip. But would she not have found it easier to come to terms with events had she been able to give way to her grief?

She returned, handed him a tumbler that was three parts full of brandy and ice, sat. 'What do you want to know now?'

'When you walked up to your brother's house on Monday morning, did you happen to notice if there was a car parked in the sitjola opposite?'

'There was one, yes.'

'Did you recognize it?'

'No, I didn't go far enough up the road to see more than the top half of it above the stone wall.'

'Have you the slightest idea what was the subject of the violent row?'

'As I think I said before, none whatsoever.'

'Your brother hadn't mentioned to you anything which had happened or had been said

95

by or to him which conceivably could have led to so fierce an argument?'

'In the past few months he's seen hardly anyone except a couple of close friends and it's impossible it could have been anything to do with either of them.'

'Do you know of anyone who actively disliked him?'

'An expatriate community like this one always has its quota of backbiting scandal-mongers and suddenly disintegrating friendships. But Justin ... Well, he was the kind of person who didn't arouse sharp emotions in other people.'

Yet it seemed he had aroused a very violent rage in someone. 'You told me he wasn't wealthy, but would you say he was comfortably off?'

'That all depends on your terms of reference, doesn't it? Compared to some of the people out here, he was a pauper; compared to me, he was comfortably off.'

'Would you know what happens to his estate?'

'I have a copy of his will, he had a copy of mine. I am his sole beneficiary.'

'Do you have a rough idea of how much his estate will amount to?'

'By today's standards, very little. When he lived in England, his only capital was his house, his only income the museum pension and the old age pension. He decided, wisely, not to use the money he gained from selling his house to buy another one out here, but to buy himself an annuity which would greatly increase his income. He spoke to a broker and asked what would be the best kind of annuity which would . . .' She became silent.

He waited patiently.

'Even though I often bullied him for his own good, he was always very fond of me. He knew how hard up I was because of the frightening rise in the cost of living out here, and that while he could help me financially—as he did—while he was alive, if he died before I did and all his capital had been invested in an annuity, he'd not be able to leave me anything. So he told the broker that as well as the annuity, he wanted to take out some form of life insurance that would ensure that if he died within ten years—which he reckoned would see me out; I hope he was right—I would benefit by inheriting a capital sum. Because of his age, the insurance was very expensive, but he didn't mind because he was making as certain as he could that I'd be all right.'

'Did he tell you how much the insurance was for?'

'Twenty thousand pounds. I suppose that gives me a motive?'

'A motive?' he repeated, his mind not on his words.

'For having killed him.'

He was startled. 'Señorita! Not for one second could such a possibility be considered.'

'It's not unknown for siblings to murder.'

'Had you committed so unthinkable an act, would you have insisted—as you have done right from the beginning—that it had to be murder and not suicide? Would you not have done everything possible to make me believe that it was suicide? No, señorita, if your brother was murdered, the one person who could not be the murderer would be you.'

★   ★   ★

The first telephone call was at ten-fifteen the following morning.

'The deceased died as a result of a single shot fired when the muzzle of the gun was within one centimetre of the temple. The skin surrounding the entrance hole was burned the typical grey-brown colour and there was the expected smeary coat of powder residue. The bullet remained embedded in the back of the skull.

'The site of the wound is such that it could have been either self-inflicted or occasioned by another party.

'The deceased's hands have been tested for powder tattooing. There are traces on both hands.'

'What's that?'

'Both.' There was a pause and then the speaker said, his tone now ironic: 'So what do you make of that?'

Alvarez was about to say that it was impossible when he remembered that two shots had been fired. Even so . . .

'There are areas of bruising on the shoulder, but these are consistent with his having fallen from a chair to the ground. He was in reasonably good physical condition, having regard to his age, except for a past injury to his skull.

'He had ingested a considerable amount of alcohol shortly before his death and the concentration in his blood was around point two per cent. That means he was past the delightful stage, but not yet at the dead drunk one.'

'Can you distinguish whether it was grape or grain alcohol?'

'That problem's with the lab boys and you'll have to get the answer from them.'

Alvarez thanked him, rang off, drummed on the desk with his fingers. He checked in the telephone directory for Phillipa's number, dialled it. 'Señorita, I must apologize for bothering you yet again, but I need to know something. Was your brother right or left-handed?'

'Left-handed. Father tried to make him

99

change, but only succeeded in making him stutter.'

'Could he use his right hand more easily than a right-handed man can usually use his left?'

'He was never able to write right-handed, but there were other things he trained himself to do right-handed because that was easier. Why do you ask?'

'There is something which has to be answered and it matters which hand he favoured.'

When the call was over, he slumped back in the chair. If it had been suicide, then Burnett must have wanted to make certain he did not mistake his aim and would have fired the fatal shot with his left hand. So was it even remotely feasible to imagine that he'd have fired the first, and exploratory, shot at the wall with his right hand? Against his will, Alvarez began to envisage a scene. The man with whom Burnett had had such a bitter row in the morning had returned that night, his anger increased rather than abated. Burnett, frightened, had sought to defend himself with the revolver. There had been a struggle, the intruder had managed to get hold of the gun and had shot Burnett. He had then set out to hide his murder under the guise of suicide. Knowing that when one fired a gun one was normally left with a powder tattoo, he had put the gun in the dead man's hand and manipulated it so that a second shot, aimed at the wall, was fired ... Never stopping to

100

remember what previous observation should have told him: Burnett was left-handed.

CHAPTER TEN

Traffic rang at a quarter to one. 'About your inquiry re red Mercedes on tourist plates. There are seventy-five on the island.'

'Hell! It'll take days to check up on that many,' said Alvarez gloomily.

'Have you any further details that might help to cut down the numbers?'

'Only that the man who saw it made a point of how big it was.'

'Then it could be one of the larger models rather than a 190. Let me check what difference that would make.' There was a long pause. 'That would leave sixteen cars, ranging up to a 560 which by all accounts is big enough for an oil sheik and his four wives.'

'Give me the names and addresses of the sixteen owners, will you?'

When the call was over, Alvarez stared down at the list. It seemed reasonable to suppose the car was owned by someone who lived close to Llueso, simply because most car journeys were short ones. Yet against that, the señorita had not recognized the man's voice and since she probably knew everyone locally who was rich enough to have such a car, this suggested a stranger from another part of the island. What could have brought a stranger to argue so bitterly with a man who had virtually become a recluse? Again, what motive for murder could a stranger have?

It was, he thought sadly, a familiar experience. After much laborious work, both mental and physical, he propounded a sequence of events which logically fitted the facts—only to discover subsequently that logically such a sequence could not have occurred. Chasing around the circumference of a circle to discover where it began . . .

★   ★   ★

Some two kilometres beyond Santa Lucía, Alvarez turned off the tarmac on to a dirt track. As the car bounced on the rough surface, he slowed right down, cursing because a man could not hope to keep his car in pristine condition when travelling so rough a surface. A notice with the name Ca'n Heal, shaped as an arrow, pointed off to the right. Happily, this new track was metalled and he no longer strained his ears to hear a spring snapping, a shock-absorber falling off, or the sump's being ruptured. The track passed through a belt of trees, mostly pine, then straightened to line up on a house. He whistled. This foreigner had bought a piece of Mallorquin history. Not even in his wildest daydreams had he ever imagined himself living in such a mansion; when he'd been young only the aristocracy had owned such properties and even if a frog could turn into a prince, a peasant could never become an aristocrat.

He parked, climbed out of the car. The garden was a banked mass of colour, overwhelming in its extravagance; many of the flowers were familiar, but others he had never seen before; several of the flowering trees were covered in such a profusion of blossom that they looked theatrically unreal; the large lawn, a deep green, had been newly mown. He wondered how much water was needed to keep all these plants, trees, and lawn, alive and flourishing in the height of the summer and could only come up with the answer that it was a prodigal waste of resources that took one's breath away.

He crossed to the wooden front door, panelled in one of the traditional Mallorquin square patterns. Age had cracked yet toughened the wood, repeated applications of gas oil had darkened it, and the sun had baked it. For centuries, that door had closed off the harsh outside world from the few inside who believed the luxury of a pleasant, refined life to be no more than a right...

The door was opened by a young woman,

wearing a white apron over a blue frock, whose manner was as pert as the expression in her eyes. 'Is Señor Heal in?' he asked.

'No, he's not.' She showed him no respect, having judged him by his appearance.

'When do you expect him back?'

'What's that to you?'

'Cuerpo General de Policía.'

She was not now frightened, as anyone might have been twenty years before, but she had become wary. 'Well, I'm sorry, but I just don't know when he'll return, except it'll likely be before eight since he told Carolina he'd be eating here tonight.'

'Is Señora Heal in?'

'There's no señora; leastways, not one that lives here. Not yet.' She giggled.

'Is there any other family?'

'The señorita, his daughter, was here earlier, wanting to talk to him; I don't rightly know whether she's still around.'

'Perhaps you'd find out? I'd like a word with her if she is here.'

'You'd best come in, then.'

He was shown into a very large room; once the ballroom? he wondered, uncertain whether a manor house would have had one. It was filled with furniture, hangings, carpets, display cabinets, and paintings, all of which to his uneducated eye looked valuable. It was, he decided, a room to make a man very careful not to belch aloud.

The far door opened and a young woman entered. 'Good afternoon. I understand you are . . .' She searched for the word in Spanish.

'Inspector Alvarez, señorita,' he replied in English. He preferred women to be dressed smartly, but had to admit to himself that she lost nothing through wearing a loose-fitting linen shirt and faded jeans. Perhaps that was because she was beautiful in a way that owed nothing to glamour and everything to character. Both the maid's attractions and hers were obvious, but the maid's raised images of lust while hers called forth only honourable thoughts . . .

'Is there some way in which I can help you, even though Father's out?'

He jerked his mind down from the heady heights of knightly chivalry. 'I would like to ask the señor a few questions concerning his car, but the maid said he's out. Perhaps you could answer them?'

'I doubt it. I don't live here and I only came along to . . . Well, like you, I wanted a word and didn't know he was out.'

There was, briefly, a note of bitterness in her voice. An unhappy relationship between father and daughter? 'Señorita, it may be possible that nevertheless you can help me. The señor owns a red Mercedes on tourist plates. Does it have darkened glass?'

She frowned slightly. 'Why d'you want to know?'

'I need to identify the owner of one such Mercedes because he may be able to help me.'

'Help you in what way?'

'With an inquiry I am conducting.'

'I can tell you for certain that Gerry's not been involved in any road accident.'

'There is no suggestion of that.'

'Then why . . .' She did not finish the question. After a moment, she said: 'I can't see that it's a state secret. Yes, his Merc does have tinted glass.'

'Since he lives reasonably close to Llueso, I imagine he drives there or to the port quite frequently?'

'That sounds reasonable.'

'And he'll know a number of other foreigners who live there?'

'Look, you'd better be a bit more specific about why you're asking these questions.'

'There has been an unfortunate incident in Llueso. Señor Burnett has died in unusual circumstances. Now, it is necessary for me to find out exactly what happened and the owner of a large red Mercedes on tourist plates, with tinted windows, may be able to help me. If it was the señor's car in Llueso on Monday morning, he almost certainly will be able to.'

'I can give you the answer now, it won't be his. He was here all morning.'

106

'I see . . . Still, it'll be best if I just ask him to confirm that. I will return here tomorrow morning at about eleven. But if that's not convenient, will you ask him to telephone me to say what time will suit him?'

She nodded.

'Perhaps you could give me some paper and a pencil so that I can write down the telephone number?'

She walked over to the nearer door. She moved with the unconscious grace of a fawn; beneath those casual clothes there must be slender limbs of ivory . . . He cursed himself for such crude, sensual thoughts. Put a swine in a castle, he still had swinish thoughts.

When she returned, she handed him a small pad and a ballpoint pen. He wrote down the telephone number of the post and his name, handed back pad and pen.

'I still don't understand . . .' She tailed off into silence. 'All right, I'll tell him or else leave a message.'

He said goodbye and left, making his way back into the huge entrance hall and out to his car.

CHAPTER ELEVEN

Alvarez parked in front of Ca'n Heal and climbed out into the burning sunshine. In a bed beyond the lawn, a man was tying tall-stemmed flowers to bamboo stakes. Even in the heyday of the aristocrats, he thought, no labourer had ever been employed solely to grow and tend unproductive things; they might have lived in luxury while all those about them were in abject poverty, but they'd never lacked a sense of values.

He crossed to the front door and rang the bell. A middle-aged woman opened the door and he introduced himself.

'I'm sorry, but the señor's not here,' she said. 'He had a telephone call and had to go out suddenly. He said he'll be back as soon as possible and would you mind waiting?'

It was far more pleasant here than in his stuffy office. She showed him into a much smaller room than he had been in the previous day, furnished in a less overpowering manner.

'Would you like a coffee; or something stronger?' She was dumpy and wore glasses that gave her an owl-like appearance; but she had a quick and ready smile. She spoke Mallorquin with the harsher accent of the west coast.

'I'd not say no to a coñac.'

She brought him a brandy and when it became clear he would like to talk, she settled in one of the brocade-covered armchairs and accepted a cigarette.

She smoked in a nervous manner, constantly scraping the ash away into an ashtray, as if it were something she did not do very often. 'The señor's all right to work for, just so long as you do exactly what he wants. I said to Frederico, maybe you are right and he's wrong, but don't go on arguing, just do it his way. It's the man who owns the mule who says when it works. But he went on arguing. I've never met a man so stubborn.'

'Who's Frederico?'

'He worked in the garden along with Rafael until Thursday, when he was sacked. I said, the señor's a man who knows exactly what he wants and he's paying to get it. If you can't understand that . . . Frederico couldn't.'

'I met the señor's daughter yesterday.'

'She's nice. Mind you, if she wants something, she can be just as tough as him. But normally she's friendly and has a bit of a chat, which he never does. Wants to keep his distance from the likes of us.'

'What makes you say she can be hard at times?'

'As to that, you've only got to see the look that's sometimes in her eyes or the way she holds her chin. Or are you like my Fernando

who only ever sees one thing in any woman?'
She chuckled. 'But if you'd any doubts, you
ought to have heard 'em last night, having a
tremendous row. I thought to myself: For once,
señor, you're getting as good as you give.'

'What was it all about?'

'Can't say, not speaking much English and in
any case, I only heard 'em from the kitchen
when I went there to get something. You see, I
wasn't cooking a meal because the señor was on
his own and sometimes when that happens he
says he'll just have something cold and I leave it
ready for him.'

'But you said he wasn't on his own, his
daughter was there.'

She shrugged her shoulders. 'I suppose the
señorita turned up unexpectedly. I mean, if
he'd known she was coming to dinner, he'd
certainly have asked for something cooked and
Fernando in his white coat and gloves, serving.
Even when it's his own daughter, the señor
wants things done in the grand manner.'

'You're quite certain it was her?'

'I heard her, didn't I?'

'You said, not very clearly.'

'Fernando saw her car outside.'

'Then there's no doubt . . . Where's she living
now?'

'Used to be in France, with her mother, and
she visited here from time to time, but recently
she's been on the island, living with a painter

over at Costanyi. Maybe that's what they were arguing about. The señor's had more women here than I could count easily, but he doesn't like his daughter acting the same way.'

Her words shocked Alvarez. He had seen Alma in a virginal light and to discover she was living with some painter . . . It was, of course, the destruction of perfection he found so painful, not the fact that she had a boyfriend . . .

'The painter's been here a couple of times; trying to sell his paintings to the señor, like as not.'

He tried to speak normally, but was conscious that his voice had roughened slightly. 'Is he one of the long-haired louts who call themselves artists to avoid working?'

'I wouldn't know about that.'

'From the way the maid spoke when I was last here, it seems the señor's getting married soon?'

'That's right enough what the lady thinks! Looking at her makes me wonder if he really knows what he's letting himself in for.'

'How d'you mean?'

'She's eyes in the back of her head and says exactly what she wants. If he thinks he'll fool her while he carries on with other women, he's got a surprise coming!'

'If that's his idea, why get married?'

'Who knows why anyone marries anyone?' She chuckled. 'When I look at Fernando now, I can't remember why!'

He smiled, although her words made him sadder than before. Perhaps the attraction of maturity was nothing but a fallacy, perpetuated by mature men. 'I suppose the señor entertains a lot?'

'That he does and it's only the best gets served. Like the last dinner, when it was lobster to start with. Imagine what that cost!'

'Not unless you give me a calculator ... Tell me, have you seen an English señor here called Justin Burnett?'

She thought for a moment, shook her head.

'Have you ever taken a telephone call from him?'

'I can't remember doing so. Of course, most times it's Fernando or Carmen, the maid, who answer the phone because I'm busy with the cooking.'

'Would you do me a favour? Go and ask your husband and Carmen whether Señor Burnett ever phoned here.'

She looked curiously at him, then stood, stubbed out her cigarette, left.

He finished the brandy and carefully placed the glass down on the coaster so that it did not mark the highly polished occasional table. If he were living in this house, he'd furnish it very much more simply ... Fool! he told himself scornfully. If he were living in this house, it would only be as one of the servants.

She returned. 'Neither of 'em's ever heard the name. Comes from round here, does he?'

'From Llueso.'

'Then the señor'll probably know him, since he goes there regularly.'

'Was he there Monday morning?'

'Must have been. Always goes then to get the Sunday paper.'

He looked at his watch. 'Won't be long to lunch.'

'I can't think where the señor's got to. He said he'd be back just as soon as he could be.'

'I'll hang on just a little longer.'

'Maybe you'd like another drink while you're waiting?'

'Maybe I would!'

★　　★　　★

The forensic laboratory rang the post as Alvarez was preparing to return home for lunch.

'The alcohol drunk was grape, not grain.'

Alvarez silently cursed his fate which forever seemed intent on wrapping the mantle of disorganization about him. It was murder, not suicide. Burnett had been drinking, but not from the bottle of whisky on the table. So either there had been a bottle of grape alcohol—coñac?—on the table and the whisky had been substituted for it, or there had been nothing because Burnett had had several drinks, but

113

had not left the bottle out, perhaps obsessively tidy even at such a moment. There could be no point in such a substitution, so it was safe to say that there had been no bottle on the table before the whisky had been put there to give the impression of his having drunk to gain sufficient careless courage to blow out his brains; placed by a man who did not know that he disliked whisky or that he was left-handed . . .

* * *

A technician rang soon after Alvarez had returned to the office in the late afternoon.

'We've compared the two examples of typing. The typeface is similar, but two different machines were used. There are enough pertinent characteristics to make that quite certain.'

One more corner of the pattern slotted into place.

* * *

The fingerprint department rang at half past seven.

'There are no dabs on the revolver but then, like I said, there weren't going to be any.'

Experts were always so certain, Alvarez thought. Perhaps that was what made them

114

experts. 'And the bottle and the glass?'

'Both wiped clean.'

'Thanks a lot.'

It was, surely, the clinching proof since it ruled out the possibility—however remote—that before his death Burnett had drunk whisky, perhaps as a gesture of contempt aimed at himself. It was impossible to believe he would have bothered to wipe down glass and bottle before committing suicide.

Obviously, Alvarez decided—trying to find an excuse for not doing so, and failing—he must ring Salas. But before he did, it might be as well to fortify himself. He opened the bottom right-hand drawer of the desk and brought out a bottle of brandy and a glass and poured himself a generous, and hopefully sustaining, drink.

The plum-voiced secretary said that Salas was in his office. It was not, Alvarez decided, his lucky day. 'Señor, Señor Burnett did not commit suicide, he was murdered.'

'Of course.'

'But why do you say that? I mean, I've only just been given the final proof...'

'The moment you assured me that beyond any shadow of a doubt he had committed suicide, I could be certain he had been murdered.'

CHAPTER TWELVE

Alvarez looked at his watch and noted with pleasure that half the morning had passed. He settled back in the chair and stared without curiosity at the morning's mail which he had not yet bothered to open. Dolores was cooking Sopa Mallorquina for lunch. In the hands of a tyro, the vegetable and bread soup could resemble prison gruel, but in the hands of an expert it became a dish fit to be served on Mount Olympus. His sense of contentment blossomed. It was Saturday. Superior Chief Salas was so superior that he seldom worked on a Saturday afternoon and therefore there would be no need to cut short the afternoon's siesta . . .

Reluctantly he brought his thoughts back to the more immediate problem of Burnett's murder. There was really no case against Heal, although he was the only possible suspect at the moment; nothing to prove that the red Mercedes parked in the sitjola had been his, that he had returned late that night, or to suggest a possible motive. Phillipa Burnett had said that she had not recognized the voice of the man who had been arguing so angrily with her brother, but that was before a name could be given to the unseen person. Identification was an odd process and quite often it needed a trigger to set it off; a person's mind would be blank until prompted and then suddenly it became filled with details. Of course, to prompt could be to risk a false identification, but only if a person were easily misled and that did not describe the señorita.

Forty minutes later, he parked outside Ca'n Pario. Phillipa was out on the patio, reading, a glass on the wooden table by her side.

'You must have heard the bar open.'

'Señorita, I assure you I had no idea . . .'

'Of course not. How could you know that an old woman like me frequently risks perdition by drinking on her own? I was only pulling your leg. Sit down and tell me whether you'll change to red wine or stick to coñac?'

She stood, appearing ungraceful because her frock was voluminous and made her look very much larger than she was. She went indoors, returned with a tumbler which she handed him. She sat, suddenly slapped her left wrist with her right hand. 'The mosquitoes are voracious. I told that old fool, Tomás, that he'd lost all the fish in the estanque, but he wouldn't listen and now the mosquitoes are breeding like flies, if that's not rather Irish.'

'They are bad everywhere this year, señorita; even in the village we are plagued by them.'

'Well, you won't have come here to talk about mosquitoes. Has . . . Have you learned anything?'

117

'Perhaps, but I cannot be certain yet, which is why I'm here now to ask you something.'

'What?'

'Are you friendly with Señor Heal?'

'I've met him at parties, but I'd never say I was friendly with him. Frankly, he's the kind of person one has as an acquaintance, an amusing acquaintance, but not as a friend. My father used to say that a gentleman remained a gentleman even though he wore a cloth cap, a cad remained a cad even though he wore a topper.'

'You are saying that the señor is a cad?'

'That is what my father would have dubbed him; amusing, witty, but indisputably a cad. However, many of the other foreigners who live here find him a very nice man. It's all a question of standards.'

'Are yours the same as your father's?'

'I hope so. I believe that a man is who he is, not what he owns.'

'Did your brother know him?'

'Not to my knowledge. Justin, even when at his most gregarious, never liked cocktail parties.'

'He might, of course, have met him somewhere other than at a cocktail party?'

'Possible, but unlikely. Heal is welcomed by people who respect wealth, my brother was welcomed by those who respect honest intelligence. Why is this of any importance?'

118

'I have learned something which makes it likely that it was Señor Heal whom you heard at your brother's house on Monday morning.'

'Impossible.'

'How can you be so certain?'

'Heal's painfully cultured tones are unmistakable.'

'When a person is excited, he can sound different from normal.'

'I've been thinking about that voice. It's possible the speaker was a foreigner.'

'But Señor Heal is a foreigner.'

She started, looked disturbed. 'Yes, of course. I'm very sorry, that was a stupid thing to say. I do apologize.'

'Señorita, there is no need. All I was trying to do was to make certain what you meant.'

She ignored him. 'There is every need to apologize. As I say to anyone whom I hear complaining about the way something is done on this island, this is the Mallorquins' land and they can do things however they want and if a foreigner finds that objectionable, it's up to him to leave ... What I was trying to explain, very clumsily, was that the man spoke English with an accent; he was probably not a native Briton.'

'Could you suggest what nationality he might have been?'

'No.'

'You've definitely never heard him before?'

'Never.'

'Was there a second voice which might have been Señor Heal's?'

'No. Why do you keep mentioning him?'

'There was a red Mercedes parked in the sitjola.'

'So you mentioned before.'

'It was probably his.'

'All I can tell you for certain is that the man I heard was not Gerald Heal.'

He was too polite to point out that her quality of hearing might have deteriorated because of her age and he lacked the courage to suggest that, having once given her opinion, perhaps she was determined not to be seen to change it. And there was, of course, the faint possibility that another man had borrowed Heal's car or had been driven to the house by Heal...

Satisfied that there was nothing to be gained from further questioning, he settled back and enjoyed the brandy.

*   *   *

He returned to the office fifteen minutes before he could, in all honesty, leave to go home and enjoy the Sopa Mallorquina Dolores had promised. He decided to use up the time by telephoning Heal and demanding the other come to his office on Monday morning. On the face of things, any interview was not going to be easy because Heal was plainly a clever man. But

120

clever men could make mistakes if they were over-conscious of their own cleverness.

He dialled Heal's number and the call was answered by Carmen. 'If the señor's in, tell him I'd like a word with him,' he said.

She gasped. 'But haven't you heard?'

'Heard what?' He hadn't an inkling of what could have happened, but instinct suggested his weekend was about to be ruined.

'The señor's been killed in a car crash.'

*　　*　　*

The mountains provided a different world from the coastal areas. Here, nature remained the ruler, powerful and antagonistic. Once, in some areas, there had been cultivation carried out along terraced slopes, but very few were now willing to labour so hard for so miserable a reward or to live in such isolation. One could drive for kilometres along tortuously zigzagging roads and not see a single inhabited building.

Fervently wishing he did not suffer from altophobia, Alvarez stood at the edge of the unfenced road and stared down at the crushed Mercedes which lay fifty metres down the very steep rock slope, hard up against a massive boulder. 'Was he dead when they reached him?'

'Too dead to say hullo.' The traffic policeman was young and determined to prove himself tough and unimpressionable. 'No one knew

121

he'd gone over the edge until a couple of cyclists noticed that tree.' He pointed at a small pine whose trunk had been shattered when the car hit it immediately after leaving the road.

'Fancy cycling up here!'

'Preparing for the round-the-island race.'

They were welcome. 'What was the time?'

'They saw the car just before half past three in the afternoon. The dead man had a gold watch—they say that that must have cost a few hundred thousand pesetas!—which was broken and that had stopped at twenty-five past twelve.'

'Was he wearing a seat-belt?'

'No. Not that it would have done him much good if he had been, at the speed he must have been travelling.'

Alvarez turned to stare up at the very sharp left-hand bend roughly a hundred metres from where they stood. A reasonable judgement was that a prudent driver would not take that corner at more than thirty k.p.h. Obviously, Heal had come round it at a very much greater speed. Because he was the kind of man he was and in a powerful car? Or because quite suddenly he could not slow down? The car must have begun to slide. A skilful driver would normally have corrected the slide by using the wheel and maybe a mere dab of the brakes, an unskilled one would have panicked and slammed on the brakes as hard as he could. There were no marks on the road, proving the brakes had not been slammed on. Either the driver had overrated his skill or by then the car had been travelling so fast—at a speed not even a Finnish rally driver would contemplate—that no degree of skill could hold it on the road.

'You're going to have to get the car into Palma.'

'Are you loco? Get that wreck back up here, on to the road? How?'

'You're a bright bunch; someone will work out a way.'

'Look, a foreigner with plenty of booze inside him comes round a corner too fast, loses control, goes over the edge, and kills himself. That's his misfortune. And if the insurance company wants to look at things, that's up to them, but they can work out what to do.'

'I want the car taken to Traffic . . .'

'Then the order will have to come from someone a lot higher up the ladder than you are. We're not rupturing ourselves dragging that back up on to the road just on your say-so.'

Mustering what dignity he could, Alvarez returned to his car. He switched on the fan to clear the oppressive heat which had built up even though both front windows had been wide open, lit a cigarette, and stared across the wooded valley at the range of bleak mountains on the far side.

Heal had become a possible suspect in a

murder case. Now, he had died in a crash. Coincidence? Instinct and experience suggested a connecting thread ... The señorita was convinced that the man she had heard in her brother's house had not been Heal. But despite her refusal to accept the fact, when a man was gripped by a violent emotion, his voice could change in character and tone and become difficult to recognize; the 'foreign' accent could well be no more than evidence of such a change. The odds must be that the car outside Burnett's home had been Heal's. A strong-willed, highly successful man, certain of his own superiority, he could have turned to murder more easily than most. The very wealthy were often overtaken by the I-am-God syndrome which led them to believe they had a right to take any action that was necessary to ensure that their will was done. It was realistic to envisage Heal as the murderer of Burnett.

If Heal had murdered Burnett, he must have realized that it was essential for his own safety that, since the police had identified his car, he appeared to give them his full and unstinted cooperation. Yet, knowing he had an eleven o'clock appointment with the detective in charge of the case, he had left the house beforehand and an hour and a half afterwards had still been forty minutes' drive away. What could have been so vitally important to him, if he was the murderer, to make him prepared to take the risk of antagonizing the detective?

*   *   *

Thirty minutes later he rounded one last hairpin bend to reach the floor of a valley which led out to the central plain. With no more precipitous drops to worry about, and only light traffic, his mind returned to the case. If it was confirmed that the Mercedes's crash had been engineered, Heal had been murdered. The two murders would surely have to be connected, at the very least through their motives. Yet he'd uncovered no motive for Burnett's death because it seemed the only person who could benefit from that was his sister; and not only had it been in her interests for the case to be named the suicide it had first appeared to be, it was almost impossible to believe her capable of fratricide. Even if one stretched one's imagination to breaking-point, how could her financial motive for her brother's death have any connection with a motive for Heal's death? What could have entwined the two men's lives when they were so totally different in every respect and, it seemed, might never have met?

Another twenty minutes' driving brought him to Llueso and he crossed the torrente near the Roman bridge. He parked outside the lottery shop, went in, and invested in six entries in the primitive lottery. On the brief drive from

125

there to the office, he pondered the problem of how to spend the hundreds of millions of pesetas one of his entries would bring him.

He telephoned Salas. 'Señor Heal has been killed in a car crash in the mountains and since he is the only possible suspect in the murder of Señor Burnett—'

'Goddamn it, you do this deliberately!'

'But . . .' Alvarez became silent, accepting that his superior chief was incapable of appreciating the fact that he had little or no say in the course events so often took. 'Señor, in the circumstances it is essential that his car is examined by Traffic to see if it was sabotaged.'

'I'm surprised you think it necessary to point that out.'

'But it is fifty metres down below the road and will be very difficult to recover. Traffic are refusing to act without an order from someone superior to myself.'

There was a long pause. 'Correct me if I'm wrong, but is it not a fact that at the moment there is no hard evidence to suggest whether the crash was the result of accident, suicide, or murder?'

'That is so, señor. But the fact that Señor Heal had become a suspect in Señor Burnett's murder suggests—'

'Suggests to someone of a rational mind, given to preferring simplicity to complexity, that if he were the murderer, then on this drive

126

he was either so mentally preoccupied with the consequences of his crime that he did not exercise the care so essential in the mountains or that he was overwhelmed by guilt and decided to commit suicide.'

'From what I've learned, he was a man so certain that whatever he did was justified that he'd never have become dangerously pre-occupied or suffer that strong a sense of guilt.'

'What motive is there for his murder?'

'I'm afraid I've no idea at this stage beyond the fact that it must be connected with Señor Burnett's murder. But I'm certain it will come to light in the course of future investigations.'

'That, surely, will depend on who is doing the investigating? Very well, I'll give the order for the car to be retrieved.' He rang off without another word.

*　　*　　*

Juan and Isabel were in the living-room, watching television. Alvarez settled in one of the free chairs and stared at the screen, but soon lost interest in the heroic deeds of the cartoon characters. Accept that the señorita was wrong and that the man who had had a row with Burnett had been Heal. What had the row been about? How could a retiring, insignificant, weak-willed man so infuriate a brash, self-important millionaire, whom he might never have met before, that the latter became violently angry?

Something caught his attention and caused him to look round. Dolores was standing in the doorway of the kitchen and staring at him with an expression of deep concern. Why was she worrying about him now? ... And then he realized why. Ever since it had been clear that he was dealing with a case of murder, not suicide, he had been overwhelmed by perplexing problems. But she, with a woman's instinct for foolishly mistaking a man's emotions, believed that he'd become so abstracted because he was yearning after Alma. Why would she never grant him emotional maturity?

As he pictured Alma, he experienced a resentful sadness; why did a man have to grow old?

CHAPTER THIRTEEN

Traffic rang on Tuesday morning.

'We've examined the car from end to end. It suffered major damage in the fall, especially to the underside when this struck a very large boulder. As a result, while we can report that both brake lines ruptured, we cannot say for certain whether they had done so prior to the crash.'

'Does that mean you can't be certain whether someone sabotaged the car?'

'Officially, we can't; there's no conclusive evidence on that point. Unofficially, I will go so far as to say that we have found marks on the brake lines which do not seem to be consistent with impact forces. But understand this: I'm not saying that we're reasonably certain the car was sabotaged even if we can't supply the legal proof, I'm merely pointing out that it could have been.'

Alvarez thanked the other, rang off. So it was still impossible to be certain Heal had been murdered, but instinct and logic said that he must have been. How to confirm instinct and logic? Uncover a motive for his murder and show that this motive was inextricably entwined with the motive for the murder of Burnett...

★   ★   ★

The laboratory reported less than an hour later.

'Death was due to severe crushing with resultant heavy damage to the brain and internal bleeding; death would have been virtually immediate. There were several areas of heavy bruising on the body, all consistent with the accident. There was a deep wound in the

129

right forearm, caused by a projecting piece of metal.

'The deceased had been drinking and the concentration of alcohol in the blood was approximately point one per cent.'

'How would that have affected him?'

'Impossible to be specific since each person's tolerance is different. But you could say he was in the delightfully dreamy state. If he was a regular, but by no means excessive, drinker, he would have been chatty, a little carefree, but probably nothing more obvious.'

'What about his ability to drive?'

'One drink slows reactions slightly, several confuse them seriously. Up in the mountains, with switchback roads and hairpin corners, the amount he'd drunk would normally be called dangerous.'

After he'd rung off, Alvarez made some quick calculations. Because Heal had left his home relatively early, it seemed reasonable to suppose that he had not had any drinks before doing so. The bars in Laraix catered for pilgrims and bus tours, therefore were not likely to be the kind of places to which he would go. Then either he had had the drink with him in the car or whoever had earlier telephoned had brought it—with the aim of getting him sufficiently under the influence to dull his senses and miss or ignore any preliminary warnings of mechanical trouble in the car? Why would he have drunk so freely when he knew he had to return home and face a suspicious detective, probably made far more suspicious because he had failed to be there at the prearranged time?

Why had the murderer murdered? Because he knew Heal had murdered Burnett and in some way that knowledge threatened him? Because Heal knew that *he* had murdered Burnett? Because Heal knew why Burnett had been murdered?

* * *

Because the region was completely undeveloped, the drive into Costanyi sent Alvarez's mind back to his youth when he'd worked in the fields, helping his parents, and at the end of each day had been so tired he could hardly eat, even though he was forever hungry.

He parked outside a bar, went in. By-passed by tourism Costanyi might be, but inside there was a colour television set, switched on throughout the day; at least there were no space machines or juke boxes and his coffee and brandy cost less than half what they would have done at a tourist bar in the port. He asked the man who served him if he knew the whereabouts of an English artist who lived nearby and, after the man had spoken to his wife, was given rough directions.

He retraced his route to the outskirts of the

131

village, then took the first side road. The land was rocky and of very poor quality and there was no irrigation, so that many of the fields grew only almond trees, while there were belts of land too rough even for them where grew only scrub bushes and the occasional pine. Near one such belt, he disturbed a small covey of partridges, something he had not seen for many years.

The caseta, without electricity or telephone, was set in the middle of a field. Outside were parked a Citroën 2CV, which looked as if it had escaped from a breaker's yard, and a white Ford Fiesta, on one rear window of which was pasted the form which marked it as a hire car.

As he climbed from the Ibiza, a man stepped out of the caseta. He shielded his eyes with his hand as he stared at Alvarez, but made no move. Alvarez crossed the uneven land. 'Señor Selby?'

'Well?'

'Is Señorita Heal here?'

'What's that to you?' he demanded with arrogant antagonism.

Hardly handsome, thought Alvarez critically and with a certain satisfaction; features too heavy, expression too sullen, and dress too carelessly casual. 'If she is here, señor, I would like to speak to her.'

'But what if she doesn't want to speak to you, señor?' Selby sneered.

'I am afraid that it is necessary, despite the great sadness she has suffered. I am Inspector Alvarez of the Cuerpo General de Policía.'

'A detective? . . . Are you the one she spoke to the other day?'

'That is so.'

'You asked her about Burnett. What's his death got to do with her now?'

'I will try to explain that when I speak with her.'

Selby hesitated, as if wondering whether to deny Alvarez's right to question Alma, then abruptly turned and went back into the caseta.

The other's manners, thought Alvarez, were not his strong point. Determined to show that a Mallorquin detective's manners were very much better, he called out: 'May I enter?' before he stepped inside. His first impression was that the main room of the caseta was so filled with a jumble of easels, canvases, paints, rags, bottles, books and magazines that there was no room for humans. But a second impression identified an easy chair and a settee and a small table against the far wall just big enough to allow two people to eat at it.

Selby went through the doorway on the south side of the room, slammed the door shut behind him. As he waited, Alvarez examined those canvases which were facing outwards. Most of them featured landscapes, though a couple were of buildings only. The Mallorquin countryside,

133

especially if gnarled, twisted olive trees were growing in it, was a favourite study for the dozens upon dozens of artists, amateur and professional, who lived on or visited the island. Although much of their work would have made a chocolate-box-maker cringe, some of it was attractive in an undemanding way. Selby's paintings, Alvarez reluctantly decided, were in a totally different league. His work possessed a quality, difficult to define but immediately recognizable, which added history, emotion, tragedy ... He moved on, stepping around a cardboard box to look at another three canvases which were propped against the wall. When he could see the first one clearly, he drew in his breath with an audible hiss. Selby had painted a naked Alma with such sensuality that she was erotically alive. Alvarez experienced embarrassment and then anger; embarrassment because the picture fuelled desires, anger because here was a man so lost to decency that he'd painted a picture of her that others would leer over.

Selby returned and stood to one side of the doorway. Seconds later, Alma appeared. Her eyes were red and puffy and her hair needed brushing; she was dressed in shirt and jeans and the shirt was badly creased.

Alvarez, hoping she could not guess what he'd been looking at a moment ago, said: 'Señorita, I am deeply sorry about your very sad loss. I much regret disturbing you at such a tragic time.'

'Then why do it?' demanded Selby roughly.

She murmured something, looked appealingly at him and put her hand on his arm.

How could she give herself to such a coarse bear of a man? wondered Alvarez. For the modern generation, it seemed love was not simply blind, it was perversely blind.

'It's all right,' she said wearily. She moved forward and cleared the books and magazines off one of the chairs, motioned to Alvarez to sit.

Once settled on the chair, he became very aware of the fact that if he looked to his right, he would be able to see her naked portrait.

She cleared a space on the settee, sat. After a moment Selby joined her. He said: 'What's it you want to know?'

'First, I must tell the señorita something.'

'Why not tell her, then?'

'It is my very sad duty to have to say that it is possible that Señor Heal's crash was not an accident.'

Alma's voice was high. 'I don't understand.'

'The braking system on his car may have been tampered with in order to make him crash.'

'Impossible!' said Selby.

'Unfortunately, that is not so.'

'You're saying somebody deliberately killed him?' asked Alma.

'I am having to consider that possibility.'

'Oh my God!'

Selby leaned forward. 'That's a load of cod's. Gerry was driving like hell, as always, and went over the edge.'

So Selby knew that he had been a very fast driver! 'Señorita, at the moment there can be no certainty what happened. So now I have to ask you, can you name anyone who may have disliked your father so much that he would have wished to kill him?'

She shook her head.

'Please think about it very carefully...'

'She's just answered you,' interrupted Selby.

'Señor, since the known evidence is not yet conclusive, one way I can try to find out what happened is to discover whether there is someone who possessed a very bitter grudge against the señor. If there is such a person...'

'There isn't, so that answers that.'

'It really would be much better and quicker if you would allow the señorita to speak for herself. I have to know the answers to my questions and so the longer they take to answer, the longer I have to distress her.'

She looked up. 'But Guy's right. There really isn't anyone. I ...' She stopped and tears welled out of her eyes and rolled down her cheeks.

'All right, that's enough,' shouted Selby. 'You can just clear off.'

Alvarez hesitated.

'I said, bloody clear off.'

Art had never been a favourite subject of his, thought Alvarez as he stood, accepting the fact that it probably would be best to leave. 'I am so sorry, señorita...'

'I'm ... I'm all right now.' She brushed the tears away from her cheeks.

'You're not all right,' contradicted Selby.

'I'd much rather get it over with. Don't you understand...'

'No, I bloody don't.'

'Perhaps,' said Alvarez, 'you have a reason for not wishing the señorita to speak to me?'

Selby swore violently. He stood, hands bunched, heavy face scowling, clearly longing to hit out and vent some of his fury. Reason checked him. He turned, kicked out of the way a book that had been lying on the floor, stamped out through the front door.

She said: 'He ... he sometimes gets very worked up.'

'So I would imagine, señorita.'

'I suppose it's what's called the artistic temperament. And then he's had the terrible disappointment because of the exhibition. That could have meant so very much to his career. Please try and understand that he doesn't really mean a lot of what he says, it's only his temper speaking.'

'I understand perfectly,' he answered

gallantly and incorrectly. 'Señorita, this is very disturbing for you, so perhaps it would be best after all if we talked another time?'

She shook her head.

He remembered Carolina's telling him that within her character there was steel. The thought came that perhaps in truth there was more steel than heart; he immediately cursed his malign imagination. 'Then will you please think again and tell me if there's anyone who could possibly have disliked your father so much that he, or she, might have wished to kill him.'

She did not answer for quite a time, then said: 'I just can't believe there's anyone who could have hated him that much.'

'Have you seen a great deal of him recently?'

'Quite a bit. Even though he and Guy . . . They didn't . . .' She stopped again.

'Didn't get on well together?'

'Gerry used to like Guy, perhaps because Guy was always prepared to say what he thought and stick up for what he'd said; Gerry respected strength and despised weakness. But when I came to live here . . . He could be incredibly old-fashioned for someone who lived a very liberated life.'

'Your father's attitude towards Señor Selby turned to one of dislike?'

'He said . . . What's it matter now what happened?'

He wondered if the possible implications of what she was saying were lost on her; or was it a case of clever artlessness being employed to try and suggest complete innocence? He decided to change the line of questioning. 'Señorita, when I saw you at your father's house, I explained that I wanted to ask him some questions. And I asked you if he could have been in his car in Llueso on Monday morning and you said no, he was at home all the time. But Carolina has told me that he always drove to Llueso, or the port, on a Monday morning to get an English Sunday paper. Why did you not tell me that?'

'Because ...' She nibbled her lower lip. 'Because it was obvious you thought he might know something about Justin Burnett's death and that frightened me.'

'Why should it have done?'

'Gerry had been gritty for days and it was obvious that something was wrong. At first, I thought it was that woman.'

'That woman?'

'The Contessa Imbrolie.' Her tone had become scornful.

'But it was not?'

'It was nothing to do with her, as he told me in no uncertain terms. How he could ever have thought that she ...' Her scorn gave way to distress. 'It doesn't matter now that it would have been a disastrous marriage. I wonder if she'll shed a single tear?'

'Does she know of your father's death?'

'I've no idea.'

'Where is she now?'

'She returned to Italy because of something to do with the house—or that's what she said. She never made any bones about preferring Italy to Spain and wanted Gerry to go and live with her there; he loved it here and expected her to move to the island. She'd have given him hell until he fell in with what she wanted. For someone as smart as he, it's incredible how blind he was to the kind of person she really is. I suppose it was the title. He had everything but an assured background. You wouldn't think that in these days anyone would have given a damn about that, but he did. He saw himself married to a contessa and couldn't see he'd also be married to someone with ice in her veins who wanted a tame poodle for a husband ... God, you must think I'm a prime bitch!'

'Never, señorita.'

'It's just ... What the hell!'

'Do you know her address and telephone number?'

'I think I've got them somewhere.'

'Would you give them to me?'

She nodded, went through to the bedroom; she returned, handed him a sheet of paper.

'Thank you. I will see that she is given the very sad news ... When you learned that your father's unusual behaviour was not on account

140

of the contessa, what did you think?'

'I stopped worrying and kind of forgot all about it until you mentioned Justin Burnett. Gerry ... Well, he'd told me he was going to see Justin on the Monday morning and the way he was all tensed up made it clear it was important.'

'Did he mention why this should have been?'

'No. But since he didn't know Justin, there could have been only one reason.'

'What was that?'

'Because Justin was an expert in Greco-Roman artifacts.'

There were times, Alvarez decided, when one could be so blind that one failed to see a sign in fluorescent paint immediately in front of oneself. 'He needed some advice?'

'He must have done.'

'Can you say why?'

'I can guess. He had bought something from Simitis and wanted Justin's opinion of it.'

'Who is Señor Simitis?'

'Gerry occasionally bought things from him. He's a dealer in antiques. For my money, a dealer in antiques looted from graves. I can sense if anyone's basically rotten and he is. I warned Gerry, but he only laughed at me. He was so certain he was too clever to be taken in by anyone.'

'Does Señor Simitis live on the island?'

'He certainly has a house here, but I've no idea where.'

There were sounds from outside and Selby stepped into the room. He glared at Alvarez, his heavy chin thrust out. 'Then you're not finished?'

'Very nearly, señor ... Señorita, I understand you were at your father's house on Thursday night. Did he mention either Señor Simitis or Contessa Imbrolie?'

She stared at him, her expression shocked.

Selby said loudly: 'She wasn't near her father's place on Thursday.'

'But her car was seen there and she was overheard ...'

'I don't give a damn who saw or heard what. She was here all evening.'

Alvarez said sadly: 'Señorita, do you agree that that is the truth?'

She nodded.

He stood, his thoughts becoming even more bitter as he reviewed the possible reasons for her lie.

CHAPTER FOURTEEN

Carmen led the way along one corridor, round a corner, and half way down another corridor. 'Here's the señor's study.'

Alvarez stepped past her to enter the large

room, darkened because the shutters were closed. He opened the shutters as she left. The study looked out on to the courtyard and for a while he watched the fountain, whose jet seemed to cool the air even in the study. Then he turned. There was a large desk, two metal filing cabinets, a half-filled bookcase, a table with a word-processor and printer on it, and three shelves on which were stacked stationery. He crossed to the cabinets. It soon became clear that Heal had been a precise and tidy man when dealing with business affairs and all the papers were carefully filed. He removed any file, the title of which suggested the contents might interest him, put these on the desk.

One hour and forty-three minutes later he reached for the telephone, dialled. When the call was answered, he asked to speak to Señor Vilanova.

He identified himself. 'I'm investigating the death of Señor Heal . . .'

'Investigating it—why?'

'Because we cannot yet be certain of the cause of the crash.'

'Is that one way of saying it may have been deliberate and he was murdered?'

'It's one of the possibilities.'

The lawyer whistled.

'I want a word about his will. I have a copy of a Spanish one which you drew up and had registered in Madrid. Do you remember the contents?'

'Not off-hand.'

'The property on the island is owned by a company registered abroad and the will leaves his interests in the company to his wife and daughter in equal shares. Among his papers are two further wills and these deal, respectively, with assets held by nominee companies in other countries. Once again, the wife and daughter are sole beneficiaries. I've been able to make a very rough calculation of the total worth of the assets and the figure's nearly three billion pesetas.'

'As much as that! I realized he was rich, of course, but I'd no idea he was that rich.'

'Had he recently asked you to draw up a fresh will?'

'He said he was remarrying as soon as his divorce in England was granted and wanted to alter his bequests.'

'According to some handwritten notes, he intended to cut out his first wife and daughter and leave everything to his new wife.'

'As far as I can remember, that was the gist of things.'

'Could he legally cut out the two from his Spanish will?'

'As a foreigner and with the property owned by a company registered abroad, in practical terms the answer is that he could ignore the Spanish requirements to leave a proportion of his estate to his direct heirs and wife.'

'He could have disinherited both of them?'

'That's right. I remember now trying to persuade him to leave both the first wife and daughter a reasonable proportion of the estate, but he became quite angry and told me that if I wouldn't do the work, he'd find someone else who would.'

'But as far as you know, no further will has actually been drawn up and registered?'

'I certainly have not carried out the work.'

Alvarez thanked the other, rang off. He stared out through the nearer window at the fountain's jet. When he had asked Alma about Thursday evening, she had been shocked to discover that he knew about her visit to Ca'n Heal. Selby had hurriedly given her an alibi and she had gratefully accepted the lie. People did not lie unless they had cause to do so...

Murder, as he was constantly reminding himself, normally called for a motive. A half-share in three billion pesetas was a motive that might strain a saint's rectitude.

It was easy to visualize Selby as a murderer. Given a motive, he would have little hesitation in sacrificing another man's life. Traditionally, artists were selfish; Selby would have been selfish whatever his trade. He needed success, and history showed that success had often not come even to a genius until too late ... But in an age when the image was more valued than

145

the substance, when the third-rate could be disguised as first-class by media exploitation, a painter with a great deal of money could promote himself into fame...

Alma was besotted by Selby—even to the extent that she allowed him to paint her in the nude. She had been described as having steel in her character; love and steel made a formidable combination. In the face of Selby's demands, had she agreed to go along with him in the murder of her father?...

Alvarez jerked his racing thoughts to a stop. He was forgetting. Since logic said that the two murders were connected, if Selby had no motive for murdering Burnett, it was unlikely he had murdered Heal. If he had not killed Heal, Alma had not condoned his actions and although she had rowed with her father the night before his murder and had lied to try and conceal that row her lie had nothing to do with her father's death.

Alvarez stood and walked over to the nearer window. The tinkling sounds of the water soothed his thoughts and made him realize how stupid it had been even to consider the possibility that a woman of Alma's character could be an accessory to her father's death.

* * *

Alvarez spoke to Pons, who was kneeling on a

sack and working on a motor-mower just inside a large stone shed which stood a hundred metres from the western side of the house. 'Are you having trouble?'

'What's it look like?'

'Like you don't know very much about motor-mowers.'

Pons hawked and spat. 'No more I do, but the señor said that since I was the gardener, I mend the mowers. Wouldn't spend the money on getting the garage to do the work.'

'The richer they are, the more difficult they find it to spend.'

'Are you just bloody right! Every time the minimum wage goes up, it's a fight to get him to pay the extra ...' He stopped as he remembered that Heal would resist no more wage increases. He was a short, stocky man, with a thatch of grey hair that stuck up at all angles above a weatherbeaten face.

'There was another chap working with you, wasn't there, who got the sack?'

'I told Frederico that's what would happen.' Pons grunted as he moved until he could stand. Something fell to the ground and it took several minutes, and much swearing, to find a small screw; he put this on the petrol tank of the mower. 'He's a young fool who's never learned to keep his head down. When a señor's paying the wages, he's always right. But Frederico had to assert himself and argue and didn't even have

147

the sense to shut his mouth when the señor became really angry. "I'm entitled to my say." Look where that say got him!'

'Had he worked here long?'

'Less than a year. And you can call it work if you want, but I don't. He could make a quarter of an hour's job last half the day.'

'I suppose the sack upset his pride?'

'It did that all right and him and the señor had as good a shouting match as I've ever heard. Him in Spanish, the señor in English. Couple of daft buggers, not understanding what t'other was saying. Still, in the end Frederico understood one thing, right enough. He'd been sacked.'

'I imagine he lives locally?'

'Comes from the village, same as me.'

'Whereabouts in the village?'

Pons scratched the back of his thick neck with a dirt encrusted forefinger. 'Calle General Lobispo.'

★ ★ ★

As were so many villages in the interior of the island, Santa Lucía was built on a hill. When the Moors had been a constant threat, raiding small communities and sacking and slaughtering, a hill had offered both a vantage-point from which to gain an early warning and a certain degree of natural defence.

The streets were narrow and the inhabitants seemed unaware of that fact; as he entered a one-way street, Alvarez was almost run into by a woman on a Mobylette, travelling in the forbidden direction; when he was half way along, a child rushed out of the house and across the road and only by braking violently was he able to avoid a collision. The street led into a small square and he parked in the first available space, deciding that for once walking was preferable to driving.

The inhabitants of Santa Lucía seemed even more parochial than those of other villages and he became angrily certain that it was not mischance which caused him to be given the wrong directions to Calle General Lobispo three times—his speech marked him as being from the north and a forastero and therefore a person to be despised and, perhaps, even feared a little. He saw a Renault Five with the markings of the municipal police, parked outside a bar, and he went in. Two policemen, in their summer uniforms of light blue shirts and dark blue trousers, listened to him, then reluctantly admitted that the road he wanted was two up.

The road from the square was not steep, nevertheless by the time he reached Calle General Lobispo he was breathless. Perhaps, he decided, as he wiped the sweat from his forehead and face, he really should cut back on his smoking and drinking . . .

No. 14 was in the middle of a long row of side-by-sides which directly fronted the road; the shutters and door had been newly painted and **three** window-boxes were filled with climbing geraniums in different colours. The front door was open and he stepped through the bead curtain into the entrada, called out. A short, dumpy woman, with the acquiline features and dark complexion of Arab ancestry, entered from the room beyond. He introduced himself and said he wanted a word with her son.

She hesitated, gave him a look in which suspicion and dislike were mixed, left. There was only a short wait before Frederico entered. In his early twenties, he was dressed in a T-shirt which bore a message in English of such vulgarity it was certain his mother had no idea what it meant and the ubiquitous jeans. His features were similar to hers, but his complexion was even darker.

'You've heard that Señor Heal has been killed in a car crash?' Alvarez asked.

Frederico shrugged his shoulders.

'You haven't heard or you don't give a damn?'

'What's it matter which?'

'Quite a lot, if it turns out that his car was sabotaged.'

Frederico was shocked out of his sullenness.

'He sacked you last week. Did you decide to get your own back by killing him?'

His mother ran into the room. 'No!' she shouted. 'Never!'

Alvarez was not surprised to discover that she had been listening; he would have been surprised had she not been.

'On my mother's grave I swear he couldn't do such a thing.' Her voice became shrill; gone, with all the volatility of the Mallorquin character, was the sullen resentment which she had previously shown and now she pleaded openly and with all her strength. 'Inspector, believe me. I beseech you, believe me.'

Frederico's fear was increased by his mother's. 'I wouldn't never do such a thing.'

'But you had one hell of a row with him when he sacked you?'

'Of course I did. I mean, he just didn't know what he was on about. Some plants can't do in the full sun and that's all there is to it, but all that silly bastard ...' He stopped as he realized that in the circumstances his choice of words was unfortunate.

'What did you do after he sacked you?'

Frederico looked bewildered by the question.

'Where did you go?'

'I came back here, of course.'

'And then?'

'I went out.'

'To where?'

'To the bar.'

'How long were you there?'

'I . . . How do I know?'

She said: 'He was there all evening and when he came back he was so tight he couldn't go upstairs to bed and had to sleep down here.'

'Did you have a thick head in the morning?'

'I was bloody ill.'

'I told him,' she said. 'You drink like that and what d'you expect? I gave him some of my medicine, but it didn't do him no good.'

'When did you go out again?'

'Not until the evening.'

'Wouldn't eat any lunch,' said his mother. 'I said to him, why go and drink . . .'

Alvarez only half listened to her. If they were telling the truth, Frederico had had no hand in the death of Heal.

CHAPTER FIFTEEN

Because the telephone directory was divided into towns and villages, it was necessary to know where a subscriber lived before one could find his name in the alphabetical list; Spaniards found the system logical, foreigners saw in it yet one more proof that Spain was separated from Europe by more than the Pyrenees. Alvarez began his search with Palma, ten minutes later found the entry he wanted under Sant José. Gerasimos Simitis lived in Ca'n Kaïlaria.

Should have been Ca Na Kaïlaria, he thought pedantically as he shut the directory. He checked the time. If he left now to drive to Sant José, which lay beyond Palma, he could not arrive before seven—his siesta had been rather a long one—and there would be no hope of returning home until well after nine ... The evening was not a good time to question a man; far better leave it until the morning.

★   ★   ★

Because of clever salesmanship, the urbanizacíon of Sant José was known internationally as a haven for the rich; one could own a house there, or visit friends, and when back in Britain remark on the fact without apologizing for having gone slumming. Lots of lovely people owned property there; a few pleasant ones did as well.

Alvarez braked, turned off the road and drove slowly up the gravel path to come to a stop in front of an elaborate porch. He climbed out of the car. The house was typical in that it lacked any architectural imagination, had asymmetrical roof lines, and was poorly built, but it was very large and in such a situation was probably worth a hundred million pesetas. He rang the bell and, as he waited, stared at the view. Because he was on rising land the sea was clearly visible, almost as brilliantly blue as computer-enhanced travel posters would have it. He revised his estimate up to a hundred and twenty million. Foreigners always paid extra to be in sight of the water. Yet when he'd been young, to live where the sea could see one had been held to be unlucky; perhaps because so many fishermen lost their lives.

A maid, young and with a slender body, but with heavy features which culminated in a bulldog jaw, opened the door. She showed him into a room to the right of the high-ceilinged entrance hall and this, because of the way in which it was over-furnished rather than for its contents, reminded him of the larger sitting-room in Heal's house.

Less than two minutes later a man hurried in, one hand held out. 'Inspector Alvarez, a pleasure to meet you.' His Spanish was only just accented. He shook hands with enthusiasm. 'Please sit down. And you will permit me to offer you some refreshment?'

Alvarez liked to boast that he never judged until he knew the whole man, yet honesty compelled him to admit that he did not always live up to his own boast. Because a man had wavy dark hair—styled, dyed?—a pampered skin that clearly received constant attention, a mouth which smiled too hard, because he dressed with such elegance, and tried to be so welcomingly pleasant, were not good reasons to dislike him on short acquaintance. He disliked

Simitis on sight.

'I can offer you coffee, tea, a very delicious tisane, whisky, gin, brandy...'

'A coñac, thank you, with ice.'

'Cognac, armagnac, Spanish brandy, or Javito from Hungary which is little known, but which I can highly recommend?'

'One of the local brands will do fine.'

Simitis crossed to the near wall, with a skipping movement, and pressed a bell. 'Please do sit down, Inspector. As they say where I was born, a man who stands keeps his head nearer heaven, but his feet grow tired.'

The only chairs, gilded, looked as if any weight of consequence would fracture their gracefully curved but spindly legs. Alvarez hesitated.

Simitis made a sound that was halfway between a high-pitched laugh and a giggle. 'They are very much stronger than they appear. Only last week, a lady who weighs perhaps twice—no, let me be tactful, one and a half times—as much as you, settled on one without any disastrous results.'

As Alvarez sat, carefully, despite the assurance, the maid entered. Simitis asked her to bring the drinks. After she'd left, he crossed to an ornately inlaid clover-leaf table and picked up a silver cigarette box. 'Do you smoke? These are Virginian, these Turkish; those are for Parisians who are nostalgic for the scent of the metro, and those are made for me by a man in Athens who used to supply the Royal Family before they were so ungraciously rejected.'

Alvarez chose one of the Athens cigarettes. It proved to be made from the smoothest of smooth tobaccos.

Simitis sat. 'Now, to what do I owe the honour of this visit?'

'I'm investigating the murders of Señor Burnett and Señor Heal.' He spoke with deliberate bluntness, hoping to pierce Simitis's egregiously fulsome manner. He was disappointed.

'You are saying that both were murdered?'

'I am.'

'My God!' He clapped his palm to his forehead. 'Shocking! Abominable! A nicer, more talented man than Señor Heal one could not hope to meet. Sadly, there is much truth in the saying, The gods envy youth because that is the one gift they cannot grant themselves. And like mere mortals, that which they envy, they destroy . . . But I digress. You are investigating two shocking murders. How can I help you? Ask me anything. Nothing would give me greater satisfaction than to bring to justice the wicked person responsible.'

Before Alvarez could say anything, the maid returned with two crystal glasses on a silver tray. She handed one glass to Alvarez, the other to Simitis, left.

Alvarez drank. The quality of the brandy suggested that it was Carlos I. 'Did you know Señor Burnett?'

'I met him once, perhaps eighteen months ago. I had a small Roman brooch which I believed dated from the first century BC, but which a self-styled expert insisted was from the second century AD. Knowing that Señor Burnett was an even greater expert on Greco-Roman artifacts than on eighteenth-century paintings, I arranged to meet him and ask him for his verdict. He agreed with me.'

'You haven't seen him since?'

'No, although quite recently I did put a small commission his way as a mark of my respect for his scholarship. Perhaps you know his book on Roman body armour?'

'I don't.'

'If you ever have the chance, read it. The breadth of scholarship is outstanding. And now the poor man can write no more. Clio has lost a great disciple. And he was murdered! How vile men's actions can be! How true that the tragedies of life lie in the past, not the future, because the past cannot be altered.'

Alvarez hastened to check the flow of words. 'You also knew Señor Heal?'

'Indeed. How can one adequately express one's grief at the thought of such a loss?'

'How well did you know him?'

'A question which, like so many, has two

sides. The first is largely a philosophical one. Can one man ever know another well? When it is extremely difficult to be certain what one's own reactions will be under all possible emotional states and all possible circumstances? But it is the obverse side which I am sure you are interested in. How close a relationship with Señor Heal was I honoured with? Can I suggest any reason for his being killed? Can I name someone so wicked, so lost to all decencies, he might have carried out the dastardly act?'

Alvarez's dislike for the other flourished. Beneath the endless flow of words there was mockery. Simitis looked with scorn on a detective in crumpled clothes who so clearly was unused to Carlos I brandy and royal cigarettes.

'I will try to answer the questions. My relationship with Gerald Heal began as a business one; but I pride myself that it soon blossomed into friendship. He was a man I greatly admired, both professionally and privately.'

'What business did you have with him?'

'From time to time I sold him works of art; works of the finest quality.'

'You're a dealer?'

'You may call me that. I buy from those who seek money and sell to those who seek beauty. I think of myself as a benefactor.'

'From whom and where do you buy?'

158

'Inspector, Inspector, what a question! Every trade has its little secrets.'

And his secrets would not bear the light of day. 'Had you recently sold Señor Heal something?'

'Indeed.'

'What?'

'Part of Priam's treasure. Resurrected a second time!' He giggled. He drank, drew on the cigarette. 'You naturally know the history of that treasure?'

'Just remind me.'

Simitis brought a mauve silk handkerchief from his trouser pocket, wiped his lips, replaced the handkerchief. 'King Priam, son of Laomedon, ruled over Troy at the time of the Trojan War. When Troy fell, he was slain. So Homer told us. Nonsense, said the experts. Homer was not one bard, he was many, the *Iliad* and the *Odyssey* were written centuries after the events they were supposed to depict, and the stories were myths; no Troy, no wooden horse; Priam had not taken charge of the body of his son, Hector, killed by mighty Achilles; Odysseus had not wandered for ten years while Penelope wove and unwove; Agamemnon had not survived the war only to return home to be murdered, and his son, Orestes, had not in revenge murdered his mother and her lover.

'One man refused to believe the experts. He

said there had been a Trojan War, as Homer had declared. Since he was not a scholar, but a businessman, he was ridiculed. But Heinrich Schliemann was crazy enough to spend his own money in search of Troy and because the gods love madness, they led him to Troy. He excavated the city and found King Priam's palace and finally King Priam's treasure. (Or so he claimed. Experts say it was not heroic Troy he found, but an earlier city; the treasure dated from before King Priam's time. Why should one believe them now, when they have been proved so wrong before?)

'There were silver vases and knives, gold diadems, ear-rings, and thousands of gold rings and buttons. What to do with this fabulous treasure? Schliemann smuggled it out of Turkey and later presented it to the German government. In the last World War, during the time that Berlin was occupied by the Russians, the collection disappeared and from that day to this it has never been seen again. Does it still exist? Almost certainly not. In an act of unsurpassed and unsurpassable vandalism, the gold and silver was melted down and sold for what it would fetch—a millionth of what the treasure had been worth.'

'You said you sold Señor Heal a part of the treasure. How could you do that when you've just told me it disappeared?'

Simitis giggled. 'Trust a detective to point that out!'

'You sold him a fake?'

'Of course.'

'You admit it?' Alvarez could not hide his surprise. He'd have said that Simitis was the last man willingly to admit he was a swindler.

'Inspector, do you imagine that I alone know the facts? Everyone with the slightest breath of romance in his breast knows them; every lover of the heroic past longs to be told that the collection has been recovered; every heart which beats with cupidity dreams of rediscovering the treasure. From the beginning of my love-affair with the past, I have been offered pieces from King Priam's treasure. Travel east through Turkey and in village after village there will appear a button or a ring from it. Peasants in Armenia, Azerbaijan, Georgia, Dagestan, Kabardino-Balkar, will show you pieces and ask so many roubles that the head spins. All are fakes. Most are crude and could deceive only a naïf who wishes to be fooled, but very, very occasionally such a piece is a work of art and it is the man who made it who is the naïf because he is an artist and could make a fortune if he worked legitimately. One such piece, a gold diadem, was offered to me a few months ago by a Kurd. He swore by all his ancestors that it was genuine and could not believe that I was not to be fooled. The price descended from the realms of romance to the point where I decided that for such a modern work of art, which this was, it was not excessive. I paid him what he was then asking. And the poor fool was as delighted at having bamboozled me as with the money I gave him.

'I brought the diadem back and had it here, mounted on a square of crimson velvet set on the mantelpiece. It was so beautiful that it was possible to believe a miracle had come to pass and the treasure of King Priam had, in truth, been rediscovered.'

Alvarez looked across at the mantelpiece above the large open fireplace, and visualized the gleam of gold against the crimson background. He tried to remember exactly what a diadem was.

'Señor Heal dined with me one evening. As was to be expected, when he entered the room, his attention was immediately drawn to my new acquisition. He asked me about it. I teased him and said that it was from King Priam's treasure ... But it was not a joke that could last because he was a man not only of taste, but of excellent judgement. So I soon admitted that it was a fake since I did not want him to suspect me of trying to fool him. Later, he said he wanted to buy the diadem. I refused because I had grown to like it very much. You see, although I naturally always want the genuine article, if that is impossible I am content to possess a fake which is as perfect as the original and only lacks its

162

years. He would not accept my refusal, but demanded I name a price. A man who makes his living from buying and selling cannot afford to buy but not sell simply because his emotions are involved. Nevertheless, I named a very high price, consoling myself with the thought that if he agreed, not only would I make a handsome profit, I could always return to my seller and ask for another copy to be made. Señor Heal paid me what I'd asked. Never have I regretted a deal more.'

'Regretted or rejoiced?'

'I do not understand.'

'It's my guess you rigged the whole set-up.'

Simitis smiled, but his dark brown eyes expressed hostility. 'You are very direct. Some might even call you rude.'

'Possibly.'

He stood, hurried out of the room with his restricted, skipping stride.

Alvarez finished his drink. It had been a standard confidence trick, playing on another man's greed and conceit, carried out by an expert. The diadem had been displayed in a manner that must attract Heal's attention. He'd examined it. Then Simitis had laughingly confessed that it was a fake. But was it really a fake? An extremely self-confident man, ready to believe himself far cleverer than he was, Heal had become convinced that the diadem was of such superb workmanship that it had to be genuine and it was Simitis who was mistaken. So Heal had decided to buy this fake, believing it to be genuine, and had eagerly paid several times what it was worth, silently laughing at the man who, unknown to him, was laughing at him . . .

Simitis returned with a sheet of paper. 'This is a copy, Inspector. Naturally, should it ever become necessary, I can produce the original.'

It was a photocopy of a receipt, signed by Heal, for a modern reproduction in gold of a Trojan diadem. The price had been fifty thousand pounds. Alvarez handed back the copy receipt.

'Would you now like to withdraw the ridiculous allegation you made earlier?'

'There are two ways of suckering a man. The easier is to fool him into believing something is genuine when it is a fake; the more difficult is to fool him into believing it is genuine, but that you, the person trying to sell it, have not the wit to realize that it is genuine.'

'The receipt proves that I did not fool him.'

'It shows that it would be very difficult to prove you did.'

'Perhaps you should remember, Inspector, that I have friends in high places.'

Alvarez was about to reply that so did monkeys, but checked the words. Sadly, it was probably true that Simitis did know important people with considerable influence. Even though Spain was now a democracy, a mere inspector was easily disposed of . . .

'And now, since I have important business to conduct, perhaps you'll excuse me?'

Alvarez stood. 'Before I leave, señor, I have to ask two more questions. Where were you on the thirteenth of this month? That was a week ago last Monday.'

'Why should the answer be of any interest to you?'

'It is the day on which Señor Burnett died.'

'You think it might have been I who killed him?'

'I have to consider all possibilities.'

Simitis went over to the right-hand of two small, matching desks, opened the flap, picked up a diary. He flicked through the pages. 'I was in Madrid. A man of your suspicious disposition will no doubt wish to verify that, so I suggest you ring the Hotel Don Pepe. What is the second question?'

'When you mentioned Señor Burnett earlier on, you said you'd met him once and later on had put a small commission his way. What does that mean?'

'My business has brought me into contact with a multitude of people connected with art, in the broadest sense, most of whom are, I am happy to say, prepared to accept that I am an honest man. One such person is Señor Joan Pravos, the owner of Galerías Mugar, one of the

165

major art galleries in Barcelona. He mentioned to me that he needed an expert's opinion on the work of an artist who lived on this island. I am interested in paintings but certainly no expert on them so I suggested he contact Señor Burnett who, as you may know, was interested in paintings before he turned to Greco-Roman artifacts.'

'Who was the artist in question?'

'I have forgotten his name.'

'Could it have been Guy Selby?'

Simitis shrugged his shoulders.

'What was Señor Burnett's judgement on the paintings?'

'I have no idea.'

Alvarez thanked the other for his help, managing not to sound too sarcastic. Simitis did not shake hands.

Back in the Ibiza, Alvarez started the engine, made a three-point turn, drove down to the gateway. A couple of cars passed and then he was free to draw across the road and start the journey back through Palma to Llueso.

Some things were becoming clearer, others more opaque. Heal had bought the diadem, having been cunningly bamboozled into believing it to be genuine. He had taken it to Burnett for verification, but Burnett had declared it to be the fake that Simitis had named it. A man who believed himself to be extremely clever, bolstered in such belief by his great wealth, contemptuous of less fortunate people, Heal had been desperate to evade the truth. Illogically, he had vehemently argued with Burnett, trying to make the other reverse his judgement; perhaps he had even tried bribery.

Yet however certainly the facts now identified Heal as being the person who'd rowed so fiercely with Burnett, Phillipa flatly denied it could have been he. How to make sense of this? Was he missing something vital? If so, what on earth could that something be?

CHAPTER SIXTEEN

Inspector Magnasco rang Alvarez from Sienbasso. He spoke in Italian, Alvarez answered in Spanish, and both were perplexed. By mutual agreement, they switched to English.

'I go contessa's house and I speak servants,' said the inspector, whose English was not of Linguaphone standards. 'He is not there.'

'What's that?'

The Italian inspector spoke rapidly and after a moment's bewilderment, Alvarez appreciated the fact that the other switched genders and 'he' was the contessa. It seemed that over the past fourteen months, the Contessa Imbrolie had had a handsome male friend, considerably

167

younger than herself; her friend had a passion for gold trinkets and fast cars. On her sudden and unexpected return from Mallorca, she had found him in the company of a young woman of extraordinary beauty. There had been a fierce row, following which the beautiful young woman had left, the handsome male friend had swapped his three-year-old Alfa Romeo for a new Porsche, and the contessa and he had gone on holiday to the Seychelles, leaving the Tuesday before Heal's crash.

Say one thing for the rich, Alvarez thought, their lifestyles were different.

★   ★   ★

He dialled the Hotel Don Pepe and spoke to the assistant manager. An hour later the assistant manager rang back.

'One of the waiters served Señor Simitis dinner in his suite on Monday evening.'

'Does he know what time this was?'

'Near enough to nine o'clock.'

'Thank you very much for your help.'

He replaced the receiver. If Simitis had been in Madrid at nine o'clock, it was extremely unlikely that he could have been in Llueso at midnight.

★   ★   ★

Salas said, over the telephone: 'Let me make quite certain that I understand. You are requesting permission to fly to Barcelona in order to question the owner of an art gallery; the reason for this request being that you believe he may be able to help with your investigation?'

'Yes, señor,' replied Alvarez.

'Yet when I ask in what way may he be able to help, you cannot give a reason.'

'In this particular case, it is rather difficult to explain . . .'

'My impression is that in every case you undertake, you find it difficult to explain. Presumably, the gallery owner knew Señor Burnett?'

'I rather doubt it.'

'Then he knew Señor Heal?'

'I don't think so.'

'Has he recently visited this island?'

'I've no reason to think he has.'

'Then how can he possibly be in a position to assist you?'

'The thing is, in the course of my inquiries his name has cropped up.'

'And that is reason enough to visit him? Then perhaps I should hope that the next name which crops up is not one belonging to a person who lives in New Zealand.'

'I have a feeling that he is important.'

'You have a feeling? That is different!

Everything is explained!'

'Sometimes a hunch ...' He trailed off into silence.

Salas spoke wearily. 'I can see only one solution. Follow your hunch and fly to Barcelona. But you will make the journey in the most economical way possible and you will not present the cost of a meal at the Ritz on your expense sheet. Is that quite clear?'

'Yes, señor.'

The connection was cut.

Alvarez had begun to sweat and he used a handkerchief to mop his face and neck. It had been a very close run thing and there had been a moment when he'd thought that he was going to have to name Selby. To have done so would have been to implicate Alma. And although he accepted that love could make a strong woman weak, he still fought against the possibility that love could have forced her to condone her father's murder.

*   *   *

Dolores, standing by the side of the dining-room table, stared with consternation at Alvarez. 'You're ... you're going to Barcelona tomorrow?'

He nodded.

'Santa María!' she murmured. Unexpected happenings always disturbed her; she liked today to be yesterday, tomorrow to be today.

'I'll be back in the evening.'

'You're returning the same day!' This made her even more upset. By her standards, a trip to Palma was still a major event; to set out to make the return trip to Barcelona in one day was almost to challenge the Almighty.

'You look as if you need a drink to cheer yourself up.' He expected her to refuse, but she didn't. Hastily, he poured out two brandies and went through to the kitchen for ice.

She took one glass from him and drank. Then she looked at him, her lustrous dark brown eyes filled with concern. 'Enrique, it's because of her that you're going to Barcelona and returning on the same day, isn't it?'

'In one sense, yes; but not in the way you're thinking.'

'No? I'll tell you exactly how I'm thinking. That a woman's heart is pierced by thorns when she sees a man who she loves making a fool of himself; when she can see the precipice which lies ahead of him, but he cannot; when she shouts a warning, but he closes his ears. I am thinking that when he has fallen and wounded himself, it is not the woman who lured him to the fall on whom he calls for help, but it is to the woman whose warning he refused to heed.'

'You've got it all wrong.'

'Is it really that easy to forget all the times in

the past that I have seen you blinded by a chit of a woman?'

'You've been watching too many soap operas. It's nothing like that.'

'It is exactly like that every time a man lusts after a woman.'

'I'm not lusting and have another drink and stop seeing everything in terms of high tragedy.' He drained his glass, stood, held out his hand and without a word she handed him her glass.

When he returned, he said: 'You can tell me. Can a woman be made evil by love?'

Her indignation was immediate. 'Only a man could ask so stupid a question! If a woman is loved—if there is any man left who can love and not lust—she is made good, not evil.'

'There have been women who have done terrible things because of love.'

'Because of lust.'

'Can you ever really separate the two?'

'A woman can always separate them.'

'The señorita is a woman who can love deeply. Yet the evidence is suggesting that the man she lives with may have committed a very great evil. If she loves him deeply, could she because of that condone his evil even though knowing it to be evil?'

She had only listened to part of what he had said. 'She lives in sin with another man, yet you still lust after her?'

'Can't you understand that I've never lusted

after her? That was all in your imagination.'

'The yearning in your eyes was not imagination.'

'Despair, not yearning; despair because although my heart tells me she's innocent, the facts suggest more and more strongly that she shares the guilt.'

He had been speaking calmly, without the bitter emotion there surely would have been had he been vainly in love with the chit of a foreign woman. She experienced a sweeping sense of thankfulness which had to find expression. She would, she decided, prepare something special for supper.

He spoke quietly, his tone uncertain. 'Sometimes I don't know what my job really is. Am I just a servant of the law or am I a small part of justice?'

She would buy some jamón serrano.

'If I am the former, I should not concern myself with the consequences of what I do; the measure of those must be someone else's responsibility. But if I am the latter, I must worry and if I can see they may cause an injustice, I must do everything in my power to avoid that happening.'

She still had time to cook a piece of lomo.

'If all the facts point in one direction, but one believes the sign they give has to be wrong, how justified can one be if one ignores them? Is failure to apprehend the guilty as great an injustice as the apprehension of the innocent? How far can one be blamed for one's own weaknesses? I can say that you must never be guided by evil, but you may not be as strong as I and therefore cannot fight it as hard. Do I really have the right to blame you when through no fault of your own you cannot meet my standards?'

The larger of the nearby bakeries might have an ensaimada con crema Catalan; the whole family loved them.

'Suppose I uncover the final piece of evidence which identifies her man as the murderer, can I even begin to justify the withholding of that evidence because I am so certain that she could never willingly follow evil and I know that if he is accused, so must she be, if not as a principal, then as an accessory?'

She said: 'I must go out to the shops and buy some food for supper.'

Only an incompetent detective would ever imagine there could be answers to such questions.

★   ★   ★

As the plane gathered speed on the take-off, Alvarez, his eyes tight shut, decided that he'd rather be in the centre of the Palma bullring, caping a seven-hundred-kilo bull with unshaven horns, than where he was. But beyond a dangerous rumble from the undercarriage as this was raised, nothing happened and eventually he opened his eyes, deciding that perhaps he was to be allowed to live a little longer. He tried to catch the attention of an air stewardess, to persuade her to serve him a very large brandy even though the flight lasted only half an hour.

★   ★   ★

His knowledge of Barcelona was scanty (he had visited the city only twice before), but he knew that the inhabitants would be united in their desire to swindle him. When he left the old terminal building at the airport and climbed into a taxi, he made certain the meter was starting at zero and he closely watched the route they took into the city, even though he had no idea which was the shortest.

The traffic was little denser than it was during the rush hour in Palma, yet it seemed to bear down on him until he wanted to tell the driver to slow, but the latter appeared to be practising for the Spanish Grand Prix; the buildings were little taller than those in Palma, yet they seemed to become skyscrapers which choked off all clean air . . .

They turned on to the Diagonal, then off it, and abruptly they were in a world that was welcomingly familiar; people had time to sit at pavement cafés, a city employee, brushing down the pavement, leant on the broom and contemplated either infinity or a crack in the pavement, a state policeman placidly watched a car park in front of a Parking Prohibited sign, and a gipsy woman, too tired to beg, sat on the pavement, leaned against a wall, and closed her eyes.

The taxi came to a halt. He climbed out, checked the meter-reading, and gave a tip that on the island he would have considered over-generous. He was unsurprised when the driver sneered at his parsimoniousness.

The gallery had a single show window and in the centre of the display area stood an easel on which was a large canvas that, to his Philistine eyes, depicted the track of an inebriated spider. He went inside. The paintings along the walls suggested more busy spiders while small sculptures, set on pedestals, lacked even that much definite form.

The gallery was L-shaped and there was a desk set at the point where the two arms joined, behind which sat a woman of indeterminate age. He introduced himself and said he wanted to speak to the owner of the gallery. Being a cultured Catalan, she would have liked to have misunderstood his Mallorquin, but was inhibited from doing so by the knowledge that he was a detective. She said she'd find out if Señor Pravos were free. She went through the doorway behind the desk, returned almost immediately. 'He can spare you a moment.'

The office was large and very elegantly furnished. Pravos was small and very elegantly turned out. His black hair was styled, his hands manicured, and his recently pressed linen suit was of the same delicate shade of blue as the wallpaper. There were three rings on his fingers, but none in his ears. He made Alvarez feel lumpenly dressed, despite a clean shirt that morning. When he shook hands, the feel of his skin was like soaped silk. 'My assistant says you're a detective from the Baleares?'

'From Mallorca.'

'Then sit and tell me, what brings a detective from the Island of Calm to this temple of art?'

Alvarez sat in front of the large desk, on which stood a small sculpture of priapic origins. 'I believe you're friendly with Señor Gerasimos Simitis?'

'I am acquainted with him, certainly. Why do you ask?'

'Because I need to know more about him. Is he honest?'

Pravos was disconcerted. 'You're clearly a man for whom the world is a place of definite values! Shall I say this: I am certain he is quite incapable of stealing any of the paintings in this gallery.'

'You asked him about the work of an artist who lives on the island?'

'That is correct.'

'Why did you do that?'

'The matter is confidential.'

'Not when you're talking to me.'

'Very well, I will tell you. I am a man of considerable taste and judgement, possessed of a desire to lead the public towards the light. It is part of my mission to introduce art to the ordinary man in the street, to switch on a torch in his mind and soul; another part of such mission is to discover artists whose worth has not yet been recognized and to introduce them to the newly-born art lovers. Sadly, the tasks are not easy. The ordinary man is unadventurous as well as ignorant and can only be persuaded into fresh realms when his curiosity is aroused by some form of publicity. I championed a certain artist for no little time, but without success, until it was decided that he would gain publicity by setting out to break the world record for pole-squatting. Of course he failed to equal St Simeon's forty-five years; nevertheless, since he was a native of this city, he received considerable publicity and people came to view his work and to buy it.

'Lacking such initiative an artist can, of course, gain the necessary publicity by a judicious use of money. One may bitterly regret that the world in which we live is a commercial one, but one cannot escape that fact and so when I was approached by a totally unknown artist who requested an exhibition for which there would be full financial backing, I was ready sympathetically to examine his work. It proved to be of a character which normally does not attract me, yet it unmistakably displayed talent. I agreed to his request. Later, it appeared that the gift of sponsorship had been withdrawn. I was left with no alternative but to cancel my offer.

'I then received a visit from a young lady who vehemently demanded that, despite the loss of financial backing, I honour my promise of an exhibition. On my pointing out that the financial situation made this impossible, she replied that art was not to be measured in pesetas ...' He sounded surprised. 'She was a very persistent young lady; quite un-Spanish. And in order to gain relief from her vehemence I was forced to admit that I had seen merit in the artist's work and I would like to hold an exhibition of it, but I added that it was necessary to gain some form of pre-exhibition publicity. En passant, I mentioned the artist who had attempted, but failed, to win the record for a pole-squat. Regrettably, she failed to appreciate that this was an example, not an instruction, and began a tirade on art and Mammon ... Let me confess, Inspector, that things reached such a pass that in order to regain some peace I promised that if I thought that despite a lack of advance publicity there was a chance of the exhibition being successful, I would after all hold it. I don't think I have ever before met anyone of such fierce and pugnacious determination...

'Not long afterwards, I was talking to Señor Simitis, with whom I have occasionally done a little careful business, and I mentioned my problem and asked if he knew the artist's work. He didn't, but suggested that if I wanted a further opinion on it, I should speak to Señor Burnett, who lived on the island.

'I telephoned Señor Burnett and offered him a small commission to contact the artist, look at his work, and judge it. He agreed to this after making it clear that it was years since he'd dealt with paintings and that then his interests had lain with the eighteenth century.

'His report was brief, but explicit. He didn't particularly like the work, yet he had little doubt that the painter had an unusual talent. But he thought the quality of the work to be a subtle one and unlikely to be recognized at first sight by the ordinary person. In the face of such a report I naturally had to bring to an end any possibility of an exhibition.'

'Who was the artist?'

'I forget his name, but it will be in the records.' He stood, went over to a filing cabinet, slid out the top drawer, and searched through the papers. 'Guy Selby,' he said, having difficulty in pronouncing both names.

CHAPTER SEVENTEEN

The tapas bar ran for three-quarters the length of the long, narrow space; in the last quarter were half a dozen tables for those who preferred not to eat at it. Alvarez made a final choice of a portion of baby octopus in a piquant sauce, carried the plate, a glass of white wine, knife and fork, over to the only vacant table.

He ate, his mind far away. It must have appeared to Selby that Burnett had scorned his work and ruined his chances of an exhibition that might well have made his name and ensured fame and fortune. So here was a motive for his murder—the revenge of the artist whose pride was not to be measured by normal, logical standards. And since Burnett had been murdered, there could be little doubt but that Heal's death had been murder and here was the motive of a fortune, to be gained through Alma, which would be lost if Heal lived to marry the contessa. Only Selby had a motive for both murders ... How could there be the slightest justification for continuing to withhold his name from the superior chief? Yet once he was named as the prime—the only—suspect for both murders, inevitably Alma must be implicated ...

He finished the plateful of mixed fish,

prawns, mussels, octopus, squid, and berberechos and then returned to the bar for a second course of liver, kidneys, meatballs, diced pork, and garlic stew. He asked for a glassful of red wine.

Back at the table, he resumed eating and thinking. When he returned home, he would have to report fully to Salas. As a consequence, Selby and Alma would be questioned vigorously and probably be arrested. The thought of Alma suffering the degradation of jail made him feel as if about to choke...

He suddenly realized that there were still two lines of inquiry which he could legitimately and defensively pursue. Even if neither should now prove to be of any account, it was as well to remember the old Mallorquin saying: Never rush, leave yourself time to enjoy tomorrow. Who knew but that tomorrow might not bring something which would delay or even deny the inevitable?

He ate a meatball and for the first time became fully conscious of how tasty were each of the dishes. It might perhaps be an idea to have a second helping...

* * *

Alvarez, standing by the side of his desk, stared down at the ringing telephone. Even though it was Saturday, the caller was likely to be Salas,

182

demanding a report on the trip to Barcelona.

He left and went downstairs, past the duty cabo, and out into the road. He walked up the shaded side to the square and unlocked his car, switched on the fan to cool the interior. As he waited, he stared resentfully at the tourists who sat at tables set outside the three cafés which fronted the square. All they were interested in were beach and booze. Not one of them would give a solitary damn if Alma were convicted of being an accessory to murder ... If only he could find proof of her innocence; if only he could forget that she had lied about that visit to her father's house; if only life hadn't taught him that when a person lied it was because there was cause, and the more desperate the lie, the greater the cause...

The car had cooled and he settled behind the wheel. He reversed, turned, and drove out of the square and on to the old Palma road. Ten minutes later, he arrived at Ca'n Pario.

'Even by local drinking standards,' said Phillipa, 'you're early; unless, of course, you've come for merienda?'

He smiled, having learned that her sharp, biting manner was not intended to be as discourteous as it often sounded. 'I am early, señorita, because I am here to invite you to lunch in Palma.'

'Beware the Danaans whose hands proffer gifts ... What do you want from me?'

183

'I would like you to listen to two men.'

'Who?'

'The first is Señor Gerasimos Simitis.'

'He sounds very Levantine. I visited Rhodes in the nineteen-twenties and had my handbag snatched. That cured me of believing, unlike my poor brother, in the superiority of Eastern Mediterranean civilization.'

'I doubt very much, señorita, that you risk a repeat of so sad an occurrence if we visit Señor Simitis. He is exceedingly wealthy.'

'You believe that to be a guarantee of his honesty?'

'It is a guarantee, surely, that he will not snatch your handbag unless convinced that it contains a great deal of money?'

'You clearly understand human nature . . . Have you had merienda?'

'I've been too busy.'

'Then we shall both enjoy it now. Sit down while I go inside and make coffee.' She went indoors.

He sat. There was a suspicion of a breeze, just sufficient to tremble the vine leaves so that the sunlight which escaped around their edges danced. Cicadas were shrilling and somewhere fairly close, perhaps in the palm tree at the end of the garden, a bird which he could not identify was singing; a cock, finding sufficient energy despite the growing heat, crowed a challenge; dogs barked; far away, so that the noise became pleasant rather than intrusive, children were shouting as they played in a pool; from much nearer came the metronomic sounds of an irrigation unit; several humming-bird hawk moths were examining flowers on a lantana bush and the beat of their wings held a note of frenzy ... When he died, he hoped it would be out in the open, amid such a scene of beauty as this.

She returned with a tray on which were two mugs of coffee, milk, sugar, two glasses, a bottle of 103 brandy, and half a coca. 'Please help yourself.'

He took one of the mugs, added sugar and milk, cut a slice of the coca, and poured out a brandy. She gave herself a brandy at least as generous as his. 'You told me who the first man is, but didn't name the second?'

'A painter. Señor Guy Selby.'

'I've not heard of him.'

'I am told that his work is talented, but he has not yet managed to become at all well known. He is a friend of Señorita Heal's.'

'Of Alma? Breeding's an odd thing. Who would have expected a man like Gerald Heal to have had a daughter with the natural charm of Alma? Why do you want me to meet the two?'

'To discover if you can identify one of them as the person you heard quarrelling with your brother.'

'Why should it have been either?'

'Señor Simitis would have found your brother too honest.'

'If a Levantine, that goes without saying. And Selby?'

'It would not have been a question of honesty, but of taste. Your brother did not like his paintings sufficiently well to believe they would have an immediate appeal to the general public.'

'He was very conservative in all his tastes.'

'So will you come with me to Palma to meet Señor Simitis and afterwards to enjoy lunch; and to continue from there to Costanyi?'

'Costanyi? I haven't been there in more than thirty years. I suppose I won't begin to recognize the place.'

'I think you will discover that little, if anything, has changed.'

'There's somewhere which has escaped the blight of tourism? Then let us lunch there and not in Palma.'

*   *   *

Alvarez braked to a halt in front of Ca'n Kaïlaria. Phillipa said: 'What an ugly, pretentious pile of a place! Presumably, the Levantine was a friend of Gerald Heal's?'

'More a business acquaintance.'

'Two of a kind. It is extraordinary how really

186

vulgar people choose really vulgar houses to live in.'

'But Señor Heal ... Have you never seen his home?'

'He restricted his invitations to royalty and those he thought might be of use to him.'

'He lived in a noble manor house.'

She was not to be denied. 'Then he will have succeeded in vulgarizing the interior.'

They left the car and crossed to the front door. The same maid whom he'd met on his previous visit opened it and showed them into the large sitting-room. Phillipa, unashamedly curious, began to examine the contents and she was looking at the hallmarks on the base of a silver pheasant when Simitis entered the room. He, exhibiting perfect manners, carefully failed to notice what she had been doing.

He crossed the floor, right hand outstretched. 'Inspector, please excuse my tardiness in greeting you, but unfortunately I was in the middle of a very important telephone call and not even for you could I cut it short.' He shook hands vigorously and there was no hint in his manner that their last meeting had ended bitterly.

'This is Señorita Burnett,' Alvarez said.

Simitis turned, half bowed, switched effortlessly to English. 'Dear lady, it is a very great pleasure to receive you in my humble home.'

For a moment it looked as if she were about

to say something, but for once she showed a measure of discretion and remained mute, merely acknowledging his fulsome greeting with a curt nod of her head.

'Señorita Burnett's brother was very tragically killed almost two weeks ago,' said Alvarez.

'Now I understand why the name was familiar . . . Dear lady, please accept my deepest and most sincere condolences at a time of such personal tragedy.'

'Are you a Levantine?'

The question bewildered him. 'I . . . I regret that I do not understand.'

'Were you born in an eastern Mediterranean country?'

'Indeed; in Kylos, on the pearl of an island of Saphos. Perhaps you know it?'

'No.' She gripped her handbag a shade more tightly.

His bewilderment grew in the face of such hostility, but he tried to remain the gracious host. 'Permit me to offer you both some refreshment. I have just had a couple of cases of Dom Pérignon delivered—'

Alvarez interrupted him. 'That's kind of you, but we're here to ask a couple of questions and then we have to hurry away. Did you go with Señor Burnett to look at Señor Selby's paintings?'

'I did not.'

'Have you met Señor Selby?'

'Never.'

'Then thank you for your assistance.'

'Do you mean, that is all?'

'Yes.'

His expression had sharpened and his eyes were diamond bright. 'Then I'm surprised you didn't just telephone me and so save yourself the trouble of coming all this way.'

'It's been no trouble.'

'You do understand, Inspector, I have never met Señor Selby?'

'So you've just said.'

Simitis hesitated, then reverted to his previous egregiously fulsome manner. 'Surely I can persuade you to do me the honour of staying just long enough to enjoy a little champagne?'

They left. Phillipa was silent until they were driving up to the elaborate gateway, then she said: 'Men like he always make me feel I need a bath. I suppose he's in some sort of racket—drug-smuggling?'

'I don't think so. That would be too risky. He trades in ancient works of art, almost certainly buying them from peasants who have looted ancient tombs and selling them to men with money who are prepared not to ask questions.'

'He sold Gerald Heal looted treasure?'

'A diadem, supposedly part of King Priam's

treasure which Señor Schliemann found at Troy and later smuggled out of Turkey. Perhaps you know the story?'

'Of course. Justin used to dream of finding the treasure even though he really believed it couldn't still be in existence. Not because of its monetary value, of course, but its historical worth. Gerald believed the diadem was genuine?'

'Señor Simitis is a clever man and he sold it as a fake, making certain Señor Heal believed it to be genuine.'

'You're saying that he made a fool out of Gerald?'

'That is so.'

'Then even though he's a Levantine, he's clever. You believe Gerald took the diadem to my brother to ask him to confirm that it was genuine, don't you? Justin would have said immediately that it was a fake.'

'Which is why it seems reasonable to believe that it was Señor Heal whom you overheard having that row with your brother.'

'But it wasn't.'

'Indeed, señorita. And knowing it wasn't, I've been trying to identify who else it might have been. Señor Simitis might have been frightened by Señor Heal's anger on discovering how cleverly he'd been fooled and he may have tried to get your brother to moderate his judgement; if your brother could be persuaded to say it might not be a fake after all, but if it was, it was the finest he'd ever seen, then Señor Heal might not be nearly so angry because his self-esteem would be far less wounded.'

'The man I heard was not the Levantine.'

'You can be certain?'

'Quite certain.'

'His voice is very slightly accented.'

'The man I heard had a voice which was more accented.'

Alvarez drew out into the centre of the road to overtake a parked car. 'If I can remember correctly, señorita, you originally described the voice as only lightly accented?'

'Well?'

'But now ... Well, you're saying it was more than that.'

'I'm saying nothing of the sort. It's a question of relativity. When I first described the voice as accented, my point of reference was a typical foreigner speaking English; you speak very fluent English, but your accent is unmistakable. The man I heard had less of an accent than you. The Levantine, however, speaks an almost accentless English—it goes with the oily appearance. Relative to him, the man I heard had a stronger accent. So you see, I wasn't contradicting myself because I'd forgotten what lie I'd told you.'

'I could never have imagined such a thing.'

'Really? I thought it was a detective's job to

regard everyone as a liar until proved otherwise.'

CHAPTER EIGHTEEN

They came out of the bar-restaurante into the
blazing sunshine and crossed to the Ibiza,
parked under a shade tree. He unlocked the car
and held the passenger door open for her, went
round and settled behind the wheel. 'I shall
treasure our meal here,' she said. 'I have a file
of good memories and when I need cheering up,
I take one out and enjoy it. Today is going into
that file.'

'I am so glad, señorita.'

'My name's Phillipa. Señorita is for people
one does not like.'

'Or whom one respects.'

She gave her short, barking laugh. 'There's
little enough cause for respecting me. When I
die, I'll not be leaving behind anything
worthwhile.'

'You will be leaving memories which others
can take down and enjoy.'

'Good God, we really are becoming
sentimental!'

He was disappointed by her response because
it seemed to criticize. He started the engine,
backed.

She had read his thoughts. 'I often wonder which is better, to be taught to eschew sentiment, as we British are, or to be taught to welcome it, as are you islanders. I suppose that depends partially on whether one is young or old. Sentiment's bad for the young, because it leads them into emotional thickets, but good for the old, because it comforts.'

She had not, he gratefully accepted, been criticizing him. What she'd said had been prompted by her need to live through the grief of the death of her brother on her own because that was what she had been taught to do. Thank God he was part of a family who would always share, and so lighten, tragedy!

When they reached the caseta, it was to find that Selby, who was stripped to the waist, was outside in the field, painting. He carefully did not take any notice of them, not even when they walked across.

'Good afternoon, señor,' Alvarez said.

'What the hell d'you want now?'

'First, I would like to introduce Señorita Burnett.'

'Burnett . . .' He turned and stared hard at Phillipa, palette in his left hand, brush in his right.

''Afternoon,' she said briskly.

'You're . . .'

'Justin was my brother.'

It was several seconds before he realized that

193

some words of condolence would be appropriate. 'I was sorry to hear about it.'

'Thank you.'

Alvarez did not need to be a detective to be able to judge that they disliked each other on sight. 'Señor, when Señor Burnett came here and saw your work, what did he say about it?'

'Who says he came here?'

'Señor Simitis.'

'And just who the hell's he?'

'A dealer in antiquities who suggested to Señor Pravos, the owner of Galería Mugar, that Señor Burnett should look at your work.'

'You've been nosing around.'

'It has been necessary.'

'Why?'

'Because my brother was murdered,' snapped Phillipa.

He had not the ease of social manner to extricate himself from the position in which his crude behaviour had placed himself. Resentfully, he jabbed at the painting with the brush.

Alvarez looked at Phillipa and she shook her head. The man she had heard had not been Selby. Alvarez was not surprised.

'I'm going to go for a walk,' she said. 'In which direction is the sea? Over there?' She pointed.

Alvarez waited for Selby to answer, then said sharply: 'Well?'

194

'Goddamn it ... The dirt track which goes past the house leads to the cliffs.'

'Thank you,' she said, using politeness as a way of castigating his bad manners. 'I won't be long.' She went down to the track, turned left, and marched on and out of sight, a stoutish, shapeless figure who carried with her an air of indomitable determination.

'Now, señor,' said Alvarez, 'perhaps you will tell me what Señor Burnett thought of your paintings?'

'Christ! How am I supposed to work with these constant interruptions?'

'Until the murderer is discovered, I am afraid you will have to find a way.'

'Because you're so thick you think I had something to do with it?'

'You are the only person with a motive for both murders.'

'What motive had I for killing that stupid old buzzard?'

'You are, perhaps, referring to Señor Burnett?'

Selby realized that yet again he'd allowed his tongue too much freedom. 'He didn't know a damn thing about modern art.'

'Would you hold that to be cause enough to justify his murder?'

'No, I bloody well wouldn't. I didn't kill him.'

'Yet because of him, you lost the chance of an

195

exhibition at a very important gallery.'

'He didn't know anyone had painted anything worthwhile after the end of the eighteenth century. He wouldn't begin to understand what I was trying to do and there was as much point in him trying to evaluate my paintings as there would be in your doing so. But just because he was biased, ignorant, and had a totally closed mind, doesn't mean I bloody killed him.'

'If he'd recommended your paintings, the gallery would have exhibited them. Had they done so, you might well have begun to find commercial success. Then you wouldn't have had to rely on someone else to keep you.'

He threw palette and brush to the ground. 'Alma doesn't bloody well pay a peseta towards my keep.'

'Who does, then?'

'Back home, I worked as a waiter, a barman, even a bloody doorman, to make enough money to come out here and paint, because that's all I've ever wanted to do.'

'And you still have plenty of capital left?'

'That's none of your goddamn business.'

'On the contrary, it has become my business because if I find that you have spent nearly all of it, then clearly your need to find more elsewhere is urgent; your resentment at losing the possibility of an exhibition in Barcelona must have been much more acute; your bitterness when Señor Heal reneged on his agreement would have been much stronger; and your relief much greater when Señor Heal died before he could change his will, disinheriting his wife and Señorita Alma.'

Selby was about to answer when they heard a car. A white Fiesta, bouncing heavily on the rough track, came to a halt near the Ibiza. Alma climbed out, shielded her eyes with her hand, then hurried across. Worried by Selby's expression, she said, her voice strained: 'What's happened?'

'He's accusing me of having murdered your father and Burnett,' he said violently.

'No!'

'According to him, I'm the only person with a motive for both murders.'

'That's utterly ridiculous.'

Alvarez said: 'I am sorry, señorita, but it is not ridiculous. It is the truth.'

Selby said sneeringly: 'I murdered Burnett because he gave my paintings the thumbs down and your father because he was about to change his will and you wouldn't be able to keep me any longer.'

'But I've never kept you; you wouldn't let me do that even if you were starving.'

'How d'you get that through a foot-thick skull?'

She appealed to Alvarez. 'Please, you must believe me. Guy wouldn't do anything so

197

horrible. He couldn't kill someone just because that person didn't like his paintings, he couldn't have killed my father. He was almost glad when he heard Gerry was going to change his will and stop my allowance because of the contessa. Her ... he's stupid about money. He's so much pride that he won't acknowledge that a relationship should be a partnership ... Why won't you understand that an artist worries about art, not money?'

'Señorita,' replied Alvarez sadly, 'there was one murder which makes it virtually certain there was a second one and it is my job to identify and arrest the murderer.'

'But why come here and make such filthy accusations about Guy?'

'Only he had a motive for both murders.'

'I keep trying to tell you, it doesn't matter how many possible motives, he couldn't kill anyone. I know he can be difficult, I know the way he talks.'

Selby interrupted her roughly. 'You're wasting your time, forget it.'

'I can't! I won't! It's no good trying to pretend you're nice and pleasant and therefore couldn't hurt a fly. You're often bloody-minded, rude, boorish. But that's because you're an artist and you hate anyone and anything that gets in the way of your art and ... Oh my God!' she murmured, belatedly realizing what she'd just said.

Where did art cease and greed begin? wondered Alvarez sadly.

'Please try to understand,' she pleaded. A thin flutter of wind briefly twitched her dark, curly hair and she instinctively reached up to recapture a few errant strands. 'All I was trying to say was that he's only difficult because all the time he's attempting to do a little more than he can presently achieve and that means he becomes terribly frustrated. But that's not the same sort of frustration that you're talking about, the kind that would make him kill ... Gerry was my father. I liked him, even loved him, in spite of the way he treated my mother. Guy couldn't deliberately hurt anyone I love.' She began to cry and as the tears slid down her cheeks, the harsh sunlight was refracted in them so that she seemed momentarily to be sparkling with colour.

'Señorita, if all you say is true, why did you lie to me? A person lies when there is something to hide. What must you hide from me?'

'I've never lied to you.'

'Sadly, you have.'

Determined to reassert himself, Selby said violently: 'If she says she didn't, she bloody didn't.'

'The señorita's car was at the señor's house the evening before he died. The housekeeper identified the voice of the woman she heard as the señorita's.'

'I don't care who says what, I'm telling you that Alma was here all bloody evening.'

Alvarez experienced fresh bitterness. Selby's ruthless selfishness had drawn Alma into a situation from which she could not hope to escape unscathed. 'Señor, I regret I am unable to believe you. Therefore you will give me your passport and I must warn you that any attempt to leave this island without official permission will be a criminal offence. Tomorrow morning at ten o'clock you will attend at the headquarters of the Cuerpo General de Policía in Palma, where you will be further questioned concerning the deaths of Señor Burnett and Señor Heal . . .'

'You can't!' cried Alma.

'No one can regret this more than I, señorita. But I have my duty to perform . . .'

'I swear I wasn't at Gerry's that evening. I was here.'

'Then who was using your car? Whose voice could be so like yours that Señora Anzana is certain it was you?'

She went to speak, checked the words, gestured towards Selby, who muttered something wildly. 'It was my mother.' There were many more tears as she whirled round and ran into the caseta.

★   ★   ★

Phillipa walked up to where Alvarez stood by his car. 'Oh dear, I've obviously kept you waiting. Not for too long, I hope?'

'No, señorita. It has given me time to think.'

'You see, the path took me to the top of a cliff which I recognized because of the lighthouse. It's where, very many years ago, a boyfriend and I once stood and ... As I've said before, nothing can be as boring as an old woman reminiscing about her youth, so let's leave it. Well, what happens now?'

'We return to Llueso.'

'You gathered, of course, that the uncouth young man here could not have been the person I heard?'

'Yes, I did.'

'He has a northern accent, but that's not the kind of accent I meant.'

'I understand.'

'Then do you now have any idea who was rowing with my brother?'

'No, señorita, I don't.'

She climbed into the car and settled. She did not speak again until they had reached the road beyond the dirt track. 'Has something rather unpleasant happened? You look so ... so bewildered.'

He answered her honestly. 'I just don't know whether it is pleasant or unpleasant.'

CHAPTER NINETEEN

Alvarez drained his glass, put it down on the desk. As a buzzing fly circled it, he came to a decision. He reached down to the right-hand bottom drawer, brought out the bottle of brandy, and refilled his glass. There were times when a man needed considerable moral support.

Ten minutes later, he spoke over the phone to the plum-voiced secretary and said he'd like to have a word with the superior chief. That, he thought as he waited, was a lie.

'I've been expecting a report from you for days,' snapped Salas.

'I arrived back from Barcelona rather late, señor, and on Saturday I had two important meetings. Yesterday was Sunday...'

'I am well aware of what day of the week yesterday was.'

'Yes, señor.'

'Then arrange your thoughts and keep to essentials. Can you now name the murderer?'

'I'm afraid not.'

'You assured me that if you went to Barcelona and questioned a gallery owner, you would at long last be able to solve the case.'

'The information he gave me seemed to make things clearer but ... On Saturday afternoon I questioned another witness and her evidence has complicated everything.'

'It will not have needed her evidence for that to happen. Who is she and what's her evidence?'

'The daughter of Señor Heal.'

'Has she arrived on the island for the funeral, when that's allowed to take place?'

'The fact is, she's been living here for some time now.'

'Then why have you never mentioned her in any of your reports?'

Alvarez, all too well aware of how one wrong word could lead Salas to suspect the truth, said: 'But you have many times pointed out, señor, that there is no need to bother you with inessential details. Until now, there was little reason to suppose that her part in the case could be of the slightest importance.'

'What has changed?'

'I've learned who it was who was arguing with her father the night before his death.'

'You'd no idea she could be an important witness, yet at this late date you discover it was she who was arguing with her father...'

'No. I have discovered it was not she.'

'And that is important?'

'Yes, señor.'

'Then perhaps you also find it of great importance that neither was the person concerned the Duchess of Alfera?'

'It was her mother.'

'Who also was not arguing with her father?'

'Who was.'

'Her mother was having an argument with her father, the night before his death? I would agree with you, that is important. So why has it taken all this time to discover so important a fact?'

'Because she wasn't on the island at the time.'

'Who wasn't?'

'The mother.'

'But . . . but if she wasn't on the island, in God's name how could she have been having an argument with him in his house?'

'I may have put things slightly clumsily. I did not think she was on the island at the time. Perhaps it would help to explain things if I started at the beginning?'

'If that is not asking for the impossible.'

'I did learn early on that on the previous evening there had been a heated argument, but I could not determine who had been the lady concerned. But when I discovered that she was not the daughter and the mother, who wasn't on the island, was, and since Señor Heal was murdered the very next morning, if, of course, it was murder which I think one must logically accept since Señor Burnett was murdered, then surely it has to be of great importance? I hope it's all clear now?'

'I feel it will prove less wearing to answer in

the affirmative.'

'So I would like to question her if I may?'

'The daughter?'

'The mother, señor.'

'You feel you need my permission to question a witness?'

'You did seem rather concerned the last time.'

'You've questioned her before? But you said you've only just discovered her identity.'

'You were concerned the last time I went to Barcelona, señor.'

'What's Barcelona got to do with the mother who's here on the island?'

'But she isn't; she's returned home.'

'To Barcelona?'

'No. That's not where she lives.'

'Alvarez, I will confess that a little while ago, I'd have said it was impossible to confuse the issues any further. That was to deny your talents. Please, in the simplest form imaginable, what is it you're asking?'

'For permission to travel to Rostagne, señor, to question the mother.'

'Granted.' The connection was cut.

Alvarez replaced the receiver. He felt proud of the way in which he'd steered his superior chief away from the embarrassing question of why, if he'd known about the heated row the night before the murder of Heal, he'd not originally reported the matter so that the daughter could have been questioned at length and in depth.

★　　★　　★

'To France? You're going to France?' Dolores stopped stirring the contents of a saucepan and used the back of her hand to wipe away the beads of sweat on her forehead.

'There are only three flights a week to Toulouse,' said Alvarez, 'but I'm in luck and there's one tomorrow. I have to change at Barcelona and it's almost a three-hour wait, but I was talking to the sargento at the post and he says that there's a very good restaurant at the airport. Their cold quail in sauce are absolutely delicious.'

'You've only just been to Barcelona.'

'I know, but this is how the case keeps going. It must be a bit of a shock, so why not let's have a drink to help us get over it?'

'Can't you see I'm busy? And there's no need for you to have one either; you're drinking far too much.'

Who was it had first said that familiarity bred contempt? He could have added that it also bred abstinence, thought Alvarez sourly.

CHAPTER TWENTY

Alvarez drove along the undulating road in the Escort hired at Toulouse airport and savoured the green, lush fields which provided a sharp contrast to the sunburned, browned countryside he had left. Gascony. Home of the finest gastronomy in France. A Carlos I brandy was delicious, but who would dare weigh it against a thirty-five-year-old Trepont Armagnac?

He turned left at a crossroads. Above all, this was the land of space. So much space that trees grew on land which could have produced cash crops. Here, a farmer could walk for hundreds of metres and still own the soil over which he trod.

He reached a notice which named Rostagne, rounded a corner, and saw, built on and around a hill, the village; similar in form to many of the inland villages on the island, yet even at a distance clearly dissimilar in character. He turned right. The road became a lane, at first bordered by trees, then by fields. He passed a farmhouse in front of which was a large flock of ducks and he remembered something that he was astonished ever to have forgotten. Ducks were to this part of the country what geese were to Périgord. There were those who claimed that

207

the livers from the specially bred and fed ducks made goose pâté de foie gras a second-rate dish. His mouth watered at the prospect of finding out.

A man was working a tractor in a newly harvested field and Alvarez stopped the car, climbed on to the verge, and shouted across to ask where La Maison Verte was. The man removed his beret and scratched his head. Was that where the English lady lived? Then the house was just along the road, on the right.

La Maison Verte was an old, one-storeyed house set in a rising field which reached up to a small copse that crowned a hill; since the windows and doors had been painted a light blue, the bricks were a quiet red, and the tiles a grey-brown, the name had become a misnomer. On the left of the track up were several long rows of lavender bushes and the air was scented by these.

The land on which the house was set was level and he parked in front of the garage. As he crossed towards the front door, this was opened by a woman. He'd built up a mental picture of Tracy Heal. Alma in twenty-five years' time. Dark, curly hair beginning to silver, the attractive, unusual face matured, perhaps the inner strength slightly more apparent, the same overall impression of sympathetic understanding. Only the strength was there. Tracy's face was more immediately and conventionally attractive, sharp, and she had used considerable make-up to try to hold back the years; her clothes were designed for fashion, not comfort; her stylish shoes had heels so high that they were absurd in the countryside and Alma would never have worn them; her face expressed a self-centredness not seen in Alma's. 'Madame Heal?' he asked in French.

'And you're the Spanish detective. Are you on your own?'

'I thought it best.' He should, of course, have contacted the French police and obtained their permission for this meeting, but then a local detective would have accompanied him and everything said would have been known officially. He still hoped against hope that he was going to learn something that would enable him to bring the case to a conclusion without publicly having to involve Alma.

'Presumably you're not intending to stand there for the rest of the day?'

He followed her inside and was unprepared for the violence of the contrasting colours with which the beamed sitting-room, with open fireplace, had been decorated and furnished. She noticed his expression. 'Michel Rimaux at his most innovative,' she said dismissively, bored by the necessity of having to enlighten a pedestrian mind.

He supposed it was because of his stolid peasant background that he far preferred colours which soothed rather than jarred.

'D'you want something to drink?'

'Thank you, that would be very nice...'

'Have you ever had Floc?'

'I don't think so.'

'It's the local apéritif, so you'd better try it.' She turned, crossed in front of the fireplace to the far doorway, went through.

A very determined woman. One who would bitterly resent being disinherited. He sat on a chair covered in a bright yellow material and looked round the room. There were three paintings, in which everything was distorted, set in luxuriously sized and styled gilt frames, many silver knick-knacks of no practical use on the mantelpiece, and a glass-fronted display cabinet filled with figurines; the multi-coloured curtains looked hand-woven, the carpet could have hung on a wall as a tapestry of futuristic design. She was clearly a woman who spent money freely.

She returned with a tray on which were two crystal glasses set in delicate pewter stems. He took one, thanked her, drank. 'It is delicious.'

'I like it.' There was therefore, her tone suggested, no room for any guest's disliking it. 'Well, why are you here?'

'I am investigating two murders which have taken place...'

'Good God, man, I know all that!'

'Presumably your daughter's phoned and

explained things?'

'She's tried, but she's useless at explaining, especially where a man's concerned.'

'You refer to Señor Guy Selby?'

'Naturally. I don't suppose you can explain how, after bringing her up to have the tastes of a lady, she can see anything in a lout like him?'

'I have been told that he is a good artist who may well develop into a great one.'

'If he paints a second Last Judgement, it won't make him any more socially acceptable; you can't make a silk purse out of a sow's ear, even if you feed the pig on truffles. After meeting him, I asked Alma why she'd picked on a man who's both a boor and a bore. If one has to go slumming, at least try to do it with some style ... I expect you smoke?'

'Indeed, yes, but permit me to...'

'There are some on the table. You can give me one.'

She might have been brought up in the finest society, he thought, but it seemed she'd never been taught to say 'please'. After carrying the brass cigarette box across to her, it became clear that neither had she been taught to say 'thank you'.

She drew on the cigarette, blew out the smoke. 'As far as I could understand from Alma, you're here because of the row I had with Gerry?'

'That is so.'

'What about it?'

'I would like to hear what it was about, what effect it had on the señor . . . all that sort of thing.'

'All that sort of thing,' she repeated in sneering tones. 'I suppose you imagine that because I had a row with him, I murdered him. Well, there were times enough when I'd have liked to have done just that.' She drained her glass, looked across. 'You're a very slow drinker.'

'I was just . . .'

'Drink up.' She waited impatiently, then took their two glasses to refill them.

After handing him back his glass, she sat. 'Did you ever meet him?'

'No, I didn't.'

'Then you missed a real bastard, figuratively as well as literally.' She drank deeply. 'There's something which mystifies me. Just how in the hell did I ever come to marry him? I wasn't all starry-eyed, like my daughter, and I knew men professed eternal love only when they couldn't get a woman into bed in any other way . . .

'He'd charm. By God, he'd plenty of that when he thought it worth his while to exercise it. And a really sharp sense of humour. He used to mock people and always hit a painful spot dead centre. When I met him, he'd money; nowhere near as much as later on, but enough to dress in decent suits, drive snappy cars, patronize the right restaurants. He'd an air about him. When he said jump, even a head waiter jumped and it takes a good man to make them shift. But his god was ambition and he'd nothing but contempt for people he'd stepped on on his way up. I sometimes think that maybe it was the challenge that really attracted me. Even sensible women are supposed to be masochists who yearn for the challenge of rescuing men from their degradations: the drunkard from his drink, the womanizer from his women, the cad from his caddishness...

'He saw personal relationships in the same light as business ones—you either broke your competitor or were broken by him. But I wasn't going to be broken, so married life was one long fight. I'm a good fighter.'

It seemed he was expected to comment. 'I'm sure you are.'

'That's why he respected me. He'd married me for a background—I gave him a touch of class—but I made him respect me.' She drained her glass. 'I knew he was rolling every female fool enough to fall for his charms, but I didn't create scenes, I gave him the refined ice-box treatment. Once I told him I wasn't sharing my bed with a man who hadn't enough taste even to keep his screwing up-market. Did that make him furious!' She stood, crossed to where he sat, and held out her hand. 'You're the slowest drinker I've met for a long time.'

He emptied his glass, handed it to her. He watched her walk to the doorway and noted the care with which she moved. At a reasonable guess, she'd been drinking before he'd arrived.

She returned and sat without handing him his glass and he had to go and collect it from her. 'Did you separate some time ago, señora?' he asked as he returned to his chair.

She shrugged her shoulders. 'God knows! Sometimes seems a lifetime, sometimes seems like yesterday. The final act was when he decided he'd prefer the company of a woman whose daddy had gambled away the estate. Twenty years younger and all mincing affectation, but she was Lady Mary something or other and his Valhalla was filled with the noble aristocracy.'

'What happened?'

She laughed, with little humour. 'It was like a French farce. He went to Miami on a property deal that went sour and came back suddenly. He found Lady Mary in bed with a plain Miss. It wasn't the lesbianism that disgusted him, it was the common touch.'

'After you'd separated, he made you an allowance?'

'You think I'd have let him get away without? I'd have had the lawyers on to him in a second and they'd have blackened his image until he'd have looked more at home in a loin cloth. He knew that and since he was still in

214

business, he didn't dare take the risk.'

'But recently he'd decided to remarry, after obtaining a divorce, and both you and your daughter were to be cut out of his will and, I understand, your allowances were to be stopped?'

'Because that's what the bitch of a contessa demanded. She'd got him by the short and curlies because of her title. Men always want more. He could buy almost anything a man could wish for, so he yearned for something money can't buy—background, breeding, the *je ne sais quoi* which separates the gentleman from the herd. Since he couldn't buy it, he tried to do the next best thing: associate with it. Contessa Imbrolie. I always think of her as Contessa Bogie. She gets up my nose. Have you met her?'

He shook his head. 'She left the island to return to her home in Italy.'

'I can picture her down to the last plunge of a neckline that in all decency and respect for age should be feet higher. Maybe it's a pity he didn't live to marry her. He'd have found out what a real bitch of a wife is like.'

'You did know that when he remarried, you were to be cut out of his will?'

'Alma told me. It didn't seem to matter to her, but then she's never been serious about money. The young of today can be such fools. It was largely her fault, I suspect.'

215

'How was that?'

'Because she moved in with an artist from a back-to-back background who hadn't two pennies to rub together. If that sort of thing amused her, why didn't she have the sense to keep the news to herself? She knew her father. Gerry jumped on top of any woman who'd open her legs, but he demanded that his females led the lives of Caesar's wife; or the life that Caesar thought his wife was leading. He wanted his daughter to stick to men who moved to Eaton Square via Eton. What did she expect would happen when she turned up with someone who was straight out of *Coronation Street*? He was so furious that he listened to all Contessa Bogie had been demanding. D'you know what message he sent through Alma? It was time we learned to stand on our own two feet. Christ, I could have—'

'Killed him?'

She drank. 'I've already answered that. And yet ... Give me another cigarette.'

He crossed to the table and picked up the box, handed it to her, helped himself to a cigarette before replacing it. 'When you went to the island, was it to try and persuade him to change his mind?'

'I said that if he carried out his threat, I'd make him regret it.'

'How did he react to that?'

'The bastard laughed. Said he'd bought the

best possible advice and there wasn't any way either Alma or I could ever get our hands on a single penny more of his. He jeered at me . . . How well do you understand people?'

'Occasionally, señora, I manage to do so.'

'Then you'll appreciate that for him our relationship was always a battle. He had to prove that he was stronger than I. So all the time I fought him, he hated me for denying him his triumph, yet he had to respect me. But when he boasted that I'd never get a penny more of his, I . . .

'The most vicious thing about money is that it rusts away one's self-respect, but one doesn't realize that until too late. It wasn't as if I were facing penury. I've some money of my own and I could hope to find a job where languages and maturity count for more than youth. But I've grown so used to eating at the best restaurants, wearing fashionable clothes, living where and doing what I want, that all the strength had been rusting away. Instead of telling him to go to hell, I began to plead, to try to trade on our past life together. I demeaned and betrayed myself. But a strange thing happened. He didn't answer me with contempt, he answered me with sympathy. Perhaps he'd been wrong in listening so uncritically to the contessa; the past grew responsibilities that should always be honoured in the future. I expect you can guess why he acted like that?'

'No one's ever totally rotten, señora, and your admission that you could fight no longer called on his sympathies. It's even possible that had you not fought him so hard when you were together...'

'What in the hell are you talking about?'

He said, flustered: 'But you asked me why he was sympathetic instead of bullyingly triumphant...'

'In truth, you don't know a damn thing about people. You're soft-centred, always looking for the happy ending. He could always produce the charm when he wanted, just like turning on a tap. And he was so good at it that he actually had me—me, his wife, who knew exactly what kind of a bastard he was—believing that here was one leopard who'd actually changed his spots. He took me out to the best restaurant on the island, complimented me on my clothes, mentioned a little diamond clip in a jeweller's in Palma that would suit me perfectly... I was staying in a hotel near Alma, but in a hell of a lot more civilized area. When Gerry suggested coming up to my suite for a last drink, I agreed. How d'you like this, Contessa Bogie? ... He'd read me like a book. There was I, responding to his charm, believing that after all he'd behave like a gentleman instead of his more normal self, offered a chance to make a tart out of the Contessa Bogie ... How he'd been laughing to himself! Making a fool out of two women at the same time as he pleasured himself . . . Later, he became bored so he cut things short. Told me he'd been thinking things over and had decided to leave everything as it was and goodbye . . . What I'm asking you is how can any man be such a pure-bred bastard as to lead me on simply for the pleasure of kicking me back in the mud?'

'I cannot begin to understand such a person.'

'Then you're not much of a detective, are you?' She had begun to slur the occasional word.

'Was this before or after you went to his house?'

'Before. Why d'you think I went there?'

'I'm not certain.'

'Tell the truth and shame the devil. Like the bloody fool I can be, I was still hoping to salvage some self-respect. In the event, I lost my temper and behaved like a fishwife and that made him even happier because he's always been envious of my manners; mine come naturally, his called for very hard work.'

'Do you know what the time was when you left his house?'

'What does it matter?'

'It might be important.'

'Nothing's important. Drink up.'

'I think I've probably had enough.'

'Good God! Are you a man or a TT mouse? Don't they teach you to drink in Mallorca?'

'Señora, regretfully, I have a job to do. So if you would just tell me...'

'Certainly I'll tell you. But if I don't particularly want to be bothered to do something, I don't do it unless I'm charmed into it. So if you want to continue with such a boring subject, you'll have to charm me. And that means that first you get me another drink.'

He stood. She was at the awkward stage of drinking and if he wanted further cooperation he needed to humour her, even if to do so might result in her becoming confused.

'The bottle's on the table in the kitchen,' she said, as she handed him her glass.

'Where is the kitchen?'

'Into the hall, down the passage, and the second room on the right.'

The kitchen seemed to be equipped with every labour-saving device that had ever been invented. As he refilled their glasses, he wondered if, since she often ate out, she used half of them. He returned to the sitting-room.

He sat. 'You had this row on Thursday night...'

'Do you think I'm the complete bitch? A lot of men do.'

'Then they are very stupid.'

'Excellent! My soft-centred detective from Mallorca has hidden talents. I think that when you really want, you can probably be charming. Where shall we go to eat?'

'To eat?'

'If you're to charm a lady effectively, you have to take her out to dinner in a candlelit restaurant when you can murmur sweet compliments between sips of champagne. I think the Auberge du Mail. Michelin has not yet discovered that they should be awarded another two stars and so the chef is still trying desperately hard.'

'I don't think I have the time . . .'

'You want to know when I left Ca'n Heal? . . . Imagine a man so presumptuous that he names his house after himself. It would have been a coat of arms next.'

He drank.

'Charm me, I said, not bore me with silence. I can't stand silence.'

'I'm sorry, but I was thinking how sad a life you've had and how you deserve something infinitely better.'

'Speak on, O charmer!'

★　　★　　★

They left the restaurant and walked slowly across to the hired Escort, their arms linked and neither of them quite certain who was gaining support from whom. Alvarez searched his pocket for the keys, finally found them. He unlocked the passenger door and held it open for her.

'If a man has manners,' she said, 'it doesn't matter if he has a face like Quasimodo's.'

Did that mean she thought he looked like Quasimodo? He settled behind the wheel and she rested her arm along the back of his seat so that her fingers brushed his neck. 'It's a long, long time since I enjoyed a meal so much,' she said.

'It was truly delicious.'

'I wasn't talking about the food.'

Despite all the wine, champagne, and armagnac, she was not slurring her words any more than she had been much earlier; for his part, he no longer gave a damn what Salas's reactions might be when he saw the cost of the meal on the expense sheet.

He drove carefully, very conscious of her fingers on his neck. Did she realize they were tracking his flesh, sending shivers down his spine? . . . They left the road and drove up to her house. 'It's been a wonderful evening, Tracy.'

'Yes, it has.' Her fingers became more active.

'But now I must be on my way after asking a couple of questions I should have asked earlier . . .'

'Which I will answer once we're sitting down and enjoying a last drink.'

'I don't think . . .'

'Good. At this time of night, no one should think. Come on.'

222

He followed her across to the front door and watched her open her crocodile handbag for the key. She would never see forty again, or perhaps even forty-five, but her figure could have masqueraded as thirty. She'd changed into a cocktail dress before they'd gone out and this fitted her with seemingly artless perfection and her small breasts were tastefully outlined...

'You've gone silent again,' she said as she opened the door, stepped inside and switched on the hall light. 'What are you thinking?'

'That I shan't be sorry to get to bed.'

'I should hope not.'

He wished his mind were not so salacious that he read into her words an inference that could not have been intended.

They went through to the sitting-room. 'There's only one thing we can possibly drink now,' she said. 'I have a bottle of special armagnac that is kept for special guests on special occasions.'

He watched her leave the room and again noted the grace with which she moved. Earlier, she had spoken of a leopard changing its spots; there was much of the powerful, sinewy grace of a leopard about her.

She returned with two balloon glasses, well filled, and handed him one. As he warmed it in his hand, he said: 'Will you tell me now...'

'No, my dear soft-centred but very persistent Inspector, I will not tell you now. One drinks

223

armagnac of this quality with fitting reverence, not as an irrelevance.'

'But I have to know...'

'And so you shall, in good time.'

'The trouble is...'

'You're troubled?'

'The hotel doesn't have a night porter and they said they always lock all doors at midnight.'

'What a second-rate place you're staying at ... So you can see no alternative to leaving here very soon?'

'I'm afraid not.'

'What a plebeian lack of imagination!'

CHAPTER TWENTY-ONE

Alvarez awoke in bed to find he was on his own. He stared at the ceiling. Even at his age, life could still play a joker.

Tracy came through the doorway. She was wearing a flimsy nightdress which revealed broad vistas yet provocatively concealed details. 'If sound sleeping is a sign of a good conscience, you're a candidate for sainthood.' She climbed on to the bed and pulled back the sheet. 'And yet, like St Augustine, I see you're not ready for that blessed condition quite yet.'

They sat on either side of the table in the small
dining-room and breakfasted on warm
croissants, salted butter from Normandy, wild
strawberry or black cherry jam, and coffee. She
ate the last piece of croissant on her plate,
looked across. 'You're sure you can't stay for a
few days?'

'I'm afraid I must get back.'

'It's probably as well.' She saw his
expression, reached across the table and briefly
put her hand on his. 'Surely you've learned that
while sorrow can last a lifetime, happiness never
outlasts days? We've both had a wonderful
surprise; let's always be able to treasure it. If
you stayed too long, I'd sooner or later bitch
and then you'd remember me as you first
imagined me to be and I would stop seeing
Lochinvar ... Much kinder happiness cut short
than destroyed.'

'That's being horribly pessimistic.'

'Have you spent your life an optimist?'

He shook his head.

'Of course not. Only fools are lucky enough
to be optimists ... When do you have to leave?'

'I need to be at the airport by five-thirty.'

'We'll lunch here so that you can discover
that when I say I'm a wonderful cook, it's not
just an empty boast. Gerry used to say ...

Goddamnit, why do I have to bring his name up?'

'If you hadn't, I'd have had to.'

'Those bloody questions! D'you still think I murdered him?'

'If he'd been killed with a knife in the middle of a violent row, I might; but his death was plotted by someone cold and calculating and therefore not by you.'

'I suppose I can accept that as a sideways compliment ... What are the questions and then for God's sake let's forget him and think only of ourselves until you have to leave.'

'Do you remember what the time was when you left Ca'n Heal on that Thursday evening?'

'No. But I may be able to find out.'

'How?'

She said, for once speaking almost hesitantly: 'I keep a diary and have done ever since I was young. But at the beginning of the new year, I burn last year's diary so that I never have to relive all my mistakes. Does that make me quite crazy?'

'Only very lonely.'

'You bastard! You really know how to go for the jugular.'

'I'm sorry...'

'Don't be, so that I can remember you as the only man I've known who tells the truth.' She stood, left.

He stared out through the window at the land which sloped up to the trees which covered the

226

crown of the hill. There'd been a fierce desire on his part to stay for the few days she'd suggested, but some instinct had urgently warned him not to. A similar bitter pessimism to that which ruled her life?

She returned, a large cloth-bound book in her right hand. She sat, opened the book at an embossed leather marker, turned back several pages. 'Thursday, the sixteenth—that's the day, isn't it? I'm not going to read out most of what I wrote because I need to keep some shreds of pride ... I drove over to Ca'n Heal, lost my temper, had a flaming row with the bastard, then drove straight back to the hotel. I wrote up the diary almost immediately after returning and the time was ten-thirty, so I suppose I left him at about nine-thirty. Now, is there anything else you want to know?'

'Did you see Señor Heal on Monday the thirteenth?'

She turned back more pages, read. 'In the morning, yes.'

'When?'

'Does it matter exactly when?'

'It could be very important.'

'Damn it! ... All right. He spent Sunday night with me, at the hotel, left after breakfast and didn't come back until the evening.'

'He was with you Monday evening?'

'All night.'

'You're absolutely certain of that?'

227

'How many more times d'you want me to tell you?' Her voice had sharpened.

'What sort of state was he in on Monday when he returned?'

'More bloody-minded than usual.'

'Did you gather why?'

'He mentioned something that had happened; I've forgotten what it was.'

'Try and remember.'

'What the hell does it matter now?'

'It does.'

Her expression became sullen. 'Give me some more coffee.' She pushed her cup across.

He filled her cup with the last of the coffee in the pot.

She added sugar and milk, suddenly said: 'I'm sorry, I'm bitching sooner than even I expected. But I don't want to go on and on talking about him; I want to forget he ever existed. I want to enjoy the few hours we've left together.'

'Remember what happened and then you can and will.'

One croissant remained in the wicker basket and she picked it out and put it on her plate, but instead of eating it she began to pluck off pieces which she teased between forefinger and thumb. 'He'd had a row with someone. Half life's about rows, isn't it?'

'Who was the someone, what was the row about?'

'I don't suppose he ever said. All that's certain is, he didn't get his way. There was never any mistaking when that happened.'

★   ★   ★

Alvarez sat in the upstairs restaurant in the old terminus at Barcelona airport and stared out through the window at a plane that was taxiing ready to take off. The quail were delicious, but he wasn't concentrating on them as he should. Coincidences bedevilled most investigations, largely because it was often difficult to identify them correctly. Investigators were by training loath to accept coincidences, preferring a definite and deliberate linkage to relate two events; but they happened. So on that Monday morning, coincidentally Heal might have had an argument which ended in his failing to get his way with someone other than Justin Burnett. But . . .

CHAPTER TWENTY-TWO

'Enrique,' said Dolores, 'you're not eating.'
He started.
'Is something wrong?'
'It's just that I was thinking.' He stirred the hot chocolate, dunked a piece of coca in it.

'Ever since you returned from France, you've been thinking.'

'There's small wonder in that!'

She couldn't make out whether his thoughts were pleasant or unpleasant since one moment his expression suggested the former, the next, the latter. Was it, or wasn't it, that foreign woman again? Despite his denials, was he in fact still lusting after her?

Jaime came into the kitchen. He yawned.

'You're going to be late for work,' Dolores said.

He crossed to the table and cut himself a large slice of coca. 'It's going to be a scorcher today, you mark my words.'

She was grateful for the chance to vent some of her angry frustration. 'My husband is brilliant! In the middle of July, when there has not been a cloud in the sky for weeks, when it is like a furnace even before the sun rises, he can foretell that it is going to be a hot day!'

'All right, all right, I was only remarking. What's suddenly got you all fired up?'

'Men.'

'Where would you be without us?'

'Much happier.' She picked up her purse from the table. 'I need to buy some meat from the butcher since I have two men who demand hot food every day because they do not have to do the cooking. Make certain that whoever's the last to leave, locks up. If either of you can remember anything that long.' She left the kitchen, head held high.

'The hot weather always gets her like this,' said Jaime, as he cut himself another piece of coca. 'I mean, what's she really got to complain about?'

Alvarez nodded.

'You're in a talkative mood, I must say!' He ate. 'Well, I suppose I'd best get a move on. It's rush, rush, rush, all day long. Doesn't give a man time to live.' He stared at Alvarez. 'At least for some it's rush. For others, it's sit on their backsides and get paid for it.'

Alvarez finally spoke. 'What's that?'

'Nothing, mate; just sweet bloody nothing. But if you don't move soon, you won't get to the office before it's time to come back for lunch.' He left the kitchen and a moment later there was the sound of the front door being shut with unnecessary force.

Alvarez emptied the last of the hot chocolate from the jug into his mug, lit a cigarette. He sighed. No matter how much it further complicated the present complications, no matter that it would probably lead him along paths he feared to tread because of where they must lead, he was going to have to accept that on that Monday morning Heal had quite definitely been the man who had rowed with Burnett.

Surely Phillipa must have recognized his

231

voice, however heated he'd become? And even if one were somehow able to accept that under extreme emotion he might have sounded very different from normal, there was no way in which his voice could have gained a foreign accent. She had been lying throughout—a fact confirmed by the way in which she had originally claimed the voice she'd heard had been very lightly accented, then had changed that description when asked if Simitis could have been the man.

Why should she have lied? To protect Heal? When she'd always despised him because he was so pretentiously false? An emotional attachment? To ask the question was to realize it was ridiculous. Could her motive have been financial—blackmail? Over what? In any case, blackmail was one of the more filthy crimes and she respected old-fashioned honour. Bribery? Virtually the same answer. There seemed to be no feasible motive for her having lied, which strongly suggested that she had not. But the premiss was that she must have done ... She'd been mistaken, rather than had lied; an old woman, slightly hard of hearing, the foreign accent existing only in her mind. She had heard Heal, but not clearly enough to be certain and a false accusation would be an iniquity, however much she disliked the man. Heal had rowed violently with Burnett, left when Burnett refused to misidentify the fake, and that night had . . . That night he had been with Tracy . . . Alvarez hastily moved his thoughts on. Heal could not have murdered Burnett. Which reintroduced Alma and Selby . . .

★   ★   ★

'It seems,' said Salas over the phone, 'as if you have actually managed to make some progress.'

'Unfortunately, señor, I am not so certain that I have.'

'You are heir to one of your many hunches or are reluctant to discern order beyond the chaos?'

'I don't think things can be as straightforward as they're beginning to look. Assume the murderer was Selby. Alma Heal must . . . Well, at the very least she must have known of his guilt. She would have been in a terrible state—her father murdered by her lover. In that case, her mother would inevitably have appreciated that something terrible had happened to her daughter and when she heard about her husband's death she would have guessed what. Would she then have given her husband an alibi for Burnett's murder when to do so must make it that much more certain that Selby would be accused?'

'With more experience, Alvarez, you would know that women are strangers to logic. You will bring in Selby for questioning.'

233

'But, señor . . .'

'And the daughter.'

'I appreciate that the evidence suggests she must have known what was happening, but I'm sure she didn't. And if she didn't . . .'

'Clearly, it is not only women who are strangers to logic. Equally clearly, you also suffer from an extremely restricted memory since it's only a moment ago that you were saying the daughter must have known of his guilt.'

'Only if one assumed Selby was the murderer.'

'An assumption which comes easily. Clearly it was she who made the telephone call which drew Heal up into the mountains when he should have been seeing you. You will bring them both in tomorrow morning. Is that perfectly clear?'

'You don't think it might be an idea to wait . . .'

'Prevarication is the last refuge of the incompetent.' He cut the connection.

Alvarez slumped back in the chair. He'd tried, but this was the end of the line. As, of course, it should be. Two cold-blooded murders. If Alma had been some hard-bitten female, would he have hesitated about arresting Selby? What kind of detective allowed his personal emotions to guide his actions? (What were his emotions? He had, now it must be admitted, initially fallen in love with the daughter. He had gone to bed with the mother. It sounded like incest. Mother of God, a man could unwittingly complicate his life!) He was betraying his duty all the time he refused to accept the truth . . .

And yet . . . Strip away all emotions and become a proper detective. Phillipa had not been mistaken, she had lied. One lied when there was motive to do so. What had been her motive? It surely could only have been the money she would inherit under her brother's will. But this, by extension, was to name her the murderer of her brother and, since everything pointed to the fact that the two murders were linked, the murderer of Heal as well. Her only motive for the latter murder could be that Heal knew that she had murdered her brother. Knowing this, would Heal have remained silent—why defend someone he must guess disliked him? And would he have allowed himself to be lured up into the mountains where it would be much easier to murder him . . .

This was to heap absurdity on top of absurdity. So back to the beginning and accept only what was known to be true. Phillipa was a woman of old-fashioned standards who had loved her brother. Then nothing could or would have induced her to murder him. Further, she would do everything within her power to bring his murderer to book. She had heard Heal have a very heated row with her brother in the morning, her brother had been murdered that night; every tenet of logic must suggest to her that Heal was the murderer. Her every instinct would have been to denounce Heal, not protect him by lying. That lie made nonsense of everything . . .

Suddenly he realized that if it made nonsense of everything, it must make sense of something. She had lied in order to make certain Heal was *not* arrested for murder. But because she would never have done that had she believed he could be the murderer, it followed that she was certain he was not. Then she had to know the identity of the murderer.

★   ★   ★

He parked his car and walked round to the front of the caseta. Phillipa was not outside, but the door was open so he called through the bead curtain.

She answered from upstairs. 'What is it?'

He moved back and sideways until he could look up through a gap in the vine. 'It's me, señorita.'

'Thirsty?'

'I need to talk to you.'

She stared down at him for several seconds, then abruptly stepped back to disappear from sight.

236

He waited, wishing himself anywhere but where he was. She came through the bead curtain and out on to the patio. 'You may need to talk to me, but presumably you can do that equally well with a drink as without?'

He nodded.

She returned inside. He sat down on one of the patio chairs and thought how sad it was that in an imperfect world it was so often the nice people who suffered and the nasty ones who prospered.

When she came out, a tray in one hand, she was wearing a flower-print frock, smarter than anything he had seen her in before, and she had used a trace of make-up to very good effect. She handed him a glass of brandy in which were three ice cubes. 'I didn't ask you what you'd like, but I imagine that you're a man whose tastes don't change.'

'I am afraid that that is so.'

'Why apologize? The world was a much happier place when there was far less change.'

'I think, happier only for some.'

'Of course. But I've learned one thing about life and because I'm old, I can say it. There will always be those who have and those who have not, whether under capitalism, socialism, communism, or any other ism. Yet the more people are fooled into striving after equality, the harsher the inequality they eventually suffer. But you haven't come here to hear my reactionary political views, have you?'

'I'm afraid not, señorita.'

'More fear?'

'Because I hate to cause unhappiness.'

'I hope you won't feel offended if I say that you really are a most extraordinary man? When I first met you—please excuse an old woman's frankness—I thought you rather dull and probably not over-bright. But as I've come to know you, I've discovered someone who knows far more about the world than most, who cares deeply about the things which used to matter, such as honesty, decency, and other people's feelings . . . Damn it, I'm sounding patronizing and that's the last thing I intended.'

'To me, you merely sound very kind.'

She stared out at her garden. 'It's no good going on trying to stave off the inevitable. You know, don't you?'

'I think so.'

'I was afraid you'd find out. If you'd been full of your own cleverness I wouldn't have been worried, but you search for the good in other people, which means that sooner or later you learn what each one of them truly is. When you know who a person really is, you know what he or she can or cannot do. When did you finally become certain?'

'I did not understand until Señora Heal told me that Señor Heal had definitely had a row with someone on the Monday morning. Unless

238

that was an extraordinary coincidence, it meant that you had been lying when you say that the man you'd heard had definitely not been Señor Heal. But I could, of course, have guessed a long time before if I'd been clever.'

'Why?'

'There are two reasons. You said your brother had been brought up to be religious and therefore he could never have committed suicide. But he had rebelled against his upbringing since, as he saw it, it had betrayed him and therefore it was likely that he would have forsworn religion. But even if that is doubtful, the second reason is more certain. He died in the dining-room, and not the study. In the majority of suicides, the suicide takes his life in the most comfortable circumstances that his method allows. The señor would have been very much more comfortable in the sitting-room, but he chose the dining-room. Why? I think it was because of the books.'

'You're quite right, of course. He hated those books, yet he brought them out here because he didn't dare get rid of them. In them, he saw the library of our youth and the brooding authority of the father who'd made him a weak man. If it had been I, I'd have killed myself in the library as a gesture of defiance; he never could defy his father, not even long, long after his father was dead.'

'Why did he commit suicide?'

239

'After the car accident he suffered recurring headaches which became more and more severe. He returned to England to see the specialist who'd originally operated on him and after certain tests a tumour on the brain was diagnosed. The specialist wanted to operate and remove it, Justin refused because he was quite certain that any operation would leave him immobilized, a cabbage.'

'Then his suicide was an act of strength, not weakness. It was not his own pain which drove him to it, it was the thought of the pain he would cause those who had to look after him.'

'I should have known you'd see it in that light ... Ever since it happened, I've been trying to console myself with the same thought.' She closed her eyes.

'Will you tell me all that happened?'

She opened her eyes. 'There's little enough to tell. I rang him early on that awful morning because I was so worried. There was no answer. I went up to his house and let myself in and found ... If there'd been the slightest chance of his being alive, of course I'd have called an ambulance. But it was horribly obvious he was dead.' She shivered. 'But instead of terrible grief blanking out my mind, it seemed ... it really seemed as if someone were talking to me. With his death, all his pensions and his annuity stopped and his estate consisted only of the contents of the house and the life insurance.

But life insurances contain a clause which excludes payment on suicide, so he wouldn't even be leaving that. And this voice went on to say that for years he'd been helping me directly and indirectly and all that must now stop and I'd be considerably worse off than I have been. Perhaps I'd have to leave my little house because I could no longer afford to live on the island. But with the money from the life insurance, the few years I can have left would be very much easier, not very much more difficult. I could buy some new clothes, a new refrigerator, I could once again eat out and choose the nice dishes, I could offer friends hospitality, I could go back to England to see my cousin's grandson.'

Her expression had suggested many emotions, one of which had been surprise. He judged that this had been her surprise at discovering how desperately she longed for a small touch of extra comfort at the end of her life.

'I've always been an omnivorous reader, enjoying anything well written, whether a classic, an autobiography, or even a crime novel. It's extraordinary what arcane knowledge one can gather from books. I knew that when a gun's fired, marks are left on the skin of the person who fired; that an expert can tell whether a bullet came from a particular gun; that a gun usually doesn't carry fingerprints, although most people believe that it does...'

He wondered at the cold-blooded courage she had had to show to overcome so shocking an experience. A moralist would probably claim that greed had strengthened an already forceful will-power; he preferred to believe it was her knowledge that she had a right to spend those remaining years in dignity and that there were times when a right could justifiably be enforced by less than righteous means.

'I had to give the impression that someone had killed Justin, then tried to hide the murder by making it look like suicide. He'd killed himself with one bullet and because of where he'd shot himself I was reasonably certain no one would be able to tell whether the shot had been fired by a right-handed or a left-handed man. Because he was left-handed, there would be powder marks on his left hand, but a murderer would probably not know that he was left-handed and so would try to make it seem he'd fired the fatal bullet with his right hand. That would mean there'd be powder marks on both hands, but I was hoping people would think there'd been a struggle and Justin had been shot by the murderer who, too excited to realize that Justin was left-handed, had tried to set the scene to make it seem Justin had fired one shot to check the gun was working and then had killed himself with the second one.'

'Which is what I did think.' Suicide disguised

as a murder disguised as a suicide. So cleverly carried out that if he had not tried very hard to prove Alma innocent and had flown to France, he would probably never have realized the fact. 'So when it became probable that Señor Heal was being suspected of the murder, you had to deny it was his voice you'd heard in case he was falsely accused.'

She asked, in a faltering voice: 'Have I been guilty of a crime?'

'I'm afraid you have, señorita.'

'I may be sent to prison?'

'I . . . I do not know,' he lied.

CHAPTER TWENTY-THREE

Alvarez sat at his desk and stared at a fly which buzzed backwards and forwards along the wall and for the moment lacked the inquisitive intelligence to continue another metre to the right to find the open window. It was his duty to telephone Salas to report that it was now established that Burnett had committed suicide. But then he would not only be exposing the señorita to a criminal prosecution, he would be ensuring that even if, on account of her age, she escaped a prison sentence, her last few years would be spent in the deep shadow of not-so-genteel poverty.

Of course, if he were really honest he'd have to admit that his reluctance to telephone was not solely occasioned by his feelings for the señorita. Salas was going to ridicule his entire investigation. . .

There had never been the certainty that Heal's death had been murder, only the strongest probability that it was because it had to be directly connected with Burnett's murder. But since Burnett had committed suicide, could there be any connection? Had Heal's crash been accidental and the damage to the braking system of the Mercedes been caused by the crash, not caused it?

What possible motives for Heal's murder remained? Alma and Tracy Heal stood to gain the fortune which they had been within weeks, perhaps days, of losing. Through Alma, Selby might gain the artistic success which so far had eluded him and which, if he could not find a source of capital, might well forever continue to do so. Simitis? He had a signed receipt for a reproduction diadem and so no one could legally prove he had swindled Heal. More, had the fake diadem been the motive for the murder, it would surely have been Heal who would have murdered Simitis, having been outwitted by a man he could not legally attack? The Contessa Imbrolie? Quite apart from the fact that she had almost certainly been thousands of miles away, it had been totally in her interests for Heal to live long enough to alter his will in her favour.

So if there had been a murder, only Alma, Tracy, and Selby, had a motive. Could Alma have committed patricide or have kept silent had she known who had murdered her father? Selby, of an unattractive character but no fool, must have known that she could never countenance so despicable a crime and that if he had committed it and she had learned this—which surely she must—she would have nothing more to do with him and so the whole reason for his crime would be nullified. Could Tracy, more emotionally at risk than she would ever admit, plan so cold-blooded a murder, even if her husband had so clearly shown how he despised her?

No, none of those three could have murdered. Therefore there had been no murder, the crash had been an accident. And now he was going to have to admit that to Salas. He summoned up his courage and reached out for the telephone, stayed his hand. Once again, he was in danger of forgetting a basic rule of self-preservation. When admitting a mistake, always provide an excuse.

Heal had been very concerned over something. On that Friday morning, when waiting to be questioned by a detective—and even a man innocent of any wrongdoing suffered some apprehension in these circumstances—he had been lured away from his house by a telephone call. So couldn't it be suggested that he must have been murdered by the unknown caller for an as yet unknown motive? Salas wasn't fond of unknowns; he might well point out that Heal, arrogant and knowing he had not murdered Burnett, wouldn't give a damn about skipping an appointment with a mere local detective . . .

Alvarez leaned back in the chair. It gave a man a headache trying to sort out a confusing and confused life.

★   ★   ★

He awoke, yawned, and reluctantly accepted that nothing had changed; he was still faced with the necessity of ringing Salas. Perhaps if he concentrated on Burnett's suicide, he could divert Salas's attention away from the mistakes over Heal's accident? Then, with some degree of resigned surprise, he realized that even now he had not yet cleared up every query raised by Burnett's suicide . . .

Phillipa met him at the gate of her garden. She had changed since the morning and now wore a frock that was old and carefully darned; her make-up had weathered, adding to her years. 'I suppose you've come to arrest me? Then I'd better change out of my gardening clothes.'

246

'No, señorita, all I'm here for is to ask you a question.'

'Oh! In some ways, I'm sorry.' She spoke as firmly as possible, but could not prevent a slight quaver to her voice. 'The waiting is beginning to be rather trying ... You'd better come in. Please mind the zinnia, which I was about to tie up.'

He opened the gate and stepped inside. A red zinnia with two enormous flowers had flopped and he carefully stepped over it. They sat.

'Señorita, originally, when you claimed your brother's death could not be suicide, you said that the suicide note had to be false, he could never have written it. The letter was not typed on his machine. Did you make it up, deliberately writing in a strange style?'

'Not exactly.'

'In what way?'

'I typed the note you found. When Justin bought his typewriter, he bought a similar one for me. The typefaces appear to be exactly similar, but I knew an expert would find differences. But what I wrote was correct.'

'The words were the same he had written?'

'Yes. I know I told you he couldn't have used so florid a style, but sadly that wasn't true. He so often tended to be grandiloquent, unfortunately especially when some reserve was called for. I remember that one of the few times we had an unpleasant row was when I criticized an article he'd written for laymen on Roman lamps. Another person's scholarship is really only acceptable if it's presented simply and in terms which make the ordinary reader feel he could be just as smart if he really wanted to be.'

'Then what did the message mean?'

'I don't know.'

'"But immortality can defeat death." D'you think that could be a reference to the book which the señor wrote which, I have been told, was very good.'

'A professor in America said that in his own field it was the finest work he'd ever read . . .' She stared into the distance.

He waited, but she did not answer his question. 'The translation of the latin meant that if one sought his monument, one had to look around. What was there in the dining-room or the rest of the house which could provide that monument? Was there, perhaps, another manuscript he hoped to be even more scholarly successful than the first?'

'There was nothing like that. He hadn't written a word since he came to live on the island. Perhaps it was a reference to the letter.'

'What letter?'

'That was by the typewriter. I burned it since it probably confirmed his suicide.'

'Didn't you read it first to find out?'

'Certainly not!' She spoke indignantly. 'It was addressed to the coroner. I have never opened, let alone read, a letter addressed to someone else unless I've been given permission.'

In an odd sort of way he found that perfectly logical. Even while breaking rules most would hold to be sacrosanct, she had carefully held to others which might have seemed to be of no account. 'If that letter had merely been giving his reasons for committing suicide, it really wouldn't have been any sort of a monument, would it? That is, not one that he would want remembered for years.'

'I suppose not.'

'And why did he mention Paris? You told me he'd never been there, but might there have been a lady whom he'd never mentioned?'

'When he was young, he would never have risked Father's wrath by enjoying the company of a cocotte—had she been respectable, he'd have brought her home since Father was very broad-minded about foreigners. Once he was married, he'd never have been given the chance. When his wife died, he was too old.'

'Then why should he have mentioned Paris?'

It was some time before she answered, her mind having slipped away to other thoughts. 'I suppose it's more likely he meant the person than the city.'

'How d'you mean, person?'

'Brother of Hector, abductor of Helen.'

'I'm sorry, señorita, I do not understand.'

'They didn't make you translate passages from the *Iliad* or the *Odyssey* at school? The Trojan War. Paris was stupid enough to prefer the most beautiful woman in the world to the rule of Asia or renown in war, so he threw Aphrodite the golden apple. His reward was Helen, wife of Menelaus. When he abducted her, the thousand ships were launched and the Trojan War began. He was responsible for the deaths of so many; Hector, Priam...'

'Priam?' said Alvarez with sudden excitement.

'Paris was the second son of Priam and Hecuba and for some reason was brought up by a shepherd on a hill. He married ... I've forgotten her name—Justin would have told you immediately. But at least I can remember that you like brandy with ice.' She stood, went into the caseta.

Priam's treasure! If you seek my monument, look around you. A letter, burned before it was read. A fake diadem, supposedly from the treasure found by Schliemann and looted from Berlin by the Russians...

Here was another motive for Heal's death and it was because of this that he had been murdered. His murder was connected with Burnett's suicide through the motive...

She returned, put two glasses down on the table. 'Has something happened?' she asked curiously.

'Yes, señorita. I think that I have just learned something very important.'

'What?'

'Perhaps I might explain later, when I have thought about it more.'

She was not really interested. She drank. 'Will you tell me something?'

'If I can.'

'D'you think I'll have to share a cell? You see, I've lived on my own for so long that I'm sure I'll feel very uncomfortable if I have to be in other women's company all day and all night.'

'Please do not consider such thoughts.'

'But I must. And at my age, that sort of thing is a worry.'

'Maybe you will not have to discover the answer.'

She looked at him with a sudden, desperate hope.

★   ★   ★

He sat at his desk. Had he had a good education, he might have understood the truth a lot sooner. Or even if he had had the nous to appreciate that Burnett, steeped in the past, would tend to think in the past and would prefer sibylline riddles to straightforward statements . . .

When Simitis had decided to swindle Heal by

employing the old dodge of appearing to be the sucker, he had overlooked one very important fact: Heal possessed the natural gift of being able to appreciate quality. Simitis had artfully exhibited the diadem and gained Heal's attention and later the sale, never appreciating that Heal had instinctively judged the diadem to be genuine. Simitis had been the fool, not Heal, because he had not recognized the truth when it had been in his hands.

Heal had taken the diadem to Burnett to be authenticated, knowing that if he were right then he owned one of the most valuable ancient artifacts in the world, as great as anything from Tutankhamen's tomb. And if the source from whom Simitis had bought it could be identified, there was a chance that other pieces, or even the whole collection, could be recovered. The fortune at stake was beyond computation.

Burnett had authenticated the diadem. And immediately there had been a violent row. Heal naturally needed the news of this fabulous discovery to be kept secret while efforts were made to recover the rest of the treasure; on the other hand, Burnett wanted the kudos of becoming known as the man who had identified the lost treasure and he didn't give a damn what Heal stood to lose by early publication. Heal, able to judge how weak was Burnett's character, had threatened him with unimaginable agonies if he so much as breathed a word to anyone. So there was Burnett with immortality (on his terms) within reach, yet a hideous fate (it would never have occurred to his craven soul that Heal might be bluffing) if he reached for it.

He'd always been a coward and when a tumour on the brain had been diagnosed, he'd refused an operation. Every day he must have seen death closing in on him; every day the headaches had grown more and more insufferable, except that he had had to suffer them unless he either submitted to that operation or committed suicide, which needed more courage than he could find ... More, that was, until he realized that suicide offered him the only way of claiming immortality while escaping Heal ...

*   *   *

Alvarez parked in front of Ca'n Kaïlaria. He rang the bell and the maid opened the door. She said that the señor was in and showed him into the sitting-room.

Simitis, this time in a light grey suit, hurried into the room. His manner was abrupt, not fulsome. 'Inspector, I am a very busy man and I simply cannot accept these repeated interruptions. I have told you all I know—'

'Not quite.'

He crossed to stand in front of the fireplace, hands clasped behind his back. 'Does that mean that you intend to continue with your ridiculous accusation that I cheated Gerald Heal?'

'Only that you thought you had. It took time to discover that you hadn't.'

Simitis could not conceal his sense of shock. 'When you were offered the diadem as part of Priam's treasure, you laughed scornfully and told the seller that this was the hundredth time you'd been told that. But what neither the seller nor you realized was that this time it happened to be true. Some, if not all, of the treasure had survived. The looters in Berlin had recognized, even if only dimly, that the pieces were worth more than their melt-down value, and so they'd decided to hide them, intending to sell them as works of art when life became settled. Obviously, they were never able to do this. Probably they were liquidated. Stalin was suspicious of any Russian who'd seen the truth of the West. The treasure was once more lost.

'Recently, at least one piece of it has been found again and the finder, probably recognizing the craftsmanship of the diadem but not its true history, naturally wanted as much money as he could get and so named it as part of Priam's treasure. Equally naturally, you derided such a provenance and bargained until the price suited you; since the seller believed he was lying, he was ready to accept such a price. With the diadem yours, you set out to swindle Señor Heal ... Only he was a lot smarter than

254

you and became instinctively certain it was genuine. So he allowed you to think that you were fooling him, while in fact he was fooling you. Once his, he took it to Señor Burnett for authentication.

'Later, Señor Heal was in touch with you, not to boast—much as he'd like to have done—but to tell you what had happened. Señor Burnett had authenticated the diadem, but had been so excited by the discovery and what that would mean to him that he had wanted to publicize it immediately, careless of the fact that this would prevent any further pieces being bought at a fraction of their worth. He'd managed to frighten Señor Burnett into silence so effectively that the poor man committed suicide. And it seemed that Señor Burnett had left behind no word of the discovery. Speed became of the essence. Were there more pieces of the treasure extant and, if so, how to recover them before the world learned the truth?

'You were possessed by two exceedingly strong emotions and it would be interesting to know which was the stronger—your anger or your greed. You hold yourself to be the smartest of men, but had been made a fool of. If somehow this potential fortune could be all yours, you could walk with billionaires. And if at the same time you got your own back on

255

Señor Heal, then your cup would be overflowing.

'You telephoned Señor Heal on the Friday morning and said you'd made contact with the seller of the diadem who was on the island and wanted to discuss further sales. No doubt, you gilded the lily by saying that it was certain most of the treasure was intact and that if the two of you acted very carefully, you'd be able to buy everything. Naturally, that captured Señor Heal's enthusiasm and so he saw nothing peculiar in a meeting deep in the mountains—all parties needed absolute secrecy.

'When he arrived, you drew him away from his car. My guess is, you said you were due to meet your contact off the road, perhaps in the ruins of an abandoned building. That gave your hired accomplice—you'd never find the courage to do such work yourself—time to sabotage the Mercedes.

'When no contact turned up, you said there'd been some sort of a hitch, but the other man was bound to be in touch again. Señor Heal left, frustrated, perhaps even a little suspicious of events, and in consequence of high emotions and the drinks with which you'd plied him, he drove even more furiously than usual. At one of the most dangerous parts of the mountain road the brakes failed, he went off the road and was killed. The fortune was yours and yours alone.'

'Prove it!' shouted Simitis.

'I can't.'

256

He stared at Alvarez, fear giving way to amazement, amazement to calculation.

'Not right now. But if I start a full investigation into all your movements, if the incoming and outgoing passenger lists of every aircraft during the relevant times are examined and your accomplice identified, if every person who was on the mountain road on the Friday is asked if he or she saw you or your car, if a thousand and one further avenues of inquiry are followed, then sooner or later I shall uncover the leads that name you the murderer.'

'If?'

Alvarez was silent.

'How much do you want?'

'The name and whereabouts of the man who sold you the diadem.'

Simitis's voice became scornful. 'So that you can try and get everything for yourself? You, a peasant on this flea-speck of an island, have dreams of becoming as rich as Croesus? Take what I offer you, ten million pesetas, and continue living, in easier circumstances, the kind of life for which you're suited.'

'I'm not interested in the treasure.'

'Then why d'you want the name?'

'So that I can give it to the director of the Museum of Humanities. He can try and recover the treasure for Mallorca.'

'You must be crazy. If I pass on the name, I lose everything...'

257

'You have already. Either you give it to me or I intensify the investigation until you are named the murderer. And until your arrest, you will spend every minute of every day knowing that fate is getting closer and closer and that soon you will be arrested, tried, and be sent to prison. Think what prison must mean for a man of your refinement. How will the crude peasants of this flea-speck of an island treat so elegant a señor as you? Can you hope to survive their rustic ways? And you will not even have the consolation of knowing that when you finally leave prison—should that ever come to pass—a fortune will be awaiting you. Refuse my deal and I'll tell the world the truth and the treasure will be found by others.'

'No one will believe you.'

'They will when they examine the diadem which Señor Heal bought from you ... Fight me and you gain nothing, lose everything; act with me and while you gain nothing, you lose nothing. As an educated, clever, refined man from the great world beyond, do you think you really have any choice?'

CHAPTER TWENTY-FOUR

Salas said over the phone: 'The two men had a fight?'

258

'Yes, señor.' Alvarez stared at the glass on his desk in which there still remained a generous measure of brandy, his nervousness growing with every second. He readily recognized that he was far from a clever man, yet if he were to save Phillipa from prison he now had to pull the wool over Salas's eyes—and Salas was surely a very clever man or how else could he have become a superior chief? 'Señor Burnett was a very nervous and excitable man. He owned this old revolver and produced it to threaten Señor Heal. My guess is that in his excited state he appeared far more dangerous than he was and Señor Heal, desperate to save himself, tried to gain possession of the gun and in the struggle it inadvertently went off. That was the first bullet, which hit the wall. Señor Heal then managed to force him to drop the gun. However, perhaps with the strength which comes to weak people when they are desperate, he got hold of the gun again and the struggle was resumed. Tragically when the gun was fired a second time, the muzzle was pointing at his forehead.'

'There were powder marks on both his hands.'

'He was left-handed, but he could do far more with his right hand than the average right-handed man can do with his left. His sister has confirmed that fact.'

'If that's what happened, how did the whisky get on the table?'

'As can be readily appreciated, finding himself with a dead man and remembering the violent row they had had that morning, Señor Heal panicked, believing he would be found guilty of murder.'

'Señorita Burnett denies it was he who had the row with her brother in the morning.'

'The señorita is old, a little deaf, and very stubborn. It now seems she did not hear as clearly as she has claimed. Having first denied it could have been Señor Heal's voice, she was very reluctant to admit that it might have been.'

'You still haven't explained the whisky or the suicide note. And what was the row about?'

'Horrified by what had happened, Señor Heal took the only course of action which then seemed to him to offer any chance of escaping being tried for murder. He set the scene to make it look as if Señor Burnett had committed suicide. But because he did not know the dead man, he had no idea that here was one of the few Englishmen who never drank whisky. As to the suicide note—it is meaningless. Señor Heal was a self-made man from humble beginnings who had become very rich and, like many such, he had an exaggerated respect for people of scholarship. He imagined that Señor Burnett would write a suicide note in the most grandiloquent of terms and that is why he typed what he did on his own machine—by sheer luck he had a similar one—little realizing that his choice of words made it clear that it could not have been composed by the dead man.'

'What were they arguing about?'

'A gold diadem which Señor Heal had bought and which he believed had come from Priam's treasure and therefore was very, very valuable. He wanted Señor Burnett to authenticate it, but Señor Burnett was reluctant to do so then and there. The final argument that evening, when Señor Heal had returned, was probably fuelled by Señor Heal's offering a large sum of money for an unreserved and immediate authentication of the diadem. Señor Burnett would have been outraged by such an attempt to corrupt his academic honesty.'

'Where is this diadem?'

'I expect it is either in the safe in Señor Heal's house or in a bank . . .' He stopped.

'Well?'

'I'm not quite certain how to put this, señor.'

'Rationally.'

'I have spoken to Señorita Heal about the diadem and she feels that it carries bad luck for the owner. I find it difficult to believe this is possible . . .'

'Does it matter what you believe?'

'She thinks it would be dangerous to risk such bad luck and since the diadem is of the greatest historical significance as well as value, would like to present it to a museum. She mentioned that her father had so liked living on this island that she was sure it would be his wish to present it to the Museum of Humanities in Palma. That would, of course, be wonderful not only for the island, but also for Spain. However, I have the feeling that . . .'

'What?'

'If her father's name were to be blackened by a further and prolonged investigation into the case, if too much evidence were made public and this cast her father's image in a dubious light, she might be far less eager to present it to a museum here, but might well decide to present it to one in her own country.'

There was a long pause, then Salas said angrily: 'How can all this evidence be suppressed—well, not be published—if Heal was later murdered and his murder was directly connected with such events?'

'Señor, you will remember that the assumption that Señor Heal had been murdered was largely based on the belief that Señor Burnett had been murdered. But we now know that Señor Burnett's death was accidental. Further, there was never firm evidence that the car crash had been deliberately engineered; all Traffic could say was that the damage to the brake systems could have been sabotage. Now that we know everything, we can for the first time clearly see the course of events. Señor Heal was trying to hoodwink the law and, being an intelligent man, he would realize that if his

262

deception were exposed he would be under even deeper suspicion of having committed murder. In the face of such danger, with a mind filled with foreboding and fear, perhaps panicking, what more natural than that he should drive even more furiously than usual? In the mountains, that is so often fatal.'

There was no immediate and contemptuous comment from Salas. As the silence lengthened, Alvarez reached for the glass.

*   *   *

Alvarez sat within sight of the portrait of a naked Alma, but even more than before he took care not to look at it. 'Señorita, I have come here to explain certain facts. Your father was present when Señor Burnett died.'

She gasped and Selby reached out to grip her hand. 'Are you saying ... Are you saying he killed him?'

'We cannot be entirely certain of some of the details, but we can be quite sure that Señor Burnett's death was not deliberate. The two were struggling when Señor Burnett had his gun, the gun went off and the second time killed him. There was no intention on your father's part to kill Señor Burnett.'

'And Father's death?' she asked in a whisper.

'That was accidental. Desperately worried by the fact that he had tried to conceal his presence at Señor Burnett's death, and by what he had done to try to suggest that that had been suicide, he did not concentrate on his driving. In the mountains, tragically, that can be fatal.'

'Both deaths were accidental?' asked Selby.

'Officially, we will call Señor Burnett's death accidental for the sake of the señorita. But I have to say that had Señor Heal lived, we might well have had to charge him with manslaughter as well as an attempt to pervert the course of justice.'

'That's great! Accidental death twice over, yet the last time you were here you called me a double murderer.'

'Certain evidence was not known then and it did appear—'

'Only to someone who's bloody blind. What I'm saying is—'

'Just for once,' interrupted Alma, 'don't say it.'

'You expect me to listen—'

'In silence.'

He was so astonished, he became silent.

'Señorita,' said Alvarez, 'somewhere among your father's possessions there should be a gold diadem.'

'That's a kind of a crown, isn't it? There's one in his safe.'

'That was the cause of the fatal argument; but for that, both señors would be alive today. It has also brought bad luck to other people. I am very worried that if you keep it, it will do the same to you.'

'Like the Hope diamond?'

'That sort of thing's all a load of cod's,' said Selby loudly.

'Señor, I do not think it is safe to be so quickly scornful of such things.'

'Goddamnit, this is the end of the twentieth century, not the beginning of the tenth! We've stopped believing in witches and warlocks.'

'Señorita, I have to tell you that the diadem is not only of very great historical interest, it is also very, very valuable. Now, of course, it belongs to you and your mother. I am asking you not to keep it, however valuable, but to present it to a museum. And since your father lived here on the island, you might wish to present it to the Museum of Humanities. Perhaps it seems difficult to give away something so valuable, but even without it you both will inherit a very considerable sum of money from the estate and will be able to lead comfortable lives. I am old enough to understand that moderate wealth is not dangerous to those who own it, but very great wealth is.'

Selby said: 'Her old man owned this thing which is worth a lot of money and you're suggesting she gives it away because you reckon it carries bad joss and also it's dangerous to be megarich?'

'Yes.'

'I just don't believe I can be hearing right. I mean—'

'Guy,' she said, 'dry up.'

'I'm not going to have him sit there, trying to make a fool out of you—'

'Right now, it's you who's being the fool.'

He swore violently, stood, charged across the room to go outside.

'I'm sorry,' she said.

'Señorita, there is no reason to apologize.'

'Considering he's an artist and so should be alive to all the nuances, it's surprising how blind and deaf he can sometimes be. Right now, I suppose it's because there's money involved. That always scrambles his mind ... There's an awful lot you haven't said, isn't there?'

'Nothing of any real importance.'

'Everything of real importance, I'd say. But I really would be a fool if I ever thought you'd tell me exactly what that is.' She stood. 'You'll have a drink, won't you?'

He looked towards the outside doorway. 'Would it not be best if I left?'

'Because of Guy? He'll be back in a while, the explosion over and all calmed down. You don't like him, do you?'

'If that is true, it will be because I think he may not make you as happy as you now believe he will.'

'How sweet you can be! Mother's absolutely right.'

'Your mother?'

'I rang her to find out how she was. She talked about your visit in very glowing terms. She hopes that one day she'll meet you again.'

*   *   *

'You really mean it?' asked Phillipa, her voice little more than a husky whisper.

'Indeed,' answered Alvarez as he stood on the patio.

'I'm not going to have to go to prison?'

'Señorita, if you forget everything except that you are slightly hard of hearing and very stubborn, you will not go to prison and your brother's life insurance will be honoured.'

'I . . . I can hardly believe it. Oh my God, it's been a terrible nightmare and now . . . Was it all so very wrong of me?'

'Wrong means different things to different people, but I think that to you and me it means the same thing. It was not wrong of you.'

'I . . . I don't know what to say. Yes, I do! I've a bottle of Codorníu Ana I've been saving for a special occasion. We will drink it now.' She hurried into the house, flustered, far from her usual self-controlled self.

He sat down on one of the chairs and stared out at the garden and listened to the sounds of his beloved countryside. The opposite to wrong was right. There was right in the world when good prospered and evil suffered. The two señoritas, each in her own way, would prosper. Simitis would suffer, far more than if he had merely been jailed, because for the rest of his life he was going to have to live with the agonizing memory of the immense fortune which had so nearly been his, but which he had lost through his own clever cupidity. And the insurance company, called upon to pay out on a claim for which they were not legally liable? If taxes and death were two certainties in life, a third was that all insurance companies prospered . . .

Photoset, printed and bound in Great Britain by REDWOOD PRESS LIMITED, Melksham, Wiltshire

Spinning Wheel's

Collectible Iron, Tin, Copper & Brass

Spinning Wheel's
Collectible
Iron, Tin,
Copper & Brass

edited by
Albert Christian Revi

CASTLE BOOKS

739
REV

Published Under Arrangement With Ottenheimer Publishers, Inc.
Printed in the United States of America

Introduction

Suprisingly, metalwares of all kinds have appealed to both men and women. Objects of iron, brass, copper and tin have been fashioned in simple and very sophisticated designs; their uses were often utilitarian, but some of the most decorative designs have been lavished on even the meanest objects.

Realizing the universal appeal of metalwares, simple and elaborate, the Editors of *Spinning Wheel* have met collectors' needs by publishing authoritative articles by well-known authors, collectors, and museum curators. This book is a compilation of selected articles about iron, brass, copper, and tinwares. More than that, it represents the very best information available on these subjects.

Iron, brass, and copper were known to the ancient Egyptians; they were used throughout the early eastern and western cultures, including China. Tinwares are, by comparison, somewhat late arrivals. But the production of tinware became widespread soon after its introduction, and more particularly in the late 17th and early 18th centuries.

For some years before the Revolution, American colonists depended on England for most of their metalwares—especially brass, copper and tinware. Soon the colonials were establishing their own metalworking shops and dependence on England for such supplies diminished rapidly. While metalware shops sprung up here and there throughout the colonies, there appears to have been more produced in Pennsylvania, based on the preponderance of signed examples extant. Even so, brass, copper and tinware continued to be imported from England and France as late as 1890. The sophistication of European designs was preferred to the less elaborate productions made in America. Since this was the case, we have covered all metalwares, both domestic and imported, in this book.

Albert Christian Revi, Editor
Spinning Wheel
Hanover, Penna. 17331

Table of Contents

18th Century Iron Furnaces

by HENRY J.
KAUFFMAN

Fireback for woodburning fireplace. Photo courtesy Metropolitan Museum of Art.

THE pre-eminent position of Pennsylvania in the modern world of iron and steel is well known and all people quickly recognize names as Bethlehem, Lukens, Midvale, Carnegie, Laughlin and Jones, but only those who have made a study of eighteenth century iron making in Pennsylvania are familiar with names such as Durham, Warwick, Elizabeth, Hopewell, Cornwall, Martic, Mary Ann and others. Despite the importance of the early iron industry in Pennsylvania, it should be pointed out that the industry did not have its beginning here for the first recorded attempt to build a furnace occurred at Falling Creek, Virginia, but it was doomed to sudden failure because of an Indian massacre when all the buildings were destroyed before iron could be produced. The first successful establishment occured at Saugus Center near Lynn, Massachusetts in 1685, sixty-four years after the Virginia attempt. Massachusetts can claim another seventeenth century furnace and numerous eighteenth century ones, but from the standpoint of numbers and importance of their products Pennsylvania had more eighteenth century furnaces than any of the colonial areas.

The reason for the location of the furnaces is very easy to explain, for Pennsylvania was particularly blessed with the raw products to produce the iron. In the first place there was an abundance of ore, particularly in the Lancaster, Lebanon, Berks, and Chester County areas, some of which is being mined today at Cornwall. The old furnace at Cornwall is in an excellent state of preservation and is a historical shrine under the control of the Historical Commission of Pennsylvania, but its adjacent ore pit continues to produce a rich grade of iron ore and has been worked constantly from the day of its opening in 1742. It is one of the most important sources of magnetite ore in America and due to its proximity to the surface much of it can be loaded by shovels into trucks and conveyed to the crusher. Copper, silver, and gold are among the important by-products secured from the mine. Most of the other mining

Iron master's house at Hopewell Village. Kauffman photo.

areas have fallen before the importance of the great sources in the Great Lake region and with the exception of the Cornwall area most of the eighteenth century iron producing areas have attained a museum status.

In addition to ore, a fuel was required to produce iron and Pennsylvania was particularly endowed with an abundance of virgin growth. The farmers of the Palatinate were attracted to Pennsylvania by the stories of the rich river valleys and walnut trees, but it was the beech, black oak, ash and white oak that attracted the iron masters. Beech was regarded as the best for charcoal and much must have fallen before the axes of the skilled European woodchoppers. It was chopped to length, skillfully piled in a tapering shape like a tepee and then covered with mud. A smoldering fire was nurtured until the wood had turned to charcoal, the operation requiring constant attendance for if the fire secured draft and broke through the mud the entire pile would quickly be consumed by flames. A small opening was allowed at the top which provided a place to start the fire and a source of a bit of oxygen to keep it smoldering. It was imperative that an adequate supply of woodland adjoin each furnace and the woodland was included whenever deals effecting the transfer of the furnace occurred.

The problem of iron making was further solved in Pennsylvania with the presence of incalcuable quantities of limestone for flux. Poured into the top of the furnace in well regulated ratios with the ore and the charcoal the limestone was always needed to make the operation a successful one. Limestone was a willing slave of the iron master for he not only used it for its chemical properties, but it is possible that the furnace itself may have been built of it and lined with a more fire-resisting brick or slate. His residence could also have been built of the same material and Southeastern Pennsylvania can still point to a few eighteenth century homes that have not fallen to the axe of fashion or modernization.

There was also a need for skilled craftsmen to build furnaces and homes and despite the fact that most of the furnace owners were Englishmen it is not likely that they allowed the skill of the German immigrants to go unnoticed. Several industries in England were developed by German skill, such as textiles, copper and brass, and it is likely that the Germans had quite a hand in Pennsylvania where their mechanical skill could supplement English capital. A great deal was required beyond the furnace, for in addition a dam had to be built, runways to the furnace constructed and water wheels as big as twenty-five feet in diameter had to be constructed and installed. These wheels tripped the ends of a huge bellows thereby creating the cold blast that was required for high temperature and the fusing of the ore. Later the bellows were replaced by pressure tubs and the water wheels were replaced by steam power in some furnaces while other furnaces became obsolete and closed before any renovations were made.

It becomes obvious that the details of running a furnace required a complete and almost self sustaining village and in Hopewell Village near Reading, Pennsylvania, it is known that a small group including woodchoppers, colliers, teamsters, blacksmiths, moulders, and wheelwrights lived in the shadow of the big house on the hill where the iron master lived. It is also possible that this group would include cabinetmakers, cordwainers, coverlet weavers, carpenters, and perhaps a wood carver or a pattern maker to supply patterns for the stove plates or other products of the furnace.

The sociological aspect of this small village appear rather depressing for it is likely that all these people lived in what is known today as "company" houses, they traded at a "company" store, and their entire economy was regulated by a scale that was very unlikely to favor the worker. The workers' lot was considerably improved over his Earlier European status, but it must have been mostly on the mental side for his greatest advance was in the little likelihood of war and pillaging.

Beyond these skilled and semiskilled groups lived another group of which not much is known but records frequently refer to the slaves and indentured servants that were connected with the furnace. By 1722 indentured servants were arriving at the port of Philadelphia in great numbers who were sold at 10 pounds each to serve a period of three or four years. In addition there were Negro slaves and Indian laborers who received nothing but the barest necessities for anything beyond that which would have permitted them to save and flee their master thereby causing endless trouble, as was sometimes the case.

Recently a number of meagerly marked graves have been found which appear to be the graves of obscure workers at the Martic Furnace. In a patch that is completely covered with undergrowth the small gravestones are almost completely lost because of lack of interest and loss of identity of the occupants. Such is the fate of the workers, but the monuments of the iron masters are huge stone houses with bronze plaques enumerating their contributions to humanity.

The eighteenth century furnaces were comparable to two distinct units in todays industrial production. They were first and essentially furnaces producing iron, frequently pig iron which was then moved to a forge and by the use of water power and a large hammer the pigs were reduced to a size that was useful to the local blacksmith for making articles of wrought iron. Secondly, they were also foundries for before the furnace and under a roof lay a large area of sand with flasks where the cast articles of the day were made. Among the articles were mortars, betty lamps, kettles, cannon, pots, frying pans, tea-kettles, cannon balls, other hollow ware, stoves, firebacks, and stove plates.

Little remains of the products of the eighteenth century iron furnace for the twentieth century collector, but the one item which is available is most intriguing, although it is a bit cumbersome to collect——stove plates. These parts of five-plate stoves like much other Americana were left to rust and disintegrate until interest was aroused in them. Then they came to be regarded as one of the choice possessions of the Pennsylvania Germans and only they appear to have used them in America. Reminiscent of their European prototypes the German natives of Pennsylvania demanded that the English furnace owners supply their wants and produce a stove similar to the ones they had used in their homeland.

The stoves consisted of five plates, bolted together, two sides, a top and bottom, and one end, thereby leaving an aperture which was inserted in a wall opposite a fire place in an adjoining room. The wide space on the edge of the plate illustrated permitted the stove to be inserted into the plaster of the wall, without imparing the completeness of the design. The end opposite the wide space or the front end of the stove was supported by bricks or some sort of fired earthenware which would not mar the floor, or conduct heat too readily. The stove was fired from the fireplace of the next room which also provided a chimney for the exit of the smoke. These were known as non-ventilating stoves and had no opening into the room which they heated.

No mystery surrounds the origin of the stove for it is definitely known that the Pennsylvania plates had European ancestors which were used throughout Germany and Scandinavia. The English never used stoves at this time but resorted to the use of open fireplaces such as the ones used when New England was settled. It is not known if the first American plates were cast from European plates or from wooden patterns, for many European plates were brought to America, some bearing dates that antedate any casting activity here. Most early plates, the first American one being 1726, consisted of two areas with a horizontal line going through the center of the plates. Above the line was a biblical scene such as the Delilah and Samson plate illustrated or numerous other motifs such as The Temptation of Joseph, Abraham and Isaac, Susanna and the Elders, Adam and Eve, Mary and Martha, and David and Jonathan. In some cases these motifs were presumed to be copied from the wood cut illustrations of a German Bible or in most cases were the artists interpretation of the text below. The text in the lower part of the early plate was usually in German and explained the motif at the top. The plate of the later six-plate stove had a conventionalized flower motif in the top part, and the bottom portion bearing the name of the iron master such as H. Wilhelm Stiegel, who also added Elizabeth Furnace or more frequently only the date indicating the time that the plate was cast. Most of the dated plates occur from 1760 to 1770.

The six-plate stove followed the five-plate stove and differed chiefly in the respect that it was moved away from the wall and had a stove pipe for ventilating, plus an opening in the front or side plate to insert wood and remove ashes. It frequently stood on cast iron legs and slightly resembled the later ten-plate stoves which are sometimes found in Pennsylvania kitchens today. Hopewell Furnace is known to have made plates for six-plate stoves but due to its late establishment (about 1760), and the fact that the art of stove plate making was in the decline, the well known example bearing the name of the iron master Mark Bird with that of Hopewell and 1772, the plate shows little of the earlier art in its decadent flower motif.

Although one plate pattern of wood is extant today there seems to be little doubt that patterns for all the plates existed and by some curious turn of events nearly all have been destroyed. These patterns were pressed in the sand in front of the furnace and when the furnace was tapped the molten iron flowed in shallow gutters to each opening, the entrance being closed when the shallow pit was filled. This technique accounts for the rough texture on the back of all plates and for the slight discrepancies in the thickness.

Similar to stove plates and often confused with them are the firebacks which were formed in the same manner as the stove plates and in Pennsylvania often bore similar decorative motifs. Due to the early establishments of furnaces and the frequent use of the backs by the English, it is presumed by some authorities that some firebacks were cast in New England prior to 1720 when Cole Brook Dale Furnace was started in Pennsylvania. They bear no relation to the stove which they slightly resemble but were used exclusively for decorative purposes and for reflecting heat in the back of wood burning fireplaces. They were continued in use beyond the time of the five and six plate stoves and were probably used throughout the colonies wherever there were English residents and there was a need for a fireplace.

The specimen illustrated has a sun with divergent rays in the area above the motif, in the center is the band indicating the name of the furnace.

A cast iron five-plate stove, dated 1760, with Biblical quotation "Las Dich Nicht Gelyssten Deines Neststen Gut" (Thou shalt not covet they neighbor's goods).

Early American Stove Plates

by LESTER BREININGER, JR.

A STOVE PLATE is a side, actually a section, of a jamb stove, more commonly called a five-plate stove. Numerous mid-18th century Germanic houses in America had a large, centrally located fireplace. A "hole" in

This fine stove plate, along with its side partners, front plate, and bottom plate, were covering the chimney of a spring house until they appeared at a farm sale in Pennsylvania in the spring of 1971. It appears to depict the Biblical story of the five wise virgins who trimmed their lamps and awaited the arrival of the bridegroom. Collection Lee Leister.

the back opened into a rear or side room, normally a parlor-type room. Projecting into this room from the back of the fireplace was an iron box consisting of five sand cast iron plates. These were bolted together and rested on a square cut stone or a brick column on the floor.

This arrangement, in essence, acted like a radiator. Logs burning in the

fireplace or in the stove itself would heat the room with no dirt caused by wood being carried, ashes removed, or even, hopefully, from escaping smoke.

The top and bottom plates of this stove were usually of plain iron. The front and sides were quite often decorated. Designs of arches with tulips and hearts abounded. Others were religiously inspired. Verses from scripture often accompanied by vivid portrayals of Biblical events (i.e. The Lord's Supper, the Wedding at Cana, and Adam and Eve) were quite popular. One of these plates admonishes "Las Dich Nicht Gelyssten Dienes Heststen Gut" (Thou shalt not covet . . .). The name Wilhelm

A badly rusted example showing four figures at table, one at the top of the stairs, and one drawing wine from a jug. The inscription states, "The first sign Christ 'did,' turned the water into wine, John the second chapter."

A fine example of "Dutch" embellishment, dated 1760. Courtesy Historical Society of Berks County.

plates were used as elevated platforms for fires in smoke house, wash house and other outbuildings; some appeared as stepping stones; others were placed under rain spouts to prevent washing; and still others were scrapped.

While a visit to the Mercer Museum in Doylestown would convince most people that all the stove plates in existence are in that collection, some plates still become available to collectors. (See *The Bible in Iron,* by Dr. Henry C. Mercer, happily, again in print.)

An excellent stove plate dated 1742 turned up last year at a public sale. It had been used as the base of an ash pile in a cellar fireplace. Fortunately, it was face down and the fires had not obliterated the design. More recently one was discovered at a Berks County farmhouse. In winter it was propped against the cellar window, in summer merely moved against the solid cellar wall.

Like gold, stove plates are where you find them. A piece of iron sticking out of a mud bank interested a muskrat trapper who proceeded to discover a stove plate; only one-fourth protruded, but it was sufficient to catch his attention. While an old outdoor bake oven was being torn down to make room for a garage, another stove plate appeared. Another was merely set against a smoke house about four inches deep in mud. Others have literally gone to pieces while serving as stepping stones.

Probably the best find was at the Sweitzer home in Brecknock Township, Berks County. While remodeling his ancient dwelling in 1907, a jamb stove was torn out to be eventually discarded. This stove was acquired by the Historical Society of Berks County (Reading, Pa.) in 1909 and is now on display there. This is one of the few original plate jamb stoves in existence. However, the original bolts and fastenings had been discarded. Most stoves in museum collections are composite ones.

One of the most distressing things to a stove plate collector's heart is the kind of information found in a ledger from Charming Forge. A bar iron forge in Berks County, once owned by the

Bortschend (William Bird shines) also appears on it. The word "shines" probably refers to his exceptional ability to produce such decorative plates. Bird was an ironmaster of Berks County who died about 1760.

Probably the most collectible stove plates were made by Henry W. Stiegel, colonial ironmaster and glassmaker of the Lancaster County Elizabeth Furnace. The subsequent invention, attributed to him, of the ten plate stove in 1765 (a self contained stove with an iron base, stovepipe and oven) dealt a death blow to the fancy, decorative stove plates.

With the demand gone, artistry withered. Though James Old of Chester County Reading Furnace, among others, was still producing stove plates in 1786, they are usually quite unimpressive and were evidently merely replacement parts of jamb stoves still in use in the older homes.

As the use of these stove plates was discontinued, the plates were put to other uses. Some were just set against the back of the fireplace. This practice is still so common, even among antiques collectors, that a goodly number of persons think these plates were originally made as fire backs. Many

Iron Stove plate depicting "The Flight Into Egypt"; ca. 1755. Courtesy Historical Society of Berks County.

legendary "Baron" Stiegel, it operated from 1750 to 1886. From an account of 1843 it disposed to one F. Sellers, in January of that year:

	Old Stove Plates		
Tons	Cwt.	Quarters	Lbs.
2	15	1	17
6	0	21	

(The hauling credited to his account at .75/Ton.)

Undoubtedly other people besides Mr. Sellers found a profit in reclaiming these old stove plates. The scrap drives of World War II took an additional toll of the remaining stove plates.

They are getting scarce nowadays, but because they are quite large, 21 x 23 inches being a common size, heavy, 70-90 pounds, and cumbersome, they are not enjoying the popularity of some other collectibles. Collectors who do have them, besides using them as decorative fire backs, often frame and mount them on the wall in the hallway, entranceway, or stairway. As early examples of our country's resourcefulness, artistry, and skill in metal working, they deserve a greater interest in their study and preservation.

Cast-iron comfort with an old wood-burning Victorian stove of elegant design.

Collecting Cast Iron Comfort

by FLORENCE THOMPSON HOWE

OLD STOVES, in today's electric-
ally operated space-age, are fast
becoming as obsolete as the horse and
buggy or the milkman. Should world
conditions create an oil shortage, as
was the case in the second World War
in the early 1940s, these old wood-
burning stoves could become the pot
of gold at the end of the heatless
householder's rainbow.

Hopefully, no such situation will
arise. But these antique heat makers
still have a place, even in the normal
programs of the "affluent society."
There's cast iron comfort for you in
the old wood-burning stove in a
hunting cabin or a fishing shack; in
a guest cottage or studio at your summer place; or even in the ell of a
remodelled farmhouse in a cold cli-
mate. Installed as stand-by equipment,
they do a job for you in remote areas
where electricity suffers frequent
"outages" from storms. They'll keep
your water pipes from freezing or,
used as auxiliary heat, cut your operating cost on your main heating
system in extreme weather.

But where could you buy a stove

today? Not at a city hardware store.
At the antique dealer's, the secondhand shop, or the country auction,
perhaps. So it's good to know something about these old stoves before
you buy.

Philadelphia pattern stoves were
introduced in New England in the

Wood-burner with Gothic facade and dainty
cabriole legs made in Troy, N. Y.

PHILIP WILLCOX,

Has received an additional supply of

Cooking

AND

Open

STOVES

which with his former stock makes his assortment as extensive and complete as can be found at any store in the county. The above Stoves he *does not sell on commission* but *buys* them *for* CASH at VERY REDUCED PRICES, which enables him to sell them *lower* than they can be bought at any commission store in this town.

STOVE PIPE,

all sizes, constantly on hand in any quantity. New FIXTURES made to old stoves, and all other work in his line of business furnished at short notice.

Also, will be kept constantly on on hand a large and complete assortment of IRON HOLLOW WARE, at low prices.

Purchasers are respectfully invited to call before they buy, at the Brick Store, one door west of the Bank, State street, where they may exchange most kinds of *Country Produce*, CASH, or *good credit*, to the best advantage, for any of the above articles

Springfield Dec 13   iu71

In 1827, Phillip Wilcox advertised stoves, stove pipes, and iron hollow ware.

early 1800s, some of them are dated "1774." Stumble onto one of these and you really have a collector's item. They were box stoves with an oven over the fire. The only boiler hose was in the bottom of the oven. Castings weighed from 700 to 800 pounds and appeared to have been made by pouring the metal into an open flat mold. There was no rim on the pipe-hole by which to secure the pipe, but a wrought-iron rim of a half-inch

thickness with a flange for support was fitted to the hole to form the union between the stove and the pipe.

A Philip Willcox stove is worth picking up, too. Philip Willcox was a stove-maker and an early merchant (1823) in Springfield, Massachusetts.

Wood-burning stove with hearth and brass finials on top made by Philip Wilcox. First quarter 19th century.

The "Economy" wood and coal heating and cooking stove manufactured by Comstock, Castle & Co., Quincy, Ill., ca. 1880.

Wood-burning stove of sheet metal bears manufacturer's identification "Reeves/Dover/Copper Alloy."

He thought well of his merchandise, for in one of his advertisements he says:

PHILIP WILLCOX

Respectfully informs his friends and the public that he has just received from New York an assortment of E. Hoyt's highly approved patent COOKING STOVES. The above mentioned stoves are so constructed as to convey the steam arising from the boilers (which is admitted to be almost the only objection to cooking stoves) directly into the pipe without the least inconvenience to the cooking; also the extreme heat that arises directly from the fire passes off, which renders it equally as pleasant and as healthy as an open Franklin; with the addition of his patent oven. They are considered by those who have had them in use, superior to any stoves offered to the public.

Willcox also advertised in 1826, stove-pipes, live geese feathers, and fan and side lights, probably for the old front door, "filled to any pattern." He announced, too, that "PEDLARS will be accommodated with a good

assortment, and at low prices." And believe it or not, he said he had "a bathing-tub to let."

Styles and decorative design in 19th century stoves usually related to the furniture of the period. Delicate Victorian filigree often reflected a mighty hot fire. There were some of the New York-born "parlor" stoves that were positively Gothic in feeling. Others, notably those made by the Shakers in Connecticut, were chaste and simple, with ornamentation reduced to the least common denominator. These little Shaker stoves, low-slung, long and narrow, with duck feet, would not be out of tune with contemporary decor.

The Franklin stoves used often today in lieu of fire-place heating, carry much of fireplace charm, but throw out more heat because not so much is lost up the chimney. Franklin himself said of his device: "My common room, I know, is made twice as warm as it used to be with a quarter of the

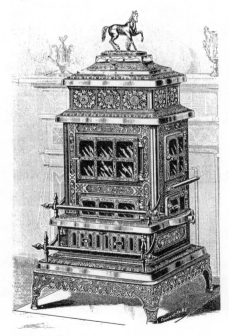

"The Ivy," manufactured by The Richmond Stove Co., Norwich, Conn., 1882. Decorated with Low's Art Tiles, bronze and nickel trimmings.

wood I formerly consumed there."
(This he wrote in 1744!)

Antiques dealers report that there is
still much interest in these old stoves.
Prices vary, of course, with their age,
condition, and desirability either for
functional use or decorative antiques.
One of the most delightful of the
later stoves is an early model of the
Florence oilstove, a rococo little
number topped with a slide-out plate
and grill. Called "Florence Favorite,"
and dated "1871," it is only 18 inches
high. It is not a wood-burner, but it
throws out a lot of heat on a gallon
of oil! A forerunner, doubtless, of our
present-day portable, though much
more engaging in appearance, it is
really a desirable old stove. It was
made by the Florence Mfg. Co. of
Florence, Massachusetts, almost a
hundred years ago.

Early oilstove (1871) made by Florence
Manufacturing Co., Florence, Mass.; height
18 inches.

Universal Base Burner No. 50, manufactured
by Co-Operative Stove Works, Troy, N. Y.,
1883.

Beauty in Wrought Iron

Some Pictures and Notes Concerning Items Well Worth Collecting and Using.

Sugar Auger. An item of utilitarian beauty of the sort that was all in the day's work for our accomplished ironsmiths, or blacksmiths. Most of us think of blacksmiths in terms of our own memory; as horseshoers. But it was this type of artisan who made all the beautiful wrought iron of our early days.

by CARL DREPPERD

THE first iron wrought in what is now our country was mined and melted at Saugus, Massachusetts, early in the 17th century. It was bog iron, "mined" by dredging out the lumps of almost pure ore in neighboring bogs, mires and fenns. Not until the rich deposits of Penn's colony were opened by Cornish and Welsh ironmasters did iron become a staple of Colonial manufacture. In fact, so great were the deposits of Pennsylvania and so active the production that England put an embargo on it; it couldn't be shipped to England in exchange for other goods. Not until the great western deposits in the Great Lakes region were discovered did the Grubb mines in upper Lancaster County yield the palm for American ore production.

Ironsmiths "ironed" a house by making everything that went into its building, including the hardware, the shutter holdbacks, snow birds, beam heads, H and HL hinges, rat tail hinges and foot scrapers, latches, lifts, locks and keys. These men also wrought cabinet hardware, and innumerable other items. For example, look at that beautiful three pronged, curling, screw which originally had a cross-handle of wood. What is it? The piece is beautiful because it is a perfect tool for its use. It is a **sugar auger.** When sugar was made in the old fashioned way, syrup was crystallized and poured into cone shaped molds for small packages of up to 40 pounds, and in barrels containing up to 250 pounds.

These molds, and barrels, were drained as the solid sugar formed, the drainage being "syrup" or molasses. Then, when ready for market, the sugar was as hard as a bone. You had

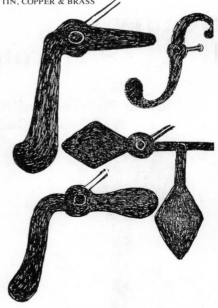

Foot scrapers. The two top ones are of the type that were driven in a wood step tread, or set in stone treads, anchored in lead. At center, a scraper to attach to the side of step, level with tread. Bottom, a scraper set aside of step riser, or at a wall corner.

Shutter Holdbacks. Top, the Swan's Head, and the "S" types, noted used from Queen Anne Period. Bottom, Later, and simpler forms, used to the 1850's, but noted on many mid to late 18th century town and country houses.

to gouge it out of barrels, loosening it . . . and so, the sugar auger was devised. The cones were not augered. They were formed with a hanging cord in them, and were cut apart with (1) Sugar cleavers and (2) Sugar nippers.

Pictured also are some excellent examples of wrought iron as used in home building, all of which are explained in the captions. This little essay is an introduction to "old wrought iron" which we have had in mind for some time. In fact several

friends of ours have undertaken the compilation of a monograph on old iron which would show most of the available kinds and sorts of pieces known to have been made from the late 1680's right through to the 1880's. So if you want more on this subject, please let your wishes be known by the simple expedient of dropping us a postal card. We hope a thousand of our many thousands of readers will want more about this most fascinating category of collecting and an item of antiquity that is bound to increase in interest, and in value, down through the years.

The Charm
of Cast Iron

by HENRY J. KAUFFMAN

Heart-shaped waffle iron thought to be 18th century and of Pennsylvania origin.

Unmarked mortar and pestle. Many of these were made in America in the 19th century. Only a few bear the imprint of the maker. Kauffman Collection.

THE COLLECTING cognoscenti, whose specialty has been the artifacts of the 17th and 18th centuries are now turning to those of more recent origin. The products of Paul Revere, Henry Will, and Thomas Savery seem to have vanished, and what was once regarded as nondescript is now moving slowly to the center of the stage.

The logical solution for the embryonic collector is to begin acquiring commodities which have been back stage or are just emerging from the wings to show up in recent antiques shows and prestigious shops. Objects made of cast iron fit into this category; some early trivets and Hessian soldier and andirons are now regarded as good company for objects made of silver, pewter, or blown glass.

A limitation inherent in objects made of cast iron is that the material itself cannot claim an ancient heritage. None was found in the tomb of King Tutankhamen, nor did the Greeks use it in building the Parthenon. Cast iron is an invention of the late Middle

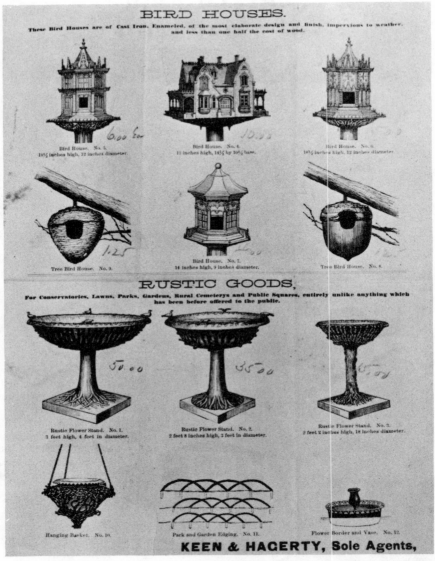

BIRD HOUSES.

These Bird Houses are of Cast Iron, Enameled, of the most elaborate design and finish, impervious to weather, and less than one half the cost of wood.

Bird House. No. 5.
18½ inches high, 12 inches diameter.

Bird House. No. 4.
12 inches high, 18½ by 10½ base.

Bird House. No. 6.
18½ inches high, 12 inches diameter.

Tree Bird House. No. 9.

Bird House. No. 7.
14 inches high, 9 inches diameter.

Tree Bird House. No. 8.

RUSTIC GOODS,

For Conservatories, Lawns, Parks, Gardens, Rural Cemeterys and Public Squares, entirely unlike anything which has been before offered to the public.

Rustic Flower Stand. No. 1.
3 feet high, 4 feet in diameter.

Rustic Flower Stand. No. 2.
2 feet 8 inches high, 3 feet in diameter.

Rustic Flower Stand. No. 3.
2 feet 2 inches high, 18 inches diameter.

Hanging Basket. No. 10.

Park and Garden Edging. No. 11.

Flower Border and Vase. No. 12.

KEEN & HAGERTY, Sole Agents,

Bird houses and "Rustic" goods made of cast iron were sold by Keen & Hagerty of Baltimore, Md., in the late 19th century.

Ages and a virtual newcomer among the substances of which important objects are made. If a blob of cast iron did appear in a bloomery before that time, it was thrown away because technicians did not know what to do with it.

By American standards, however, it is old, almost as old as the earliest settlements, for in the 1640s a furnace was built at Saugus, Massachusetts. It has recently been rebuilt so that anyone who visits it may see how metal was cast "in the good old days." Incidentally, Saugus was the first capitalistic venture in the New World, a fact which has little relevance to its production of artifacts. Up to now, only one product remains which can be attributed to it with any degree of confidence, but as objects of cast iron become increasingly sought after, others may be found.

Throughout the 18th and 19th centuries, many furnaces were operating along the eastern seacoast, producing pigs of iron as well as numerous finished objects such as cannons, cannon balls, skillets, griddles, trivets, kettles, firebacks, stove parts, and mortars and pestles. Over the years, most of these products had been relegated to scrap heaps or the bottoms of wells. Some of them have been rescued and given places of prominence in private collections and museums. Unfortunately,

Waffle iron of cast iron decorated with Pennsylvania German motifs. Kauffman Collection.

Trivet of cast iron marked on the back "W. B. Rimby, Baltimore, 1843." Notice the use of Pennsylvania German decorative motifs. Osburn Collection.

Tulips decorate this cast iron trivet. Marked on the back "W. B. R. 1843." The flat surfaces on the designs were created by wear, probably sliding of a flat-iron across its surface for many years.

Three-legged iron kettle with the name of the maker, Sampson and Tisdale, cast into its side. This firm was listed as "foundrymen" in New York City in the first half of the 19th century. Kauffman Collection.

only a few of these fascinating objects can be identified as the products of a particular furnace or foundry since the name of the facility which produced them was rarely imprinted by the pattern maker or foundryman.

Possibly the most desirable products of the furnace in the collector's view are firebacks and stove plates. To make these, patterns of wood were pressed in a bed of sand in front of a furnace; after the furnace was tapped, the cavity was filled with molten iron. In this way the details of the pattern were dramatically duplicated.

A fireback was a single sheet of iron placed against the back wall of the fireplace to promote the reflection of heat into the room, a function for which a masonry wall was quite ineffective. Before the 1760s, when stove pipe came into common use in America, a Pennsylvania stove consisted of five plates, the open end being inserted into the rear wall of a fireplace in the adjoining room. The wood was fed into the stove through the fireplace, and both the stove and the fireplace used a common chimney for the disposal of smoke. Many of the side plates of the stoves were decorated with designs with Biblical themes. An authoritative book, describing these

stove plates in great detail, was published in 1914 by their most avid collector, Henry Mercer. It is aptly called *The Bible In Iron*.

Several furnaces were famous because they produced military "materiel" for the American Revolution, but such products are a bit clumsy to collect, and few of them have survived. A cannon which was rejected because of imperfections lies on the casting bed at Cornwall Furnace, near Lebanon, Pennsylvania. Such identification is unusual. In general the lack of identifying marks has caused a certain apathy among collectors regarding the owning of such objects.

A number of so-called gypsy kettles survive, ranging in size from quite small to very large, which bear the names of the furnaces where they were cast. Although the large kettles cannot be regarded as household collectibles, the small ones fit well into this category; a perfect example might be regarded by some collectors as an object of considerable charm. In addition, a number of signed teakettles survive; these are attractive, particularly if they are suspended with a tilting device, which permits the pouring of hot

Cast iron facade on a building at Front and Arch Streets, Philadelphia, Pa. It is reported that the front on a nearby building is hinged so that the entire facade can be swung outward.

water from the kettle without removing it from the fireplace.

A profusion of trivets has survived; however, most of them might be regarded as "late," and few of the earliest examples are signed. W. B. Rimby, a foundryman working in Baltimore in the 1840s, made several attractive models, some of which are signed and dated. Doubtless other signed examples survive; however, those by Rimby are particularly pleasing. His use of Pennsylvania folk art motifs suggests that many of them were made for merchants or peddlers operating in Pennsylvania.

Frying pans, andirons, mortars and pestles, and similar objects frequently bear the imprint of their makers. Some

of the cast iron balusters and porch posts used in the South were made in the North and shipped to such ports as Charleston and New Orleans. When the gold rush was at its height, entire houses of cast iron were shipped to California where they were assembled in a few days; they proved to be completely adequate for miners who were "in a hurry."

Finally, in the middle of the 19th century, entire buildings were constructed of cast iron, some of them being many stories high. The most famous structure was the Crystal Palace in London which housed the great British Trade Exhibition of 1851. A few buildings in America employed a facade of cast iron. A number of them survive in the Front and Arch Street area in Philadelphia. Though one can collect such items only photographically, they remain an interesting facet of American industry and architecture and are well worth preserving as typical of an era when America was solidly built.

Cast iron tea kettle marked "I. Savery, New York." An 1842 business directory for New York City listed J. Savery and Son (William) as merchants located at 113 Beekman Street. Shelburne Museum Collection.

Friends of Cast-Iron Architecture

The Friends of Cast-Iron Architecture are seeking new members who want to see that cast-iron buildings are recognized and appreciated. Honorary co-chairmen of the group are Henry-Russell Hitchcock and Sir Nikolaus Pevsner. Dues for becoming a Friend are $2.00. Write: Mrs. Margot Gayle, Chairman, Friends of Cast-Iron Architecture, 44 West 9th Street, Room 20, New York, N.Y. 10011.

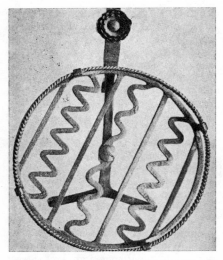

Handwrought Iron Trivets

by DICK HANKENSON

HANDWROUGHT iron trivets of the eighteenth and early nineteenth centuries — and a few were known to be in use in America as early as the seventeenth—stood in the fireplace or on the hearth to hold a pot or kettle whose contents were to be kept warm. They were of all sizes and shapes — triangular, round, rectangular, even of irregular design. They were made with high legs and short legs — the high-legged trivets were the earliest type—with handles, and without handles. Some were made at home by the man of the house; most were fashioned by the village blacksmith. Either the housewife suggested a design for her trivet, or the blacksmith followed his own ideas. No two are found exactly alike.

Many methods of decoration were used. In some cases, metal was heated in the forge, bent into shapes and twisted for artistic decoration. Trivets are found with inserts of iron, or even copper, cut in fancy shapes. Sometimes these inserts were hammered attractively.

Trivet legs and feet were often very fancy. Some were twisted and flattened; more were welded to the body

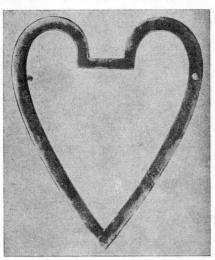

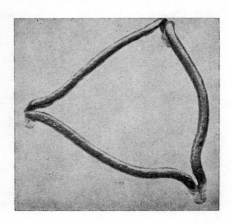

ILLUSTRATIONS

Counterclockwise from top:

Rare Lazy Susan with unusual railing of twisted iron. Body is of forged pieces welded together; side supports for railing are riveted to body, bent over railing. Legs are forged and bent, welded together; short handle has applied 3-piece rosette. Large loose rivet allows turning.

The rim here is a flat iron strip; center bars and legs are each one piece, riveted to rim.

Early "Heart" design; body forged of one piece and welded at point; legs riveted to body.

Forged of round iron, three separate pieces are used, with legs bent down. All pieces forge-welded together.

Intricate detail is shown here; crossbars are mortised into body, legs bent down, rattail handle used. Design is hand-cut with cold chisel.

Three separate pieces of square iron are forge-welded together; legs and body are formed of the same pieces.

by the forge-welding process. In this, the metal was heated in the forge to a very high temperature; a little flux was added; and the two pieces of metal were joined by hammering them together on the anvil.

Occasionally trivets were found with the legs riveted on. Here, a hole was made in the edge of the body, the shaped leg inserted, and the protruding end pounded until it was riveted tight. This method was also used when an insert was added as part of the body.

Handles were frequently ornate, and disclosed a fine quality of workmanship. Rattail ends were made by heating the iron and drawing the metal to a point by hammer and anvil.

Wrought iron stands for smoothing irons, also called trivets, were in early use. They are most often found in triangular shape, though they were made in other shapes, too. About 1830 cast iron trivets appeared, and by 1850, the handwrought iron trivet was well on its way to oblivion.

Wrought iron trivets, pictured, from the author's collection, indicate various types and shapes that may be found, and should be cherished.

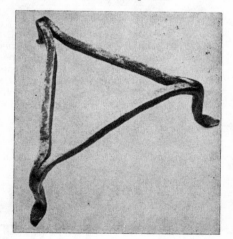

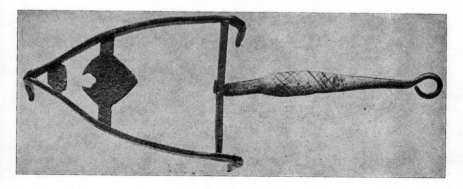

Left, top row: Star and leaf form from a Dutch smoothing board; Heart and keys with Ying-yeng or Chinese Swastika center, scalloped edge; Star and circles, with openwork saw edge. **Bottom row:** Star and hearts, openwork, ribbed border. Note the pointed oval separating heart at the bottom. This clue would seem to indicate the design is lifted from a Dutch carved spoon rack; Star and loops; with open saw edge; Star and circles with scalloped edge. None of these trivets have handles. They range in size from four to eight inches in diameter. All are cast iron.

Cast and Wrought Iron Trivets

by HUGO DARMSTAETTER

THE sheer and unalloyed pleasures that lurk in collecting little things in the field of antiques is a discovery which, perhaps, every collector must make for himself. While it is quite true that my own collecting habits and activities are in the field of furniture, the birth of my collecting and its continuation is due to my mother who, in some twenty years, collected over seven hundred, all different, cast and wrought iron trivets or stands. Her collection, while of little things, is on the heavy side. Yet I have been told by more than one decorator of note that this collection, accumulated piece by piece, would make a series of most interesting interior walls by mounting the trivets against an oyster-white background.

The cast trivet for flatirons was made in so many different designs by so many large and small ironfounders from the early 1800s down to the early 1900s that the total production must have reached an astounding figure. In the research thus far conducted, it would seem that every iron foundry of record, at some time or other in its history, cast a number of these objects, either as original designs by their own pattern makers or as copies of trivets made by some other foundry. It has been said that if a foundry cast stoves, grates or parts, it also cast trivets. With this production established, in theory at least, who can say it is only theory when we view the infinite number of trivets that have survived the years? To say the total production was a million a year for a hundred years might even be an understatement. Yet now these trivets are getting scarce, and some of the really early examples are quite rare. We may even agree that the term unique, or one-of-a-kind, can be applied to certain examples.

It would seem a rather hopeless task to attempt a tabulation of what foundries made what trivets, and when. Very few of them are marked except those designed as advertisements for the foundries. Often a stove works supplied each distributor or retailer with hundreds of trivets, to be passed out as advertisements for the stove, and as gifts to buyers of stoves. These trivets, generally, are marked and carry the name or some insignia of the foundry. But many really lovely trivets are unmarked. The same thing is true of the wrought iron trivets which, generally earlier than the cast iron ones, were the individual work of artisans at the forge. It goes without saying that every wrought iron trivet is an individual production and that even though it may have been made over and over again as a type, it is doubtful if any two so made, even by the same smith, are precisely alike. The temptation to vary the designs, if ever so slightly, while hammering and welding thin straps of iron, generally caused the worker to add his own individual touch.

But since these trivets do exist in numbers that puts them within the realm of deserved classification, it is quite logical that an attempt be made at such classification, using the facilities of one of the larger collections to start with. Since I have fallen heir to such a collection I have, tentatively at least, the fol-

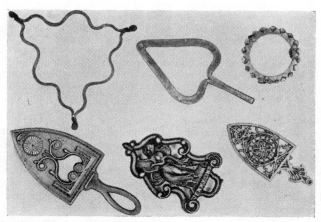

Above, top: Wrought iron Triangle form trivet with flat button feet; Spade, or heart-shape, of wrought iron; Small Circular, or wrought iron, with bossed rim. **Bottom:** Spade, with classic molding, chrysanthemum and crescent, and loop handle; Rocaille Spade shape, with thumb hold. Displays classic Muse of Music and bears legend "Jenny Lind"; Late Spade with "church-window" decoration and Eastlake handle. Bottom row are all of cast iron.

Above, top row: Circular, wrought iron, high footed; Spade, wrought iron, with five cut-out hearts and stamped in legend "FORGET ME NOT"; Ovoid, with points and scrolls. **Center row:** Spade, with simple loops, bearing legend of Patent, and the "patent" a waxing roller just above the openwork handle; Geometric, six circles looped to form stars, and loop handle. **Bottom row:** Circular, wrought iron, with flat button feet; Triangular, with scrolls, and pan handle, wrought iron; Horseshoe, cast iron, openwork date is 1894.

lowing to offer as a contribution toward a classification of patterns. Certainly this task is not exactly a picnic. But we do have the inspiration of Mrs. Ruth Webb Lee who, with courage worthy of an army general, understood . . . and accomplished . . . the Herculean task of classifying all patterns of pressed glassware.

The first attempt at classification should, it would seem, separate these trivets into basic shapes. This, then, is an attempt at such general classification:

Disc, or Circular: Trivets of round shape. Known with and without handles, some very plain and simple and others highly ornate, resembling the so-called Pennsylvania barn symbols, butter molds, et cetera. The vast majority of these very ornate circulars seem to have been cast in New York state foundries, from designs found on carved woodenwares of the Netherlands.

Geometrical: Under this broad category would fall combinations of circles, triangles, squares, and allied forms regardless of the pattern achieved. Known with and without handles.

Heart: A variant of the spade shape, but showing a clearly outlined heart form, known with and without handles.

Horseshoe: One of the favorites with foundries of the latter half of the 19th century. Rarely without handles, frequently with advertisement of maker, but known in a wide variety of decorative styles, all within the horseshoe shape.

Ovoid: Oval shapes with either rounded or pointed ends, with or without handles.

Spade: This shape is obviously designed for use as a flatiron rest. The body of the trivet is spade-shaped, and generally has a handle at the blunt end of the spade. Many spades had cameo portraits of famous people in low relief.

Gridiron: Many varieties, some looking like waffle irons and others like standard gridirons. Known with and without handles.

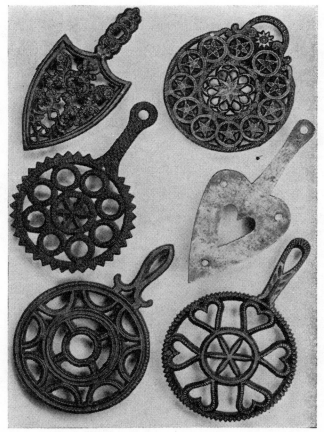

Above, top row: Spade trivet, with armorial scrolls and rococo handle; Circular, with thirteen stars in smaller circles and ten-pointed star at base of stub handle, marked "E. R. Manley". **Center:** Circular, Dutch star and eight circles, saw edge, pan handle; Wrought iron heart with heart cutout and long, or "pan" handle. **Bottom:** Circular, with simple geometric openwork and scroll handle; Circular, six hearts and star with serrated edge and pan-handle. All cast iron except where specifically designated as wrought.

Square: Solid or openwork, with or without surface ornamentation, some with handles but generally without handles.

Star: A rare form. Made with and without handles. 3, 4, 5, 6 and 7-pointed star examples are known.

Triangle: Not a variant of the spade shape, because handled examples are known with handle affixed to a side and others with handle affixed to one of the points. Those with handles are generally in the form of an equilateral triangle.

With this simple recitation of basic forms comes a descriptive problem comparable only to the task that faced Mrs. Lee. Rather than attempt formalized recitation here—for my task is not yet one quarter done and these presented constitute the very first publicity yet released—I will attempt secondary classification as captions under each of the illustration groups.

Toy Trivets to Treasure

by MARGARET H. KOEHLER

THROUGHOUT HISTORY, children have learned by using their own tiny replicas of adult's things. Originally trivets were used to hold cooking pots over an open fire, and later as a resting place while these pots cooled. In more recent times, trivets—in this instance sadiron holders—were made to hold heavy flatirons, and a century or so ago little girls learned how to iron by working on their doll's clothes with miniature versions of their mother's irons and holders.

Some years ago, Mrs. Madeline Thompson started collecting old trivets. One day she found a toy trivet just 3 inches long at an antiques shop. She purchased it for her collection and, as so often happens, one tiny trivet led to another. Before long, she had accumulated several miniatures of their larger counterparts. Mrs. Thompson discovered that toy trivets ranged in size from as little as 2¼ inches long to as much as 5 inches long, and came in a wide variety of shapes and designs. The miniature flatirons too, were just as varied in size and shape. Most toy trivets were made of cast iron, but a few brass ones have been found, also.

Apparently some of the larger miniature trivets were not designed initially as playthings for children; possibly they were salesmen's samples. These were sometimes listed in old catalogs as "half-size" trivets and are fairly easy to detect since they are too large for a toy iron, and too small for a full-size iron.

Collecting toy trivets can inevitably lead to the collecting of other iron toys. One of Mrs. Thompson's favorite iron toys is a tiny coal stove, complete with an array of miniature pots and pans. It occupies a prominent place in her kitchen and seems to compliment her collection of toy trivets.

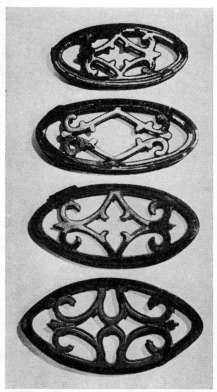

Oval-shaped toy trivets range in size from 3 inches long (top) to nearly 4 inches long (bottom); those shown above are made of cast iron.

This sturdy little sadiron, just 3 inches long, rests on a trivet 5½ inches in length.

A rare duck-shaped sadiron, 2 ½ inches long, rests on a "Cathedral No. 4" trivet, 3 ½ inches long. In 1865, these were offered "Painted in four colors."

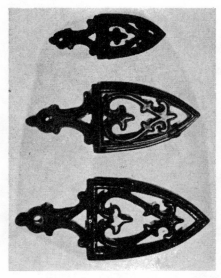

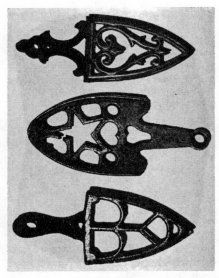

Cast iron toy trivets in the "Cathedral No. 3" pattern can be found in lengths of 2 ¼ inches (top), one of the smallest, to 3 ⅝ inches (bottom).

Some "not quite miniature" trivets measure from 5 inches long (top) to nearly 6 inches long (center); the "Cathedral No. 5" trivet (bottom) is 5 ½ inches long.

Bootjacks

by WILLIAM PALEY

A BOOTJACK, like a footscraper, usually had its place near the service door of the house—often doing double duty as a doorstop. Its primary function was to assist in removing the high, tight boots, which were fashionable in the eighteenth and nineteenth centuries, without the inconvenience to the wearer of stooping or of soiling his hands. Not only were bootjacks made for gentlemen but for ladies as well, as evidenced by the adjustable and the double-ended types. The Industrial Revolution with its increasing emphasis on travel, and the Civil War which necessitated it, brought about the invention of the small portable and folding bootjacks.

When low-cut, laced shoes became popular late in the nineteenth century, bootjacks, like the boots for which they were designed, became obsolete. Many have survived, however, and some interesting examples can be found in cast and wrought iron, brass, and wood. The several illustrations accompanying this article show a variety of types that can be found.

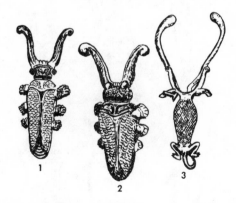

Illustrations drawn by the author.

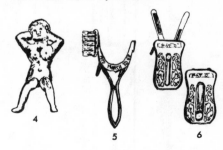

Key to Illustrations

1 and 2: Two versions of the iron beetle bootjack. *3:* Of brass, with two movable mandibles which clamp over the instep of the boot as the heel is forced into place.

4: Variously known as "Naughty Nellie" or "Naughty Lady." *5:* Equipped with a stiff brush and handle for removing caked mud and cleaning boots; this piece is marked "Patd. March 3D 68." *6:* As the prongs retract, the fore-legs fold back against the body making this a very compact portable bootjack.

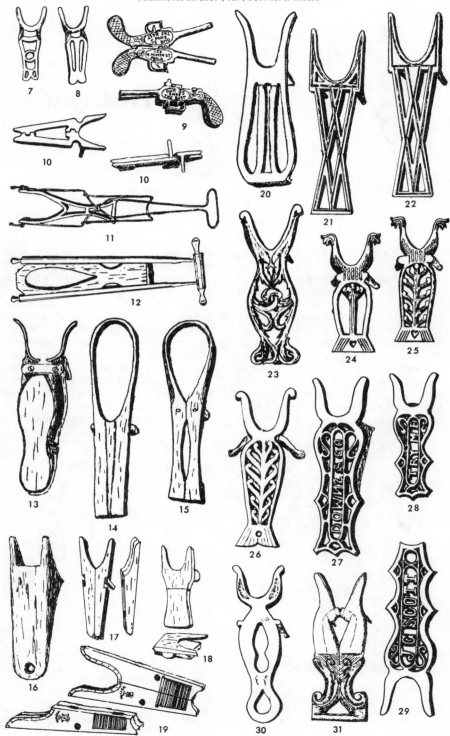

7   8

9

10

10

11

12

20

21

22

23

24   25

13

14   15

26   27   28

16   17   18

19

29

30   31

7: A small, lightweight iron boot-jack. *8:* One like this is shown in the Bennington Historical Museum; like most iron bootjacks, it is late 19th century. *9:* A realistic pistol when closed, and a bootjack when open. *10:* Another lightweight folding piece.

11: Of cast iron and wire, this boot-jack was designed for someone who could not bend or stoop. The long wire handle can be operated from a standing position, and a wire clamp holds the heel firmly in place while the boot is being removed. *12:* The loop in this oak bootjack was designed to hold down the instep of the boot as the foot was withdrawn.

13: An ingenious combination of wood and iron. As pressure is applied by the free foot, the metal prongs close tightly about the heel of the boot. *14 and 15:* Neatly made hardwood bootjacks.

16: Bootjack carved from one piece of oak. *17 and 18:* Two folding boot-jacks made of walnut.

19: The opening for the heel is bound with leather to prevent scuffing the boot; a strip of rubber provides a firm grip for the free foot. *20:* A large, heavy cast iron bootjack.

21 and 22: Differ only in the design around the heel opening. *23:* A fairly common entwined scroll pattern, cast iron.

24 and 25: Variations on the same design. *26:* The fishtail design is somewhat refined in this example.

27, 28 and 29: Cast iron bootjacks marked "Downs & Co.," "Try Me," and "J. G. Scott."

30: Cast iron bootjack with shoe design in center. *31:* Two boots form the heel-grip for this cast iron boot-jack. The initials "G. R." are impressed on the back. *32:* A decorative, but sturdy cast iron bootjack.

33: A rather crudely cast iron boot-jack. *34:* A simple design in a cast iron bootjack. *35:* Cast iron in a plain vertical design.

36: Designed for use as a wrench or a bootjack. *37, 38, 39 and 40:* Heavy cast iron bootjacks. *41:* Cast iron with a pleasing heart design.

42: Very early cast iron bootjack with heart motifs. *43 and 44:* Two different forms with similar designs.

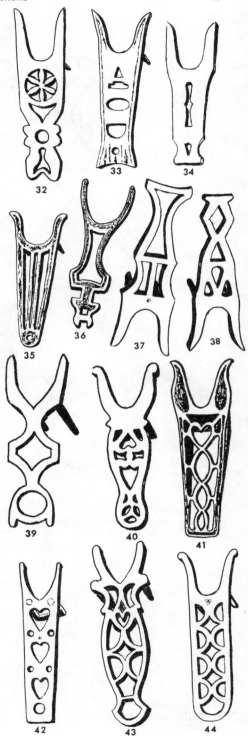

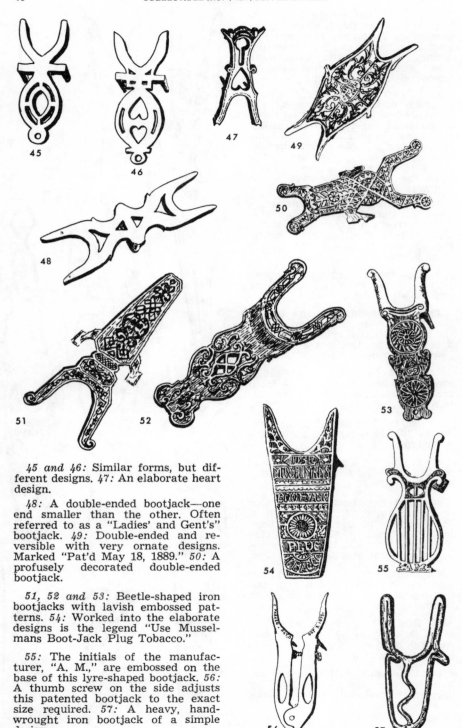

45 and 46: Similar forms, but different designs. *47:* An elaborate heart design.

48: A double-ended bootjack—one end smaller than the other. Often referred to as a "Ladies' and Gent's" bootjack. *49:* Double-ended and reversible with very ornate designs. Marked "Pat'd May 18, 1889." *50:* A profusely decorated double-ended bootjack.

51, 52 and 53: Beetle-shaped iron bootjacks with lavish embossed patterns. *54:* Worked into the elaborate designs is the legend "Use Musselmans Boot-Jack Plug Tobacco."

55: The initials of the manufacturer, "A. M.," are embossed on the base of this lyre-shaped bootjack. *56:* A thumb screw on the side adjusts this patented bootjack to the exact size required. *57:* A heavy, hand-wrought iron bootjack of a simple design.

"Oven" andirons; hollow, with slides for baking potatoes inside

Pre-Stove Cooking

by EDWIN C. WHITTEMORE

BACK THERE in the 1600s and the 1700s, how did your Great-great-great-great-grandmother Hepzibah and your Great-great-great-aunt Piety do the cooking? What were the conditions they had to work under? What were the big differences from today?

First of all, there was no semblance of a constant, steady, even heat. Stoves were not used until the early 1800s, and then only by a few. They were not at all common until the middle of the century. So the source of heat for cooking was the fireplace, roaring hot one minute, ashen and cool a little later. A fundamental problem in cooking was constant readjustment to varying cooking temperatures.

Secondly, there may not have been fire there when you wanted it. There were no electric switches, no gas spigots, not even matches. Lighting a fire with flint and steel by means of the family tinder box was both tricky and tedious, and often took more than a half hour to do. Thérefore, fires were, so far as possible, made perpetual by constant feeding with fuel, skillful banking at night and when not in active use.

Thirdly, there was no refrigeration. The cool depths of the dug well and the corner of the backyard brook helped, but in a limited way.

Fourth, there was no running water. Very occasionally an ingenious home-owner would draw water from a hillside spring to his kitchen by gravity, but this was rare. Water had to be dipped, pumped, lifted and carried—carried in endless repetition.

How in simple terms did those industrious early housewives actually perform the cooking processes, prior to the arrival of the cook stove? There were really two distinct periods, not definable so much by date as describable in terms of the living habits and facilities that created two separate eras. Here are the distinctive marks of the two:

A. The period of: Wooden chimneys, clay lined—Hearths with limited capacity — Wooden lug poles — Dutch Oven baking.

B. The period of: Brick chimneys—Hearths with huge capacity—Iron lug poles—Built-in-chimney baking.

Because of primitive conditions, strictly local sources for the materials, and limited labor supplies, the early years were shy of building materials such as brick. Great wide boards, 30 inches wide and wider, were sawed by hand in the pit, fashioned into chimney form and lined with clay which baked hard, dry, and fire resistant.

Across over head would be a long, freshly cut pole, often of swamp maple which, being green and moist, would last for months before drying out and burning. This lug pole, so-called, was usually about five feet above the floor of the fireplace, the hearth. From it hung all manner of "S" hooks, trammel hooks, either ratchet or tongued, and on them in turn were the various kettles and pots in all manner of shape and size.

On the hearth itself was another series of utensils, all on legs, most with pad feet, ready to be moved forward and back, to and fro, amid the hot coals and the warm ashes to get more or less heat as needed.

Baking in this early period was most often done in a tightly lidded heavy iron pot. Most authorities agree this is the true "Dutch oven," though

the name has often been used for other devices also. This Dutch oven had legs and, most important, a lid so strong and nicely fitted that not only could the oven be set in among the hot coals, but hot coals could also be heaped upon the lid. All kind of baking was done in it.

The second period presents the same theories and practices, but slightly more refined. Brick, made locally or imported as ship's ballast, was used to construct fine big solid fireplaces and chimneys. Iron was being "worked" in the colonies, so the perishable wooden lug poles give way to various types of iron lug poles and back bars, firmly and permanently implanted along the upper reaches of the fireplace.

In place of the Dutch oven, built-in bricked ovens handled the baking. These were large and small; often in a domed beehive shape, at one side, at both sides, or to the rear of the fireplace. They were connected to the chimney with an independent flue.

Of course, neither Dutch ovens nor built-in ovens were always used. It would not be uncommon to push a bed of hot coals and ash to one side of the hearth and bury potatoes directly in it to bake. Andirons were there to hold up the burning logs, and one ingenious person fashioned hollow "box" andirons. The front ends slid forward revealing attached interior trays. Potatoes were put upon them and the trays slid back within the andirons for baking.

Cooking Processes

The actual processes of cooking fell

Top to bottom: large iron skimmer or strainer; pothook with wooden handle; average-size skimmer; wooden toddy ladle.

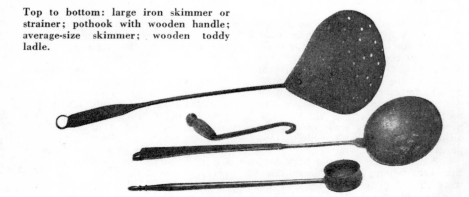

Small tin reflector oven with spit adjustable to many fixed positions; wire potato
boiler or basket.

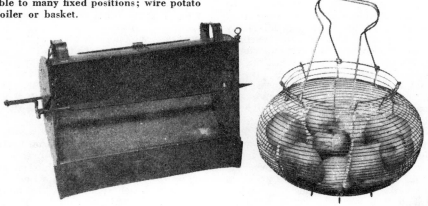

into the same categories as they do,
today:

Roasting. In the earliest times the
bird or piece of meat was simply suspended from the front edge of the
fireplace and made to revolve. Sometimes a child was assigned to this
task. Sometimes the busy housewife
twisted the suspending cord at handy
intervals, letting it "unwind" itself in
the opposite direction. Later, revolving spits were used, operated by a
descending weight as in a grandfather's clock. There were also mechanical key-wound spring-driven
"jacks" for the purpose and, on more
occasions that one first realizes, a
spit operated by a treadmill on which
a dog ran.

Proper capture of the maximum
amount of heat and the increased
availability of tin produced the reflector oven, or tin kitchen, or hearth
kitchen, as it is called. Sitting on short
legs, a giant hood with curved back
and open front faced the fire. Across
it ran a wrought iron spit or skewer
which was manually turned a little
at a time as necessary. Suitable holes
in the tin sidewall, and a properly
placed hook or position-setter beside
the spit, made many positions possible. To conserve heat there was a
hinged "peep hole" in the curved back
wall. Through this, the cook could
observe how the roast was doing
without turning the whole reflector
oven. These reflector ovens came in
various sizes from about twelve to
twenty-four inches.

Baking was chiefly accomplished

in the Dutch oven, the built-in-brick
chimney oven, and reflector ovens.

Toasting is a form of roasting.
There were many toasters. some of
them exceptional examples of the fine
work that a blacksmith could do in
decoration with iron. As a group they
were characterized by the various
methods of turning or flipping the
carrying unit (the toast holder, etc.)
so that each side could be exposed to
the heat without changing the position of the toaster handle which
naturally was kept where it would
not get too hot to manipulate.

Broiling, where the meat, fowl, or
fish to be cooked was brought close
to the heat, is the method where the
juices are of great volume, and to the
colonists these juices were of great
importance. Consequently, every effort was made to catch and save them.
A broiler may have been stationary
or revolving, and it was often made
with grooved arms leading to a
reservoir area. The revolving feature,
as in the toaster, placed the material
near to the flame without having the
handle get too close; it also provided
an adjustment for greater or less
heat, the ever-constant problem with
an uneven heat supply.

Boiling and *Stewing* call for the
same procedures, but with more or
less heat. A variety of pots and kettles
were used, often of iron, also of copper
and brass. Portable, they could be
used anywhere within the fireplace.

It should be pointed out that the
huge 8 foot, 10 foot, and larger fireplaces were rarely used for one huge

enormous fire. Actually, the sides and corners of the hearth were often used for a bench or small settle so that members of the family could really sit within the chimney for warmth. It would also be a common experience to find two or more fires within the same fireplace at the same time—a medium sized one in the center, perhaps, while a low burning heap of red coals might be performing another cooking process to one side. So there were big pots, little pots, covered pots, open pots, pots with bails, pots with side handles, almost always on legs.

Frying has changed little over the years. In the early days the problem, as in the other methods of cooking, was in the varying degrees of heat available, and in the practical problem of handling the hot pans over an open fire. One s o l u t i o n was the long-handled wrought-iron frying pan, a common item. More rare and more interesting were the revolving frying pans on legs, with a handle. Actually, there were a great many kinds, sizes, and styles of fry pans in the equipment of early kitchens. Interesting note — there were almost never any small ones.

Comes the Crane

The crane which replaced the lug pole, and which became such an important central unit of hearth or fireplace cooking, is said to have been an American invention, but that is questionable. The crane is the horizontal arm suspended from the side wall of the fireplace and swinging out as desired into any one of many positions. It gradually replaced the lug pole, often was supplementary to it.

The manner in which a large heavy duty crane was installed in a fireplace explains why the original suspending rings or pintel units are rarely rescued from old houses even though the cranes are. There were usually five thicknesses of brick to the wall of the fireplace. The pintel pins not only went through these five layers but also had right angle terminals. The stock was heavy iron bar stock. They could not have been removed without tearing down the chimney!

In some homes there was another built-in cooking unit — an iron kettle set into brick, much as the oven was built. With a fire and flue of its own, or taking its heat from the chimney which it abutted, the built-in or "set" kettle was used primarily as a source of hot water, for "scalding" pigs, and for other tasks calling for a large container of hot liquid.

Food and Equipment

There was romance, variety, and ingenuity connected with products accessory to the cooking processes. Salt was done without, was made from sea water, even imported, until sources of salt were developed in this country. Spices were obtainable through import, being compact and of high value, and were used even more than they are today. Sugar was scarce, came in heavy cones and was cut into chunks with special sugar cutters, then pulverized in crushers. Only city folk had it. Those in the country depended on honey, molasses and maple syrup.

There was variety and ingenuity, too, in the tools or equipment of the cooking area, crude as they may have been. There were all sorts of ladles,

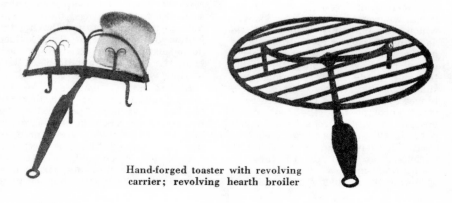

Hand-forged toaster with revolving carrier; revolving hearth broiler

strainers, and dippers; there were herb drying racks and herb grinders. There were sieves with wood frames and lovely plaid-design woven horse-hair mesh. There were graters, large and small, simple and complex. There were rotary apple parers and potato parers. There were lard presses, food choppers, countless different sizes and shapes in mortars and pestles. There were large and small pot hooks of iron, or wood and iron, with which hot containers could be handled. Wood and iron were the usual materials but brass and copper were also used.

"Mixture" dishes were the order of the day — porridges, stews, broths, mush, and hash. A big kettle was kept simmering over the fire almost continuously, and a newly-shot rabbit or squirrel would be dressed and popped into it. Because potatoes disintegrated if cooked too long, they were often placed in a globe-like potato basket of wire, and set down into the simmering kettle, being removed when done, as the whole simmered on. Similar contrivances were used for foods such as eggs. There was considerable of this cooking-within-cooking.

To accompany the meal, the beverage was very often beer or hard cider, both of which were normally preferred to water. The table was extreme simplicity. There were wood and horn spoons, no forks, few knives, much eating from the fingers.

Iron Match Safes

Six of the sixty-six match safes in the Dickinson Collection.

SOMEONE has said that over 500 different categories of interest wait upon the collector who takes the plunge. The more we visit the homes and offices of collectors of the unusual, the more we think the anonymous commentator missed the mark by 500 categories, at least.

Mr. Harry P. Dickinson is a manufacturing jeweler who, perhaps, tiring of gold, silver and platinum, turned to cast iron. He wanted something "little" to collect; again, perhaps something not too far removed from his own association with small but precious items. One day, on Cape Cod, he bought an unique little hinged box on a hanger which they told him was a match safe.

Now he owns between sixty-five and seventy cast iron match safes, all different. The most unusual one is a Church match safe, featuring a Gothic arch, in outline, with a Gargoyle from Notre Dame serving as the container, the cap being hinged and serving as a lid. Another intriguing one is a miniature grinding mortar, issued as an advertisement for the maker of the Grinding Mills, located at Easton, Pennsylvania. There are two and three tiered examples which, Mr. Dickinson says, were made to accommodate both live and burnt matches. Thus far, this collector has not started on mechanical match safes, but there are such items; there are storks, pelicans, monkeys and other beasties who gyrate, peck and pick into a slot and lo, up they come with one match.

Clockwork Roasting Jacks of Iron and Brass

by DAVID CLARKE

CLOCKWORK roasting jacks, those handsome and ingenious little machines whose purpose was to turn the meat roasting before the open fire, were in use in the first half of the 19th century. Apparently most of them were made in Sheffield, England, and from the scarcity of examples to be found in America today compared to the number available in England, it would seem they were in more common use in the mother country.

These efficient kitchen aids hung from a shackle or bracket fastened to the chimneypiece. The roast was hung on the hook below. Sometimes a jack is found to which has been added a small cast iron wheel with several hooks below which could carry a number of steaks or other small items at once.

These little machines were cased in well polished sheet brass and bore the maker's name on a decorative stamped brass label. They were provided with an iron clock key, and the keyhole was given a neat swinging coverplate.

The jack made by Linwood is the type most usually found today. Another variety, made by Chesterman (still a prominent name in Sheffield engineering circles) used a slightly different movement in a case of squatter shape. The Restells Patent Jack, manufactured by E. B. Bennett, was of banjo shape and had a permanently fitted brass winder in the center of the casing.

John Linwood seems to have been the most prolific maker. His clockwork movement seems crude, yet in reality it was a triumph of design over the limitations imposed by the materials and technology of the period. The designers, not having an efficient thrust bearing available to support the load,

Linwood-made jack hangs from a typical brass bracket fixed above the fireplace, and shows wheel attachment from which steaks or small items could be hung.

had to devise a mechanism with the minimum of friction in order to conserve the energy of the spring and so make a long running machine.

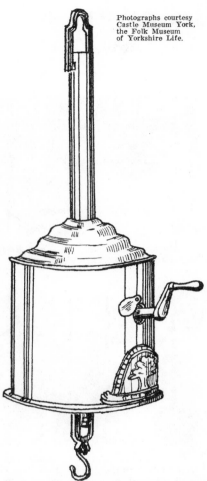

Photographs courtesy
Castle Museum York,
the Folk Museum
of Yorkshire Life.

vertical pin which is the pivot of a quadrant driving through a train of gears to the final hook. It is this hook with its concentric pinion that is suspended by the silk.

A refinement usually included was a spring loaded clutch at the hook to prevent it from turning when the jack was not in use.

The jack was made to work for long periods under difficult conditions without attention. Today they are eagerly sought by connoisseurs of clockwork as well as collectors of culinary equipment.

Most usual type of clockwork roasting jack found today. **Author's collection.**

This was done by carrying the load on a skein of silk thread anchored at the top of the tubular extension. This could not, of course, twist more than a few times before offering resistance and the rotation was therefore reversed after every two or three revolutions. There was an added advantage in that a governor was not required to control the speed, the meat just revolved gently to and fro.

This movement has an anchor type escapement reminiscent of that in a long case clock. The spring drives the escapement wheel through a pair of gears. The teeth on this wheel impinge alternately on projections from a

This jack works above a "hastener", or sheet iron Dutch oven, which was placed in front of the fire.

Household Ironwares

by DORIS S. WOOLF

MOST collectors of early Americana respond to the homely appeal of household items in wrought and cast iron. From visits to museums, historic houses and antiques shops, we are familiar with the intriguing list of collectible ironware —the firebacks and stove plates; fanciful toasters and grills; long-handled skillets and slices with their charming terminals; toddy sticks and tongs; skimmers, ladles, and spoons; quaintly shaped teakettles, Betty lamps, and the relatively rare lacy-handled posnets. Although these numerous hearth and culinary items that have come down to us have, for the most part, lost their purely utilitarian value, they are rich in historical significance and useful decorative accessories in creating early-day atmosphere in the increasingly popular Early American home.

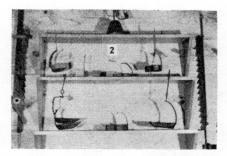

2. *Collection of ratchet lights and Betty lamps; rush light on top shelf.*

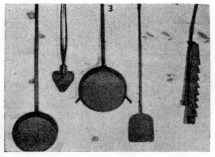

3. *Long-handled skillet, Pennsylvania heart-shaped waffle iron, three-legged skillet, peel or slice, saw-toothed trammel.*

1. *Top shelf: Rush light, mortar and pestle, lamb door stop, "bee hive" string holder, charcoal stove iron. Middle shelf: Lacy-handled cast-iron posnets. Bottom shelf: 18th century handled pot for open hearth cooking, covered Dutch oven, wood-burning stove kettle.*

History proves that iron was the first native metal utilized by the colonists. In 1630 a rich deposit of bog-iron was found at Saugus, Massachusetts, near Boston. A company was founded and a hammer, smelter and a foundry were set up for producing both wrought and cast iron. Thus was born one of the earliest New England industries. The

enterprise flourished and supplied our first colonists with the necessary pots, kettles, hinges, locks and latches and the impressive battery of fireplace equipment that was seen on every hearth at this time, when all cooking and heating came from the log fire on the open hearth.

During the first years of American colonization, fat-burning Betty lamps, not much changed in form from the ancient Roman lamps, were used; later, when candles were dipped at home, the smith's business grew even more brisk in the making of iron candlesticks. The original Saugus foundry expanded and established other forges in 1648 and 1652 at Braintree and Raynham, Massachusetts. With expanding colonization and the new forges, the production of our collector's items grew enormously—to such an extent that there are enough of these simple, delightfully wrought iron pieces for every one of us to possess at least a few of them. And to own an item of 17th or 18th century American iron is to provoke an interest in the history and origin of man's use of this least expensive and most adaptable of all metals.

From the standpoint of style and design, the best American iron was made from the time of the Revolution to the end of the 18th century. After 1800 there was a rapid decline in the production of American hand wrought ironwork, except in Pennsylvania where the ancient traditions of the blacksmiths continued to flourish and the production of excellent ironware continued as late as the mid-19th century. Because of the persistence of Pennsylvania smiths to continue the old methods and the lingering traditions in other Eastern states, despite the advancement of the Machine Age, collectors of today enjoy abundant examples of early American ironware.

5. *Hearth display: round revolving grill, toggle-arm pipe tongs, Betty lamp, double Phoebe lamp, spatula, spoons, peel, fork, "spider", trivet, and kettle.*

4. *Collection of grills, toasters, wrought iron handled bed warming pan, short trammel.*

Wall Lavabo of agate-enameled stamped sheet iron, made by the Central Stamping Company of Saint Louis, Missouri, 1889, for the Western Cottage trade.

Wafer Irons   *by MARY EARLE GOULD*

A wafer was a form of unleavened bread used in religious ceremonies. As early as 1358, a wafer iron used in making wafers was mentioned in an appraisement of goods belonging to an English gentleman:—"one pair of irons for the Eucharist." The wafers were used with wine at the sacrament of the Lord's Supper.

A wafer iron (or tongs) is a utensil with two hinged parts, fashioned of iron by the blacksmith. It has two round plates or heads, measuring about six inches in diameter and the handles are three feet long, such as were on all implements used in the fireplace. Some early irons bear a seal with three locked hearts surmounted by a cross enclosed within a circle, and an anchor with ornaments imitating leaves. Some have a crucifix or a sacred monogram. All of the irons show that they were used exclusively in ceremonial services.

Among the bride's gifts was a wafer iron, with the date of the marriage and the initials of the giver, usually the groom. This gift was an omen of good luck. One such wafer iron in the author's collection, is (illus.), marked 1785 with the initials W C M. There is a heart and scroll on one head and on the other two hex marks and a simple scroll. These incisions were not cut in the reverse, so the dates and initials on the wafer iron were not as they should be on the wafer. The art of reversed stamping was doubtless of little concern in those early years.

The wafers or wafer cakes were made by a waferer and two or three irons were sufficient in supplying a community for any ceremony. It must have been a tedious task for one man to manage the irons and make a great number of cakes. The iron was first heated over a charcoal fire or in the embers of a fireplace, before the batter was put into the heads. There are rests in some collections of early implements on which any long-handled iron could be held while cooking over the fire. These rests are frames with three or four legs from which extend an arm on which the handle of the iron rested. The wafer iron or the

waffle iron was extremely heavy and these rests relieved the worker from holding the implement over the hot embers. A dealer in the cakes was called a wafer, or it was a wafer woman who sold the cakes.

As the years went on, the types of wafer irons changed and various shaped heads appeared, being oval as well as round. A short-handled wafer iron shows that the wafers continued to be made when stoves replaced open fireplaces. There is a projection on this type of iron which rested on the rim of the stove hole, and the handles are short. (see illus.)

In this country the wafers were used in the home as well as in the church. The irons were made by local blacksmiths and the patterns on the

(Left) Early wafer iron dated 1785, initials WCM, two hex marks and heart. (Right) Later wafer iron with short handles and a protruding nub which rested in stove hole.

heads were flowers, initials and dates, and the necessary hex mark. This hex mark was supposed to keep away evil spirits, (witches in particular) and was used on doors, tools and utensils, expressing the confidence of the owner for his protection against evil spirits.

A rule for making wafers or wafer cakes is given in a cook book called Two Fifteenth-Century C o o k e r y Books. "Waffres — Take the womb (belly) of a luce (full-grown pike) and sethe here wyl and do it on a mortar and tender cheese thereto, grynde them togethir; then take flour and white of Eyren (obsolete word for eggs) and beat them togethir and look that the eyrcun (iron) be hot and lay thereon a thin paste and then make waffyrs and so on."

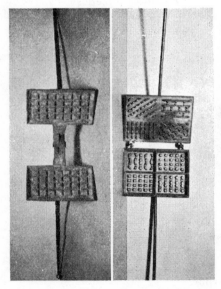

Early waffle irons. The one on the right has different patterns in each section.

From a cook book of the early 19th century, it would seem that wafers continued to be used. By then their use was for home as well as for church ceremonies. A rule reads:— "Dry the flour well which you intend to use, mix a little pounded sugar and finely pounded mace with it; then make it into a thick batter with cream; butter the wafer irons, let them be hot; put a teaspoonful of batter into them, so bake them carefully, and roll them off the iron with a stick." Sometimes the rolled wafers were filled with whipped cream and sealed at the ends with a preserved strawberry.

Waffles and waffle irons are more commonly known today than wafers and wafer irons. In the early centuries, there was a Waffling Sunday in Sweden similar to the Wafering Sunday of old England. On that particular Sunday, the people of the communities went from one home to another and were served waffles. It was a social gathering of the communities connected with their religion.

A rule for waffles used more than one hundred years ago reads: — One quart flour and a teaspoon salt. One quart sour milk with two teaspoonsful melted butter in it. Five well-beaten eggs. A teaspoon or more of salaratus, enough to sweeten the milk. Bake in waffle iron. Waffle irons well oiled with lard each time they are used.

The old waffle irons have oblong heads, with a block pattern. The irons were hand wrought by the blacksmiths. When the manufacturing of iron tools came about, the shape of the waffle iron became more fancy and these were stamped with a date or with a number. Many irons are in the shape of a heart. One of the illustrations is an early hand wrought iron with both heads alike, while another illustration has eight section with a different pattern in each section.

Such records of the early years bring to us of the 20th century a history of that first Mother's Sunday. Three hundred years ago, the observance was established. Love, honor and respect brought about the day and in our modern custom, there should be that same love, honor and respect.

Iron Apple Parers

by ALAN ANDERSON & WILLIAM THOMAS

Fig. 1: Unmarked wooden parer, only slightly different from the model patented by Reuben and Amos Mosher, in 1829. On display at Huntington (N.Y.) Historical Society.

APPLES WERE a staple commodity in early 19th century New England and other settled localities in America. They were pressed into cider, dried, strung, made into apple butter and apple sauce. They were fried, stewed, baked, cooked into pies and other pastries, like dumplings and Brown Bettys. Since so many of these edibles required that the apple be peeled, ingenious Yankees were quick to invent and put into use mechanical apple parers.

The earliest American parer now known is a wooden one designed and

Fig. 2: Improved Apple Paring and Slicing Machine, 1856.

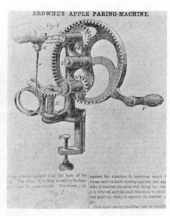

Fig. 3: Browne's Apple Paring Machine, 1855.

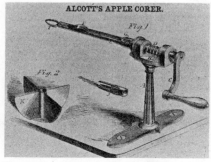

Fig. 4: Alcott's Apple Corer, 1859.

Fig. 5: Manufactured by Goodell Co., Antrim, N.H.; patented March 18, 1884.

built around 1750. Until about 1849, when cast metal parers appeared, apple parers were made of wood, except for the metal knives.

The first recorded U.S. patent for a parer was granted to Moses Coates, Downing Fields, Pa., in February 1803. In the next 35 years, several other patents for wooden parers were issued. They went to S. Crittenden, Connecticut, Aug. 1809; Willard Badger, Massachusetts, Feb. 16, 1809; Cyrus Gates, Rutland, Vt., Dec. 15, 1810; Reuben and Amos Mosher, Saratoga County, N.Y., Dec. 28, 1829; A. Glendenning, Loudon County, Va., Sept. 9, 1823; Cyprian C. Pratt, Paris, Me., Dec. 28, 1833; Daniel Davis II, Tolland County, Conn., March 14, 1834; Robert W. Mitchell, Martins Hill, Ohio, April 13, 1838; and J. W. Hatcher, Bedford County, Va., Feb. 3, 1836.

Most of these parers operated on the same principle, but all had variations acceptable for patent rulings. Skilled home craftsmen, copying patented models on their own lathes, produced many personal variations. Yet the parers all achieved the same end. The apple was impaled on a fork and by simple or complicated means, was skinned by the rotation of the parer with a knife blade held against it.

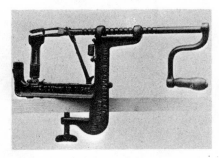

Fig. 7: Manufactured by Goodell Co., Antrim, N.H.; no patent date appears on it.

Fig. 8: Unmarked; possibly a copy of one of the Goodell patents.

Fig. 6: Also manufactured by Goodell Co., patented March 24, 1898, marked "White Mountain APE"; designated as the "Turntable '98" model.

Fig. 9: No manufacturer's name on this, but the patent dates of May 5, 1858, June 7, 1870, and March 26, 1872, appear.

Fig. 10: Patented by H. Keyes, June 17 and Dec. 16, 1856.

Fig. 11: No markings; possibly a metal variation of Julius Weed's wooden parer and slicer.

Fig. 12: Known as the Turntable Apple Parer, this bears the same patent dates, June 17 and Dec. 16, 1856, as the Keyes model, but also carries the name of Lockley and Howland.

Some parers operated by direct drive; some by belt drive; others had a coupling of a large wooden wheel with ratchets engaging a small wheel carrying the apple fork; still others employed multiple gears to speed up the apple and the paring operation.

The *Scientific American* for December 1, 1849, carried an illustrated account of what appears to be the first patented metal parer. Juliu(s) Weed of Painesville, Ohio, was the holder of the patent, dated July 31, 1849. (Fig. 13) Though partially constructed of wood, the principal mechanisms were of metal. Its special feature was that it not only pared, but also cored and sliced the apple.

In the August 11, 1855 issue, *Scientific American* showed Browne's Apple Paring Machine. (Fig. 3), invented by J. D. Browne of Cincinnati, Ohio, who called it "a very compact and simple machine for paring apples and other fruit."

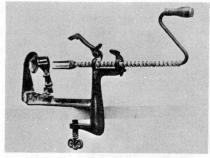

Fig. 14: No markings; possibly a variation of the Goodell Co. parer.

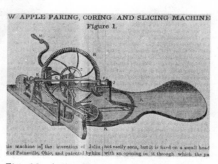

Fig. 13: Julius Weed's invention, patented July 31, 1849.

Alcott's Apple Corer (Fig. 4) was shown in the April 2, 1859 issue of *Scientific American*. The article accompanying the diagram stated, in part: "This machine may also be made into a parer by placing the three pronged holder, J, over I, and placing the apple upon it, it can be pared very quickly by hand."

The only other parer illustrated in *Scientific American* appeared March 22, 1856, and was listed as the Improved Apple Paring and Slicing Machine. (Fig. 2) The accompanying

Fig. 15: Manufactured by C. E. Hudson, Leominster, Mass.; patented Jan. 24, 1889.

Fig. 16: "Made only by the Reading Hardware Co., Reading, Pa.; patents dated May 5, 1868, May 3, 1875, Oct. 19, 1875, Nov. 14, 1875, May 22, 1877.

description shows clearly the operation of this model and all others similar to it:

"The machine is small nearly all its parts being of cast-iron the whole weighing only 2 lb. 10 oz. The contrivance is secured to the table by means of the clamp, A, and to this is attached the standard, B, by means of the strong joint at B, which permits the careening of the machine both right and left. E is the driving wheel, motion being given by means of the crank to all the parts. Upon the face of the driving wheel E, is an inclined scroll, R, upon which one end of the rack bar, G, glides; this rack connects with, and gives motion to, the loop gear H, which supports and guides the spring rod, I, upon which is affixed the paring knife, J.

"The machine being careened, as shown in the cut, an apple is placed upon the fork, K, when by rotation of

Fig. 17: Patented Oct. 6, 1863; no other markings.

Fig. 18: Similar to the Goodell parers, but unmarked.

the crank the driving wheel, E, gives motion to the pinion, E, and thence to the fork and apple, while the scroll, F, acting through the rack bar, G, upon the loop gear, H, the paring knife, J, is thereby passed, during the rotation of the apple, from its base around to its outer end, and effectively pares the apple, when the outer circuit of the scroll, F, having passed the end of the rack bar, G, the coiled spring attached to the other and lower end of the rack bar, contracts, and returns the rack bar, loop gear, spring rod, and paring knife to their original positions in readiness to repeat the operation of paring.

"Without removing the apple from the fork the machine is now careened in an opposite direction, when the pin, L, which secures the loop gear, H, within its socket, comes in contact with the tripping post, M, causing the partial revolution of the loop gear, and thereby withdrawing the end of the rack bar, G, from the scroll, F, thus permitting the backward rotation of

the crank and driving wheel, together with the fork and apple. The slicing arm, N, which is the one hinged to the standard, B, and sustains the slicing knife, O, is now swung by the left hand and pressed lightly against the apple, which is thereby cut into one continuous slice or ribbon, leaving only the core, in cylindrical form upon the fork.

"The careening of the machine perfectly accomplishes the separation of the slices from the parings, while the parabolic curvature of the slicing knife produces such a formation of slices that they do not pack closely together while drying and yet are not in the least objectionable for immediate cooking. This is a novel contrivance; that it works well we know from actual experiment. More information may be obtained, by letter, of the proprietors, Maxam and Smith, Shelburne Falls, Mass."

The rest of the parers illustrated are from the collection of Elsa Anderson of Huntington, N.Y. They give a fine display of the varieties of metal parers available. Only the advent of cast iron made this variety and large production possible. Notice in this assemblage of parers the useless complexity of some, and the utter simplicity of others. All had one single purpose, the paring of apples as quickly as possible.

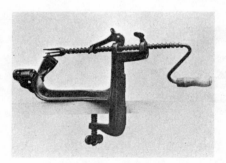

Fig. 19: Similar to the Goodell parers, but unmarked.

Early Iron Lighting Devices

by EDWIN C. WHITTEMORE

IN THE earlier types of lighting devices, it is noticeable that a high percentage are of a sort where the position of the light can be raised and lowered in relation to the person using it.

Lighting collectors are often crudely awakened, and even disappointed, the first time they actually test an early lighting device. Observed in a dark room, the light is amazingly insignificant; it can be compared to that of a wooden kitchen match or a small candle. This slight amount of illumination given off by rush lights, Betty lamps, grease lamps, etc., probably explains the great attention given to the adjustability of the light to a desired level. The user wanted it placed where it would do him the most good!

What to Look For

An interesting approach to the study of early lighting is to examine the many types in terms of classifying them according to the methods of this up-and-down adjustment. There are eight easily recognizable types, and a lighting collection that included at least one of each would be outstanding.

In simple terms, these are the eight classifications:

1. Dependence on what the lighting fixture rests upon. *Example:* a tin Ipswich Betty Lamp with its weighted cone base.

2. Dependence upon the point from which the fixture is suspended. *Example:* wrought iron loom light with vertical bar to hang down from nail or peg at variable heights.

3. Dependence on varying the height of the suspending unit. *Example:* the trammel-type fixture with paired members that can shorten or lengthen the vertical height.

4. Dependence on spiral-cut or screw-type central unit around which the candle or lamp carrier rests. *Example:* the sought-after revolving candlestand with crossbar.

5. Dependence on friction wedging. *Example:* a candle-carrying crossbar held to any position on a vertical shaft by a wedge.

6. Dependence on the spring tension of metals. *Example:* a hog-scraper iron candlestick. The movable platform holding up the candle stays where it is put by tension between it and the wall of the tube.

7. Dependence on spaced notches or holes in the vertical member. *Example:* a slot-type vertical candlestand.

8. Dependence on turnscrew wedging. *Example:* a crossbar candlestand where the bar rests on a separate turnscrew, fitting into the vertical member.

Left to right: iron hog-scraper candlestick (#6); table or miniature revolving candlestand (#4); wood-based candlestand of the 17th century with spiral-cut iron top section (also #4).

The Conestoga wagon at the Pennsylvania Farm Museum at Landis Valley was made in 1812. Still in possession of its original parts, it clearly shows the skill of the blacksmith who "ironed" it.

Conestoga Ironwork

by PHYLLIS T. BALLINGER

IN THE days when our nation was young, and a principal source of food for its exploding population came from the rich farm lands of Lancaster County in southeastern Pennsylvania, Conestoga wagons carried tons of produce to the bustling cities and returned with dry goods to be used in rural areas. The wagoner was the only person to direct these vehicles, and the responsibility for its maintenance was entirely his own.

The wagon was equipped with all that was required to keep the vehicle operative. A tool box, always painted blue, the traditional color of the wagon bed, was attached to the left side of the wagon. Its hinges and hasp were often ornate, usually symmetri-

cal, and always firmly riveted for extra strength. The decorative ironwork on the tool box is considered the height of the blacksmith's craft, for it is here that one finds the most handsomely wrought of all the "ironing" on the wagon. The padlock was of like quality, sturdy but artfully made. The feed box, which hung on the rear of the wagon, was another item which was reinforced with decorative ironwork.

Approximately 15 x 20 x 7 inches, the tool box contained such things as an extra doubletree pin, utility hammer, pincers, nuts and bolts, snap rings, "S" links for repairing chains, bridle bits, and horseshoeing equipment. If a repair had to be made along the way, the wagoner built a fire by the roadside, used the tire of the wagon for an anvil and became his own blacksmith. Although he developed considerable skill in working with iron, the wagoner's work is clearly discernible from that of the professional blacksmith. This can be seen in examining chains used on the wagon. Some, made in very intricate linking patterns, have an obviously replaced link interrupting momentarily the beautiful design of the original.

While these artful chains, fashioned by the blacksmith, greatly appeal to collectors, the somewhat clumsily repaired links also appeal to those who are captivated by the romance of the period. They call to mind the trials and tribulations of the wagoners, and the great contribution made by these men to our country's growth and well-being.

Among other ironwork found on Conestoga wagons which are eagerly

Wagon jacks, made by the blacksmith who did the "ironing" on the Conestoga wagon, are among the few dated tools to be found.

Interesting ironwork can be found on Conestoga wagon tool boxes.

Drawings of various decorated axe rests. Affixed to the hound tree of the Conestoga wagon, they combined utility with artistry.

stamped into the metal with a star punch, adding a flourish to the overall design. At times the date was outlined with intricate border designs.

The strips of iron, the rear hound plates, the coupling pole pins, and the stay chain hooks were sometimes wrought with artistic touches, too. On these, hearts and tulips, snake heads or the entire body of a coiled snake are to be found over and over in slightly different forms.

No discussion of the ironwork found on the Conestoga wagon would be complete without mentioning the wagon jack. This was used to raise the wheel high enough to clear the ground when repairs were necessary; it was also used to free a wheel from a rut in the road. Approximately 24 x 7 x 3 inches in size, it was standard equipment for the wagon and when not in use it hung on the rear axletree. Made on the principal of modern jacks with rachet type expansion, it cradled the spoke or axle and lifted a considerable weight when the handle was turned. Two spurs on the base of the jack precluded any chance of its slipping while in use.

Straight and curved chisels in various sizes and a circular punch were used to hammer in the initials and numbers found on hound bands and wagon jacks. These simple tools, which the blacksmith made himself, produced quaint effects that collectors find desirable.

In the writer's collection is a wagon jack dated 1859 which was found at Intercourse, Pa. Having survived the Conestoga wagon for which it was originally made, it was used to repair farm wagons for generations. This jack has an interesting though not uncommon feature in connection with the date. The numeral "1" is made with two "Js," the second reversed and with a line joining them to form the letter "H." It has been suggested by Henry K. Landis who, with his brother George, founded what has become the Pennsylvania Farm Museum at Landis Valley, Lancaster County, Pa., that this symbol represented *Jahr Herr Jesu,*—"in the year of our Lord."

collected today are the axe rest, the collar placed on the tongue of the wagon (frequently called the "hound band"), the ornamental piece that was placed on the end of the tongue for a practical purpose, and the stay chain hooks.

The axe rest was an object upon which the blacksmith could again display his skill in making decorative ironwork. Floral patterns, geometric designs, or little scrolls can sometimes be found on this piece of equipment —the writer has seen one in the shape of a nicely proportioned fish.

The hound band often had initials cut into it, and the year the wagon was built. On some, the date was

The same marking can be found on old chests, date stones, and cast iron stove lids.

Our jack now leans against the fireplace in the den where it recalls legends of a colorful era in American history. After removing the rust and dirt which had accumulated over a period of years, we gave the jack a protective coat of wax. One antiques dealer suggested that we spruce up the old iron by removing the rust with steel wool, cover it with old fashioned black stove polish, and then buffing it to a dull luster.

Western movies, TV shows, and novels have made us conscious of the Conestoga wagon and the part it played in the development of our nation. For about 100 years, from 1740 to 1840, these "ships of inland commerce" were seen in great numbers. One contemporary writer, Morris Birbeck, said, in 1817, "About 12,000 wagons passed between Baltimore and Philadelphia and this place [Pittsburgh] in the last year." By 1840, however, railroads and canals had taken over the freight traffic, and the Conestoga wagons were slowly pushed into oblivion. The accoutrements of the wagon, its fancy ironwork, and the charming little hames bells, which have a story of their own to tell, have now become collector's items.

Illustrations courtesy of the Pennsylvania Historical & Museum Commission, Harrisburg, Pa.

Portable Early Iron Footscraper

AS A RULE, early iron footscrapers were firmly embedded in the brick or stonework of steps or stoop. They were adjuncts of the house and belonged to it forever. This one, of hand-wrought iron, from the collection of Mr. Ray O. Hill, Beaver Falls, Pennsylvania, is portable, mounted on a solid, very heavy block of wood. It could be carried from door to door, wherever it was most needed, or from house to house. Apparently it was set this way originally, a makeshift to suit someone's particular needs.

Such a mounting is well adapted for use today when household moves are many and frequent, and a collector who treasures an early footscraper may want to use it, but hesitates to affix it permanently.

A Sampling of Sad Irons

by A. H. GLISSMAN

T HE TERM "sad iron" is of ancient descent. The words "sad" and "sorrowful" existed together in English usage in the 14th century, and we find Chaucer using the word "sorrowful" in its present day meaning. "Sad," however, could mean "solid, dense, compact, or heavy," a meaning now obsolete. "Two grete ymages of golde sad," was written in the 14th century, and another early chronicle, ca. 1330, refers to "with iron nayles sad, his fete was schod."

About 1388, Wyclif in translating the Bible from Latin to English, gave Exodus 38-7 as "Forsoth thilke auter was not sad but holowe."

The word usage wore well; more than two hundred and fifty years later, in 1641, a book on farming advised, "Short barley strawe is the best for stoppinge of holes, because it is sadder and not soe subject to blowe out with everie Blast of winds, as other light and dry strawe is."

As for "sad iron," the earliest printed English reference appears to be in Babbage's *On Economy of Machines and Manufactures,* published in 1832, in which he refers to "sad irons and other castings." The following year, in 1833, J. Holland, in *Manufacturing Metal,* wrote, "Dealers commonly distinguish these useful implements by the terms: sad-iron, box-iron, and Italian iron," indicating that

the term was by no means a recent one.

Appreciation is expressed to Mr. R. K. Blumenau, History Division, Malvern College, Worcester, England, for historical background on the term "sad iron." Additional comments may be found in the *Oxford University Dictionary,* edited by Sir James Murray, 1914 edition.

MEXICO

1. The large handles of these "tattle-tale bell" irons are hollow and contain a ball which rings when the iron is moved. The story goes this was to tell when the maid was shirking; actually, when the handle is gripped, the bell can no longer be heard. All are handmade, and each is different.

2. 19th century, handmade. Many flowered irons come from Mexico. Though they resemble love token irons, the Spanish or Mexican groom never gave his bride something to work with as a wedding present; friends might do so, and he might later on.

ENGLAND

3. 19th century English irons had a sad base but hollow handle.

4. Charcoal burner, mid-19th century. Brass heat shield is decorated with British seal showing lion, unicorn, and crown, and the name "Victoria."

FRANCE

5. Late 19th century commercial launderer, used on a cast iron stand with a small ironing board mounted on it. A bar with a spring tension hooked in the hole in front of the handle to add pressure.

ALSACE-LORRAINE

6. Box iron, 17th century, possibly earlier. Small pieces of leather remaining on the original wool cover of the handle indicate it was once leather covered. This style of long pointed iron is typical of the Alsace-Lorraine section, famous in early days for its ironworks, also of Switzerland. It was heated by an iron slug, warmed in the hearth. Usually a couple of extra "heaters" were kept in the fire.

SWITZERLAND

7. Early 19th century, with shield and white cross of the country as decoration; asbestos heat shield was added later.

HOLLAND

8. Thin brass charcoal burner of the type used in Holland since the 18th century. Sad irons and charcoal burners of the heavier cast iron were introduced in the latter half of the 19th century.

GERMANY

9. Box iron, 18th century; brass shell, iron handle; iron slug, partially shown, was heated in the hearth and inserted in iron.

10. *Left,* charcoal iron, ca. 1800; still being made, but with "K" on the handle instead of "G". *Right,* Japanese reproduction, with thin coating of highly polished brass.

AUSTRIA

11. Alcohol burning travel set, ca. 1860-1900; many were sold in the U.S. around 1900. Trivet (upper right, in case) is for the tank and burner, which can be removed by lifting out if iron gets too hot.

RUSSIA

12. Made in Lindengraph, ca. 1790-1800, this iron has two heaters. In later years, the pin was hinged and was part of the cover; handles were also made in decorative styles.

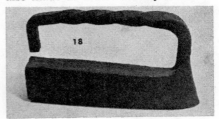

CHINA

13. Charcoal irons were known in China before the time of Christ. This one is very old, though the inscription on the side, referring to one of the four lakes of China and a wall built by Tu Wing Loy, has not yet been satisfactorily translated. Handle is not original, but was carved from horn and installed later.

14. Beautiful replacements of ancient Chinese irons, strictly for tourist trade; they are soldered and would fall apart if heated; some are very old, some are new.

15. Japanese reproduction of a Chinese iron, very large; handle holder is roughly brazed on; handle tilts too high for comfort or use.

CEYLON

16. Charcoal or wood burner, 11" long; weighs 13 lbs.; handmade of heavy brass. This type was used for hundreds of years in parts of Europe and Asia, and is still being used.

KOREA

17. Charcoal iron, brass with teakwood handle. In the Orient, the kimonas were separated by pulling a string so they could be ironed flat with pan-shaped irons. They were then put back together and the wrinkle made in assembling was touched up with the tiny iron, which was heated over the charcoal in the pan.

UNITED STATES

18. Tailor's goose, 18th century, handmade from one piece of iron. Open end of handle allowed it to be hung on a rod over an open fire with the ironing surface next to the hot coals.

19. Polishing iron, made by M. A. N. Cook Company; first patented in 1848.

20. Charcoal iron by Cummings, Taliaferro and Bless, patented 1852; also made under the names "Cummings and Bless," and "Bless and Drake." Bless was known for the manufacture of tools for the housewife, and he was connected with several factories in different states; all built irons. The Bless and Drake plant at Newark, N. J. manufactured irons until about 1900. Bless used as a trademark Hephaestus, the Greek god of ironworkers; and the whisk-

ered, hairy head of this ancient god appeared on the dampers of his charcoal irons.

21. Combination smoothing and

fluting iron, ca. 1870, by Bless and Drake, also made by Cummings and Bless. The height of the smokestack was lowered about this time.

The Sensibles

21x. Sensible, patented Sept. 19, 1871, shows early detachable handle.

22. N. R. Streeter & Co., Groton, N. Y. made their Sensible irons in several types for different uses, from at least 1871 to 1908. At left, 1-lb. iron which a hatter used as a tolliker,

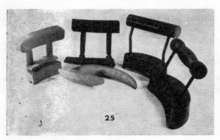

though this size was also used by children and as a salesman's sample. Next, a 7-lb. sad iron dated 1881 on handle; in front of it, a 3-lb. iron, 1871. Right rear, smoothing iron, dated 1908; this has a sheet of asbestos through the center; lower front, a sleeve iron.

23. Sensible sleeve iron, 1888.

24. Sensible smoothing iron, 1908.

25. Hatters' irons, called tollikers or shackles, were used to mellow the hat rims; they came in many shapes and were made by many companies. They took very little heat, and many had wooden handles and handle posts like the two at left, built by M. Mirrer Co., New York, since 1900. Two on right are of a style built for over a hundred years. The lying-down example is all wood, and quite modern.

26. Asbestos Sad Iron, dated 1900. The large one is a smoother; small one, a flounce iron. Removable skirt and handle was lined with asbestos to hold heat from the hand. The Asbestos came in a variety of sets composed of three irons to one handle.

27. "Neplusultra," patented 1902, burned a coke nugget which was sold by its maker, the National Iron Distributing Co., 817 Foss Ave., Drexel Hill, Pa. It was improved and called "Onlyone." Patents were issued in 1914, 1924, and 1932, with slight changes in pattern.

28. Tailor's steam iron, 14-pounds, manufactured by Peth Pressing Process, Buffalo, N. Y., was first patented Sept. 20, 1910. Steam was produced from a boiler, usually in a back room; the finger button released the steam which entered through a hose leading to the larger pipe; the surplus was expelled through the small pipe and carried by the exhaust hose outside the building.

29. The Royal, which burned kerosene; kerosene irons usually have two adjustments.

30. Early Coleman, which burned alcohol, ca. 1900.

31. Hot Point travel iron, by Edison Electric Appliance Co., Inc., patented Feb. 6, 1900 and Aug. 15, 1905, has flat contacts for extension cord. It boiled water, heated two curling irons, and the holder folded into a trivet to hold iron while ironing.

32. Hot Point 20-lb. tailor's iron,

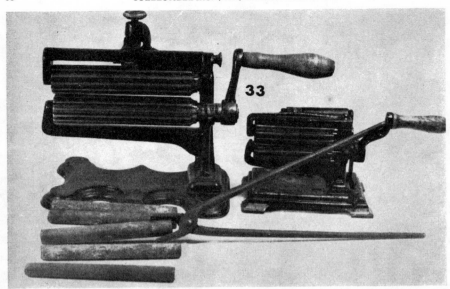

first patented by Edison Electric Appliance Co., June 11, 1910, used 110 volts and had a High, Low, and Off setting on the switch.

33. The large Crown and the smaller Eagle fluting irons were both patented in the 1870s.

35. In earlier days, a Chinese launderer held and blew water from his mouth on the clothes being ironed. Americans frowned on the practice; hence the blow can, about the turn of this century, to be held in the mouth while ironing.

36. Trivet with folding point.

Polishing and Smoothing Irons

by A. H. GLISSMAN

1B

POLISHING and smoothing irons have been known in England and France since the early 19th century. It is believed that such irons originated in France, but as yet no proof for this premise has been found. Among the irons shown in our illustrations are some made in America in the mid-19th century. The pictures are all from the Glissman collection of irons, one of the largest and finest in the United States, which contains many examples of polishing and smoothing irons.

Figure 1 A: The iron on the left was listed in an 1899 English catalog as a "polisher." The two irons on the right bear the legend "M.A.B. Cook, Pat. 1848" (patented in America by Mary Ann B. Cook, Boston, Mass., December 5, 1848). In her patent papers Mrs. Cook stated that the convex shape of the heel and toe of her iron made it ideal for "smoothing and polishing shirt bosoms." To polish the fabric, the iron was tilted forward on its heavy convex toe; the additional weight at this portion supplied the pressure needed for polishing. The flat surface of the iron, which was thinner, held just the right amount of heat required for smoothing the material.
Figure 1 B: (At Top) Illustrations which accompanied Mrs. Cook's patent papers.

1A

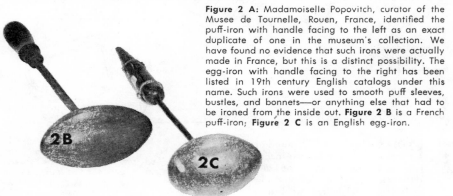

Figure 2 A: Madamoiselle Popovitch, curator of the Musee de Tournelle, Rouen, France, identified the puff-iron with handle facing to the left as an exact duplicate of one in the museum's collection. We have found no evidence that such irons were actually made in France, but this is a distinct possibility. The egg-iron with handle facing to the right has been listed in 19th century English catalogs under this name. Such irons were used to smooth puff sleeves, bustles, and bonnets—or anything else that had to be ironed from the inside out. **Figure 2 B** is a French puff-iron; **Figure 2 C** is an English egg-iron.

Ball-irons (**Figure 3 A**), egg-irons (**Figure 3 B**), and mushroom-irons (**Figures 3 C and 3 D**) were mounted on stands and called "standing irons" in various catalogs. There were many shapes made, each one given a special name to fit the shape. Originally, these irons were heated in hot coals and wiped clean before use; around 1900, steam was used to heat these irons. Electric irons of this type can be purchased today, complete with a stand that clamps onto the ironing board. English catalogs illustrated such irons from the early 1800s to 1925. The early irons weighed from 2 to 8 pounds each; they were used to iron puff sleeves, bustles, and bonnets. The mushroom-iron can be removed from its base and used as a smoother.

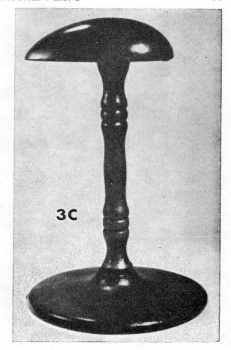

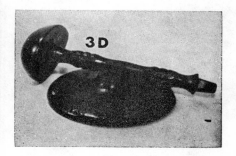

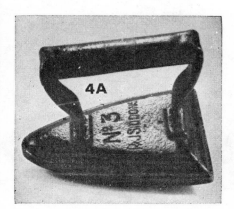

The convex-bottom polishing iron (**Figure 4 A and 4 B**) was made by the J. J. Siddons Company, England, prior to 1928. The present manager of this firm, who has been in their employ since 1928, cannot recall such irons being made there in his time. Unfortunately no records of Siddons' early irons are available, but it is known that they produced irons from 1846 to 1941.

Irons with checkered soles, like those in **Figure 5 A**, were designed to produce the most friction with the least amount of pressure. The most popular shape resembled a hatter's iron. The French style usually has a diamond-patterned corrugated sole like the one shown in the center of **Figure 5 A**. Irons of this design were brought to Mexico by the French during their invasion of that country, in the mid-19th century. When the French were forced to leave Mexico, in 1867, they left behind many of these irons. Consequently, smoothing and polishing irons of this type can be found in Mexico from Guadalajara to Mexico City. Some have the name of the manufacturer on them; others do not; most weigh about 4 pounds.

The iron shown at top center in **Figure 5 A** is marked "M. Mahony, Troy, N.Y." It was patented by Michael Mahony in November 1876 (Pat. No. 184,881). The iron shown at top right in **Figure 5 A** is marked "Geneva" and was made in Geneva, Ill. Another smoothing iron in the author's collection, marked "Genoa," came to him from Genoa, Italy.

The smoothing iron at far left in **Figure 5 A**, and in **Figure 5 B**, has a convex sole and a wrought iron handle; it was made in England in the last half of the 19th century.

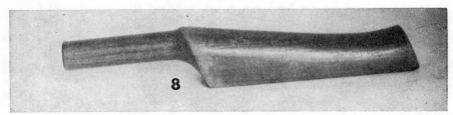

The object shown in **Figure 8** (Above) is a cable splicer's tool used to smooth and pound lead around a splice made in a lead covered cable. A tool of this description has recently been incorrectly identified as a smoothing device for pressing and drying damp clothes.

Illustration from Michael Mahoney's patent for an "Improvement in Sad-Irons"; the smooth projections produced the much desired gloss on linens.

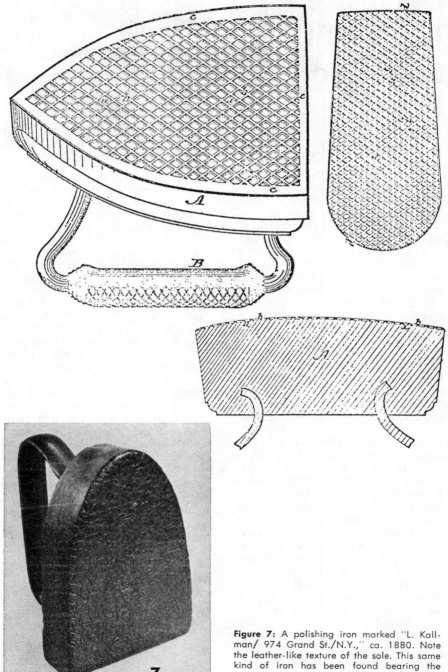

Figure 7: A polishing iron marked "L. Kallman/ 974 Grand St./N.Y.," ca. 1880. Note the leather-like texture of the sole. This same kind of iron has been found bearing the name "M. Mahony"; we believe this iron was manufactured by Mahony for L. Kallman.

Decorated Tools of Iron and Steel

by CARROLL HOPF

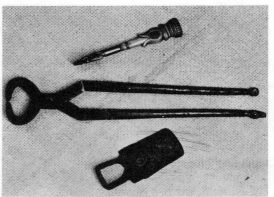

WEBSTER'S DICTIONARY defines the word tool in part as: "Any implement or object used in performing an operation or carrying on work of any kind, esp. where the implement or object is used or worked by hand." One can conclude from this partial definition that there are many different artifacts which may be correctly called tools, from carpenter's planes, chisels, and adzes to finely executed utensils employed by a seamstress for sewing together cloth.

The merit of any tool is quite naturally judged upon its functional value when used in the given task for which it was designed. The functional quality may be analyzed in terms of how well a particular tool withstands the stress and strains encountered when in use, and the quality of the finished task. Here we must assume that a tool, a sharp axe for example, in the hands of a competent person, would perform superior to a dull axe as far as determining the quality of the completed job. Durability and performance, we can say, were and are today the required requisites of a desirable tool. With emphasis placed upon above criteria during the tool making process, whether by hand processes before the advent of the industrial revolution or by mechanical means thereafter, it seems apparent that little emphasis was extended towards superficially decorating tools in general. The seemingly substantial numbers of undecorated tools from both eras which have survived to present day also bear out this statement.

These three tools share one common characteristic in that they are each decorated to some degree. The small wrought iron grubbing hoe (bottom) has a heart motif stamped into the iron. It is only 5¾" long. The farrier's pincers (center), for removing nails from the shoe and hoof of a horse, displays more intricate embellishment consisting of a dog's head and faceted ball at the end of the handles. Farther up each handle it is decorated with fine chisel work. The initials E.M. are stamped into a circular medallion. They supposedly belonged to a blacksmith who worked in Clay, Pennsylvania, in the late 19th century. The pincers are 16" long. The handle of the pastry crimper (top) is carved from bone and displays a tulip motif with cross hatching; the crimping roller is made of iron, while other metal parts are brass. Overall length is 7". Hoe and pincers are from the author's collection; crimper from the collection of The Pennsylvania Farm Museum.

Tools exhibiting some form of decoration — carving, molded or cast, wrought, punched, stamped, engraved, or by other means — may be thought of as reflecting traditional as well as contemporary cultural values of their respective periods. As such they be-

Included in an assortment of tools necessary to carry on the trade of coppersmithing would have been several stakes of different shape and size over which sheet copper was hammered into shape. Today stakes are difficult to locate on the antique tool market. As numerous as they must have been, one can only surmise that many were sold for scrap iron as coppersmiths went out of business. The stamped decorative pattern and date of 1833 makes this example particularly interesting. Overall height is 15½". Length is 25". Collection of The Pennsylvania Farm Museum.

Of German origin, the flax hetchel is decorated with geometric motifs incised in the wood with a compass. Traces of blue and orange remain in the motifs. The hetchel is an important tool in preparing flax fibers for spinning. Fibers were first pulled through the iron teeth set farthest apart. This not only straightened out the fibers but left coarse strands caught in the teeth. The finest flax thread was spun from fiber still remaining in the hand after being pulled through the set of fine teeth. Coarse fiber was spun into heavy tow material used for sacking.

The hetchel is 30½" in length and probably dates from the first half of the 19th century. Author's collection.

come valued documents contributing to a better understanding of social and material culture history.

Assembling a collection of decorated tools can be a prolonged experience both interesting and educational. The accompanying photographs illustrate an assortment of embellished tools from agricultural artifacts to sewing items. Comparable examples are yet to be found on the general antiques market. It probably will take some searching to find unusual examples, but after all, isn't that half the enjoyment of antiques collecting.

The broad axe was indispensable for hewing and dressing logs after they had been cut down. It was used with two hands and generally had a handle less than 24" long. Broad axes exist in various form; some examples, as this one (top) have the blade sharpened only on a single side of the axe, hence the term "chisel-edged" blade. Others are sharpened on both sides and are "knife edged." Overall size and shape varies extensively. Broad axes are sometimes found with decorative stamping as this example illustrates. The date 1835 can be seen immediately above the two horizontal grooves. The splitting wedge (bottom) exhibits a particularly unusual stamped design. The patterns on both tools were applied by the use of a hardened metal die with the pattern cut in relief. Overall length of the broad axe is 11"; the wedge is 9½" long. Collection of The Pennsylvania Farm Museum.

Hatchets

by HENRY J. KAUFFMAN

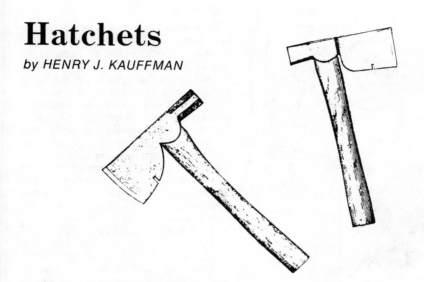

TODAY'S COLLECTORS OF tools are particularly interested in those used for shaping wood; there were many of them, used over a long span of years, and a great number have survived in a remarkable state of preservation. The axe seems to be considered of most importance; it is probably the oldest of tools, and it offers a multitude of variations. One would expect the hatchet to claim like interest and importance because of its similarity in shape and function. But not so!

Tool historians and collectors alike have relegated the hatchet to undeserved obscurity. W. L. Goodman in *The History of Woodworking Tools* did not even include the word in the index to his book. While the hatchet probably reached a higher status in America than in Europe, it was far from unknown there. This writer once discovered a marvelous example on the Left Bank in Paris.

The earliest reference found to the hatchet is in *Mechanicks Exercises* by Moxon, published in 1703. One entry suggests the hatchet was a light tool, basiled (beveled) on one side only, and used with one hand. Continuing evidence through the years indicates that the hatchet was a hewing tool and, at least in earliest times, did not have a facility for pulling nails. Because the inner surfaces of small boards on furniture of the 17th and 18th centuries were

finished by hewing, a small tool for such a purpose would have had wide use.

There was doubtless some overlapping in the use of a hatchet and a hand axe. Yet an illustration in *Mechanicks Exercises* shows a tool which clearly resembles a lathing hatchet of modern times. It is called a "Mason's Tool" and described as: "A lathing hammer . . . with which the laths are nailed on with its head, and with its edge they cut them to length, and likewise cut off any part of a quarter *(sic)* or joyst, that stick further out than the rest."

Thus it is evident that at the beginning of the 18th century the tool was used for both nailing and splitting. The lathing hatchet pictured with the above description was narrow so that it could be used to drive nails in the corner made by the ceiling and the side wall. Its function as a hewing tool can be discerned since one side of the tool is flat, the bulge of the handle being entirely on the opposite side.

An example of a similar tool, but with a canted handle, is in this author's collection. Mercer does not mention this type in describing the hatchet in his *Ancient Carpenter's Tools*. Possibly due to the often small nature of its work, it did not require such a handle. While Mercer's description confirms that there were hewing hatchets, most of the nine which he illustrates appear to be small axes.

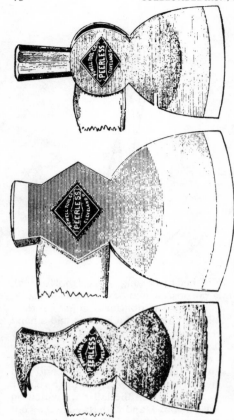

Illustrations from the tool catalog of T. B. Rayl & Co. of Detroit, Mich., probably dating late 19th century. These focus attention on different styles of hatchets. Most of the claw type were manufactured in the late 19th century and early 20th century.

The hewing hatchet in this author's collection was made by welding two slabs of iron together and edging the bit with a piece of steel. This procedure was followed because iron was cheap and easily welded, both properties lacking in steel. After the steel edge was ground away from many sharpenings, a new piece was "laid" on the edge, providing an adequate tool for many more years of use.

Also in regard to the hatchet used as a hewing tool, *The Cyclopedia: or Universal Dictionary of Arts and Sciences,* by E. Chambers, published in London in 1751, reads: "HATCHET: a joiner's instrument wherewith to hew wood.

The hatchet is a smaller, lighter sort of ax, with a basil edge on its left side; having a short handle, as being to be used with one hand."

In 1753, a *Supplement* of the same publication gives other uses for the tool. It is the only reference found which suggests its use as a weapon. "HATCHET (cycl) a small ax, used by pioneers, who go before to prepare the ways for an army, by cutting down hedges, bushes, styles, or gates. The grenadiers carry some times a hatchet by their side; and French dragoons, who have but one pistol, have a hatchet hanging at their saddle-bows, on the right side."

The hatchet was always a one-handed tool, but its modern function as a household and carpenter utility tool was unknown in the 18th century. Mercer says of it: "While the larger broad axe held its own through the 19th century, this little, basiled, one-handed tool, with or without a pounding poll, owing to the increased abundance of ready-prepared lumber dressed in the planing mills, fell out of use after 1830, while two other forms of the hatchet, used for rough-surfacing, splitting, chopping, and nailing, became more and more the continual companions of the carpenter."

A 19th century form of the hatchet, not recognized by Mercer but illustrated in the business catalog of T. B. Rayl & Co. of Detroit, is the half hatchet. It had less spread in the bit than the full shingling hatchet but more than the narrow lathing hatchet. Mercer evidently never made this distinction since he classes the half hatchet with the lathing type.

Although half hatchets are not a common form, some at least were made in the 1860s and 1870s by Beatty who worked in Chester, Pennsylvania, and had a salesroom in Philadelphia. As a trademark he used his name, "Beatty," and an impressed representation of a cow. Often the cow was so lightly impressed that it is difficult to find.

The full shingling hatchet is the tool most people envision when the word "hatchet" is mentioned today. Among the examples pictured here is one with an intaglio impression of two undecipherable letters. It has a contracted head for driving nails, and a slit in the bit

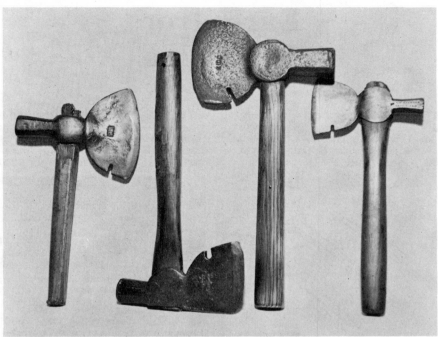

Four hatchets of interest to the tool collector. The first on the left is a so-called shingling hatchet with an intaglio stamped mark which cannot be deciphered. The second is a half-hatchet with the name "Beatty" and the outline of a cow impressed in the metal. The third is marked "C. Kidd" who worked in Baltimore in the second quarter of the 19th century. The last one is marked "C. W. Bradley" whose location is not known; this latter tool was purchased in Connecticut.

to pull nails. It is made of iron and on its edge was "laid" a piece of steel for cutting purposes.

The *Index of Patents*, issued from the U. S. Patent Office from 1790 to 1873, lists only six patents granted for hatchets while more than one hundred were issued for axes. Although there seems no clear cut difference between a hatchet and a small hand axe, a hatchet, generally speaking is a small tool, designed for use with one hand, with a contracted stud or poll for driving nails and a facility for pulling nails. Considerable research remains to be done before the hatchet story is completely told.

Early Iron Hardware

by RAYMOND F. YATES

HARDWARE is a guide to dating old furniture, and the collector should learn to recognize the nails, screws, hinges, drawer pulls, and the like used on truly old pieces.

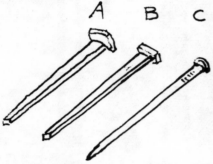

A, old crude hand-forged square nail, 1700-1800; B, machine-cut nail, 1810-1890; C, modern wire nail.

NAILS: The earliest nails used in both house and furniture construction were hand-forged, and were usually made by "nailers" who worked at home. These square nails were forged, one by one, from high purity "Russian iron," which did not rust. About 1830, nails were made by machine; these, too, were square. Since square nails were used as late as the 1880s, when the modern round nail was introduced, the sight of a square nail-head on a piece of furniture is not convincing proof that the piece is old.

Really old square nails are much cruder than the machine product. The blanks had to be heated, then shaped and headed. Hand-forged nails show hammer and anvil marks; the surfaces are rough; the heads are anything but perfectly square or oblong. They rusted very little, while machine-made nails rusted badly. If the collector carefully examines old hand-forged nails, he will quickly learn to recognize them. Such nails were used only on primitive pieces, mostly of pine. Early cabinetmakers who worked for the carriage trade did not use nails.

SCREWS: The removal of a screw and careful inspection of it by the collector—a small magnifying glass is helpful—will often help him date a piece of furniture. The crude hand-made wood screws used before 1830

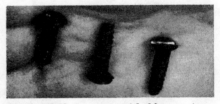

Old hand-filed screws with blunt points; some were used to 1830s.

are easily identified. The spiral threads are hand-cut with a three-cornered file; the slots on the screw heads are shallow and often badly off center; the ends are blunt instead of sharply pointed. To start the screw into the wood, a hole was made by a gimlet. The blunt-ended wood screw was inserted into it and driven home with a screw driver. Modern sharp-pointed, perfectly uniform, machine-made "gimlet screws" began to be manufactured during the 1840s by the American Screw Company. While the presence of hand-filed screws usually means a piece of furniture is a real antique, furniture fakers have been known to switch screws in an effort to fool experts.

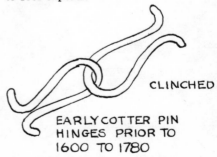

CLINCHED

EARLY COTTER PIN HINGES PRIOR TO 1600 TO 1780

HINGES: Hinges vary a great deal. The earliest forms appeared in New England on blanket chest lids. Some were no more than pieces of cowhide nailed in place. Such leather hinges are difficult to date; farmers have used them for years. Cotter pin hinges, also used on pine blanket chest lids, were made with iron wire, and can be as easily reproduced with a piece of modern iron wire as leather hinges can be replaced with an old bit of harness. Blanket chests with original cotter pin hinges are rare.

Butterfly and rattail hinges, hand-wrought by blacksmiths, were used during the eighteenth and early nineteenth centuries. Rattail hinges were usually employed on blanket chest lids. Similar hinges were manufactured from the 1840s through the 1860s, the machine-made hinges being smooth with no hammer marks. However, one must remember that modern

The H and HL hinges were made in brass as well as iron. From 1760 to 1800, brass hardware was seldom used on anything but formal carriage-trade furniture. It was imported from England until the Revolution. After that, local craftsmen began to copy it for use on mahogany pieces in the Chippendale, Hepplewhite and Adams styles which they were creating from English design books.

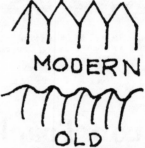

Sharp accurate screw threads on modern machine-cut bolt; crude threads made by hand with a file, before 1830.

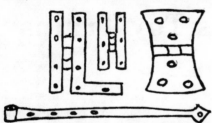

Old hand-forged hinges: left to right, HL, H, butterfly; below, rattail.

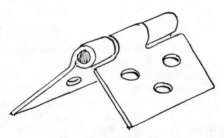

HAND-FORGED HINGES 1725-1800

hinges alone do not date a piece; worn-out hinges could have been replaced by original owners. Instances are known where an early owner had himself removed fine brass hardware to install a set of later Sandwich glass knobs.

HAND MADE DRAW PULL POST – BRASS 1750-1820

DRAWER PULLS: Some of the earliest drawer pulls were lathe-turned wooden knobs. These cannot be classed as hardware unless they were attached with wood screws, which have their own story to tell as to date. Many wooden knobs or pulls were held to the drawer front with a dowel pin glued in place; these are usually early ones, although this is not a positive clue to dating. All screws and bolts used to hold early metal drawer pulls to drawer fronts were hand-cut. The screws with their crude threads are especially easy to recognize.

"Cannon Ball Train," the largest iron toy train made by Ives, Blakeslee and Williams Company, in 1893.

"Michigan Central R.R.," a scarce nickle-plated iron toy train believed to have been made by either the Kenton Hardware Company, Kenton, Ohio, or the Grey Iron Company, Reading, Pennsylvania (?), ca. 1910.

Iron Trackless Toy Trains

by EMMA STILES

WIDELY SOUGHT BY COLLECTORS today are the trackless iron toy trains which first appeared in America in the late 1870s. These trackless trains were string-pulled, hand-pushed, or mechanical, the mechanical locomotives housing a strong clockwork movement.

Made of cast, as well as malleable iron—the malleable being earlier and most rare — locomotives and molded cars were cast in lengthwise sections. Molten metal was poured into sand molds, which were removed when the metal had cooled and solidified. Joining the seams, adding the axle and wheels completed the car.

The first iron trains were rather stiff in style, more or less copied from earlier tin types; many were virtually scale models. From 1880 to 1890, they grew more refined and more elaborate. They continued to flourish up to about 1930. By then, the models were generally smaller and less detailed.

Locomotives were sold individually, as were extra large freight and passenger cars, measuring more than 17 inches long, and wholesaled in 1893

at $13.50 per dozen. Locomotives and tenders were sold as a unit; but most often the complete train consisted of locomotive, tender, and one, two, or three cars. The tender, of course, always came with a complete train, but seldom was a little tag-behind caboose included. Locomotives pulling one freight car and one passenger car were called "combination trains."

Most freight cars were gondola-like; many carried a brakeman standing in each open car. Large closed freight cars were manufactured with movable side doors; these are considered rare today. Vestibule, observation, and passenger cars were also made.

The Wilkins Toy Company of Keene, N. H., in their 1911 toy catalog advertised "coal freight trains"— locomotive, tender, and one, two, or three coal cars. These were enameled, embossed, and decorated. "P.R.R." in high raised gold letters covered the entire sides of each coal car. A movement of lever to either side of the coal car opened swinging doors in the bottom, allowing the load to dump;

returning lever to normal position closed the doors.

The terms of the Wilkins Toy Co. stated "All shipments F.O.B." They made no allowance for breakage, nor guaranteed delivery. Their goods were packed in regular crates or cases as specified and if ordered differently or in less quantity, a higher price would be charged for special handling. Of the 32 trains in their 1911 catalog, only two included a caboose.

Ehrich Brothers, Eighth Avenue, New York, N. Y., advertised in their 1882 winter mail order catalog a solid iron toy train—locomotive, tender, and two freight cars, painted red and black, packed in a sliding-cover wooden box at 95 cents, but stated shipment would be made by express.

The Ives, Blakeslee and Williams Company, 294 Broadway, New York City, whose factory was in Bridgeport, Conn., displayed a most attractive line of iron toy trains in their 1893 toy catalog. Locomotives had been included in the Ives toy production since the 1870s. The Ives company was the great pioneer in the iron toy field and where it led, others followed. Competitive imitations, lacking the finer detail and castings of the Ives models, appeared a year or two after Ives introduced some new toy.

In their 1893 catalog, Ives introduced an entirely new and original steel passenger train with observation car. It was 58 inches long; the locomotive and tender were iron and japanned black; the passenger coaches were of steel and painted in brilliant colors.

In the same catalog, Ives advertised their new model, the "Cannon Ball Train," the largest iron train made, with locomotive, tender, closed freight car and vestibule car. The number "189" was embossed in an oblong panel on both sides of the tender; "Union/*/Line/*" was embossed on the right front side of the freight car, and "Capacity 50,000 pounds" on the back side. The decoration was reversed on the opposite side. Printed in raised letters on the passenger car were the words, "Limited Vestibule Express." Despite its lettering, the passenger car was of the non-vestibule design. The locomotive was an extremely accurate representation of the real thing. The details on it extended to tiny bolt heads, cast on the side rods. When coupled together as a unit, this large cast iron trackless pull-train measured almost five feet long. It wholesaled at $54 per dozen. Three trains, packed for shipping in a wooden crate, 13 x 20 x 32 inches, weighed 104 pounds.

Another special train advertised by Ives that year was the celebrated White Train or Ghost Train, 41 inches long—

The manufacturer (s) of these iron toy trains could not be identified, but they are typical of the types made in the late 19th century and can be found in various sizes.

"Baltimore & Ohio" iron toy train attributed to the Wilkins Toy Company, ca. 1900.

locomotive, tender, and two white vestibule cars. It wholesaled at $21 per dozen; one dozen, packed in a crate, weighed 198 pounds.

The least expensive four-unit passenger train in the Ives 1893 catalog was called "The Hero." It was 14 inches long and sold at $4 per dozen. The least expensive four-unit freight sold at $2 a dozen; it, too, was 14 inches long. Of the 13 complete trains displayed in their 1893 catalog, not one showed a caboose.

The Carpenter Line of Toys catalog, a 5x7 inch, 22-page, paper-cover pamphlet, reprinted by F. A. O. Schwarz of New York for the Antique Toy Collectors Club, carried a good selection of iron trains. Though the date of the original catalog is not given, patent dates appear under each picture. One freight train listed five patents and re-issue dates between May 4, 1880, and May 13, 1884. The name Williard & McKee, 21 Park Place, New York City, presumably the distributors, appeared on the front cover of the catalog.

There is some mystery in connection with the Carpenter toys, for no one yet has been able to pin down a manufacturer's name or address for them. Apparently Carpenter farmed out his work. Patent No. 227216 for a toy train was issued to Francis W. Carpenter at Rye, N. Y., on May 4, 1880, and Patent No. 298446, for a toy railroad, to Francis W. Carpenter at Harrison, N. Y., on May 13, 1884.

Of the five complete trains displayed in the Carpenter catalog, not one came with a caboose.

The Hubley Manufacturing Company, Lancaster, Pa., in their 1906 catalog, advertised train "No. 60-½"— locomotive, tender, and two passenger cars, polished copper oxidized." It weighed over 12 pounds and was 43 inches long. There were 14 complete trains shown in the Hubley catalog; of these only three pulled a caboose.

The most desirable of the early iron locomotives, aside from the very large pieces, are 2-2-0 models, lettered "Big Six" or bearing the patent dates May 4, 1880, May 25, 1880, June 8, 1880, Aug. 16, 1881, or Aug. 19, 1884. Models bearing these patent dates were **manufactured until about 1900 by J. & E. Stevens Co., Cromwell, Conn.,** as well as by others.

Of the 1915 period, the largest size cars, 15 inches or more in length, any of the model street cars, and the iron electric-type locomotive are the most desirable.

The little locomotives with the tender cast integral and only one pair of movable wheels were staple designs in virtually every line for more than 40 years and are quite common. To entice children to play with the trains, parents called, "Johnnie, come pull the puffers." The subsequent puffing noise that was heard issued not from the train but from its proud owner's pursed lips.

Cast Iron Fire-Fighting Toys

by MARCIA RAY

THE ARCHIE Stiles family collects just about everything—antique baby buggies, horse prints, old post cards, horse-drawn sleighs and carriages, beer steins, powder flasks, old banks, and shaving mugs. They even have a complete antique barber shop. On their place in Meyersville, New Jersey, they keep an antiques shop, a museum, and a pet farm, too, with tame deer to pull carriages, a trained rooster, and ponies.

Among their favorite collectibles are their iron toys, and they are especially proud of their fire-fighting equipment.

Cast iron fire-fighting toys, when they came on the scene in the 1870s, were comparatively plain. Through the 1880s, they became more elaborate and extraordinarily realistic. Many fire-fighting toys were scale size; some measured almost 3 feet long. Hitches were made with one, two, and three horses; some horses could be unhitched from their shafts. Various

means were taken to provide a galloping motion for the horses. Some horses were made whose four legs moved independently of each other when the toy was pulled along. Fine quality engines carried miniature removable axes, water buckets, and an extra supply of ladders.

Toys Illustrated

The five toys pictured —Fire Chief Wagon, Hose Reel, Steam Pumper, Fire Patrol Wagon, Hook and Ladder — were featured in the 1893 catalog of Ives, Blakeslee & Williams Co., 294 Broadway, New York, whose factory was at Bridgeport, Connecticut.

Featured also was the Mechanical Fire Engine House, an exciting handsome toy with a powerful clock movement. The entire front of the house was made of cast iron, as were the windows and cornice. The roof, floor,

Toys from Ives, Blakeslee & Williams Co., advertised in their 1893 catalog.

and sides were of wood. It measured 8½x12x15½ inches, and wholesaled at $5. The clock motor was set above the doors on the inside front of the house. The directions were to "wind as you would a clock; pull out the stop wire on outer side of the house; after the bell has struck one-two, one-two, three, the doors fly open and the engine dashes for the fire."

The sides of the Chief's Wagon, drawn by galloping horses, were covered with bold embossed letters, reading CHIEF. The Hose Reel carriage had four wheels; hose reel carts were made with two. The hitches consisted of one, two, or three running horses; realistic hose was wrapped round and round the free turning reel.

The Steam Pumper, a mechanical fire engine with racing horses, 5x7x19 inches, was made with a clock motor. When wound, the two small wheels in front of the boiler and the pump work rapidly, imitating an engine at work. These sold in 1893 at $36 per dozen, wholesale.

The Fire Patrol Wagon — with a driver on the front, and 6 cast iron firemen in uniform sitting on the side benches, ready to leap out at the first sign of smoke — had an embossed FIRE PATROL, covering both side panels. The Hook and Ladder, with running horses pulling the Hook and Ladder truck, carried driver, tillerman, and ladders.

The company also advertised in this same catalog a "great new addition to the toy fire brigade — two iron extension ladders, 18 inches long, 4 cast iron firemen in bright uniforms, and one length of rubber hose with nozzle, packed in a neat box." It wholesaled at $5 per dozen.

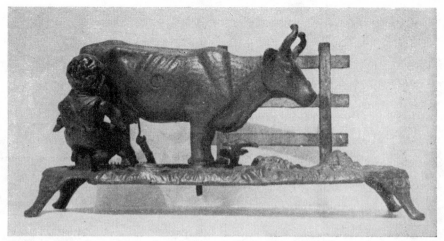

Kicking Cow: Press flower-shaped lever and cow flips tail, kicks stool, farmer with bucket lands on back in grass. Product of Stevens Foundry, Cromwell, Conn. (1888).

Mechanical Iron Banks

by WILLIAM H. MONTGOMERY

ANTIQUE mechanical banks have long been collectors' items. Today they are being so assiduously sought by bankers and financial institutions as well as established collectors that the casual collector may find them so scarce as to seem almost un-obtainable. Prices, too, have spiralled to such fantastic heights as to discourage the newcomer from the thought of acquiring a sizable collection. However, at least *one* antique bank, either a good mechanical or a good still, is within range of every

Bad Accident: Lever operates mechanism to send boy leaping from behind bush to frighten mule and upset cart with watermelon-eating farmer. As wagon falls, boy retreats, coin under wagon seat falls in body of wagon.

collector's purse and province and belongs in every over-all collection of Americana.

These banks, which reached their height of popularity in the 1870s and 1880s, though some were made earlier, and others as late as 1915, were primarily toys rather than objects for the encouragement of thrift. Nearly all of them can be operated by pressing the lever or knob without the necessity of depositing a coin. Because most of the banks were of iron, shatterable if dropped, it is no wonder that a majority of those manufactured have been broken. The chipped and worn paint on many remaining attest to hard use through the years.

A large part of the charm of these old banks stems from the fact that they are pure Americana. Even the substance of which they were manufactured, iron, was not plentiful enough in other countries to be used in children's toys. However, iron foundries in the United States found toys profitable, and employed really good artists to design the banks and plan the concealed mechanisms which made the parts move. The designers used many familiar figures in their choice of subject. Banks appeared featuring such typically American sports as baseball, football and bowling, or such popular types of entertainment as magicians, Punch & Judy Shows, performing animals, and acrobats. They ranged from a Preacher in the Pulpit bank to popular comic strip characters, like Uncle Remus, the Katzenjammer Kids and the "Shoot the Chutes" bank with Buster Brown and Tige.

Many of them portray a raucous humor, with people getting into accidents, often with animals as the cause of the trouble. Butting goats, kicking cows, bucking mules and buffalo provided slapstick comedy. The animals are generally well-proportioned and pleasing to the eye, and the people, lovable and good-humored, never seemed to mind much when they are knocked over to stand on their heads or lie flat on their backs. Often the exaggerated facial expressions are very funny. The old bank designers, in their zeal to make the children laugh, created masterpieces of humor which have fascinated generations of adults as well.

Always Did 'Spise A Mule: Grinning jockey holds coin in mouth, press of lever pitches him forward over mule's head, depositing penny in base of bank. Upside down grin seems to become expression of pain (1879)

The prices of old mechanical banks vary a great deal depending on their rarity. While the "Kicking Cow" and "Always Did 'Spise a Mule" are perhaps equally attractive and similar in action, the "Kicking Cow" is much more rare. John D. Meyer's book, copyright in 1952, prices this " 'Spise a Mule" bank at $22, and the Kicking Cow bank at $200!

The Dentist bank, pictured, was originally sold by the manufacturer for $8 a dozen. The selling price listed by Ina Hayward Bellows in her *Old Mechnical Banks*, published in 1940, was between $20 and $30 each. In 1952, John D. Meyer in his *Handbook of Old Mechanical Penny Banks*, set the current price at $165. In April, 1955, a catalogue published by David Hollander, New York, offering for sale a number of mechanical and still banks from the Chrysler Collection, listed the same bank, in fine condition, with original paint at $350. It is a safe guess that today's spiralling prices will seem low to a future generation.

In the parlance of the trade, "O.P." means "Original Paint" and "O.F.," "Original Finish." A bank is said to be in "mint" condition if it still has all

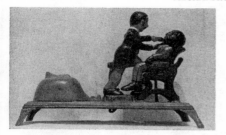

Dentist: A penny slipped into dentist's pocket as he stands poised for action, and a press of lever, sends him backward, tooth in forceps, while coin flips into gas bag. Simultaneously patient and chair tip backward.

or virtually all of its original paint. Of course, a bank which is "mint" is worth more than the same bank in a badly faded condition, or with much of the paint gone or badly chipped. However, most collectors want nothing whatever to do with a bank that has been repainted. Hence an old bank, even with little or none of its original paint left is more valuable than if repainted. Many repaint jobs are crude in both conception and execution, but even the most expert restorer, bent on deception, would find it as hard to repaint a bank in the original colors to fool a connoisseur of banks as to counterfeit money to deceive a Treasury man.

Non-experts who contemplate buying a mechanical bank would do well to seek the advice of experienced bank collectors in order to avoid the pitfalls of buying a repainted job, worth, perhaps, only a fraction of the price asked, or of paying a too high a price for one of the less rare banks.

It is to be remembered that some of the most attractive mechanical banks are the cheapest because they were immensely popular and sold in the largest numbers. Rarer banks may be those which were more fragile, or ones with less popular appeal which were manufactured in small

quantities. Some of the rarest of all are ones which a manufacturer put on the market only to find he could not sell them advantageously and withdrew the model after a comparatively small number had been made.

Magician: Theatrical figure, on platform labelled Magician Bank, at operation of lever, lowers hat over coin placed on table. When hat is raised, coin has disappeared through magician's legs to base of platform. (1882)

Mammy & Child: Originally advertised as Baby Mine: Baby kicks as Mammy feeds coin placed on spoon into outsized mouth of child. Will swallow up to 25¢ piece. Second slot in Mammy's apron is unusual feature. (1884)

Collectible Still Banks

by WILLIAM H. MONTGOMERY

(Photos by Doris Montgomery)

PENNY banks of pottery, glass and tin appeared early on the American scene. Poor Richard's adage "A penny saved is a penny earned" was taken quite literally, and as soon as the first copper pennies were minted in 1793, enterprising glassmakers and potters had banks ready to hold them.

Sometime after 1860, cast iron banks appeared. Though a few still banks in iron antedate the mechanical banks, it was not until the late 19th and early 20th centuries that the still bank achieved mass popularity.

That many of these still banks are scarcely fifty years old seems not to detract from their interest to today's collectors, but rather to add by this very "lateness" a certain nostalgic charm. Makers of still banks, as of the mechanicals, turned to the fads and fancies of the day for inspiration, and it was not so long ago that Black Beauty was on every bookshelf, the Flatiron Building was the place to see in New York, Mutt and Jeff were in the Sunday funnies, and performing animals made Circus Day memorable. Iron still banks, cast in such pleasant molds appeal both to those who "remember when" and to those whose "Grandma had one!"

Earlier still banks were usually of two pieces of metal, bolted or screwed together, to be opened by removing bolts or screws. Around 1895, safe and building banks appeared, which were opened by working a combination on the door. This type was popular as late as the 1920s.

Many attractive forms are being currently issued by banks and thrift institutions which reflect today's interests. One such features an airplane, others Daniel Boone, David Crockett, Captain Kidd and such.

The modest collector, with a fascination for the America of the past seventy-five years and an eye to a collection that is due to increase in

value, may well find it profitable to follow the familiar slogan "America Banks on Banks".

From the funnies, *Mutt and Jeff, Mama Katzenjammer* and her incorrigible boys were popular subjects. Best known of the many famous building banks is *New York's Flatiron Building. Rough Rider Teddy Roosevelt,* about to charge San Juan Hill, is earlier and more difficult to find than a Trick pony bank, for instance, but still attainable. *Black Beauty,* is now one of the rare still banks. So is the *Liberty Bell,* patented 1875, and sold at the Philadelphia Centennial. Printed history, pasted on wood base, describes it as "Bailey's Centennial Money Bank."

Ornamental Iron Works

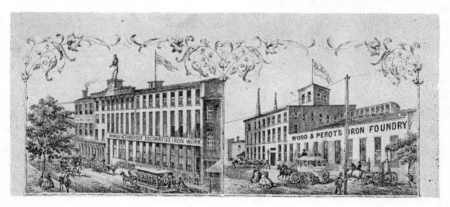

THE rarity of any print has many aspects. Take the above lithograph by Ketterlinus of Philadelphia. It measures only 7 x 4¼ inches, but is packed—literally packed—with important historic information. And this is the story it tells: The Wood & Perot Iron Foundry of Philadelphia sold so much ornamental ironwork to New Orleans customers they erected a branch foundry in the Louisiana Metropolis. That New Orleans foundry is pictured at the right of the print; the Philadelphia works on the left. At both foundries the following items were manufactured: Iron railings for cemetery enclosures, public Squares, Churches, and Private Residences. Iron Verandahs, Balconies, Bank Counters, Stairs (in every variety), Mausoleums, or Tombs, Chairs, Settees, Tables, Tree Boxes, Hitching Posts, Lamp Posts, Brackets, Statuary and all other Iron Work of Decorative Character. Drawings were furnished to those who wish to make selections.

The view of the New Orleans factory of Wood, Miltenberger & Co., shows the Cathedral spires in the background and a steam fire-engine, dray and omnibus on the street. The Philadelphia Foundry, with its gigantic iron statue, is pictured on its Ridge Avenue facade, with the double track horse-car line. The next time you admire the iron lace of the Vieu Carre, chances are you'll be admiring ironwork made at both Philadelphia and New Orleans by the same company. The New Orleans foundry was set up over a century ago.

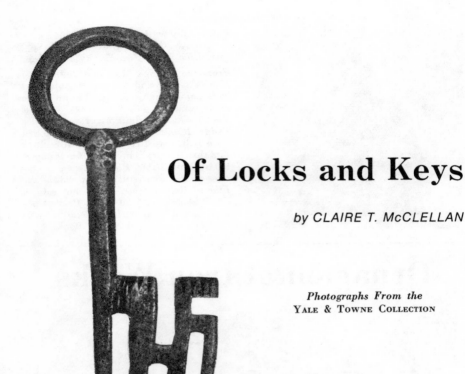

Of Locks and Keys

by CLAIRE T. McCLELLAN

Photographs From the
YALE & TOWNE COLLECTION

IN MOST developing civilizations there comes a time when a stone rolled before a cave, a thong tied to a doorpost, or the recitation of an incantation no longer serves as adequate protection for man's person or accumulating possessions. At this point bars and bolts usually appear. There remains the problem of securing these so that no one but the owner may have access to the property, and locks and keys supply the answer. Evidence that man has met this need in similar ways has been found in the remains of early cultures in many parts of the world—though the results have differed greatly in appearance.

Lock historians agree that the first key-operated locks were probably those in use in the Nile Valley, 4,000 years ago. Such a device was pictured in temple frescoes at Karnak. The earliest actual example of this "Egyptian type" of lock and key was unearthed at the site of the palace of Sargon, near the Biblical city of Nineveh, during the excavations in Asia Minor in the mid-19th century. Its finder, the Italian archeologist-

artist Joseph Bonomi, the younger, described the great wooden lock, and said that its key was "as much as a man can conveniently carry." Such keys somewhat resemble oversize wooden toothbrushes, the "bristles" being pegs to lift falling tumblers in the lock. Locks of this type have been used until very recent times in Mediterranean countries and are still to be found in rural areas.

The huge bronze keys slung over the shoulders of Homeric Greeks were little more than hooks to lift the door bolts, but the Greeks made a significant contribution to lock development by placing these bolts inside the door and using a keyhole.

Among the Romans, lock development progressed rapidly. Skilled metal workers, familiar with all the locking mechanisms then extant, they perfected several designs and made much use of movable locks with keys small enough to be worn as finger-rings. Keys were often given Roman brides to signify their rights to household possessions, a custom surviving for centuries in Europe.

The iron locks of Rome went with

the Legions wherever they carried the Roman standard, but little remains of them except their bronze hasps, bolts and keys, which have not succumbed to rust. Keys in particular have been found in numbers, partly because the cult of the Persian god Mithras was a popular one among the Legionnaires (100-400 A.D.) and one of its rites was the burial of a key with the dead. When Vesuvius covered Pompeii in ashes in 64 A.D., a locksmith's shop was preserved for future study. In it were found doorlocks, padlocks, ornamented keys, and what appears to be a "skeleton" key.

The latter was probably for the smith's use on *warded* locks, introduced into Roman culture by the Etruscans. These are locks in which obstructions or "wards" are placed within the lock, and the key bit has to be cut to pass them in order for

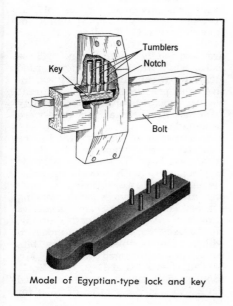

Model of Egyptian-type lock and key

the bolt to be retracted. This type of mechanism became the prototype of European locks for many centuries. All of us are familiar with warded locks, since they are still in use where security is not too essential.

Medieval metalwork is famous for its great beauty, and locksmiths' guilds were exacting. An apprentice was forced to spend ten years before submitting the "masterpiece" that, accepted, would qualify him as a

journeyman. Wealthy merchants, bankers, and nobles spent great sums on locks and keys. It is said that Henry II of France had a series of locks made for the apartments of his mistress, each with its own key, while he alone held the "master key" to unlock them all! The lacy heraldic designs of locking devices became more and more elaborate; and a key— sometimes of precious metal — was thought a suitable gift for a monarch to bestow on a favored subject.

Dr. Williamson, in *The Amateur Collector,* published in 1924, tells of a Countess in the reign of the Stuarts, Lady Anne Clifford, who kept a local smith constantly employed fashioning locks for her to give friends, favorite tenants, and local churches. Some of these great rectangular locks with their keys bearing the countess' initials and date were still in use at the time of the book's publication.

Medieval and Renaissance locks were usually ponderous. Great iron keys unlocked dungeons; brass ones with vintage motifs were favored for wine cellars. The chatelaine of manor

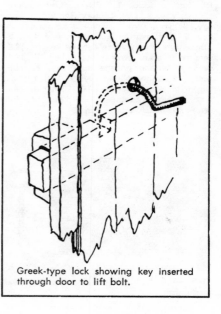

Greek-type lock showing key inserted through door to lift bolt.

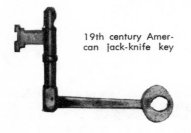

19th century American jack-knife key

or castle carried a ring of keys at her belt for linen press, storeroom, chest, and cabinet—and to give visible evidence of her station in life. Locks were generally too costly for the poor, who had little to protect in any case.

While appearing formidable, European warded locks were fairly easy for the skilled "picker" to open. To foil these, locksmiths came up with dummy and hidden keyholes and with trick devices that might alarm the household with bell or explosion, or even trap, brand, or shoot the would-be thief tampering with the lock. In spite of these precautions and the severe punishment meted out to thieves, lockpicking continued.

Occasionally European lockmakers had added a lever tumbler to the warded locks, but it was not until the latter part of the 18th and early 19th centuries that several English locksmiths invented devices of far greater security. The patents of Robert Barron (1778), Joseph Bramah (1784), and Jeremiah Chubb (1818) are especially noteworthy. These locks, while much safer than warded locks, were complicated, very expensive, and practical only where great wealth was involved or security essential. All locks at this time were handmade.

At the time of the Crystal Palace Exposition in London in 1851, locksmiths on both sides of the Atlantic had come up with models of great ingenuity, and were trying to pick one another's devices with varying degrees of success. Dr. Andrews (Solomon Andrews, Perth Amboy, New Jersey, ca. 1836) had a model in which both tumblers and key bits could be rearranged at will. Mr. Newell (Newell and Day, New York, 1850) made a successful key-operated bank lock after his offer of $500 for

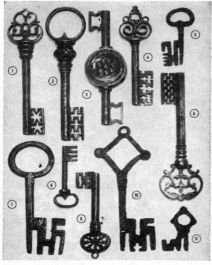

Gothic, Renaissance, and Baroque keys, all for warded locks. **1.** 17th century German cabinet key. **2.** 16th century German cabinet key. **3.** 16th century German passage door key. **4.** 17th century German cabinet key. **5.** 8th century Merovingian cabinet key. **6.** 17th century German passage door key. **7.** 10th century German pasage door key. **8.** 15th century German cabinet key. **9.** 16th century North Italian cabinet key. **10.** 13th-14th century Austrian passage door key. **11.** 8th century Frankish cabinet key.

18th cent. prison lock, wards and spring lever mechanism.

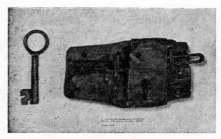

Semi-mortise passage door lock, 17th century.

Lock placed on the West Gate of the Holy Sepulchre in Jerusalem by the Crusaders in 1099 A.D.

Multiple lever Chubb-type, ca. 1863

Linus Yale, Jr's early pin-tumbler cylinder lock of the 1860s.

anyone able to pick an earlier model had been won. Thousands of patents for locks and improvements were taken out from the time of the American Revolution until the 1920s; some are more interesting than practical. Many of them, however, incorporate the principles in general use today.

A noteworthy example is that of Linus Yale Sr., a maker of bank locks. In 1844, he patented a household cylinder lock, embodying the old "Egyptian" pin-tumblers mechanism. His son, Linus Yale Jr., originally an artist, perfected this in patents of 1861 and 1865, adapting it to the machine production methods coming into use in the industrial age. He formed a partnership with an engineer, Henry Towne, but died just before the formal opening of the factory of the company that still bears his name.

Other early firms, some still in business, are Evans and Watson, Philadelphia, 1852; Russwin, New Britain, Connecticut; and Sargent and Company of New Haven, Connecticut, which celebrated its 100th birthday recently.

American ingenuity and production methods have discouraged foreign competition in our own country, and American locks are an important export item. An Ilco-Lockwood model (Fitchburg, Massachusetts) went with Sir Edmund Hillary to the top of Mt. Everest; and an unusual recent photograph shows an African chieftan wearing very large and heavy padlocks made by the Master Lock Company of Milwaukee as earrings.

"Old Western Jail Keys" from Coryell County, Texas, Jail, built 1875. Largest, 6" long, for front door; next largest for back door; smallest for strongbox; others for cell padlocks. All are Chubb-type.

Collection: Jim Miller, Gatesville, Texas

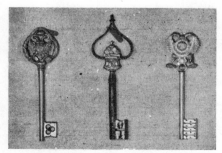

Large, ornate Chamberlain keys, presented by European rulers to court officials, 16th century on. Key at left was given Maria Theresa of Austria. Today we still give visiting dignitaries "a key to the city."

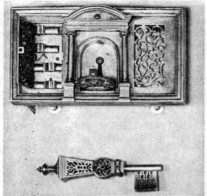
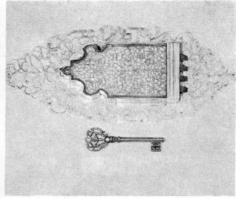

Masterpieces, left to right—Rim lock, 16th cent., French; keyhole cover and left mortise opened by pressing button in lintel. Lock with 4 bolts, 18th cent., French. Door lock, brass plate engraved in German: "Invented and made into a masterpiece by Johann George Popp, 1756, Furth, Germany." To qualify as locksmiths, apprentices submitted masterpieces such as these—after ten years or more of training.

Padlocks were made by both the early Chinese and the Romans. The former seem to have been the innovators of the keyless or "combination" padlock, in which a series of manipulations is necessary to free the hasp. This principle was introduced into Europe around the 16th century, and is still used on safes, vaults, and some modern padlocks.

The derivation of the word "padlock" has been the subject of speculation. Webster's *New World Dictionary* attributes it to the Middle English "padde" or frog, as suggested by the shape of some locks; others have suggested it comes from the attempts to foil the "footpads" or "pads", Medieval thieves. The latter view seems more reasonable, considering the numbers of Oriental and Roman padlocks made in the shape of fish, birds, animals, and mythological figures.

The literature of locks and keys is extensive, containing hundreds of volumes of many dates and in many languages. Some notable libraries of them have been formed; best known are those Mr. William McInerney, the Historian of the Associated Locksmiths of America, and Mr. Robert Nelson of the Mercer Lock Company of Philadelphia, who also has an extensive collection of antique locking devices. A book recommended for the average collector is *The Story of Locks* by Walter Buehr (Chas. Scrib-

ner's Sons, 1953), whose readable text and charming illustrations by the author give insight into both the working and history of locks.

All collectors should endeavor to see the traveling exhibits of the famous Yale and Towne Collection, which includes many noteworthy collections acquired by this pioneer American firm. They are booked through the American Federation of Arts, and the public relations department.

Keys are interesting and attractive objects, as decorators have discovered. Ornate or plain, large or small, and of a great variety of materials, all keys have a mission — they move an obstacle or series of obstacles that prevents something from being opened. They are worth collecting in themselves; and are found in increasing numbers in antique shows and shops.

A word of caution: it seems that there are numbers of large wrought-iron keys now being made in Mexico, "aged" in lye, and sold to unsuspecting dealers and collectors as "Old Western Jail Keys." Had there been as many jails as there appear to be keys, it might almost seem there was one for everybody living west of the Mississippi before 1900! Bought cheaply, these keys are interesting, however, since most of them are handmade replicas of old Spanish and Mexican Colonial keys still to be found South of the Border. Some, of course, are genuine.

Since lockmakers are constantly improving both the precision and quality of their products (famous artists have been employed by Yale and Towne to design their hardware), a farsighted collector might do well to add some of these present day items to his collection. A recent news story told of a "great-grandmaster" key unlocking all 524 doors in the new Health, Education and Public Welfare Building in Richmond, Virginia. There were "grandmaster" keys for all the doors on any one floor; the most unusual of all was the key that worked on every lock while the building was under construction—but once any room had been unlocked with its regular key, this construction key would no longer work on the lock. Surely some lucky collector will eventually get this item!

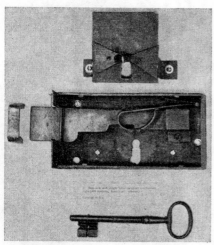

Late 18th cent. single lever tumbler.

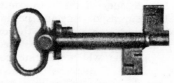

Double-bitted key, with hollow shank holding second key, German, 17th cent.

Large key for spring mechanism lock, 17th century, German

Door Knockers and Porters

by CYRIL BRACEGIRDLE

I T WAS not until late in the 16th century that doors began to have knockers of any kind. The monasteries and cathedrals of the Middle Ages invariably carried on the main door a lion's head with a ring through its mouth. These were not true knockers, since there was no boss against which the ring could be struck; indeed, their principle use seems to have been to enable any wrong doer, fleeing from the soldiers or an enraged mob, to claim sanctuary by grasping the ring since they were then technically within the protection of the Church.

These rings were, however, the direct ancestors of the knocker. In the last decades of the 16th century, the blacksmiths of England began to make similar iron rings for the ordinary domestic door, and provided a metal plate on which the ring could be hammered. Sometimes the knocker took the shape of a mallet in imitation of the wooden mallet which Elizabethans often hung on a nail beside the door for visitors to knock with and make their presence known.

One of the earliest types of mass-produced knockers consisted of a simple iron piece swinging from pivots attached to a metal plate. These proved an incitement to young hooligans to test their muscles at the sport of knocker-wrenching. Sometimes after a night of revelry whole streets would awaken to find their knockers lying in the roadway. Largely because of this, the simple pivoted rapper went out of fashion.

More elaborate and secure knockers, made of cast instead of wrought iron, were developed. Animal head shapes became fashionable with the rapper swinging from mouth or nostrils. There were rappers in the form of fruiting vines, or a hand grasping a

Spanish knocker in chiselled iron; late 16th century.

Victorian cast iron knockers from an illustrated catalog of hardware, ca. 1850.

bar. A classical vogue from the 1760s brought the vase shape, also Egyptian sphinx heads; and in 1839 the firm of Coalbrookdale, in the English county of Shropshire, introduced castings which could be hand-chased and highly burnished. A collector's item today is the knocker bearing a diamond-shaped mark which shows that the design was registered sometime between 1842 and 1883.

Along with knockers came the door porters, or door stops, most of which are of iron or brass and date from 1775 onwards. That was the year in which John Izon and Thomas Whitehurst of England patented their invention of the rising door hinge which caused a door to rise slightly as it opened and then to close again unless held—a boon even today, as any housewife with thick carpets will know.

The arrival on the domestic scene of the rising hinge undoubtedly helped to force the development of the door porter. Early examples were often in the shape of a basket of flowers, or a lion's paw. Often they were quite large and heavy. A crouching lion or sphinx could be up to 15 inches in height and weigh 3 to 5 pounds. Aristocrats had porters made in the form of their coat of arms.

In the mid-19th century, porters in imitation of celebrity figures appeared; there was the Duke of Wellington in a cocked hat. Admiral Nelson, and Queen Victoria in coronation robes. Punch and Judy shapes were popular,

English cast-iron door porter; mid-Victorian period.

Cast-iron door porter- symbol of an "Englishman's Castle." Ca. 1870.

as also was a knight with sword and shield in symbolization of the guardian of the "Englishman's castle." The rarer items eagerly sought by collectors today are obelisks in Derbyshire marble. There are also domes in a clear green glass with elongated air bubbles trapped inside; these were made in Bristol and Nailsea.

Often the best sources from which to acquire knockers and porters are the sales of old houses, though the dusty recesses of English junk shops can also yield surprising treasures.

The invention of the electric bell effectively put an end to the manufacture of door knockers and porters.

Late Victorian door knockers; some, like the second from the left in the top row, have the name of the resident engraved on a plain surface.

Paul Revere, Brass and Coppersmith

by CARL DREPPERD

MUCH has been written about Paul Revere, including Esther Forbes monumental "Paul Revere & The World He Lived In", published by Houghton Mifflin, 1942. This being the case, practically all articles and commentaries of the past decade have been so many twice-told tales, told all over again. New material on Paul Revere has indeed been scarce, but recently two happenings of importance make another essay on Paul Revere almost mandatory.

In 1788 Paul Revere acquired an iron furnace which he converted for the casting of bronze church bells and cannon. His first cast bronze bell was pulled from the sand of its mold and core in 1792. On that day Paul Revere entered a new business and became an active partner in the stabilization of our new nation. In 1794 he received an order to cast howitzers of 8.25 inch bore for the army. Our great wooden ship of the line, The Constitution, was then in process of building. The copper bolts required to build, and the copper to sheathe this frigate were ordered from England. Upon arrival, certain of the bolts were found to be of the wrong size. Revere remade them.

In 1800 he admitted that he had discovered the method of making copper malleable and rolling it hot. His first customer was the Commonwealth of Massachusetts, which purchased 7675 pounds of copper sheathing and 789 pounds of copper nails to cover the State House dome. The Commonwealth paid the bill quickly enough for Revere to meet his payrolls, while the Federal government lagged far behind and wondered whether it was necessary after all to give orders to our own

productive facilities when it was so much easier for a bureaucrat simply to order the copper from England.

When Massachusetts paid Revere over $4000 for the copper for the State House dome he plowed the money back into copper production. His next job was to re-copper the Constitution and thus, for the first time, a U.S. ship was re-coppered with United States made sheeting.

In 1803 Revere did something that perhaps shocked the smart boys of the nation's capital. He told the Secretary of the Navy that he found it difficult to procure stocks of new or old copper, that merchants were not in the habit of importing it. He therefore suggested that the ships of the U.S. Navy purchase copper at Smyrna and bring home a number

Paul Revere & Son,

At their BELL and CANNON FOUNDERY, *at the North Part of* BOSTON,

CAST *BELLS*, of all fizes ; every kind of Brafs ORDNANCE, and every kind of *Compofition Work, for* SHIPS, &c. *at the fhorteft notice ;* Manufacture COPPER into SHEETS, BOLTS, SPIKES, NAILS, RIVETS, DOVETAILS, &c. from *Malleable Copper.*

They always keep, by them, every kind of *Copper 'roftening for Ships.* They have now on hand, a number of Church and Ship Bells, of different fizes ; a large quantity of Sheathing Copper, from 16 up to 30 ounce ; Bolts, Spikes, Nails, &c of all fizes, which they warrant equal to Englifh manufacture.

Cafh and the higheft price given for old Copper and Brafs ·   march 10

Early View of Boston. That dense smoke on the horizon is from Paul Revere's Foundry. The date of this print is 1788. It is views of this kind that make collecting Industrial and Commercial Americana a most interesting pursuit.

of tons. The first U.S. vessel to do this was the Constitution. The copper business was launched.

In 1804 Joseph Warren Revere, son of Paul, was made a partner in the business and given a one-third interest in his father's property, then valued at $16,200. In this deed Paul Revere, the father, is listed as a "gentleman", and his son Joseph Warren as a bell and cannon founder. Paul Revere continued as a gentleman should who still owned a two-thirds interest in a business. He acted as chairman of the board, so to speak, and sent his son abroad on a fact-finding visit to the copper-making countries of Europe—England, Wales, France and Scandinavia. In 1805 Joseph Warren returned to continue the expansion of the infant industry founded by night rider Paul Revere.

The business, if it didn't boom, certainly made excellent progress. Off its rollers came copper to roof public buildings and private dwellings, and stock for the merchants of Canada, the New England states, and the Atlantic seaboard. Coppersmiths were calling on Revere for sheet copper and technical advice. Robert Fulton wrote to Revere in 1808: "I am informed you have a mill for roleing of copper and that you furnish it in any size. I wish to have

a quantity of 12 pound to the square foot and should be glad to know your price and when it could be delivered." This was copper for the boiler of the world's first truly successful steamboat, the Clermont. From then on Fulton turned to Revere for the boiler copper of his every new steamboat and the records of the company indicate business to the volume of over $10,000.

Revere, of course, was being undersold by the British copper producers and, in Revere's opinion, imports were encouraged by our Treasury's laxity of tariff provision. Revere spoke for a 17½% duty on all copper except pigs and bars, and said that plate should be included as manufactured copper. Because of a twisted interpretation of the law, he had to pay full tariff on scrap copper sheathing that had been taken from ships in foreign docks!

Thus began an industry which, by the time of the War of 1812, found the U.S. Navy ready for action because we had copper for ship bottoms and bronze for guns.

Perhaps, from a collecting standpoint, nothing more need be said except that every collector should do his best to procure a copy of "Paul Revere—Pioneer Industrialist" and read the story from cover to cover. This is a booklet the like of which should be published by every company in America. If there be any who say they are so late in point of time that they have no antiquarian background, let them hide their heads in shame. Every business in America has an antiquarian background, either objectively or subjectively. When that background is brought to light it exposes facts which make the history of business a revelation and not a lot of mumbo-jumbo.

Early American Brass and Copper... and its makers

by HENRY J. KAUFFMAN

Typical Pennsylvania teakettle, signed by W. Heiss, 123 North Third St. Philadelphia, in rare 6½″ diameter size. Most are 8 to 10″ in diameter; a few are 12″.

THE QUANTITIES OF copper and brass wares found in antiques shops in this country focus attention on the fact that though pieces may look alike they are not always equal in value. All copper teakettles, for example, appear essentially the same wherever they were made. While there is little difference in the value of imported English and Scandinavian kettles, the average American copper teakettle is worth a great deal more than either. This conclusion applies in a general way to all antiques, but it is recognized more acutely in the field of copper and brass because of the difficulty in determining the place of origin.

The historical perspective of coppersmithing in America might start as early as 1738 when Peacock Rigger advertised in the *Pennsylvania Gazette* that he was located in Philadelphia, "in Market Street, near the Sign of the Indian King," where he made and sold all kinds of copper work.

In the *Pennsylvania Journal* of September 4, 1766, Benjamin Harbeson announced he had removed his shop to the corner of Laetitia Court. He listed him-

self ready to serve on reasonable terms in such copper work as "stills, brewing coppers, sugar boilers, copper fish kettles, teakettles, boilers, soap coppers, brass and copper washing kettles, stew pans, frying pans, capuchin plate warmers, brass and copper scales, warming pans, chafing dishes, chocolate pots, copper ships' stoves, silversmith's boilers, brass and iron candlesticks, brass cocks of all sorts," and various items of London pewter, bell metal, and tin.

This imposing list of objects made by one man before the American Revolution indicates that there was a sizeable production of these objects at that time. Not all coppersmiths who worked at the trade until about 1850 made as wide a range of objects as Mr. Harbeson. However, styles changed very little as long as these objects were made by hand. The function of stills, for example, changed little throughout the period; hence the shapes remained much the same. The same is true of skillets, stewpans, warming pans, and the like.

It is important to note that many of

the objects named in early advertisements in America have never been found or identified with a maker. The writer has never seen, definitely attributed to an American maker, brewing coppers, sugar boilers, soap boilers, washing coppers, copper ships' stoves and other of the items enumerated. Objects he has seen that have been positively identified as American products include one or two each of warming pans, liquid measures, stew pans, skillets, half-bushel measures, many copper kettles, and hundreds of copper teakettles.

A number of large copper kettles for making apple butter were made by the Schaum family in Lancaster, Pennsylvania. However, this particular use has never been found listed among products made by an 18th or early 19th century coppersmith. Kettles for making apple butter were not lined with tin as most other vessels were. Schaum kettles, made until 1926, were widely distributed through the country by Sears, Roebuck & Company.

The scarcity of stills, signed or un-

Copper frying pan made in Philadelphia, though maker's name cannot be distinguished. Possibly made by Bentley, a Philadelphia craftsman who made interesting forms and signed many pieces.

Copper measure by Holmes & Evans, Fisherville, N. H. Measures of copper are common, but signed ones are very rare. The sets were used for selling liquor to the retail trade at distilleries.

Unusually attractive brass warming pan with maker's intaglio stamp under group of holes near top showing initial "C" and a possible, though indistinct "A P." Surprisingly few warming pans, either of brass or copper, were signed, though almost every coppersmith of the 18th century mentioned them in his advertising. It is Mr. Kauffman's opinion that those which do exist with name of craftsman engraved on the lids are imported. Of the 3 marked pans in his own collection, none can positively be attributed to an American craftsman. One has an intaglio stamp with initials "I W" on the hinge, which might be interpreted as Joshua Witherle, a coppersmith in Boston in 1789. However, attribution of this type is precarious.

FRANCIS SANDERSON,
COPPERSMITH from LANCASTER, living in
GAY-STREET, BALTIMORE-TOWN, a few
Doors above Mr. *Andrew Steiger's*,

MAKES and fells all forts of COPPER-WORK,
viz. ſtills of all ſizes, fiſh and waſh kettles,
copper and braſs, brewing-kettles, faucepans, coffee
and chocolate pots, ſtew-pans, and Dutch ovens. He
ſells any of the above articles as cheap as can be imported from *England*, and carries on his Buſineſs in
Lancaſter as uſual. He likewiſe carries on the TIN-
BUSINESS in all its branches. Country ſhop-keepers
may be ſupplied, either by wholeſale or retail, and all
orders ſent from the country ſhall be carefully executed.

Advertisement from the *Maryland Journal and Baltimore Advertiser*, August 20, 1773. Sanderson worked in Lancaster, Pa. before the Revolution, later in Baltimore. At least one signed piece is known; others may exist in the Pennsylvania-Maryland region.

signed, is curious, considering how many were made and how widely they were used. Of the half dozen the writer has seen, only three were marked.

It must be obvious to the reader that this perspective on early coppersmithing is focusing directly toward Pennsylvania. Though coppersmiths were working all over the Colonies, more signed pieces have been found by Pennsylvania craftsmen than the rest of the country put together. It may be that more Pennsylvania craftsmen signed their products, but it is the writer's opinion that the bulk of 18th century coppersmithing, and a great deal in the 19th century, was done in the Keystone State. A small number of New York coppersmiths signed their work, and there are scattered examples from New England and the South, but the main route for signed pieces seems to be from Philadelphia to Pittsburgh. Perhaps John Getz of Lancaster signed more pieces of copper ware than any other American coppersmith.

In identifying objects of copper and brass, a connoisseur may know styles well enough to attribute unmarked objects to American craftsmen or to European sources. For instance, teakettles with a hinged lid on the spout are regarded as foreign; no American examples are known. This need not mean that one signed by an American craftsman

may not be found tomorrow. Such an exception will not greatly change the conclusion, for principles are not established on one or two exceptions.

The only sure method of identifying an American object of copper or brass is by finding a *bona fide* name of an American craftsman on it. A name alone is not proof of American production as a number of European craftsmen placed their names on their products. In the columns below are listed some of the craftsmen known to have worked in sheet copper and brass in America, with an identifying date. Any of their names *might* be found on an early brass or copper piece.

John Morrison's mark on handle of copper teakettle is a rare impression; hardness of copper and large size of stamps produced few such nearly perfect impressions.

Some American Coppersmiths
from Contemporary Records

Apple, Jacob	Philadelphia	1852
Apple, Philip	Philadelphia	1811
Attlee, William	Lancaster, Pa.	1790
Babb, John	Reading, Pa.	1806
Babb, Mathias	Reading, Pa	1796
Bailey, William	Maryland & Pa.	1770
		-1800
Beader, Henry	Harrisburg, Pa.	1820
		-1826
Benson, John	New York	1841
Bentley, David	Philadelphia	1842
		-1852
Bigger, Peacock	Philadelphia	1740
	and Annapolis	-1750
Bintzel, Daniel	Philadelphia	1842
Bintzel, William	Philadelphia	1852
Blanc, Victor	Philadelphia	1811
Bratzman, Andreas	Reading, Pa.	1813
Brotherton, E.	Lancaster, Pa.	1806
Brown, Thomas	Philadelphia	1852
Bruce, John	Baltimore	1850
Buchanan, James	Pittsburgh	1818
Buckhard, Peter	New York	1841
Carpenter, Alfred	Boston	1848
Carter, John	Boston	1848
Chessen, George	Philadelphia	1811
Clark, Forbes	Harrisburg, Pa.	1814
Clemm & Bailey	Baltimore	1784
Coltman, J. W.	Boston	1848
Cook, John	Philadelphia	1811
Cropley, John	Philadelphia	1852
Cunningham, Wm.	New York	1841
Darby, William	New York	1841
Davis & Wiley	Pittsburgh	1837
Deich, John	Philadelphia	1840
Delaney, John	Carlisle, Pa.	1792
Dickey, Isaiah	Pittsburgh	1837
& Co.	Maryland & Pa.	1770
		-1800
Diller, Samuel	Lancaster, Pa.	1869
Dusenbury, Thomas	New York	1841
Dverter, Wm.	Lancaster, Pa.	1869
Eicholtz, Jacob	Lancaster, Pa.	1810
Eisenhut, John	Philadelphia	1811
Eisenhut, John D.	Philadelphia	1852
Fisher, Charles	York, Pa.	1832
Foos, Jacob	Lancaster, Pa.	1869
Forrest, Jacob	Lancaster, Pa.	1869
Gallagher, P.	Boston	1848
Getz, John	Lancaster, Pa.	1817
		-1835
Gould, Joseph	Boston	1848
Graff, Joseph	Philadelphia	1852
Grauel, Daniel	Philadelphia	1811
Grimes, James	Pittsburgh	1837
Haldane, James	Philadelphia	1765
Hammett & Hiles	Philadelphia	1840
Hannah & Launy	New York	1841
Harberger, Henry	Philadelphia	1811
Harbeson, Benjamin	Philadelphia	1790
Harbeson, Joseph	Philadelphia	1766
Harbeson, Joseph	Pittsburgh	1807
Harley, Francis	Philadelphia	1840
Hasler, John	New York	1841
Heiss, Goddard	Philadelphia	1852
Heiss, Wm. Jr.	Philadelphia	1852
Heller, Henry	Philadelphia	1840
Hemmenway, B.	Boston	1848
Hill and Chamberlin	Boston	1848
Howard & Rodgers	Pittsburgh	1837
Hunneman & Co.	Boston	1848
Hutton, William	Philadelphia	1840
Jewell, Charles	New York	1841
Keefer, J & F.	Pittsburgh	1837
Kidd, John	Reading, Pa.	1790
		-1800
Knox, Edward	New York	1841
Kower, John	Kutztown, Pa.	1841
Leacock, William	Philadelphia	1840
Lee, William	Philadelphia	1852
LeFrentz, George	York, Pa.	1783
Lightbody, Collin	New York	1841
Lindsay, David	Carlisle, Pa.	1792
Lock & Cordwell	Boston	1848
Loring, A. B.	Boston	1848
Loring, John G.	Boston	1848
Lyne, John	Harrisburg, Pa.	1811
Lyne, Robert	Philadelphia	1800
McBride, John	York, Co. Pa.	1783
McCauley, John	Philadelphia	1800
McCoy, Neil	York, Pa.	1784
Megee, George	Philadelphia	1840
		-1852
Meredith, John	Philadelphia	1840
Miller, F.	Chambersburg, Pa.	1800
Miller, Jacob	Harrisburg, Pa.	1820
Minshall, Thomas	Middletown, Pa.	1802
Morrison, John	Philadelphia	1790
Noble, James	Philadelphia	1840
Oat, George	Philadelphia	1852
Oat, Israel	Philadelphia	1852
Oat, Jesse	Philadelphia	1811
Oat, Joseph	Philadelphia	1840
Oat, Joseph & Son	Philadelphia	1852
O'Bryon, Benjamin	Philadelphia	1840
Orr, Robert	Philadelphia	1800
Peters & Co.	Philadelphia	1811
Pier, Benjamin	New York	1841
Potter, James	Philadelphia	1790
Raborg, Christopher	Baltimore	1785
Read, W.	Philadelphia	1840
Reed, Robert	Lancaster, Pa.	1795
Reigart, Henry	Lancaster, Pa.	1803
Rink, Miller H.	Philadelphia	1840
Roberts & Son	Philadelphia	1840
Roberts, Israel	Philadelphia	1811
		-1852
Roberts, James	Philadelphia	1852
Rulon, Jane	Philadelphia	1852
Schaum, Benjamin	Lancaster, Pa.	1790
Schaum, Peter	Lancaster, Pa.	1790
Schoenfelder	Reading, Pa.	1803
Seffron, George	York, Pa.	1789
Shenfelder, Asop	Reading, Pa.	1838
Shuler, George	Middletown, Pa.	1803
Simons, John	Philadelphia	1852
Stafford, Spencer	Albany, N. Y.	1794
Steele, George	Hartford, Conn.	1790
Stoehr, Daniel	Hanover, Pa.	1787
		-1863
Strickler, Issac	Philadelphia	1811
Sweet, William	New York	1841
Thayer, Cornelius	Litchfield	1785
Thompson, John	Harrisburg, Pa.	1814
Tophan, Reuben	Philadelphia	1800
Town, John	Pittsburgh	1813
Trueman, Thomas	Philadelphia	1790
Tryon, George	Philadelphia	1811
Upperman, John	Lancaster, Pa.	1811
Varley, Abram	Marietta, Pa.	1814
Waters & Milk	Boston	1848
Weitzel, George	Lancaster, Pa.	1830
West, Jacob	Philadelphia	1840
Whitaker, Robert	Philadelphia	1811
Williamson, Isaac	New York	1841
Winter, Jonathan	York Co. Pa.	1788
Witherle, Joshua & Co.	Boston	1789
Witman, John	Kutztown, Pa.	1804
Wright, John	New York	1841
Yeates, Edmund	Philadelphia	1811
Youse, George	Harrisburg, Pa.	1807
		-1814

Ornate brass wall sconces and standing pulpit lights for one or two candles. These ranged in price from 6 to 12 schillings each.

Old English Brasses of the Late Georgian Period

by BENJAMIN EDWARDS

Clock brasses, capitals, bases, etc., for wooden columns.

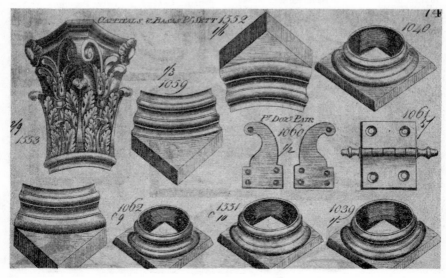

WHAT is a "rapper?" "Rapper," in the England of 1825 meant what we call a knocker; a door knocker. In case anyone wonders, whether or not these items entered our country from England as early to mid 19th century imports, the answer is yes, and in great quantities. In fact they have never ceased to enter. From at least 1900, they have entered as reproductions, made by reputable old firms. Perhaps reproduction is not the correct term. Certainly, in some cases, brass items have been made in the same way, from the same pattern, for a century and a half, by the same firm. Therefore the proper term would be continuous production and not reproduction. Furthermore, a surprising number of rappers and other brasses are now entering the country as antiques—for they date prior to 1830.

Fully to understand this brass situation it is necessary to know that Birmingham, England, has been a brass and cutlery city for lo, these many scores of years, adding up to three or more centuries. Birmingham brass barrels for pistols and guns have been imported since, it is said, 1700. There are other experts who insist that Eltweed Pomeroy, the early gunsmith of the Pilgrim Company made pistols with barrels of "Brummagem Brass".

The fact of early or late making of brass items in traditional forms, and of modern castings from ancient patterns, cannot be determined by textual demonstrations. One must know brass, patterns and sources. Late productions, shipped here as new goods, will have country of origin marking . . . or should have. But old items are now coming in as imports sponsored by a small army of keen dealers who tour England and the Continent at some profit, just buying glass, china, and brass items of antiquity for resale.

The illustrations selected for this text are direct from the original catalog of a Union of Birmingham brass founders who sold goods for domestic use and for export. You will find their

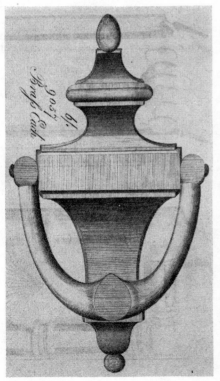

So-called Colonial rapper, actually of the Adam period, and hand and shell rapper.

clock balls, capitals, bases, and hinges on many American clocks. Similarly, you will find "rappers" on many old American homes, and the sconces and lighting fixtures still used in untouched early homes and properly in certain restorations.

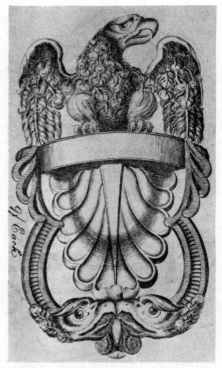

Eagle brass door rapper which cost 9 schillings in 1825. In bronze or cast iron the price was 3 schillings.

No. 1

Brass Trivets—
The Old and
the New

by WILLIAM PALEY

No. 2

Back of No. 1

No. 3

IS IT POSSIBLE to distinguish between old trivets and modern reproductions? Many collectors of old
trivets are frustrated by the difficulty
experienced in doing so; others simply
avoid collecting brass trivets entirely,
realizing that it is so easy to "age" a
modern one.

In response to several recent re-
quests for help, here are a few guides:
1. On the authentic old brass and
copper trivets, since the work was
hand-done, the legs almost invariably
pierce the tops. (No's. 1, 2, 6, 7, 9, 10,
11, 12, and 13.) The top will be of
sheet metal of uniform thickness
which may be from 1/16 to 3/16
inches. Cast brass trivets are not
common, but when found, the legs
are cast integral with the top (No.
14).

2. The top of an old trivet is quite
often warped and uneven as a result
of holding heavy objects, of being
used as a stepping stool, and of being
dropped, thus bending the point. (No.
12, and No. 13 detail.)

3. The uniform application of bangs
and nicks is suspect. There are certain places where a trivet will usually
get marked, depending on the type of
use it has had. (See No. 7) I have one
trivet which was obviously used as a
hammer to drive a nail. One edge is
badly scarred; otherwise it is unmarked.

4. The upper surface of the trivet
will be much smoother than the underside. (No. 1 detail.) The smoothing effort was concentrated on the

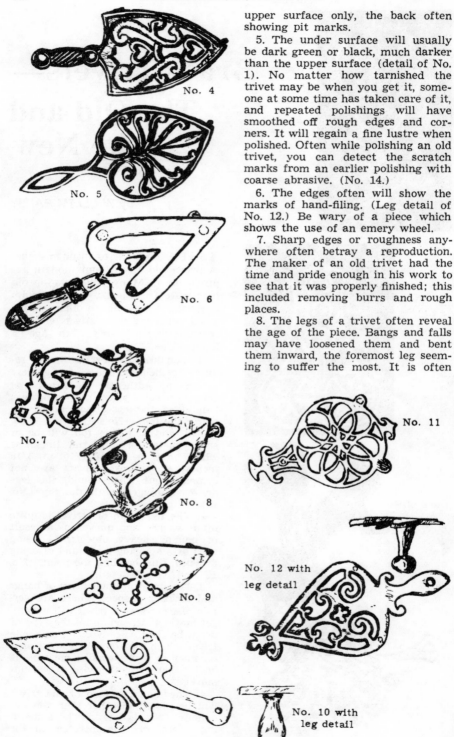

No. 4

No. 5

No. 6

No. 7

No. 8

No. 9

No. 11

No. 12 with leg detail

No. 10 with leg detail

upper surface only, the back often showing pit marks.

5. The under surface will usually be dark green or black, much darker than the upper surface (detail of No. 1). No matter how tarnished the trivet may be when you get it, someone at some time has taken care of it, and repeated polishings will have smoothed off rough edges and corners. It will regain a fine lustre when polished. Often while polishing an old trivet, you can detect the scratch marks from an earlier polishing with coarse abrasive. (No. 14.)

6. The edges often will show the marks of hand-filing. (Leg detail of No. 12.) Be wary of a piece which shows the use of an emery wheel.

7. Sharp edges or roughness anywhere often betray a reproduction. The maker of an old trivet had the time and pride enough in his work to see that it was properly finished; this included removing burrs and rough places.

8. The legs of a trivet often reveal the age of the piece. Bangs and falls may have loosened them and bent them inward, the foremost leg seeming to suffer the most. It is often

more bent; its forward edge is more worn and rounded. (Detail of No. 1.) The same applies to the outer edges of the other two legs. Uniform rounding of all edges of all legs is suspect.

9. Become familiar with the patterns being reproduced, and the characteristics of these trivets, their size and weight, type and length of leg, where and how they have been marked by their maker, since honorable makers of reproductions will stamp their product. Be suspicious of seeing several brass trivets of the same or varying design, all with identical aging characteristics, at the same time, in the same place. Old brass trivets are not likely to be found that way.

10. No single one of the above points, but a combination of all of them is the best way to identify an old trivet. Sometimes, even with all of these in mind, you cannot be sure. Some dealers, unfortunately, give trivets a bath which removes all dirt and aging from front and back.

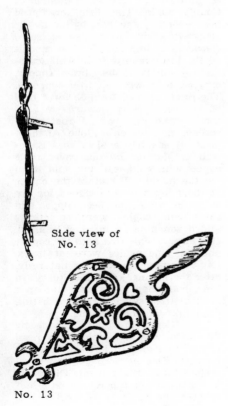

Side view of
No. 13

No. 13

No. 14

KEY TO ILLUSTRATIONS

No's. 3, 4, 5; Three of the most commonly reproduced designs in brass as well as in iron.

No. 6: A wooden handle is almost a sure indication of an old trivet. The rosewood handle and brass ferrule make this brass heart trivet distinctive.

No. 7: The three legs which had worked themselves loose were ineptly tightened by hammering the trivet surface leaving dents.

No. 8: A rather clumsy, hand-made brass stand with handle, legs, and lugs brazed to the heavy sheet metal body, and the entire trivet coarsely hand filed.

Brass trivets with dowel-type iron legs, such as *No. 9,* or turned iron legs, like *No. 10,* that pierce the surface are old. Most brass trivets have brass legs. The pendulum-style trivet *(No. 11)* has three mismatched legs; quite often a loose leg was lost, and a substitute was added.

No's. 12, 13, 14: A popular design was often copied by different craftsmen, leading to slight variations. The hole in the handles of *No's. 12 and 14* are later improvements on the earlier *No. 13.* The earliest of the three, *No. 13,* is of thinner brass than some trivets and hence, as the side view shows, has been bent out of shape. *No. 14* is of cast brass with integral legs and body.

Eagles of Brass, Copper and Zinc

The Centennial Eagle of Bakewell &
Mullins, made at the Salem, Ohio factory
of this firm. It is the same type of eagle
that decorated the parapets of Centennial
Buildings, 1876.

by CHARLES MULLINS

MANUFACTURED BY
BAKEWELL & MULLINS,
SALEM, OHIO

EAGLE COLLECTING is no longer a limited cult. Neither is it a vogue. It is a growing pursuit which no longer draws the line at carved wood eagles by the mass producer, Bellamy or the itinerant ne'er-do-well Schimmel. Now our eagle collectors seek any and all eagle forms, whether weather vanes, architectural decoration, ship figure heads, overdoor or hatchway pieces, or just room decoration. The collectors cannot, somehow, concern themselves over and seek for rarities in Eagles such as the magnificent examples carved by Dr. Grier, by Benjamin Rush or Samuel Skillin. Instead they must, to be successful collectors—and a successful collector, some believe, is one who achieves possession of the object of his quest—find eagles that were made in sufficient quantities so as to survive in great enough numbers to be found.

One important such a source of eagle manufacture was the Architectural Ornament Works of Bakewell & Mullins, at Salem, Columbiana County, Ohio. This firm, organized over a century ago, had, by the 1880's, achieved a line of eagles of some considerable importance. They modeled the birds boldly, from well sculptured originals, of sheet brass, copper, or zinc, over wrought iron supports. The prices ranged from $5 for a bird of 12″ wingspread, upwards to $210 for an "Old Abe" with 9 foot wingspread, mounted on a globe. At these prices it is fairly evident that Bakewell & Mullins did not cover their eagles with gold leaf, but sold them "in the metal". Therefore the eagles of sheet brass were designed for use as made, while the sheet copper and sheet zinc eagles were sometimes gilded, sometimes painted, or bronzed. It is also possible that both the copper and the zinc eagles were, at times, left unpainted, to weather naturally, after the manner of lead statuary. In time, both copper and zinc take on a dark mottled surface of greyish tint, not unlike weathered stone.

The "Centennial Eagle" made by this firm was available with head turned to right, to left, or straightforward. This permitted symmetrical architectural arrangement. This eagle was available on a perch, or on a half sphere. The size was 47 x 48 inches.

On perch, the price was $30; on half sphere, $32.

The "Trade" eagle, with 6 foot wingspread was probably designated as trade type because it was designed for use as a sign. It should be remembered that "Eagle" was a favorite business name. Many towns had an eagle works of some sort or other. Some had an Eagle brewery, some an Eagle chair factory, Eagle soap works, Eagle pharmacy, Eagle mirror works, Eagle pottery and so on.

The firm also made a gigantic Mural Eagle with 14 foot wingspread. This was an eagle in low relief, wings outspread, head thrust through a 13 starred wreath, one talon supporting the U. S. Shield, the other grasping arrows and ribbons. When tightly affixed to a wall, this eagle could be treated as a carving, or pargetry decoration; it was, however equally applicable to an exterior wall, especially within the confines of a gable, or similar architectural area. The price of this grand eagle was $200.

Bakewell & Mullins made "Old Abe" the major eagle of their collection. This bird, with 9 foot wingspread, was available on the type of base shown (actually the upper area of the field of a shield), or mounted on a half sphere. Old Abe is depicted in his most famous pose, that of the living standard carried by Wisconsin troops in the War-between-the-States. This

Top, "Old Abe"; center, "Trade Eagle" and bottom, the Mural Eagle for interior or exterior walls. All illustrations from original art supplied by the manufacturers, and used in the 1880's.

is not a fairy tale. Old Abe was a live eagle, trained to sit on a perch carried in a parade. When the Wisconsin boys were mustered in the Union Army, Old Abe was taken along and carried as a living standard in battle. He became a very famous bird indeed; was exhibited at the Centennial and has had a place in the Wisconsin State Capitol building. The price of this Old Abe was $200 perched on the shield top, and $210 perched on a half-sphere.

Weather Vanes

by ALBERT CHRISTIAN REVI

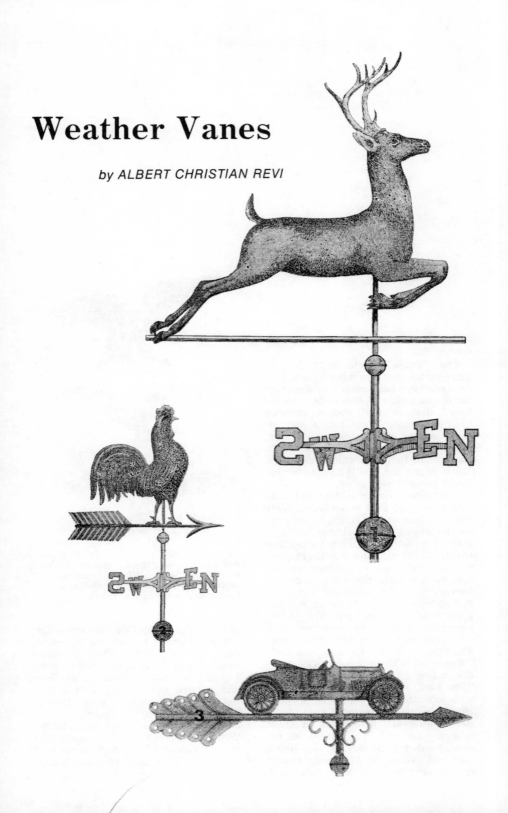

E VER since they were elevated to the classification of "Folk Art" and "Primitives," early handmade weather vanes have become too difficult, and too expensive, for collectors of modest means to acquire. As a result, many people have begun to collect weather vanes produced after 1850, using them for decorative purposes inside and outside the home.

About 1928, E. G. Washburne & Company, at that time located at 207 Fulton Street, Brooklyn, New York, published a catalog of their weather vanes. Some of the designs shown had been carried over a period of several years, but the catalog indicated that new designs—like the car weather vanes—were in the offing at all times. Illustrations of gilded, full-bodied and swell-bodied animals—cows, bulls, deer, dogs, horses, roosters, sheep, hogs, eagles, and fish—predominated, but there were also designs featuring sloops and schooners, windmills, and a quill pen. Silhouette weather vanes made of flat copper, finished in gold leaf or statuary bronze, or any special color, were shown on the last few pages of the catalog.

The E. G. Washburne Company was established in 1853, and un-

1. Gilded deer; swell-bodied and full-bodied models in 20″ and 30″ lengths. 2. Swell-bodied roosters of gilded copper were produced in various sizes—14″, 18″, 24″ and 28″. 3. Gilded, swell-bodied runabout mounted on arrow 26″ long. 4. Windmill, 18″ high, rod with fence and dog, 42″ long, were made of copper finished in gold leaf, statuary bronze, or any special color. 5. Cardinal point designs identified with commercial manufacturers of weather vanes. Top to bottom: L. W. Cushing, J. W. Fiske, W. A. Snow, E. G. Washburne, R. Watkins, and two unknown manufacturers whose vanes are often seen. (Illustration from **Weathervanes and Whirligigs**, by Ken Fitzgerald.) 6. Full-bodied sloops and schooners of gilded copper, 36″ and 48″ long. 7. Gilded quill pen weather vanes ranged in size from 1½ to 6 ft. long. 8. Flying ducks, in silhouette, 30″ long. 9. Silhouette of milkmaid and cow, 30″ and 47″ in length.

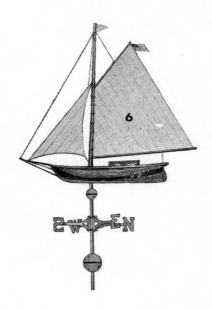

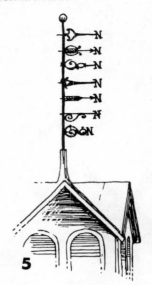

doubtedly they manufactured many unusual weather vanes, both before and after their 1928 catalog was printed. The firm was listed as the Washburne Weather Vane Company in the 1965 edition of the New York City Directory, but no mention of it was found in subsequent editions. Ken Fitzgerald's new book, *Weathervanes and Whirligigs* (Clarkson N. Potter, Inc., Publishers), gives Washburne's present address as 85 Andover Street, Boston, Mass., and advises that new "old" weather vanes can be purchased from the company, or from one of their distributors.

5

Tin Cookie Cutters, Molds, and Sconces

by ALICE WILT STRAUSS

One of a pair of early tin sconces with high narrow back bent forward to form hood. Author's collection.

FOR many weeks before Christmas the Pennsylvania Dutch housewife was busy making preparations for the holiday season, for the festivities did not end on December 26, but were carried over into the weeks that followed. She had to be well supplied for her holiday entertaining. There had to be cookies for the friends who came "putzing," and cookies and coffee and home-made wine to serve to the men who came on New Year's Day to "shoot in the New Year." The Christmas cookie was as traditional with the Pennsylvania Dutch as the Putz or the tree.

Only at this particular time of the year did the "fancy" cutters come into use, and from the rolled dough came stars and angels, household and farm animals, birds and flowers. Some of these cookie figures took their places on the tree with the candy canes and popcorn strings, but most of them were used for the holiday entertaining.

Many of these "fancy" cutters are still to be found, some in fine condition, and collectors are gathering them up to use, or simply to add to their collection of primitives, as examples of a type of life which is fading into history. But the tradition of the Christmas cookie is still observed in many sections of the Dutchland.

Conflicting stories have been told regarding the inspiration for the designs on these cutters, so without proper authentication it would be difficult to state definitely what prompted the choice of patterns. Some folks say the star, the angel, the camel, sheep, etc., were inspired by the figures of the nativity, and the Germans' love of the Putz. But other designs not associated with the Christmas characters are found as frequently as those mentioned. These must have had their origin elsewhere.

The horse was a favorite subject and is found in standing or running position. The pig, sheep, goat, donkey, cat, and the dog in a variety of breeds, would indicate that the tinsmith derived many of his ideas from the farm. He used also the rooster, the hen, the duck, and birds which are not easily recognized.

The eagle, which is a favorite Pennsylvania Dutch pattern, is considered one of the most desirable by collectors. But the tinsmith must have looked to other sources as well, for the forest animals have turned up on the cutters—bears, lions, foxes and others. The deer, though not as common as the barnyard animals or some of the others, is found often enough to make the search for the unusual worthwhile.

It has been suggested that these out-of-the-ordinary cutters were a necessary in-

Rare cookie mold about 20″ square; pudding mold; cheese mold. Owned by Ruth Briggs, Rockford, Ill.

vention of the tinsmith when he found his customer already well-supplied with cutters in the conventional patterns. In the very early days the housewife's only opportunity to obtain her tinware was through the visit of the itinerant tinsmith. Traveling from farm to farm, the tinsmith would produce, on the spot, the items needed by each family. Perhaps the housewife had her own ideas about the designs she wished on her cutters. Or perhaps, as was suggested, she was well supplied with the usual array and wanted something unusual.

Most of the cutters were small, the largest being, perhaps, not more than six or seven inches long, although pictured with the pudding mold, is a rare cutter measuring about twenty inches square. The figure is a rabbit. The earliest cutters

were without handles, but most of them had "air holes."

Some of the patterns had two sets of cutting edges. The outside edge cut through the dough, while the other cutting edge was not as deep and served to make an impression on the surface of the cookie. Thus instead of the cookie being merely a figure in outline, interest was heightened by the addition of features on a man or woman, for instance, and by the details of the clothing. Some of the figures most eagerly sought by the collectors are the Colonial horseback rider, the Revolutionary soldier, the Indians, men or women; Uncle Sam, Mennonite figures and other historical figures representative of the progress of the period.

But the cookie cutters were not the only collectible examples of the tinsmith's art.

Collection of cookie cutters showing: horse standing and running, deer, dogs, lion, pig, eagle, 2 other birds. Owned by Ruth Briggs, Rockford, Ill.

There were the tin coffee pots of the early nineteenth century, the only decoration being the design in punched tin. Unlike the designs of the punched tin food safes, those on the coffee pots were not punched through. The pattern showed up in a series of raised dots on the surface of the pot, and it was applied to the tin before the tin was shaped.

The tin pudding molds and cheese molds could be as useful today as they were in the nineteenth century. A good boiling to assure cleanliness, perhaps a bit of solder on loose joints, and the mold would be as good as new. A punched tin lantern might add a decorative note to a home furnished in Early American, but its usefulness for lighting should not be depended upon. However, there are many tin candlesticks which could be useful, and some of the wall sconces. These sconces were made in several different styles and frequently can be found in shops, though pairs are getting pretty scarce.

Most decorative of these were the mirror sconces. These consisted of a round tin plate, slightly concave, which was covered with small mirrors set in "S" circular pattern. This plate hung against the wall, and a bracket at the base held the candle or candles. The mirrors, reflecting the light, produced a pleasing effect and also increased the efficiency of the fixture for illumination. Another type of wall sconce was similar to the one described above but was without the mirrors. This had a round tin plate, much like a pie tin, which hung against the wall, and was usually plain except for a fluted edge. The candle bracket extended from the base. Still another type had a high narrow back bent forward to form a hood. This hood was usually fluted.

Not infrequently the itinerant tinsmith was called upon to produce a particular piece to suit the whimsy of a housewife— a small box for trinkets, a decorative mirror frame, or even a toy or two. Exhibited at a show a few years ago was a doll house which had been brought from the Pennsylvania Dutch country. The exhibitor explained the house had been made on order by an itinerant tinsmith, and it is fun to let one's imagination roam a bit and picture the delight of some little girl years ago, when she awoke on Christmas morning to find the beloved Putz, and the pretty tin doll house beneath her tree.

Tin Candlemolds

by DONALD R. and CAROL M. RAYCRAFT

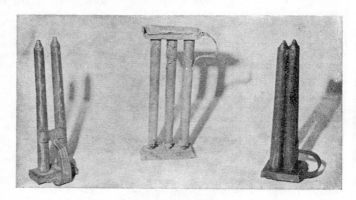

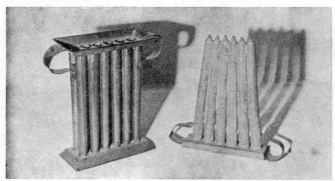

Above: Tin molds with 2, 3 or 4 tubes were used by American house-wives in the early 19th century. Below: A rare 12 tube copper candle-mold; early 19th century. Tin candlemold with an unusual arrangement of its 6 tubes; early 19th century. Authors' collection.

IN HIS definitive study on early lighting devices, Arthur Hayward (3) comments, "candlemolds a few years ago were very plentiful and lightly valued, but the demands of collectors have become so insistent lately as to practically sweep the market here."

Mr. Hayward's statement is familiar to collectors of early lighting, primitives, and country antiques and accessories. The difficulty in acquiring candlemolds is further emphasized when one considers that Hayward's comment was made over 40 years ago. His book, *Colonial Lighting*, was first published in 1923 and a second edition was issued in 1927.

Erwin Christensen (1) writes that "candlemolds tell at a glance how candles were made. It (the candlemold) is purely utilitarian yet extremely attractive." Candlemolds vary greatly in size and shape, ranging from single tube molds to molds containing as many as nine dozen or more tubes. The most common candlemolds contain 4, 6, 8, or 12 tubes. Candlemolds are usually constructed of tin. However, early pine framed pewter molds containing from two to three dozen tubes are available. Candlemolds made of copper are scarce, though much later than the framed pewter molds.

Among the most sought after candlemolds are molds with an odd number of tubes or those with an unusual arrangement of tubes within the mold. Most candlemolds are rectangular in shape. Among collectors the most sought after mold is the rare round candlemold. This mold has the tubes within it arranged in a circular fashion rather than in a rectangular or square pattern. The authors recently witnessed a round 12-tube mold sell for $180 at an auction.

Candles were considered a great luxury in colonial America. A prime request when the colonies were being supplied with British goods was for tallow and candles. The major difficulty in making candles in colonial America was finding a substitute for beef tallow. Cattle were not plentiful in the colonies until the late seventeenth century. Among the several substitutes for the scarce tallow were wax from the honey combs of wild bees and spermaceti.

Spermaceti is a waxy substance obtained from the head of the sperm whale. It was found in a thick, oily form. Whale fat and blubber also

were a source for spermaceti. The spermaceti emerges as a mass of flaky white crystals. As much as 12 to 15 pounds of spermaceti could be gathered from a single sperm whale. Mary Earle Gould (2) writes that "a candle made from spermaceti wax gave as much light as three tallow candles and a flame four times as large." The mid-eighteenth century found a number of Eastern coastal cities with street lights illuminated by spermaceti candles.

Tallow made from fat found near the kidneys of cattle was considered to be of the highest grade for use in making candles. Tallow makers used

A rectangular 36 tube tin mold used in the 19th century by itinerant chandlers or candle-makers who traveled the rural areas selling their wares. Collection Mr. & Mrs. John Curry.

a number of processes to obtain this substance. One common manner was to cut suet (hard, light fat found around the loin and kidney areas of cattle) into small pieces and heat it in large iron pots until the fat melted. It was then dried and the residue pressed until all the tallow was extracted from the tissue.

The most sought after substance for making candles undoubtedly was the bayberry or candleberry. Bayberry candles emit a fragrant aroma when lit, and burn quite slowly with little smoke. Miss Gould reported that bay-

Square 48 tube tin mold of the early 19th century. Some molds were made with as many as 120 tubes. Authors' collection.

berry picking reached such heights that laws were passed prohibiting the picking of the berries before a set date.

In his work, *The Ballad of William Sycamore,* Stephen Vincent Benet touched upon his dying character's lasting memory of early frontier living:

"And some remember a white starched lap,
And a ewer with silver handles,
But I remember a coonskin cap,
And the smell of bayberry candles."

The berry is found growing in clusters on the stem of the bayberry shrub *(Myrica pensylvanica)* which grows along the Atlantic coast and as far west as Louisiana. The berries were carefully picked, slowly boiled, and skimmed repeatedly until the wax took on a light green color. Bayberry candles were used only on special occasions and were expensive when purchased from a traveling candlemaker or chandler. The cost and relative scarcity of bayberry candles was due to the great amount of berries needed to make a single candle. A bushel of berries produces only four

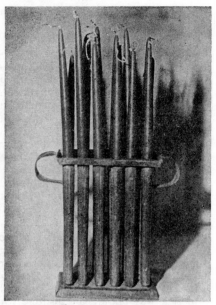

A rare 18 tube tin mold demonstrates its decorative possibilities when used as a candelabra; early 19th century. Authors' collection.

or five pounds of bayberry wax. Scientists today make use of the bark of the bayberry root in making a drug that shrinks tissue.

The productivity of the housewife-candlemaker was highly dependent upon the weather conditions outside her door. The months of September, October, and early November were considered the best time for molding candles. The fall months were advantageous for reasons other than the weather. Normally, cattle were butchered at this time and the tallow was readily available. A single candlemaking day could produce enough candles to light many a dank, dark winter's evening. It was possible for a housewife to make as many as four to five hundred candles in a day if she possessed a number of large molds.

The wicks used in making early candles were usually made from loosely spun cotton. Four to eight strands of the spun cotton were twisted together into a single wick. The greatest difficulty in molding candles was keeping the wicks taut within the tubes of the candlemold.

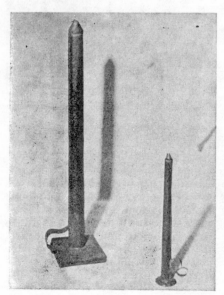

Left: Tin candlemold used to make large altar candles for churches; height 21". Right: Early 19th century single tube tin mold with fluted base; height 9½". Molds with 1, 2 or 3 tubes are more difficult to find. Authors' collection.

After the tallow was poured into the molds it took from a quarter to three-quarters of an hour to harden. When the candles were ready to be taken from the individual tubes the mold was dipped into a tub of hot water. The hot water loosened the tallow on the inside of each tube and the candles emerged from the mold unscathed.

After the candles were removed they were stored in the cellar of the home for from three days to a week. The candles were then stored in wooden, and later tin, candle boxes.

Bibliography

1. Christensen, Erwin. *The Index of American Design.* New York: Mac-Millan Company, 1950, p. 92.
2. Gould, Mary Earle. *Antique Tin and Tole Ware.* Rutland, Vermont: Charles E. Tuttle Company, 1958, p. 104.
3. Hayward, Arthur. *Colonial Lighting.* New York: Dover Publications, 1923 (revised 1962), p. 78.
4. Coffin, Margaret. *History and Folklore of American Country Tinware, 1700-1900.* Camden, N. J.: Thomas Nelson & Sons, 1968.

Hitching Weights

by F. M. GOSLING

FIG. 1

FIG. 2

THE IRON weights shown here were used in lieu of a hitching post or hitching rail in the days of the horse and buggy. A leather strap, approximately 4 feet long, with a snap attached to each end, was fastened to the weight by one of the snaps and the contrivance carried in the buggy. When no other means of tying the horse was available the driver lifted the weight by the strap, placed the weight in front of the horse, and snapped the other end of the strap to the bridle. A driver could leave any well behaved driving horse secured in this fashion and be reasonably sure the rig would be in the same location upon his return.

From time to time someone brings up the question, often with tongue in cheek, as to the correct name for these weights. Included in the answers will be "curb weights," "hitching weights" and "tether weights," not to mention what they were called when accidently dropped on someone's toe.

Perhaps hitching weights would fit them best. A search through 6 old hardware and mail order catalogs showed a listing in only one, a Montgomery Ward & Co. catalog of 1902-1903 in which they appear as "Hitching Weights, 16 lbs. price 50¢."

The top of Figure 1 reads "S H Co./12." Figure 2 bears the wording "N Lansberg & Son."

Oddities in Early American Tinware

by CARROLL HOPF

THE COLLECTOR of antiques has a wide choice from which to make his personal concentration. If, for example, he elects Folk Art as his interest, he may generalize and collect objects in such diverse media as iron, wood, pottery, or glass, or he may specialize in some particular category. The photographs here represent a specialization of artifacts fashioned from tinplate.

Tinwares are made of thin iron sheets coated with tin. The tin retarded rust and provided a bright, easy-to-clean, sanitary surface. By present day standards, the tinplate objects pictured here can be classified as oddities, or at least in the realm of the unusual, when compared to the ordinary everyday

This particular form of ear trumpet is advertised as the "Miss Greene Hearing Horn" in the 1901 Sears, Roebuck & Co. catalog. "Its peculiar formation is especially adapted to gather in sounds and convey them audibly and distinctly to the ear." It has a black japanned finish and measures 18¼" in length. **Collection of Miss M. Carrie.** (Photo by Poist)

The tin shaving mug is probably contemporary with pottery and porcelain examples which also bear an appendage to the side. It is interesting to note the variance in the appendages. Many are in circular shallow bowl form added at the top of the mug; in this form the lather was raised from soap. The other type of appendage, as shown here, was fitted onto the side and extends the height of the mug. This probably served as a storage receptacle for the shaving brush. Measuring 4¼" high and 3¼" diameter, this example dates from the last half of the 19th century. **Penna. Farm Museum Coll.**

utensils fashioned in tin over the years —the pails, dippers, measures, and canisters that were made in abundance.

All of these examples are products of local tinsmiths who, along with various other craftsmen, once formed an important segment of our rural society. In addition to being unusual in form, each piece reflects a high degree of skill and expertise of craftsmanship on the part of its maker.

Good tinware of high quality may still be found on today's antique market. Approximately half of the items illustrated were purchased within the past four years.

"Mr. & Mrs. D. W. Van Auken, From Reform School" is inscribed on the crest rail of this delightful tin chair. A decorative twisted banding is applied to the top of the crest rail, center splat, and around the seat skirt. The chair has never been painted. Probably dating from the last quarter of the 19th century, it has an overall height of 35". **William Penn Memorial Museum Collection, Harrisburg ,Pa.** (Photo by Karl G. Rath)

That our ancestors were a thrifty and saving lot is well attested by this pitcher, mended with a tin handle. The humble repair is ably done and expresses someone's skill as a worker of tinplate. The pitcher is an earthenware type quite common during the middle decades of the 19th century. It is banded in blue and white slip and of English origin; 8" high, 6" diameter. **Penna. Farm Museum Coll.**

Molds for puddings and jellies are found in a multitude of shapes and forms. A collection of the many forms is in itself a very rewarding effort. A horseshoe form, as this example, is probably scarce when compared to the frequency other shapes are found. It is 7½" in length, 7⅜" in width, and 2" deep; dating probably from the last half of the 19th century. **Penna. Farm Museum Coll.**

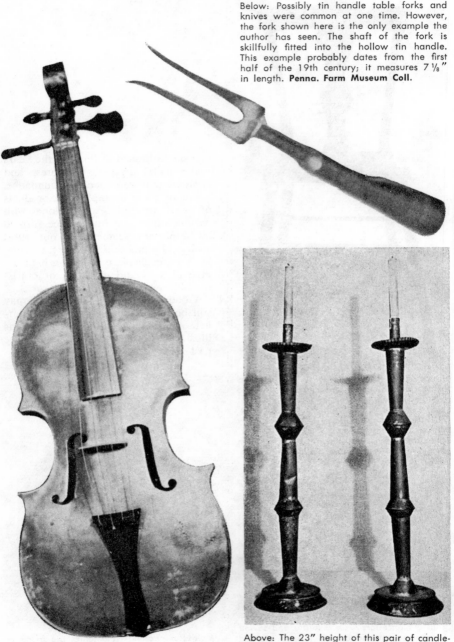

Below: Possibly tin handle table forks and knives were common at one time. However, the fork shown here is the only example the author has seen. The shaft of the fork is skillfully fitted into the hollow tin handle. This example probably dates from the first half of the 19th century; it measures 7 1/8" in length. **Penna. Farm Museum Coll.**

Above : The tonal quality of this tin fiddle is admittedly not as fine as that of a wood fiddle. No pertinent information is known concerning this example—why it was made of tin, where it was made, or by whom. The perfect state of condition attests to its being well cared for through the years. Its length is 22". **Penna. Farm Museum Coll.**

Above: The 23" height of this pair of candlesticks makes one suspect they were made for use in a public building, perhaps a church. A good sense of design and proportion is exhibited in the interesting form of the shafts. The bases are sand filled. Dating from the first half of the 19th century, they were discovered in Berks County, Pennsylvania. **Author's Coll.**

Of early 19th century origin, this bird cage may well have housed a quail, cardinal, robin, or any other bird small enough to fit in it. Completely made by hand, it has a sliding up and down door, two bars of which extend through the top of the cage. It is 13" high; 9" in diameter. It was discovered in central New York state. **Author's Collection.**

Below: Upon several occasions tinplate containers similar to the illustrated examples have been referred to in contemporary writings as "measures." Certainly they may have served this purpose; however, their cylindrical form and side-mounted strap handles at the top are derivative of the drinking mug form used in the latter 18th and early 19th centuries. It may well be that they were used as drinking vessels. Respectively they measure 6" and 9 5/8" high by 4" and 5" diameter. Both probably date before mid-19th century. **Penna. Farm Museum Coll.**

Above: Tin Horns are generally common items. The majority are straight forms measuring anywhere from 12″ to over 4 ft. in length. They were used frequently by coach and stage drivers, peddlers, and on the farm to hail the men in from the fields. This example is unusual for its rectangular form. It emits a powerful one-note tone. Probably dating mid-19th century, it measures 23″ overall length. **Penna. Farm Museum Coll.**

Below: A genuine "Whatsit," this ambiguous looking tin object has puzzled all of the experts we consulted in an attempt to determine its name and use. It consists of two shallow disc-shaped containers connected by two hollow tubes. The larger container, 16¼ inches in diameter, has a screw cap closure, so obviously some kind of liquid was poured into this object; the smaller disc-shaped container has no opening. Its overall length is 26½ inches, and both containers are about 4 inches in depth. The author would welcome any suggestions about its use and origin.

Far right: Tin pipes would seem impractical for smoking tobacco, and it's quite possible that they were actually used by children to blow soap bubbles. Some people believe they were intended as tin anniversary gifts. Certainly very precise workmanship is revealed in its making. The example shown is 7 inches long, and was probably made in the last half of the 19th century.

Right, center: This tin Leader Box originates from the Mohawk Valley in upstate New York, and quite probably from the Fort Plain area.

Applied crimped banding and a star motif add extra interest to the overall form. There was at one time a quarter moon applied next to the star.

Leader Boxes originally served the functional purpose of connecting house gutters to downspouts. Their use explains why so few are found today; many have rusted to pieces right on the houses. This example probably dates from the second quarter of the 19th century. It measures 22″ high. **Privately owned.**

Left below: A tin kerosene lamp, circa 1870, exhibits construction features found in earlier whale oil and fluid burning lamps. Notably the sand filled base and the conical shape reservoir are reminiscent of earlier lamp forms. We cannot dismiss the idea that this lamp may have been converted from whale oil to kerosene. It stands 12″ high and measures 4¼″ in diameter around the base. **Penna. Farm Museum Coll.**

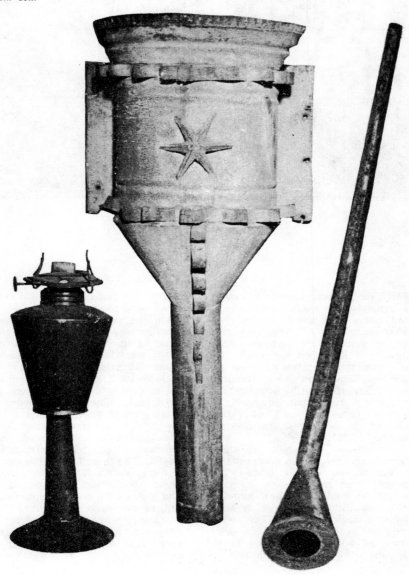

Kitchen Tinware

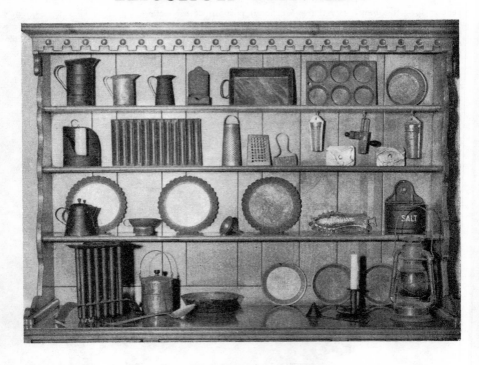

by LOUISE K. LANTZ

THE early nineteenth century cook, accustomed to kitchenware of cumbersome iron and heavy pottery, welcomed the advent of the tin-plated iron or steel called tinware. Quite literally, it lightened her work; today's thin weight products were beyond imagining. The tinware pictured here, from the author's collection, embraces a time span of nearly a hundred years, from hand-crafted pieces of the early 1800s to patented gadgets of 1911.

First on the top shelf are three sizes of measures, handmade, probably by the master of the house. The hanging wall match safe, so convenient to hold the many matches needed for oil lamps and coal or wood stoves, is factory made. These were produced in quantity and in wide variety of designs. Next are a heavy single-handled early bread pan, a muffin tin patented in 1874, and a small deep pie pan.

On the second shelf is a shielded candleholder, home-crafted, to be hung by its brass ring, or set solidly on its wide base. The breadstick pan makes 12 sticks; others may make 6, 8, or 10. The handled round vegetable grater is hand-punched, probably early nineteenth century; the factory-made grater beside it is of the same period. The handled chopper with corrugated blade is one of six different shapes in the author's collection. The three hanging graters are nutmeg graters. The center one, with wood knobs, was patented in 1896 and guaranteed not to "clog, tear the fingers, nor drop the nutmeg." (The nutmeg is held tight to the grater by a spring on the side, and is grated very fine, distributed evenly and entirely, leaving no waste.) The backed cookie cutters, in shape of duck and fish, are handmade. Many other intriguing shapes are to be found, with a hole or two for poking out the cut cookie.

The third shelf boasts three fluted-rim cake pans; a small coffee pot with heavy copper bottom; a funnel for filling canning jars; a smaller funnel advertising C. D. Kenny Co. (an old Maryland grocer); a fish-shaped aspic mold; and a hanging salt box.

Bottom Shelf

On the bottom shelf is a graceful 12-hole candlemold, from the collection of Mary Keefer. Next come a covered, bail-handled lard pail, and a deep heavy cake pan with tapering sides, sometimes called a corn pone pan. A well used stirring spoon is in front. The first of the three pie pans advertises the Baltimore Pie Bakery, last listed in City directories in 1911. In front is a tin candleholder, with an extinguisher near by, and a Dietz lantern. The lantern, commonly used outdoors and in the barn, was often handily hung by the kitchen door.

Other interesting old tin-plated kitchen articles to be found without great difficulty are tart and patty pans, tube cake pans, japanned bread boxes, rotary flour sifters, egg beaters, dippers, colanders, scoops, serrated-edge bread knives, spatulas, drip pans, doughnut cutters, fruit and vegetable presses, even dustpans!

The molds here pictured may be characterized as follows: *Top row:* **Geometrical,** swirl, cornear and pineapple, from J. & C. Berrian, c. 1848. The high molds are for ice cream. *Center row:* Lion top, fig cluster, ice cream column and sheaf of wheat. *Bottom:* Rose, pineapple, and grape molds. All the large molds here pictured are jelly molds, said to have been either imported or made by Stoughtenbaugh of Brooklyn, N.Y., mid-19th century. Actually, Yarnall of Philadelphia was selling the same type of molds in the 1840's.

Primitive Tin Graters and Strainers

Above: The two types are positioned for grating. *At left:* Reversed for use as strainers.

Two types of strainer-graters. One is box-like with pierced tin bottom; the other is a piece of pierced tin set in a plank.

by EDWIN C. WHITTEMORE

TWO OR three hundred years ago, household utensils in most of America were made of iron, pewter, or earthenware. Iron was heavy and brittle, and it rusted. Pewter was heavy and dentable, and it melted. Earthenware was bulky and heavy, and it broke. They were not ideal materials for items to be given hard use, in contact with cold liquids and hot fires.

It is easy to see why "tinware" was accepted so quickly, and became popular so very fast. Actually, the term "tinware" is a misnomer, for tinware, as we know it, is actually sheet iron on which layers of tin have been deposited. Often 85 percent of the total content is iron.

Tinware was developed in Germany in the 1500s, moved quickly to the British Isles where there were both rolling mills and a supply of tin ore. In England, tinplate, and tinware items made from it, were produced in the early 1600s. In the early 1700s, the American colonies started importing both finished tinware items and the rolled tinplate sheets from which to fabricate household utensils.

Tinware actually did not need much of a push for housewives accepted it willingly. It was shiny and sparkling, the "poor man's silver." It was light; it stood heat; it could easily be fashioned into many types of items. It was relatively inexpensive; it did not crack or melt; it resisted rust, and could easily be mended by soldering.

The special category of "pierced tin" housewares is one of the most interesting in the tinware field. Immediately we think of pie safes with pierced tin panels, foot warmers, lanterns, graters, colanders, and related items.

Usually the tinplate was pierced before the item was assembled. A sheet of tinplate of the required size was cut from a flat sheet and placed, still flat, on a suitable surface, such as a sheet of lead, a pine plank, or even hard wet sand, packed solid. Then, with a hammer and nail, or better, a hammer and sharp edged chisel, the worker pierced the sheet in various designs, simple or intricate.

If a nail was being used and hit-or-miss designs employed, the result was most varied. With a more skillful artisan, using a sharp chisel, the result could be quite delightful. Most often the piercings were slots or dots, but with special cutters, other design elements were incorporated, such as stars, half moons, and crosses. Related to piercing was the simpler "embossing," where patterns were accomplished without cutting completely through the tin.

Piercing was done in the tinplate for functional reasons as well as for design. In lighting devices such as lanterns, it let oxygen in, heat and smoke out. In graters, the rough side became the work side, the rough edges of the pierced holes doing the grating. As a strainer, the smooth side was a practical workable surface which provided drainage.

We show here two examples of an ingenious household device depending on pierced tinplate—the combination grater-strainer. Both sides of the tinplate are functional in the same piece. In the boxlike example, a sheet of pierced tinplate covers one whole side. Placed with the rough side up, it serves as an excellent grater for cabbage, carrots, and potatoes when they are being grated to make coleslaw, to color butter, and in making starch. Turned to the other side, it becomes an excellent strainer or colander of good capacity for washing vegetables and such.

The other example, made from a plank, is identical in function, but with smaller capacity, and probably represents a buried improvisation.

These combination grater-strainers are very collectible. They may be used for their original purpose, or simply hung on the wall for decorative effect. They may be wired with a low-wattage bulb to give a soft and patterned light in a special location, such as a hall or infant's room. They represent an interesting group of the "practical primitives" which are becoming more and more popular with collectors.

Tenth Wedding Anniversary Tinwares

by GLADYS REID HOLTON

Tin fans fashioned for 10th anniversary gifts. The larger is 17" long overall, 12 5/8" in diameter; the smaller, 8" in diameter has a 15" long chain attached to the handle, designed to be hooked to milady's belt. Both fans show signs of use.

THE CUSTOM of "celebrating wedding anniversaries has of late years been largely practiced," wrote John H. Young in 1881 in *Our Deportment, On the Manners, Conduct and Dress of the Most Refined Society, Compiled from the latest reliable Authorities.* "They have become a very pleasant means of social reunion among the relatives and friends of both husband and wife. Often this is the only reason for celebrating them and the occasion is sometimes taken advantage of to give a large party of a more informal nature than could be given under other circumstances. The occasion becomes one of the memorable events in the life of the couple whose wedding anniversary is celebrated. It is an occasion for recalling the happy event which brought to each a new existence and changed the current of their lives. It is an occasion for them to receive congratulations upon their past married life and wishes for many additional years of wedded bliss. Upon this occasion the married couple sometimes appear in the costumes worn by them on their wedding day."

Ten years later, in 1891, Richard A. Wells, in *Culture and Dress of the Best Society,* was still extolling the celebration of wedding anniversaries as "one of the pleasant customs which is coming into general favor," and adds, "Special anniversaries are designated by special names indicating the presents suitable for each occasion."

For the tenth anniversary, designated as "Tin," he suggested: "The invitations for this anniversary may be made upon cards covered with tin foil or upon the ordinary wedding note paper with a tin card enclosed. Those guests who desire to accompany their congratulations with appropriate presents have the whole list of articles manufactured by the tinner from which to select.

"A general frolic is in order at the tin wedding. It is an occasion for getting together old friends after 10 years of married life. Gifts are usually in the form of kitchen utensils—tin candlesticks, tin fans, tin ornaments, even tin tables and chairs are offered as gifts. These cause much merriment as well as showing the ingenuity of the giver."

Today's 10th wedding celebration would be exciting if Mexican tinware were used for table settings and decorations.

Tin has been a valued metal since ancient times. The early Egyptians sought sources for tin in countries outside their borders. The inhabitants of Mesopotamia obtained their supply from mountains in the northern part of their own land. As the world widened, deposits of tin were found in the Balkans, Bohemia, Brittany, and northern Spain. Tin was found in England, in Cornwall, and some historians believe this was one of the

Folding fan, with 12 10-inch sticks and two guards of pricked tin, including the letter "B" in the design; mount of paper with watercolor paintings of two sailing ships.

Left: Tin flower vase, 8 ⅞" tall, 3 ½" diameter at top and base. Right: Tin bouquet or posy holder for carrying a corsage, 6 ½" long, 1 ¾" at the opening.

primary reasons the early Romans invaded and occupied that land.

In those early days tin was used primarily in the manufacture of bronze. By 2000 B.C. it was being smelted and refined, and eventually bars of more or less pure tin replaced raw tin ore as a trades goods.

In colonial America before there were rolling mills, sheet tin was imported from England. Sheet tin was made principally of iron, therefore subject to rust and corrosion. To preserve the metal, tinsmiths and dec-

Marshall of Philadelphia advertised that he "produced plain, painted, japanned, and planish tinware." (Planishing is the light hammering of metal to produce a smooth surface.) In 1832, 11 shops in Stevens Plain, Maine, produced a total of $27,300 worth of tinware. Soon enough tinwares became "everyday common."

By the 1880s and 1890s when articles of tin were decreed as 10th wedding anniversary gifts, donors

Lined tin jewel box, 4 ½ x 3 ½ ", 1 ¾ " deep.

Dressy tin comb for the hair, 6" long overall, 6" wide.

orators of tinwares painted their goods or used a finish known as "japanning," a technique which had come to America from the East via England. Japanning was achieved by applying several coats of asphaltum over the surface of the bright tin. One coat produced a thin, transparent, light-brown finish; additional coats resulted in a darker, more opaque finish.

Connecticut was one of the early centers for the training of tinsmiths. As the supply of tinplate increased, larger quantities of tinware were produced. On April 27, 1767, Benjamin

went to great lengths to provide something "different," and ingenious tinsmiths seemed never to run out of ideas for fanciful handmade remembrances to "cause merriment."

Wedding Anniversaries

1st — Paper	7th — Woolen
2nd — Cotton	10th — Tin
3rd — Leather	15th — Crystal
4th — Books	20th — China
5th — Wood	25th — Silver
6th — Candy	50th — Gold
60th — Diamonds	

Painted Tinware, Pontypool, and Painted Toleware

by CARL DREPPERD

Pair of Directoire, painted tole jardinieres, in green and gold. Date is c. 1795, or perhaps as early as 1785. The square bases are marbleized, the flaring quadrangular vase-form painted with griffons, torches, and vine in gold. Between the jardinieres, a pair of scalloped edge plant pans of Charles X period, c. 1825.—Illustrations courtesy of Parke-Bernet Galleries.

Many Collectors have been Confused, and Understandably So, Over the Accurate Nomenclature for Some Collectibles. To Clarify One Group Which has Long Suffered Misnomers, Here is the Actual Difference Between . . .

SOME months ago a commentator on things antique in a Metropolitan paper referred to common painted tinware as toleware. "The peddler's gift to collectors" was his phrase. This writer had confused the term "tole-ware" with "tinware," an error in nomenclature all too prevalent, but which in essence is comparable to confusing Dresden with Nippon, or Chippendale with Hitchcock. Like many other and more grievous errors in print this one, perhaps, was only a reflection of the error in the minds of most collectors in respect of the meaning of painted tin, and toleware.

Tole is a French word meaning *sheet iron* or, *plate of steel*. An item of tole is nothing more or less than an item made from sheet iron or sheet steel. If the item is tin plated, it is to be characterized as *tinned tole,* or *tin-plated tole*. If the item is painted and decorated, it is *painted tole*. Since it is *painted tole* that is almost invariably meant when the term toleware is used, it would be well, first to study the genesis of this ware.

Painted tole is the result of an effort to make a decorative, non-breakable ware imitative of enameled ware (enamel on copper or some other metal, as Cloisonne, or Limoges) and comparable to fine ceramics. Some of the finest examples were made during the age of its beginnings, the period of Louis XV. The objects made ranged in size from the minute to the gigantic; from snuff box to bath tub! Lamps, bowls, lavabos, candlesticks, boxes, trays, table tops, painted by the most accomplished fine artists of that day were made of sheet iron for the Royal, the Noble and the wealthy. The high place popularity of *painted tole* continued through the century 1750–1850. And so we find examples reflecting the styles of Louis XV, Louis XVI, the Directoire, The Empire, Charles X and Louis Phillipe. The painted tole of the last period was of course of Louis XV revival style; the style we call Victorian. It should be remembered for all time that painted tole was a luxury item. The sheet iron itself was cheap. Its fabrication into objects was the work of master smiths. Its painting, after the coating with many layers of ground, carefully rubbed and baked, was by artists like Louis David and Virgie Le Brun. It was sold in the Rue de la Paix . . . but never vended by peddlers. Of that we may be certain.

Pontypool ware is the English equivalent of painted tole. Pontypool is a town in Wales where iron was wrought into sheets and finally rolled. Here, also, sheet iron was first plated with tin by application of the molten silvery metal. But Pontypool ware could be either plain sheet iron, or tinned sheet iron in its first phase of being. What made it a ware rich and rare was its painting by accomplished artists of the stature of Angelica Kauffman, and Francesco Bartollozzi. Pontypool ware attained high vogue in England during the great classic revival staged by the Brothers Adam. It, too, was luxury ware of high price. Again, we may be sure, it was never peddled by itinerant vendors. Was it sold in the American Colonies? Was Painted Tole known and enjoyed here? Indeed yes. But in the homes of Royal governors and the mansions of the rich and well-to-do. No lane and by-way peddler ever had it for sale.

Painted tinware was the cheap imitation of painted tole and Pontypool. There is no cause for wonder about this. The imitation of luxuries, as cheap products, was a phenomenon in every field. Even the highly prized silver lustre ware of this day—as an antique—was once nothing more than the cheapest of imitation silver. In the case of painted tinware, (meaning painted tinplated sheet iron objects, or even untinned sheet iron) the imitation got cheaper and cheaper; the painting less and less imitative of painted tole and Pontypool. Finally it became a matter of quick striping and slap-dash. Yellow ochre took the place of gilding; the palette shrunk to black, green, yellow, red and blue.

As the cost of production dropped to pennies per object, this painted tin became a peddler's stock in trade, along with unpainted, tinned sheet iron ware and utensils. Since the peddlers wares when painted cost a bit more than plain tinned wares, resourceful people bought the plain and painted it themselves. Some of this ware is quite well painted. And now, to pile error upon error, some people call this home painted tinned sheet ironware folk art!

For those who desire to be fairly precise in their use of terms, these simple definitions should be helpful:

Painted tole, or toleware: To be applied only to French, fine painted sheet iron wares made as luxury items.

Pontypool ware, or Pontypool: To be applied only to English, fine painted sheet iron wares made as luxury items.

Painted tinware: To be applied only to cheap or good painted, tinned or plain sheet iron wares made for popular sale, or home painted.

Japanned in America

by JOHN C. VITALE

Among the more desirable items in japanned tinware are "Coffin" trays, which derive their macabre name from the shape of contemporary caskets. Top: Japanned Coffin tray with gilt decoration. Bottom: Japanned Coffin tray with Chinoiserie decoration in reds and browns on a bottle-green ground; border in gilt. Both ca. 1830. (Courtesy Cleveland Public Library.)

ALTHOUGH the early New England Yankee is frequently accused of having been exceptionally "Puritan" in his tastes, one of the first crafts to take root in the American Colonies was the highly decorative art of japanning. Consequently, today, during the period of rising interest in American culture, the term —*Japanned in America*—has become extremely popular. It describes a golden moment in the broad cultural panorama of American folk art.

Japanning, like so many early American art forms, first became popular in England. During the 18th century trade with the Orient was flourishing, and the English tea merchants, ever alert for a new item to lure the public, brought back a wealth of elaborately lacquered tea chests and metal trays from the mysterious Orient. Impressed by the beauty of the designs, English craftsmen immediately began imitating these wares. Instead of painstakingly applying countless layers of lacquer—as was the custom in the Orient—the English craftsmen speeded up the process by using an asphaltum varnish solution that could be applied in one layer. When heated, the asphaltum dried to a brownish-black, partially transparent and similar in tone to the Oriental lacquer.

In Pontypool and Birmingham, where the new craft first took hold, the term "japanning" was used to identify the art, stemming from the fact that these imitations looked as if they had been "made in Japan."

When it was introduced in America, "japanned" articles won instant favor. Those who could afford the luxury of imported japanned tinware welcomed the highly decorative pieces with their romantic Chinoiserie motifs. For a moment in history, the japanned tinware helped the New England housewife escape from her cocoon of innocence and isolation.

So popular was japanned tinware in the Colonies that the craft was destined to find a home in America. Boston became the first center for America's japanners with nine industrious craftsmen working at this trade. Such cities as Salem, Newport, and New York all had at least one japanner working in the area.

One of the earliest and most skilled japanners in Boston was Nehemiah Partridge. During the 18th century, when it was customary to practice more than one trade simultaneously. Partridge operated a small apothecary shop in "Treamount" Street and practiced the relatively new art of japanning as a side line. In 1713 he announced in the Boston *News Letter* that he did "all types of japanning at reasonable rates." For years, Partridge, and his contemporaries in Boston—Ambrose Vincent, Joshua Roberts, Stephan Whiting, and Robert Davis—supplied the needs of the local housewife.

Unfortunately the art of japanning was a slow and laborious process, and each article had to be carefully prepared, then baked; two or three coats of asphaltum were often required to achieve an opaque and almost black effect. Consequently, although a constant market was available to the japanner, many died insolvent.

Despite the fact that japanning was far from a lucrative trade in early New England, its popularity continued to gain momentum. Many gentlewomen, charmed by the delightful qualities of japanned tinware and furniture, desired to learn the craft. To satisfy this need, teachers of the art came forward. One such teacher was Joseph Waghorne.

Long recognized as a skilled japanner in both England and Colonial America, Waghorne announced in the Boston *Gazette* in 1739 that he "would teach Ladies to Japan in the newest Method invented for that Purpose, which exceeds all other Japanning for Beauty." When sufficient interest had been aroused among the young ladies of Boston, the dashing Waghorne opened a school for japanning on Queen Street. Each of the artistic "scholars" were charged the sum of £5.

With the continued interest in the art of japanning it was inevitable that the craft would develop into a large scale business of manufacturing. The man destined to accomplish this goal was Edward Patterson. Patterson, a Scotch-Irish imigrant, who arrived in town with 18 cents, opened a factory for japanning tinware at Berlin, Connecticut in 1770. Long before, however, Patterson—aided by his brother William and his sister Anna—had begun working imported sheets of tin into cooking utensils at home, using wooden mallets. They first accumulated a stock, then sold it from door to door in Berlin and near-by settlements, carrying their wares on their backs.

Upon opening his factory, Patterson employed local women skilled in the craft. Although far from being as capable of matching the skilled work of the Oriental craftsmen, these women developed a forthright style of painting using both freehand methods and stenciling. Dynamic brush strokes and the use of bold primary colors became their identifying trade marks. The technique of japanning employed by Patterson's skilled women was basically simple. They began by working out designs in gold-leaf patterns. Next the design was painted in with clear varnish, or with lamp black and gold size. Baking the decoration to a hard finish was the last step.

Patterson's output of tea trays, pans, kettles, and every other kind of household tinware was prolific, but it was not until much later that mass production methods entered the field of decorated tinware. This feat was reserved by chance for Oliver Filley of Bloomfield, Connecticut.

Like Patterson, the industrious Filley began his career as a tinsmith and part time peddler. He was acquainted with everyone connected with the metal industry in the state of Connecticut. When the opportunity presented itself, he bought the patent rights to a machine designed for working tin. The price was $20. With such a machine at his disposal Filley's production of tinware far surpassed that of Edward Patterson. In a steady and endless stream, trays, toys, and a vast assortment of small, decorated tinwares poured from the Filley factory. All were charmingly japanned in bright colors.

Because of Filley's tremendous output it became necessary to find new markets for japanned tinware. To accomplish this the Yankee peddler was called into service. Known commonly as "Sam Slick from Pumpkin Creek," the walking peddler began carrying japanned tinware into the deepest parts of New England. Within a few years japanned wares became the fastest moving commodity carried by the Yankee peddler. Soon the names of Patterson and Filley were known far and wide. Consequently, the mark which they and the scores of other lesser lights in the field of japanning left upon the American scene was a lasting one.

Fig. I

Fig. 2

Fig. 3

20th Century Childrens' Tins

by ERNEST L. PETTIT

AS SOON AS machinery to make tin cans was developed, between 1860–70—up to then they had been made tediously by hand—other tin containers, especially for food stuffs, came on the scene. Merchandisers discovered early that art work on the new tins helped sell the product they contained; that decorated containers had special appeal to children— youngsters like to play with them, keep little trinkets in them, gather berries in them, or use them for lunch boxes; and that what children clamored for, parents usually bought.

As new techniques in printing and stamping appeared, designs and decorations in tin containers advanced. A young visitor at the 1876 Centennial Exposition in Philadelphia might have spent his pennies for a half-pint tin pail of peanut butter, undecorated except for the embossed lettering which identified both the product and the place of purchase. By the 1890s, boys and girls were begging for the gay tin Schepps Cocoanut can, printed in glowing colors with a monkey-in-the-jungle scene. Since the bright tin was advertising on the grocer's shelf, the name of the product or its maker was never omitted in its decoration. Sometimes the can maker's name appeared in tiny letters close to the top or bottom rim. Without this line, exact identification of the tin maker is impossible.

Gradually pasteboard packaging took over, and fewer products were put out in tins. The many small factories which had been engaged in making or printing tins for local areas went out of business or were absorbed by larger companies.

Early tins for children are delightful to own, but not particularly easy to find today. The colorful tin containers manufactured in the first half of this century are more plentiful. Though less distinctive, being quantity-made, they can add time-span to a collection of earlier examples or form the nucleus for an engaging "late" collection.

Fig. 4

The six tins pictured here, designed specifically for children, encompass the period from 1900 to 1944. Not all of these were made to hold a specific product. Produced in quantity by large companies, they went to stores which either filled them from stock, usually with confections of some sort, or sold them empty for Santa Claus or the Easter Bunny to fill at home.

Fig. 5

Key to Illustrations

Fig. 1—Armour's VERIBEST Peanut Butter came in this pail-type tin featuring a bail handle. The lettering in blue and white; the Mother Goose characters are in natural colors; the background is orange. It is $3\frac{1}{4}$ inches high, $10\frac{1}{4}$ inches in circumference, and was manufactured by the Continental Can Company of Chicago, Illinois, ca. 1900.

Fig. 2—This octagon-shaped box, $2\frac{1}{4}$ inches high, $5\frac{1}{2}$ inches long, and $4\frac{1}{4}$ inches wide, is illustrated on the top and sides with the story of The Three Little Pigs. The background shades from pink on the edges to white, with the figures in natural colors. It was made in Mansfield, England, by the Metal Box Company, Ltd. (B. W. & M. Branch), ca. 1930.

The forerunner of this company was established in the 1890s, and was known as the metal box making firm of Barringer, Wallis & Manners. In 1921, the union of this firm with Barclay & Fry and Hudson Scott produced the Allied Tin Box Makers, Ltd. In 1922, the firm name was changed to The Metal Box & Printing Industries. In 1930, the company be-

Fig. 6

came the Metal Box Company Ltd., and as such exists today.

Fig. 3—Oval in shape, this box is entitled on the cover "Peter Rabbit on Parade." In natural color, Peter Rabbit and his friends—Unc' Bill Possum, Herry Hop Frog, Sally Sparrow, Happy Jack Squirrel, and others —march around the sides of the tin. This box, 2¼ inches high, 12½ inches in circumference, was made by the Continental Can Company and carries the trade name of TINDECO.

Originally TINDECO was the trademark for the Tin Decorating Company of Baltimore, Maryland, a company owned by the American Tobacco Company for many years, and which manufactured tins for the packaging of that company's tobacco. When the American Tobacco Company sold TINDECO to Owens Illinois Glass Corporation, it became the Owens Illinois Can Company, a subsidiary of the glass corporation. In 1944 Owens Illinois Can Company (TINDECO) was sold to the Continental Can Company and is now Plant No. 9 of that corporation. The trademark TINDECO is no longer in use on its containers.

Figs. 4 and 5—Both of these are rectangular in shape, 2¼ inches high, 4½ inches long, 2½ inches wide. Both are Christmas tins and feature a carrying handle. *Fig. 4* has a red background with "Merry Christmas from Santa" printed on the cover. The Mother Goose characters are pictured in natural colors. Scenes on the sides are encircled by holly wreaths.

Fig. 5 has a blue background with "Twas the night before Christmas" printed on the lid. The front panel shows Santa arriving; the top has him climbing down the chimney; and the back pictures a fireplace with stockings hung waiting to receive him. Both of these could have been purchased with or without contents. Each has the trademark TINDECO stamped in the bottom panel. I am of the opinion these were made by the Owens Illinois Can Company, ca. 1930–40.

Fig. 6—This Circus Club Mallows tin is cylindrical in shape, 7 inches high, 9¼ inches in circumference. The caricature represents a circus baboon. He is attired in a bright yellow jacket, brown pants, red vest, white shirt with blue stripes, and a green necktie. The pull-off lid is his sporty yellow hat. There may have been similar tins made to represent other animals of the circus world. The Whittal Can Co. (non-existent since about 1930) made this tin, which originally held marshmallows, for the Harry Horne Company Limited (now Harry Horne Limited) of Toronto, Canada.

English Biscuit Tins

by HELEN McGOLDRICK

Fig. 1: *Bird's Nest* was enormously successful in 1908.

Fig. 2: *Golf Bag* celebrated the advent of women on the golf course.

> Webster lists *"Bis'cuit. 1. A kind of unraised bread, plain, sweet or fancy, formed into flat cakes and baked hard; commonly called 'cracker' in the United States."*

WHEN THE PRESTIGIOUS Victoria & Albert Museum in London sponsored a show of biscuit tins last Christmas, the imprimatur was finally put on this distinctive English manufacture as an important collectible in the decorative field. The 200 tins in that exhibition are a tiny portion of a collection that goes into the several thousands gathered and owned by an Anglo-American who wishes to remain anonymous.

Much of the information on biscuit tins—who designed them, how rights to them were reserved, etc., has been lost. Many of the biscuit companies have been subject to "take-overs" within the last five years, and records, along with thousands of old tins, have been destroyed in these amalgamations. So, as interest was growing in this country in biscuit tins as col-

Fig. 3: Two of a large selection of bags that appeared over the years; *Fishing Creel* (left) and *Satchel* (right).

lectibles, the records of the names, dates, designers, quantities, etc., were being destroyed by the biscuit manufacturers themselves for "lack of space to house them."

Happily, the anonymous gentleman who owns the enormous collection has many of the facts in his files, among the most important being the proper names and dates of thousands of tins. Unwilling himself to capitalize on his collection, he has been most generous with time and information to make this article possible. His hope is that new collectors will interest themselves in the ways in which both the graphic design and the shapes of the tins reflected the artistic styles and the times in which they were issued.

Perhaps it all began back in the 1830s, when Thomas Huntley, a baker, offered his biscuits and buns to the passengers on the Bath to London coach when it stopped at the Crown Inn in Reading. So good were his wares, that travelers frequently wrote back asking that he send biscuits to them in other cities. To accommodate them, Thomas called on his brother, Joseph Huntley, a tinsmith and ironmonger, to make boxes in which the biscuits might be sent safely.

From this beginning grew two large fortunes and two world-famous businesses. Thomas' bakery became Huntley and Palmer; Joseph's tins turned into Huntley, Bourne and Stevens, tin box makers.

Actually, other manufacturers had

Fig. 4: *Bluebird* resembles a caricature and is actually more green than blue with a large red beak.

begun to sell their products in tins, and these boxes, whether for biscuits, tea, sugar, or whatever, had paper labels. In some cases a tin metal label was soldered on, but biscuits universally came with paper labels. As paper labels were often damaged by dampness, by rough handling on long journeys, or in the stores, the need was for a permanent way of indicating their contents.

In 1868 the joint efforts of the companies started by Thomas and Joseph Huntley achieved a milestone in packaging by introducing the first transfer printed tin (*Figure 8*). The process used was one patented by Ben George (Benjamin George George) of Hatton Garden. The design was by Owen Jones, an influential architect and designer of the time, who had a retainer from Huntley and Palmer for doing display cases and other design elements for their business. His first landmark tin had a design of arabesques and carried for the first time the Royal Warrant "By appointment to her Majesty the Queen." It is done in red, blue, and green.

Despite this great step in the elimination of paper labels, transfer printing could also suffer in shipping from serious movement of the cargo. Several years later, Barclay & Fry invented a direct method of printing on tin by offset lithography. Within another five years tins could be embossed and decorated with great elaboration. (Despite these advances, some paper

Fig. 5: *Greuze Tea Caddy* is one of many designs using famous paintings as a theme, in this instance Jean Baptiste Greuze's "Milkmaid" from the Louvre's collection.

labels were used well into the 20th century.)

From then on English biscuit tins had two purposes. The first, of course, was to protect the contents in shipping; the second, to lend both a decorative note to the furnishings of a home and a practical note since the empty containers could be used for

Fig. 6 , left: *Book* was copied from a 1704 edition of "Het Boek Der Gebede" in the British Museum's collection. **Right:** *Literature* was a single tin simulating eight books; such fake books were extremely popular in homes that contained only one real book—the family Bible.

Fig. 7: The romance of the rose covered *Log Cabin* and *Windmill* appealed to all but the sophisticate.

something other than biscuits. As years went on they served as sewing boxes, substitutes for clocks, candlesticks, picture frames, mantel ornaments, vases, fruit bowls, mirrors, toys and games, and repositories for all sorts of items.

Tins came in the form of Sevres vases, Louis XVI caskets, clock and candelabra sets, golf bags, cottages, windmills, binocular cases, handbags, fishing creels, false books, stacks of plates, and birds. They reflected the changing tastes of the times—from Owen Jones' opening arabesque through Chinese and Japanese motifs, Chippendale, the romanticism of Indian and Eastern settings, Art Nouveau, and Art Deco—with an overwhelming interest in the activities of the Royal family.

By the 1880s the tins could be shaped, embossed, and colored in elaborate style. In the 1880s and 1890s they became very elaborate, very ornate, and designs tended to be themes of current events, fashions, in a sense, of the year. There was no limit to the digressions from the cube or square permitted the unsung designers who worked for the tin manufacturers.

Generally speaking the tins are most interesting graphically and for their elaborate decoration up to 1900. Then began the period of imitating life. Tins looked like everything they were not. After World War I they began to be utilitarian; toys like "Perambulator" (*Figure 9*) or "Kitchen Range" for little girls; games such as Peek Frean's "Cocoanut Shies." Huntley & Palmer put out handkerchief boxes and an egg-stand in 1928. (Interestingly, only two designers' names are known out of the thousands of tins designed over this 60-year period, Owen Jones, and then, 60 years later, Mabel Lucie Atwell, the well-known English artist who worked under commission for Crawford & Sons in the 1930s.)

Biscuit tins were sold most widely during the Christmas season; being a double gift of food and an attractive container. They were largely bought as gifts by the middle economic class. The so-called Great Houses never had them; they were too small for the great quantities needed in such large households. Catalogs for the tins came out once a year—sent to the retailer by the biscuit company. (The biscuit company bought from the tin box maker.) The retailer chose the tins he santed and also specified the filling he desired in each tin.

The "Specialty" tin was the largest one offered. Then there were "Juveniles." This refers to size of tin, rather than to subject of design, and they were designated Juvenile 1, 2, 3, and 4. Miniature tins were made filled with "mechanical" biscuits, molded in shape, similar to animal crackers. Commemorative flat miniatures celebrated Royal weddings, birthdays, and Queen Victoria's Jubilee. The Lusitania, celebrated as a giant step forward in ship building, appeared in a miniature. The British Empire Exhibition of 1924, the Wormley Exhibition of 1924, the Prince of Wales' visit to India in 1920, the State Coach tin of Jacobs in 1937, the coronation of George VI and Elizabeth, the Silver Jubilee of George and Mary, the Exposition tin of 1900 of Huntley and Palmer, and the coronation tins for Edward in 1902, all were represented.

One of the most unusual tins is a miniature put out by Huntley and Palmer for the Paris Opera, containing a picture of the Opera on the tin. It was sold in the lobby of the Opera House and never anywhere else.

At the height of the craze for biscuit tins there were some 60 com-

Fig.10:*Grandfather Clock* is a very nice imitation in tin of much admired Chinese lacquered furniture; painted in black and gold with some little highlights of green and blue.

Fig. 8, right: The milestone tins issued in 1886 by Huntley & Palmer, the first to appear without a paper label and the first to carry the Royal Warrant. **Far left:** *Fireside* is decorated on four sides and the cover with Kate Greenaway figures.

Fig. 9: *Perambulator* with red haired baby appealed to grand-mothers and children alike.

panies actually making biscuits, but there were 125 companies selling biscuits under their own name. The tin makers had competition for their wares and the most prestigious company would have the novel tin first. When they relinquished it, the rights would be sold to a second company. Thus the same tin could be used by many different companies. The famous little red trunks, for instance, were sold by 12 different manufacturers at various times, and we know that tea and sugar cubes were also sold in that same tin! The Sun Dial, used by Huntley and Palmer in 1893, was being used as late as 1928 by William Crawford & Sons.

Titles of tins would also reappear. For instance, the "Pheasant" was used in 1890 and again in the 1930s. Every tin has a correct title. Throughout decades of tin box manufacture, reproductions of famous paintings, reflecting the tastes of the period, were used.

By the 1930s the spiralling costs of manufacture caused the containers to be restrained in shape and design, and their appeal now rests in the gay colors and the wide range of subjects pictured on them.

Some notable tins, easily identified, with dates they were first issued:

Fireside (*Fig. 8*)—Huntley & Palmer, 1890

Polo (Polo and four other sports)—Huntley & Palmer, 1890

Carriage Clock—MacFarlane & Lang, 1899

Library—Huntley & Palmer, 1900

Literature (*Fig. 6*)—Huntley & Palmer, 1901

Picture Frame—MacKenzie & MacKenzie, 1903

Bagatelle (a game)—Jacobs, 1904

Plates—Huntley & Palmer, 1906

Bird's Nest (*Fig. 1*)—Maker unknown, 1908

Satchel (*Fig. 3*)—Maker unknown, 1908

Log Cabin (*Fig. 7*)—S. Henderson & Sons, 1910

Blue Bird (*Fig. 4*)—McVitie & Price, 1911

Golf Bag (*Fig. 2*)—Maker unknown, 1913

Camera (box type Brownie)—Maker unknown, 1913

Book (*Fig. 6*)—Huntley & Palmer, 1920

Windmill (*Fig. 7*)—Huntley & Palmer, 1924

Kitchen Range—Maker unknown, 1926

Egg Stand—Huntley & Palmer, 1928

Grandfather Clock (*Fig. 10*)—Huntley & Palmer, 1929

Perambulator (*Fig. 9*)—Huntley & Palmer, 1930

Coconut Shies (a game)—Peek Frean, 1931

Greuze Tea Caddy (*Fig. 5*)—Carr & Co., 1936

Walnut Tea Caddy—Wm. Crawford & Sons, 1937

Fishing Creel (*Fig. 3*)—Maker unknown, undated

Collecting Early Barbed Wire

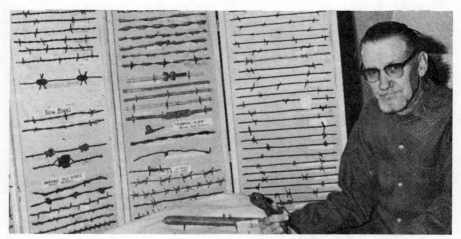

SINCE L. D. Martelle of Pierce, Nebraska, began collecting samples of barbed wire in 1940, he has found more than 250 different types. They have come from some 20 states and several foreign countries. But his collection is nowise complete, he says, for there were at least 400 different kinds of barbed wire made.

When he began his collecting, he was doing shelterbelt work with the Forest Service at Columbus, Nebraska. He had made a good start on his collection when he was sent to Haiti in 1943 to supervise the clearing of 3,000 acres of jungle land and the setting out of rubber plants. His choicest souvenir of Haiti was, of course, a piece of barbed wire! Back in Nebraska with the U. S. Department of Agriculture in soil conservation work, he continued his search.

"Why barbed wire? Mostly because it's a link to the past," says Mr. Martelle. "Barbed wire made it possible

to settle the West. With barbed wire, the settlers for the first time were able to fence cattle adequately and eventually to turn to purebred livestock. The early samples are really something, but the inventors had the right idea."

LaSalle, Illinois, was the cradle of the early barbed wire boom, for there the idea for it was born when Julian Smith, in 1867, patented the first barbed wire. Though Mr. Smith's "spool wire" was never produced commercially, it led the way to other types which were.

Four principal manufacturers quickly sprang to action—P. T. Glidden, Charles F. Washburn, Isaac L. Ellwood, and Jacob Haish. Among the first types was the single wire with clamped-on barbs, the fencer doing the clamping. When Mr. Glidden brought out the two-strand twisted type, his competitors gave way. That is the only type manufactured today.

Two New York Makers of Early Tinware

by MARCIA RAY

Benham & Stoutenborough
Glen Cove, Long Island

Illustrations of tinware from the catalog of Benham & Stoutenborough, ca. 1870, indicate the variety and excellence of their wares.

IN TERMS of shop practice, the making of what is called tinware or tinned tole begins with the 18th century technique of hammering to shape over molds, anvils, and stakes, and reaches to the beginning of mass production when the "drop" process was used. This process, briefly, involved the use of heavy shaped drops of polished cast iron (sometimes wrought iron) directed in their fall upon a piece of the metal laid over a corresponding negative, or female, die.

The first objects made by E. Ketcham of Brooklyn, N. Y., by this process, were one-piece dairy bowls. (History of the firm indicates Charles Hodgett and William Taylor, practical tinsmiths, were among the founders, ca. 1850.) By 1865 they had perfected the technique to the point of making seamless tinware with sides varying only fifteen degrees from vertical. At that time Ketcham also developed the retinning process by which an extra coat of tin was added to the already tinned wares shaped in one piece, to cover all stresses, strains, and breaks in the original plating. Production was at high peak in 1876, with shipments

being made to all points in the United States, Mexico, and South America, and even to England and the Continent. Items of major antiques status produced by Ketcham are the planished wares which looked, originally, almost like silver, and the japanned wares, ornamented "in the very highest style of the art"—trays, coolers, toilet sets, and cake closets.

Andrews & Benham, tinsmiths, formed a partnership in 1840 at 111 John Street, New York, for the production of tinned tole and japanned tinned wares. When M. Stoutenborough, employed in 1846 as an apprentice, became a partner in 1860, the firm name changed to Benham & Stoutenborough. They moved to Glen Cove, Long Island, where they began *printing* decoration in colors on japanned wares with flexible blocks! Later they used lithography, applying the lithographed design on the sheets before forming into objects—substantially the same technique used today. Of high interest to collectors are their beautiful jelly molds, color-printed toilet wares, toilet stands, hand decorated coolers and water cans. Less well known are the tin tubes they made to hold nitro-glycerine, for use in the War between the States.

E. Ketcham
Brooklyn, New York

Oyster Dish.

Hip Bath.

Coffee Urn.

Polished Teapot.

Cake Closet.   Well Bucket.

Chafing Dish.

Plate Warmer.

Illustrations from E. Ketcham's catalog, ca. 1870, showing japanned and plain tinware for most every use.

Classic Examples of Early Tinplate and Tolewares— 1780 to 1840

by CARL DREPPERD

PERHAPS AT NO time in the history of collecting has tin-plated sheet iron, and plain or planished sheet iron ware (properly termed "tole" only when unpainted or unplated) been so popular with so many collectors. This, in turn, has resulted in the uncovering of many objects which, again in turn, pose a question as to their original purpose and use. In a broad scale research effort to determine, without question, the original names for such items, we have had exceedingly good fortune. We have found an illustrated catalog of such wares by a manufacturing exporter of England who had the rare good sense to designate every item he pictured, and to picture every item he produced. Thus the documentation is complete and unimpeachable.

This manufacturer, Tozer, of London (1780-1840), exported considerable ware to the United States, from the end of the Revolution. Here it became far more than a semi-luxury item sold in the more exclusive housewares stores; it became the prototype ware, the model ware, copied to some extent by every manufacturing tin and sheet iron smith (whitesmith) working from our earliest Federal era down to at least the 1880's. Many items became staples with our makers, a fact proved by comparing the price listings of Tozer with our American tinsmiths' price books and catalogs.

While the names given for the various objects shown here indicate their use, some require a bit of explaining: A Turbot pan was used to steam fish. A Batchelor's Broiler hooked onto a hob grate and was used to broil small birds, et cetera. A Breakfast Pot was a room service item—the pot proper for tea, the box-like cover for bacon, eggs, toast, et cetera. Candle Safes are candleholders, the candle burning within the pierced walls; it was also used to heat gruel, milk, or some other hot beverage.

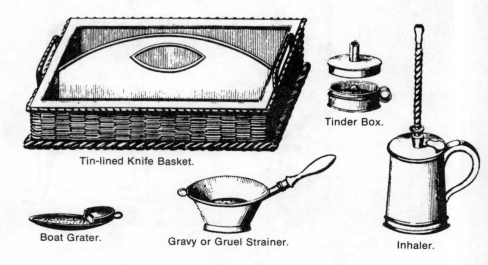

Tin-lined Knife Basket.

Tinder Box.

Boat Grater.

Gravy or Gruel Strainer.

Inhaler.

Hash Dish and
Burner.

Lantern with
horn windows.

Writing Candlestick.

Spice Box, round.

Oblong Tea
Kettle and Stand.

Cheese Toaster, planished.

Japanned Beer Jug.

Chocolate Pot.

Cheese Toaster for water.

Cheese Toaster.

Block Tin Stomach Warmer.

Oval Kettle.

Hanging Lamp.

Sugar Box, round.

Tea Cannister, square.

Large Candle Safe.

Bread Tin.

Sugar Box, square.

Oblong Dish Cover.

Bed Pan.

Ale Taster.

Spice Box, square.

Wine Mulling Pot.

Pannekin.

Treacle Can.

Milk Measure.

WITHDRAWN

Juliet's Nurse

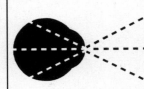 This Large Print Book carries the
Seal of Approval of N.A.V.H.

JULIET'S NURSE

LOIS LEVEEN

THORNDIKE PRESS
A part of Gale, Cengage Learning

GALE
CENGAGE Learning·

Farmington Hills, Mich • San Francisco • New York • Waterville, Maine
Meriden, Conn • Mason, Ohio • Chicago

GALE
CENGAGE Learning·

LIBRARY OF CONGRESS CATALOGING-IN-PUBLICATION DATA

Leveen, Lois, 1968–
    Juliet's nurse / by Lois Leveen. — Large print edition.
      pages ; cm. — (Thorndike Press large print historical fiction)
    ISBN 978-1-4104-7755-2 (hardcover) — ISBN 1-4104-7755-X (hardcover)
    1. Large type books. I. Title.
PS3612.E9233J86 2015
813'.6—dc23   2014045623

Published in 2015 by arrangement with Atria Books, a division of Simon & Schuster, Inc.

Printed in Mexico
1 2 3 4 5 6 7 19 18 17 16 15

*For MIO
and BMOP,
who do not like to read novels
(If you happen to read this one, I hope
you recognize in it the things I learned
from you.)*

PART ONE

1360–1363

ONE

Two nights before Lammas Eve, I go to bed believing myself fat and happy. You will think me a fool for being so deceived, at my age. But in our hearts, we all wish to be fooled. And so we make fools of ourselves.

For months, Pietro and I have finished dinner with a sampling of his latest confections: candied cherries, quince marmalade, muscatel-stewed figs. Though he still cannot afford sugar, Pietro's begun gathering honey from hives in the groves and fields beyond Verona's walls. This frightens me, for I was badly stung as a child. My face swelled so large, villagers crossed themselves when they passed me, as though I was a changeling. But whenever Pietro returns from his hives he hums like he's a bee himself, insisting this will be his good fortune at last. With the honey, he can make, if not the bright, hard confetti candy the apothecaries offer, at least such treats as we might sell ourselves.

Though I warn he'll put us in the alms-house by squandering any of the precious spices for our own pleasure, each night I let him pull me to my feet and feed me an un-named delight. Standing close behind me, he covers my eyes with one broad hand, and with the other slips some new delicacy upon my tongue like a priest placing a commu-nion wafer. "Why do you look for a sting," he asks, his words soft in my ear, "where there is only a sweet?" So I swell not from the sharp sting of a bee but with the many dainties he's made from their honey. Or so I believe, my body spreading and slowing while the spring's warmth deepens into the summer's heat.

The delicate flavorings my husband brings to my mouth seem to sharpen my sense of smell, so that I cannot abide any off odor. I scrub and air everything in our meager rented rooms. And the week before Lam-mastide, I launder our linens. Every coverlet and pillow-casing, all the sheets stored within our musty marriage-chest — they get such a laundering as I've not found time to do in many a year, killing every louse, flea, and bedbug upon them. It's three days' work, and I struggle with each basketful of bedding as I walk to the public fountain, and even more when I carry the linens wet and heavy back to the Via Zancani, and haul them up the ladder to our roof. Once they're hung along the wooden window-rod under the bright July sun, the sheet-corners catch on the wind like the black-tipped wings of the gulls chasing each other over the Adige River.

My Pietro has never been one to waste a clean bedsheet — nor even a new-swept table-carpet or a leaf-strewn patch of ground within a sycamore grove — without taking me upon it. And so every night of the week, he climbs on me with the same merry lover's zest with which he connived me of my maiden-head thirty years before. About this, too, I fool myself: that we could laugh and lust as though we are still such youths as when we first lay together. As though we'd never left the countryside to enter city gates, and the plague had never come.

For seven nights, we sleep snug and satisfied on those sheets. Until the earliest hours of the day before Lammas Eve, when I awaken to find the bedding soaked.

Pietro is a man who rouses neither quickly nor easily, so I give him a knee to where I know he'll most remember it. "You pissed the sheets."

He wakes, and swears, and says, "It's not

11

me who wet it." Pushing off the coverlet, he traces the damp spot with the cinnamon-smudged nail of his stout finger. The stain forms a little sea around the buxom island of me, yet reaches not halfway under him.

Fat and happy. Could I believe myself those things, and nothing more? Could I think myself only old and corpulent, glad just to rut with the same hoary goat I long called beloved husband? In the months of shortened breath within my tight-pulled dress, had I not felt the truth of what was happening?

I had not. I could not. Until Pietro traces it on the sheet, and him still not understanding what it is.

Now it's my turn to swear. "By my holi-dame, go get a midwife."

He's more stunned by this second, spoken blow than the first, physical one.

"Husband, will you not see? It's not age that's stopped up my bleedings these seasons past." I pull his hand onto me. "It was a quickening, so long done that here's my water, broke. Blessed Maria and Sainted Anna, I am about to birth a child."

This brings him full awake. He kisses the last of the words from my mouth, and kisses my full belly, and kisses each of my broad haunches. The glad fool even kisses our puddled sheets, he's so pleased at the news.

"A midwife," I remind him, as the church bells ring for lauds-hour.

He dances his way dressed with even greater glee than that which with he usually undresses me. The way he sways and hoots, it seems as if he's still drunk on last night's wine, until he stops before the picture of the Holy Virgin suckling her babe. He crosses himself three times and mutters a prayer to her to keep me well while he is gone. Then my great bear of a husband, forgetting to duck his head, smacks his broad brow hard upon the beam above the doorway. He reels like a buffoon before galloping down the stairs and out into Verona's still-dark streets.

Alone, I look to the Virgin, not sorry it is too dim to make out her familiar features. Whatever apprentice painted her had no great gift, for she is a cockly-eyed thing, the black pupil within one pale blue orb gazing down upon her infant, and the other looking straight out at whoever passes before her. Pietro gave her to me when we married. At twenty he knew no better than to pick her, and at twelve I knew no better than to find her lovely. In the decades since, I've fancied myself worldlier, snickering at her ill form. But there's no snicker in me

13

now, as I ask the most unlikely of mothers how this could be, and will she bless me, and why do my pains not come, since my waters are already loosed. It's a one-sided conversation, like all I ever have with her. Lonely and terrified, I lie flat on my back, kneading the thick flesh of my sides but afraid to touch my belly. Waiting for Pietro, and the midwife, and my own last and least expected infant to arrive.

"No birthing chair?"

By the time Pietro returns, the day's light is already stealing into the room, and there's no hiding that the midwife he's brought is gnarled like a walnut, with a palsy shaking her hands and head. I cannot imagine where my husband unearthed such a decrepit creature, though I suppose we are lucky that at such an hour he found anyone at all. She sends him away as soon as he shows her in, leaving only me and her assistants, twin girls so half-witted the pair of them do not seem the equivalent of a singleton, to listen to her complaints — the first of which is the absence of a birthing chair. Her only solace in hearing I have none is to say it is just as well, as I am too fat for a baby to escape me seated upright.

Next, she demands to know when my last

bowel movement was. Too many days past for me to remember, is the best I can answer. I've not marked each bodily passing like it's some holy feast. Not with such wind, such colic, and such loosing and then stopping-up of bowels as I've had these years past. Why keep careful count of all the troubles that time, that thief of youth and health, works upon my body? We are not wealthy. Though Pietro would insist on seeking out physick and apothecary if ever I spoke of these ailments, I know such things are beyond our means. So I've taken what comfort I could in having Pietro's honeyed sweets in my mouth, and tried to find in my husband's doting some relief, if not remedy, for everything I suffer.

The midwife seizes on my constipation as though it's the only care either of us has in all the world. Displaying a gleaming desire to purge my bowels, she sends one twin off for common mallow, borax, and dog's mercury to be boiled into a soup, while she sets the other to rubbing chamomile and linseed crushed in olive oil into some hidden nether place where front and back join between my legs. It's not hard to tell which of those girls she favors.

Only when at last I shit to her satisfaction does she turn her attention to delivering my

15

child. She produces a small dowel for the kitchen-twin to coat in chicken fat, then has the other twin open me with it so the midwife might survey my insides. She tells me to scream, loud as I can. I do not find this hard to do, with a fat-coated dowel shoved in me. I shout till I am hoarse, which finally brings on the first birthing pains. A fine trick that, no voice left for howling just when you want to howl most.

From time to time, my banished Pietro calls up from the street, saying he has a gift for me. One twin or the other runs down, returning first with a tiny woven pouch containing a Santa Margherita charm, then with a marten's tooth, then with a wooden parto tray rubbed so smooth with use, I cannot make out which sainted mother is bearing which holy babe in the scene painted upon it. Though I curse the money-lenders and the marketwomen so eager to prey upon my worried husband, I wrap my hand around charm and tooth, and tell the twins to set the tray where I can easily see it. Fourteen years it's been, since he last had cause to lavish me with parto gifts. A dozen years since, in my maddened grief, I burned up all the ones he'd ever given me upon a plaguey pyre. I can feel the heat of that fire now, am bathed in the sweat of it, as I beg Santa Margherita and the figure on the parto tray and our cockly-eyed Holy Virgin to make this baby come.

The day is already past its hottest when Pietro sends up three eggs. One tawny, one spring-sky blue, and the last a purest white. The midwife spins the eggs one by one atop my belly, snorting with approval when each comes to rest pointing to my woman-parts. Pricking a hole on the top and bottom of each egg, she bids me blow out the yolks. The twins fill the first shell with amaranth, the second with fennel seed, and the third with sow thistle, each of which the midwife says I am to rub upon my breasts every night to keep my milk thick and plentiful. Setting the shells in a variegated row beneath the Virgin's picture, she beats the eggs till the golden yolks stain all through the glossy whites. In the next pause between my pains, one twin feeds me raw egg swirled in red wine. As I struggle to keep the loose, thick mixture down, the other twin greases my nether end with the rest of the eggs combined with oil of dill, while the midwife lights a votive and mutters an abracadabra of prayer.

After the candle burns low, she orders me to kneel wide-kneed on the floor. The twins heap pillows behind me, and the midwife instructs me to arch back over the pile until my head touches the worn wooden floorboards. I tell her I saw an acrobat once that might have contorted backward like that, but he was a strapping young lad, which I most certainly am not. The twins each grab one of my shoulders, stretching and pushing according to the midwife's commands, until I'm as close to that improbable position as a woman my size and age can get.

Once I'm stretched neck to knees like racked linen, the tight globe of my belly pointing up, the midwife lays one icy hand atop the great mound of me, and works the other inside. Palsy shakes her so furiously, I feel the tremors deep within me. I lie folded back like that until my shins are numb, my back cricked, and the upside-down world no longer unfamiliar, before her bony hands jiggle the baby loose. I swear it stands straight up within me, my belly-button a brimless cap upon its hidden head. It balances like that a short minute, then pitches down again facing the opposite direction. But still, it will not push its way out of me.

All my other babies, conceived as they were from Pietro's randy youth and my ready young womb, were eager to press their way into the world. Nunzio came just two months after quickening, and Nesto only

18

three. Donato barely brought me any birthing pains, and Enzo kicked and pushed himself out while Donato was still at my breast. I'd not begun to bleed again before I was carrying Berto, so I cannot say how many months he grew inside me, though it seemed a scanty few. And Angelo, my littlest angel, began to drop from me as I bent to blow out a candle, and was halfway into the world before we had the wick relit. But this baby feels the slowness of our ages. Though I try to fill the time with hopeful prayers, I cannot help but think of certain horrors. The widow in the village where I grew up, who swelled four years before she was delivered. A young bride startled by a fox on the way to her wedding bed, who bore a pointy-faced child whose body was thick with reddish fur. The cousin of Pietro's who birthed twins, one as perfect as an orchid bloom, the other a ghastly bluish-purple beast.

The midwife quizzes her assistants on what they think she ought to try, to pry the baby from me. "Girdle the laboring mother with vervain leaves gathered before dawn on the feast day of San Giovanni," recites one. She sounds quite convincing until, picking with a grimy fingernail at a freckle on her chin, she adds, "Or is it plantain

19

leaves, gathered at evening on the feast day of San Giorgio?"

The second twin shakes her head. "Have her wear her husband's shoes upon her hands and his pants upon her head," she insists. "Perch his hat upon her abdomen, while she recites the name of his mother, and his mother's mother, and her mother before her, backward, and begs forgiveness from all their saints."

They go back and forth like that, until at last the midwife claps them each on the ear with a satisfying smack. She informs them that it is time to fumigate my womb, as the smoke from a fire of salt-fish and horse hooves should surely get the child moving. This, I think, is clever true. What being would not vacate where it lay, once the stench of herring and hoof reaches it?

We have some small bit of salt-fish in our store, but as I've never found much call in my kitchen for horse hoof, one twin is sent off for that, while the other scrounges up the last of our apples. This is a disappointment for the midwife, who would prefer an artichoke. I'm not sure it matters much, as she shoves it inside my behind, saying it will tip the womb to help slide the baby free.

But it does not, and neither does the fumigation. The day turns to slant-light, then twilight, then dark, and still the baby is not born. The midwife mutters incantations over me while the twins doze in a heap in the corner and Pietro, having snuck back inside, snores from the kitchen floor. In these small hours, I sink into a wet chasm of pain. Muddy, bloody walls undulate high on either side of me, threatening to cave in if I struggle too hard to claw my way out. From this place I pray, not to the Sacred Madonna or any of the blessed saints or even to the Most Holy Trinity, but to my own child. *Come out to me, dearest lamb. If the world is so cruel you are frightened of it, I will hold you, and protect you, and teach it to love you as I already love you.* Words I dare not say aloud but form in my mind, so that my little one alone can hear.

By the next ringing of matins bells, I fear there is no baby in me. Had I not bled four days in a row, some time this past spring? But as the sun slowly rises I feel that my belly is indeed full, though what is waiting to be birthed is not a new babe. It must be one of my well-grown boys, come back to claim the mother-love that floods through me once again, a love I thought I'd buried in the single grave that swallowed all of them. In such delirium, I do not mark the new ways in which my body is stretched and twisted by the midwife's apprentices, what is rubbed or dripped or shoved onto or into the varying parts of me. I come to my senses as the sext bells ring at midday, to find myself standing with an arm over each twin's shoulders, the three of us walking a circle like blinded mules turning a mill-wheel. We grind on and on for hours. When, bathed in sweat and mad with thirst, I beg for water, the midwife gives me only wine. But when I plead to be numbed by wine, all I get is tepid water. You can pray to God and holy saints for compassion, but do not bother to ask it of this midwife.

It is the afternoon of Lammas Eve when the baby finally arrives. A daughter, the first I ever bore. I am so grateful when she passes from me, I croak out an exhausted, "Ho-sanna." But "Susanna" is what the ancient midwife hears. She bathes, swaddles, and bundles my babe. Worn as I am, I can barely raise my head to steal a glimpse of my precious girl before the midwife calls out the window for Pietro, who she chased back out of the house at daybreak, to take Su-sanna to be baptized. Then she orders one twin to shove hellebore petals up my nose until I sneeze the afterbirth into the other twin's waiting hands.

■ ■ ■ ■

Delivered of my daughter, I sleep. When I wake the night is late, the fire out, the room empty. I might believe the laboring and birth all a dream, but for the soreness between my legs, the animal stench of blood and sweat and secundine that hangs in the dark. And the terrific ache that swells my breasts, my hardened nipples ready for Susanna's mouth. Swollen and tender, I hear Pietro's sobs filling the dark house.

A man will cry for joy when his wife has born his son. A softhearted man will even weep astonished tears over the delicate beauty of a new daughter. But this animal sound Pietro makes is different. I know it, and the knowing stings spear-sharp through my waiting breasts.

This is why the midwife sent her off so quick, that my child's tiny soul might fare better than her tiny body would. What ill-formed thing did the midwife sense in my newborn that, with a mother's heart, I missed? I cannot know. And I'll not forgive myself for not knowing.

In my sleep, I'd clutched the Santa Margherita charm in one hand and the marten's tooth in the other. Cupping my belly against the crude stigmata they've pressed into my palms, I wonder how, in all the months my daughter lived in me, babe and mother a single breathing being, I'd not let myself know her. Such a fool I was, not to even admit that she was there. And now, when I most crave her, crave the hungry suck with which she would crave me, she is gone.

What's tomb is womb. That is what the holy friars preached when Death with his plaguey army robbed us of so much, more than a decade past. Worms will turn dead leaves, dead trees, dead men into new soil. But what can worms do for a living, grieving woman?

Let the brown-frocked friars tremble with awe over how the tomb of earth sprouts seedlings. Such wonders are no comfort when you birth a babe who dies.

When next I wake, the room is filled with golden light, and all Verona smells of yeasty bread. It is Lammas Day, a harvest feast. Sown seeds reaped as grain, then ground and baked to rounded loaves. Pietro, red-eyed and bewildered, kneels beside our bed, tearing small pieces of the blessed bread. Dipping some in honey, some in wine. Feeding each to me. Could anything be so sweet against the metallic taste of grief?

24

A Lammas Day procession winds past, its drums and shouts and trumpets echoing against the tight-packed buildings, resonating across our floor and up our walls. After the noise passes away, Pietro slips his hands beneath me, his palms warm against the ache across my back. "Susanna is —"

I shake my head, cutting him off. I will not let him say the word. Will not make myself listen to it.

Why could we two not just be alone, like we'd been the seasons past, and happy? But there they are, the portrait of the Holy Madonna suckling sacred babe upon our wall, and some saint or other being newly born upon the parto tray that holds the honey, bread, and wine. Icons of what we cannot have, blessed mothers such as I'm reminded I'll never again be. The plague that stole our other children laid half the city dead. But this fresh loss comes to us alone. This is grief's great trick: you think you have faced the worst of it, not dreaming of all that is yet to come.

Somewhere outside a lonely kitten mewls, and my milk begins to run. Pietro catches the first weak drops on his pinky finger, a too-delicate gesture for a lustful husband. He wets a cloth and washes me, dresses me, rebraids the great length of my hair, and covers it. Then he guides me to my feet, and leads me down the stairs and through Verona's crooked streets. Sore and stiff, I move slowly. But what aches most drives me on, as I hold Pietro's arm, repeating to myself the promise he whispered as he lifted me from our bed. There is a baby waiting. Needing me as much as I need her.

We leave our familiar parish, Pietro guiding me past the towers and guild-halls and churches that mark the way to the Piazza delle Erbe. Even with the merchant stalls closed up for Lammas Day, the air hangs fragrant with basil, rosemary, and fennel, the last reminding me that I left my herb-filled eggshells behind. But I'll not turn back. I need no remedies, no potions. I need only a child to draw out what is already thick in me.

We cross below the Lamberti tower, to where the piazza narrows into the Via Cappello. This parish is not a place I ever come, for what have I to do with the Scaligeri princes and the wealthy families who guarantee their power? Nothing. Until today. This holy-day when, stopping midway along the Via Cappello, my husband raises a grand carved knocker and swings it hard against the wooden door. The door opens, and beneath an archway tall enough to admit a man on horseback, I enter Ca' Cappelletti.

The Cappelletti house does not smell of yeasty Lammas Day offerings, nor of the goods sold in the herb-market. There is no hint of the fetid waste that fills Verona's streets or the hogs roaming loose to feed upon it. Those odors cannot breach these walls, thick as a cathedral's. I breathe in the miracle of it, as a house-page no older than an altar boy nods a curt dismissal to Pietro, then leads me alone through the cool air of the ground floor, perfumed by the household's stores of wine and grains, cured meats, hard cheeses, and infused oils. I follow him up stone stairs to a storey so full of wool carpets, fur robes, and lit perfumers, their rich smells settle as tastes on my tongue. The walls and even the wooden ceiling beams are painted with holy images here, and exotic beasts there, and everywhere repeating shapes and dancing patterns that dizzy me.

We wind past the great sala and through the family's private apartments to an intimate corner of the house. The page stops before a heavy pair of curtains, scraping agitated lines along his neck and stammering out that he's not bidden to go any farther. I part the curtains and, passing

27

between their woven scenes of hinds and hares frolicking in some imagined forest, I enter the confinement room.

A maid-servant weaves through the room with trays of roasted capon and sweetmeats, serving a dozen gossiping women who circle around the new mother's bed. Most of the guests wear jeweled overdresses heavily embroidered with the crests of the city's finest families. The others have the full-skirted habits of Verona's wealthiest convents. No one notices me enter, except a sharp-eyed midwife's assistant, who slips a swaddled bundle into my arms, whispering, "Juliet."

Juliet — a little jewel. No ruby, no sapphire, no diamond could dazzle more. My little jewel and I are as eager for each other as young lovers. Settling upon an enormous pillow on the floor, I cradle her in one arm, loose my milk-soaked blouse, and offer up a breast. She takes it with such lively greed as makes me smile. When she's sucked that, and then the other, to her satisfaction, I lay her down before me on the silken cushion. I snug her head between my calves, her swaddled feet tucking into my plump thighs, my thumbs tracing the soft smooth of her tiny cheeks. Sainted Maria, the very sight of her bursts my mother-heart.

Juliet is my earth, and I am her moon, so

caught in our celestial sphere we exist entirely apart from the rest of the bustling confinement room. Invisible even to the new mother lying in the parto bed, who lifts her slender arm, coral bracelets jangling down her wrists. With no more signal than that, silver goblets and flasks of trebbiano are brought out for the guests. Bright maiolica bowls appear, their lids hiding spiced stews. Trays come piled with sponge cakes and marzipans and fine salts. All eaten with a set of delicately worked silver forks brought by Prince Cansignorio's aunt, who repeats to each woman who arrives how they were chosen from the Scaligeri inventories by the prince himself.

I care nothing for the lavish confinement gifts, nor for any of the room's fine furnishings, except the heavy silver tub in which I wash Juliet, and the iron brazier over which I warm the swaddling bands to wrap her. To tend, to touch so little a living delight. I lean close to smell the delicate baby scent of her, and know it is my milk on her breath, my kiss on her downy hair. *Dearest lamb,* I whisper with those kisses, *do not worry or wonder what all those other noises are, who makes them and why. They do not matter, now that I am here. Here for you.*

■ ■ ■ ■

Juliet has a ferocious hunger, rousing herself six or seven times during our first night to nurse. I do not bother to lace my blouse, keeping a breast ready so that she'll not cry and wake the house. But to feed her, I must be fed. In some quiet hour, hungry from her hunger, I steal up to the table beside the parto bed, where remnants of Lady Cappelletta's supper remain. A taper flickers beneath a portrait of Santa Margherita. Is it any wonder the saints favor the rich for offering up such extravagant devotions even while they sleep, when the rest of us can barely afford to keep a candle lit upon a worktable when we are full awake?

In the dancing light, I pick the darkest of the meat. Even cold, it is the finest I've ever eaten. I close my eyes, sucking poultry-flesh from bone, savoring the flavors until I feel another set of eyes upon me. Lady Cappelletta's.

I slip the purloined bone inside my sleeve, so I'll not be called a thief. But well-fed as Lady Cappelletta is, she does not seem to mark what I've taken.

She stares at my untrussed breasts. "Is that what they do to them? Suckle like piglets till they fall flab?"

Standing so close beside her parto bed, I see she is hardly more than a child herself, consumed by girlish fear at what her body is, what it will become. "Time will do what time will do," I say. "No one stays" — I peer at her and make a careful guess — "fourteen forever."

She looks down at the bumps that even after pregnancy barely bring a curve to her nightshirt. "I'm already turned fifteen."

"An age when bud turns into bloom." An age that is but a third of my own. Her face, her neck, are smooth as a statue, her bead- and braid-strung hair shining. Lady Cappelletta is that beauty the poets call a just-plucked rose, and gossiping old dowagers call a coin that's not yet spent. Wondering that this is not enough to please her, I add, "And blessed that your child is healthy." She cannot know what those words cost me.

"So what if it is?"

"Not it," I say. "She. A beautiful daughter of a beautiful mother."

Some hard emotion pulls at the edges of her pretty mouth. "Who should have borne a son."

"You are young. There will be sons yet."

"I am young, but my lord husband is not." She shudders when she speaks of him.

"Neither is he patient."

Surely tonight all her husband's thinking of is how much it costs to dower the daughter of so fine a house — that will shrivel more than a man's impatience. But who am I to tell her so?

"He'll climb right back upon me," she says, "to make a son."

Fear tinges her words. Perchance it's more than age that makes them ill-matched. He must run hot, as men do, and she cold, as I for one do not. Although never having seen her husband, I cannot say whether there is anything in him that might please any woman. Especially one barely out of girlhood.

"The midwife will tell him he must wait, as all men do," I say, thinking of how Pietro brought me here out of our marriage bed.

Her fingers, heavy with pearl rings, tug at the gold-and-garnet cross that hangs around her neck, then turn the coral bracelets upon either wrist. Extravagant talismans, doubtless from her husband's family, which no one thought to unclasp at night so she might sleep in comfort.

She's sorely in need of mothering herself, new mother though she is. I could sit upon this grand bed, stroking her hair and whispering soothing words until her hands lie calm. I might tell her that many a wife whose husband gives her no pleasure in the getting of babies still finds great joy in the children she's borne. But Juliet begins to stir, and I turn my back to the parto bed to take up the child who is my charge.

Two

For the first five weeks, I see nothing of the Cappelletti compound except the confinement room. But Lady Cappelletta is not wrong about Lord Cappelletto's eagerness to make a son. The day after I arrive, her breasts are bound in squash leaves to dry their milk and keep her fertile. And at five weeks to the hour of when her labor ended, her husband — who's not bothered to make a single visit to the confinement room — orders her brought back to their marriage bed. The fire in the confinement room is put out, the parto linens and sumptuous wall-hangings folded away for when she'll bear again. The handsome walnut-and-ivory cradle, with its fine white Levantine silk and gold-fringed coverlet, is moved through the family apartments to what will ever after be Juliet's room.

Her own room. Bigger than the one in which my whole family slept, and hung with fabrics I cannot even name, fabrics so mysterious and beautiful I know they're not from Verona or Mantua or any land where anyone I know has ever been. It has art like a grand parish church, paintings of the Blessed Maria and the Sainted Anna, and a niche as big as a man filled with a statue of San Zeno. All smile their holy approval onto a bed that's wide enough for a bride, a groom, and half their wedding party. The headboard and footboard rise so high, it's like a little fortress when the bed curtain closes around them. Outside the footboard sits a cassone-chest longer than I am tall, its sides and cover carved with chubby angels. When I open it, the woody scent of rosemary seeps from the dresses stored inside. Garments sized for a child of two, of four, of six, each more elegant than the next — a bishop's ransom worth of clothing, waiting for my tiny Juliet to grow big enough to wear. And beside the massive bed, a narrow, low-slung truckle-bed for me.

Juliet's chamber glows with light, a perfect setting for my little jewel. There is a window that stretches from below my knees to high above my head, broad as my open arms. My fingers are greedy to touch its thick, warbled panes. Real Venetian glass, nothing like the waxed-cloth windows on the Via Zancani.

These panes are set within a heavy frame hinged to swing wide, to let in air from the Cappelletti's private arbor. In all the years I've lived among the city's crooked, crowded streets, I've never known that such trees grow within Verona's walls, their ripe fruit so fragrant. This is what the rich have: the prettiest smells in all the world, and the means to close out even those whenever they want.

It is a bright September day, so I keep the window open while I sit in a high-backed chair and sing to Juliet. I sing, she sleeps. Surely no harm if I sleep too, dreaming the golden sun is Pietro come to warm me, inside and out. It's a dream so real, I wake certain I feel the very weight of him, and find a poperin pear lying in my lap.

I might believe Pietro is here withal, when I see that. *Pop-her-in,* he calls the bulging fruit, wagging a pear from his breech-lace whenever I bring some home from the market. But shut within the Cappelletti compound, it cannot be Pietro who pranks me.

A boy of nine or ten perches on the bottom of the window frame, watching me. His light brown hair falls in loose, soft curls to his chin. His face stretches long for a child's, as if the man in him is already struggling to make his way out. His arms and legs are thin and strong, although not pinched by work like my sons' were. He pulls his head high and announces, "I am the king of cats."

I've not forgotten how to manage a playful boy. Picking up the pear by its round bottom, I wave the peaked tip at him. "A cat who hunts fruit instead of mice?"

"Cats climb," he says with feline pride. "I heard whistling outside our wall. When I climbed over to see what it was, a man asked if I would bring that to you."

I ask who the man was, as if I do not already know.

The boy describes my strong bull of a husband to the very mole above his left eyebrow, while I bite deep into the pear. "He said to tell you that if you like that, he has something even juicier for you to eat."

Though I blush, the child seems ignorant of what charming filth Pietro bade him speak. "How did you know to bring this here, to me?"

He laughs, raising both knees and rolling back. Backward out the window. My heart goes cold, the pear-flesh stuck in my throat.

But in an instant two small hands appear on the bottom of the window-case. The child vaults himself into the chamber, turns a somersault, and leaps up. "I am Tybalt, king of cats. I climb, and I jump, and I know all that happens in Ca' Cappelletti." He struts back and forth like the Pope's official messenger proclaiming the latest Bull. "That is my cousin, and you are her nurse, and tomorrow is the Nativity of the Blessed Virgin, and before you go to be shriven the man will meet you, and he will give you three almond sweets to give to me, as long as you give your sweets to him."

"Tybalt my king of cats," I say, careful to hide my surprise that Pietro has trusted this strange boy to bear me these naughty tidings, "how clever you must be, to keep such delicious secrets."

The mention of secrets sets off another round of acrobatics. "I know every hidden passageway in Ca' Cappelletti, and which alcoves to stand in to overhear what somebody is saying." He gives his narrow chest a proud thump. "I've climbed all the way to the top of our tower, as high as the campanile of Sant'Anastasia. The perch is filled with rocks I carried up myself, some as big as a man's head, to throw on any enemies who pass below."

"Any enemies?" I raise the pear to my mouth, to hide my smile.

"The Cappelletti have many enemies," he

says. "Because we are so brave and pious."

A man makes more enemies being cruel and quick-tempered than brave or pious. But there's time enough for this Tybalt to learn such things, so I only nod and tell him I can see how gallant he is, and bid him finish off the pear as his reward.

He takes the knife from his belt, assaulting the pear as though it has offended his honor. He carves the pale fruit-flesh with the same coat-of-arms that is painted along the corbels and patterned in golden thread into the Cappelletti linens. Neither Pietro nor I were born to families who had so much as a surname, let alone a scroll-worked crest to herald that name to all the world. But the Cappelletti coat-of-arms is a bewildering thing. Unlike most shields one sees around Verona, which feature eagles or dragons or other formidable beasts, this one boasts only a peaked mitre-hat.

"Does your family make hats?" I ask, though I doubt that even the most gifted milliners could ever amass such a fortune as built Ca' Cappelletti.

Tybalt scores the air with his dagger to correct me. "Not hats, chapels. Our family endowed so many of them with all we earn from our lands, Pope Innocent III himself decreed we should be named for them."

"I see the joke," I say, the word for the Pope's mitre-hat sounding in our Veronese dialect almost the same as the word for chapel.

"It's not a joke," Tybalt insists. "It is a shibboleth."

I do not know what a shibboleth is, cannot guess why Tybalt's so proud that some long-dead Pope gifted his Cappelletti ancestors with one. But from the way he swaggers out the word, I know how best to answer. "A shibboleth. How clever."

This brings another smile to the boy's face, and he lists the names of a half dozen bygone emperors, telling me how they hated the Popes and the Popes hated them. How this emperor warred against that Pope, and the next Pope plotted against the subsequent emperor. On and on for a hundred and fifty years, the Cappelletti always siding with the Pope, supplying knights and horses to capture whole towns from rival families named Uberti and Infangati and Montecchi. A catalogue of bloody conflicts this Tybalt's been taught to recite like a poet singing a love-ballad.

How much easier it is to be poor than rich. We are too busy scrambling to find enough to eat each day to worry ourselves over the centuries' worth of slaughtering that consumes a boy like Tybalt, who chews thick slices from the pear as he schools me about his esteemed relations. His father is Giaccomo, and Juliet's is Leonardo, and they are brothers. Very cunning, very courageous, and very rich, ever plotting against anyone who dishonors their noble family. Just like all the Cappelletti who came before them. When I ask which man is the elder, Tybalt laughs and tells me they are too old for anyone to remember. From this I figure that his father must be the younger, for an older brother never fails to impress his son about his rightful place in the family line.

"And your mother?" I make my words sound light, so they'll not betray my worry. Tybalt's mother cannot be near so young as Juliet's, to have a son of his age. If she is cruel or jealous, she will make life hard for her sister-in-law. And for Juliet, and me.

"My mother is with the angels." Tybalt turns to throw the pear core out the window. He keeps his back to me, his voice unsteady as he tells how his mother passed just before Michaelmas, birthing his sister Rosaline.

Not yet a year gone. The air of death still lingering in the confinement room when young Lady Cappelletta was brought in for her own recent childbearing.

"You must love your sister very much," I

41

say, to ease any resentment Tybalt might have for the baby whose birth brought the death of their mother.

"I've never seen her. My father sent her away to be nursed, so that he'd not be reminded."

Only a man could have such sentiment: to love a departed wife so much, he banishes the child she bore.

Juliet stirs in her cradle, giving a little cry as if to confirm the folly of men. Every wisp of her first golden hair has fallen out. But even bald as an ancient abbot, Juliet is still my beauty. I take her into my arms, telling myself I only want to check her swaddling, to be sure each limb is wrapped tight.

Tybalt sees how needy I am just for the feel of her. "My uncle thinks my father is a fool. He says not even a daughter should be sent off as a newborn."

Much as I agree, I know better than to confirm aloud that his father is a fool. Instead, I motion the boy close and place his tiny cousin into his arms, hoping she'll make up for the sister he does not know. He wiggles one of his small fingers before her face, and she smiles up at him. "You must protect your cousin Juliet, and your sister Rosaline."

He nods, touching that same eager finger

to where his knife hangs at his waist, as if he might need at any moment to ward off some grave threat. My Pietro was a motherless boy, and it was the love of his doting older sisters that taught him to love me. Why should I not give this serious, tumbling Tybalt more to care about than almond candies and ancient feuds?

Juliet sleeps heavily our first night in her bedchamber, but I am wakeful, worrying over how I will contrive a way out of this room and away from Ca' Cappelletti, to meet Pietro. How I miss my husband's snores, the way even in sleep his great bear-paw of a hand cups my rump or hip or the soft curve of my belly. We've never been so long apart, even after my other lying-ins, for we have but one bed. When each of our sons was born, Pietro placed the newborn boy on the bolster above our heads, and entertained me by translating their gurglings into wild tales of where they'd been and what they'd seen before coming into this world, as one by one our older boys dropped off to sleep. He spun weeks and weeks of such stories, filling the nights until I was well again.

All that fills the night in this great chamber is the sound of Juliet's small breath, and the church bells counting off the three hours between compline and matins, then the three between matins and lauds. And in between the tolling, the songs of the nightingales in the arbor. Their trillings have barely given way to the first morning lark's insistent chirps when, without so much as a knock, a man strides into the chamber, the dangling ends of his broad silver belt clanging with each heavy footfall. He's of great girth if no great height, and as anyone but a blind man can tell from every gilded stitch upon him, rich. With a rich man's surety of all that is his due, he demands, "Where is my Juliet?"

My Juliet. Hearing him say those words makes me despise him, detesting how his silvery hair grows thick from his ears and nose yet thin upon his head. Holding my milk-sodden nightdress closed, I fold back the coverlet and reveal my darling lamb, perfect in her sleep.

He lifts her up, away from me. I feel the warmth go out of the truckle-bed, the slight hollow where she lay chilling into an abyss as Lord Cappelletto cradles her in his arms. His liver-colored lips kiss her creamy cheek, those bristly nostrils widening to take in the precious scent of her.

His thick fingers draw a tiny cap from his

doublet pocket. It is a deep indigo, worked with gold. A perfect miniature of the elegant headpiece Lady Cappelletta wears, though with fewer rows of pearls. Too delicate in its silk and jewels for an infant. But when he puts it on Juliet's new-bald head, she strains against her swaddling as though she means to raise her own tiny hand to settle the cap in place.

"Juliet Cappelletta di Cappelletto," he says to her. Not in some foolish cooing singsong, like my doting Pietro would. But Lord Cappelletto's deep voice betrays an adoration that does not seem to fit a man who'd not bothered to make a single visit to his wife's confinement room.

"Your milk is fresh?" He asks me this the way a man fingering his coin purse might inquire about the strength of a plough-ox.

"It came the same day she was born." I turn my back to him as I lace my nightdress, to keep him from surveying me in the way I've surveyed him. Though in truth he's not raised his gaze from Juliet.

"You sent your own child off?"

This is what he thinks of me. That I would pay some peasant in the hills to take my just-born child, so I could earn a few soldi more by nursing his. I turn to him with a stare that could vinegar whole casks of wine.

"Susanna was not sent, she was taken." I cross myself. "God rest all Christian souls."

He crosses himself, repeating my prayer before adding, "I christened Juliet for my most cherished, departed mother, God keep her in His rest." This surprises me. I'd not known she'd already been baptized, being but a day old when I came to her. He presses a thumb gently to her forehead, just as the priest must have done. "The prince himself stood for her, and so did Il Benedicto."

Two godfathers, and well chosen. Prince Cansignorio Scaligero is the most powerful man in the city, having killed his own brother this winter past to seize the rule of Verona. And Il Benedicto is the most pious, as resolved to be poor as the prince is to be rich. Il Benedicto owns nothing but a haircloth shirt, sleeps in the doorway of whichever church he finds himself nearest to when the curfew bells are rung, and eats only if some stranger, moved by some mixt of guilt and charity, presses food on him. No one knows his true name or his family or where he came from, nor why he chose, longer ago than anyone can remember, to evangelize in our streets. Some say Il Benedicto is too devout to abide the petty corruptions of a monastery. Others whisper he's too unschooled to be allowed to join a religious order. But not one of the tens of thousands of souls in all Verona doubts that this pauper is the nearest of us to God. No man could do better than this calculating Lord Cappelletto has, guaranteeing his family the protection of both God and government by binding his daughter to such godfathers.

His daughter, their goddaughter — but my darling lamb. And easier for me to scheme a way out of Ca' Cappelletti with her, now that I know how much Lord Cappelletto wants the world to think him pious. "Bless the saints," I say, and I do bless them, for giving me my chance to see Pietro, "if she is already baptized, she can join the children's procession for the Nativity of the Blessed Virgin." Making myself as big-eyed as a cow, I offer to carry her, if his lordship wishes it.

He purses those liver lips, unsure. So I add, "Il Benedicto leads the procession, kneeling." It is only a guess, but surely a good one, as Il Benedicto never misses a chance to inspire Verona with his bloody-kneed piety.

"Make sure Il Benedicto blesses her on the steps of the Duomo, once everyone is assembled just before the procession starts," he tells me. "And carry her toward the front of the cortege, near Prince Cansignorio's favored nephews."

I nod my feigned obedience. What trouble is it to me to keep her close to the swaggering little counts, at least until I can slip away to see Pietro?

But Lord Cappelletto will not leave me and Juliet be. He points to the empty cradle, with its sumptuous layette. "My daughter is not to be taken into a servant's truckle-bed."

"She naps in the cradle. But nights are long for a child to be alone." As they are for a full-grown woman. "If I keep her close, she'll not cry."

Juliet gurgles a smile at him. Already she knows how to rule a man. Nestling against Lord Cappelletto, she softens him from an imperious father into something closer to a doting grandpapa. "I suppose if Juliet prefers it, you may put her down for the night in her bed, and lie there yourself," he says. "Only until she is old enough to mind you sleeping beside her, but that will be some time yet."

Some time. I hold his words tight in my chest, guarantee of all the hours they promise I'll have with Juliet.

My breasts are hard and full again, and I reach for my nursling, needing her to suck the ache away. But before Lord Cappelletto will let me have her, he says, "Make sure Juliet wears the Cappelletto headpiece, always. Not only when you take her out, but whenever she is awake."

He means for me to know she is above me. But surely it is only him who is above, too certain of his superiority to see that silk and pearls and all King Midas' piss-streams of gold could not equal the worth of what flows between my milk-babe and me.

Juliet begins to work her mouth into the demanding circle I know so well. As her lips curl in and out, I wait, knowing that when the first cry comes Lord Cappelletto will have to give her back to me. Only I can give her what she most wants. What she truly needs.

When you make the circuit of a city's churches following a kneeling supplicant, you move with God's glory, but not with God-speed. The Nativity Day procession forms a snake of many parts, slithering slowly away from the Duomo, a thousand Ave Marias swallowing the rhythmic slapping of the Adige against the city's edge. Juliet begins to fuss as soon as the cortege turns south. By the time we reach the Chapel of the Sainted Apostles, her tiny lungs hit full howl.

You might think the celebrants of the birth of the Holy Mother would greet an infant's cry with *alleleuia* and *amen*. But we're surrounded by a rivalry of mamas, each trying to push their little ones closer to the head of the procession in the hope of winning the Blessed Virgin's favor. Or at least of having something to brag over, when they gather tomorrow at one or another of the city fountains to haul water home for their daily round of chores.

Marking what tart looks and bitter murmurs we get for disturbing the solemn rite, I pinch Juliet's swaddled bottom to be sure she'll keep up her wailing, which I take as my excuse to steer us out of the piazza. Once we're free of the crowd, I slip the jeweled cap from her head, hiding it in my sleeve so no one will know her for a Cappelletta as I carry her toward the Via Zancani. Toward home.

Pietro meets us in the doorway, gathering me and Juliet together in his big arms, his thick chest absorbing the last of her howls. "How I've missed you, Angelica," he says, guiding us inside. "These have been the loneliest weeks of all my life."

He's kept house as best he can in my absence, which even in what little light steals through the waxed cloth that covers our window-holes, I see is terribly. This should please me, for what woman is not glad to know how helpless her husband is without her? But here in our dim little room, the loss of Susanna cuts even more sharply than it has during all the weeks I've been gone.

In the familiar nest of our marriage bed, I bury myself against Pietro, and he buries himself inside me. As though we could lose our freshest grief in pleasure taking. This is the crudest comfort we can offer each other, and like beasts driven by their heat, we take it.

After we are spent, I lie in Pietro's arms with Juliet at my breast, breathing in the warm scent of the straw mattress. For a few precious moments, it is as if Susanna lived, and we are a family. Until the noise creeps into the room. A steady, droning buzz, coming from the opening to the roof, a sound I know in my bones.

"You brought a hive here?"

"It's too quiet, all alone." His voice tremolos against the hum of the bees. "Not in all the years of my army did I ever think this house could be so quiet."

Pietro's army. That's what he called our boys. Half a dozen sons, each a head taller than the next, from Angelo, not yet two years and squirming in one of his older brother's arms, to Nunzio, at fifteen already of a height to look Pietro directly in the eye. These little rooms could hardly contain them all, and whichever way I turned I'd find one of the older boys tickling a younger one until both shrieked with joy, or one of the littler ones stomping and strutting in proud imitation of his bigger brothers. If Enzo began to sing, soon enough you'd hear a chorus, and if Berto let slip some wind, the others would join in to make a stinking cacophony. Once when I sent Donato to bring my loaves to the public oven, he passed a preacher who drew a crowd by imitating a tree-frog's call, and for months afterward our home sounded with a pond's worth of ribbiting. This little house was never still, never silent, with Pietro's army. Until, within a single ugly week, every one of them was dead.

I tell Pietro that all day the Cappelletti compound is noisy as a little village. "But at night, if I wake, I hear only Juliet. Her breath." I shift her from my breast and lay her down between us, show him how I turn my head over hers, holding a cheek above her dainty nose and milk-wet mouth to feel that breath on me. Then slowly, slowly, I lower my head onto her chest, laying my ear over her heart. Careful, always, not to burden her tiny body with the weight of me. How many hours I've held myself like this, just to be certain of her during the darkest of night.

When I lift my head, Pietro props himself on his elbow and rests his own cheek onto Juliet's small body. He closes those beautiful eyes of his and listens, squeezing my hand with gentle pulses that echo the beating of her heart.

Lying entwined with them beneath the portrait of the Holy Madonna, all I want is to feel her cockly-eyed blessing on us. But I cannot ignore the bizz-buzzings shimmering up my spine. "You know it frightens me to have bees so near."

Pietro drops my hand and rolls away from me and Juliet. "They may be near, but you're not." Lying on his back, he stares up at the ladder-hole to the roof, watching the bees crossing above.

I wish now that Lord Cappelletto shared his sorrowful brother's sentiment. But with all his prideful love for Juliet, he'd never allow her to live in the cramped quarters of a wet-nurse. Not when he could summon any of a hundred peasant women to Ca' Cappelletti, to nurse her there.

All around the city, churchbells begin to ring. Knowing the Virgin's procession must be nearing its end, I rise from our bed. I pull my veil and my gown and Juliet's pearl-beaded headdress from where they're heaped with Pietro's clothes, and begin to dress. I count out three almond comfits to bring Tybalt, leaving all the rest behind as I bid my husband good-bye.

Before returning to the Via Cappello, I carry Juliet to the Franciscan friary, ready to cover her innocent ears while I confess the bitter-sweet pleasures I've just taken with Pietro. Though the Pope may go to Babylon and back proclaiming that it's a sin to revel in any pleasures of the body, the Franciscans are forgiving sorts, if you make sure to sprinkle *blessed husband, conjugal duties,* and *matrimonial bed* throughout your shrift. Even so, I'm careful in my choice of confessors.

Friar Lorenzo fancies himself a man of never-ceasing learning. He is writing a treatise on marital relations. Or so the rumor goes, the whispered explanation for why he leans so eager an ear to any penitent who divulges what Friar Lorenzo in his chaste state cannot know directly. Lovesick boys, naughty girls, and many a full-grown man or woman wearing well-rumpled shift or smock — they all warm the cool air of Friar Lorenzo's stone cell with details of their hot lusts. Although the friar is a thin man, practically swimming within the folds of his cassock, he has rather large ears even for a cleric. Between those ears brims the greatest gift for a penitent, a natural history of healing herbs and cordials. When a lady finds herself more harmed than charmed after a visit from the raunchy Mab, in the space of the same shrift with Friar Lorenzo she can confess her sins, be forgiven, and be dispensed some flowery decoction to rid her lips of what blisters she earned playing her lover's trumpet. No wonder Friar Lorenzo is regarded as a treasure without equal in all Verona.

"God give you peace, Angelica," he greets me. "It's been so long since you've come to be shriven, I'd not known which to fear for more, your mortal body or your immortal soul." He lays a hand of blessing on Juliet. "But I see what has kept you away. Lord Cappelletto has already made several generous altar-gifts to celebrate this new member of the Church, and he honored me by choosing my hand to sprinkle her holy baptism." He smiles encouragement at me. "A pleasure, always, to absolve a sin."

I take the holy hint, telling him I hope I'll not disappoint him, having only an hour's worth of lovemaking with my husband to confess. He nods gravely, urging me to unburden myself of every copulatory detail. When I finish, he raises a single eyebrow and asks if that is all.

I bow my head like a dog caught helping himself to a cutlet while the cook's back is turned. "I deceived Lord Cappelletto. I let him believe I only intended to take Juliet to join the procession for the Blessed Virgin. Which I have done. Before I did Pietro."

"And what else?"

"Only Pietro."

"No other bedmate, of course not. But what other sin, my child?" Friar Lorenzo would call even Methuselah himself *my child,* if they ever happened to meet. "Not only in deed, but in thought, we sin."

He means my darling lamb. He can mean only her, for what other secret do I carry? "Sometimes when we are closed up alone together, I imagine she is my own. My Susanna."

Though he hunted for a sin, I mark from the way he pinches at his ear that he does not care to catch me at this one. It was Friar Lorenzo who baptized Susanna, and blessed her shroud. He's the one who told my grief-struck Pietro of the Cappelletti being in need of a wet-nurse, then arranged the terms of my service with them. "Never question the wisdom of God, or of Church," he tells me. "Do not deceive yourself or the child, about what she is and to which family she belongs."

Wise though Friar Lorenzo is, at this moment I realize all he'll never know. Whatever lusty pleasures I take with my husband, he finds forgivable. But my wishing my dead daughter alive, a mother's most urgent desire — that the celibate cleric cannot possibly understand.

After I bow my head, bend my knee, and say my penance, I step from the friary into an afternoon grown gray. When the first fat drops of rain begin to fall, I stop beneath a narrow archway, steadying my back against the rough stones while I slip Juliet inside my dress to keep her dry. As we make our way through the crooking streets to Ca' Cappelletti, she nestles into the warmth of my body. Nothing comes between us. Nothing.

THREE

Every house has its rhythms, and the first I learn of Ca' Cappelletti's is this: Lord Cappelletto rises before the morning bells. He dresses and washes in the dawn's first streaks of light, then breaks his night-fast in the sala beside Juliet's chamber. By the time the prime-hour bells toll, he's guttled himself full. He comes in and takes Juliet from me, holding her so long that when he hands her back she stinks of Lodi cheese and liver pie. Then he rushes downstairs to hear the first of the day's news cried through the streets, before he disappears into some corner room on the ground floor.

"We're free of him," I tell Juliet, though by my mickled saints, I'm as bound as she is, as I wrap her in fresh swaddling. Shut up in this chamber hour upon hour, as two days, three days, four days have passed, all the same.

But as I rock Juliet in her cradle late in

the morning on the fifth day, I see Tybalt crawling out the window opposite, on the far side of Ca' Cappelletti. He slithers on his belly across the kitchen roof, then inches atop the arched entry to the arbor. Passing hand-over-hand along the ledge beneath Juliet's chamber, he pulls himself in through her window.

He carries a toy bird in his mouth, which he drops at my feet. "The king of cats has brought a present for his cousin."

"Even a cat can use a door," I tell him.

"My tutor pushed a cassone against the door, to keep me at my lessons while he goes drinking at the tavern."

Tybalt can escape a room. His tutor can escape the Cappelletti compound. All I can do is stare out the window at what grows within the walled-in arbor. "When your father learns you've disobeyed your tutor —"

"My father is in Mantua, serving at the court of the Gonzaghe. And my uncle is in his study buried in accounting books, except when he's called away to some meeting of the prince's council. And my aunt is in her bedchamber, always in her bedchamber." He pounces on the bird-toy, tossing it into the air and catching it in his mouth. "But now you're here to play with me."

Though the bird's feathers are real, its eyes are dull beads. Flightless, lifeless — like I feel, cabined here.

But I see what the bird-toy cannot: how to play Tybalt by letting him play with me.

"We could have a hide-and-go-a-seeking," I say, "if we could find a place far from your uncle and your aunt."

Tybalt puffs his chest like a blackcock grouse before a hen. "I know the best hidey-hole in Ca' Cappelletti. No one will look for us there."

He pulls back the wall-hanging beside the statue of San Zeno, straining under the weight of the thick weave. Underneath, where I expect bare wall, there's a door with a bolted lock.

A whole world opens off this chamber, and I'd not known it. A world that surely must be full of wonder, if the door is hidden, and barred to me.

Tybalt bids me hold the wall-hanging while he draws his dagger. He works the pointed tip into the lock, twisting it this way and that until the metal working clicks into place.

The door swings open, revealing not gold or marble or any sumptuous thing, but only the interior of the Cappelletti tower. Dank and bare, and of no interest to me. But Tybalt snatches Juliet from her cradle, whisking her through the heavy-beamed doorway. Bounding up the stairs, he calls down to me to hurry.

Inside the tower it's dark, the air a damp chill. The walls are thicker than my Pietro is tall, narrow lines of sunlight barely stealing through the sparse bow-slits. The winding steps are worn shallow in the middle, and the wooden landings groan beneath my weight. I keep my shoulder pressed against the rough stone wall to steady myself. But the stairs stretch on and on like nothing I've climbed. Not since I was Tybalt's age, herding my family's flock up and down mountainsides.

As I rise, my calves burn. And then my thighs. Hot pain twinges across my hips and up my back. I'm not caught halfway up to Tybalt, and already there's no breath left in me.

"I cannot," I call to him. Or try to, gasping out the words.

Not that it matters, as Tybalt pays me no mind. "I'm old enough to climb to the top," he says, "and so are you." As though age is only what makes us able to do, and not what steals the doing from us.

His footsteps grow fainter the farther I am left behind. I'll not be stranded here, partway between unseen ground below and whatever lies above. Not stop to imagine what might happen to Juliet in this dark place, without me to protect her. And so I cross myself and snail up the steps after Tybalt.

My head is light by the time I reach the final landing. But the landing is light too, bathed by the sun pouring through the arched openings that crown the tower. I'm like a blind man startled to regain his sight, blinking at all the bright as I pick my way across the wooden platform. I gather Juliet from Tybalt's thin arms, the tiny warmth of her spreading against my chest.

"Let me show you," Tybalt says. He pulls me to the tower's edge, where I see the city as I've never before seen it, stretching below as though Tybalt, Juliet, and I are angels looking down from heaven.

I know Verona as I do my own body. Every labyrinthed passage and each loose paving stone along my parish streets. The smell of tanneries, of public ovens, and of offal-piles. The snorting hogs upon the piazze, and the rush of the Adige beneath the bridges. But I've never imagined this: that I could stand as tall as the church campaniles, watching the city's roof tiles glint in the sun, the people and animals moving between them as small as crawling insects. The world spreading beneath me glows with the sublime beauty you see in paintings of the Annunciation. And that same holy terror that widens the Blessed Virgin's eyes and flushes her cheeks beats sharp within my own awed breast.

A golden-bellied thrush soars by, so close I lose my footing. I grab at Tybalt to catch my balance, ripping his silken doublet. As he reaches out to steady me, sunlight catches the flesh beneath the tear. It's raised in angry welts, his torso purpled with bruises.

"Who did this to you?"

"Did what?" He asks as though the beatings come so regularly, there is nothing astonishing about them.

My finger circles his discolored skin. Still child-soft, despite the ugly mark. "Who hits you, Tybalt?"

"My tutor, of course. He says that I am slow with Latin, and with the abacus. But he's the one who's slow, and dull. Why should I be bothered with book-lessons, when I can teach myself to jump and joust and parry like brave knights do?"

Pietro's army was true enough to its name, our boys staging epic battles or wrestling like the gladiators of Ancient

Rome. But not one of my unschooled sons ever earned a bruise in the way Tybalt has.

No matter how hungry we were, Pietro never put any of our boys to work for masters who beat them. "You cannot treat a boy like he's a beast," he'd say, "and expect he'll grow up to be a man." Having spent his childhood coddled by his sisters, Pietro saw no need to allow anyone to cuff and thrash his children. Having spent my childhood terrified by my father's beatings, I agreed. But despite all of our indulgence, not one of our boys ever grew to be a man. Who knows what Tybalt, born to wealth and power yet marked with what my sons never had to bear, might come to be?

I tell Tybalt I must sit and nurse Juliet. I let him lead us back down the tower stairs and into our chamber, as I carry her wrapped within my careful arms. I'll mend his doublet while she sleeps.

Lord Cappelletto dines in the sala just before sunset, offering barely a word to his wife, who sits on one side of him, and endlessly haranguing his nephew, who's seated on the other. He speaks of ventures and profits, which bore the boy, and sieges and skirmishes, which thrill him. Lord Cappelletto tells Tybalt that he must learn to move the silver king upon the chessboard in the corner of the sala with cunning care, if he's ever to understand how his uncle moves the young prince who sits upon Verona's throne. Through all Lord Cappelletto's endless lecturing, I'm made to stand beside the table holding Juliet, so that if he happens to look up from his meal, he may gaze upon her.

Though the aromas of the rich foods growl my stomach, I get not one bite of what the Cappelletti eat. When Lord Cappelletto lets out a belch to show he's had his fill, the preening serving-man rushes forward to clear the trencher, and without a word I am dismissed. As soon as we're outside the sala, the serving-man sneers at me, scooping through their leavings with his bare hand to gull whatever he can for himself. I carry Juliet back to our chamber, where I find my own meal: overly boiled farina that's grown cold long before I dip my spoon to it, which I'm to wash down with a jug of wine that's so diluted it tastes more of well-water than of grapes.

It's no mystery what makes a rich man rich. They have what we poor do not: money. This money of theirs is not like what we earn with honest sweat. It has its own magic, by which it is forever making them more of what they've already got. When Pietro and I first came to Verona and were in want of a place to sleep, we pawned everything we'd brought except a single cooking pot, yet had barely enough to rent a narrow little house from a man who was so wealthy he owned more buildings than all his relatives could ever inhabit. Every year since, the rent on our house has come so dear that the landlord grows richer and richer while we stay always poor.

Living within Ca' Cappelletti, I realize a rich man's food is not unlike his money, for I'd swear I can see Lord Cappelletto growing fatter while I am always famished.

So in the middle of a morning hour when he is gone from the compound, and Lady Cappelletta is yet in her bed, and poor Tybalt is at what no right-minded person would call the mercy of his tutor, I gather Juliet in my arms and steal down from our chamber. The autumn day is dry, and the air in the courtyard smells of the acrid odor of olives being pressed to fresh oil, mixed with the heavy must of strong wines aging in barrels in a nearby storeroom, and the fragrance of loaves baking in the Cappelletti oven. The bready scent draws me to such a kitchen as I've never imagined any house could have. Set in its own stone building, it

66

has two open fires along with the oven, and pots of every size hanging from the ceiling and stacked along the walls. A table as big as an ox-cart sits in the center of the room ringed with mysterious jars and jugs, its top covered with sprigs of fresh-pulled herbs.

The man standing at the table does not glance up when I enter. He's got the drawn face of a hare, the skin beneath his eyes shaded from want of sleep. His quick-bladed mincing of parsley does not slow, even while I complain my food's too bland.

"That's no fault of mine," he says, snorting in all the sharp, sweet, thick flavors of the meal he's making. "Lord Cappelletto told me you're not to have any sauce or spice, no hint of flavor that might taint your milk."

This is how I'm spoken of, like I'm some cow being pastured. "I nursed six sons while eating savory dishes, and none of them —"

"None of them is Lord Cappelletto, who is the man who pays my wages." He reaches for a head of garlic, and, sliding his thumb up the dull side of the blade, begins to peel it. "Meager wages they are, for everything I'm got to do to get his meals cooked, the arbor fruit and all the vegetables that are brought in from his country estates preserved, and a winter's worth of meats cured.

They do not keep a man-servant in this house I can trust to send to the market to buy a decent round of cheese, or a pantry-maid with sense enough to keep the mold from growing on it once it's brought back here."

Cribbed as I've been within Juliet's chamber, still I know the truth of what he says. Tybalt's tutor is not the only hireling seeking his own pleasures. The serving-man'd slurp the dregs out of a dead man's cup, or so I suppose from how often his face is flushed with drink. The maid-servant is such a doltish thing she truckles more grime into a room than she ever manages to clean out of it. Tybalt tells me there's no need to grumble over her, for she'll doubtless be gone in a month or two, like all the other maids before her. And whenever I catch sight of the house-page, he's scratching so furiously at himself that I'd not let him within twenty paces of Juliet, to keep whatever infests him away from her, and me. For all the poor are in want of good masters, it's the wonder of Ca' Cappelletti that the rich can be so in want of good servants. A fine riddle that proves for me to puzzle over whenever Juliet's soiled swaddling needs washing, and I must haul up the water bucket from the courtyard well myself, balance the tub above the brazier fire in our chamber to heat it, scrub the strips of fabric clean, and lay them in the sun to dry, all before my babe cries once more to be fed.

"Lazy and insolent," I say, to show him I agree. "It must be trying for so skilled a cook to have to rely on them."

He pitches the peelings into the fire with a flourish, as if to confirm how worthy he is of my compliment.

"So skillful a cook," I continue, "could easily prepare a bowl of hearty broth, and send it up to me with fresh bread and oil. And a bit of cheese, which after all is made from milk. Surely that would do no harm."

For the first time, he raises his eyes to take me in. "Lazy and insolent," he repeats. "And witless as well, if you think I take orders from a common servant."

My quick tongue is ready to tell the cook I'm not some common servant. But Juliet wriggles in my arms, and in the moment I take to soothe her, the cook turns his back to me to toss the garlic into a sizzling pot upon the fire. Then he bends to stir the parsley into a bubbling sauce, and a hole gapes in his breeches, revealing a hairy part of him that I'd just as soon not see.

What use is it to argue with such as him?

I carry Juliet out of the kitchen. Before I

make my way back upstairs, I slip into the arbor. Though the trees are nearly bare, I hunt out the last three apples that've fallen from the branches. Closed up again in our chamber, I gobble the fruit so fast, my stomach twists in pain. But I'm not sorry to have eaten my fill, defying Lord Cappelletto despite the cook.

From the time I could first grasp my mother's skirts, I've always done my part of a household's work. I began as any girl does: mashing herbs, shelling beans, and kneading dough, though soon enough I was stirring ashes back to fire, drawing water by the bucketful, and tossing scraps to hens and hogs. By the time I was eight, I could lay a trap to kill the mouse that'd gotten into our grain, or tell with a single whiff when the cooking oil was near to turning rancid. I stank of manure when the fields were tilled, of lye when we did our laundering, and each night of whatever simmered in the pots I stirred. There was not a chair in my father's house for anyone but him, so I stood even through the long hours when I spun and sewed.

Once Pietro and I were married, I'd barely finish one chore before I had to set my roughened hands to the next. To keep my husband and our growing army of ever-hungry sons fed took such hours of buying and storing and preparing food, there hardly seemed enough light left in the day for all the scrubbing and salting, sieving and weaving, sorting and mending a household requires.

I'd not imagined during any of those work-worn years that one day I would sit for hours in a high-backed chair within an ill-run house with nothing to do but watch a single infant sleep. Would I have believed then that I could feel as dulled by it as I do now? But we are what our life makes us. Hard as I've always had to work, I've never been any good at being idle.

Besides, in the hole exposing the cook's hind-part I glimpsed a portent of something I'll not let come to pass. And so I plot my way into Lady Cappelletta's chamber. Young as she is, younger than five of my six boys would be if they lived, still she is the lady of Ca' Cappelletti. Whatever else the gulling, gadding, tippling, scratching servants do, or do not, to look after the larder and the cleaning and the grounds, the household linens are her responsibility. If she'll not tend to them, by spring not a one of us will have a proper cloth to wipe withal when we relieve ourselves, nor hose or breeches to lace back up once we are done.

This does not occur to Lady Cappelletta until I come into her chamber carrying the spindle, needles, and hoops that Tybalt hunted up among his mother's things. "We should begin while the light is still strong," I say. She's a-bed, eyes red above her lovely cheeks. She nods, barely, and I busy myself with lifting the lid of the nearest linen-chest and surveying its contents, while Tybalt carries his cousin's cradle into the chamber.

Lady Cappelletta grows so distressed at Juliet's presence, I mean to distract her with some comment about how much needs mending. But before I can, Tybalt plucks up her cap and puts it on his head. Letting it fall in front of one eye, he lifts Juliet from the cradle and dances her in her matching cap along the edge of the broad bed, warbling nothing-such words as Lady Cappelletta laughs. This is Tybalt's gift, to himself and to us. Hungry for a mother's love, he mines affection from this aunt who shows none for her own child, just as easily as he does from me, bereft of every child of my own. By the time his tutor calls him to his lessons, Lady Cappelletta is, if not delighted to be left with Juliet and me, at least willing to abide us along with her household duties.

At first she and I speak only about the inventory of linens, what tasks we need to do. I've always liked to work the spindle, the certainty of the spinning, dropping, and catching as wool or flax turns to yarn. The weight and rhythm anchor me. She is more suited to the needle, her young eyes and slim hands working such delicate stitches as I'd never manage. We are ill-matched in many ways, Lady Cappelletta and I, but that is what makes us well-matched for our tasks.

As the weeks of autumn pass, the wool oil seeps into my hands, its sheepy smell staying with me even when I sleep. I begin to spin stories while I spin thread, stories of tending my family's flock when I was a girl. I tell them as cradle-tales for Juliet. Lady Cappelletta shows no sign that she listens, until I soothe Juliet through one colicky suckling by recounting an early blizzard that caught me and my sheep the year I turned twelve. The storm was fierce as well as sudden, purpling the sky and turning the world so dizzying white I'd not believed we'd ever find our way back to my village. I was shivering as much with fear as cold, when a rowdy band of hunters happened across the hill where we'd been stranded. Three of them eyed my plumpest sheep, debating which one to kill off for supper. But the fourth smiled kindly as he eyed me instead, and he convinced the others he'd lead the flock back to my family, for what he was sure would be ample reward.

"Reward it was, and he took it long before we reached my father's house," I say, shifting Juliet from my left breast to my right. Is it any wonder the scent of wool moves me to tell such tales, given how at Pietro's gentle urging I bade my virtue fond farewell before an audience of baaing sheep? "We were married before the spring snowmelt, and soon enough I was at my own lambing."

Lady Cappelletta looks up from her sewing as though she's noticing me for the first time. "You've borne children?"

"Barren women cannot suckle." Does she really need me to tell her such things? "And neither can virgins. Except for the Sainted Maria."

She listens only for what she wants to hear. "Sons? You've been delivered of healthy sons?"

I tell her my children were all boys, and all born healthy. "Except the last, which was neither. God rest them, every one." I mark the sign of the cross against my face and chest, before pretending to busy myself with unraveling Juliet's soiled swaddling.

Hard as it is to speak of all my lost little ones, what pricks most is how Lady Cappelletta disregards their deaths. "How? How did you make sons? If I can bear just one . . ."

I made sons easily, without thinking of it. Made them with Pietro, in all the warmth and strength of his youth. Not a bit like Lady Cappelletta, with her repulsion over the getting and having of babies, nor like Lord Cappelletto, bulbous and spotty with age.

"I did not lie too long in bed," is what I say, "either before my husband came to me, or after." True enough, for each boy I bore only increased the load of my household work.

She nods at my words, though giving up the hours she spends under her bed's rich, heavy covers'll not come easily to her, even if all she does instead is sit robed in furs sewing before the fire. Still, she might as well stop wallowing about like a sow in the mud. So long as a wife loves her bed only when her husband is far from it, she'll not help herself in the getting of a son.

"And I ate sparingly." Again, the truth. We were often hungry, more with each mouth we had to feed. But that's not why I say it.

75

Lord Cappelletto is a man whose opinions grow as his hair does, only where you'd least want to find them. Though I'd not dare raise a plaint with him about what the cook told me, I take some small pleasure in forbidding Lady Cappelletta from having her fill of all the foods that are forbidden me.

She gives another nod, though this one is slower, worry widening her amber-flecked eyes. "The apothecary sent balsam and peony seeds. Not to take by mouth, but to put inside me, there." She gestures toward her lap. "Lord Cappelletto read a treatise by a very learned physick, which says that this will help."

Apothecaries. Treatises. Reading. If people put their faith into these things, is it any wonder they never get around to the making of children? The only remedy I've ever known, ever needed, was simply doing what we without money always do, to take a little pleasure in our lives. We romp, and we rut, and we leave it to the saints to decide when the babies come.

"Plant salves? Flower seeds?" I snort at the idea that those are what she needs inside her. And then I tell her things she'd never imagine, about how to draw a husband's salve and seed into her. I let my eye catch bolster, carpet, pomander — whatever lies around the chamber. Imagining some copulatory use for every object, I describe these acrobatic feats as though they're common practice to all but her. I do not know if any of the acts I describe make a womb more likely to form a boy. But seeing how she looks at me, like a veal-calf watching its fellow herd-mates being slaughtered and then eyeing the butcher as he turns, knife in hand, its way — that's grand amusement to me.

"And if your husband, once he is in that position, can balance with his left leg up," I say, "then you might reach across and slip your mouth about his —"

A small, horrid gurgle cuts me off.

Juliet, my dear babe, shudders in my lap.

She's open-mouthed, her breathing stopped. Her face a ghastly blue.

Blue against the indigo of the cap that, unswaddled, she's pulled from her head. The silk border of the cap is wet. The last two pearls that rowed its edge are missing.

I crook my littlest finger into her tiny mouth and pry out a pearl. Tossing the precious bead to the floor, I fish my finger in again. But in the small, wet cave of her mouth, I cannot feel the second pearl.

I lift her and turn her upside down,

smacking the heel of my hand hard against her back. Nothing. Not a whimper, not a gasp. Not any sign of the deadly jewel.

Lady Cappelletta shrieks. But I'm too terrified to utter a sound.

I turn Juliet face up again and bend closer over her, opening my mouth to cover hers, and her nose as well. I suck in, as deep as I can. Deeper than I thought I could. My great, fat body fills with what I suck from her. A grim reversal of how her small, delicate body has grown these past months with all she's sucked from me.

Suddenly something thumps against my gullet. The pearl, freed from her throat, hits so hard within my own I nearly gag into her mouth. Juliet begins to struggle, kicking and swatting, straining in her desperate will to breathe. But the air's sucked so tight between us, I cannot lift my mouth from hers.

I work my tongue within my mouth, rolling the pearl forward as I pull fresh air in through my nose. Pinning the pearl between my tongue and teeth, I push this breath deep into her. Push myself in that one great breath away from her.

Juliet howls as I spit the pearl into my palm. She's red-faced and wailing, inconsolable. I'm glad for it. I do not know how many nights the sight of her, blue and still, will haunt me. But for now, I relish this lively, angry red of her, proof that she's not gone to join my other little ones.

"What have you done to Juliet?" Lord Cappelletto rushes in, shouting as though Ca' Cappelletti is under sling-and-arrow siege.

"Saved her," Tybalt says, vaulting into the chamber after Lord Cappelletto. "It was amazing, Uncle. My cousin could not breathe, so the nurse did it for her."

Lord Cappelletto's roiling anger boils off in a vapor of worry. "Could not breathe? Is she ill?"

"She choked on a jewel that came loose from her cap," I answer, letting my gaze drop to the once elegant headpiece, crumpled and saliva-soaked at my feet. I want to make him feel that it's his fault, for ordering that an infant wear such a thing.

"I was in the antecamera, practicing my lute, and I saw it all," Tybalt says. "The nurse was giving lessons to my noble aunt, just as the tutor does to me. My cousin turned blue as a spring sky, and the nurse turned her back to the carmine of the prince's pageant-robes."

His half-lie hits me like a shaming slap. I'd not heard a single pluck of a lute string, and if he'd been practicing in the antecamera, how could he see Juliet turn veiny blue? Tybalt must have snuck close to listen to all the filthy things I told Lady Cappelletta. Filthy things I was so consumed with telling, I'd not noticed him — just as I'd not kept careful enough watch over Juliet.

The boy slips something from his sleeve, holds it above Juliet, and slowly lowers the end into her mouth. Her face puckers around it, and she gives suck with that same determined mouth-tugging that makes my nipples ache. She's so pleased with what she tastes, she forgets her sobs. Her angry fists relax, and the red seeps from her face.

Tybalt shines with boyish pride. "I knew a candied orange peel would make my cousin happy. Candies always cheer me. That's why the honey-man gave these to me."

I understand who Tybalt means, but Lord Cappelletto does not. He asks if a honey-man is something like a straw-man.

Tybalt laughs and does a little straw-man dance, as though he has muscleless limbs propped up by poles. "The honey-man's not made of honey," he explains. "He's a maker of it. Or he is a keeper of the bees that make it, and then he makes it into this." He shakes a rainbow of candied fruit pieces from his sleeve. He smiles at his own treasure-stock, but then his face wiggles into a frown. "The honey-man asked if he might keep a hive inside our arbor. May he, Uncle? He says our trees will bear better fruit, which he can candy for us."

Lady Cappelletta's tongue pinks out between her lips, as though she's tasting first one and then another of the candied strips of fig and pear and lemon that sit in Tybalt's hand. Knowing my husband offers more tempting treats than hers ever will, I say, "I heard once of a treatise that said children fed on honey grow both sweet and rich." I keep my eyes on Tybalt and Juliet as I speak, though I mean the words for Lord Cappelletto.

They hit perfectly upon the mark. He waves a hand, the way a wealthy man does to show he spends money with no great consequence, and informs us he is having a dovecote built in the arbor, so Lady Cappelletta can be kept on a breeding diet of dove, and capon and gosling, and eggs and hens of every sort. "This honey-man shall come and place his hive beside the dovecote, in exchange for whatever delicacies please Juliet and Tybalt." He wraps one wrinkled hand around Juliet's tiny fist and with the other tousles his nephew's long curls. Then he plucks up a ruby strip from the boy's store of candied fruit, tossing it between those liver lips as he leaves the chamber.

The moment he's gone, Lady Cappelletta gestures Tybalt to her, taking careful stock of the sweets that are left. She chooses one to eat right off, and three more to hoard beside her sewing things. Tybalt turns to offer me a share, but I busy myself with getting Juliet reswaddled. I bend my head low as I unravel the fresh winding strips, to hide my worry about bees being kept so close, and my flush of anticipation for the visits of the man who'll come to tend them.

But then I notice the army of tiny purple specks beginning to appear on the bottom half of Juliet's face. They form a wine-colored version of the beard and mustache Prince Cansignorio wears. They say the Pope himself ordered the prince to grow the hair on his face, to make public penance for killing his hated older brother to become Verona's ruler.

I do not need the Pope in far-off Avignon to tell me that what stains Juliet is not her guilt. It's mine. I barely emptied my mouth of smutted words before I laid it onto her. Though Tybalt convinced Lord Cappelletto that I saved her, these marks across her face will ruin her, if they remain. What man would marry a beard-besmirched girl, no matter how large her dowry?

But I see still worse in those purple prickles. They are ghostly reminders of God's tokens, the plaguey black specks that spread their way across the lean thighs and muscly arms of my boys, and of countless others like them that the pestilence stole away.

Not Juliet. Not so long as I breathe will I watch the breath seep from her. Tucking a blanket to cover her discolored cheeks, I place my gentlest kiss between Juliet's puzzled eyes and ask Lady Cappelletta's leave to take the infant to the Franciscans, to offer a prayer of thanks that she is saved.

I'm barely through the door of Friar Lorenzo's cell before I am begging absolution for my soul, and some herbal remedy for Juliet's body. "I cannot absolve you," he says, pressing the tips of his long fingers together, "until I know your sin." Man of God and science that he is, he bids me repeat every filthy thing I said to Lady Cappelletta, making me admit which are things I've done myself with Pietro, and which were only my depraved imaginings.

When at last I finish, he asks, "And the bead, did you say it was, on which the child choked?"

Surely he knows what I said. Friar Lorenzo

never forgets a detail that's confessed to him. "Pearls, two of them."

"Where are they now, these pearls?"

I picture where the crumpled cap dropped during my frantic effort to save Juliet. But I do not know what's become of the jewels she sucked from it. "They must've fallen somewhere in Lord and Lady Cappelletti's bedchamber."

His nose twitches like he's a hound scenting rabbit. "Can you find them?"

I cup a hand around the cradle blanket covering Juliet's bare head. She feels so small. Even more fragile than she was on the day when I first met her. The day I lost Susanna. "Can you not offer her some cure without them?"

"A cure? Of course, of course." He does not even bother to examine her before going to his cache of petals, leaves, and seeds. He grinds up some sickly-sweet smelling remedy, which he spoons into a pouch, securing the drawstring with a tiny cross. He tells me to mix two pinches of the herbal with a thimble-full of still-warm goat's milk and rub the paste onto Juliet's chin and cheeks, first thing in the morning, again when the sun is at its highest, and finally after it sinks entirely from the sky. Three times each day I am to pinch and mix and rub, until the guilt-rash goes away.

"Come back then, with the pearls. As a token of thanksgiving to the Holy Church that she is spared."

This many pinches, that many times a day for who knows how many days, and all the while needing to hide Juliet's besmirched face from even Tybalt's curious eyes. My muddled brain is so occupied with trying to remember all of that, it's only after I leave the friary that I stop to wonder where I can get warm goat's milk. Though hogs and chickens, donkeys and wild dogs fill Verona's streets, there's not a goatherd within the city gates. And if Friar Lorenzo knows of some miracle that turns solid cheese back to flowing milk, he's not shared it with me.

But I'll not let Juliet bear that mark. Back in Ca' Cappelletti, I lay her on her big bed. I loose the string that holds the tiny cross and drop two quick pinches of Friar Lorenzo's powdery herbal into a thimble. Pushing off my dress, I squeeze myself like I'm a goat, catching my own warm stream of milk to mix the paste. I coat Juliet's face with it, praying to Sant'Agata to leach the stain from her. I do the same come evening, working with an apothecary's care.

The measuring and mixing vex me even in my sleep, and I wake early, urging Juliet

85

through her suckling so I can begin to work my flow into the thimble.

A cart wheel thumps across the courtyard stones, and Tybalt calls from the far side of Ca' Cappelletti, "The honey-man is here."

I drop the thimble and hurry my lacings closed. Hugging Juliet against me to smother her startled cry, I hie through the sala and down the stairs into the courtyard. But I stop short when Pietro, who's pulling a handcart, turns to me.

I cannot kiss him, cannot even let on that I know him. Not here, where the pompous cook or the prickling page or any other member of the household might peer out and see us. Lord Cappelletto forbids the wet-nurse even a sprig of parsley. He would never tolerate any of her husband's humors tainting her milk.

I nod toward Tybalt, who's dancing with excitement atop the curved ledge of the courtyard well, and say, "You might have sense enough not to wake the whole house, banging about at this hour."

Pietro answers my scolding by shaking a handful of honeyed walnuts out of his pocket and offering them to Tybalt. "Do you know what a swarm is?"

Swarm. Such a soft-sounding word, to carry such threat of stinging.

Tybalt leaps to the ground, stretching himself before Pietro, eager to show off. And even more eager to earn the candy. "That's when bees attack," he says.

Pietro draws back the sweets, shaking his head. "There's no danger in a swarm. They are how new hives are made, like the building of a new church when a parish gets too crowded. When a hive becomes too full, the queen leads some of the bees out to look for a new place to live. That's when the honey-man husbands them. He must make sure they survive in their new home." He pulls the canvas covering off the cart, revealing a log as long as his outstretched arms, capped on each end. "There was a queen whose hive was at my house. But now, she's here."

His words sting in a different way than any bee could. The sting's made all the worse because I do not dare reply, not here.

"Show him where to set the hive in the arbor," I tell Tybalt, "so you and Juliet can watch the bees from her window." And I can see the beekeeper when he comes to tend them, without the rest of Ca' Cappelletti knowing.

I lead the way, settling Juliet onto the bench beside the new-built dovecote while Tybalt and Pietro maneuver the cart through the narrow archway into the arbor. A person could stand within the Cappelletti courtyard all day and not suspect what lies on this side of the passage, hidden behind the kitchen and the chapel. Pietro surveys the copse of fruit trees, amazed, before lifting the hive-log from the cart. Broad-shouldered though he is, still he staggers under the weight of it, his face reddening as he sets it on the ground.

"The honey-man needs a cup of something," I say to Tybalt. "Fetch him some trebbiano."

Tybalt pouts. "I want to see the bees."

"I'll keep the bees sealed in the hive until you're back," Pietro promises.

Tybalt smiles and tumbles off. He's barely out of the arbor before I'm in Pietro's arms. I close my eyes, savoring the feel of his big hands on me, the taste of my mouth on his.

"Angelica, where can we —"

"The boy will be back in only a minute."

Pietro pulls me tighter, as though he means to take me right here, in that single minute. By my troth, were I a younger woman, I might let him.

But age has made me one who savors more slowly. And now that I have Juliet — secluded though the arbor is, I'll not risk having one of the feckless servants bumble in and discover us.

Juliet's chamber is just above us, over the chapel. And beside it is the tower, its dark stair hidden to even the most curious eyes — but opening right into her chamber. "Come to me through there," I say, pointing to the low arch at the bottom of the tower.

I press myself against him for one more kiss, then hurry to the bench and take up Juliet. Crossing back through the courtyard, I climb the stairs to the sala and spirit one of the dinner knives from the credenza. Back in our chamber, I set Juliet in her cradle, making a quick bow to San Zeno before I pull back the wall-hanging. I kneel before the tower door like a penitent before his priest, my lips moving not in prayer but in impatient oaths while I tilt the knife into the lock.

Once the metal working turns and the door heaves on its hinge, I turn back to the window. Pietro is crouching before the hive, Tybalt beside him. My husband points, explaining as he used to do with our boys. Tybalt nods, hungry with questions. But I'm hungry, too. I swing the window wide and wave at Pietro.

He twists a fat cork from a hole in the log. The first bees fly out, turning one loop in the air and then another. As Tybalt spins beneath them, following their paths, Pietro crosses to the tower, his feet quick on the worn stone steps. He is barely in the room before he's inside me.

"Tybalt?" I ask, worried the boy might burst in on us.

"I told him he must count the bees." Pietro runs kisses from beneath my ear all down my neck. "That will occupy him, while I occupy something else." He pulls himself nearly out of me, then plunges slowly in again. Over and over, working up his whetted rhythm, setting off the first tremors deep within me. But as I thrum with pleasure, the prime-hour bells ring.

"Lord Cappelletto." I gasp out the name.

Pietro goes limp inside me. "Angelica, you've let Lord Cappelletto —"

"No. Never." I cannot find words fast enough. "He's a shriveled old thing. But he'll be coming here now, to see Juliet."

I push my husband off me so fast, he rolls to the edge of the broad bed. I give him one more shove, sending poor Pietro tumbling to the floor, and whisper for him to stay there. Working my way back to the other side of the bed, I pull Juliet from her cradle just as the door from the sala opens and

Lord Cappelletto stalks in for his morning visit.

I tip my head, making doe-eyes at Juliet in a grand show of my innocence. Only then am I reminded: the prickle marks still taint her.

"She's just started to give suck." I pull Juliet to me, rubbing my breast against the corner of her mouth. She burrows into me as though she is a rooting pig, and I work the folds of my nightdress to hide her face from Lord Cappelletto.

But he jabs a hairy-knuckled finger at something behind me. "What's that?"

My throat tightens as I turn. Pietro is pressed against the bottom of the bed, hidden from view. The tower door is pulled shut, covered by the wall-hanging. But there, at the feet of the statue of San Zeno, is the dinner knife.

"Tybalt brings things in to play," I say. "He'd invent a broadsword out of anything, to pretend that he's a knight at jousting."

"The Cappelletti have foes enough for him to raise a blade to when he comes of age. But our family silver is not for a child's play. Have Tybalt —"

"Is that the crier, already coming up the Via Cappello?"

Lord Cappelletto, ever impatient to calculate how to turn the day's first news to his family's advantage, forgets whatever was about to trip from his wagging tongue. He makes his daily retreat through the sala, his footsteps echoing down the stairs and into the entryway to Ca' Cappelletti.

Pietro pulls himself back onto the bed. "This is no way for a husband to be with his wife."

"This is the only way for a wet-nurse to be with her husband." I wrap my hand around him, careful not to disturb Juliet. It has never taken much to firm Pietro, and our months apart serve in my favor. As soon as Juliet's had her fill of me, he lays her on the bolster above our heads, as though this was our bed and she our babe.

But once he and I are done and laced back up again, Pietro kneels beside the bed, taking my hand to his lips. "Now that I've a hive here, and the other at our house, I'll harvest more honey and more beeswax. When I sell the wax and what I make with the honey, it will bring enough to pay our rent and keep the two of us, all year."

I am not a stupid woman. I know that when a man contracts to hire a wet-nurse, and another to let his wife serve as one, there is hard bargaining over how much money passes from one to the other, though no one bothers the milk-mother with such details. Whatever Friar Lorenzo said and did when Susanna died to bring me and my nursling together, it was set down as so many soldi to be paid each month by Lord Cappelletto. A sum that is delivered to Pietro by Friar Lorenzo, who keeps some tidy portion as his brokering fee. But what ties me to Juliet is worth far more than money.

"It will be summer before there's honey and beeswax to be harvested," I say. And although I'm not the kind of woman who holds her tongue before her husband, for once I do. I'll not remind him now that it's far longer than that before an infant is weaned. Two years, two and a half — does he not remember how it was with our boys? Would I want any less than that for my last darling?

Before he can answer, the door from the tower creaks open. Tybalt pushes aside the wall-hanging, bounding his way into the chamber as he recites all the many things he's noticed about the hive. How some bees fly, and others crawl along the ground. And some stay within the hive, pushing out the dead. He grabs my husband by the hand, pulling him back into the tower, down the stone steps, and outside.

I leave the window open, listening to their voices in the arbor as I fish the thimble from the bedclothes and prepare Friar Lorenzo's remedy for Juliet.

I've not forgot what else Friar Lorenzo told me I must do. I must bring him those pearls, to give grateful thanks to the Holy Church that Juliet is saved.

I remind myself of this as I sit with Lady Cappelletta in her chamber. While my thick fingers spin a steady rhythm and her thin ones sew, my eyes rove like unleashed beasts, searching the stone floor.

But I cannot find those wayward pearls. Not that first day. Nor the second. As the nones bells ring on the afternoon of the third day, something finally catches my ever-roving gaze. Some lustrous thing wedged within the pebbly crack between two of the large floorstones. Juliet stirs in the cradle, and I reach my foot out to rock her. But I'll not let my eyes leave that spot, certain it's a pearl.

"It must tire you, working such a fine stitch," I say to Lady Cappelletta.

She nods, letting her needle dangle as she rubs her eyes. I sing a slow lullaby about a fast-growing swan, pretending it is meant for Juliet, watching as Lady Cappelletta becomes the bird I sing about, her long, slender neck too delicate to bear the strain of holding up her pretty head.

Once her chin dips down, I say three silent Pater Nosters. When I'm sure she's deep in her sleep, I slip from my chair and lower myself to where the pearl lays. My breath stills as I work a thick forefinger and my fatter thumb into the crevice. The pearl is curved and smooth, and the rough floor-stones scrape my knuckles raw as I pry it loose.

Tucking the gem inside my dress, I survey every inch of all the rest of the floor. But search as I might, I cannot find the second pearl. Just yesterday, Marietta took her leave of Ca' Cappelletti. Or Maddalena, maybe she was called. The latest of the serving-maids, she'd not stayed long enough for anyone to be certain of her name, and was gone so quick there'd not have been time to shout it after her even if we'd known it. Perhaps it was the weight of a pilfered pearl in her pocket that carried her away so fast, well beyond anywhere Lord Cappelletto, let alone the wet-nurse, might find her.

When Juliet and I lie at night in her great bed, I roll my own purloined pearl in my palm, imagining how much it might bring at one of the money-lender's stalls. Who knows how far Pietro and I might travel on that sum, what of the wide world we could discover together. But precious as the pearl is, it is nothing compared to Juliet. No more than a small, hard sphere beside my warm, soft girl.

I go early the next morning to make my shrift. Friar Lorenzo greets me with his familiar "God give you peace" as I pull the blanket from Juliet's head to show him how the purply prickle has faded.

"So dark." His words confound me, until I realize that he does not mean her face. He means her new-sprouted hair.

In place of the blonde down she was born with, this hair is as coarse and dark as mine. And her eyes — they've darkened too, so slowly I've not noticed, from their first pale gray, past Lady Cappelletta's amber, to a deep brown that matches my own. "It must be your milk," he says.

I'm not a woman who blushes easily, not even in a friar's cell. What use is such coyness before your holy confessor? Still, my cheeks redden as I wonder how he knows that I used my own milk to concoct his remedy for Juliet. "The hair came in before that," I say.

"Before? You've nursed her since she was born."

I realize too late that he'd not known. Not until I half-told what now he makes me tell in full. I silently beg forgiveness, not from my saints but from Juliet, as my guilty tongue betrays how I milked myself to heal her, a secret only she and I should share.

Friar Lorenzo frowns and mutters something about seething the flesh of a kid in the milk of its mother. As if goat stew has anything to do with my darling girl. "Remember your place, Angelica. You are only her wet-nurse."

How could I forget my place when it's with Juliet, always with Juliet? I'm the one, the only one, who wakes with her and sleeps holding her, the one who's given up Pietro and my little house and my whole life for her. The one who suckles her, and saved her. "Only her wet-nurse," I repeat, nodding. There's much of Juliet's heart that only her wet-nurse can know.

I draw the pearl from my belt-purse and pass it to Friar Lorenzo.

"Only one?" he asks. That same *only.* Always it is that same *only,* when he speaks of what I am, and what I do, and what I bring.

With a quick tug of his purse string, Lord Cappelletto gives the Church far greater offerings than this lone pearl. Altar-gifts to celebrate Juliet's birth. The cost of a month's fresco painting to commemorate a saint's day. A handsome sum of silver coins, that God might favor the commencement or completion of some business dealing in which Lord Cappelletto has an interest. He'd drop a diadem's worth of pearls into Friar Lorenzo's waiting palm, for he gladly tithes from his vast riches. And, eager to best every other noble family in Verona, even more gladly brags of it.

But this thanksgiving gift for saving Juliet comes from me, alone. I searched and searched, and found the pearl. And if it was any sin to take it, surely it is absolution to give it over to the Church.

"I prayed to the Holy Mother to help me find the pearl Juliet choked on, and she did," I say. "Only one, so that must be what the Blessed Maria knows the Church should have."

Friar Lorenzo looks at me. Looks, I swear, into my very soul. Then he pockets his precious gem and sends us back to Ca' Cappelletti.

FOUR

During all the years I ran my own house, I never relished how I had to hurry my dough to the city ovens for baking, or bargain for every bent coin's worth of household necessities I bought in the market. How I hefted dirty pots to the fountain, scrubbing them while I sweated under the sun's heat or shivered with the winter's cold or soaked to sodden in the rain that might come any time of year, then hauled them home filled with whatever water we'd need until I returned to the public fountain the next day with another load to clean. With so many tasks pulling me through Verona's teeming streets, I never saw the joy in any of them, until passing the winter within Ca' Cappelletti.

There are braziers to heat every room in this house, and at least the itchy little house-page never lets the woodpile dwindle. But the smoke-thick air that hangs inside is rough in my throat. So rough my eyes tear, and I long to walk in the bone-chill of the fresh winds blowing off the Adige. Instead, I'm shut away like some lord's jealously guarded wife, going out only when I can give excuse to see Friar Lorenzo. And how often can a wet-nurse tell her employer she has sins she must confess?

Juliet is as restless as I am, angry that I can do nothing about the teeth tearing their way out of her gums. Why a babe of six months needs teeth at all, I cannot say, when surely I'm enough to feed her. Or would be enough, if not for the pain those teeth bring her. Sore and sullen, my beloved nursling shoves my breast away like I am no comfort to her.

Only Lord Cappelletto savors these dark days. Some of his seed seems to have settled in his wife, and he's as pleased as she is sick with it. He thunders in as we sit with our sewing, carrying a gilt chest nearly as large as Juliet's cradle. The sight, or perchance the smell, of him makes Lady Cappelletta heave into the bucket that now is always beside her. While he waits for her to finish, he beams just like Tybalt does whenever he has some new trick he wants to show us.

"I've brought your dowry jewels."

"They are not mine," Lady Cappelletta says. "They are yours." Her voice is uncertain. As though she fears that for all her retching, she and the jewels are about to be packed up and sent back to whatever family cared so little for her happiness, they married her off to this old mule.

"They are mine so long as you are mine, and I shall choose which ones you'll wear, and with which gown, on the palio-day."

"The foot race?" Lady Cappelletta eyes go so wide, perhaps she worries that he means for her to run the course herself. A fine show it would be, her huffing along among the teams of well-oiled men nominated each year from the city's assorted parishes to compete in the race, named for the green palio-cloth that's awarded to the winner.

But that's not the spectacle Lord Cappelletto means to make of his pretty young bride. "Prince Cansignorio is hosting a palio-day banquet for Verona's hundred richest men, and their wives. There'll be more than one family there to whom we owe a century-old grudge, and I'll not be outshone by any of them."

He unlocks the little chest, selecting a pile of gold buttons and silver-set gems for us to sew onto her gown and sleeves, and an even larger pile we're to attach to his robe and doublet. It will be no easy thing to work so many fancy stitches, with the palio-day only a week away. But when Lord Cappelletto snaps the chest shut and departs, I'm glad to take up a needle, and to have Lady Cappelletta do the same.

Verona's palio-race has been run along the campo outside the city walls for a hundred years at least. Longer than the Scaligeri have ruled Verona. But Lord Cappelletto's boasted to Tybalt about how he advised Prince Cansignorio, who is ever eager to surpass the brother who ruled before him, to extend the length of this year's race all the way to the Piazza dei Signori. And to richen the prize. The new prince will gift the winner not only with the traditional palio-cloth but with three whole bolts of pale blue samite, thumb-wide bands of gold and silver woven through the thick fabric. Also a riding horse bred from his royal stable, and a brace of fatted geese. Before the race begins, there will be endless delights for the gawking eyes of any who line the course. Musicians. Jugglers. The prince's whole menagerie paraded by. Perhaps an exorcism, if Providence will send some bedeviled soul for the saving. Prince Cansignorio promises Verona a celebration to make even the bishop forget it is a Lenten Sunday.

I, of course, am no bishop. So while Lord and Lady Cappelletti vie with rival nobles for the favor of the prince's table, I'll steal away to watch the race with Pietro, cheering as we always do for our parish-runner. I deserve an excursion outside Ca' Cappelletti, beyond the city gates. And tetchy as Juliet's grown from teething, perchance a few hours of fresh air, and fresh sights, will distract her.

Verona's narrow streets ring thick with different languages on the palio-day. Not just the dialects of Venetians and Tuscans, or Sards and Calabrians. The air is heavy with the guttural languages spoken by those who come from across the Alps and far to the North, as well as the rapid, jagged rasps of Arabian traders. There are those who say the world is broad and wide, and those who say there is no world without Verona's walls. Today it seems that both are right: the broad, wide world throngs within the city walls, separating me from Pietro. As the inns empty of foreigners, I push through the crowded streets, Juliet tight in my arms, and Tybalt close by my side.

He appeared in Juliet's chamber this morning, just after his aunt and uncle left for the prince's castle. Chittering away while he watched me braid my hair, ready my overgown, and slip on my veil, never considering that I might not intend to bring him with me. This is my own doing. From the first day nimble Tybalt came into Juliet's chamber, I've taught him to funnel his love for his dead mother and his sent-away sister onto her. He entertains her for hours on end, delighting in filling her with delight. It is always the bitterest of sweetness to see them together, for he is of an age somewhere between Nesto and Donato, and offers Juliet the same tender affection my sons showered on their littlest brother, Angelo.

How could I leave Tybalt behind? He is so lonely. So sensitive. And he is the closest companion I have within Ca' Cappelletti, as I whisper when I remind him that our outing is to be an especial secret, just between him and me, and Juliet.

Tybalt marvels at the throngs who are turning out for the race, bowing his head in reverence to the clusters of dark-robed priests and priors, then gawking at the eager hands of pickpockets and prostitutes. But even such wondrous distractions do not keep him from asking, "Will my father be here?" as we cross beneath the massive portraits of San Zeno and San Cristoforo that decorate the city gate.

Tybalt's widowed father has been in Mantua longer than I've been at Ca' Cappelletti. Tybalt asked for him on All Saint's Day, on Christmas Day, on the Feast of the Epiphany. Even, out of habit, on a few lesser saints' days. Always there is a letter, with his father's seal. Letters so full of sentiment, Lord Cappelletto refuses to read them aloud, leaving little Tybalt to struggle to decipher his father's ornate script. Though I cannot read a word, I learn from those letters what Tybalt is too young to understand: why his father left him. Too attached to the dead wife whose features show in her living son. Too afraid to cherish the boy, lest he be lost as well.

"Do you see Pietro?" Better, I reason, to distract Tybalt with a question that will delight him, than to give his own question the same-again answer that shadows even his happiest days.

Pietro comes to check the hive in the Cappelletti arbor as often as he can, though still not as often as I want him. Whenever he appears, Tybalt follows him like a waggly-tailed pup, reporting all he's observed of the bees since Pietro's last visit. Young though he is, Tybalt's no fool, and when he asked me how I knew the honey-man, I made him cross his heart and swear upon his much-cherished honor to keep the answer to himself. But when I then confided that Pietro is to me what Lord Cappelletto is to Lady Cappelletta, Tybalt laughed and said this could not be true, for his uncle and aunt never smile at each other as Pietro and I do. What else we do we are careful to keep from him, and with each visit, Pietro crafts evermore elaborate challenges to distract the boy long enough for us to sneak our time together in Juliet's broad bed. Or upon the stone floor of her chamber. Or against its carved-wood door. By my troth, there's not an inch of that room that Pietro and I've not explored as we explore each other, hurrying ourselves to be done before Tybalt bursts in to show off the latest king-fisher feather, or goat horn, or bear claw that Pietro bade him find.

At my mention of Pietro, Tybalt scrambles ahead, searching out the spot along the edge of the race-course where my husband has stretched a bedsheet for us to sit upon as we watch the day's entertainments. It is one of my better sheets, just the thing a man would choose to throw onto the ground, never mind how people to either side will grind their filthy soles into it. A year ago, I would have carped at Pietro for ruining a sheet this way. But now I sleep on far finer linens, stitched with the Cappelletti seal by Lady Cappelletta's own hand. My worn bedding, my musty marriage-chest, the few tiny rooms of our rented house — they've become part of another life, the life I had before I had Juliet.

Tybalt runs to Pietro, who catches him up, swinging the boy in his two strong arms so that Tybalt somersaults high in the air before tumbling onto the sheet with a laughing shriek. Pietro, already red-cheeked and purple-tongued, offers me a swig from a three-quarters-plump wineskin As he lays his stubbly cheek against Juliet's smooth one, he slips a hand inside my dress, rubbing with his thumb in a way that sends shivers all through me.

I give his hand a playful slap. "Best not set a pot to boil, if you've no way to let off its steam."

We settle on the sheet sitting one inside the other like a set of stacking bowls, my back warming against Pietro's broad chest and his big legs curving snug around my hips, passing the wineskin between us to ward off the February chill. Though the ruby barbera's not of so fine a quality as what fills the casks at Ca' Cappelletti, at least it's not watered down like the pale trebbiano Lord Cappelletto allows me to be served.

I pour some of the barbera onto my pinky and rub it along Juliet's aching gums. The wine, and being out in the brisk air, soothe her. She coos at the bright scarf I bob before her, while Tybalt runs along the edge of the raceway, doubling back every few minutes to report on what spectacle of minstrels or stilt-walkers will soon parade before us.

I wait until the boy is out of earshot to tell Pietro about Lady Cappelletta. "It's a mystery how a woman can eat so little yet vomit so much. At least, it is a mystery to her." I lift the wineskin in toast to her ignorance. "I told her it's a sure sign she is carrying a son, a strong boy who wants her belly all to himself. I can be kind to her, when I have a mind to."

Pietro leans back, letting cool air fill the space between us. "What kindness is there in lying to her?"

"You do not know that it's a lie. It might be a son. Or a daughter. Or a hairy mole. Or an overly bilious humor. Or a clever ruse to keep her husband from her bed, though I doubt she is capable of that." How can Pietro chide me? "Why not let her believe she carries his heir, if that makes it easier for her to suffer these months of constant retching?"

He reminds me the rich are spiteful. "If she does not bear the son you've promised, she may take her disappointment out on you."

"Until she bears a son, her husband has her in such a qualmish state, she's not able to do much hurt to me, or to anyone else." I hope this will prove true, that there will be a healthy boy to please the father and relieve the mother, before Juliet is old enough to notice how Lady Cappelletta looks at her.

"I'll make some ginger comfits, taffied with honey and almond milk, for you to give her when her stomach needs steadying."

I do not care to have my husband thinking up treats for Lady Cappelletta. "The Apothecary Guild will come after you, if you start making medicines."

Mischief plays along his face. "Perhaps you can demonstrate what punishment you think the guild master should demand?" He pulls me close, his breath warm. "I miss you, Angelica. The smell of you, the taste of you. That perfumed bed in another man's house — that's no way for us to be together." He draws Juliet away from me. "Let Tybalt watch her for a little while."

It's more than wine that's stoking my husband. Stoking me, too. And it's true, Tybalt is devoted to Juliet. If I tell him to count out the number of monkeys and baboons to her as the prince's gilt-caged menagerie parades by, and to make up a fabulous story to tell her about each of the prince's lions, he'll do it, whether I am watching over his shoulder or not. Perhaps when he reappears, Pietro and I might —

A curse and a splintering crack split the air. Four of the young men who've been calling out bets for the palio-race swear and jump on a fifth, who's broken a cudgel over one of their heads. The foursome topples the culprit, and all five tumble in a mass of angry arms and legs onto our sheet. The broken cudgel swings wildly, smashing the side of my face.

Something jagged catches inside my cheek, and salty blood thicks into my mouth. I spit one molar and then another onto the bedsheet, as a crowd of gangly, coltish youth, some barely past their boyhood, swarm at us.

Pietro pushes Juliet into my arms, wrapping himself around us as he tries to pull me to my feet. But it's impossible to stay standing amidst the angry surge.

Hundreds of them, there suddenly seem to be. Some coming from the campo and others pouring out from the city gates. All of them swinging fists, clubs, whatever they can grab, while decent people struggle to shove their way clear.

I bend over Juliet, my body the only protection I can give her. Pushing my tongue against the bloodied gap on the side of my mouth, I hold to her like a half-drowned person clings to a floating log, as everything we have with us — our bedsheet, the scarf, and my lost teeth — are swallowed up in the press of bodies.

It's impossible to see more than a few arms-lengths in the direction we last saw Tybalt run, away from the city toward where the race was meant to start. I realize there's no way Pietro and I can keep Juliet safe if we try to go after him. And I'm too afraid, for her and for myself, to send Pietro off alone.

A mother of sons knows which boys have to be watched every waking moment — and some sleeping ones as well — to be kept from trouble, and which might wander off but will always return, none the worse for their adventures. Though cat-like Tybalt loves to leap, he always lands on his paws. Or so I've believed. But who knows what might become of such a trusting boy in the midst of a fist-ready mob.

Terrified families pour into the race

course. The frenzied mob, hungry for more space in which to fight, follows. Pietro half-pulls, half-carries me in the other direction, into the sycamores edging the campo. The grove seethes with shrieking children, frightened mothers, and uncertain fathers. Near us, a trembling girl of twelve or fourteen sobs. Her mother kneels before her, trying to work some tuck in the girl's torn gown to cover her tiny breasts and belly, which have been badly pummeled in the fray. I turn away and seek the only comfort I can think of, leaning against a thick-branched sycamore to nurse Juliet.

My poor lamb must be half-starved, for she drinks me in as she's not done in the weeks since her teething started, those new-sharp teeth shooting a delicious pain through my too-full breast.

Pietro watches her suck with eyes full of wonder, the way he did when I suckled our sons. When I curse the brawlers, he says, "They are just boys. Their blood is still so hot from the pleasure-filled nights of Carnival, they seek mischief even now that it is Lent."

"Not all boys are so hot-blooded." Our boys, I mean. They might have tussled with each other, but Nunzio and Nesto both had Pietro's tender heart. They kept their younger brothers from any real harm. Except once, that once. It was Berto who led them to it. Or maybe Enzo. I was never sure, for none of them would tell me how it happened. And before I could wheedle or harangue it out of them, death stilled all their tongues. For months afterwards, I pleaded with the saints, cataloguing all I'd do if they would give me back my sons. Even just one or two, if I could not have them all. Who cares which was the first to lead the others into danger?

"It must have been a group of Florentines who started it." I cannot understand what Pietro means, until I realize he's talking not about our boys, but about the brawlers. He repeats what everyone around us is saying, about a bridge in Florence where the young men gather by torchlight to fight. Not ten or twenty of them, as might come to blows in any God-fearing city, but eight or nine hundred at a time, some barely old enough to grow hair on their chins, or anywhere below. All punching and stabbing at once, until they cannot tell friend from enemy in the maddened fray.

"This is not Florence," I say. Verona's not suffered such fighting in years. Not since Prince Cangrande II put down a rebellion early in his reign, ordering every soul in the city into the Arena to watch as he hacked off the heads of a half dozen conspirators. I'd buried my face against Pietro as each condemned man was blind-folded. Like the kneeling, bare-necked culprits, I'd not known when the first axe blow would fall. Though my stomach leapt at each thwacking execution, what haunted me more were the scores of others Cangrande II tortured and left dangling from the old Roman bridge over the Adige. Their cries echoed through the city for three days and three nights as they begged Death to take them, while ravens plucked at their bloodied bodies.

But in the sound and sight and smell of their agony, the rest of Verona knew ourselves safe. After that, the only blood shed in our streets was what Cangrande II ordered to amuse himself. Ambushes followed by savage beatings, mostly. Or a quick-plunged blade of assassination. Such attacks were plentiful, to be sure, for he was a brutal man, but they were aimed only at whatever noblemen the prince deemed too powerful. A prudent mother could easily keep her children locked at home until each spurt of violence was over.

But Cangrande II is dead. And though no one mourned him, not even his widow nor

114

either of his mistresses, as I shiver in the sycamore grove I realize no one knows if Prince Cansignorio is man enough to keep the city's peace. Cansignorio, after all, has never killed anyone aside from his own brother. And after that, he fled to Padova until he was certain he'd be welcomed back as Verona's new rightful ruler. What good is a prince who cannot keep a youthful mob — or the warring Milanese or wily Mantuans — at bay?

Bells ring from inside the city walls, one angry peal answering another. Word spreads through the sycamores that the Franciscans are making their way out to the campo. Walking bare-footed in brown-robed pairs and chanting in Latin, as though godly incantations can stop a fist or club mid-swing.

All at once, the earth itself begins to rumble. Worry rounds Juliet's eyes as hundreds of horse-hooves thunder against the ground. The angry rhythm sets off a wave of anticipation throughout the grove. Prince Cansignorio must have sent his knights at last. Whether he rides at their head, as the older generations of Scaligeri did, or sits drinking from golden goblets with his wealthy guests, none of us in the grove can guess. But we listen with care to the crashing lances of a hundred mounted knights, and the tormented shrieks of whoever is in their path.

At last the sounds of fighting die away, and the brigade clatters off. Families all around us gather themselves, convincing one another they feel safe enough to leave the sycamores and make their way home. But I cannot take Juliet back to Ca' Cappelletti. Not without Tybalt.

The barbera burns in my belly, my head aching from its vapors. Why did I bring him withal? Why, having brought him, did I not keep him near? Tybalt is neither my child nor my charge. But he's a tender boy. And he is Juliet's cousin, the only nephew of her powerful father. How could I risk not only his little neck but also every tie I have to her?

Juliet, squirming in my arms, begins to cry for Tybalt. By my heart, I know the half dozen ways she shares any unhappiness with me. She cries when she is hungry for my breast, and she cries when her swaddling becomes too full of piss and shit. Cries from colic, though not often, given what Lord Cappelletto lets me be fed. Cries from the cold or the heat or the aching in her gums. Cries when she is too long in her mother's presence. And cries when she is too long from her cousin's.

I somehow believe Juliet's sobs will draw Tybalt to us. When they do not, my wine-soaked worry deepens. "What if —"

Before I can give voice to all I fear, Pietro cuts me off. "He strayed away before the fighting started. We'll find him, and you'll see he's fine."

Pietro is a hopeful man. But that can sometimes wear upon a wife. He knows I have no patience for being told everything is fine, when in truth neither of us can tell how well, or how awfully, something might turn out.

Walking out from among the trees, we pass brawlers and innocents alike, dragging their mauled selves from the campo. Those too hurt to walk howl for friend or stranger to take mercy on them. The gilded cages of the menagerie lie toppled on their sides, the whimpers of the frightened animals inside swelling into the cacophony of human shouts and cries. But we see no sign of Tybalt and no trace of where we sat when he last left us.

"There's no place for him to find his way back to." I raise my voice to make myself heard above Juliet, whose wailing grows louder the longer she longs for her cousin, who could be halfway to Villafranca by now.

Or drowned in the Adige. Or carried off by ransom-seekers. "And no way for us to know where to look for him."

"So we will look in all directions," Pietro says. He starts to walk in a circle. Not a perfect round, but an ever-widening curve that slowly grows to take in a greater and greater area.

I taught him this trick years ago. Whenever a sheep strayed off, I'd spiral farther and farther around my flock until I found it. But sometimes what was left to be found was only the mauled remains that a bloody-fanged wolf had left behind.

Pietro keeps walking, the distance between us growing as he circles away. I'm not the sort of wife who follows anywhere her husband leads. But then he begins to whistle. He knows I cannot stand him whistling when I'm worried. I cut in a sharp line across his curving path, scolding him to pray instead, or just to shut up entirely. Anything but that cheerful whistling, which does not seem right until we find Tybalt.

"Until," he repeats, meaning to assure me the boy will be found. Pietro slips an arm around me, and we walk side by side. Curling our way beyond what was crushed in the brawl, we cross winter-bare fields, Juliet inconsolable in my arms. We've walked for who knows how long, my throat aching from calling for the lost boy, when Pietro stops. He hears first what I, soaked in Juliet's crying, miss: the matched cries of Tybalt, pitched as high as those of his baby cousin.

Tybalt is tucked in the crook of an olive tree. Pietro reaches up, murmuring gentle words until the boy crawls into his arms. His big hands run over the teary child, and he shrugs to let me know neither flesh nor bones seem broken.

"The brawl is over." Pietro cradles Tybalt to his chest as I cradle Juliet to mine. "The mob is gone, it's safe to come back with us now."

Tybalt tips his head up. "What brawl? What mob?"

"Never mind about that," I say. I pass a hand through the boy's pretty curls, as much to reassure myself as to comfort him. "Why were you hiding?"

"The other boys said I could not win."

My relief at finding Tybalt ebbs back into worry. "What other boys?"

"There were five of them. We had a contest to see who could piss the highest. I made an arc just like a fountain, I should've beat them all. But one of them, who was smaller than me but wore a fur-trimmed carmine

119

cloak just like the prince's, said I'd not win unless I could make myself into a statue the way he can."

I work the edge of my tongue in and out of my fresh-cracked toothhole, trying to dull the throbbing edge of pain as I puzzle through what Tybalt means. The boy he met must be Cansignorio's nephew, Count Mercutio, who's been sent by the prince's conniving sister and her calculating husband to Verona to serve in the court of his ruling uncle. Everyone knows why, though no one dares say it out loud: if Cansignorio cannot make a legitimate heir, this Mercutio might one day rule our city. Unless he somehow provokes his living uncle, and thus meets the same fate as his murdered one. Such are the prospects of a royal boy.

"Even counts and princes cannot turn themselves into statues," I say, thinking Tybalt is confused by the tombs of the Scaligeri, which rise high above the churchyard of Santa Maria Antica, each with a sculpted likeness of the man whose remains it covers. The sarcophagus of Cangrande I is topped with a statue of the prince astride his horse, his sword sticking up from his lap in such a way that Pietro snickers whenever he passes it, saying all of Verona can see in that extended member why Cangrande I was called the big dog.

"This one can," Tybalt insists. "After he shook his last piss drops off, he turned like marble down there. I shook myself and tried to turn to stone, too. But I could not."

I cannot help but smile at the idea of Mercutio swinging his little manhood at Tybalt like a miniature version of the rock-hard sword sported by the death-statue of Cangrande I. It's welcome relief after all the terror of the brawl to laugh at the way small boys tease each other.

As we walk back to the city gates, Pietro provides the talk that Tybalt's father is too far off to give. If only we could pass a ram tipping its ewe, or a mastiff mounting a bitch in heat. But you never happen upon those things when they are most convenient, and so Pietro gestures wildly to illustrate his explanations. Though I walk a little ways off in the hope Tybalt might forget that Juliet and I are here at all, I mark the way he tilts his ear, struggling to understand what turns a man hard as stone, and softens him back up again.

To me, those things are far easier to grasp than what would bring youth not half a dozen years older than Tybalt and Mercutio to such bloody conflict, leaving the campo

121

trampled, the palio-race unrun, and who knows how many innocents hurt or killed.

FIVE

Shad, eel, perch, carp, pike, trout. Pickled, salted, smoked, breaded and fried. In the forty meatless, milkless days of Lent, the cook dishes up so much fish for the Cappelletti, I swim the Adige in my dreams. I visit whole underwater kingdoms as I sleep, a twitch of what are no longer my human hips sending me gliding headlong through mysterious dark channels. My scales shimmer in the cool rush of river-water, and I want to stay weightless and submerged forever. Until the night between Maundy Thursday and Good Friday, when a whole herd of gaping-eyed sea monsters chase me in my sleep, sinking fangs into my guts as I struggle to swim free. I wake gasping for air, beached on Juliet's big bed.

I need to relieve myself. There is a filth bucket beside the bed, where I'm meant to empty my bladder and bowels. But I just dumped and scrubbed the bucket after supper. Rather than soil it again so soon, I make my way through the dark sala to the privy closet in the antecamera outside Lord and Lady Cappelletti's bedchamber. It's the first private necessary I've ever seen, and I sneak into it whenever I can. Shutting myself inside I always feel, if not like a queen upon a throne, at least like a fat hen on her roost. It holds the cleanest waste pot in the house, the maid hauling off the contents three times a day. Which you'd think is often enough.

Yet as I approach the door, the stink wrenches my stomach halfway to my mouth. Lord Cappelletto must have filled the privy with who knows what ill-humorous excretions. Surely I'd do better to go back to my own bucket.

But then I hear the whimpers. Small, wounded sounds, more of fear than physical hurt. A noise I first heard from a neighbor's puppy, not at the moment my father smacked it hard between the eyes for digging in our field but when, seeing the stick swung high once more, the animal sensed it was about to be struck again.

Pushing open the door, I realize the stench is not of piss or shit. It's rot. The fetid rot of human flesh, which hung so heavy during the great pestilence that no one who lived

124

then can ever forget it. It's coming not from the high-sided privy pot, but from Lady Cappelletta, who lies curled into a sweat-soaked ball on the cold floor.

This is my luck, to escape sea monsters in my sleep only to wake to this.

I kneel in the doorway, one hand covering my nose and mouth, the other gently pulling free the thick locks of Lady Cappelletta's hair, on which she's sucking.

"I reek," she says.

It is so true, I do not bother to disagree. "Where is the pain?"

"Gone. Since last week."

"A week past, and you've not yet sent for the midwife?"

"Lord Cappelletto calls for the midwife, when it is my time." Her eyes swim up, then down, uncertain. "Is it my time?"

Fifteen and lady of a grand house, yet she's still more of a child than I ever had the chance to be. Already delivered of a daughter, she knows less of bodily things than I did even before my first babe quickened in me. I'd tended a herd. Watching my flocklings tup then lamb, I formed some vague understanding of the relationship between the two. Learned, from watching, all the troubles there were to worry over. I saw lambs come out feet first. Or two-

125

headed. Or, twisted up within a bleating, terrified mother, not at all.

"If you're in pain, the midwife should come."

"But I'm not in pain, not since last week."

"That is when she should have come. Now it may be too —" I catch myself. What use is there in lecturing? I lay a careful hand across the rise of her belly. "Has it moved since then?"

She shakes her head, keeping her eyes from mine.

It's not that she does not know. It's that she'll not admit to herself what she knows.

"And the smell, when did that start?"

"Just the last day."

"Have you bled?" I ask, and she nods. "But nothing else has come out?"

She cocks her head at me, like a slow-witted horse.

I try to make my words gentle, but what is the use? "It needs to come out of you."

"They die if they come out too early, that is what my sister told me when she gave me my bridal-chamber instruction. I must keep it in me. Lord Cappelletto needs his heir."

A privy closet is no place for prolonged debate, especially when its inhabitant is putrid. And too terrified to understand what's happening to her. I brush Lady Cappelletta's feverish cheek, wondering how long she's hidden here trying to deny the death inside her. This is the difference between us. I lost an infant I'd not even known I carried. She carries an infant she'll not admit is lost. The two of us, huddling with our separate griefs in this tight space.

"Lord Cappelletto waited this late to marry," I say. "He can wait a little longer to make a son."

"He did not wait. He had sons." Her voice drops. "It is not his fault if I cannot make a healthy boy. His first wife gave him three sons, before she ever had a daughter, as he likes to remind me. He still calls for her in his sleep, thirteen years after the plague took them all."

I slump onto my heels, feeling the weight of what Lord Cappelletto survived. To lose all one's children, this most terrible grief I know too well. But to endure it alone — that I cannot imagine. I would have thrown myself into the same shallow grave that swallowed my sons if Pietro had not held so tight to me, his grief as great as mine. I can only pity Lord Cappelletto for whatever twisted curse of luck kept him alone alive. And Lady Cappelletta — though she'd hardly been out of infant swaddling when the plague ravaged Verona, the ghost of it yet hovers over her marriage bed, festering its way inside her.

"The midwife must come, and maybe a surgeon, too." What more can I say to make her understand? "It's already dead, and must come out of you. To be buried, like his others." I add the last part in the hope of convincing her that Lord Cappelletto will be moved to sympathy by this new loss. But we both know her dead issue cannot be buried in his family tomb, or any consecrated ground, its unbaptized soul condemned to who knows what eternal fate.

She grabs my hand, crushing my fingers with a surprising fury. "She took it. I know she did." She speaks with a lunatic's urgency. "I hate her."

"Who?"

"Juliet."

What is she saying in her madness? "She's just an infant."

"Not the brat, the other one. The one he named her for. His dead wife. I hear it every night: Juliet, most cherished, departed mother. Even in his sleep he taunts me with it, to remind me of what I'm not."

So this is why she loathes my Juliet. A treasured jewel named for a wife Lord Cappelletto may have truly loved, the mother of all he'd lost. All the things he's given my dearest lamb — ivory-inlaid cradle, pearl-trimmed cap, grandly godfathered christening-day — such weak talismans against what he and I and everyone who lived through that awful time knows can so quickly snatch breath and life and joy away.

When death decides to come, neither wealth nor piety can stop it. We know this, and yet we bargain with our saints and ourselves, every moment of every day trying to deny the one great truth of life: loss. It is a fool's bargain, but still we make it.

"You are his living wife," I remind her, "and you've given him his only living child." Given me my only living child as well. A child I need to protect. Protect even — especially — from Lady Cappelletta. "Let them take what stinks of him from you. As long as you survive, that is all that matters."

She gives the slightest nod and eases her grip on me. I fold her fingers around the garnet-studded cross that hangs on a thick chain around her thin neck, to give her something to hold to once I leave her.

She slips the bejeweled cross-piece into her mouth, sucking like a child and rocking herself back and forth. Unsound body, unsound mind. You need not be a midwife or a physick to know which is the harder to salve. I unbend myself, my legs tingling and unsteady as I go to wake Lord Cappelletto.

When I part the curtain around their marriage bed, I see in his sleep-softened face some tender thing I've never before noticed in him. Not so gentle-hearted a man as my Pietro, but one more touched by sentiment than I'd thought Lord Cappelletto to be. A frescoed Virgin covers the wall beside the bed, watching over him like a doting mother over her own slumbering son.

But where care lodges, sleep cannot long lie. I shake him awake. As he makes out my face, he grunts with alarm. "Juliet?"

"Juliet is fine. But Lady Cappelletta —"

"Is it the child she is carrying?"

It's true, this wife means no more to him than the pried-open oyster means to the man that seizes a pearl. Or the man who, seeking a pearl, finds none. "The child is already gone."

The softness sags out of his face, and I recognize the same old man who was too superstitious to visit the confinement room.

Before I can say more, he slips from the bed and kneels beneath the painting of the Holy Madonna, grabbing my arm and pulling me down beside him. His insistence startles me, until I think of how many nights, and days, he must have knelt alone after losing his first Juliet and all their little

130

ones. Word for word I match his prayers, taking comfort in our nearness as we implore the Blessed Maria to keep safe the soul of his never-to-be born babe, along with the many souls of those others taken from us. All our plague-dead children. His first, beloved wife. And Susanna, my terrible fresh loss. Almost too much to bear, such doubled and trebled grief, until I utter that one comfort, the name of our living love. The two of us entreat the Sainted Virgin to keep little Juliet with us and well. "And Lady Cappelletta, too," I say, crossing myself and waiting for Lord Cappelletto to do the same.

He does, calling her Emiliana. It's the first time I hear her Christian name. Those pretty syllables seem to shimmer from his stale-breathed mouth. He calls on Santa Margherita, and the Virgin Mother, on his own patron saint and on Lady Cappelletta's too, praying she will prove fecund. I know that whether we fare well or ill, it's only by the saints' intervening grace, and even the apothecaries will tell you the Pater Noster and Ave Maria are the surest cure. But how long ought a man keep beseeching the heavens to let his wife birth new life, while she lies alone and terrified within a privy closet? I give off a little cough, interrupting

Lord Cappelletto long enough to squeeze in a quick *amen* and hoist myself to my feet.

"Amen," he repeats, rising and calling for the page to fetch Verona's most respected midwife, to rid Lady Cappelletta of what she's lost.

Prince Cansignorio and his household ride on horseback at the head of the Easter procession, while all the rest of Verona walks. Or nearly all. Lord Cappelletto strides. Having maneuvered his way to a position right behind the prince's family, Lord Cappelletto wears an expression I first caught sight of while peering out from behind my mother's skirts when Luca Covoni, who owned our village, came to collect my father's rent. A tightness around the jaw to convey impatience at being bothered with such petty matters, a tightness that barely masks what shows in the darting, bulging eyes: a deep sense of pleased possession, as though Covoni owned not just the land, but all of us who lived and labored on it. Striding in the wake of the Scaligeri horses, his vair-lined velvet robe secured by a broad silver belt that wraps twice around his great girth before dangling nearly to the street-stones, Lord Cappelletto exudes the same entitled air, but with an assurance that a man like Luca Covoni, whose hems remained caked with manure from the fields and dirt from our peasant floors, never had.

Tybalt and I follow like a pair of pack-donkeys, me bearing Juliet and Tybalt carrying the silver chalice that will be the Cappelletti's paschal offering. Both held so high that every noble family who walks behind us, and all the less-than-nobles who line Verona's streets to watch the grand procession, see them.

Lord Cappelletto's tasseled hat has slid to one side, revealing his balding pate. Tybalt giggles at the way the glinting sun dances on the sweat that slicks that feeble, hairless spot. But no one else is close enough to notice. And if anyone wonders at the absence of Lady Cappelletta, surely they cannot imagine the state she's in. From the time the midwife arrived with her hooks and pliers, not all the aqua vitae in the city could quiet Lady Cappelletta's screams. I glugged back a good quantity myself in the hopes it might at least dull my hearing, but it's been no help. I've kept Juliet and Tybalt as far from her as I can, though in truth there's no place in all Ca' Cappelletti where her maddened howls do not reach.

But passing outside the compound's walls brings me no solace. A dozen brutal fights have bloodied Verona's stone-paved streets since the palio-day riot. I've not left Ca' Cappelletti during these deadly weeks, and now the slightest jostling from those behind us in the cortege, or the press of the crowd watching us pass, shimmers fear across my back. As the trumpets heralding the prince sound against the buildings that line our route, I'd swear I hear in their reverberations some echo of cursing and crossed swords. The silver chalice flashes like an upraised dagger, and with every turn we make, I wrap myself tighter around Juliet, certain the day's uneasy peace is about to burst.

Following so close to Prince Cansignorio offers faint comfort. Several years shy of thirty, he's barely older than the palio-day brawlers and, it seems, no wiser. Lacking his brother's lust for control, he's not bothered to quell the violence. Mayhap he believes that as long as Verona's bloodthirsty youth are killing one another, they'll be too busy to raise a blade against him. Though the city is in want of peace, he offers only a grand show of his own supposed piety, pledging a thousand candles to each church and chapel in the city. He leads the Easter procession on a three-hour circuit for all Verona to witness his enormous waxy offering, as though we are too stupid to realize that princes pay their tithes out of poor men's taxes.

At last, we reach the Duomo. As we face the rippled marble columns framing the cathedral's entry, the crowd sways before its arches and peaks, its windows carved with more beasts than Noah could've fit within a fleet of arks. I wish I could set my rump upon one of the stone griffins flanking the door and settle Juliet onto my lap, for at eight months she's grown heavy as a good-sized sack of grain. But what do Cansignorio or Il Benedicto care for a woman's suffering? Neither of them offer any balm for my throbbing feet and aching shoulders, as they stand in the shade of the cathedral, taking long turns addressing the crowd. Blessed, the poor are told they are, though not a one of them — with their dirt-streaked nails, callused hands, and bodies still bent from whatever toil swallows the other six days of their week — will gain entrance to the Duomo. Not today, a day so sanctified that prince, counts, lords, and all the new-moneyed merchants turn out in their finest silks and furs, velvets and jewels, to command places in the cathedral. It is Easter. Christ is risen, and so are the profits of every fabric dealer and goldsmith in the city.

135

I wonder where Pietro might be among the gathering. This was the one hope I carried when I left Ca' Cappelletti: that he and I would find some way to find each other. Foolish wish. For how can I tell if my husband is one of the tens of thousands of people crowding the streets that fan out from the Duomo, when I face only the back of Lord Cappelletto's balding head and the Scaligeri horses' behinds?

The prince's nephews ride two astride the same horse, a broad black beast that, as if to add an *amen* to Il Benedicto's final blessing of the crowd, lifts its tail and looses a mound of slick, brown dumplings onto the cathedral steps. The younger of the boys, the one called Mercutio, digs a quick heel into the horse's flank. The beast turns sideways just as the liveryman steps forward to lift the child from the horse. Swinging his far leg across the animal's hindquarter, Count Mercutio thrusts himself into the liveryman's arms with such force the servant stumbles back into the steaming turds. Sliding across the mound, he loses his grip on the boy, who manages to crash, hands outstretched, into the ample bosom of the bishop's niece.

Surely the liveryman will be put out from service, and probably from the city walls, for such clumsiness, though I see it's all the boy's doing, a prank to amuse himself during the solemn monotony of Easter morning. Tybalt stares at Count Mercutio, worry edging his face. Count Paris, the prince's other nephew, still atop the horse and clutching its mane to keep from tumbling off, mirrors Tybalt's expression. As though each of them knows that while this bit of Mercutio's fun is at the liveryman's expense, next time it might be at theirs.

Lord Cappelletto gives a quick nod to Tybalt to make haste as he follows the prince's family through the massive cathedral doors. Tybalt looks longingly at me, but I give his shoulder a loving push. Shifting Juliet from one hip to the other, I make my way to the smaller northern door with the other women.

In all my decades in Verona, I've never been inside the Duomo. I always offer my confession in Friar Lorenzo's cell, Pietro and I going to full Mass no more than once or twice a year. And that we did at San Fermo Maggiore. Nesto insisted the communion wafers there tasted better than any others he ever had. We laughed when he said that, thinking it a sinless sacrilege for a child to believe such a thing. After he died, I took what small comfort I could in feeling the same circle on my tongue he'd been so adamant about having on his.

If I were at San Fermo now, I would make my familiar way along the nave, slip through the side door in the upper church and down the stairs, passing the corridor that leads to Friar Lorenzo's cell to head instead into the lower church. There, in the cool dark air, I could nestle Juliet to my breast and nurse her as I used to nurse my boys, under the watchful eyes of my most beloved saints. But the Duomo is as strange to me as a Mohammedan's temple. Spread broader and rising taller than San Fermo, the grand cathedral does not make me feel like an angel ascending to heaven — more like a tiny churchmouse dizzily scurrying across its vast, patterned floor. Scores of candles burn upon the altar. Watching them glow, I try to feel Pietro near, to believe it is his bees who birthed the wax that drips, liquid hot, before the image of Our Lord and Savior.

Though I know by rote my Ave Maria, Pater Noster, and Pax Domini, the rest of Mass remains a mystery to me. Not so Lord Cappelletto. Even from across the nave, I mark the proud way he intones in Latin along with the cathedral priests. He pulls sanctimoniously on Tybalt's ear whenever the boy's eyes start to wander to the sculpted swords that frame the rood screen, or the painted scenes along the side-walls of bloodied martyrs glorying in their righteous torments.

Once the last prayer sounds against the cathedral walls and the congregation rises from our knees, the priest signals for the acting out of the Passion, which features a live lamb and three donkeys — a spectacle beyond anything the Franciscans over at San Fermo ever offered. The woman beside me strains to get a better view of every hollow between the would-be Christ's ribs and the shimmering oil on his anointed feet. The Crucifixion is so realistic, I wonder if instead of pardoning a criminal in honor of the holy-day, Cansignorio means to start a new tradition by having this one sacrificed.

But no, the pretend Savior survives long enough to be entombed and then rise up. For what inspiration would there be in death, common as that is? The miracle is in the Resurrection. Or ought to be, though in truth I notice Mercutio snickering and Tybalt slumping with disappointment when they see how the priests playing the Roman guard conspire to block the congregation's view while the pretend-Christ clumsily replaces his brittle band of thorns with a golden crown. Holy chicanery it is, yet it impresses the thousands of Veronese pressing in behind us, whose rippling murmurs of awe fill the cathedral.

After the congregation has gasped and oohed to the bishop's satisfaction, he gives a final benediction and disappears into the sacristy. Cansignorio and the counts follow, Lord Cappelletto close on their heels. He hurries Tybalt along with him, the boy struggling to keep the chalice raised high as a score of men who are the most trusted of the prince's allies swarm forward with the various treasures they are gifting to the church.

The last of them is barely through the rood screen before the congregation begins to press its way from the cathedral, eager to trade piety for pleasure. But I must wait for Lord Cappelletto. Slipping a finger into Juliet's needy mouth, I murmur, "Yes, dearest lamb," matching my words to the familiar, urgent rhythm with which she sucks: three insistent squeezes, then a pause, and then three more. Kissing her dark hair, I smell not the delicate baby scent I crave, but the dank, spicy incense that fills the Duomo. At last the cathedral bell begins to ring, and the bells of all the churches across Verona answer, their high- and low-pitched peals dancing across the city's tiled rooftops. Lord Cappelletto reappears, barely flicking his eyes to me to signal that I am to follow after Tybalt, who's scurrying at his heel.

As soon as we return to Ca' Cappelletti, Lord Cappelletto orders every trencher in the house set out in the sala. There is cabbage loafed with eggs and garlic, savoried with marjoram, mint, and walnuts, baked heavy with Piacentine cheese. Mutton is served stuffed with pork bellies, parsley leaves laced through the meats. Next come liver pies and veal tortes, and platters of aspic shimmering with whole peppercorns and slivered cardamom seeds. Lord Cappelletto possesses the same gusto for breaking the Lenten fast that he'll soon have for breaking wind.

Although Lady Cappelletta still lies raving in the parto bed, he does not seem to mark her absence as he holds Juliet upon his lap and catechizes Tybalt about which men who knelt and worshipped nearest them in the cathedral are allies to the Cappelletti, and which are enemies. He talks full-mouthed of a seducer kidnapping a dowried girl away from her lawfully bound fiancé, or of a drunken insult shouted at a gambling table, quizzing Tybalt about what revenge should be exacted for each wrong, never mind that they were committed three generations past.

The more Lord Cappelletto talks, the more he drinks, until he's had wine enough to drown the Venetian fleet. He pushes first a goblet and then a trencher toward me, and orders me to drink and eat my fill.

But for once, I've no appetite. I'm thinking of the lamb stew I always made for Easter, which my Berto especially loved. Donato teased him as we walked home from church one year, saying there'd not be enough for Berto, which made the younger boy cry. Nothing we said or did could calm him, until Nunzio hoisted him onto his shoulders and ran the whole way home, letting Berto dip a spoon into the cookpot before the rest of us had even turned into the Via Zancani. I'd not believed I could bear to taste that stew again after the pestilence stole our sons, but still I made it that first Easter and ladled out a bowl for Pietro. Pulling me onto his lap, my husband tore off a piece of bread, dipped it into the soup, and begged me to have it for Berto's sake. Every Easter since, we've eaten it like that, with each mouthful recalling another memory of our lost boys. But this year Pietro must be having who knows what for his holy-day meal, alone in our house or out among strangers at some public tavern, his pocket full of honeyed sweets I cannot taste.

Sometime during the week past, a splintered fish bone slipped beneath the tooth that sits beside the gaping hole left by those I lost in the brawl. I push my tongue at the stuck bone, letting the pain throb into my gum and flash along my jaw as I watch Lord Cappelletto giving Juliet tastes of this or that from his finger. When a pinkieful of lemon pottage makes her throw up — not the soft milkish spit she trails every day on me but thick gobs of undigested food — I reach fast for her, glad for the excuse to carry her back to our bedchamber.

Tybalt follows after us. I wish he'd chirrup out some joke or song to cheer me despite myself. But he sinks onto a high-backed stool set against the far wall, plugging his nose with his fingers while I wash Juliet and replace her puke-covered swaddling with fresh bands. He watches like a cat outside a mouse hole until I nurse her to sleep.

"What's the Order of Santa Caterina?" A funny question, even for a boy as odd as Tybalt.

"A convent." The truth. But from the confusion that pulls at his curious eyes, I can see that like so many of life's truths, it's

143

of no particular help. Not until I explain, "A place where nuns live."

This Tybalt understands. He clasps his hands against his chest, fluttering his eyelids and pulling his cheeks taut in mimicry of the dourest abbess, and parades around the room. Then he asks, "What does *weaned* mean?"

I crook an elbow around Juliet's head, to protect her from hearing such a word. "Weaned is when a child grows too big for nursing."

He nods like some great sage. "When they're weaned, they go to the convent."

His words catch me cold. "When who's weaned? Who's going to a convent?"

"It's what the bishop said, when Uncle bade me give him the silver chalice." He screws his voice into a perfect imitation of the bishop's haughty tone: "We shall keep a place at the Cloister of Santa Caterina. Send her as soon as she is weaned."

Something sharp jags inside me. "You're sure that's what you heard?"

Tybalt puts a hand to his heart, swearing on his most prized possessions: three marzipan wise men he's been hoarding since Christmas.

"Was he looking at your uncle, or at another man?"

"He looked at the chalice. It was heavy, and I had to carry it for hours, until he took it from me."

I curse that chalice, which I mistook for a mere paschal offering, never guessing it was the first piece of a convent-dowry. Now I see that the silver goblet is like Juliet herself — a sacrifice Lord Cappelletto will gladly make, bargaining with God to give him a son.

Tybalt's words still turn in my head hours later, as I fall into a tormented sleep in which I dream I search all through Ca' Cappelletti only to discover my girl gone, and Lord Cappelletto laughing over some swollen-headed boy who fills her cradle. This boy is so hideously deformed, his face cannot be called human. He has a spiderish number of arms and legs, which spill out of the cradle onto the floor. Even as I dream, I can hear Lady Cappelletta howling as she lies wakeful with wild-eyed fear that she'll never deliver a living son. Or maybe she howls from the grim realization of all that it will take for her to bear one.

During the next months, I lose more teeth. One into a thick cube of veal fat, another to such rotting that Lord Cappelletto pays his barber to pull it from me. I lose teeth, and

Juliet gains them, two tight little rows rising from her gums. Tybalt and even Lord Cappelletto marvel when Juliet opens her mouth and the light flashes on those perfect teeth. Such marvels only taunt me, consumed as I am with what Tybalt never should have told.

Friar Lorenzo, sensing I'm keeping some secret, presses me each time I return to be shriven. I make careful catalogue of every hour I snatch with Pietro, when I stop at the Via Zancani on my way to the friary and whenever he comes to tend the bees at Ca' Cappelletti. I accumulate randy acts to repent, knowing that I'll not confess to the friar what really burdens me. Not tell him how I hate the thought of Juliet being taken from me and sent to a convent, consigned to the same celibate life he lives. What use would it be to confide what is not my sin, when I know already how he will answer? I am only a wet-nurse. A woman who is not to question God or Church or Lord Cappelletto.

So I'll not question, not aloud. Only when I'm alone, with Juliet burrowing asleep against me, do I silently wonder how long we will be able to keep our precious milk bond — and what I will do to protect it.

Six

Although Lord Cappelletto waited five weeks from when his wife was delivered of her first child before taking her again, she was brought back to their bed only five days after the midwife removed her second, dead one. I thought Lady Cappelletta would cower from him like a caged animal. But instead she shrilled out demands that he mount her once, twice, three times each night, which he was glad to oblige. In the days afterward, she'd remain in bed and rave for Tybalt, of all the household, to come and place a hand upon her stomach and say whether he felt anything stirring there.

What could Tybalt feel at such moments but frightened? The boy who loves to stage bloody battles with toy soldiers, and who eagerly recites every gory detail of a dozen assassinations undertaken by long-dead Cappelletti to avenge their honor, yet who delights in making up songs and tumbling-shows to entertain me and Juliet — this same boy has learned to hide whenever he hears his aunt call. So, for his sake, I go to her instead.

She's not pleased when I come into her bedchamber carrying Juliet with me, as if it is the child's fault, or mine, that she was born a girl. "Where is Tybalt? He is the only one in this whole household who cares for me."

I open my mouth to assure her that's not so. But what good would such lying do her? She's barely older than Tybalt. They might have whiled these last years of childhood as contented playmates if she were not married to his uncle, her lonely fate already settled.

I balance Juliet on my hip while I open the window covering to let the newly warming spring into the room. "Lord Cappelletto chose you for his wife."

"He chose me in payment for a debt."

This seems to me more of Lady Cappelletta's madness, for what man marries a debt-slave, instead of working her for what is owed? But when I turn back toward the bed to tell her so, she cuts me off.

"Lord Cappelletto was visiting one of the Scaligeri castles on Lake Garda. He rode out upon a hunt, and one of the hounds got loose and killed a hind on my family's lands. My sister loved that hind and wept to find it slaughtered, so when our cousin discovered the bloody-mouthed dog, he slit its throat, to please her. Not long afterward, a serving-man from the hunting party came near, calling to the dog. My cousin laughed and told him it was dead. But Lord Cappelletto, as a guest of the Scaligeri, demanded the life of whoever killed the hound. Our family priest advised my grandfather to send away my cousin, and offer Lord Cappelletto a wife instead."

She fingers the edge of the coverlet, as if she's trying to pull loose the thread that binds her to her husband. "I thought he ought to have my sister, for if she'd not wept over the dead hind, the hound would never have been killed. But my father said she was promised to one of the lords in Padova, and he did not care to jeopard what he'd already given for her dowry. So I was delivered to Lord Cappelletto."

A deer, a dog, a daughter: are the rich so muddle-headed from all they possess that they think such things are equal, and ought to be traded one for another? Yet this must be what Lord Cappelletto believes, pledging Juliet like a sack of tithed coins to the

Church to please the saints into giving him a son.

When Pietro first made of me a wife, I'd stir myself awake in the smallest hours of the night, watch his sleeping face by whatever moonish sliver rose, and whisper out all the grateful love I felt. Whatever we might declare by day, only in the night, when slumber dulled his ears to me, did I dare show how desperate I'd been for anyone to care for me as he did. Not until Nunzio was delivered of me and exhaustion stole my strength and made me cling to any sleep I got, did I stop rousing myself like that. By then it mattered not. Cradling our first son, Pietro knew the full measure of the ferocious love I felt for him, and I knew he felt the same for me. Lady Cappelletta's wakeful nights and red-eyed days offer no hint of such joy for her.

I nestle my sleeping Juliet into a chair and bring the work basket to Lady Cappelletta's bedside. "Your father must have thought it well to marry you to an ally of the Scaligeri," I say, though such alliances are made only to serve men. If Lady Cappelletta's gained anything by the match, it could only be in measure against how awfully her own family may have treated her.

I search through the basket for a hoop

from which emerald-green and ruby-red silk threads dangle. It's the budding floral hedge she was embroidering before the child died in her. But when I hold it out to her, I see her hands are still too twitchy to work a needle.

I sit beside the bed and begin to fasion the slow stitches myself. This is how we'll pass the days. I can care for Juliet, and do the household's sewing. The hare-faced cook will prepare the meals. The cleaning and tending will fall to whatever worthless servants wander in and out of employ within Ca' Cappelletti. But there is one wifely duty that Lady Cappelletta alone must perform.

Through the nights that follow, whenever I hear her desperate pleading for her husband to make his heir upon her, I wonder whether that hind was better off. At least its end came quick, and someone wept for it.

It's the height of summer, but Tybalt does not seem to notice the day's thick heat as he chases a capon around the dovecote, trying to slip one of his out-grown stockings over its squawking head. His father's most recent letter made mention of the expert falconry practiced by the Gonzaghe courtiers. Tybalt read the letter to Juliet and me

151

over and over so many times I can recite it back like a traveling peddler calling out his wares. Tybalt's convinced himself that if he can train a bird — any bird — to sit upon his arm, cast off, and return with some wormish kill, surely his father will come back to see such a feat, or send for Tybalt to go to Mantua to show off his prowess, such as the boy imagines it to be.

I should rescue the stocking, and the dishcloth he cut up for jesses, and the ribbon he's fashioned for a leash. Should consign them all to my work basket, which grows fuller every week. But how can I deny the self-sworn protector of Ca' Cappelletti a chance to play at manhood?

"Look at the castrated little cock," I laugh to Pietro.

"Tybalt may not have a falcon, but the bird runs, and flies, yet it will return." Pietro pinches one of the scarlet-orange blooms on the pomegranate tree, pulling it free without losing a single delicate petal. He dangles the flower in front of Juliet, who opens her pretty pink lips and squeals "usss, usss." It's her first word, or will be once she learns to say it right. I let Tybalt believe it's *cousin,* though I'm sure she's really saying *Nurse.*

Pietro lets the flower drop. "You hold too

tight to her, Angelica. At that age, our boys
—"

"She is not like our boys." Why must I
even say it? Our boys never looked upon
trees like these. Never knew their father to
tend bees. Never saw him cut honeycomb
from a hive, as he's just done. As he did
with not a single of his own half dozen sons
to help, but only little Tybalt.

I'd watched the two of them from inside
Juliet's bedchamber. Even with the window
pulled tight to keep the bees out, I could
not help but imagine the dizzying smell of
ripe fruit going soft in the midday sun. And
intermingled with the smell of fruit, a
smudgy waggle of smoke, which tapered
into the sky from the torch Pietro'd lit to
keep the bees at bay. Through the wavering
air, I saw how he unsealed the lid from the
cut-log hive, deftly slicing and lifting out
the combs. How he broke those combs into
the deep-sided pot that Tybalt held for him,
to begin the slow process in which the wax,
which Pietro will trade to a chandler, rises,
while the thick honey sinks.

Even with a cloth covering his face, Pietro
sang while he worked, to show me he has
no fear of bees. He is a barrel-chested basso,
and his timbrous notes wavered against the
panes as if they meant to steal their way

into the room, as Pietro has stolen his way inside the half dozen times he's come to Ca' Cappelletti to check his bees.

After Pietro culled what he wanted from the hive, he replaced the cover on the hewn log. And then my husband dipped his broad thumb into the honeypot and pulled it back out glistening, closing his eyes as he sucked off the golden liquid. At last, he opened those beautiful eyes and dipped his thumb again. This time, he held it up, slowly waving it at me.

My mouth watered for that sun-colored honey, and so I disappeared from the window, carrying Juliet through the tower passageway and down into the arbor.

Pietro pulled me around the side of the dovecote, holding me close as he slipped that thumb into my mouth. But Juliet wriggled in my arms like a kitten wrapped in a drowning-sack, separating Pietro's chest from mine.

I'd taken a half-step back from Pietro, tasting apple and pear and pomegranate, my tongue coated with all the fruits of the arbor condensed into the warm honey, as I commented on Tybalt and his capon.

But Tybalt's not what my husband's thinking of. "It's been a year, Angelica. Time to loose the child's swaddling."

A year. A birth, a saint's day, Christmas, Lent, Easter. Each was Juliet's first. Each, aside from birth, is what Susanna never had. Every holy-day, every season, I feel it.

The first year is the hardest. That is what the black-veiled crones say, the ones who gather like sharp-beaked crows at a stranger's graveside, cawing unasked-for advice at the mourners. The brown-frocked friars, if they bother to murmur any sort of comfort, will say as much as well. But no one says aloud what my mother-heart cannot unlearn: hard as the first year is, harder still is what happens in all the years that follow, when part of you forgets for a moment here or there what you've lost, even as the rest knows that in your deepest bones you can never for a day, an hour, an instant, forget.

I still catch sight of Donato or Enzo or any of my boys, out of the corner of my eye. Sometimes I see them at the age they were when death snatched them, and sometimes as the age they'd be now, every one of them grown tall. Sometimes they're some age in between, so I'm not certain from the fleeting features which son I saw, those beautiful lost faces blending one into another.

But not Susanna. She stays ever a newborn babe, still covered in our shared blood, as she was in that too brief moment when first and last I glimpsed her. If Juliet's grown and gained this year past, it's only in measure against Susanna. How can I be glad for that? Why wish this last child grown enough to be taken from me and sent off to live among cold-humored nuns? Swaddled, she is safe. Suckling, she is satisfied. And so am I.

"It is for Lord and Lady Cappelletti to decide when she is ready to be unswaddled." Even as I say it, I know how Pietro might argue back. Lady Cappelletta has no notion what a child needs. And when have I been eager to obey Lord Cappelletto? Pietro might point out these things, or things much like them, and I ready myself to answer as soon as he does. But instead he says what I never expected to hear.

"We could have another."

My tongue swells in my throat, too full for me to speak. All I can manage is to shake my head. Shake it as though to keep what he says from landing in my ears.

We've never spoken this way, uttering out-loud plans for making babies. There'd been no need for such talk during those first laughing days of lusty love when we made Nunzio. Nor in the fifteen years that followed, when our little house filled with growing boys. And after we lost our sons, I never dared say to Pietro, nor did he dare say to me, that we should make another. This was what the pestilence taught, a lesson too terrible to ever forget: it was not for us to decide what child we got, when they came, and when they were taken.

Month after month, I'd watched the moon grow full, wishing, hoping, my belly would grow with it, but all that swelled me was time, and wine, and sweets. And then, long after I'd given up waiting: Susanna.

Did Pietro say anything to me, or I to him, to make her come? Could we have said anything to make her stay?

This past year, the year since she was lost, is the only time I ever let the getting or not getting of children govern how Pietro and I indulge ourselves. There are countless ways for a wife to please a husband, and a clever husband can match them one for one in the pleasing of his wife. Pietro's not ever remarked on how careful I've become since entering Ca' Cappelletti to keep his seed from landing where it might quicken in me. Not because I do not want his child, but because I cannot bear to lose the child I already have.

For this is what wealthy men dread most in a wet-nurse. I've seen women with smaller waists and faces far gaunter than mine standing in church doorways, milk soaking through their gowns while some sneering notary takes their testimony. But each woman and every notary and anyone who happens by — all know such a woman's sworn-to-God statement will do no good when the court hears the suit her employer has brought against her. The merest suspicion of pregnancy is grounds enough to break a contract with a wet-nurse, no matter if it proves false or true. I'll not take such a risk with Juliet.

I love Pietro. But with what foolishly deluded heart can my husband believe that he and I might yet see even one child raised and wed, when we have buried seven children dead?

"It was you who brought me here," I remind him. "You set your mark on the nursing contract, hiring me away."

"It was Friar Lorenzo's idea, not mine," he says. "He told me there was one other baby born that day in all Verona, and by God's grace the family was in want of a wet-nurse." My strong Pietro quivers like a too-shorn sheep. "I waved his words away, thinking I could not bear to let you go. But when I saw how your body ached, like my own heart, for our dead daughter, it seemed the only way to stop your weeping. The only comfort I could give to you."

I pull Juliet close against my heart, feeling the weight of how much my husband loves me. "You were right, Pietro. She's my comfort for all we've lost. Just as you wanted her to be."

"As I wanted, and you needed, a year ago." He dips his little pinky into the depths of the honeypot, then traces my lips with the golden liquid. Dots it on my sweat-damp brow, his finger lingering between my eyes like Friar Lorenzo offering Ash Wednesday absolution. "But now I need you home with me again."

Instead of answering with words, I lead him into the tower and up to Juliet's room. Laying her in the cradle, I bid him gather back the sun-warmed honey with tongue instead of finger. He savors that and more from me. For the first time in a twelve-month, I let him spend himself deep inside me, and I shiver with the pleasure of it.

Afterward, I steal to the privy pot, as though his seed means no more to me than what else is squatted out here. I mouth a silent plea to the Virgin Mother. *Sacred Maria, you who did not bear your own husband's child so that you could raise the one God gave to you* — a shrewd opening, to remind her of our likened states — *I beg of you, take pity on me. On me, and on Juliet. Most Holy Madonna, keep us together, always.* Then I rouse Pietro, telling him it's time for him to take what he's harvested back to the Via Zancani.

But the pleasures I steal with my husband are not the only delights I must keep secret. Come nightfall, while Tybalt and the other Cappelletti sleep with bellies full of the evening's meal of roasted capon, I do what I've never so much as hinted to anyone, even Pietro or Friar Lorenzo, I've long been doing. I unwrap the swaddling bands, letting Juliet's arms and legs spring free.

She gurgles with pleasure at the rush of air. I match her throaty purrs, nuzzling the delicious plump of her legs and arms, cupping my belly against the soft bottoms of her feet.

This is my secret joy, and hers. It started one half-mooned night before the Pentecost, when I awoke to her crying over having soiled herself. I unswaddled her and wiped her clean, but in my exhaustion I fell back to sleep before binding her arms and legs again. I dozed and dreamt and woke to Juliet grabbing at my hair and ears. She even wiggled her curious hand into my gaping mouth to touch my broken teeth and full, wet tongue. When I laughed, she folded herself and stuck her own toes into her mouth. I gobbled up her other foot, humming as she squealed. In that delicious moment, I knew the same pleasure she'd known months before, my mouth as full of her as hers has been of me.

We slept again, entwined like vines heavy with ripe grapes. When sun and lark roused the house the next morning, I reswaddled her, pressing a finger first to my lips, then to hers. She nodded, sure and solemn, as though she knew we needed to keep anyone from suspecting how free she'd been.

When the next night came and I took her into bed with me, she looked up with such expectation in her dark eyes, I could not leave her bound. I woke terrified through those first weeks, fearing her limbs would go crooked because they were not kept wrapped tight. For that is all we ever hear: the tighter the swaddling, the straighter the arms and legs. But the fear that comes with morning's light is nothing compared to what I feel in the dark, once her arms are free and she reaches for me, or when she tests her uncertain legs by stepping against my thighs. We are lovers of the purest kind, for what greater love is there than the one between a mother and a milk-babe? Happy nights, when we take such simple, secret pleasures.

Swaddled, she is safe. Suckling, she is satisfied. That is all Ca' Cappelletti, or Friar Lorenzo, or even my own dear Pietro need know.

SEVEN

When Juliet is nearly a year and a half old, Prince Cansignorio comes to dine. Lord Cappelletto, eager to please his powerful guest, lets Carmignano flow by the cask, and I do not miss the chance to drink my fill as I hold Juliet for her royal godfather and the other guests to admire. The prince has brought a half dozen musicians with him, and they play different styles of song, some brightly plucked upon the lute and some heavy with the viol's melancholy, to match each course as it's served. While I soothe Juliet by swaying to the melodies, Cansignorio sits at the table-head drinking down one round of the Cappelletti's wine after another. Lord Cappelletto twines compliments over his regal guest until the prince interrupts and, with a tongue heavy as wet wool, announces that he's sent counselors to every ruling-house within a month's travel by horse or sail. They're seeking a woman not too old, not too ugly, with not too many brothers in her powerful family, to become Cansignorio's holy wedded wife.

Lord Cappelletto raises his goblet before anyone else can. "To a goodly, Godly match."

The prince nods and drains his cup once more, as Lord Cappelletto leans forward to suggest that Cansignorio's good fortune would be best served if, before any dowry is negotiated, he dismissed a certain maladminstering Uberti, appointing Lord Cappelletto to oversee his treasury instead.

Though the prince waves in wine-flushed agreement, all Europe knows it's not only by the size of the dowry-portion that a ruler values his wife. I see it in how Cansignorio looks at Juliet, eyes full of pity for Lord Cappelletto, and something else for Lady Cappelletta, who still cannot produce a son. Eggs are eaten, herbs are applied, prayers are said. But nothing quickens. Her blood has stopped and started three times in twelve months, what is purged from her each time not even formed enough to bury beside her other lost one. The fault cannot be in the stars, or something gone off in the year's grain, for bellies spread all over Verona. The prince's mistress is thin and carrying high, so that not even the bishop can pretend not to notice that Cansignorio will have another bastard long before he ever takes a bride. Lord Cappelletto takes careful note, commissioning a finely worked silver dog with sapphires for its eyes as a gift of congratulations to the prince, and an even more ornate silver-and-sapphire cross for the altar of one of the chapels in the Duomo as penance for his envy.

While the thickest of winter's fog twists through Verona's streets, Lord Cappelletto sends the nittish house-page searching through the family's storerooms. It takes a half-day's hunt before he barges into our chamber bearing such a contraption as I've never seen, a thick wooden ring etched with the Cappelletti crest, held up by four carved legs set on a larger ring balanced on wooden wheels. "Girello," Lord Cappelletto calls it. He orders me to unswaddle Juliet and set her inside the frame, as though she's a cork being fitted with feathers for a game of shuttlecock, and he means for me to bandy her back and forth.

Juliet has no need for this strange machine of which Lord Cappelletto is so fond. She is ample-limbed and dimple-fleshed like me, not wan and sullen like Lady Cappelletta. I know how ready her chubby legs are, a sturdy match to her plump, impatient arms. I'd bid Tybalt to teach Juliet to walk as my boys taught their younger brothers, for a ready babe will give toddling chase to an apple rolled along the floor. Pietro's army roly-polied an entire orchard's worth of apples between the six of them. I baked each bruised fruit with parsnip, fig, and turnip, seasoning the mixture with anise, fennel, and a touch of mustard. Then I chewed with my own mouth the portion to feed whichever boy was just out of swaddling. The whole neighborhood could smell the scent, imagine the taste of one of our sons learning to walk.

But Ca' Cappelletti fills only with the dull, grating sound of wood wheels along the stone floors. Juliet careens in the girello, dark eyes flashing wonder at how she can make herself go. But then comes the pause as she turns, looking back to make sure I'm following. I am all she seeks, and she ventures in her walker only so far that she can please herself at being able to waddle her way back to me again.

As Juliet masters the girello, Lord Cappelletto tells me the page is to take the cradle from her chamber. He says it is to make more space for Juliet to practice walking, but from the way his scheming tongue darts at the spittle that gathers in the corner of his mouth, I can tell this is a lie — or at least not all I'd have of the truth.

I piece the fuller truth together hours later when I stand in the sala window, straining in the last of the day's light to sew a border of Damascus cloth onto one of Tybalt's doublets. It is a lurid violet, as costly for the vivid color as for the exotic fabric. Tybalt begged for it in imitation of the new fashion the prince's nephews wear. Lord Cappelletto, ever wanting to outdo his noble rivals, happily indulges anything that ties his household to Cansignorio's. Never mind how my eyes strain to work such careful stitches, attaching the border to a garment that Tybalt, already long in the leg, will soon outgrow.

As I pierce the needle into the precious Damascus cloth, I catch sight out the window of the house-page. He's bearing the cradle along the Via Cappello as though Lord Cappelletto has ordered him to float an infant Moses down the Adige to some unknown pharaoh. But no, just before the page reaches the Porta dei Leoni, he turns into a humble doorway.

It's the house of a pursemaker. He is a man with maybe six, maybe seven daughters. I can never keep track as they pass back and forth on their household errands. However many they total, you do not need an abacus to tally that there are too many of them for a pursemaker to dowry.

Wide-hipped and young, those daughters are. It flashes on me like a lightning bolt: Lord Cappelletto means to have his pick, trying one and then another to fill that cradle with a son.

I store away the discovery like Tybalt stores candies in his sleeve, though it gives me something more sour than sweet to chew. I draw Juliet out of the girello, saying I must go to San Fermo to be shriven, though we head first to the Via Zancani.

"You cannot warm two houses with only one woodpile," I say, after I've shared the gossip with Pietro. Lord Cappelletto will never have heat enough to make a son in his marriage bed, if he spends himself among the pursemaker's daughters.

Pietro, who has heat enough for an iron-maker's furnace, swings himself before me. "But if your fire's big enough, who knows how many pots you can bring to a boil."

My husband is a merry man. It's a truth I treasured when he and I had every night together, for we always made good use of them. But the stolen hour here or there we've had these seasons past to take our quickest pleasures — they are like crumbs of stale bread to a starving man. And worse, to a starving woman.

There are undowried daughters up and down the Via Zancani, the same as on the Via Cappello. And Pietro can easily find time as he travels from hive to hive to stop among the prostitutes who ply their trade in the sun-bleached stands and shadowed corridors of the Arena.

"Have you been bringing many pots to boil?" I ask.

He pulls me to him. "One pot is all a good cook needs to make the most savory of stews." Burying his face in my bare belly, he runs those big hands above and below, touching and then tasting all the places he knows well. What we make is more savory than stew, fills me more than whole loaves of bread. We lie so long together, I have to skip my shrift, carrying my sins along with the precious taste of Pietro on my tongue. The smell of him lingers on me as I bear Juliet through the wintry streets, clinging to Pietro's promise that he passes solitary days and nights while I am gone.

Back in Ca' Cappelletti, Lady Cappelletta is wearing a new gilt-and-emerald brooch and a puzzled look, not sure what to make of her husband's sudden generosity. I remind her it is a rich man's duty to purchase such sumptuous things, for how else are the silver-smiths, gem traders, and silk merchants to keep their families fed?

It's true Lord Cappelletto wants all Verona to know he is a rich man. But there are other things he'd not have his wife know, and that is why he buys what he believes will distract her. During the next months, the Cappelletti wardrobes swell. But Lady Cappelletta's womb does not. Whether the same can be said of the pursemaker's daughters, I cannot tell, their bodies hidden beneath new cloaks as they scurry along the Via Cappello.

The year's first snow does not come until the middle of February, falling just past dawn in great fat flakes that make Juliet press her nose against the cold glass of the window. Tybalt would carry her out into the courtyard still in her nightclothes if I did not stop them long enough to bundle her, and him, and myself as well. Outside, the chill air tingles against our skin, as Tybalt insists we turn our faces up to the sky, open-mouthed like three baby birds waiting for worms to drop from their mama's beak. Juliet giggles at the silver taste of falling snow, but whimpers with disappointment when she watches the flakes melt into moist nothing in her cupped hand. Tybalt lifts her up, spinning with her in his arms until she laughs once more.

A man's boots crunch along the entryway. It is Pietro, come to check how the hive is faring in the blustery cold. Juliet wriggles free of Tybalt and totters toward my husband, half-singing and half-panting, "Po, Po, Po," in perfect imitation of the tone with which I call Pietro's name when he and I lay together. Why does this surprise me? She's heard it enough times, when I've given her a top or doll or just a pot-spoon to bang against the floor, anything to distract her while my husband and I take our tumble. "Po," she says again, insistent, reaching up her arms.

Pietro scoops her up, planting a warming kiss on her reddened ear. But as she shrieks another joyful "Po," Lord Cappelletto appears behind my husband.

"What's this?" he asks.

I'm not sure which distresses him more, to find Juliet outside at this hour and in such weather, or to see her beaming at the beekeeper with a grander version of the same adoring look Lord Cappelletto believes she saves only for him.

"Where have you been so early, Uncle?" Tybalt asks, juggling snowballs. The four perfect rounds arc up, only to smash apart when he tries to catch them.

Lord Cappelletto blinks once, twice, as though he is trying to conjure the right answer, then says, "A business matter. For the prince."

But his clothes are dry, his cheeks pale, not the wet and pink they'd be if he'd come all the way from the prince's castle, or even one of the lordly palaces that line the Piazza dei Signori. He must have passed the smallest hours of the night at the pursemaker's house, hoping to slip back here before anyone noticed he was gone.

My teeth ache in the wintry air as I reach for Juliet. I mean to hurry her inside, but when I take her from Pietro, she shrieks, "Po, Po, Po," so fiercely that Lady Cappelletta rushes down into the courtyard, asking whether the house is under attack.

"Such a bright child." I speak as though Juliet's recognizing Pietro should please the Cappelletti. "She knows it is the beekeeper, and she asks for a little honey."

I pray the mention of sweets will distract Lady Cappelletta as well as Tybalt, just as surely as needing to deceive Lady Cappelletta will distract Lord Cappelletto.

Pietro, who never comes to Ca' Cappelletti with an empty pocket, pulls out a bundle of candies and passes them to Lord Cappelletto, who doles them to his wife and nephew, and to Juliet, like a guilt-faced priest giving out the sacrament. Lady Cappelletta shivers, blue-lipped in the cold, and lets her husband drape an arm around her, guiding her inside. I follow, carrying Juliet back to our room without any farewell to my husband, who is already answering a new round of Tybalt's never-ending questions.

A child will parrot whatever it might hear, and who knows what the consequences will be, for the child or for the one whose words she innocently repeats. When I was a girl — older surely than Juliet though I could not say how much older — I repeated what I'd heard my father say a hundred times: *pox-faced son of the Devil.* His hateful name for our hated landlord. Yes, a child too easily recites what it does not understand, and that is how I spoke those words when Luca Covoni appeared one summer day to take his share of my father's harvest.

He repeated them, looking not at me but at my father. And before my father could respond, Covoni said the rent on the land we worked would be doubled the next year, and every year thereafter.

Covoni had barely left before my father grabbed a metal cooking spoon and began to beat my face with it. When I asked what I'd done wrong, he bared my buttocks and swung the spoon against that tender flesh, whacking out each syllable of *pox-faced son of the Devil,* demanding I never mock him again.

Though I'd always been quick with words, I'd not known what it meant to mock. And this I must have protested to him. For next he screamed he'd take a knife to my very tongue and cut it loose for all the trouble it caused. My mother went out, leaving me to his rage — or so I thought. She reappeared clutching a clay jug she'd hidden in the root cellar. Even I could smell the heavily fermented contents as she uncorked it. Wine made my father cruel enough. Surely with such evil spirits in him, he'd kill me.

But once he started to drink, he could not stop. By the fifth swig, or the sixth, he'd lost interest in me. My mother just had time to whisper a single command to me before he shoved her down onto the bed. She smiled at him, but she kept one eye on me to make sure I did as she bade, running to my aunt's house on the far side of the village. It was three days before she let me back. My father's rage had faded, though the angriest of the red welts he'd laid on me were still raw. That was my first lesson in the value of keeping things unspoken, or carefully half-told.

I'd not lay a hand on Juliet, would not even threaten it. But by the look upon Lord Cappelletto's face when she called for Pietro, I know I must quell what's dangerous in her mouth, just as surely as my father did what was in mine.

The day is bright from sun and snow, too bright for spinning schemes. I wait until night settles like a great shadow over Ca' Cappelletti. Then I teach Juliet to do what I hope will keep us in Lord Cappelletto's highest graces.

I let her grow hungry and hungrier, before I untruss my left breast. I dance it above her, watching her watch the nipple slick with milk. As her mouth opens, I take her chin in my other hand, gently working her jaw up and down as I say, "Papà."

"Po," she says. "Po," reaching for me with greedy hands.

I pull away. "Papà."

"Pa-po." Closer, but still not close enough.

"Papà, Papà, Papà, Papà, Papà, Papà, Papà." I repeat it so many times it begins to sound like none-such speech to me, until at last she says, "pa pa."

"Yes, my darling girl, yes." I let her take me in her mouth, indulging her only long enough to dull the ache I feel from being too full of milk. Then I pry her from my breast and make her say "pa pa" again, before I let her drink her fill.

I go to sleep thinking myself quite clever. But when I wake, Juliet is kicking at my ribs, calling "pa pa, pa pa," as she pounds her hands against my breast. That is what she thinks "pa pa" means.

This will please neither Lord Cappelletto nor Lady Cappelletta.

Lord Cappelletto's grown so full in the gut, there's a pouch within the household sewing basket filled with buttons he's burst loose. I slip one of the silver buttons stamped with the Cappelletti crest into my blouse, and, sure the saints will smile at such ingenuity, let it settle into place between my breasts. When I gather Juliet to me to nurse, she discovers the button, clutching it with one hand while the other cups the great globe of me that fills her mouth. I kiss her hair, then kiss the hand that holds the button, whispering, "Papà." Every time she nurses, she finds the button, wrapping greedy fingers around its shiny surface and singing out, "pa pa," before she latches onto me.

I bide our time until the prince next comes to dine. While he brags of the fine bride he's at last contracted for — who will come from Naples with a good dowry, a grand title, and best of all, a dead father, no surviving uncles, and a sister who rules the city of Durazzo childless — I let Juliet crawl into Lord Cappelletto's lap. She reaches for the topmost of his buttons, calling, "pa pa, pa pa."

"Papà," Lord Cappelletto repeats, laughing and grabbing her insistent hands before they tear the button loose.

Juliet smiles up at him and says, "Nusskiz," which is how she demands a kiss from me. Lord Cappelletto, who always thinks he understands what he does not, bows his head and pushes his big nose toward her delicate lips, waiting for her to kiss it. I notice what no one else does: how she hesitates. But my good girl does what is asked of her. I nod, letting her know that later, once we are alone, I'll give her what she seeks.

It's harder to herd a well-pastured lamb than one that's never left its pen. Freed first of swaddling and then of the girello, Juliet tumbles and stumbles and grabs at anything she can. We go to confession just before Pentecost, and when Friar Lorenzo bends to bless her, she pulls so hard at his Pater Noster cross that the cord snaps. Beads fly loose, bouncing across the hard floor of his cell. I kneel and crawl, searching out the myrtle-scented beads. He keeps careful count until I find them all.

But Friar Lorenzo'll not scold Juliet. He lays a loving hand on her bejeweled cap and says, "Juliet Cappelletta di Cappelletto, truly you are Heaven's child."

She rewards him by snugging herself into the thick folds of his cassock and trilling out, "Fri-lore-so, Fri-lore-so." The holy celibate, beaming like a proud grandsire at how she forms his name, offers a Latin benediction to show all is forgiven.

When we leave his cell, I take her into the lower church, where she toddles up and down the aisles to touch the brightly colored saints painted upon the square pillars while I say my Ave Marias. Her delighted squeals echo against the ceiling arches, until I'd swear the icons themselves smile back at her. She insists she can make it up all the steps by herself, and though she uses hands as well as feet in her crawling climb, when she reaches the top, I stand on the landing below and clap to show her she's done well.

This sets her squealing again, and she bolts into the upper church — and comes to a smacking stop against a kneeling, sobbing woman.

I hie to them, murmuring an apology to the mourner. As I scoop up Juliet, she grabs at the woman's veil, expecting a game of peekie-boo as she pulls the dark fabric up. But my sweet girl's grin cracks into a gasp when she sees the woman's face, leaden with grief.

The woman reaches to tug the veil free. But no, her fierce hands seize Juliet, snatching the child to her.

Juliet screams. A sound of pure fear, entirely unlike her familiar squeals of joy, or impatient wailing, or frustrated sobs, or any other noise she's ever made.

"So alive," the woman says, clinging tighter as Juliet shrieks louder.

I reach for Juliet. "Let me take her, while you make a prayer for the departing soul of the one the you've lost."

"I've not lost one," the woman says. "I've lost them all."

Her grip is as tight as mine, and we stand together like a single, strange beast wrapped around my screaming Juliet, until one of the Franciscans hurries out from the sacristy as if he's expecting to combat Satan himself.

Seeing him, the woman looses her hold. I cradle Juliet to me, bearing her away, out of San Fermo and into the bright sun.

Shushing her terrified cries, I carry her toward the Adige, hoping the swooping gulls will distract her. But even when her screams subside, she'll not forget the woman.

"Who-da?" she asks, "Why-do?" — her worried way of wondering who the woman is, and what made her act so strangely.

How am I to answer? Although I'd never before seen her, I know everything about the woman's agony as surely as, in that horrible year when plague crept across this very bridge into Verona, I knew my own miserable self.

For weeks, for months, as the mysterious pestilence ravaged the city, I woke fearing I felt the gentle swell in the pit beneath my arm or between my legs. I was sure I would be the one taken, and then Pietro after me, our children left orphans. When each dawn found us well, I prayed my thanks, then prayed my beseechment that I might live to pray such thanks the next day, too.

Pietro and I lumbered like blinded mules through the deathly miasma that lay upon the city, struggling to keep ourselves and our boys clear of it. I rose at odd hours so that I could draw water from the public fountain when no one else was there. And I wrapped myself like the wife of a Mohammedan whenever I went to the market, although in truth we stayed half-starved because I feared what sickly airs might coat any eggs or grain or meat I bought.

That spring, Pietro was hired by a confectioner whose apprentices had fled the city. It was against the guild rules for a grown man to be taken into the trade, but in those dismal seasons no one bothered to enforce such statutes, for what man wants to waste what might be his last healthy day just to swear out a complaint against a rival artisan? If you've never lived through plague, you'd not believe how popular clove-soaked candied walnuts or cinnamon-sugared bozolati can be. When disease ravages innocent and guilty alike, there are those who don hairshirts and shout for repentance, and those who drop breeches and call for delights. Appetites for confections swelled along with appetites for every other bodily indulgence, and Pietro was gone long hours from us. When my chores gave me need to go out as well, I bade Nunzio lead his brothers to the roof, to play whatever games they could invent. I never would have believed this safe and right before the plague, but now I thought only of the one great harm that I

181

believed could not find them there.

Any mother of sons knows how boys will entertain themselves watching ants carry off the carcass of a wasp. From our roof, my sons saw Verona's bier-bearers crawling ant-like through the streets, first to the cemeteries and then, once there was not a single square of consecrated ground left unfilled, to any field beyond the city gates where a mass grave-pit could be dug. It was not right for children to gape at those bespotted, boil-ridden corpses being carried off. But what else could I do with them, six sons I dared not let into the street? I always barred the door from the outside, so they could not let themselves out. Returning an hour later, I'd hear their shouts and taunts, the thrumming of a ball against the wall, all the boisterous cacophony of boys kept locked inside echo-ing along the street. In happier times, a mother might scold her sons for such disturbance to the neighbors. But during those months when pestilence silenced so many, whenever I came back to my boys' noisy mischief, I kissed and hugged them hard, until even little Angelo squirmed away from me.

Half a year we lived like that. Till the autumn day I went to buy the last of the season's onions, hoping they would somehow be enough to get us through the winter. When I haggled over the brown-skinned bulbs, did I forget to beg the saints' forgiveness for my great presumption that there would be eight of us to feed all the way to spring?

As I neared our house, I heard Angelo crying as though his older brothers were tormenting him. No mother is surprised by such things, but Angelo's wail was unusually frightened, and frightening. The door was still shut fast, just as I'd left it. But what tingled in the pit of my arms and between my legs swelled to a throb as I unbarred the door and hurried up the stairs. There was Angelo, red-faced and bawling, bound to the bed with a dishcloth. I stopped only long enough to see he was unharmed, before I searched out his brothers. They were not inside, and when I called them name by name to come back from the roof, there was no answer.

I hauled myself up the ladder, but none of my boys stood upon the roof's sloping tiles. My yells sounded back unanswered from the walls of the neighboring buildings, which rose above our little house.

Somewhere Berto let out a giggle. One of his brothers smacked him back to silence before I could be sure where the sound was coming from. Curving foot to tile, foot to tile, I crept to the edge of the roof. Bracing myself against the corner of our neighbor Luigi's house, I peered out. Though the day was cold, Luigi's shutter was flung back, a patch of faded bigello caught on its hinge. I knew the fabric well. Nunzio, Nesto, and Donato each had worn and outgrown the tunic it was torn from, which now was Enzo's.

Angelo, still bound to the bed, let out a doleful cry. My foot slipped, sending a tile sliding off the roof. It smashed into the street, and Enzo poked his curious head out from Luigi's window like a ground-mole popping up from his hole. Before I could grab for him, his brothers pulled him back inside.

I could not creep hand-over-hand along the awning pole that hung across the windows, as my sons must have. Instead I crawled back up the roof and down the ladder, hurrying down our stairs into the street. Banging on Luigi's door, I called his name, and then the name of each of my naughty sons. None answered. I grabbed the latch, which lifted too easily in my hand.

Luigi was a tanner, and at first I thought the stink inside must have come from a remnant of curing hide. But climbing his stair, I knew the stench was too terrible for that.

I found him lying on the floor. His half-rotten corpse gaped with holes where rats had fed off him for who could say how long. But those devil-toothed rodents would never be so cruel again thanks to my sons, who'd taken Luigi's kitchen pestle and smashed the rats to death. Five in all, one for each boy.

How could they be so impious? As if dying unshriven and unblessed, then being chewed through like some Alpine cheese, was not enough for Luigi to suffer. Though the sight and stench of him turned my stomach, I kept my sons in that room yet longer, ordering them all to kneel and pray for the poor man's wandering soul.

But I could tell already it was too late. I did not yell, or strike, or chasten them. Neither did Pietro, when I told him that night what they'd done. We both knew that what punishment they'd suffer for their savage sport was one we could neither give nor relieve.

Two days passed before Berto began to swell. Within hours, four of his brothers did as well. We tried to keep Angelo apart from them, but where in our little rented rooms could he be hid? The pestilence took but another day to find him.

By the end of the week, every one of our dear boys was dead. Pietro bore them off on a single bier, while I cursed the saints that saw fit to let me outlive my sons.

So alive, the grieving woman in San Fermo said. So alive — the worst thing to be, when you've lost all. But the best, now, as I hold Juliet and coo her calm again.

EIGHT

The dovecote stands one year, then two. Tybalt grows bored with chasing game hens, and Juliet, at nearly age three, squeals with pleasure while swooping after them herself. Lady Cappelletta has been fed innumerable eggs and a countless weight of poultry-flesh. Was it dove, or partridge, or sparrow that at last did it? None can say. Her madness quiets as her breath grows shallow, her face swelling like the pig bladder blown full of air that my boys used to bat back and forth between them. No one speaks of it. She is too fearful. And Lord Cappelletto is too superstitious.

He hires a donkey to carry her in this year's Easter procession, while he walks before her beaming as he shows the whole city that he's finally filled her belly again. Ridden by an ass so long, she now rides one — a merry joke, though I've no one to tell it to. But some jokes tell themselves. During

187

Mass, Lady Cappelletta lets slip such a passing of wind, it echoes against the arched ceiling of the cathedral. On the men's side of the nave, Tybalt's laugh breaks nearly as loud, setting Juliet giggling as well. I pinch a look at him and a thumb on her, until they hush.

Juliet's so big, I cannot hold her as I kneel, and so she must kneel herself, though her body leans heavy into mine when she grows tired. As for Tybalt — even on his knees he's now taller than his uncle. But he still mumbles during Mass, repeating by unsteady rote as I do, with none of Lord Cappelletto's prideful mastery of Latin.

Once we are back in Ca' Cappelletti, the Easter feast spread upon the sala table, Tybalt is the first to fill a trencher, and just as quickly fills his mouth. While Lady Cappelletta, elbows propped upon the dining table, falls into a doze, Tybalt's new-long arms stretch for seconds and then thirds, emptying the serving bowls of the wild boar braised in rosemary, wine, and walnuts, and then the roasted kid stuffed with parsley, veal, and fig.

The Lenten fast is hard on growing boys, but Lord Cappelletto is harder on him still. Last month, Tybalt finally bested his uncle at chess. After all the years of losing, he was so proud he'd won, he ran to tell me and Juliet and Lady Cappelletta, and did not understand why I tried to shush him. I'd not expected Lord Cappelletto to take well to being bested, and in the days since, he's seized every chance to needle Tybalt, insisting his nephew will do the Cappelletti more dishonor than five generations of Infangati or Uberti or Montecchi have.

"Your Latin is disgracing." He jabs his dinner knife into Tybalt's trencher to take back the last lamb-and-fennel sausage. "And your tutor tells me your figures and tallying are even worse."

Lord Cappelletto's words hit Tybalt like gut punches, hunching him forward, singeing his ears with crimson shame. Juliet, frightened for her cousin, climbs onto my lap and searches out a breast for what is her comfort, and mine. I ought to carry her off, to nurse her far from Lord Cappelletto, but I'll not abandon Tybalt.

"I try, Uncle." Tybalt's voice cracks under the effort of answering. "But words or sums upon a page dance before my eyes until I'm dizzy."

"Dizzy?" Lord Cappelletto snorts the word back. "Lazy. A lazy princox, and I'll not suffer it."

I share, if not Lord Cappelletto's severity,

at least some worry over what will become of Tybalt. He does not fall in with the other boys his age, who roam the city looking for trouble. When he sneaks from his family compound, it is only to follow Pietro as he makes his circuit from one hive to another. And my husband says Tybalt's enthusiasm wanes when it comes time to haggle with the chandler or coax raw honey into carefully spiced comfits.

But anyone with sense can see that Tybalt is not lazy. He dances, and prances, and tumbles, burning with more energy every passing year. He still dotes on Juliet, so that whenever he comes into a room, she smiles at him like a coquette at a wealthy suitor. And, like that wealthy suitor's poorest and most desperate rival, Tybalt will do anything to please her. But these days, nothing he does seems to please his uncle.

I remember first Nunzio and then Nesto at thirteen, when a youth thinks he is too clever to be young, though truly he is too young to be clever. An age when he needs most what Tybalt's father is not here to give.

Broadswords hang upon the sala walls, each as long as Tybalt is tall and all decorated with the gilded Cappelletti crest. Tybalt loves to play at swords, just as his uncle loves to tally the profits of his investments

— and to outdo the Cappelletti's rival families in currying favor with Verona's ruler. "They say Prince Cansignorio has sent to Brandenburg, to hire the city's finest master-at-arms to teach Count Paris and Count Mercutio." I speak to no one in particular, though I make sure Lord Cappelletto hears.

"Who says this?" he asks.

I shrug, as if to show it's on everyone's tongue, though truly it's only on my own. I've woven it out of thin air, and now I knot the loose strands into a tidy edge. "They may only be his nephews, but Prince Cansignorio rears them as though they're his own sons."

Lady Cappelletta jerks herself awake at the word *sons*. Lord Cappelletto makes careful survey of the low spread of her belly. "I will write my brother about securing a master-at-arms. It's time someone disciplined Tybalt."

Tybalt pulls himself up at the idea of training with a swordmaster, Juliet hiccuping off my nipple to give him a milk-wet smile.

Lord Cappelletto's mouth puckers over how Tybalt's joy feeds Juliet's. And it is from those puckered lips that I hear the words, "And also time for Juliet to be weaned."

Weaned. If Lord Cappelletto took my breasts into his stubby-fingered hands, twisting like Sant'Agata's tormentors, it'd not pain me more than his uttering that word does. As though what flows between milk-mother and milk-daughter can be cut off with a single word. As though I'll let the dour cloister of Santa Caterina swallow all the light and joy of Juliet, just so he can bribe the saints into giving him a son.

I rouse Juliet early the next morning and tell her we must go see Friar Lorenzo. She knows the route as well as I. Grasping my hand, she leads me along the Via Cappello toward the Porta dei Leoni, turning south and east and south again through streets no wider than a donkey-cart. Although by night these tight passageways are so quiet you can hear the thrusting of a single vendetta-driven blade, at this hour they're crowded with women and children hauling and haggling and hanging laundry, the street more filled with noise than light. Juliet stops every tenth step to gape and wonder, wearing my patience filigree thin by the time we emerge into the bright sun before San Fermo, cross the churchyard, and duck into the entrance to the friary.

Juliet is always delighted to enter the Franciscan's cell. She raises her face, ready to hear him say how pretty she is, grown ever prettier since our last visit, though he'd not have thought it possible. Her little mouth loves to form the words *me fess* and share with him her childish misdeeds: how she's cried herself exhausted while refusing all my efforts to console her, or plucked a flower after I've forbidden it. I always nod solemnly as she speaks, repeating her odd-formed words so he can understand them. By my troth, I believe she only does such little wrongs for the joy she finds in adding her play-shrift to my weightier one, and having Friar Lorenzo in a single breath forgive us both.

But today the truest sin I have to tell is neither hers nor mine, so I'll not say it. How can I confess that Lord Cappelletto is ready to make sacrifice of Juliet? I claim impiety instead, for laughing with Tybalt and Juliet at Lady Cappelletta's breaking wind.

I bow my head and Juliet, her lip trembling with regret, bows hers, as Friar Lorenzo absolves us. "Poor Lady Cappelletta, she suffers so," I say, when he has done. "She'd do anything to be cured of such windiness. And Lord Cappelletto would give anything to have her cured."

Friar Lorenzo's great ears brighten to hear *Lord Cappelletto* paired with *would give anything*. I may not know a word of Latin, but I've long understood the mendicant order's unspoken motto: do all you can for the poor — and take all you can from the rich. It's the latter he's at now, leaning his tonsured head over his stock of petals and powders, muttering about wild celery and cowbane, then mastic, cloves, and madder root, carefully mixing in drams of who knows what else. He grinds it all into a powder, pours the powder into a pouch, and affixes a tiny cross, so Lady Cappelletta and her lord husband will know it came from him. "Three scruples," he instructs me, "to be given her with sweetened wine, whenever the windiness takes her."

I accept the Franciscan's *benedicte* along with the little pouch. When we leave his cell Juliet wants to tarry as we often do, stopping first to visit the bright saints in the lower church, and then, in the upper church, to twirl beneath the dim ones peering down from the dark ceiling. But I've no time for church and saints, when for once it's Lady Cappelletta's help I seek.

Juliet, long too big for the cradle yet still too small for a needle, has learned to make toy bird or clay horse her companion during the slow hours Tybalt is with his tutor while Lady Cappelletta and I sit sewing. But though I've told her a thousand times that what is said in Friar Lorenzo's cell is a sacred confidence between penitent and priest, Juliet proves again this morning what I often say: two can keep counsel, putting one away.

"Ma'da," she says, for the formal *madonna madre* is still too much for her little tongue to master. "Ma'da, me fess, and Nurse fess, and Friar make it go way."

Proffering the pouch, I explain, "Friar Lorenzo sends a blessed remedy to soothe your suffering," and instruct her to call for wine. Not the pale trebbiano Lord Cappelletto has her drink, but a foreign-made malmsey as red as the flush it will bring to her wan cheeks.

Three scruples, and wine, and honey to go with. One goblet and then another, and the mixture so sweet and good, she drinks down a third. All that tinctured wine calms her ill-winded humors, and soon Lady Cappelletta is giggling like a child of eight and not the woman of eighteen she'll soon be. She says Juliet's play horse reminds her of the steed that was the pride of her father's stable, telling us how on holy-days the

195

horse's mane was woven with ribbons and pearls to match her sisters' fair hair, and her own. She even sings a little song that they sang as all three girls rode upon its back. Juliet's eyes puzzle at hearing the bright melody from such a usually so sour source.

"Happy days of childhood," I say, though I know not whether she had even a dozen such days before she was married off. But I need her to help me give my Juliet such happy days — and happy nights — as she deserves, not a one of which will come to her if she is sent off to Santa Caterina. "You should tell Lord Cappelletto to get so grand a horse, so that you and Juliet and the new babe might ride like that, when the second gets as big as Juliet is now."

"I cannot tell my lord husband such a thing," she says.

Even the wine is not enough to nerve her. So I add what ought nerve any wife. "I should think there's much you'd like to tell him, for mousing after the pursemaker's daughters instead of doing his dowry-duty to you."

Though it's not my proper place to speak so, what more have I to lose than if Juliet is sent off to the nuns? But my words are like a swift-winged wasp circling before Lady

Cappelletta's brow. Her eyes cross in confusion.

"A wife must catch the rat, when her husband's on a mouse hunt." I work the spindle quick, letting my words work her. "Even Prince Cansignorio keeps his natural spawn out of the castle, now that he's got a proper wife. A husband must show public pride for his lawfully begot, church-blessed children, and send the bastards away."

This is my pretty plan. If Lord Cappelletto is in want of a child to sacrifice, let the convent devour what children he's made outside his marriage bed. Though for all I know, he's had even less luck planting his seed among the pursemaker's daughters than with his wife.

I bid Lady Cappelletta take more wine, hoping it will warm her to what I'd have her do. "Tybalt says the queen upon the chessboard uses knight and rook to keep herself protected. Just so a wife, who keeps her children near to make her husband put his duty to her first." I drop my voice to a conspiratorial whisper, though in truth there's no one near enough to hear. "I knew of a woman once, whose husband became so overfond of his natural child he took it into their home, and sent his wife and lawful children off without returning her

197

dowry-portion."

I do not add that the home was a mere shack, the wife a shrew, the dowry-portion a near-dead billy goat, and even so, the village priest declared the husband wrong and gave the wife back her rightful place — where she was made to raise her husband's bastard child along with their legitimate ones.

As we sew, I keep a steady pouring of wine into Lady Cappelletta's goblet and vinegar into her ear. When the dining hour draws near, I urge her to put on her wedding bracelets. She wears them like Tybalt does his father's castoff gorget-armor — believing it girds him for some imagined battle, though in truth it's too big to fit him.

Juliet, grown tired of her horse, begs for a length of ribbon. I give her three, and show her how to weave them into a braided diadem, which she carries into the sala, where Tybalt is already waiting. When Lord Cappelletto enters, Juliet runs to him with the bright crown in her outstretched hands, calling, "Me give pa-pa."

But he ignores the gift and does not bend for her soft kiss. "I must go to Mantua," he says.

Mantua is a spark that ignites Tybalt. "Will you see my father? When do you leave? May

I come?"

"I will go." A mere three words, yet Lady Cappelletta heaves a sigh at all it took for her to say them.

Lord Cappelletto, surprised to hear his wife speaking at all, answers, "You'll not."

But he looks full at her as he speaks, rather than keeping his eyes on his trencher, or on Tybalt, or on anything else in all the room. When a husband looks away, he is done hearing what his wife might say. But if his eyes meet hers, she may pry upon that tiny crack, if she has nerve to answer back.

All that wine has surely nerved Lady Cappelletta, though I mouth *the pursemaker's daughters* at her, just to be sure. "My dowry-gold fills your purse," she tells Lord Cappelletto. "You've no need to seek another."

Tybalt looks with wonder from his aunt to his uncle. "You're going to Mantua to get a purse?"

"I'm going to Mantua because my brother is unwell." Lord Cappelletto's wrinkled features sag under the weight of his words. But they hit Tybalt even harder.

"Will you not let me see my father?" he asks.

Before Lord Cappelletto can reply, I say, "A child is much comfort to a parent at such times."

For once, Lady Cappelletta catches the meaning first. "Your brother will want to have his rightful son with him in Mantua." She takes her husband's hand and lays it upon her babe-stretched belly. "And you will want to have your own."

It's the first I've ever seen Lord Cappelletto find comfort in this wife. "We will all of us go to Mantua," he says, just to be sure he's the one who settles it.

I gather Juliet onto my own lap, whisper *Mantua* into her ear. But before I can spin out tales of all the wonders I imagine we'll see there, Lord Cappelletto looks over, as if discovering Juliet for the first time. She beams at him like sunlight streaming through church glass, offering the ribboned crown again.

"Juliet Cappelletta di Cappelletto, we must go to Mantua," he says. He takes the crown and sets it on her dark hair. "You will stay here and be weaned, while we are gone."

I flash a look at flush-cheeked Lady Cappelletta. But she is leaning toward Tybalt, the two of them murmuring about their journey — both so caught up in their confidence, neither of them thinks of Juliet, or of me. They do not so much as mark

Lord Cappelletto waving his long-pronged fork and telling me, "The child is to be done with crying for the dug, before we return."

For all Juliet's memory and more, our days have always started with Lord Cappelletto coming for his morning kiss. But these mornings, there is no Lord Cappelletto thumping his way into our chamber, nor any chance of Tybalt climbing through the window or sneaking in by way of the hidden tower door, and no Lady Cappelletta anywhere in Ca' Cappelletti. It was a furious flurry of preparations, afternoon stealing into night, before we saw all three of them off at the next dawn. Lady Cappelletta sobered back to her usual uncertainty as her husband guided her into the wooden box of the hired carriage. She begged Tybalt to sit with her among the household bolsters and brass-hinged traveling coffers that were lain inside. But he insisted on riding upon a post-horse just as Lord Cappelletto did, one hand clutching the leathered bridle while the other waved fare-thee-well to Juliet and me.

Juliet's eyes widen with unease a dozen times a day at having all of our household routines unsettled. Again and again, I remind her that they are gone. That the sun must rise and make his way across the sky, then sink down and disappear, over and over at least a hand-count's worth of times, and maybe two or three, before they will return. Then I ask what she wants to play, and let her whims set each hour of our days. Though these may be the last we'll have together, I'd not have her know. I'll not burden her with all the grief I feel, as I hold her and offer what Lord Cappelletto demands she learn to live without.

It's more than a week that they've been away. Juliet, playing the wood-nymph frolicking among the fruit-laden trees, bids me be her fairy-queen. So I'm plumped upon the bench beside the dovecote as though it were my fairy-throne, when Pietro comes into the arbor. One of his hands curves around a sack that's tied off with a tiny cross. I realize in a chilling instant why Pietro has it, what Lord Cappelletto must have directed Friar Lorenzo to send.

As the cross catches the summer sun, my besotted lamb reaches for it. Pietro slips Friar Lorenzo's pouch to me, then flourishes his empty hand as though he's a court magician. Juliet, startled to find what she seeks gone, blinks out disappointed tears. But Pietro offers his other hand, which holds a second well-filled sack, this one smelling of cherries, clove, and cinnamon. Juliet snatches it, twirling with delight. She pulls out three honeyed cherries, stuffs them into her mouth, and resumes her frenzied circuit through the arbor.

I hate to see her cry. But I hate more to see her soothed so easily.

"What comfit will comfort her, once she's tasted this?" I wag Friar Lorenzo's pouch of wormwood at Pietro.

"The child finds other delights than the breast. So might the breast, and the rest of my beloved wife, find other delights than suckling the child."

He pulls me into the shade of the peach tree. A tender sapling when first I came to Ca' Cappelletti, these three years later it's grown big enough to bear plump fruit. Pietro plucks a peach, halving it with his bare hands. He grasps the pit in his strong teeth and spits it to the ground. Then he rubs the wet, ripe peach halves along my neck, across my collar-bone. Deep into my dress. Slicking my breasts with peach flesh, as juice pours down my belly.

His tongue follows, licking and probing. Reminding me a husband's mouth can be as needy as a nursling's. As needy, and as needed. July is hot even in this shadiest corner of the arbor, and I am hot, too.

Pietro knows it, urging my hands to the most ravenous parts of him.

I'm dancing my hips against his when a sharp shriek ruptures the air. A shriek, and then an awful silence. And then harrowing sobs that pierce my heart.

I race through the arched passage into the courtyard, Pietro following. Juliet's sprawled beside the well. Tripped over her own impatient feet, her brow cracked open.

I kneel and kiss her bloodied head. But before I can ready a breast to soothe her wailing, Pietro takes her by her tiny shoulders, turning her away from me toward him.

"Did you fall upon your face?" he asks, as though any fool could not know that's what she's done.

He waits for Juliet to snivel back a sob and nod, then says, "A child falls upon its face, while a woman falls upon her back." He laughs, sweeping her up with his big arms so she lies gazing at summer's cloudless sky. "Will you not fall backward for a merry man, when you are grown and have wit enough to know more pleasures?"

Juliet stints mid-wail. She smiles up into Pietro's winking eyes and leaves off crying. "Aye," she says, though surely she cannot know what he means, never mind how many times she's been with me when I've fallen on my back for him.

He sets her down and runs a broad thumb across the ugly lump that's swelling from her brow. "A lesson every girl does well to learn, and you'll have a bump as big as a cockerel's stone to remind you of it." He laughs again, and she laughs too. Her tears forgotten, she runs off into the arbor to play.

I lean back, letting the well-stones take the weight of me. "She's too young for talk of rooster parts, and rutting people."

"She is growing. Soon she will be grown." He sits beside me, slipping an arm across my shoulders and pulling me to him. "Why not let the girl know what pleasures she'll relish when she's a woman?"

"She'll not ever get to relish them." I bury my head against him and tell him how Lord Cappelletto plans to send her to the convent as soon as she is weaned. "He'll take her first from me, and then from every worldly pleasure. She'll wither away in a cloister, so he can have his son."

My merry-tongued husband has no words at first. But then he sighs and says, "She's his child. He may dispose of her as he pleases. You've known that all along. But if we have one of our own —"

"She is my own." The words I've never said aloud come pouring out. A flood, an avalanche. "It's my milk that's made her. The bone and muscle and soft, smooth flesh of her, they're all grown from what I give. The hair upon her head, dark as my own, and those plump cheeks. There's more of me in her than of Lady Cappelletta, or even Lord Cappelletto. Anyone can see it."

"What they see is the Cappelletti crest. Upon her clothes, and this grand house. And on the signet ring with which Lord Cappelletto will seal the papers committing her to Santa Caterina." Pietro kisses me, not with his earlier passion, but with the same gentle comfort I offered Juliet for her broken brow. "You've always known this time would come."

I've known, of course. But by my troth, I've not known, too.

Have I not said that self-deceiving is the very way of humankind? That in our hearts, we all wish to be fooled, and so we make fools of ourselves? There are coin-hungry husbands who every year contract for a different babe to be cradled at their wives' breasts, and hard-to-please fathers who will hire first one nurse, then fickly turn her out and seek another, and then another after that, so that their child ever suckles upon strangers. But what Juliet and I share is not, cannot, be like that.

I am a fool, perhaps, but even as Juliet shed her swaddling, learned to waddle then to walk and now to run, even as she's swallowed her first tastes of solid food — in all this time we've had together, I've not truly believed that Lord Cappelletto could ever be so heartless as to cleave me from her.

"I'll not lose her."

"No, you'll not. Novitiates, and even full-habited nuns, may have visitors. I'll take you to the convent whenever she's uncloistered."

How can Pietro's talk of some-day visits succor me, when I know I'd not survive the stretch of time between them? "How can I live even for one day apart from Juliet?"

"Three years, you've lived apart from me."

"And it was ten times three years that we had together first. Why can I not have even half so long with her?" My words fly sharp and heavy, like the rocks Tybalt hurls from atop the Cappelletti tower.

How can my husband argue with me over this? Does he not know what losing Juliet will cost me? Did he not grieve for our sons, and for the loss of little Susanna? Is my mother-love so different from what a father feels?

Pietro pulls himself away, rising to his feet. "Mantua is only a day's ride from here.

Lord Cappelletto may return at any time. When he does, he'll expect to find her weaned. And if she's not, he'll likely put you out at once for disobeying him. You'll get no chance to bid *God-be-with-you-and-good-bye* to Juliet. No leave to see her, even on uncloistered days at Santa Caterina. Nor ever again to visit Tybalt."

What Pietro says is true. But every syllable of it forms a taste as bitter on my tongue as Friar Lorenzo's wormwood will be upon my breast.

"I must go to Villafranca. A day's walk each way, to haggle for what spices I can afford before I harvest this summer's honey. When I'm back, I'll not come here again. I'll not keep sneaking about, stealing time with you like I'm a thief taking what is rightfully Lord Cappelletto's." He leans down and kisses my hair, letting his words slip softly into my ear. "For thirty years we made a home together, through the worst that anyone could suffer. Since you came here, I've worn my patience like haircloth, waiting to have you back again. It's time for you to be my proper wife. Let me love you near, as I've loved you every day you've been away."

I close my eyes, feeling the sun pour its stern heat across my face as I nod to my beloved husband. But he cannot see how I rub my tongue against my mouth-roof, knowing his honey-coated words'll not take away this bitter taste.

For one last night, I nurse Juliet into milk-sweet sleep. Restless though I am, waiting for her to wake and take her final taste of me, she sleeps heavily, stirring only when the morning lark twitters outside the open window, and the sun begins to stretch its golden way into the room.

"Me pick?" she asks, studying me with drowsy determination. I nod, glad for this game she's loved to play since before she had the words for it.

She opens an expectant mouth and takes in the nipple of my left breast. As she suckles, she reaches her hand up to stroke my face, drinking me in until my left breast has no more milk to give. I wait in perfect anticipation for her to reach her mouth to the ripe right nipple. Then I pull her close, savoring her last latching onto me. Wondering if ever tender hearts could break more than mine will, and hers as well, when we are forced apart.

By day's full light, I cannot deny the truth in what Pietro said. Yesterday's bruise has deepened into a hideous purpled rise above Juliet's eyes. That sight alone might be enough for Lord Cappelletto to put me out. I'll not risk disobeying what he's ordered me to do. Not anger him so, he might never let me see Juliet again. So I pray to Santa Margherita and Sant'Agata and the Blessed Virgin Mother for such strength as only women show, as I loose Friar Lorenzo's cross-bound pouch.

I was not much older than Tybalt is now, when I had Nunzio, my firstborn, at my breast. I can still remember how he crawled up my belly and found the nipple for himself. They will do that, the clever ones, in their first hour. And from that first hour, for fifteen years my milk ran for my boys. And then, when I was long past thinking I would ever suckle babe again, it came once more. Seven I birthed, and seven I nursed. But after today, not any more.

While Juliet giggles and gambols about the arbor, I sit beside the dovecote to rub on the wormwood, the godly friar's way to trick a child to stop suckling. I flinch at the first dab, expecting it to burn like salt in a fresh wound. But crueler than that, I feel nothing.

As I coat myself with this bitterest of herbs, I sense a dark form suddenly rising.

The bees — they're flying frenzied from the hive, the arbor filling with their thousand-headed hiss. They hover in a whirling mass in the hot, fruit-scented air before forming a furious, swirling cone between me and Juliet.

The slabbed bench slides beneath me, then drops away. The fast jerk flings me to the ground. Stones fly past. The dovecote cracks, birds caw. Bells across the city clang. Not rung with the pious care that calls the holy to pray, but as if some unseen demon's hand was smacking every clapper in Verona, intent on splitting all our bells to pieces.

I cling for a hellish eternity to the shuddering ground, wondering if this thundering from every side will ever end. Worried the world will no longer stand when it is done. And plotting how to drag myself to Juliet.

And then, in an instant, the earth stills. The eddying cloud of bees funnels back into their fallen hive. Birds soar from the crumbled ruins of the dovecote, screeching as they spread themselves through the arbor trees. Screams of agony seep into Ca' Cappelletti from Verona's streets. But not a sound comes from Juliet.

She's heaped on the ground. She does not sob, does not stir. Not even when I crawl near and lay a hand across her chest to feel for the quiet beating of her heart.

I pull her to me, pushing my breast into her gaping mouth. She vomits me out the instant she tastes wormwood.

"Goddamn the brown-frocked friar." The words are out before I know I've made them. Surely I'm the one who'll wind up damned, for that unholy utterance. Perhaps I already am.

The arch over the passageway to the courtyard has collapsed. I stumble over toppled hunks of marble, clutching glassy-eyed Juliet to me. The great Cappelletti crest that hung within the courtyard lies smashed upon the ground. But the well still stands. I thank the saints for it as I haul up a pail of water, the rope rough against my hands.

My legs quake so, I cannot tell whether the earth is trembling again. I scrub and scrub my bittered breasts, dipping my tongue to test the taste. Wormwood, wormwood, wormwood. I cannot rid myself of it. How can I make Juliet come back to me, to herself, without a milk-sweet breast to draw her here?

Leaving her beside the well, I scurry once more across the jagged pile of fallen stone into the arbor. I do not give myself time to think, or doubt, or fear, before bending to pry loose the lid of the cut-log hive. I plunge my hand inside, the waxy comb crumbling in my desperate fingers.

The first sting burns the wattle of flesh hanging beneath my elbow. Pain sizzles up and down my arm and across my hand, as a second bee stings, and then a third. Then too many to keep count.

I hold tight to the crushed bits of comb, zigzagging my way from the hive, shaking bees out of my sleeve. By the time I'm back in the courtyard, I'm so swollen with stings, it's hard to unfold my fingers. I slip the sticky comb between Juliet's gaped lips and beg her to take suck.

She begins to work her mouth, leaching golden honey from the wax. The sweetness soothes her, and soon she hums with pleasure. She reaches for me, squeezing my arm, which makes the stings pain even more.

We rock together in the day's heat. Cocooned in pain, and grief, and honeyed relief, while Verona's streets echo with terrified shouts reporting all the damage the shaken earth has wrought.

NINE

The servants have all gone pecking after their own pleasures since Lord and Lady Cappelletti went away, and the house-page is still not back at his post. Which means there's no warning before the horse is inside the Cappelletti gate. Lathered from being ridden too hard for too long, the beast brays as the rider jumps down. I recognize the heavy footfall on the stone path, the clanging of the broad silver belt. But I've no time to right myself and Juliet, and no means to make her swollen head and bruised face less frightful.

"Juliet?" Lord Cappelletto calls her name as a question announcing his return.

"Papa," she answers, opening her arms and raising her face in anticipation of his kiss.

What's sweet anticipation for her is sour worry for me. Lord Cappelletto left the most beautiful of daughters, and returns to find a seeming changeling for his child. All the easier for him to cast her off to a convent, and cast me from her forever.

But though he startles at first sight of her, he kneels and kisses her with keen father-love, then murmurs soft words only she can hear before kissing her again. His voice catching in prayer, he brushes his finger along her brow, gently tracing the bruise that's spread beneath her eye. "I rode straight from Mantua as soon as the ground ceased shaking, fearing you were hurt."

"Me was hurt. Me fall, and Nurse fall, and dovey-coo fall."

I seize upon what she says, nodding toward the fallen archway. "We were in the arbor when the earth quaked. The dovecote collapsed, and Juliet fell and cracked her brow. She cried for the dug, but having weaned her as you bade me, I comforted her with honey." Every word I say is true, even if things'd not occurred in the order that I tell them. But I put my whole heart into what I promise will happen next. "What's bruised on her will heal, and she'll be every bit the lovely Cappelletta di Cappelletto, pride of Ca' Cappelletti, before the dovecote is rebuilded."

Lord Cappelletto shakes his head. "It'll not be built again. Lady Cappelletta has borne a son —"

"Thanks be to God." I cross myself with my sting-riddled arm, though I'm unsure whether Juliet is saved. "A son, at last."

"Her last," he says. "Dead within the hour it came out of her, and dead she nearly was with delivering it." Grief bows his balding head. "The day we arrived in Mantua, her pains came on. The Gonzaghe sent their own court midwife along with their physick, but neither one could save my son. Nor could the physick cure my brother." He clasps Juliet tighter, nearly smothering her against the dark folds of his new mourning cloak. "The physick is certain nothing more will quicken in Lady Cappelletta's womb."

Juliet wriggles her face free. Impatient with his talk of what she's too young to understand, she mews out, "Tybalt?"

She wants to know where her beloved playmate is. But Lord Cappelletto, bound by his own thoughts, says, "He'll be my heir. I promised my brother I'd take him as my own to keep our family's fortune complete."

Heir and *fortune* mean much to a man as rich as Lord Cappelletto. But what comfort can they be to a father-hungry boy like Tybalt?

Lord Cappelletto spends the rest of the day

shut inside Ca' Cappelletti, so bereft he turns away even the prince's own messengers, though he sends out alms of loaves, oil, and wine to honor the memory of his brother, and of his last lost son. His days in Mantua have aged him by ten years, and he carries himself more burdened than the page and serving-man who, having skulked back to Ca' Cappelletti, are ordered to haul off the pieces of the crumbled archway and the fallen Cappelletti crest.

When, hours later, a carriage arrives, Lord Cappelletto himself reaches up to lift out Lady Cappelletta, grief seeding an unwonted tenderness for his nearly taken wife. She is more wan than ever, her amber eyes unfocused as he guides her gently to the ground. "Ma'da," Juliet calls, putting all a child's expectation into those two syllables. But Lady Cappelletta, flickering like a tallow-candle in a sudden wind, pays her no notice.

I kiss Juliet's dark hair, whispering that Tybalt is here, too. But what appears next is not Tybalt, though the delicate creature has his pretty eyes and poutish mouth, its well-shaped head crowned with the same long, soft curls. Juliet buries herself among my skirts, taking timid peeks at the beautiful being. A younger, softer, girlish version of

Tybalt, with none of his awkward angularity. Nor his bold curiosity. Hesitating at the carriage opening, she crosses herself and recites some Latin prayer.

Lord Cappelletto nods at her piety. "Fear not, fair Rosaline," he says. "Tybalt, come help your sister down."

Tybalt is not eager to obey, I can tell from how long it takes him to make his way to the carriage opening, jump to the ground, and turn to lower this Rosaline out. His long face is made longer by grief, and he'll not meet my eye, nor Juliet's. As the last of the day's dusk seeps from the sky, he follows Lord Cappelletto up the stairs, Rosaline holding to his arm in imitation of how Lady Cappelletta clings to her husband, all of them cloaked in mourning.

I've promised Juliet what I've not got to give: Tybalt. Long after the compline bells ring, she lies awake in our chamber, waiting. Sobbing herself sick, she begs me to bring her beloved cousin. And so I go looking for him.

Lady Cappelletta is long settled in her bed, though whether Lord Cappelletto lies beside her or spends the night hours upon his knees down in the Cappelletti chapel, I cannot tell as I sidle past the antecamera to their chamber. All is still along the loggia overlooking the courtyard, the storerooms bolted shut, the entry to the parto room left bare. Inside the apartment on the far side of Ca' Cappelletti, I find only Rosaline. She's sleeping with a cherub's guiltless grace in the ornate bed that once held her parents, though in all my time in Ca' Cappelletti Tybalt's been the only one to lay his head here.

But tonight, no part of Tybalt is in the bedchamber. Nor in the study that sits beyond it, though he so dreads his tutor's lessons, I'd not expect to find him there. From the study window I look out over the kitchen roof and across the toppled passage to the arbor, to where the moon rises above Juliet's chamber. The dark silhouette of the family tower tells me where Tybalt must be. Where I must go to find him.

Despite the score of times Pietro's climbed the first storey of the tower stair to make his unseen way from the arbor into Juliet's chamber, I've not repeated the climb to the tower's top, not since that morning long ago when I first followed Tybalt up. By day the many steps were hard enough for me, but at night they're dark as pitch. Part of me is glad for it, for the darkness keeps me from seeing what I hear: the scurrying of rats or mice, I know not which, and the night-flapping of bats above my head.

I make my way slowly, for I've not got Tybalt's taste for adventuring — although I know what's urged him up the tower stair tonight is something else, something heavier on his heart. Turning up the final flight, I see him perched like a falcon upon the ledge at the tower top.

I whistle one low note as I approach. Afraid any more than that might startle him, send him tumbling to the street so far below.

"They took him." I can barely make out his words. His body is balled tight, his face buried against the sumptuous cloth of his mourning cloak.

"Death took him," I say, though I know too well what little comfort those words bring.

"They did it. I'm not sure how, and my uncle'll not tell me. But I know. I saw the swallow-wing."

I lay a hand on his head. It's feverish hot. "How could a bird —"

"Not a bird." Shaking off my mothering fingers, he points to one tower, then another, standing eerie guard over Verona. He does not pick every tower in every parish, only those whose bricked tops are notched with curving clefts, the same as ornament the city walls, and the prince's castle.

I know the pattern as well as anyone who lives within Verona, though I suppose I never noted how each cleft resembles the wings of a swallow raised in flight.

"The swallow-wing is the mark of those who hate us, because we're loyal to the Pope." Tybalt endarts his words like an archer shooting flaming arrows. "It was on the house where my father stayed. That's why they killed him."

Burning anger in a boy of thirteen only hides the more tender thing he feels. "He was not killed," I say. "He died."

"My mother died from giving birth. My new baby cousin died from being born. But why would my father die, unless some Uberto or Montecche killed him?"

What way is there to teach a child about the randomness of death? My own sons never heard a word of it from me, not in all their youthful years. Nor in that awful week when they lay ill, each too deep in his own agony to know when another of his beloved brothers slipped from us forever. No one could have imagined a thing as awful as the pestilence, until it came. But what good would it have done us to know such a thing could happen, in the years before it did?

"My daughter died, the day that Juliet was born."

Tybalt raises startled eyes to me, as surprised to hear those words as I am to utter them. But our own pain is all we have to offer when those we love are suffering.

"I miss my Susanna every day. But every day, I know I have Juliet, and you, to love. It's what saves me from wishing I'd gone, too, when Susanna went." I kiss his head. Not merely to comfort him, but to give myself a chance to take in his boy-scent, to warm myself with what burns in him. "You miss your father, as a son should. But Juliet is downstairs, crying for you. And Rosaline will want to see you when she wakes. And I need you, and so does Pietro, because we've no boy of our own. Neither does your uncle, or your aunt. We're none of us your father, but you are our dear Tybalt. In our love you'll find your solace, the same as I found mine in you and Juliet."

He does not answer, not aloud. But he lets me help him from the ledge and lead him to the stairs. He slips a grateful hand into my sting-swollen one, and together we make our way back down.

Not knowing how many nights I've left with Juliet, I'd not waste this one in sleep.

Whenever I begin to doze, I yank myself awake to watch her, nestled through the smallest hours of the night between me and Tybalt. They whispered long together before he fell into the deep sleep that grief brings, and she into the contented slumber of a child whose disordered world has been restored.

But Lord Cappelletto is more wakeful. The nightingale is still trilling when he pushes his way into our chamber. He's so rushed he's not stopped to break his nightfast, nor even to rinse the sleep-stink from his mouth. And so it's with the stalest of breath that he says, "We must go to Santa Caterina."

"Would you break your new heir's heart?" I keep my words a whisper, to let the children cling to their final hour of limb-entwined sleep. "I found him atop the tower ledge in the middle of the night, so bereft he might have fallen." I cross myself. "Or worse, if I'd not lured him down to take condolence from Juliet for the loss of his father."

Even in the pewtery pre-dawn, I see that Lord Cappelletto's features mirror Tybalt's grief. "He was my own and only brother. All I had, after the plague had done with everyone else I loved." Lord Cappelletto closes his watery eyes. "But what comfort was I to him, when years later it was his wife who lay dead? I lost him then, to his own anguish. Now I'll never have him back. He's left me with only a boy to fill his place."

"The boy will be a man soon enough." I hear in my own words the echo of what Pietro said of Juliet. Juliet, who neither Tybalt nor I can bear to lose. "We must take care that he'll not grow bitter before he's grown. He loves Juliet more dearly than he loves himself. He'll not be able to endure it if you send her to the nuns."

"To the nuns?" Lord Cappelletto does not bother to keep to a whisper, as he repeats what I've never let on I know. His words pull Tybalt full awake, and Tybalt's stirring rouses Juliet.

I kneel beside the bed, laying one hand on her head, and the other onto Tybalt's. "Just because God's not granted you a son, is no reason to banish your daughter." Let Lord Cappelletto take whatever pleasure he'll have in hearing me beg. "Please, do not shut Juliet away in Santa Caterina."

"You're sending her back with Rosaline?"

I cannot understand what Tybalt's asked, or why it makes his uncle crumple onto the edge of the big bed.

"No one is sending Juliet anywhere," Lord

Cappelletto says. He pulls her onto his lap, as though to fend off any who might try. "I'd not even return Rosaline, if it were left to me. She is an obedient child, though not so winsome as my Juliet, and two marriages would serve the Cappelletti all the better, with what alliances a dowry as big as what I'd give would bring. But my brother would not have his daughter wed, not risk her to her mother's fate." He wraps an arm around Tybalt, holding the cousins together. "I suppose it's just as well. Rosaline'd not know how to pass back into a worldly house like this, having lived half her life already among the Holy Sisters."

Half Rosaline's life was scarce two years ago — not so long after that Easter Day when Tybalt told me what he'd heard the bishop say. The silver chalice Lord Cappelletti gifted to the Duomo must never have been meant to pay for Juliet's place in the convent. It was for Rosaline's.

Lord Cappelletto is like any man, ever wanting to produce an heir. But even in these wife-maddening years of trying to make a son, he's never stinted in adoring Juliet. My sleepy-eyed girl snugs herself against him now, and any fool can see she long ago won his heart.

With Juliet and Tybalt in the circle of his

arms, Lord Cappelletto reminds me of the painting in his own bedchamber, the Sainted Maria holding the Holy Infant and his blessed cousin the Baptizing Giovanni.

And I might as well be the ass the Holy Family rode out from Bethlehem. I'm no more than a dumb beast that Lord Cappelletto can declare he's done with, now that Juliet is weaned. For what good is it to me to keep my girl from the convent, if I cannot stay with her?

"Rose-line go way?" Juliet asks, frowning when Lord Cappelletto nods. "But you and Tybalt and Ma'da stay with Nurse and me?"

She's my true heart and reads my very thoughts: whoever comes or goes, surely Juliet and I must be together.

"Yes, my beloved," Lord Cappelletto promises. "God and saints be willing, we will all of us stay healthy and well, within Ca' Cappelletti."

Juliet smiles across her father's arm at me, and I smile back. Only when a lone morning lark begins to twitter, calling for a mate that does not answer back, do I wonder how I can tell Pietro that I'll not be coming home.

Lord Cappelletto insists Juliet join him and Tybalt as they accompany Rosaline to Santa

Caterina. It's the first time she and I will ever be apart. But by my saints, it'll be the last.

Lord Cappelletto holds her tight against him on one post-horse, Tybalt and Rosaline matching their pose on another. "Honey nurse?" Juliet asks, looking down at me.

"You'll be back before the sun makes his way across the sky, and I'll be here," I say, not betraying my worry about where I must go, who I must see, in the scant hours before she, Lord Cappelletto, and Tybalt return.

My stiff and swollen hand works clumsily when, alone in Juliet's chamber, I wind my braid beneath a veil, as any decent woman does before going out. But as I step into the Via Cappello, a crooked-back crone creeps by, bare-headed. A wimple-less mother passes the other way, herding her unshod brood. All around me, women bow uncovered heads, taking careful steps across fallen stones. Surely they cannot all be prostitutes. No more than all the boys who hold out an imploring hand today were beggars just two days ago.

Walled off within Ca' Cappelletti, I'd not imagined all the devastation yesterday's quaking caused. Full buildings felled with families still in them. Shrieks of pain and plaintive prayers from under piles of rubble. I've seen Verona's buildings stand emptied by the creeping pestilence, but I never dreamt the city would face such reversed misery. Light streams through the gaping spaces where roofs and walls have fallen away, the sun beating hard on the bruised and bewildered who, having escaped a collapse, now wander with no place to go. Teams of men, grunting like beasts, struggle to unbury the not yet dead. Plastery dust swirls in the air, coating everything with an eerie pall.

Where in all of this is my Pietro?

Consumed with fear of losing Juliet, I'd not thought what threat the trembling earth might have been to him. Pietro's so strong he's ever been my strength — but passing among these ruined buildings, I realize that the men who lie lifeless beneath them were just as hale and every bit as hardy as my husband, until the quake came.

The wooden stalls of the Piazza delle Erbe now are broken heaps, and the few who've come out to sell are outnumbered by the hungry. One old man waves a cudgel, trying to hold off a pack of children who are snatching at his wares. Two of the bigger boys rush him, pinning him to the ground while the others rifle his stock like rats scurrying onto a new-moored boat. None of those who hasten past stop to help the man. Not even me. When I glance back after I've crossed the piazza, the children have already picked his goods clean.

Turning south, I see a trio of stubble-faced youth scrambling atop the remains of the metal-workers guild hall, stuffing what they loot into bulging sacks. Such shameless thieving makes me gape, until one pulls his dagger, flashing it at me. Hurrying away, I turn into a narrow street. Before I'm halfway down it, a shriek of timber splits the air, and a house-front topples into my path. A moment later, and I'd have been beneath it.

I double-back, twisting along one tight passage, then another, improvising routes around what the rubble blocks. I've never been so lost in broad daylight, and it's more by luck than memory that I find my way to the Via Zancani.

Although most of its roof tiles lie shattered in the street, our home still stands. Only when I see the barred door do I realize Pietro's not yet back from Villafranca. I cross myself and make a quick prayer asking San Pietro, his patron saint, to keep my husband safe. Then I hurry off again.

I'm not the first to seek Friar Lorenzo's

aid today, and it's no short wait among those who line the windowless passageway outside his cell. In the press of people, there are some who share their suffering with any who'll listen, and those who keep their mouths shut tight, determined to hold what burdens them for the friar's ears alone. I fall among the latter and have no use for the former, too troubled about Pietro to take any interest in these strangers' misfortune.

When at last I step into his cell, Friar Lorenzo's customary "God give you peace" sounds wearied. He does not even wait for me to answer with *And peace to you* before he reaches for my swollen mitt of a hand and turns it over, examining my welts.

"Plantain leaf, a simple cure," he says. "If only there was so ready a remedy for what brings most Christian souls to me today."

Though the poison still singes up and down my arm, I tell him that it's not bee stings that brought me. "Pietro went earlier this week to Villafranca —"

"Well that he did, my child. The quaking there was not so great. Some cornices and lintels fallen to the ground, but not a single person needing to be buried."

The thick-cassocked friars gather news like magpies gather anything that shines, and I take comfort from his report. But so long as Pietro's unhurt, I'm not sorry that he's still far away. That I've time to plot and plan before he must hear what he'd not have me say.

"Bethanks to your wise dispensing of wormwood, Juliet is weaned, as Lord Cappelletto wished." I bow my head to show I know my place. "But his wife has lost another babe, and she'll not bear again. Poor Lady Cappelletta. So young married, and too soon marred."

I wait for Friar Lorenzo to cross himself and intone a prayer for her, before I continue. "The ones so delicate as she is often prove no better for rearing children than for bearing them. And so Lord Cappelletto wishes me to stay at Ca' Cappelletti and care for Juliet." Surely, Friar Lorenzo will wish it as well — if I make him see some especial advantage in it. "Lord Cappelletto dotes on Juliet more than most men do their daughters. Though who'd expect less from such a noble and pious man, and a most generous benefactor of the hallowed Church?"

Friar Lorenzo well knows how often Lord Cappelletto opens his purse to holy hands, and he makes quick calculation of all that it's worth to keep such a man pleased. "I'll need to draw up a new contract," he says. "Now that the child is weaned, you'll not earn the whole of Pietro's rent any longer, though as you say, I'm sure Lord Cappelletto will be most generous in what he pays to keep you."

The whole of Pietro's rent — this is the first anyone's bothered to tell me what price men put on what I am to Juliet. These three years past I've earned what in that time I lost: the cost of the home I left for Ca' Cappelletti. Each hour I stole at the Via Zancani, each time Pietro begged me to move back — all of it paid for with the very milk of me. More mine than in all the years I lived there, yet not mine at all.

"Such matters are beyond me," I say, fluttering a hand to smooth my veil. "But Pietro — he can be proud, like any man. Your godly counsel will do much to guide him to accept whatever Lord Cappelletto offers."

"I will speak to Pietro as soon as he returns from Villafranca and inform him of the new terms of your service," Friar Lorenzo says, eager to earn whatever payment he'll make for drawing up the contract.

I accept his absolution along with the pouch of plantain leaves. Taking my leave of his cell, I head to the lower church. It is the least grand part of San Fermo, yet it's always been my favorite. The paint is still being laid fresh on the frescos in the upper church, but the saints upon the columns down below are old familiars. They're always ready to hear my prayers and, if they offer nothing in response, at least they'll not ask anything of me, either.

On this of all days, I know what I need to beg of them. Of her. For it's the Holy Virgin whose favor I seek, and of all the many paintings and statues of her in Verona, it's the one in the lower church whose help I need. I know her face better than I do my own, for though I've caught an occasional glimpse of myself reflected in a puddle or a water pail, I've knelt gazing on her for countless hours. A century of fading has taken its toll on the golden crown around her head and the brightly patterned throne on which she sits. But time's not marred the pale breast where her Sacred Infant suckles. I'll beseech this Blessed Mother, who'll never wean her own Holy Son, to take mercy on me and ensure that what Pietro'll not hear from me, he'll listen better to from our holy confessor.

But when I climb down the steps, I see someone is already inside the lower church. A youth of Tybalt's years, he stands with his back to me. He's swaying and moaning, halfway between the image of my suckling Maria and a fresco of the naked full-grown Christ accepting his cousin's sprinkling baptism.

It's not the spirit that moves the youth. It's the flesh. I come up behind and pinch his ear. "Here, of all places, for the hand to be upon the prick —"

"The prick of noon," he laughs, "and sext will soon be ringing."

I raise a hand to slap such sacrilege from him, but when he turns to face me, my open palm goes to my mouth instead. It's Prince Cansignorio's impish nephew.

Though I recognize this Mercutio, he has no notion who I am. And well it is that he does not, for I'd not have anyone know I nearly struck a member of the royal household.

Mercutio wiggles his own royal member at me. "Half Verona has fallen — why not make rise what I can?"

Piety, debauchery — when the pestilence raged, there were those who chose the first, hoping to be saved, and those who indulged the second, fearing they would not. To desecrate a church with self-spilled seed — that's one extreme, to be sure. But it's said that in the sudden jolt of catastrophe, some who survive feel the dark premonition of their own eventual death. Mercutio may smirk with a youth's bravado, but I sense beneath it a desperate child's fear.

"Do not let the friars find you at that here." That's all the reprimand I can bring myself to give him, before I hurry off.

First Nunzio, then Nesto, grew to such an age, younger in some and older in others, when a mother must avert her eyes, and pretend she does not know what her son's hand does beneath his doublet hem by day and the bed cover at night. My sons indulged themselves with especial frequency, for they had Pietro's heat. Donato at all of nine was not long from discovering what already pleased the elder two. But before he did, they and their three younger brothers all were taken. Self-pleasuring, that simple sin, one among the many things they'd never know.

This Mercutio, and Tybalt, too — they're not much shy in years of those who brawl upon Verona's streets. And while Lord Cappelletto has grown keen to take his nephew as his heir, Mercutio's uncle may not be so kind. Prince Cansignorio killed his own brother to seize his place upon the throne. What chance is there that, once his sister's son comes of age, Cansignorio will deal differently with him?

The sun is at its highest by the time I turn into the Via Cappello, the sext bells tolling as I enter Ca' Cappelletti. Those sonorous tones resonate through my very bones as I wait for Juliet to come back to me.

If Juliet craves me like I crave her, she's done well hiding it, delighting in the game I've made of what I give her instead of my own milk. Bread soaked in wine. Porridged chicken fat. Barley in beef broth. I bade her close her eyes and guess what each was as I put it into her ready mouth. Such tastes, such textures for her pink tongue to learn as we sow the pleasure nursing taught us into something new.

I steal early out of bed to find some fresh delight to feed her. The air is hot and thick with fruit. I shudder, thinking of the wet peach flesh Pietro rubbed me with, just four days past. Why not share such succulent fruit with Juliet?

I hurry down into the arbor. But I stop fast before I reach the peach-laden tree. The beehive's been righted, its seal replaced. I smile and turn this way and that, dancing my skirts as I search for where Pietro waits for me. Behind a tree? Crouched by the ruins of the dovecote? Within the entry to the tower stair?

No, and no, and no again. He's not any-where. The twittering I hear is only the morning lark, not the whistling tease of my hiding husband.

Something thumps upon the kitchen roof. I look up expectantly, as though my great bear of a Pietro might be there. But of course it's only Tybalt, sprung from his own rooms and calculating whether he can leap across the fallen archway onto the ledge that leads to Juliet's window.

Catching sight of me, he bounds to the roof edge and jumps down. He lands nimbly on those cat feet, dives into an elegant somersault, and brings himself up facing me.

"Have you seen Pietro?" I ask.

"Is he here?" Hope widens Tybalt's eyes. Which tells me he's not seen my husband since before going to Mantua.

Is this Pietro's way of punishing me? To come before I've risen, or after I've gone to bed, and leave this sign that he's been without bothering to see me. *I'll not keep sneaking about, stealing time with you like I'm a thief taking what is rightfully Lord Cappellet-to's.* But what greater sneaking is there, than for a husband to come so near yet not take his willing, wanting wife?

"The hive's upright, and the lid is back in

place." I feel a fool for saying aloud what Tybalt can see with his own eyes.

Feel yet more foolish when he thumps a proud fist against his chest and says, "I righted it myself, and I put my ear to the trunk to check the hive-noise. I even swept the dead bees away and watched to be sure the rest were gathering pollen again. I did it all, without even being bid to."

Tender Tybalt, ever hungry for my praise. Or better still, for Pietro's.

"Pietro will be pleased with you." I let the compliment settle like a richly woven mantle over his broadening shoulders. "He's probably tending some of his other hives. Perhaps you can find him and let him know what you've done. Surely he'll want to come and admire it himself."

Tybalt's never been a boy who's easily put off, not by one so soft-hearted as Pietro. Let him convince my husband to come here, and I'll work my own greater persuasion once he arrives. For though I schemed to have Friar Lorenzo be the one to tell Pietro I'd not be returning home, there's that which I saved to say myself.

No lord would risk his child's wet-nurse tainting her milk by receiving her husband's seed. But now that Juliet is weaned, what objections could Lord Cappelletto have to me fulfilling my conjugal duty to Pietro, so long as it does not interfere with my caring for Juliet? Pietro and I might even enlist Friar Lorenzo to write it into the new contract, such terms as say that Pietro may come to me here, or I go to him, openly. And with a frequency we've not had these three years past.

I pluck a blushing peach from one of the fruit-laden boughs and offer it to Tybalt, then pick another to bring upstairs to Juliet. I'll ready the slices while she sleeps, so she can wake to the delicious promise of what I tasted when Pietro was last here.

Summer's sun melts the hours. They pour one into another, and still Tybalt stays gone. As the day grows hot, then hotter, sweat streaks my face and neck, bathes my back and belly. Juliet's unceasing chirruping makes my head ache. It's no ease to me when, after I at last settle my little one into her nap, the house-page comes scraping and scratching to tell me Lady Cappelletta summons me to keep her company. I cut tooth against tongue to keep from telling him a wet-nurse is no lady's waiting maid. Wet-nurse I no longer am, and to stay with Juliet, I must be whatever the Cappelletti will want of me.

Lady Cappelletta lies a-bed, still worn with the jaunce from Mantua. Or so I'd supposed, until I enter her chamber and see the vinegared way she waves me near, her wedding bracelets clattering. "Sing to me," she commands. "And not the dull religious droning Lord Cappelletto favors. I want a pleasure-song."

Surely she wants more pleasure than I can trill forth. "If you are sorrowful —"

She cuts me off with a quick snort. "What sorrows have I?"

What am I to answer? *You are wed to an old goat who's not given you a living son, and for all your beauty, even in your youth you already look more misused than I at my age do.* "None, unless you say so," is what I say aloud.

"None indeed, now that the learned physick tells my lord husband he must be done rutting with me." A newfound contempt curls her mouth when she speaks the phrase *my lord husband.* Before I can puzzle over it, her ring-laden fingers drum a quick cadence against the wooden bedstead, demanding I match a bright-paced tune to it.

I sing, fast then faster still, my breath short and shallow as I struggle to keep pace with her hurried rhythm. When the song is done, she says, "The journey to Mantua was so rough, the infant fell from me, pulling my womb out with it. The midwife and physick made me soak all night in a bath of mugwort and fleabane, before that cursed womb could be shoved back inside. They stuffed a linen full of pennyroyal and spikenard into me, to keep it in place. I was more dead than not, and begged them to let what lingered of me go."

"But by God's grace, you survived." As though she should need me to remind her of it.

"I survived because the esteemed physick did not wish to upset his Gonzaghe patrons by losing a patient whose husband is so close an ally to Prince Cansignorio." All hint of the timid girl she's been is gone, leaving instead a young woman who puts me in mind of a foal struggling to take to its legs for the first time: unsteady yet certain she's mastering something she'll make good use of. "I made the physick promise that if I lived, I'd need not suffer Lord Cappelletto to take his pleasures on me again."

"A wife's duty," I begin, as though I might yet explain the pleasures Pietro and I take in each other, to one whose husband is so ill-matched as hers.

"My duty's done. I delivered him his son.

What fault of mine if it did not live beyond the hour I bore it?" It's more than an ill-fated laboring that makes her face less soft than it once was. The calculating glint that's come into her eyes gives her a newly hardened beauty. "He's got Tybalt for his legal heir. That was my idea, though I took care my lord husband heard it from his dying brother's mouth. The boy has no mother — he'll not turn me out when I am widowed."

Her conniving is no match for my own, for though she may feel her way upon a foal's ready legs, she lacks the cunning of a mare that's run as many courses as I have. "If Lord Cappelletto makes a son outside your marriage, he might yet change his will." Might turn even against Juliet, if a canny mistress pushes him to it.

"Lord Cappelletto is firm only in his faith," she says, "his eel too slithery to seed even one of the pursemaker's daughters. He beseeched every saint in heaven to send him an heir, not believing such piety could go unanswered, until his brother's final confessor convinced him that his legitimate son's death was punishment for breaking his church-made vows to me. He'll do penance by giving dowries so the pursemaker can marry off every last daughter, and hew to his marriage vows henceforth." She gives a smile that lets the sharpest of her teeth show. "Tybalt well earned his place, conveying to me all that was whispered at his father's bedside."

I'd not have thought that Lady Cappelletta and I could be so much alike. She young, and rich, and wanting only to keep her husband from her, and I at my age plotting to find a way to draw my husband back to me. But in our choice of go-between, we are the same. Faithful Tybalt. On who else can we rely?

Lady Cappelletta bids me sing another song. While I warble it out, she tells me, "I've not forgot it was by your urging that I went to Mantua." Those calculating eyes shimmer with the same hard contempt they showed when she spoke of Lord Cappelletto. But this time, she lets me see it's meant for me. "You convinced me to try what nearly killed me. If I'd stayed safely here, I'd not have suffered any of it."

I'd not intended any harm to her. Not thought what toll my goading might take, so consumed was I with keeping Juliet from the convent. But what way have I to tell this to Lady Cappelletta?

Quick feet cross the antecamera, and in one great rush Tybalt enters the chamber. "Half the hives are harvested. But the —"

Lady Cappelletta cuts him off. "Is that a proper greeting for an heir to give his aunt?"

Tybalt drops his eyes from mine, bowing his head to kiss her hand. "God give you good-den, dear Aunt."

"When did you last make your prayers?"

"Yesterday. When my uncle and my cousin and I took Rosaline to Santa Caterina, we joined the Holy Sisters at their Mass."

"You must pray every day, as Rosaline does, for the souls of your departed parents."

Why must she pester Tybalt about his prayers, making him dwell on what he's lost, just when he has news to give to me?

"You're to go once a week to Santa Caterina, to make memorial devotions with your sister," she tells him. "And on the other days, pray here with Juliet. Rouse her now, and have her make *amens* with you."

"Juliet is tired," I say. "It's best she rest through the hottest of the day."

"My lord husband insists it's not too soon for his adored daughter to learn how one day she will pray for him, and for me, when we are gone."

Death sat so near to Lord Cappelletto the week past, he supposes its bony hand will soon reach for his wrinkled one. And so he wants to be assured of what is every parent's due: a dutiful child whose prayers will ease his way to heaven when his time comes.

"I'll make sure they do as Lord Cappelletto wishes." I rise and nod for Tybalt to lead the way from the chamber. He is the heir now. It'd not do for him to follow behind me.

But as soon as we are in the sala, I lay a halting hand on his shoulder. "Half the hives are harvested," I repeat, "but?"

"The rest are left heavy with wax and honey." He tells me how he traced and retraced Pietro's usual routes, surprised not to find him collecting from one hive or another, or making his way between them.

"Perhaps he's bargaining with the chandler," I say.

"A beekeeper cannot bargain until he knows how much wax his bees have made this season, Pietro's told me that a dozen times. It will be weeks of separating honey from comb, before he sees the chandler."

With all his heeling after Pietro, Tybalt knows my husband's business better than I do. But I know my husband's heart. I need Tybalt to bring him to me, or to discover where I might find him, so I can ease him to accept my staying at Ca' Cappelletti. "There are many ways to move about Verona, and more than one bridge crossing the Adige. You must go out again —"

Scarlet tinges his ears, his shoulders hunching into the same curve as when Lord Cappelletto carps at him.

I'll not treat Tybalt so, not add to what already grieves him. "Juliet will be glad to have you wake her," I say instead. "She misses you when you are gone."

The thought of her lifts his chest. Juliet never wants a thing from Tybalt but his companionship. Not Lord Cappelletto, nor Lady Cappelletta, nor even I can say the same.

Our chamber glows in the afternoon light as he shakes her softly from her sleep, lifts her from the bed. She kneels drowsily beside him while he stumbles through his Latin and she mumbles her made-up imitation of his prayers. Another day, I might take joy in seeing them bow their heads together. But I can barely bide myself until they utter their *amens*. If Tybalt cannot find Pietro for me, I must plot some way to seek him out myself.

I don my veil and tell Juliet, "You say your prayers so well, perhaps we should go to Friar Lorenzo, so he can hear them for himself."

"Me pray," she says, greedy for the praise she knows he'll give. "And me fess to Friar."

But the name that brightens her face shadows worry onto Tybalt's. "Friar Lorenzo bade me tell you to come see him. He told me I must not forget."

Something catches deep inside me. "When? When did he tell you this?"

"This morning." Tybalt pulls at where his doublet collar rubs tight against the fresh bump of his Adam's apple. "He called to me as I passed the friary on my way to check the first of the hives."

Friar Lorenzo must have spoken to Pietro. But if my husband leaves it to the Franciscan to give me his response, surely it cannot be a happy one.

"Fess to Friar," Juliet repeats, sliding her sweat-damp hand into mine.

"Tomorrow," I say. "Or the day after." I'm in no hurry to hear Friar Lorenzo repeat whatever angry words Pietro has for me.

Juliet tugs my hand. "Fess now."

"You said that you would go." Tybalt's voice cracks as he takes my other hand. "He'll think that I forgot."

Is this not why I hold myself from returning home to Pietro? To soothe and care for Juliet, and for Tybalt, when not another soul in all the world marks what each of them needs? With their doubly insistent grip upon me, I force myself into the Via Cappello.

Heat thrums from buildings, streets, every surface of the city, even with the sun slanting to the west. Though the cries and confusion caused by the quake have ebbed, something sinister hangs over Verona, the souls of those crushed beneath fallen buildings lingering in the heavy air. Tybalt and I hold Juliet between us, and for once I do not smile at how he keeps a ready hand upon his dagger hilt, as we seek out an unblocked route to San Fermo and the friary.

A dozen needy beings crowd the corridor outside Friar Lorenzo's cell, and I worry how I'll keep Juliet from growing tetchy until it is our turn. But I worry more when the Franciscan comes out to call the next expectant in and, seeing us, waves me ahead of those who've been here longer.

In the cool quiet of his cell, he dips his tonsured head to Juliet, keeping his eyes from meeting mine. He blesses her and takes the kiss she offers for his narrow cheek, then blesses Tybalt and tells him to take Juliet into the lower church to make their prayers.

"Me pray already. Me fess now." Even pouting, Juliet is a pure and pretty thing.

"The lower church —" I begin, but find I've no words for what I've seen Mercutio at there, not ones that I would say before Tybalt and Juliet. And whatever Friar Lorenzo has to tell me weighs thick enough in this close space, I know it's not meant for them to hear.

I join Juliet's hand to Tybalt's, and give his shoulder an easy urging from the cell, promising a comfit for every pillared saint they pray to before I come to find them. Though how I'll convince Pietro to spare me comfits to gift them when he'll not even speak to me directly, I cannot fathom.

Once they're gone, Friar Lorenzo tells me, "Hunger can turn even good men cruel. And terror brings out the very worst, or the very best, within us."

If I were in need of homilies, I'd come to Sunday Mass. "What does Pietro say?"

The Franciscan rubs at where his eyelids droop from want of sleep. "Yesterday at dusk, a mother and daughter were making their way back from the public fountain, when a brace of rowdies laid hold of them. They had no riches, nothing to steal but the few worn garments they'd just scrubbed clean. This was no satisfaction to the ruffians, who tried instead to take from the daughter what no Christian girl wishes to give. The mother screamed for them to stop. Pushing herself before the child, she begged them to take their pleasure upon her instead, and leave her daughter be. A passing stranger, hearing her, swung at the two villains, and the mother snatched the child and ran off. They found shelter in Sant'Eufemia, where the priest gathered half a dozen clerics to take them home. By the light of the clerics' torches, they came upon the man who'd been their savior. He'd been stabbed and left dead in the street."

He touches fingers to brow, to heart, to both sides of his chest. "Angelica, it is with a heavy heart but all Christ's redeeming love that I tell you the man who died so nobly was your Pietro."

"Tell him I will leave Juliet." The words twist out of me, some unseen blade tearing them from my gut. "Tell Pietro I will come home before this very day is through."

"It is too late for that, my child. Your husband is gone. I saw him for myself, afterwards."

Pietro cannot be dead. That is the truth, the certainty, that cracks open my chest, jolts me into motion. Out of the cell, away from this lying Friar Lorenzo.

I must get Juliet and Tybalt. I'll take them back to Ca' Cappelletti, then go myself to find Pietro. The Via Zancani will be seeped in evening shade by the time I reach it, the door to our house swung wide to let fresh air flow in. I'll coax the kitchen ashes into full fire, and Pietro will pour our wine, singing with me as I cook, as he always used to do. As he's always meant to do again.

TEN

"Nurse wake?"

Juliet buries a tear-streaked cheek against my neck. Beyond the curve of her head, I see Tybalt, crouching with a worried stare. Above him dark lines mark out a low-curved ceiling, the paint an eerily familiar hue. Too somber for Ca' Cappelletti, and the hard stone digging flat against my back tells me I'm not in bed. Before I can ask where we are, why we are here, a hand reaches over from my other side.

"It is well you are awake, my child." Friar Lorenzo's touch is icy as he marks a cross upon me.

It all rushes back, every wretched thing the blessed faint let me forget. "Nothing can be well. Not without my husband."

The Franciscan unfolds himself. Standing on the step above the landing to the lower church, he speaks down to me. "If Pietro is in a better place, we must be glad for that."

"Po go way?" Juliet asks. "Like Rose-line?"

The friar tugs at one of his great ears. Waiting, wanting me to say it. But I'll not.

"Pietro's dead?" Tybalt's two words explode against the arched ceiling. They shiver down the walls, rumble across the floor, and crawl up my spine, to pound between my eyes.

"Yes, my child," Friar Lorenzo says. And then, because what holy man does not love to hear himself speak, he adds, "This life is but our bitter passage to the next."

Juliet burrows tighter against me, though surely my little one cannot know what he means.

"Shall we pray for Pietro now, as I do my father? Or must we wait until the funeral?" Tybalt's voice breaks, then settles into the careful rote that years of his tutor's beatings have taught him. "My father's funeral procession had eight horses, and wound through the city for an hour, and his Requiem Mass was said in the biggest church in Mantua." He sits straighter in his mourning cloak. "How many horses will Pietro have, and how long will we walk?"

"Such processions are only for rich men," I tell him. "The bishop does not open the Duomo doors to bury one as poor as my Pietro."

Friar Lorenzo hisses at my sacrilege. "Rich or poor, every loss we suffer is God's will. He gives us mortal life that we may pray, and do good, and earn our eternal place among the righteous."

What place have I earned, refusing my husband what he begged of me: that I live with him as a loving wife should? Did he hold out hope that I was coming home? Or did he die knowing I'd determined to stay away?

Did Pietro rush at some swift-bladed ruffians because I'd left him, even left it to Friar Lorenzo to tell him I'd chosen Juliet over him?

I twist onto my side, my arms cocooning her against me. This is my comfort, and my curse: to choose this child, the single salve for all I'd lost. Not realizing I'd lose yet more.

Friar Lorenzo lays that icy hand upon the back I've turned to him. "What's tomb is —"

"Doom." I cut off his holy platitude with my hard-learned truth. I'll not let the celibate speak to me of wombs. Not when I've left Pietro without a single living child to pray for him, as Tybalt does his father, and as Juliet one day will for Lord Cappelletto. "Bury him as you will," I say. "I'll have none of it."

The cloister bell tolls, calling the Franciscans to vespers. Friar Lorenzo cannot bear to leave us without uttering a final, "May God have mercy on his soul, and on all of us."

Once he's gone, I let Tybalt lead me back to Ca' Cappelletti, where I bury myself in my own tomb, built of my guilt and my grief, and of Juliet's commiserating tears.

Hot as it is, even with the sun disappeared and the stars flung against the sweltering sky, lying restless through the night all I can think of is the rime-frosted day when Pietro and I first said farewell, and what followed from it. He'd returned to his village to give his family the news that we were to bind ourselves as married. While he was gone he sent me a love-gift. A handkerchief, of no fancy material. Just a little trifle to carry the scent of him. Or so I thought.

To a girl of twelve who has no more than chores for company, the fortnight a lover is away seems an eternity. I tucked the handkerchief into my dress so that I might always have it, have him, with me. On the day Pietro returned, he asked for it, and I slipped a hand to where I'd kept the kerchief close against me.

I did not find it. Did not even have sense enough to hide my surprise.

"What's the matter, Angelica?" he asked.

"Nothing, now that you're back." I nuzzled his chest, knowing I could well take in the smell of him, and his taste and touch, without that bit of cloth.

But he pulled away. "There is something special in the kerchief's weft I want to show you."

"You sound like a fabric merchant, trying to prove his prices are fair."

For once, he had no heart for teasing. "That kerchief is above any price. My mother wove it." This was the first he spoke to me of her. "It was the last thing she made before she died."

I saw then all it meant to him.

I bowed my head. "I've not got it."

"Go fetch it, then."

"I cannot."

"You've thrown it away?"

"Of course not. I . . ."

As my words trickled off, Pietro's voice rose. "You gave it to another?"

"Never."

"Well then, where is it?"

In the month we'd known each other, I'd never seen Pietro angry. But I'd seen my father beat my mother many a time, knocking the very teeth from her head, for far less than losing such a precious thing.

Surely it was fright that made me answer as I did. By punching my fist hard at Pietro's face.

In an instant, his much larger hand flew up. But not, as I feared, to hit me. Only to wrap my wrist in his broad palm, to keep me from hitting him again.

Whatever pain flashed along his jaw was nothing compared to the deeper hurt that showed in his eyes. My arm went slack in his tight grip.

He dropped his hold on me, turned, and left my parents' house without another word.

My mother offered me no comfort, saying only she'd raised a fool, for even at twelve I should have known better than to raise a hand to a man, whether before we were wed or after. When my father came in from the fields, she bade me tell him what had happened. He beat us both, screaming that he'd not find another one so gullible as Pietro, to marry me to without a single denaro of dowry. For what had he got to give, even to be rid of such a stupid daughter? He threw me out of the house. Not for the night, for good.

The moon was three days shy of full, and

I did what any herder does, when something is lost from the flock. I began circling slowly outward, seeking after it. Searching not with my eyes on the horizon for the low, wooly form of a sheep, but with my gaze to the cold ground, willing the handkerchief to appear.

It was no easy task. The moon was well on its descent when, crossing Agostino di-Maso's land, I glimpsed something in his pigsty. There, trudged deep into the half-froze mud, was Pietro's treasured handkerchief. How the pigs had gotten it, and why once they had it they did not chew it up entirely, I could not know. I worked the cloth free and carried it like a martyr's relic to the icy creek edging Agostino's fields. Though I scrubbed it against a rock until my fingers bled, the kerchief'd not come quite clean.

I brought it to Sant'Agnese, our village church, meaning to ask the priest to write a letter to send with it to Pietro's parish. But there was no need for a letter. Pietro had gone straight to the church from my parents' house, hoping to take holy council. Finding the priest gone, he'd slept all night before the barred church doors.

Though he'd always seemed man enough to me, at twenty he was still in truth a youth, and the softness in his sleeping face taunted me with all I'd lost in striking him. As I laid the folded kerchief on his chest, he grabbed my wrist. Full awake at once, he held me for a silent instant, as he had before stalking from my father's house. But now he pulled my wrist, drawing me down onto him. Pressing my fingers against the intricate weave of the soiled kerchief, he told me of his gentle-hearted mother and how indulgently she loved him. He said he wanted to make such a mother of me, once I was his wife. Which, when the priest returned an hour later, I soon was.

Not a hand was raised between us after that. Nor was one ever raised to the son I bore that year, or any I bore after. Even in his hottest youth, Pietro never needed to prove himself by beating wife or child. There are few enough like that, and I never forgot it was my own foolishness that almost cost me my Pietro. I always swore I'd not take such risk again.

Why did I ever leave him? How could I have let myself lose him?

I could go now. Climb the tower steps once more. Dark as it is, I could find my way up, perch like Tybalt at the tower's top, and look upon Verona. This city where Pietro and I came so young and full of hope, holding nothing but each other's hands, to build a life. A life so filled with death — our sons, our daughter. But always, we held to each other. Now, with him gone, I'll not hold on. I'll look upon the world and let myself slip free. It would be so easy to let the heavy thing inside me have its way. Let loss be the weight that carries me down, down, down, until I'll never have to bear this grief again.

I close my eyes, imagine swaying in the hot air, feeling myself fall. But something stabs sharp at my back. My eyes fly open, and I turn. The statue of San Zeno towers over me. The fishing saint of fair Verona, his unseen hook plunging deep into me. Pulling me back. Because it is forbidden to die this easy, longed-for way.

Pietro well earned his place among the righteous. And surely all our little ones are there as well. All my lost beloveds together, waiting. What would I be, to damn myself from them for all eternity? Hooked here, I'll not let myself make that last climb up the tower steps and leave this mortal life. Though by my troth, it's all I long to do.

"Eight comfits," Tybalt says, climbing in through Juliet's open chamber window sometime in the ripening morning hours

260

before the terce bells toll, "as you promised." He sets down a sack as big as a pillow-casing, casts off his mourning cloak, and slides one hand into the other tight-pulled sleeve of his dark doublet to draw out the candies. Softened from the heat, each is fragrant with some surprise of quince, or fig, or apio, and laced with cinnamon, ginger, or clove. And all of them emanating the unbearable sweetness of honey.

Juliet snatches one of the comfits. She runs to the far side of the bed, slipping it into her mouth before I can stop her.

"Where did you get these?" I ask Tybalt.

"I woke at dawn and went to the Via Zancani. I knew there would be comfits there."

"You broke into a dead man's house to steal candy?"

"Pietro always brought us sweets. He'd want us to have these." He holds the candies out to me.

I cannot bear to taste what my husband made. I do not deserve to hum with delight in his handiwork, as Juliet does, working the sticky comfit with her tiny teeth. I nod at the sack. "What else have you thieved?"

Tybalt draws up the bag, reaching in and pulling out the Virgin's portrait that hung upon our wall. The one Pietro gave me when we wed, trothing ourselves together until death forced us apart.

I tell Tybalt my cockly-eyed familiar has no place in this grand house, where fine images fresco the walls.

"My uncle says you may hang the Holy Mother here, and wishes she may bring you comfort," he says. "And he gives his leave for you to take Juliet and me with you today, when you go to the Requiem Mass."

Lord Cappelletto gives me leave to do what I'd not asked of him. I've never once spoken Pietro's name to him, and I long ago forbade Tybalt to ever mention my husband before his uncle, to keep safe my place with Juliet. But what does that matter now?

Of all the house, Lord Cappelletto's the one who might truly know my grief, because he knows his own, kneeling nightly before the Madonna in his chamber and praying for the cherished wife he lost. Yet I'd not share my most private hurt with him.

Tybalt entreated Lord Cappelletto from some belief my mourning must take the same shape as his does. It's Tybalt who wants this. Tybalt who's put on his finest garments, the seams strained from how fast he's grown, to go to the Requiem Mass.

"Afterwards, I'll finish harvesting the

hives," he says. "I'll collect the wax and honey, and separate them out. I helped Pietro enough times, I'm sure I can do it on my own. But I've no way to make comfits. When the honey's ready, I'll sell it to an apothecary who'll work with it himself, as the chandler does the beeswax."

"Is this all you can think of, honey and candles and candy — even with Pietro gone?"

"Bees die each day, but the hive goes on," Tybalt says. "That's what Pietro taught me. He said the ones who gather pollen may never taste the honey it will make. He told me it's why he loved the bees. The way they build, creating combs not for themselves but for the future brood. Like the men who lay a church's marble cornerstone knowing they'll not live long enough to pray within the finished nave." He draws a deep, wavering breath, laying a hand on his mourning cape as if to touch his own great grief. "Pietro said this is why we must take care in tending them. The hive must live, and in its life we'll find our hope."

I'd not known such things about a hive — or about my husband. Never understood why the bees that afrighted me could so comfort him. What other things had I been too afraid to hear from him? What else about Pietro will I now never know?

Tybalt urges me to braid my hair and ready Juliet, so we'll not be late. When I set my jaw and make no answer, he says, "I did not want to go to my father's funeral, until my uncle said I must. He said that we must show everyone the strength of our piety, even when we are bereaved. But the friar says we go for God, to implore him to take my father's soul, and now Pietro's, into heaven."

"Those are a nobleman's reasons, or a clergyman's," I tell him. "Not a woman's." Not a widow's.

My whole life I've seen them. You can tell which ones truly loved their husbands, some wailing and pulling hair and clawing at their own faces, and some still and stony silent as they kneel through the Requiem Mass. All listening from under their dark veils as though something in the priest's impenetrable Latin might meliorate their grief.

But what could lessen my loss, what can console me, now that it's too late to beg Pietro's forgiveness and give myself wholly back to him?

I busy myself with calling Juliet to me, dabbing her face and untangling the knots sleep worked into her hair. "We'll not go anywhere," I tell Tybalt. "The streets have grown too dangerous."

"I'm not afraid." He pulls himself tall, widening his shoulders as broad as they'll go. Which is not nearly broad enough to carry all he thinks he can.

"What good did a fool's bravery do Pietro?" I lace my words with enough venom to sting us both. "A full-grown man, and the brace of murderers left him in the street to die."

Juliet whimpers. I've pulled her hair too hard, and made her hear such ugly things. Shrinking from me, she reaches for Tybalt. He bends to her, offering her kisses and a second comfit. Distracts her with her toy bird before he straightens up again and kisses me as well, the same tender way my sons did.

"I'll go alone. I'm Tybalt, king of cats, and I'm not scared. I loved Pietro. And you said that he loved me. I'll kneel and pray the Mass for him, even if you'll not."

This is how he leaves us, Juliet playing with that beady-eyed bird while I stand at the window staring out at the hive thrumming in the arbor. Wondering over what parts of Tybalt are yet boy, and what are already man, that make him able to face what I cannot.

Tybalt is the nimble king of cats, and the

legal heir to Lord Cappelletto. But who am I? Not who I've been for more than thirty years. No longer Pietro's adored wife. Nor Juliet's wet-nurse. I gave up my husband for her — but what am I to her now? What will I be a year, a decade, hence, should God make me live so long without Pietro? What is a milk-mother to a child who's been weaned?

I'll not forget how she turned away from me, seeking solace from Tybalt instead. And worse than her turning away was the moment before, when she looked at me just as Pietro had when last I saw him — the last I'll ever see him. The same accusing look almonding her eyes, the same surprised hurt stippling her still-bruised brow.

Like a clapper smacking hard against a bell, it hits me. Rings hard at my temples, reverberates across my head, down to my heart. It makes my arms shake, and my legs. I turn from the window, sun-blind as I look back to Juliet. In two strides I'm beside her, swooping her up so quick her toy bird tumbles to the floor.

"Nurse?" She is too startled to utter any more than that, as I carry her back to the open window, hold her in the brightness of the light. And realize what surely has been there to see all along.

Her coarse, dark hair. Her deep brown eyes. Friar Lorenzo himself marked how much they are like mine. Colored by my milk, he claimed. But the shape of those eyes, how they sit in her face. The way emotions dance across her features. It is a face I know better than I know my own, and yet I've not recognized it until now.

It is Pietro's.

I know what Lord Cappelletto, with his treatise-reading, feared. It's why men draw the nursing contracts as they do: to keep a husband's humors from tainting his wife's milk, and transforming the nursling's features. But what I recognize is not just in her features. It's the child's very nature — for is not my sweet, loving Juliet more like Pietro than like Lord Cappelletto or Lady Cappelletta?

Surely this is something more than milk or taint. All these years, Lord Cappelletto's seed could no more quicken into healthy babe in Lady Cappelletta than Pietro's could help but make strong babies in me. Except for their first, and our last. How could we make something as weak as Susanna, to not live a single day, and they make such a precious, lasting jewel as my Juliet?

How've I not seen it before, not known

how truly she is mine? For surely she was mine even before she sucked the first milk of me, mine before I even knew she stirred within me. Mine, as she could never be the Cappelletti's.

Why else would Friar Lorenzo arrange for me to come here, yet howl at me, over and over, about being only a wet-nurse? Who else but he could know what happened the day two daughters were born, both brought to him for baptism, but only one survived? The priests are ever saying we must trust God's plan for us, and with all their Latin learning making us believe they always know such plans better than we ever can.

I breathe in the honeyed spice of the remaining comfits, more redolent than all the incense of a Requiem Mass. I swear by the Sacred Maria and the Holy Infant and every heavenly saint that sits among them, I still cannot believe I've truly lost my husband. That Pietro could have slipped from this life without bidding me farewell.

This is the loneliest, the most unbearable, part. To have not said one last *I love you*. To have the last we said not be a true good-bye.

But lonely as it is, I am not alone. Tybalt's father left two children, Tybalt and pious Rosaline, to pray for him. Pietro suffered six sons lost. But still she is here. Our final, secret, stolen one. Kneeling beside me in this light-filled chamber before the Holy Mother that Pietro gave me, the two of us praying as we take one final taste of his honey on our tongues.

■ ■ ■ ■

Part Two

1374–1375

■ ■ ■ ■

ELEVEN

I keep my place beside the sala window as Lady Cappelletta, Juliet, and I sew. Purblind as I've grown, none begrudge my standing where the light is better. Nor do I mind being where the view is better as well, for my aging eyes are keener for what passes below than for the stitch my needle makes. Verona's spring bustles with donkey-carts sloping off the bridge from the far side of the Adige, heading for the Piazza delle Erbe. Wine barrels are heaved into houses full, or hauled out empty. Veiled women and thick-bellied men hurry toward some urgent task, or stop to gossip in the street. The Via Cappello is like a river thick with barques and barges while I'm tethered in port, watching every thing and everyone that sails by.

But the top-gallant is here inside, Lord Cappelletto flapping as noisily within the sala as a high-masted sail in a blustery wind. "We'll serve ravioli of wild boar simmered in spring herbs, to start. Next, veal stuffed with saffroned pigeon, leek, and fava beans. Then chicken, sausage, and Lake Garda carp, layered with dates and almonds and laid inside a pie. It will be the finest wedding banquet Verona's seen since our own."

"My lord husband has forgotten," Lady Cappelletta says, without bothering to raise her eyes to his, "the feasts we ate when Cansignorio was wed a decade past."

"More sumptuous than ours, as is a prince's due. But no better than a plowman's meal before furrowing a barren field, as it turned out to be." Lord Cappelletto takes a certain pleasure in pitying Cansignorio, who has neither sons nor daughters by his lawful wife. "This may not be a royal marriage, but we'll reap plenty of delights when it comes to fig and pear composed in rosemary and anise. And almond-porridged quince, and cherry-and-rose tarts. And peaches braised with gingered honey." He smiles at Juliet. "I've not forgot who keeps a ready tooth for sweets. Do you not, my love?"

Nearly fourteen, and still Juliet blushes with full innocence. But Lady Cappelletta's own innocence is long gone. She's become well-practiced in disdain, and serves up her scorn in overly abundant portions. "We've much to do to get the trousseau finished," she tells Lord Cappelletto. "Juliet is slow with a needle, and such distractions do not make her any quicker."

Though Lord Cappelletto has all a man's ignorance of needlework, he waves away her chiding. "A rushed stitch is like a rushed courtship," he says. "What comes together overhastily is too easily undone."

Courtship and *come together* jolt Juliet. Her needle pierces a finger, and she gives a startled cry as red drops fall upon the sheet she sews.

"That's the only pricking there'll be upon that bedsheet," I say, to bring a laugh from Lord Cappelletto before worse comes from his wife. "Enough it must be for all the Holy Sisters of Santa Caterina." I add that last to remind them that the convent trousseau we're making for Rosaline'll not be truly hers, every stitch of it to be held in common among the cloistered nuns.

These months we've spent sewing, and the long night of feasting to come — all of it to consecrate what none of us would wish for ourselves. Prince Cansignorio's childless marriage is no more barren than Rosaline's Christly one will be. But Tybalt tells me his devout sister wants nothing more than chastity. At her age I surely wanted chastity

— though only in the sense I was in want of it, delighting as I did in my marriage bed. But those days are forever past, and what I am in want of now are delights Rosaline'll never know. She long ago donned habit, and as soon as she was deemed of age she happily professed her vows. This season she is fain to consecrate them, and Santa Caterina is glad for it. The convent, like all the Holy Church, dearly loves its ceremonies, for every one of which Lord Cappelletto gives generous dotal alms.

I take the bloodied bedsheet from my blushing Juliet, rubbing comfort onto her injured finger with the soft of my thumb, and hand her a pillow-casing to finish instead. "Salted water will bring such a stain out," I say, "as many a tearful bride learns the morning after her marriage is consummated."

That brings a knowing smirk from Lady Cappelletta. It goes unnoticed by her husband, who busies himself with cataloguing the esteemed guests he'll invite to feast in honor of the newly mendicanted Rosaline.

Juliet's usually so heavy in her own sleep that I may drowse late as I could wish and still rise first from our long-shared bed. But she's full awake before the prime-hour bells ring on the Sunday Rosaline is to be consecrated, kneeling before the statue of San Zeno while peering expectantly at me. As soon as I unlid my eyes, she asks, "Is my cousin a better girl than I am?"

To wake with such worries is to not know what true worry is. But my dearest lamb ever struggles to bear Lady Cappelletta's carping. And it is no easy thing for even such a light as Juliet to dwell in the shade of the ever-pious Rosaline.

I pat the sheet beside me, waiting for Juliet to settle back in bed and proffer a good-morning kiss before I answer. "Rosaline is good at being good, but it is much better to be better at much."

"Such riddles, honey nurse." She snuggles against me. "Can you not tell me if I am the precious jewel that you and my lord father Cappelletto and my holy father Friar Lorenzo all say I am?"

Why does the age that in boys brings boastful confidence in girls bring only doubt? There'd been naught like this in all my years of raising sons, or in rearing Tybalt. But Juliet of late puts me in mind of a bud you need protect, lest a sudden storm tear loose its new-formed petals before it flowers to full bloom.

"Rosaline is a tambour, taut and well put

to the task of giving off a steady beat. You are more a well-stringed lute. Full of bright notes and pleasing melodies" — I lift a lock of her hair and dance its end along her neck — "so long as the right hand plays upon you. Now, out of bed we must both be, and readying ourselves to go to Santa Caterina."

This is enough to satisfy her, though it's no full part of all that I might say of what and who she is.

When my heart first seared with the pain of losing my Pietro, I ached to claim her for my own. But what would my word have been against Lord Cappelletto, who believes with all his own heart that she's the sole fruit of his loveless marriage, the same girl the city's finest midwife delivered of Lady Cappelletta? What more proof would he need than what lying Friar Lorenzo would gladly give to keep so rich and influential a patron satisfied? For that is what I puzzled out, in my grief-filled sleepless nights: who else but Friar Lorenzo could have managed it, and why else would he have done it? To preserve a wealthy, powerful family's joy, for which they ever bestow gilded thanks upon the Church — even if it meant yet more grief for me and Pietro. With a single deceit he fooled us all, rich and poor alike. None would believe a brown-cloaked Franciscan of being so duplicitous, so what good would it have done me to accuse him? I'd not risk being sent away from her. Not hazard the tie I yet have to my daughter.

So I've forced myself to keep kneeling before my confessor, never letting the slightest sign of what I know flicker in my eye. With Pietro gone, I've need to be shriven only once or twice a year, and in those infrequent visits Friar Lorenzo's not sensed anything amiss. Harder is holding my secret from my own darling girl. Too young she was at first, to understand. Too young to keep such a confidence. And even now — how could I take her from so grand a house, and force on her a life without name and fortune? Each day her belly fills with the Cappelletti food, and their fabrics clothe her finely. Each night we sleep entwined on the Cappelletti linen. I've let that be enough, for now.

I could not love her more even if all the world knew how truly she is mine. And soon my bud will blossom to full bloom, and I'll know the time is right to tell her.

It's no easy thing to find a conveyance grand enough to suit Lord Cappelletto yet narrow enough to pass through Verona's crowded streets. Once the convent dowry is packed inside the carriage, there's barely room for four to sit within in any comfort, so it's just as well that Tybalt insists on riding post. Though the weather's warmed, he still wears his cloak trimmed in marten fur, for I've not had time to take the winter lining out and sew in this season's taffeta instead. He carries himself with the confidence earned in years of daily practice with a master-at-arms, and Lady Cappelletta smiles and admires the handsome figure he cuts upon the horse. So handsome, so admirable, is Tybalt, she must turn immediately to Lord Cappelletto and make great show of forbidding him from trotting off beside his heir. This is the closest to kindness she comes, to keep her aged husband from mounting a steed and thrusting himself into the saddle, for which surely he's grown as ill-suited as all the other mounting and thrusting she long ago forbade him. And so Tybalt gallops ahead alone, as the rest of us wend more slowly out of the city and across the river, to where Santa Caterina nestles on a gentle hill above Verona.

Slow as we've come, still Lord Cappelletto insists there's time to descend into the catacomb and clear the cobwebs from his family crypt before the convent ceremony.

Juliet cannot bear the sight of bones and begs to walk the Stations of the cloister instead. Lady Cappelletta gives her leave to do so, though she relishes the visit to the tomb herself — I suppose to be sure Lord Cappelletto's first, beloved wife remains quite dead.

I stay with my Juliet. In the near two years since she turned twelve, my girl's not been allowed to leave Ca' Cappelletti, save to make her shrift to Friar Lorenzo, or to walk behind Lord Cappelletto in a holy-day procession. A rich man's marriageable daughter is like his wife's dowry-jewels — a precious treasure to be kept under lock and key, shown only when he deems it to his family's advantage. Soft as Juliet is, it's not been hard on her to be penned in, her days filled with whatever sewing and singing I devise to divert her. But I'm glad to escape the confines of Ca' Cappelletti, to be brought beyond the city walls, and walk among the cloister garden smelling its mint and thyme and fecund dirt. To breathe in their pungent promise, and know that spring is the season of possibility.

Even Juliet senses it, laughing and pointing at plant and peacock and every pretty view. All talk of tombs forgotten as she wanders along the venerative path, infused with as much awe for what grows in the garden as for the Christly acts commemorated at each Station. I'm glad of it. Glad that even here, she is as full of love for this life as the encloistered Rosaline is for the holy hereafter. Surely God and saints'll not favor less her liveliness.

After we make our prayer at the final Station, Juliet's mouth curves into a sly smile. "I've a surprise to show you," she says, bidding me close my eyes as she steers me along another of the convent's paths. It is a contenting thing to be led by my near-grown Juliet, her gentle touch guiding me as she chitters to herself about which way she means for us to go. She stops us with a giggle, and opening my eyes I find myself facing a statue of Santa Caterina.

Towering over us, Caterina's colors dazzle in the sun. Her cheeks flush pink, the red of her lips nearly as deep a ruby as her gown. The bright green robe held by two angels above her saintly gilded crown contrasts with the deeper green of the martyr's palm she holds, which is dotted with golden dates. Her other hand clutches a dark brown torturer's wheel. Mysterious gold letters are worked into the holy book that opens at her breast.

"I came here once, when I was a girl," Juliet tells me, as though I could forget that day. "When I saw this statue, I thought that it was you."

"Me? A virgin saint?"

"Do not tease me, Nurse, for what did I know of such things?" She points to Santa Caterina's wheel. "This seemed so like your spindle, and her hair is fixed in braids like yours."

"Most of the women in Verona wear their hair in braids." Reaching beneath where Juliet's unplaited locks fall from her Cappelletti cap, I give the lobe of her ear a loving tweak. "And what I cradled at my breast was more precious than any book could be."

Soft cooing sounds from behind the statue. "A songbird," says Juliet, "and we've not a crust of bread to feed it."

"A cat," I correct her, "and he'd not be satisfied with any less than two full loaves."

The cooing turns to cawing laugh, and Tybalt steps out from where he's hid. "Is a convent walk a place to play, and are you yet of such a pranking age?" I ask, though my smile shows how glad I am to see him.

"Does the cruel virago scold," he hunches out his head and wags a finger, before straightening himself tall again, "even when a goodly man places candles before a godly saint?"

"A goodly man," I repeat, mocking him in turn, to Juliet's delight — for she and I still see the boy, the youth, that Tybalt's been, though at twenty-three he's eager to believe none can detect it. "Does that not depend on whether what you offer is a narrow taper or a well-thickened votive?"

I reach into the wooden chest he carries, feeling for the familiar shape of candles. But what I touch instead is an unexpected form. Drawing it out, I see the offerings Tybalt's brought are carved in the shape of the Holy Mother. I lift this one to my lips to offer prayerful kiss. I breathe in the sweet scent, pressing my thumb until it makes a slight burrow in the beeswax.

"Did it come from our hive?" Juliet asks.

"Harvested from the one within our arbor, and the others that I —"

The convent bell cuts Tybalt off. He nods for me to place the votive upon the altar at the statue's base and makes a quick prayer as I touch its wick to the one that already burns low there. Carrying the near-full chest in his hands, he offers one elbow to Juliet and the other to me. We slip our arms through his, walking three abreast across the cloister grounds. Honey-scent, spring, Juliet, and Tybalt — all of this warms me.

Though convent-dowries and what the

Sisters sell of their vineyards' yield keep their church well, it's not so large as some within the city. Christ, like some Mohammedan sultan, takes many brides at once, and the churchyard teems with the families of all those who are being consecrated.

"I pray you, sir, let us pass," Tybalt says to a man so broad there is no easy way around him.

The man turns and, instead of stepping aside, takes quick survey of Tybalt. "Whose son are you?"

Such a question, meant to insult any full-grown man, cuts all the worse with one who's spent so much of his life fatherless.

"I am Tybalt Cappelletto, brother to Rosaline who will be consecrated a Sister of Santa Caterina within the hour. And I should like to kneel and pray for her long service to the Holy Church, rather than standing here squabbling with you."

But the man'll not move. "You bring so small a chest of candles, Cappelletto?"

Tybalt takes a half-step forward, crooking his elbow to maneuver Juliet behind him. "I bring such a goodly store each week. Our candles burn day and night in every chapel and before every holy statue at Santa Caterina, as the Sisters say Mass for our noble family."

The man smiles as though Tybalt is a hind with one foot caught in a well-strung trap. "Fifty boxes of candles a year, is that all the Cappelletti offer?"

"Candles to keep filled the score of gifted silver candlesticks that bear the Cappelletti crest, and a wedding cassone overflowing with trousseau linens." Having risen from the catacomb and pressed his way through the crowd to find us, Lord Cappelletto takes even more than his usual pleasure in cataloguing his own calculated benevolence. "Along with silver plate for the church altar, and another two chests filled with enough of Prato's finest wool to make full-skirted habits for every Sister here. And a plot of tilling land near to Villafranca, rich soil that the Cappelletti've held for five generations, ever since it was given to us by the Pope's decree for besting some rebellious mountain peasants with unfounded pretentions to nobility."

Lord Cappelletto spits the last part, but this thick mule of a man only shrugs. "Rich dirt, perhaps, but poor compense for all the Cappelletti slaughtered by their fiercer, braver foes, in that generation and the next." He swells his belly all the larger, to be sure we cannot pass, and nods at Tybalt's wooden chest. "I suppose you may be so indulgent for a niece. Would that I could do as much for my goddaughter Augusta Infangati, who consecrates her vows today. But as a man with seven sons, I must take more care in stewarding my family's fortunes."

Son and sons, is that all this man talks about? I'd curse him and every son he has, and be done with him so we can settle ourselves to prayer. But it's not a woman's place to speak in public, and Lord Cappelletto'll not leave off so easily.

"A burden it must be, to know your family's wealth will be so divided and diminished, when the whole of it has never been even half what we Cappelletti have." He tips one ear, as though pondering some great question. "But perhaps that's not all there is to the matter. Even one as poor as Il Benedicto makes tithe out of his meager means, yet it's said the Montecchi never tally the church's portion as fully as you ought."

Marking how the name *Montecchi* shoots an angry twitch along Tybalt's jaw, I lean close and whisper to him what I dare not say to Lord Cappelletto. "A nice quarrel to have before a church, while Juliet waits to kneel and pray, as do your aunt and pious Rosaline."

The Montecche is already thundering

back at Lord Cappelletto. Tybalt cuts him off, shoving the box of candles into the man's fat gut. "I make a gift of these to you, that you may give them to the church to celebrate your goddaughter, and none of your sons suffer a pennyworth of loss for it. Come Uncle, Coz, and Nurse, let's show the Sisters of Caterina the reverence that's their due."

He ducks around the man to walk beside his uncle, taking care that Juliet and I follow unharmed.

"You were right to put your duty to Rosaline before such bickering," I tell Tybalt, when we reach the church door.

"I'd not put anything before my family," he answers. "I care not how large a man's fortune is, nor how many sons he's spawned. But I'll not forget how the Montecche insulted me, and Rosaline, and our uncle, and the Holy Church as well."

There's only so much insult given as what we choose to take. But high-born Tybalt, braised like the tenderest veal cutlet in all Lord Cappelletto's talk of family honor, will not see that. So I turn instead to Juliet. She's laid a hand upon Lord Cappelletto's arm and whispers some pleasant word to coax a smile from him. Such affection is more than his wife ever offers, and any who look upon Lord Cappelletto can see how he treasures it. Treasures her. He smiles and says, "Darling daughter," kissing her farewell then hurrying to take his place among the kneeling men, while Juliet and I join Lady Cappelletta on the women's side of the nave.

Darling she is, and daughter, too. Milk-daughter, and more, to me. Let Lord Cappelletto call her what he will. He's as blind with would-be father love as Tybalt is with hot rage over whatever slight he's sure the Montecche made. Mannish pride on either side, and Juliet and I have naught to do but bow our heads and pray among the women.

Rosaline'll not see us once the Mass is done. The stone-faced prioress nods approvingly at all that Lord Cappelletto gifts the convent, then announces that Rosaline is so moved by her newly consecrated state that she's vowed not to speak for an entire week. And she'll keep a holy fast for just as long, consuming nothing but the Host.

By my saints, this Christ is a demanding husband. To ask a wife to forego the pleasures of a conjugal bed, and have neither words nor food to fill her mouth instead.

Lord Cappelletto scowls at this proroguing of his planned feast. He's thinking of the powerful guests he's longing to impress, and of ravioli and savory pie and all the other already-prepared dishes that'll not keep another week. Lady Cappelletta, who's learned to love an evening's revelry since her husband, grown too old to dance, leaves her to terpsichore among his guests, shares his displeasure. But Tybalt's jaw softens at the prioress's pronouncement. Though I wonder what in his sister's self-denying devotions so pleases him, I give Juliet's chin a loving chuck and say, "It's just as well to wait the feast. For all we've sewn of Rosaline's trousseau, there's been little time to array Juliet, and Lady Cappelletta, as finely as we ought for such a fête."

The thought of getting up greater finery satisfies girl and woman both, and Lord Cappelletto's hairy fingers busily tally how much can be made of another week of preparations. Tybalt catches my eye with his own, endarting his gladness to me before taking his leave to untether the post-horse.

Plodding as the carriage ride is, still we arrive at Ca' Cappelletti before Tybalt. Lady Cappelletta hastens to the upper storage room and unlocks the cassone that holds the finest of the household fabric stores. "The zetani, at last," she says, pulling out a length of cloth as azure as Santa Maria's own celestial robes.

Juliet's slim fingers ripple along the velvet-embossed silk. "Does my lord father bid it, Madam?"

That she calls Lady Cappelletta by the same *Madam* as I do is comfort to me, though to hear her mouth form *father* for Lord Cappelletto always sets a sharp shard in my craw.

But *bid* is the word that catches for Lady Cappelletta. "This zetani was pawned to him in payment for some debt so long past, the color fades along the folds." She raises an eyebrow in careful calculation. "Surely even my lord husband'll not begrudge us fabric enough to make new sleeves for his dear daughter, and his wife."

Juliet raises pleading eyes to Lady Cappelletta. "Can I not have a whole gown of it?"

It's not greed but a child's innocent delight that makes my girl ask. But such innocence only draws a frown from Lady Cappelletta. Indulgent as Lord Cappelletto is with Juliet, my girl's not noticed he's harder with his wife.

"No simple stitch will pull such well-wefted cloth to proper shape," I say. "Which means we'll have enough to do to get sleeves cut, set, and sewn in one week's time."

The soft zetani scents our fingers with the rosemary that's kept it free of worm and moth, and I know my Juliet will shine in so rich a color worn against the pale yellow stripes of her gown. But it seems whatever rest I'd hoped to have once Rosaline's trousseau was done will never come, for we work long past the evening torches being lit. Although I keep a ready ear for Tybalt's return, I never hear him. Such is the man that he's become, still prancing on cat paws though he's long grown — yet oftener and oftener keeping counsel only with himself.

It's a short night's nap I get, because not long after the lauds bells are rung trumpeters pierce Verona's sleep, summoning Prince Cansignorio's most trusted advisors. Lord Cappelletto responds to the blasts like a hound to the huntsman's whistle, rushing down into the still-dark street to join the hastily called council.

I swing open the window in our bedchamber. "Why let in such chill?" Juliet murmurs, snuggling deeper beneath the bedclothes.

I do not worry her with an answer as I lean out to smell the air. No fire, no powder. The city's quiet, except for the peals of the trumpeters, the hoofbeats of their horses, and the clatter of the lords answering the call. But after I pull the window tight within its case and turn back to the room, a shiver catches me. Not of cold, but of something else. Some foreboding makes me cross myself and ask safekeeping from my Virgin before I climb once more into the bed where Juliet, fast asleep again, breathes a steady rhythm into the still room.

By the time Lord Cappelletto returns, the sun is high and the whole house is long awake. He barks down in the kitchen before storming his way into the sala.

Lady Cappelletta, practiced at ignoring her husband's moods, does not even turn her head when he enters. Juliet wraps the length of zetani she is working around her shoulders, wanting Lord Cappelletto to take some pretty notice of it, and her. "Will I not make a fine sight at the feast?"

But for once his brooding brow does not raise in joy at Juliet. "There'll be no feast," he says.

This at least works a response from his wife. "Does my lord husband not wish to celebrate our brother's daughter Rosaline's most holy state?"

Brother, Rosaline, and *holy state* — she offers all three when any one of them ought to be enough to catch his heart. But none do.

"There's been fighting," he tells her, "upon Verona's streets."

"Surely there has." I answer fast, in case his words have frighted Juliet. "As happens on so many nights, while we are safe inside."

"This was not some night-brawl in a remote corner of the city. There's blood spilt among the Scaligeri monuments in the Santa Maria Antica churchyard. Prince Cansignorio, fearing some treason, has forbidden any gathering of lords outside his council chamber until the culprits are caught."

Such is a man's reasoning, which makes everything that happens have to do with him. Cansignorio, who with cold heart and quick hand killed one brother and keeps the other chained within a prison cell, knows well how easily traitorous thoughts can turn to deeds. But with a woman's wit, I sense something else at play.

I let out one cough and then another, hacking louder and louder until Lord Cappelletto orders me from the room to take wine and water.

Needing neither wine nor water, I swallow my false coughs and head instead for Tybalt's rooms. But he's not there. Not in the courtyard. I spy him at last in the arbor, staring at the beehive.

I cannot move on so fleet a foot as he does, and, keen as his long-ago lessons from the master-at-arms have made him, he calls, "Good day, dear Nurse," without even turning.

"A good enough day for those who did naught last night. But for any who scaled the compound walls and went —"

"Will you not come close," he cuts me off, "and look at this?"

I've no use for bee watching, and he well knows it. But to talk to Tybalt, one must talk as Tybalt will, and so I edge closer to the hive. At a limb-hole of the log, a mob of bees savages some winged foe like fierce-jawed dogs tearing at a fox.

"Why do they attack one of their kind?"

"Not one of their kind," he corrects me. "An intruder, who snuck into their hive to steal their honey. Do you not see the difference?"

I'll not get near enough for my old eyes to mark it. But he leans yet closer, admiring the raging insects. "It's said the bees are more like us than the English or French or Germans. Always seeking for what is sweet — but when something goes amiss, fast to fight to defend their hive."

"A foolish sacrifice, to waste one's life just to sink a single sting."

He turns, ready to tell me I am wrong. But my gasp overruns his words. A finger-long cut crusted with blood slices his cheek. "You're hurt," I say, as if to dare him to deny it.

"It's but a scratch, and well worth the greater damage I did the Montecche."

"That pompous old man? He must be your uncle's age."

"It's not him I fought, but one of his precious sons. Less precious now, for the hurt I've done him." He smiles, and the cut snakes into an angry curve. "Insult they gave us, and injury I gave back."

Insult, ever insult. The Cappelletti honor is like that finely worked zetani. A pretty, precious thing, though in truth too delicate. The poor who cloak ourselves in coarse woollen bigello, which bears a host of blows, can only wonder that the zetani of a rich man's honor is so easily marred. And so often in need of avenging.

"Prince Cansignorio believes both insult and injury were meant for him," I tell Tybalt. "When he discovers you're the culprit —"

"He'll not know. I took care to meet the Montecche when only stars were watching, as he returned alone from a night of drinking."

Is there no way to make Tybalt see the danger in what he's done? "The Montecchi will cry for justice."

Tybalt laughs as though I've truly turned into the foolish old virago he teases that I am. "Will the man whose blood I drew denounce me publicly, and admit to all Verona how clumsily he fought, and how easily I bested him?"

He unseals one end of the log hive and daggers off an edge of comb. The bees arc around him, intoxicated by the sweet scent of their own handiwork. But none offers an angry sting. It's as if they believe him one of their own, and know he means no enmity to them.

He holds the dripping comb out to me. "Honey will keep the cut from festering. Will you not offer a careful rub and a kind word, to have me healed?"

For all the sauce and swagger with which Tybalt wields a weapon, deep within he's still the lonely child who's ever needed me. Needs me as much as I need him.

I take the comb and dab honey along the angry stripe that mars his cheek, as I tell him about Prince Cansignorio's decree. "Your uncle'll not be pleased to learn you're the cause that cancels Rosaline's holy-wedding feast."

This cools a little of his hot pride. "My sister deserves more banquets than all Verona has the means to give. But she's too saintly to care whether we feast her. And my uncle, who values naught more than the good name of the Cappelletti, must be glad to have his heir defend it."

Tybalt speaks the words *his heir* as one might speak of *his silver belt* or *his ermine-lined gown* or *the fee-simple of his landed holdings*. Lord Cappelletto's taken Tybalt as his heir, but never given in return what Tybalt so longed for from his father, and found only too briefly in Pietro.

I slip the comb into his pouting mouth so he can suck the remaining honey from it, as he learned to do when Pietro first set the hive here. I wait until I'm sure the sweetness is on Tybalt's tongue before I say, "Lord Cappelletto loves you, and Rosaline, as surely as he loves Juliet."

He chews the comb until he's worked all the golden honey from it, then spits the palish wax upon the ground. "My uncle loves Rosaline for being pious, which he hopes will bring the favor of God and Church upon our house. He loves me for matching honor to that favor, so long as my first honoring act is unwavering obedience to him. But Juliet has his purest love."

Quick as my words come, he lays a long finger against my lips before I can utter any of them. "Hush, Nurse. We both know it's true, and you know I'll not resent it." He smiles again, and the glistening honey on his cheek makes this curl of the cut appear less sinister. "Juliet is as charming as Rosaline is good. Any man might love her. Why would her father not?"

I'll not answer as I could. Not dare betray to Tybalt what I've not let anyone know that I know: who her true father was. "You'll have to stay within Ca' Cappelletti until the cut has healed, to keep clear of Prince Cansignorio's suspicion. But there'll be no hiding it from your family."

I lead him out of the arbor and through the courtyard, stopping to collect some wine before we climb up to the sala. Though for my part I might prefer some aqua vitae, wine is all Lord Cappelletto drinks. And so I pray the vin santo will be enough to calm his ire, and to let flow Lady Cappelletta's full sympathy for Tybalt, which runs as deep as my own.

It's Juliet who first catches sight of us as we enter the sala. Paling at her dear-loved Tybalt's bloodied cheek, she cries out, the zetani sliding from her lap and pooling on the floor.

Lady Cappelletta's amber eyes flicker with surprise, then horror. "Who's done this to you?"

Lord Cappelletto, who stands at the window, turns to see what's amiss. Spying Tybalt's wound, he demands, "What villain is this within my house, jeoparding our family by raising a weapon against the prince?"

I step between them. "He's not jeoparded —"

Lord Cappelletto cuts me off, pushing his way to Tybalt. "Are you yet a child, hiding behind the nurse's skirts?"

"I'm neither villain nor child." Tybalt draws himself to his full height, dwarfing Lord Cappelletto. "I raised a weapon only to defend our family. Glad I was to do it, and to pay this simple price" — he runs his smallest finger along his sliced cheek — "for the pleasure of spilling a greater quantity of Montecchi blood. Such was their due, for insulting our gifts to the Holy Church."

Lord Cappelletto's mouth sharpens to a pucker, as he takes in Tybalt's words. But then it broadens as he laughs, pulling Tybalt into his arms.

"Dry your womanish tears," he tells Lady Cappelletta and Juliet. "Tybalt's done right.

Done as I did many a time when I was of his age, to pluck the crow of the Montecchi and their allies." He claps a hairy hand upon his nephew's back, like a knight patting his stallion after a victorious joust. "Prince Cansignorio's quick to take a slight where none is given. But he's got no part in this private quarrel between families. So long as none know the part you played last night, it'll be but a short delay before the edict's lifted, and we feast for pious Rosaline. And for brave Tybalt."

It's not love of the sort Pietro showed Tybalt, that tender echo of what he felt for our own sons. But it's all Lord Cappelletto offers, and Tybalt drinks it in like a bee sucking nectar from a blossom.

One note, then the next, then yet another — they fly so swift from Tybalt's lute, I can barely draw air in fast enough to match singing to them. Together we turn such a bright tune that Lady Cappelletta hums along, one foot tapping as she sews.

Such is not enough for Juliet. Her sleeves done two days past, the needle now holds no interest for her. Bearing herself with perfect grace, she hops and turns about the sala. A pleasing sight to match each pretty song. But she longs for a chain of other dancers.

"Might not my lord father —"

Lady Cappelletta's smile sours. "Your lord father has much to do, tallying rents and tributes."

She's always glad for the long hours her husband spends in his study bent over his correspondence, and gladder still when he leaves Ca' Cappelletti entirely, which he's done much this week and a half past. Lord Cappelletto's impatient for any chance to be in Prince Cansignorio's presence, showing the Cappelletti loyal.

His going out makes harder Tybalt's staying in. After so many days with little to do but pluck tempestuously upon the lute strings, Tybalt's chin hangs, and his shoulders slope.

"Dance with me, Coz," Juliet says, "while Nurse sings for us."

But even she cannot draw off his sulk. "I prefer to dance with steel rather than with silk."

Such poetry, just to show he's still eager to spill blood. "It's dancing with steel that's gashed your face, and left you closed inside among the ladies," I remind him.

He makes no answer, which upsets me more than the bitterest rebuke. This quiet, brooding Tybalt — he steals in like evening's shadow creeping across a room, pushing out the bright, loving boy we adored. Would my sons have sullened so, if they'd lived to such an age? Would they have turned away from me, as Tybalt of late so often does?

Juliet reaches out her hands to me. "Nurse, you must make yourself my partner. Come, I'll hear no plaints about your corn-riddled feet or achy hips." She widens those familiar eyes in such a way as she knows makes it near impossible for me tell her no.

But I'm suddenly in such a sweat as if it were the height of summer, or some devil-ish spell raged over me.

"I must have water," I say, laying my needlework down and standing myself up. This is my well-worked compromise for the hours I spend in Lady Cappelletta's pres-ence: I'll not ask a by-your-leave-may-I-m'lady of her, as the common servants must. Instead, I annouce what I intend to do and set myself to doing it, unless I am bade otherwise.

"I'll go withal." Tybalt's quick onto his feet, as if accompanying me to the courtyard well offers some great respite for his restless-ness.

His coming along does not please me, for ruddied as I feel, I might plunge face and neck, arms and chest, into the water trough,

303

were he not near. Instead, I must settle for long sips from the well-cup.

Tybalt's mouth twists in thought as he watches all I swallow. "Bees need to drink, just as we do." He points through the passageway to the arbor, toward a low clay bowl near the hive that's filled with a pebbly mound over which he's poured water. "It's not rained in weeks. The other hives must be without water by now." Tipping his head, he surveys the top of the compound wall. "Perhaps tonight, I can replenish them."

"You cannot," I say. "You must not." Flushed though I am, that portending shiver shakes over me. "Your cut's nearly healed. Surely the bees can wait another week, until you can go safely through Verona's streets."

"In a week, we may have lost whole hives. Pietro's hives."

"I'll go." Why do I promise such a thing, though the bees frighten me? It's hearing how he speaks of Pietro. Esteeming my husband's memory is the one honor I understand. "If you'll invent some excuse to satisfy Lady Cappelletta, I'll go early tomorrow, when it's yet cool."

He is a sly fox and I'm the fat hen, I see that from the smile that spreads along his face as he tells me where each hive is set and how to reach them, saving for last the ones nooked within the walls of Santa Caterina. He knew I'd not let him journey so far with the prince's edict still in place.

Small sacrifice it is for me. Shut away all this time, I long to roam the city and wander through the countryside beyond its walls.

"It'll take all morning, and much of the afternoon," I say. Longer, if I dally in places of my choosing.

"You'll need to save the hours after noon to go to the Mercato Vecchio while the fabric merchants have out their finest wares."

"Do you mean for me to dress the bees, once I've watered them?" In truth, the thought of walking among those crowded stalls, bright colors dazzling my eye as my hands work their way across silk, samite, and Damascus cloth — that delights me, whatever reason Tybalt has for wanting me to go.

He takes my plump hand, raising his long arm and twirling me beneath it as Juliet would've had me do in her capers around the sala. "The bees need no more dress than a dusting of bright pollen. But our dear Nurse deserves something prettier than that old morello to wear to Rosaline's feast."

His words stop me mid-turn. For near

eleven years, I've worn naught but mulberry-dyed cloth. I've not minded my widow's weeds, bought with what was made selling off Pietro's few garments, and the scant furnishings and kitchen things we'd owned. I wear my loss for all the world to see, for it's all I've left of my happily wedded state. Or nearly all, aside from our Madonna, and Pietro's three linen shirts. Well darned they are by now, but still I ever wear one beneath my dress, the last hidden rub of him on me. Only my precious bedmate Juliet knows how I yet keep something of his against me. But even she does not suspect how I hope the dull morello worn atop those shirts washes any brightness from my face, keeps anyone from noticing the way my coloring matches her own.

I drop my hand from Tybalt's. "Sumptuous colors come at great cost. They're meant for such as Juliet, and Lady Cappelletta."

"Pick something golden, then. The color of new-minted coins, and the flowing honey that brings them." He reaches for the cup, dips it once more into the well bucket, and holds it tippling full to me. "Half all the harvests' profits are your due. Will you not spend them?"

This is a well-worn argument between us.

The boy who, through all his tutor's beatings, never cared to reckon sums has turned
into a man who faithfully tallies how much
each season's wax and honey yield, and
figures to the last eighth-denaro the half-
share he insists is mine. I've not touched
any of it, letting Tybalt store those coins
along with the wages Lord Cappelletto pays
each quarter for my minding Juliet. As
though the things I do for Juliet, I do for
money — no more than Tybalt tends Pietro's hives solely to take a partner's portion
of the little sum to be earned at it.

Another flash of heat rises over me. I accept the cup, swallowing down the water
while Tybalt reminds me for the hundredth
time that the coins sit in a box hidden
beneath the arbor-hive. The bees guard our
lucre, which is made from robbing them.
"Take all of it, if you wish. And take my
hooded cloak as well, so that at each place
where there's a hive, they'll know I've sent
you."

"And what of Juliet?" I ask. We both know
this is no journey on which Lord Cappelletto would allow her.

"I'll play the knight-gallant for her, and
give her dances as well as songs, and jousting games, and every piece of play her pretty
heart desires." Grown as he is, he's got less

patience to dote on Juliet, though she longs for his attention as much as ever. I nod to let him see how pleased I am that he'll please her.

Taking quick measure of my gladness, he asks, "And while I amuse my cousin, will you carry a message from me to Rosaline?"

The slightest crease rises between his eyes, and I begin to wonder if all the talk of watering bees or buying cloth was but a ruse, so that he could ask this of me.

"Of course." The fat hen is not so fast outfoxed, for I'm glad to be privy to whatever confidence he sends his cloistered sister. "What shall I tell her?"

"No need for telling." He draws a folded page from his doublet sleeve, already sealed with a fat dollop of blood-red wax. "I've got it written here."

"Written — for Rosaline?" Perchance the girl can read, the Sisters of Santa Caterina needing to be learned enough to spend their days bent over holy books. But to write is to keep confidence from me, and Tybalt well knows it. "There was no need for you to struggle with a pen," I say, mouthing Lord Cappelletto's ready reminder of Tybalt's flaws, "when I'd have no trouble remembering your message, and repeating it to her."

Unkind it is of me, but if the words hurt

Tybalt, he gives no show of it. "Rosaline prefers me write, so she may keep the missive and read it over in any lonely hour."

I'd not believe pious Rosaline passed any lonely hours, living among a convent's worth of company and devoting herself to her holy wedded Christ. I pack my tongue close among my well-cracked teeth to keep from saying so to Tybalt, as I tuck the letter into my own sleeve.

TWELVE

It's good I've got the girth I do. It draws up the length of Tybalt's cloak, the excess fabric folded over the twice-girdled silver belt he's lent me. A rich man's finery works like a faery-tale spell. Wrapped in it, I slip into houses as grand as Ca' Cappelletti in every parish of Verona, each with a hive within its hidden garden. There are yet more hives nooked into the very walls that encircle the city, and tucked in trees that edge the fields beyond the walls. None question me busying myself about the hives, cloaked in fine camlet embroidered with the Cappelletti crest in gilded thread.

I imagine Pietro as I go about, how carefully he must have chosen each place, how wily he was to site his hives so well. Log or cork, woven fennel stalk or wooden chest — I'd not known there were so many ways to house a hive, each selected to suit where it's placed. And nearby, always some simple dish piled with pebbles where water's meant to be.

Tybalt's talked so much of how Pietro loved his bees, I try to feel for the tiny creatures some small part of what my big bear of a husband felt. As I tip the jug I carry, the bees dance with expectant delight, the most adventurous ones touching down on one of the tiny rocks, drinking from the shimmery surface even before I'm done. It's not unlike tending a flock. Though it was my family's poverty that put me to shepherding, I came to relish roaming beyond the sinister confines of my father's house, the dull familiar of our little village. I passed happy days among my sheep, soothing any nighttime pangs of solitude by burrowing myself against a warm, woolly companion. It's comfort to think Pietro felt the same, venturing out from the Via Zancani to set one hive and then another, slowly casting a buzzing skein around Verona and the countryside beyond.

As I make the steep climb to Santa Caterina, the ruts formed on the narrow path by hoof and cart and carriage all work hard upon my feet, the borrowed belt clanging an uneven rhythm to match my unsure pace. I empty the jug in careful swigs, husbanding a few drops onto my sleeve and pressing the dampened cloth against the hot nape of my neck. The sun stays close on me, drawing his course along the sky as I rise above the city, until at last I stand before the convent gate.

Setting down the water jug, I use both hands to tug upon the bell-pull, feeling for the resistance that weighs the weathered rope, a metal answer to my effort. This is how our lives are marked and meted out. The tolling of the hours of a day, the Sunday of a week, the holy-days of a year. And then the rings like this, tolled to tell that somebody's arrived. And the other kind, rung from parish church when someone's departed. Only when I led my flock to pasture could I forget such a great and brassy sound, forget that in all the universe there was something louder than bleating sheep, or a wolfish howl, or the most fiercely raging storm. Louder than any noise I heard upon the hills.

An-gel, an-gel. In the awful time when we lost all, the death knells rang day and night, knocking my heart from its rhythmed beats and stunning the breath from me. Pietro would gather me in his great arms, so that his broad chest was all I could know of the world. Pressing his lips to my ear, he whispered *an-gel, an-gel,* over and over, matched to the pealing of the bells. Angel, each one of our boys was become, as though their souls rode to heaven on the tolls. Angel, Pietro said I was, his Angelica here on earth.

I want to hear my husband's comforting *an-gel* once again. But the high-pitched clanging of the bell upon the gate to Santa Caterina offers only a keening questioning.

Metal slides against metal, the hasp swings, and the wooden door gives way. I'm faced with a woman near my own age, or so I guess from what the wimple shows of her gaunt face. Her hands are rubbed raw, the odor of lye clinging to her.

"I'm here to tend the bees," I say, lifting the jug. She nods and turns without a word. I follow her inside, wait while she slides the hasp shut. She points me to the well and, before I've drawn the water to refill the jug, silently disappears back into the laundering shed.

Tybalt's told me where to find the half a dozen hives nestled among the convent grounds. As I bend to pour water at the first of them, set within the vineyard wall, a lone bee flies inside the gape of cloak below my chin. I stop stone still, anticipating the hot anger of its sting. But I feel instead a gentle tickle as it crawls along the curve of my collar-bone. The creature makes curious survey of my tender flesh, such as none has done since death stilled Pietro's insisting kisses. Tybalt's spoke enough of the workings of a hive that I know this bee was hatched no more than a few months past. But still I cannot help thinking of it as my husband's. I close my eyes, shutting out the world that's easily seen, and wonder if in its oddly pleasant prickling there's some message from him.

"Pietro, our girl's near grown. Lovely and loving as only we could make her. Fresh as the milk and sweet as the honey that's fed her. And Tybalt — at last to raise a boy who's lived to be a man. You'd be proud of him. But husband, how I miss you. Just as much today as I ever have." I wait, wanting for some answer. But all I hear is the steady hum of the insects entering and exiting the hive. The shivery sensation along my neck is gone, whatever bee was there flown off to join the others, unrecognizable to me once I blink my eyes open to the bright sun.

I make my way from one hive to the next, the convent grounds familiar from my recent visit, though to move about them, even to breathe the same scent of earth and plants, feels different without Juliet and Tybalt. The land slopes gently here, and at the farthest hive, I turn back to look across the low wall that encloses the convent. Spread in the valley below, encircled by the Adige, is Verona. I search for the familiar shape of San Fermo, then the soaring campanile of Sant'Anastasia, and try to pick out which of the household towers rising between them is Ca' Cappelletti.

Does a bee feel such a pull for its hive, as I do for the teeming city? Is each nectar-gatherer as devoted to its queen as I am to Juliet, that even on so short a flight, there is always the longing to be back with her?

The bee is more practiced at parting from its queen, for it takes flight each day. I've not been away from Juliet since the morning more than a decade past when, newly weaned, she rode here with Lord Cappelletto and Tybalt, to bring Rosaline back to the nuns. I still miss those first years. Sometimes I believe I'm living them again during our nights of enlaced sleep, when all the world retreats and Juliet's bed becomes a tiny ship in which the two of us drift, dreaming together.

I can feel the wonder of her at each age she's been. Tiny baby, plump toddler, fast-growing girl. The near-woman she is now. I'd keep her this age forever if I could, though part of me is impatient to see the lady she'll soon be — and to have her know

315

all she is to me.

That impatience quickens my pace to the final hive, set near the statue of Santa Caterina. But when I round the curve in the path, the water jug slips from my hands, smashing to the ground. The bees. They're everywhere. Crawling on the outside of the hive, irrupting onto the ground below it, infesting every nearby leaf and stem. Fear shivers over me as I watch the dark, creeping army. And then, in a frenzied instant, every bee alights at once. Like Biblical locusts blotting out the sky, they swoop together toward the saint.

They land upon the book she carries, which disappears beneath the writhing swarm. The great mound of bees teeming Santa Caterina's breast seems a perversing of every statue, every fresco, every image I've ever seen of Santa Maria suckling the Holy Christ.

I thought that it was you. A tremor shudders my own breast, as I remember Juliet's words. What have I to do with such an awful-omened thing?

I sidle away, too frighted to turn my back lest the bees come after me. As soon as I round a curve in the path and can no longer see them, vinegary fear pumps through my legs, and I race across the sloping grounds to the convent gate, thrust back the metal bar, and heave the hasp free. Shoving open the gate, I stumble down the winding path.

It's a clumsy-footed scramble to the city, tripping over Tybalt's too-long cloak. And over my own dripping dread. Just as I reach the Ponte delle Navi, something slams hard against me from behind, knocking me face-first to the stone span. Bone cracks as blood fills my throat.

"Dirty Cappelletto." Each syllable comes with a boot kick, the last of them pitching me onto my side.

"What's this?" Another voice, uncertain. "A maid in a man's cloak?"

"Made to pay, she'll be," the first, angrier man says. "Though what I'll thrust in her is not what I'd thrust into that knavish Tybalt."

A thud — and then a weight on me. That same man, cursing. And another, pummeling him with a wrathy, "The devil take you, for attacking a woman in broad daylight."

I try to push myself up, but the slightest lift of my head sets the world swimming. I cover my face while they brawl over me.

The shouting spreads, and the sounds of fighting, too. Like tinder igniting into an ever-growing ring of flame.

Someone grips my wrist, peels my arms

from my face. A careful finger pries my eyelid up. In the blur, I make out brown cassock, and Friar Lorenzo's great gaping ears.

He pulls me to my feet and guides me from the fray, which spills from the bridge into the piazza. Edging past the swinging fists and flashing daggers, we slip around the massive hind-end of San Fermo and take shelter in the arcaded churchyard.

The noise of the clash is muted within these holy walls. But that only makes the pounding in my head sound louder. "No farther," I say. Or try to, the words swallowed in a bloody gurgle.

It is enough for the friar to make out my meaning. He sets me upon a bench and unrolls the sleeve of Tybalt's cloak. Bunching the gilt-embroidered edge against my nose, he bids me hold it tight to staunch the blood.

I nod, but even that slight movement shoots pain through my skull. Friar Lorenzo hies to his cell, returning to offer both poultices and prayers. Neither brings me relief. With a rip of pain along my side, my stomach twists, and I heave out a putrid stream onto his holy robe.

When I croak out an apology, Friar Lorenzo waves the words away. He has all a

Franciscan's devotion to the wretched — coupled, perchance, with some scheme to appeal to Lord Cappelletto for the gift of a new cassock. He moves to make the sign of the cross upon me, but his *benedicte* is drowned out by a thundering of horses' hooves and the angry trumpets of Prince Cansignorio's royal guard.

"Thank Christ, they'll put an end to the fighting," Friar Lorenzo says.

It's true, the lance-wielding guard will scatter the brawlers. But Tybalt, who drew his sword to answer so small a slight as he imagined the old Montecche gave him at the convent, has his hot-headed match in a thousand other young men of Verona. As I mark the blood that's soaked into the gold-threaded Cappelletti crest embroidered on his cloak, I wonder whether it will take more power than the prince has, and a greater miracle than Friar Lorenzo can pray forth, to calm them all and bring a lasting peace to the city's streets.

Though Friar Lorenzo offers his arm to lead me back to Ca' Cappelletti, once we make our slow way out of the churchyard and enter the piazza, he stops to survey the handful of youth who, too wounded to run off, are being held by the prince's guard.

Each breath sears new pain into me. I long

to be a-bed and have Juliet lay her pretty head beside my throbbing one. But I'm caught quick while Friar Lorenzo weighs the worth of delivering me to Lord Cappelletto against what he might amass here. The Franciscan'll not easily forego a chance to offer succor to any who are hurt. He must want to tend the injured brawlers, and to plead with the guard to have mercy on them, which will surely earn him the favor of the young men's powerful families.

Another horseman cantors up the Via Filippini. He wears Cansignorio's own colors, the carmine of his high-hemmed doublet and well-turned leg setting off his night-black mount. It's as if an over-earnest hand has copied over the prince, creating a younger, handsomer, and less haughty version of Verona's ruler.

"Is this some new treason against my uncle?" he asks.

Nephew to a prince — surely the greatest gain is to be made by catering to him. "Young cocks, Count Paris, you know how they crow. But it's only some ancient grudge, rupturing anew. No treason is intended." Friar Lorenzo presses his palms together and bows his head as though he's begging for the count's guidance to solve a great dilemma. "I might treat both their anger and their injuries, and thus do my rightful duty to Verona's ruler by calming such disturbances to our streets, if I were not pledged to escort this goodly widow to Ca' Cappelletti."

The count, though no older than the brawlers, bears his princely connection with great pride. "I'll guide the widow," he tells Friar Lorenzo, "while you remedy the rest." He unhorses himself, leaving the reins to one of the guard, and offers me his arm. "If it pleases you?"

It pleases me to look upon such a pleasant face. And yet it pleases me not, to be bloodied and stained in his handsome presence.

"May the saints bless you for your benevolence." I lean unsteadily on him, forcing my features not to betray how badly I ache as we walk along the Via Leoni. "Surely Lord Cappelletto —"

"Sure Lord Cappelletto surely is, as I've seen often enough in my uncle's council chamber." He smiles, and despite the pain I do, too. Few there are for me to smirk with, about Lord Cappelletto's pretensions. "You are by blood or by marriage, a Cappelletta?"

That wilts my smile. "Neither," I say. What binds me to Juliet is something I cannot explain. Not to this noble stranger. Even with Juliet herself — we've no words for what we share. "I care for Lord Cappelletto's daughter."

"Is she of an age that requires much care?" He gives a curious glance to my mannish cloak.

"She's a girl for whom none can help but care. Including her devoted kinsman Tybalt, who dotes on her while I am off upon a pressing errand, gifting me his own cloak to do it in."

"A greater kindness it might have been, had he not been so generous."

Savvy this Paris is, discerning what I've not wanted to admit to myself. Tybalt put me into danger by bidding me wear his family crest while the Montecchi seethed to avenge themselves on him.

"You seem to be a man who knows much of kindness." And being a man, like all men happy to be praised. So happy that haply in lapping up my flattering he'll forget whatever he's surmised about me and Tybalt. "We've no feast fit for a count prepared," I say as we turn into the entry to Ca' Cappelletti, "but perchance we can decant some of Lord Cappelletto's finest Carmignano for you."

Before he can answer, Juliet's merry laugh rings from the loggia. "There you are, at last." She hurries down the stairs into the courtyard. "Tybalt and I spent the morning collecting blossoms from our arbor, so I could make you this."

A bright garland, worked with more love than skill, drops to the hard ground when she sees my bloodied face.

"What's happened to you?" She covers me with kisses like a mother cat licking a hurt kit, then issues a curt, "Raise a bucket from the well," ordering the count as if he's one of her family's man-servants. He wordlessly obeys. She does not notice the bemusement dancing on his lips as she undoes the fazzo-letto scarved around her neck and dips it into the water he's drawn.

I mark that, and more, as Juliet gently washes me. All the love with which I've fed her, she gladly feeds back to me. She may not have the learned friar's knowledge of medicinals, but her tenderest mercies do me more good than any holyman could.

Paris drops to his knee, gathering up the garland and offering it to Juliet. "She ought to be a-bed. Perhaps I —"

Juliet gives no notice to the kneeling count, keeping her worried eyes on me. "Are you tired, Nurse?"

"I should like to lie down, though to climb the stairs may be much for me," I say, imagining myself carried in the arms of the handsome count and laid beside Juliet in her great bed.

But Juliet, my innocent, asks, "Shall I call for Tybalt?"

The name throbs pain through me. I shake my head, which worsens the hurt, and tell her I can manage without him if I might lean upon her. She wraps her dainty arm around my thick waist and draws my hand across her narrow hip. Wrapped together, we walk like a single lopsided creature up the stone steps, Paris watching until we disappear inside.

Once we're in our chamber, Juliet unclasps my borrowed belt and removes the soiled cloak, then unravels my braids and works her own ivory comb through my hair. Undressing, undoing, freeing what's confined — her tending echoes how I've put her to bed, how many thousand times.

She settles me beneath the bedclothes and pulls wide the window, letting in the fruit-ripe arbor air, before setting beside me. "Am I a good nurse, Nurse?"

"So good that I'm a lucky sufferer."

But the lock upon the tower door turns, and my luck turns with it. Tybalt swings his way into the room. The sight of my swollen features stops him short.

"Stung?" he asks.

"Struck. By some unruly youth who mistook me in your cloak."

"Dishonorable dog." The score along his cheek pulls taut. "I'll pay him what he's due for treating you so."

This is the difference between the warmth of Juliet and the heat of Tybalt, the measure of what each will do believing they do it for me. "And what will he pay you, in return? Or pay me, or Juliet, or anyone of us?"

"It is our honor —" he begins.

"It was her blood." Juliet lays a protective hand against my cheek. "Better saved than spilled, if that's the cost of honor."

"Do not let Lord Cappelletto hear you speak so, Coz."

She draws her hand to her mouth so fast you'd think it burnt. Juliet does not bear harsh words well. Especially when they menace with the threat of harsher still from Lord Cappelletto.

"Cansignorio's nephew knows that I am struck," I say. "If he tells the prince, they'll soon discover it was you who drew the first blade."

"Who'll trust what that pleasure-loving Mercutio says? He's overfond of the Montecchi, and even the prince knows it."

"Overfond of much, Mercutio is." I flash

a look toward Juliet, to warn Tybalt not to utter any more in front of her about pleasure-loving Mercutio's debauchery, rumors of which are enough to shock all of Sodom and half Gomorrah. "But it's Paris who happened upon the brawl and brought me home. Let him advise the prince on how to settle it. He seems a fair man."

"Fair to look at," Tybalt says. "Your sight's not harmed, nor is your lus—"

"Truly, my head aches. Juliet, would you call for some aqua vitae to soothe me, and a plate of walnut-candied figs?" I take care to name a delicacy she'll crave along with the drink I want. With a devoted nod, she's off to have both brought.

Once she's gone, I tell Tybalt, "You must watch what you say when Juliet is present."

"What harm can unchaste words do chaste ears?"

I know well how easily unchastity undoes the chaste, especially at such an age. But before I can answer, something in his own words draws Tybalt's attention. "What reply have you from Rosaline?"

Rosaline — when the bees teemed Santa Caterina's breast, I forgot about his message for her. But when I tell Tybalt what I witnessed, he waves off my terror.

"A harmless swarm, flown from a hive

that's grown overcrowded because I've not been to collect their comb and honey." He lectures as though I am a thick-witted child. So when he says, "I must gather them into a new hive, and bring the missive to my sister," I do not try to stop him. I'd not realized what risk there was to me in going out wrapped in his cloak, and mayhap he'd not known it either. But if it's danger for him to lurk about Verona, that's his own doing. I'll stay safe inside with Juliet, as I'm meant to be.

As I pass back the letter, he says, "The bees are nothing for you to fear. As for the Montecchi, I'll give them more than even for the hurt they've done to you."

I make no answer as I wait for him to go. And for Juliet to return with the sweetness of the figs, and the numbing flow of aqua vitae.

Lady Cappelletta'll not bear the sight of me, banishing me from the sala like a thief from the city. What offends her is my swollen nose, though it's the smash to the back of my skull and the boot-blows to my side that more trouble me. How am I to see my own hard-used face? But I cannot help but feel the thudding ache across my head and the groaning pain in my gut — and half a dozen times a day the flashing of that feverish heat, which I might've hoped the beating had knocked out of me.

Still, I have my truest comfort, for Juliet begs leave to tend me. And so we've the days, like our nights, to ourselves.

"How do you feel?" she asks me for the hundredth time.

Like I've had my head bashed in, my body bruised, and my nose broke. But instead I say, "Funny, how sharp my smelling sense has got. I can detect each fruit and flower in the arbor, the way a keen ear perceives the separate notes within a harmony."

"Can smells make a harmony?" she asks. "Is that not a lovely riddle?"

Juliet is lovely, yet no riddle. No convolution or dual meaning in her, still taking delight in such simple games as she and I conceive for ourselves. "Rosemary and roasted veal make a harmony."

"That is taste, not smell."

"Close your eyes," I tell her. "Can you not conjure both? How the sweet-sharp rosemary scents the roasting flesh, perfuming the air around the kitchen in the hours before you sit in the sala and taste how tender and succulent the meat."

The tip of her nose twitches as I talk, her pink tongue peeking from between her lips.

I press my tiniest finger to it. Her lids fly open, and she laughs. "Tell me another."

"No." I give her only a single heartbeat of disappointment before adding, "it's your turn to tell me."

"Minted lamb stew?" So tentative, until I nod. Assured of my approval, she catalogues a rush of toothsome dishes as would do the Pope's chef proud. "Pork and ginger pie. Piacentine cheese in fennel sauce. Partridge and pine-seed ravioli. Plum and cardamom tart." Wonder wrinkles her pretty brow. "Must it always be food?"

I bow my brow to hers and slowly tilt my head from one side to the other, as though I'm rolling out a delicate crust. How that simple touch soothes us both. "It may be whatever you wish."

Her eyes rove, landing upon the statue of San Zeno. "Incense and a woolen habit," she says.

"That's Rosaline's harmony, as sure as beeswax and the steel of a Toledo blade is Tybalt's."

"And what is mine?"

"When you were a newly born babe, you smelled like softest down, brazier-warmed swaddling bands, and my milk." No need to speak of what soiled the swaddling, which I was quick enough to clean. "Now you're a rose that's freshly bloomed, a dancer's flush when the tempo's fast, and a spice-and-honey comfit."

She purrs at the first part but frowns at the last. "No more food, Nurse. We agreed to it."

To believe I agree to whatever she demands — she's not so far off in that. "And would you not eat such a comfit, if I offered it?"

She grabs at my sleeves. "Have you been hiding comfits?"

As we make mock battle over imagined candies, heavy footfalls thud their way to the chamber door. Lord Cappelletto calls, "Is my Juliet within?"

"Why not enter," she answers with a laugh, "and find out?"

She's not noticed how the man who once barged in at any hour now stops, always, when he's without to ask if she's within. Or rather, if she's noticed, she's not reckoned why. Lord Cappelletto has no worry that he might open the door to an empty room. His concern is that opening it unannounced, he might see more of his daughter than a decent father deems right, now that the bodices of her gowns grow tight across her chest. Juliet is too pure-hearted to fathom the worry her tenderly budding body could work into Lord Cappelletto — or what else it might work into another man.

If he'll not gather her into his lap as he did in years past, still he's pleased to have her give each of his cheeks a kiss. "Nurse is nearly better," she tells him, "for I've given her good care."

He nods without so much as glancing my way. "Well that you're done with it. Prince Cansignorio gives permission for us to feast Rosaline this Sunday, thanks to a member of his household who made the plea for me." I'd expect resentment to tinge such words, for Lord Cappelletto likes to believe he speaks directly into the prince's ear and needs no one to intercede for him. But I hear something else instead. A glimmering of some hope Lord Cappelletto has for even greater alliance with the Scaligeri.

"You shall wear this for the dinner, and the dancing afterward." He slips an emerald ringed in gold upon her finger. The stone is as big as a cherry and as green as the first leaves in spring. "A jewel as lovely as my Jule."

"How heavy it is," she says.

"You do not think it too archaic, I hope."

She smiles reassurance at him. "An old style, but a pretty one. Was it my mother's?"

"No. It was —" He draws a short breath.

331

"It was Juliet's."

"Another lovely riddle, that a ring can always have been mine though I've never before seen it."

I'd not let out the answer to that riddle. Not let on what I think of how he means to spoil her by gifting her his dead wife's rings.

"The color will shine against my zetani sleeves." Juliet twists the ring one way, then the other, as though screwing some un-voiced doubt into its place. "Although the pale hue of my gown'll not show it nearly as well."

"Why not have a whole dress of the zet-ani, then?" Lord Cappelletto's no wiser than a fly, carried by carefree wings into the silken tangle of her carefully stretched web.

But I'm the one who'll be mope-eyed from working silken strands to finish a new dress by Sunday. "We've no time to sew a gown," I say.

"I can buy time," Lord Cappelletto says. "A dozen sempstresses' time, if Juliet re-quires it."

Juliet takes her eyes from the ring to beam at me. But she raises a hand to her own nose at the reminder of my bruised face. "May we make it a masked ball? I might be the summer sky, in an azure gown — and my lord father bedecked in gold could be the shining sun."

She means to find a way for me to hide my face so I might join the feast. And she knows to make best case with Lord Cappelletto by letting him believe she thinks only of what ought delight him.

"Have you forgot we fête to honor Rosaline's consecration of her vows?" he asks.

"Rosaline might mask herself as virtue," I say.

"Or a saint," suggests Juliet. "Would it not honor her order for her to dress as Santa Caterina?"

"No." I answer too fast, my chest prickling with the memory of the teeming bees. "Lord Cappelletto is right." I bow my head as though begging his pardon. "Rosaline must come only as her pious self, whatever mask and costume anyone else might wear."

To be told he is right is enough for Lord Cappelletto. He does not mark how Juliet and I've bested him into consenting to a masquerade, as he nods assent.

I suppose there is some convolution to Juliet after all, though I'm the only one who discerns it. And with that same discernment, I espy the swirl of carmine in the courtyard in the days that follow, as Paris visits Lord Cappelletto's study.

I say naught of it to Juliet. Not yet. Handsome as he is, a meet match for my girl, I savor our last however long it will be, when she and I alone share such a love, a heart, a bed as we've enjoyed these near to fourteen years.

The household boils over with servants, the loutish staff familiars lording themselves over the score who're hired on just for the days of frenzied preparations. Wine barrels are thumped up the stairs to edge the sala, plate burnished till it shines, unlighted torches positioned ready to be blazed. I've never gained a liking for the cook, who begrudges every bite I've eaten in all my years within Ca' Cappelletti, and it pleases me to hear how he bellows at all hours for some inept hireling or other to fetch obscure ingredients, his kitchen fires smoking long into the night.

Even Juliet grows burdened before the week is done. Eager though she is to feel the swish of the zetani as it drips in long folds to the floor, she struggles through the hours spent holding herself statue-still as the city's finest sempstresses huddle close around her, their hurried needles flashing.

I sit nearby, my back to them to keep my bruised face hidden as I work my own needle, securing jeweled birds and enameled stars and every sky-born wonder onto the headdress that will crown Juliet come Sunday night. Lady Cappelletta twins my task, adorning the ocean-green samite that will be her headdress with mermaids and dolphins and mysterious creatures of the sea. Her gown is of the same fabric, the thick gold ribboned into the cloth shimmering like sunlight beaming upon watery waves. It's the dress she wore to Prince Cansignorio's wedding banquet more than a decade past, seamed narrower now than it was then, when her belly swelled with one of her many ill-fated pregnancies.

The dress cost so dear, I'd have thought it'd have to be the Pope's wedding banquet before Lord Cappelletto let her don it again. But for this feast he spares nothing, showing off every connection he can to the Scaligeri. Flower-entwined ladders to match their crest are set against the courtyard walls, the banqueting table festooned with marzipanned dogs like those on the Scaligeri livery, each wearing a Cappelletti cap of jellied quince. The morning before the fête, he rouses Lady Cappelletta from their broad bed before the terce bells ring, insisting she accompany him to Mass at Santa Maria Antica so they can see the Holy Sacrament raised up by the Scaligeri's priest's own hand.

He'd have Juliet along as well, but if Paris is what I suppose, there'll be time enough in years to come for her to kneel and open her mouth for regal communion. I bid her feign the heavy breath of sleep while I plead for Lord Cappelletto to let her lie in bed a while longer. "She's overworn from standing so many hours," I say. "She must rest, to look her best tonight."

This brings an indulgent nod from Lord Cappelletto, and an envious glare from Lady Cappelletta, who must wish she'd been as clever in making the case to stay a-bed herself.

But once they're gone, Juliet'll not fall again to slumber, nor let me. "How can you sleep on such a day as this promises to be?"

"Like this," I say, closing my eyes and gaping my mouth. I throw a clumsy arm atop her and make great mocking snores.

She laughs but wriggles free, waving aside my urging for another hour's doze. "Do you not recall what it is to be young, and eager for a ball to start?"

"We had no balls when I was young."

She gives one of my grayed locks a gentle tug. "Were you born in days so ancient, they'd not yet invented feasting, and dancing, and masquerades?"

"There were feasts and dances and masquerades, but not for those so poor as I was."

"Honey nurse." Her voice is thick with pity. As though to not don a fine gown was the worst suffering there was to my girlhood. "What did you have instead?"

I've always been careful not to speak to her of men like my father. What does such a pretty, petted child need know of cruelty? Instead I spin a tale of my first spring with Pietro. He still carried his hunter's bow, and we wandered together by day, and by night slept beneath the open sky. What more music did we need than his voice joining mine in song, what dancing beyond the hot rhythm of his hips against my own?

"But did you not want for company?" she asks.

"If I did, I'd fashion tiny cups of acorn caps and hazelnuts, and we'd have marmot, squirrel, and black-grouse to dine."

"Did you, truly?" The hints of woman in her melt away into a girl's delight. As though she's still of such an age to believe in enchanted beasts.

I lay a solemn hand to my heart. "Pietro and I had marmot, and squirrel, and black-grouse, and we dined." When I drop my hand and smile, she sees the joke, and we laugh at how easily I've pranked her. But before the girlish part of her fades away again, I ask, "What do you remember, of Pietro?"

"I remember a room, where I would play upon the floor. There was a man there, taller than my father, who always kept a sack of sweets. He'd come here, too. You were happy when he was here, but he was happier when you were there. How do I know that, who was happy where, when it all seems more like a dream than some true thing? If I try to conjure the man's face, it's only Friar Lorenzo's features that I see."

"Your memory plays tricks on you. Often we'd visit them both in a single day, but there's not much of Pietro in Friar Lorenzo." Yet much of him in you.

I dare not tell her that. Not yet. Such privity it would be, and thus better kept until her future is secured, and neither she nor I must rely upon the Cappelletti.

"Sometimes what I think I remember of Pietro seems only what I've heard told by you, or Tybalt." The name douses me like a hard rain, and she marks it. "Are you still cross with my cousin?"

Tybalt's held himself from us all week, haunting the world beyond the Cappelletti walls. By my troth, though it's been hard on her, I've not minded. He makes the injury done me solely what serves him — as though my bruised body is measured only by the insult to his honor. I know it's what he's learned during all the years he's listened to Lord Cappelletto cataloguing ancient slights. But there's deeper hurt in Tybalt treating me so than came from all the blows and kicks the brawlers gave me.

Perhaps I've been too soft with him these long years, believing the mother-love for my lost sons might find and fill in him the longing for his own lost mother. But all that soft has made him hard, and harsh, and ever more hot-headed. What love he's got from me and Juliet, and even Lady Cappelletta, has kept him from seeking what young men ought: the kind of love that might quell raging youth into courting, and settling to marriage.

"He's like a horse too long unbroke," I say, "that now'll not be bridled, and would throw off any who try to ride him." My pun's too bawdy for Juliet to ken it, so I offer a more sober answer. "I'm cross with how Tybalt crosses —"

Bloodthirsty shouts cut me off. The sound of metal clashing metal echoes along the Via Cappello.

"Bend your knee, and clasp your hands." I nod toward the Madonna as the alarm is rung. "Pray to the Holy Mother to keep the parish safe."

My own knees bend, though only enough to carry me from the bedchamber into the sala. The common servants have already shucked their labors and got their heads stuck out the windows to get the better view. As I jostle my way among them, calls for clubs, hook-bladed bills, and spears rise from the street. A crowd is gathering below, accursing first against the Cappelletti, then at the Montecchi, for sparking the violence. On either side of me, servants cheer and jeer by turns, as though donning Cappelletti livery has made them take their master's fight as their very own.

Blasts sound from unseen trumpets. Where the Via Cappello broadens into the Piazza delle Erbe, there's a flash of carmine. The crash of fighting ceases, and Prince Cansignorio's voice reverberates against the buildings, though by the time his words reach Ca' Cappelletti, they're too obscured for us to understand.

"Nurse? Are we safe?" Juliet has crept unseen into the sala. When turn from the window to answer her, the servants surrounding me turn too, elbowing each other

340

and whispering at the sight of Juliet still in her nightdress, no cap on her head and her hair yet held in plaits.

"We are as we were," I say. "Safe within the walls of Ca' Cappelletti."

"And my lord father, and my —"

"Safer still, within church walls." I hie to answer, to hide the truth: the fighting may well have caught Lord and Lady Cappelletti as they passed through the Piazza delle Erbe. Would Lord Cappelletto call for a long-sword to join the fray? Or tremble and cower behind his wife? Either way, surely he and she remain unharmed. Whatever sparked was fast extinguished, and the alarm that tolled was not followed by any death knells. I take Juliet's hand. "Come, we've much to do before tonight."

I guide her back into our chamber, where we braid my hair and unbraid hers, arranging mine as I always have, and hers to hold new fullness around her face. "Is it not dull, to ever wear your hair the same way?" she asks, tying a length of morello velvet to the tails of the two long braids that hang upon my back.

"Saints, widows, and happily wedded matrons all plait their hair," I say, though at nearly thirty Lady Cappelletta still wears her hair as a well-born maiden does, most locks loose, strung through with pearls and precious beads. That's her vanity, and her husband's, too. Although she's not as just-plucked fresh as when I first came, still there are few faces so fair in all Verona, an artly work kept framed by flowing tresses and the jeweled Cappelletti cap. As though beauty might be mistook for happiness. "When you're wived to a worthy man, you'll want no more fashion than to keep him faithful."

"Wived?" She pulls at my shoulder, turning me to face that face so like the one to which I was once wived.

"To a worthy man," I repeat. "Like Pietro." My heart quickens. For all the times I've spoke of my lost husband to her, I've never till now breathed to her the thought of the husband who'll be hers.

Her heart must ever match my own, for it raises a flush into her cheeks. "And where would I find such a worthy man? Shall I climb mountains and ford rivers and seek out unknown kingdoms, as would-be lovers do?"

"I've sung you too many fanciful troubadour songs, if you believe that's what real lovers do." What can I say, to ready her for what I suppose Paris will propose? For ready she must be to answer right, and too undesigning is she to imagine it herself. And yet, dare I speak of him, if I do not know his heart? But then, what heart would not want Juliet?

I'll not speak the name, and raise her hopes, before he plights his troth. I draw her hand in mine, tracing my pinkie along her palm like some sooth-telling Egyptian. "There is one nobly born, pleasing of features and true of heart, who'll see in you, and be to you, such spouse as any would be glad to get."

She giggles, flushing deeper. "You tickle me."

"And yet you've not drawn your hand away." I kiss her palm, fold her fingers to hold the kiss in place, and lay that hand between my breasts. "You've had my heart for your whole life, and soon, I promise, you'll have another. Do not forget mine, when you find his."

"I'll not. I cannot." She flutters open her fist, her fingers trembling as she presses the kissed palm against me. "Will you not come with me, when I am married?" She bows her head, unsure. "If such a thing really is to be."

"It is to be, though whether in this season or in one to come, I cannot say. You're too sweet a fruit to go unpicked." I give her cheek a gentle pinch. "And near enough to being ripe, you must be ready for it. But worry not, I'll go with you. Always and wherever." My talk of fruit sets my stomach grumbling. "We ought eat now."

"Eat now? When there's such a feast to be served in a few hours?"

This is how artless my girl is, that she would think she might eat her fill while she sits before the honored company, rather than pushing her portion around her plate without lifting a bite, to show herself dainty. I am a woman of many appetites and never connived like that myself, denying one fleshly pleasure in the hopes of garnering another. But I've watched Lady Cappelletta and the Cappelletti's noblish guests long enough to know what's expected at a so-called feast. "There's still much I must teach you," I tell Juliet, and bid her call the serving-maid to fetch from the cook a sampling so we can taste now what she'll not swallow later.

THIRTEEN

"Nurse. Nurse."

The urgent cry wakes me confused. In my dream, nurse I did. I was a six-teated creature, and each fed a mouth of ferocious hunger. An agony of pleasure, to feel those tugs upon my willing dugs. Until a seventh mouth opened onto me. Finding no nipple, it sucked against my very flesh. Sucked more than milk, for milk gives life, and this took life from me until I'd nothing left to give the other six, nothing left even to save myself. The pleasure turned to searing pain. A burn upon my skin that blazed to roast the very heart of me.

"Nurse." Lady Cappelletta is as insistent as whatever tormented my sleep. As I rise to go to her, the twinned faces of comedy and tragedy fall from my lap to the floor. It's the mask Juliet and I made to hide my marred face at the masquerade. I'd bade her find a stick we might attach to it, so I could fan it

back and forth when the sudden heat flushes over me. She went, and I waited, and in the afternoon's great warmth I dozed just long enough to dream. And to wake to this shrieking.

I hurry from our chamber through the sala and the antecamera to Lady Cappelletta, who greets me with, "Where's my daughter? Call her forth to me."

She might well have called Juliet herself, as summoned me to summon her. But Lady Cappelletta likes having someone to do what she wills.

I trudge out, calling, "Juliet, my lamb, I bid you come." But my dear lamb is like a ladybird, flitting about. My talk of courtship has given wing to her heart, and sent her fluttering to some corner of Ca' Cappelletti. "Juliet? Juliet?"

By my lost maidenhead, I grow red repeating her name until, simple as you please, she steps out from behind the heavy curtain that hangs across the entry to Tybalt's rooms. "How now? Who calls?"

"Your mother," I say. As if in this moment when she stands celestial in that zeitani, Juliet might hear me claim her as my own. But remembering the impatience in Lady Cappelletta's voice, I shake the thought from my head and follow wordless as Juliet presents herself in the antecamera to the Cappelletti's bedchamber. "Madam, I am here. What is your will?"

Lady Cappelletta smiles. Not approvingly, as loving mothers do, but disapprovingly. One of Juliet's sleeves has come loose. Her coral necklace is askew. There is a golden blush of pollen midway down her skirt. Lady Cappelletta takes silent stock of all these flaws.

I step between them. With a single swift motion, I hitch sleeve, straighten necklace, and sweep skirt clean.

Lady Cappelletta frowns at my now-yellowed hand, frowns deeper when the emerald upon Juliet's finger catches her eye. "Nurse, give leave awhile. We must talk in secret."

Secret shoots a jolt through me. What secret can she have to share if not the one I've guessed already, which Lord Cappelletto must have bade her convey to Juliet?

I ought to turn and go. Let Lady Cappelletta tell what I anticipated. I'll hear it soon enough. Juliet holds no secrets from her beloved bedmate. But it will be a long night, a lot of wine. Many guests, and jests. Hours of dancing, though I've too many corns upon my feet to join in. The house will be so thick with merriment, there'll be no time between now and dawn for me to draw Juliet aside, draw out from her what Lady Cappelletta means to share in confidence. If I'm to be of use to my girl on this auspicious night, I must know now.

I wait in the doorway like a flipped card hanging in the air before it chooses which way to flutter and fall, while Juliet pouts at Lady Cappelletta.

Lady Cappelletta'll not suffer anyone's pouting but her own. She looks as if she might order me to close Juliet up in our chamber for trying her. But she'll not. Not with the evening's esteemed guests nearly to the door, where they'll expect to find Lord Cappelletto's family turned out to welcome them.

She waves her thin wrist as though she's just remembered something. Which perhaps she has: remembered that if I'm gone and she says something that fills Juliet with grief or fear or overjoyed exuberance, she'd have to be the one to soothe her. And Lady Cappelletta is too well-primped, too eager to make her own way to the sala, to risk that. "Nurse, come back and hear our counsel."

All ears I am to hear it, but still she pretends there's some reason of her own she's kept me here. "You know my daughter's of a pretty age," she says. A pretty way for her to put it, when I know Juliet's age to the hour. By my few remaining teeth, I know it better than I know my own. "She's not fourteen."

"She's not fourteen," I say, as though Lady Cappelletta has not just said it. But I say it looking at Juliet, while Lady Cappelletta spoke looking at her own reflection in the well-polished silver tray that hangs upon the wall. As if to be assured she's not long past such years herself. "How long is it now to Lammastide?" I ask, though Juliet and I both know. We count the days each night, before we fall to sleep.

"A fortnight and odd days." Lady Cappelletta does not keep the same exacting tally as we do.

"Even or odd, of all days in the year, come Lammas Eve at night, she'll be fourteen." To the day, to the hour, I know it. Those days and hours that I'll not forget. They make me tell what once was my dearest truth, which I hold even dearer now that I know it for a lie. "Susanna and she — God rest all Christian souls — were of an age. Susanna is with God. She was too good for me." As though Juliet is not too good for Lady Cappelletta.

"Eleven years it is," I say, "since the ground quaked, the day that she was

349

weaned." As if the earth rended itself out of grief at seeing Juliet put off my breast. "She could run and waddle all about, and fell, and broke her brow."

Juliet has ever loved to hear my stories of when she was her littlest, so I tell the tale of that day. I do bear a brain for memories, and a tongue as well that loves to speak, and on I prate until Lady Cappelletta stamps a foot and says, "Enough of this. I pray you, hold your peace."

What I hold is not my peace but a pretty piece of Juliet's past, and I'm so keen to share it, I tell yet more of when she was a toddling thing, a falling girl, and Pietro saged how she one day would be a woman and fall as women do, for a man.

This brings a flush to Juliet, turning her face bright against the azure of her gown, like the reddened sun dawning into fresh sky. When I talked to her this morning of falling for a man, she hung eager on each word. But that was done between the two of us. Now, before Lady Cappelletta, she waves my words away. Dark eyes pleading above those blushing cheeks, she says, "Stint, I pray you, Nurse."

Pray I do, with all my soul. "God mark you to His grace, you were the prettiest babe that ever I nursed," I say, adding with great care to catch Lady Cappelletta's ear, "If I might live to see you married once, I have my wish."

My wish, and my felicity. We'll make a handsome household with Count Paris. And soon enough there'll be babes of my dear babe that, if I cannot suckle, I can at least succor, and raise. A lasting part of my Pietro, and a joy of my old age.

"Marry," says Lady Cappelletta, taking to my hint like a shad swimming for some worm wriggled on a hook, "is the very theme I care to talk of. Tell me, daughter Juliet, how stands your disposition to be married?"

She only calls Juliet *daughter* when there is some especial reason playing mother suits her, some praise or prize to seize herself. But Juliet slides her eyes to me and watches for my careful nod before she answers. "It is an honor that I dream not of."

True enough. Too giddy a girl to sleep this day, and why should she save only for a dream what I've told her will be waking true? "An honor," I repeat, with a wink to her. "Were I not your only nurse, I'd say you'd sucked wisdom from the teat."

Lady Cappelletta smooths the seagreen samite over her own never-tasted breasts, reminds us how often ladies of esteem younger than Juliet are already made mothers. Recalls that she herself was delivered of a babe when she was not much older. And for once says the very words I hope to hear. "The valiant Paris seeks you for his love."

"A man, young lady." This is what I say? At such a moment, to sound such a thick-witted fool. But why not be a joyous fool, to know my Juliet'll have so fine a match? Count Paris may not carry the spice-and-honey scent of my Pietro, but surely he can be something near to what my bee-sotted husband harvested. "Lady, such a man as all the world. Why, he's a man of wax."

My wax Lady Cappelletta must immediately outdo. "Verona's summer has not such a flower," she says.

A flower handsomer by far than the old shrub to which she's wed. Mayhap that is her part in this, for I'd not expect her to delight in being made a grandame, and have all Verona reminded she's no longer any summer flower herself. But to gather such a flower to her by marrying Juliet to him —

"Nay, he's a flower," I say, to pluck what's budding from Lady Cappelletta. "In faith, a very flower." I rub one pollened hand against the other, and think of all that the bees take from such lovely flowers, to make the delicious drip of honey that Juliet so loves.

But Lady Cappelletta is done with flowery talk, and makes a bookish speech to Juliet, about pens and lines and what is writ along the margins of some dull tome or other. Books? Who cares what lays between the covers of a book? What matters is what lays between the covers of a bed. To remind them both of this, I place a loving hand upon Juliet's taut belly, as if to warm her womb to what it will receive, and say, "Women grow by men."

I might add that first men grow by women, for it's time Juliet was taught how to play a pricksong so more than music swells. But better to save such talk for when we are far from Lady Cappelletta, who has no ear, no taste, for bedroom harmonies. My Juliet shall learn from me the lessons that I learned laying with Pietro, and know what pleasures a warm-humored wife can take, and give, within a marriage bed.

Footsteps sound from the compound's entryway — not just the scuttering of servants but the first of the guests already arrived. "Speak briefly," Lady Cappelletta says, "can you like of Paris's love?"

Now her eyes, like mine, are on Juliet. I cannot say what Lady Cappelletta sees, but

I see in this one moment all Juliet's life.
And all of mine. I see summation of all my
joy, comfort for all my sorrows. I remember
what it was to be such a creature, and have
that ram of a Pietro come tupping upon me.
I want such years of pleasure for her. But I
see too that she is still a tender lambkin,
not sure even how to answer without first
taking private counsel with me.

"I'll look to like, if looking liking move."
She pauses, choosing her words with care.
"But no more deep will I endart my eye,
than your consent gives strength to make it
fly."

A clever rhyme, and I reward it with
another wink, to show she's a good girl for
saying it so. Let Lady Cappelletta believe
it's her consent, and her lord husband's, Juliet speaks of. My girl and I both know what
we together can make fly.

But what flies now is one of the newly
hired serving-men. He's not been here a
week, but already he's as indolent and
insolent as any who've ever served within
Ca' Cappelletti. Rushing in, he treads hard
upon my foot before making a bootlicker's
bow to Lady Cappelletta. "Madam, the
guests are come, supper served up, you
called, my young lady asked for." He slides
his slithery eyes over Juliet. I'd have him

out for that, but, catching my glare, he adds, "The nurse cursed in the pantry, and every thing in extremity."

Cursed — hearing that, I might name an extremity into which I'd put, if not every-thing, at least the serving-man and pantry-maid and any others who dare try tell me what's my place. I've seen dozens like this one come and go in the nearly fourteen years I've been here. I'll outlast him and his impertinence. Or if I'll not, it'll only be because I'll go with Juliet when she's wed to Count Paris and become mistress of her own house.

"I must hence to wait," the servant says, as though he means to wait table, when by my holidame, I suspect what the wastrel waits is only a chance to pinch some cups, and some choice meats, and the pantry-maid as well. "I beseech you follow straight."

"We'll follow." Lady Cappelletta barely gives curt nod to dismiss him, before shoot-ing one last judging squint at my dear girl. "Juliet, the count awaits."

As soon as Lady Cappelletta passes out of the room, I grab Juliet about the waist and swing her round. Nose to nose, like a mama cat admiring her kitten's whiskers, I say, "Go, girl, seek happy nights to happy days."

■ ■ ■ ■

The cook's plucked a half dozen peacocks, stuffed them with fried oysters and spiced oranges, roasted all in belly lard, laid each upon a silver platter, and arranged the feathers back upon them. When they're served, the forty guests who've come to dine stamp their feet in delight. Iridescent feathers shimmer as knives thrust and carve the birds.

All through the sala, young men make great show of sucking meat from quills and offering them as adornment to the loveliest ladies. Tybalt did as much for me, years past. A pretty bit of flattery to an old woman. But tonight he sits somber beside the sister whose features are so like his own, except that while his are edged with truculence, hers sit prim enough they might still every wavering feather. Rosaline wears a dun-colored habit, the crucifix about her neck as big as an assassin's dagger. Though Lord Cappelletto and the other revelers raise goblet after goblet to drink her health, not a sip passes her pure lips.

I might pity the poor girl, who'll never know the delights Juliet is to find in Paris's bed. But what Rosaline cannot know, she'll not miss. She bows her head and crosses herself, over and over through the dinner, shocked at the company's indulgences. The goodly nun eats only lettuce dressed with lemon, followed by a handful of fresh grapes. Nibbling like a rabbit among hounds until she can bear no more, when she leans and whispers to Tybalt, who rises and leads her from the room.

The rest of the company makes up for her restraint. Having had our fill of peacock, we're served the flakiest of focaccia, the pastry filled with egg-basted turtledove. Next comes fig-peckers braised with four kinds of olives, then pheasants covered with fried squid, followed by veal mortadella simmered in fava beans and mint. Lord Cappelletto flouts the sumptuary law, keeping keen eye to make sure the trencher nearest Prince Cansignorio's nephew is always the first filled.

Though Juliet sits across from Count Paris, she does not raise her gaze to his, the shyness natural to her age ripening to coyness by my morning's tutelage. She tilts her head to mine, feeding me from her trencher with her own hand, like I'm her pet. Hiding my bruises behind my broad palm, I eat all that she demurs, waving off only the boar's head covered in pomegranate. Too toothless at my age to burst the rosy seeds and taste the succulence inside, I've Juliet to savor what I no longer can. I bid her nibble upon those pretty seeds as we gossip like old women and giggle like young girls, ahum with our wooing news.

When the rose water is brought in finger bowls, I fuss over Juliet, carefully turning my own ill-used face from the company while I dab at her mouth and work the silver-and-ivory pick I wear about my neck to clean her teeth. She's too grown to need such tending, but it occupies me while the lesser servants clear away the plate and push aside the tables. The diners don their masks, and I raise mine. More guests arrive already in their costumes. Lord Cappelletto drones a pompous speech about the days when he wore a merrymaker's visor, though his bulbous nose is so frightfully large it's impossible to imagine the mask that could've covered such a thing. "Thirty years, since I last danced," he says, raising an uncertain eyebrow to some other shrivelled codger, "or only some five-and-twenty?"

Who cares which it was, I wish to say, impatient for him to give lute and pipe leave to play so Juliet may prance to her finer future.

Wax or flower, whichever Paris is, he shades easily among the masked revelers. Not so his cousin Mercutio, for not by his face alone has that debaucher made himself known around Verona. Mercutio wears his doublet so short, it shows every whorl and flourish upon his gilded codpiece. He's a nearer relation to the prince than Paris is, which may prove perilous. Rumors swirl through the city of how Cansignorio plots to have his bastard sons rule after him, and all Verona knows how Cansignorio disposes of relations he deems rivals. Although it's hard to imagine lascivious Mercutio taking any interest in the throne — unless perhaps there were a shapely maiden or two seated stark-naked upon it.

The summer night grows dark, and the house is thick with torchsmoke. I try to keep sight of Juliet among the dancers, but the rings and chains move quick, and my old eyes weary with peering through my mask-holes. Searching for a place to sit, I spy Tybalt at the edge of the hall, sliding his sword in and out of its scabbard.

"Freshly stained?" I ask, nodding at his blade.

"I drew during this morning's fray, but had no time to drive my hate home before the prince's guard came calling peace."

Disappointment smolders along his face, as it did when he was but a boy, longing for his far-off father's company.

"Did I not tell you I'd no desire for your vengeance?"

"I heed you, Nurse, as I try to heed my uncle. But neither you nor he can dissuade me, when it's my sister I defend."

"Rosaline?" What sort of brute would attack a nun? "Was she —" I search for the word, imagining the folds of her habit hiding such bruises as I bear. "Is Rosaline unwell?"

"She is well." The words bring no softening to what pinches hard in him. "Too well, too fair, too wise, wisely too fair. She's caught the eye of a certain cursèd rakehell who woos and woos, and will not hear her *no.*"

This must have been what he wrote so secretly of in his letter, why he was so impatient for her reply. The wall around the vineyard of Santa Caterina is low enough for a lusty man to climb. And many a girl or woman who's shut up in a convent for want of a proper dowry would be glad for a clandestine suitor. But not pious Rosaline. She'd not be hit by Cupid's own enchanted arrow.

"What harm can unchaste words do chaste

ears?" I repeat what fell from Tybalt's own mouth, in hope it'll cool his too easy temper.

But Tybalt's like an iron held so long in the fire it glows of its own accord. "The scoundrel haunts the convent. Offers gold enough to seduce a saint, in hopes Rosaline'll ope her lap to him. To know some fiend plots to use my sister so —"

"Is only to know what moves a man." Pietro, I miss you now anew, for surely you might better speak to Tybalt of what I know he needs. Might bend his ear with more merry tales than Lord Cappelletto's droning on of family honor. Might convince him to seek a more pleasurable thrusting than what men do with swords. "It's time you thought of such pursuits yourself. Not to cast your eyes upon one pledged to chastity, but to set your heart on some hartless hind." I conjure all the love I've ever felt for Tybalt. "You've an affectionate nature. Why not make an honorable suit, and take a bride?"

"It's not for me to take, but to be given. My uncle will arrange a wife for his heir such as suits him, when he deems the time is right. I'll have naught to say about it, except to mutter the church vows when I'm told I must. What joy is there in that?"

I search across the sala, hoping to catch

sight of Paris empalmed with Juliet. Though the dancers are a blur, my own palm quakes with the thrill of imagining their hands joined. "Lord Cappelletto can arrange a winsome match," I say. "If you but speak to him —"

"I've tried to speak my part, endeavoring to tell him that this villain who would seduce my sister has dared come here enmasked to find her. And am told, *be patient,* and *take no note of him,* and *he shall be endured.* Am told I must keep the peace within Ca' Cappelletti, even with one not worthy to be granted it." He draws sword and strikes, his well-handled blade slicing a single blood-red thread from a nearby tapestry. "I'm the one who's always told to guard our honor, yet when I try am called by my own uncle a *goodman boy,* a *saucy boy,* and a *princox.*"

"Your uncle says many things that would better go unuttered, and are best unheeded." I stoop and pluck up the silken strand, looping it to form a bright bud I nestle between my breasts. But I cannot raise even the smallest smile from Tybalt. "You are a good man, and no boy. Saucy at times, but who does not prefer a sauced meat to a dry one? As proud a cock as any prince, but no princox."

Nothing I say soothes what rages in his eyes, or loosens the tight grasp on his hilt. Hoping wine will do what words will not, I go to find him a full goblet, and myself one as well. But before I can make my way back to him, I hear, *"Nurse, Nurse,"* shrilled in that voice I'm suffered to obey. I empty both goblets in swift gulps, stash them on a window's sill, and turn to present myself to Lady Cappelletta.

I'm flushed with the wine, but she's flushed with something else, the samite pulling low upon her bosom as she leans close to Paris. "Nurse, I crave —" Paris arches an eyebrow at the word, which makes her flush more — "a word, I crave a word with Juliet. Fetch her here."

Fetch, like I'm a hound and Juliet some slobbered-upon bone. But I nod and curtsy. Let Paris see Lady Cappelletta for what she is, and see me as a worthy part of Juliet's dowry. Juliet, who I find not among the dancers but, after seeking everywhere, discover in an alcove speaking to one of the masked guests, a thin and tallish fellow. "Pilgrim," I hear, and "prayer," and "book." Can my Juliet be so simple-hearted, wasting an evening's revels in such dull talk? Duller even than what Lady Cappelletta might have to say.

"Madam." I speak boldly, for surely Juliet'll be glad to be called away from such as this. "Your mother craves a word with you."

Hearing me, and realizing she's been overheard, Juliet flitters like a pale moth and is gone.

"What is her mother?" the fellow asks, his callow voice an odd match to his well-jeweled mask.

What is her mother? I might count all heaven's stars before I could count the ways I can answer that. "Marry, bachelor," I say. If he's a clever man, he'll know what I say next is as untrue as a married bachelor would be. "Her mother is the lady of the house, and a good lady, and a wise and virtuous one."

Though he's not so handsome above as Paris, nor so well-formed below as Mercutio, still he has a boyish pretty mouth below his mask, and a pair of shapely arms. I press myself close upon those arms and say, "I nursed her that you talked withal." And nursed enough wine tonight to take this stranger into my confidence. "I tell you, he that can lay hold of her shall have the chinks." Chinks of the precious dowry coins Lord Cappelletto will gift Paris, whole cassoni of which could be worth no more than her treasured maidenhead. With that bit of bawd, off I go after Juliet.

But the wine pounds in my head more steadily than my feet pound upon the floor. I'm whirled this way and that among the press of people, until Lord Cappelletto orders the musicians done and the stairway torches lit. I find my lambkin standing to the side, watching the departing guests. She pulls me near to ask who this one is, and that, just as she's done since she was a girl of six, wide-eyed at all the finery worn to a fête.

When she points to the pretty-mouthed one, I tell her I know not his name. My knowing not is not enough, and off she sends me to find out. But this guest I ask does not know, and neither does that. And so I go on inquiring, until I feel a grope upon my rump, and turning quick collide into Mercutio, who laughs and tells me the pretty-mouthed youth is called Romeo.

The name means naught to me. "What Romeo?"

"Romeo Montecche."

Such a rascal is this Mercutio, to prank me with false words. I parry back, "What man is mad enough to bring a Montecche here?"

Mercutio roars open-mouthed, and says

he is the man, and if a saucy maid will call him mad, she'll get what she deserves. With that he swats my bottom, sending me stumbling. When I right myself I keep on my way until I'm back beside Juliet.

"His name is Romeo, and a Montecche." All Lord Cappelletto's bitter railing about the ill-blood between their families ought to make the name Montecche familiar to her. But her startled eyes fill with such confusion, I add, "son of your great enemy." I take care to whisper, for if Tybalt hears a Montecche's here, and him already in such angry spirits —

But when I look about for Tybalt, he's nowhere in the room. How long is it since I had sight of him? He might be lying in wait outside for the would-be seducer. If he sees instead a Montecche passing from his uncle's house, Tybalt'll follow him into some dark corner of the city to lay sword to him. Or not to him, but them, for Romeo leaves with Mercutio and half a dozen of the other maskers. Tybalt is hot enough to try them all. Which worries me so much I only half hear Juliet reciting some verse twining hate and late, and love and enmity.

I cup a hand to my ear. "What's this? What's this?"

Even in this near-extinguished light, I feel

the warmth of her blush as she answers. "A rhyme I learned of one I danced withal."

A pretty bit of poesy from Paris, it must be. I'm impatient to have her tell it to me, that I might know what count to take of the count who courts her. But before I can bid her repeat it, Lord Cappelletto calls, "Juliet."

"Anon, anon," I answer, for I'll not make her face him alone.

We find him misty-eyed and musty-breathed, speaking of fathers and daughters and the honor it will be to unite his house with the Scaligeri. Hearing him, Juliet goes green as a spinached egg. Only my quick catch keeps her from fainting to the floor. "It's late," I say, "and the torches make for close air on such a hot night." With no more by-your-leave than that, I steer my girl away to our bedchamber.

"What've you had to drink?" I ask, when we're shut up alone.

"Naught but water. Like Rosaline."

Naught to drink, nor to eat. Weak she must be. I take my leave and hie to the kitchen, snatch from the voracious serving-man the most delicate remaining morsels, and tuck a vessel near-full of wine beneath my arm. Laden, I return to find the chamber door pulled fast to me. I call once, twice, and a third time, worrying that she's fainted. But, ear to the door, I'd swear I hear her speak, answered by a second voice sounding farther off. Tybalt, perhaps, climbed up to her window as he did so many times in childhood. Could he have found a heart for such frolicking tonight? If any could call him to it, it would be Juliet. Her bounty is as boundless as the sea, her love as deep —

Paris's wooing must be catching, for my thoughts to weave into such lovers' verse. "Juliet," I call once more, arms aching from all I carry.

The door flies open. Juliet's no longer the pale moth, nor the Florentine's greened egg. She's pinked, and pleased, and pulls me inside, and shuts the door behind me, and waves away all I've brought. Steals a look toward the moon-lighted window and asks, "Nurse, what hour is it?"

The answer throbs from my sore head to my swelled feet, paining every part in between. "So late of night, it's better called early on the morrow."

She fills a silver goblet with rubied wine, and passes it to me. "Will it be long till the hour of nine?"

I mark the pearly tooth she works into her lip, and know there's more tolling than the city's bells. Perhaps it was another man's voice I heard without, a more smitten heart than Tybalt's calling as she stood in the window as shining fair as the East's own sun. "The lauds are already rung. Next will be the prime, and after those the terce, that ring the hour of nine. Are you so well wooed, and your heart so fully won, that you forget such simple things?"

The question makes her laugh, and cry, and throw her arms around me. So furiously am I hugged, the goblet drops, splashing wine across us both. My morello hides it well enough, but the beautiful zetani's ruined.

I tut at her. "Lovestruck though he is, if he saw you now —"

I only mean to tease, but Juliet digs sharp nails into me. "What do you mean? Will he not be true, when he sees me for what I am?"

"What you are is good and goodness." I rock her in my arms, like I did when she was but a babe. "Have no worries, you've won his whole heart. If it's already early on the morrow, then by my saints, this will be the day that you are trothed to Paris."

"Paris?" The name falls like a curse from her mouth.

"Juliet, did he not please you? You dance, and trade rhymes, and hurry night into morning so you may see him anon." I meant to teach her art enough to earn a noble match. But not so much as to tease and toy, and risk losing what any girl ought be glad to get. "His love's declared, so you may trust it. If you care for him, be plain about it. Elsewise, you are unfair to Paris."

"Would that I were unfair to Paris. What do I care if he finds me fair?"

I catch her chin in my hand, look close into her eyes. It's not a flirt's pretty pout that pulls at her features. Rubbing my broad thumb along her soft cheek, I stop a tear. "So you do not love?"

"Love? Of course I love. Has my heart not rushed along with yours, each time you repeated how you felt when first you saw Pietro? All these years I believed I swelled with the very flush you did, just to hear it told. Until tonight, when at last I felt such love myself, and knew it a thousand times more wonderful than even your words could tell it." She lays her head upon my neck. All the slim of her nuzzles against the girth of me, and her heart sounds as quick within my chest as it does her own. "I do love, dear Nurse. But this love I have is not for Paris."

"Then for who?"

She lifts her head and turns half away. "What is *who*? Who am I, or you, or any of us, when love makes changelings of us?" She closes her eyes and I swear by the Madonna, she is more beautiful than I've ever seen her, standing bathed in moonlight. "What if I were not a Cappelletta? Would I still be who I am?"

"Yes." The word forms like a holy prayer upon my lips. Or more, for it is my dearest prayer answered. I search that moonlit face. Does Juliet sense at last what all these years I've held from her? "You'll always be a precious jewel, even if you're no Juliet Cappelletta."

"And what if I were the very opposite of the Cappelletti?"

"The very opposite of what they are, is the very thing Pietro and I ever were." The words that always seemed impossible to speak now melt easily from me. "Poor we were, without a name or fortune. But we loved, and were happy, and made in our happy love —"

"What if I were a Montecche?"

Her words are like a needle drawn too hard. They bunch my brow. They make no sense to me. "But you were not born to the house of Montecchi."

Some strange sentiment tremors across her. "Not born," she says, "but what if I were wed to it?"

Is there a heart that knows a heart better than a mother knows her child? For I see now what was right before my nose some hour past. "Romeo, the one you spoke withal — is he this love?"

"Romeo." She sighs to say his name. "No rose could be more sweet. No man more meet." Tears shine in her eyes, and something more shines upon her lips. "I do love, and Romeo is the one I love, and Romeo loves me."

The hard stone floor seems to shift, the very earth sliding from beneath me. Paris — such a match would he be for my girl. I could not conjure more kind, more handsome, more well-placed than he. And this Romeo, some near relation to the very Montecche who punched and kicked at me, believing I was Tybalt. Which could I possibly want for Juliet?

But when she buries herself against me and asks, "Why must I always hate where I'm told the Cappelletti hate, and love only where they bid me love?" I will my legs strong, that I may bear the sliding and the shifting. Glad as I am the Cappelletti's ancient quarrels mean naught to her, I'm gladder still when she almonds her eyes at me and says, "Surely you'd not have me wed a man who moves me any less than Pietro moved you."

To have her love as Pietro and I loved — this is the one legacy I've to give. How could I wish for her the match Lord Cappelletto makes, if it'd be no more loving a marriage than his own? Would I have her so miserable with wealth and rank as Lady Cappelletta, when I know how even on our hungriest days love fed me, and Pietro, and all of our boys?

This is the lesson the rich never learn. A full heart lasts longer than a full belly. And a well-carved bed hung with finely painted canopy and curtains is no great fortune to the wife who finds no pleasure there.

But little as I care what Lord Cappelletto wants, there's another among the Cappelletti who yet concerns me. Juliet and I've heard Tybalt curse the Montecchi long enough we both know such a wooing will not sit well with him. When I remind her of this, she smiles the very way she did when she toddled after Tybalt as a tiny thing.

"My cousin'd do better to love than hate, you're always saying so yourself. By my lesson, he can unlearn this generations-old enmity, and learn to love where love's well won. For how can he despise all Montecchi, once his dearest cousin is become one?"

It took so small a slight to drive Tybalt to

take up a sword in this ancient feud, I'd not have thought there'd be any way to convince him to lay it down again. But I want to believe that what was best in the boy can yet govern the man. If her love can temper Tybalt's hate, he'll be the better for it.

And if my body still aches with keen reminder of what vengeful wrath can wreak, what fault is it of Romeo's? My own vile father's violence did not taint my marriage. Why would Romeo's Montecchi blood stain Juliet's new joy?

"If he loves you as Pietro loved me, he'll win my consent. But first I must know if his heart is as true as yours."

"At nine, you shall know. I told him I would send to him at that hour." She's so lovestruck, she kisses my lids, and lobes, and the great wine-soaked, morello-covered bosom of me, as she says, "Your eyes must be mine, and your ears, and your heart as well, so you can judge by light of day the truth of what I feel tonight."

Judge I will. For Juliet is all to me. If I might see her married — not merely once, as I said before Lady Cappelletta hours past, but well, as she begs of me now — then truly my mother's heart will beam fuller than moon, and sun, and all the fairest stars I set upon her headdress.

FOURTEEN

Though Juliet and I barely doze a dozen winks between us, the rest of Ca' Cappelletti clings to heavy slumber. Slipping from our chamber before the terce bells ring, I move through a hushed house. The remains of feast and fête litter sala, stairs, and court-yard, the snores of lord and servants the only sounds within the compound. Despite my haste, I stop within the arbor. The bees are already in flight, scenting the morning yeasty-sweet with brood and honey, their bodies goldened by their loads of pollen. I whisper to them of what fills Juliet's heart, and mine, as though they might bear my words to my departed husband as they soar into the sky. It's all I want, to share love's happy tidings with him. But my eye catches on one of the Scaligeri-style ladders that'd been put up within the courtyard. Nestled instead beneath Juliet's window, the flowers twined to it crushed last night by Romeo's eager boot. My sore side aches as I wrestle the decoration back to its former place, so none will wonder who climbed so close to speak to her.

Stepping into the Via Cappello, I nearly collide into Tybalt, who's pulling at his glove with the satisfied expression of a cat licking cream off its paw.

"Where are you rushing to?" His eyebrow arches. Not with the boyish curiosity with which he'd pose endless questions to me or to Pietro, but with a cocksure man's quick censuring.

"Juliet suffers from last night's excitement, I must fetch remedy for her." Not one false word in that, though together they conceal the truth. "You've risen early," I add, to heave his mind from her and me, "though perhaps part of you rose late, moved by some beauty found among the fêting dancers. And having moved something in her, the part that rose first now rests, as the rest of you must rise at this hour to hasten home." With a wink, I ask, "Who is she, Tybalt?"

"Not she, but he." His chin thrusts forward, drawing his long face even longer. "I've done as my uncle bade, letting him play generous host to the rogue who'd rob my sister of her greatest treasure. But the villain's gone out from our house, and I've left a challenge at his own for him."

I wish I could run a hand through Tybalt's curls and ease away this sour humor as I soothed so many dark moods that shadowed his boyhood. But he's too old to let me lay comforting hand on him. Too old to know how young he yet is — though Juliet, younger still, may be the one who'll calm for good what rages in him. All I can do is cut short his talk of bloody-bladed revenge by pulling my veil full upon my face. Carefully covering the last of the bruises that remain from when I was mistook in Tybalt's cloak, I leave his smoldering hate to seek Juliet's new-kindled love.

The Piazza delle Erbe is already thick with vendors hawking and customers haggling. I fan away the swelting air, wondering how I'll recognize Romeo unmasked in the day's light. The only familiar face I pick out in all the thronging crowd is Mercutio's. He's perched upon the piazza fountain as if he's peering up the Madonna's statued skirts. There's barely a stitch of cloth upon him as he splashes in the spouting water, defying any who pass to chastise him for defiling the public font.

Mercutio may know no morals, but he knows well Romeo. And so I make my veiled way to him and say, "God ye good morrow." For which I get back naught but filthy bandying.

I survey his smirking companions, marking which seems to wear the mouth I met yester-eve. Easy enough to choose, as the sleepless youth wears the same doublet and hose, as well. When I artfully ask where I may find young Romeo, this very one says, "Young Romeo will be older when you have found him than he was when you sought him," before admitting he's the fellow who bears that name.

Well said that is, and I tell Romeo so. Cleverness is a rare enough trait among young men, as Mercutio himself proves, interrupting me to recite some randy rhyme that's all hare and hoar without much wit. He carries on until at last Romeo waves him and the others off.

I wait till they're well gone before I speak. "My young lady bid me inquire you out," I say, though I keep what she bade me convey to myself. I'll not open her heart to him, until I discern what he might be.

Even unmasked, this Romeo is not so handsome as Paris. Though I suppose some might find him comely, with light locks falling to his shoulders. There's a brooding in his eyes and at that pretty mouth, tinged not with Tybalt's gall but with a wistful melancholy that might easily move a heart as soft as Juliet's.

"The gentlewoman," I begin, though it startles my own ears to hear my girl called such. Did I not mark the girlish way she giggled and flushed yestermorn, when first I spoke of her marrying? Those words must've softened her eye to Romeo, and charmed her ear to whatever he whispered to woo her. "The gentlewoman is young. If you lead her in a fool's paradise, if you deal double with her —"

Suddenly I wish, if not for Tybalt's sword, at least for some steely way to show this Romeo I'll not let any hurt to Juliet go unanswered. Even a mother bird has beak and claws to defend her nest. But what have I to raise against a man?

I lean wordless toward Romeo's narrow chest, as if to show I'd peck him clean if he does her harm.

Romeo raises a knobby-jointed hand in protest. Lays that hand upon his heart and swears it swells with love for her. With quavering voice he says, "Commend me to your lady."

He's wise enough to ken I'm what will bring him and her together. Or, if I doubt, keep them apart. Surely only a pure heart can discern all I am to Juliet, when such as Lord and Lady Cappelletti still deny it.

I promise to tell Juliet well of him. "When I say how you protest, she'll be a joyful woman." That word sits easier with me now, for surely this teary Romeo will gently make a woman of her.

My answer draws his pretty mouth into a proper smile. "Bid her devise some means to come to shrift this afternoon," he says, "and there she shall at Friar Lorenzo's cell be shrived and married."

By my Sainted Maria, what am I to make of this? To honor her straightaway in holy marriage, that is as it should be. But to have them joined in the very cell where as a babe I brought her, the place where when she toddled I first modeled to her how to make good shrift — I might've been glad for it, had I not guessed years past what trickery the Franciscan performed when my girl was baptized there.

"Friar Lorenzo agrees to marry you?"

Romeo swells with youthful pride at having secured the Franciscan's approval. "He says a happy alliance it will prove, that turns our households' rancor to pure love."

I nod. Calculating as Friar Lorenzo is, I'll not be outdone by him. None knows better than I how well he holds secrets, and if he weds Juliet to Romeo, surely neither she nor I will bear any sin or blame from it. Who else would marry them, without the consent of the Cappelletti?

Romeo presses a florin into my hand with the same certainty with which a priest lays consecrated Host upon the tongue. But with my tongue I tell Romeo I'll not take even a denaro. What I do, I do not for gold or silver but for love of Juliet. And then, because I know I must win his love as well, I tease Romeo as I've long teased Juliet and, in happier times, Tybalt. "There is a nobleman in town that would fain lay knife aboard, and husband a meal of my mistress."

At this Romeo goes pale as a clout. Has no one taught him the jesting my darling ones and I've enjoyed? No matter. It's a pleasure he can learn from me, while Juliet learns other pleasures of him. "She'd as lieve see a toad," I assure Romeo, "a very toad, as see him."

I prate on about when Juliet was a prating thing, making careful study of how Romeo hangs ravenous on each word, hungering to know more of her. Before I take my leave, I remind him to keep no counsel, that we must hold this marriage secret.

He swears his serving-man is just as true to him as I am to Juliet. But how can a common servant be all I am to her? True in what I do, if not in what I've let her believe I am. Surely the time is near to tell her all, though how am I to deliver such unexpected news?

In wondering at it, I nearly miss what Romeo says next. Lovesick, he prattles as a poet might of tackled stairs and top-gallants of joy, until I discern that he means for me to meet his man a little while hence, and receive some ropes by which Romeo'll come to Juliet to consummate tonight what the friar will officiate today.

Tybalt's never needed ropes to reach our window, cat-nimble climber that he is. Nor did Pietro, directed by me to mount the tower stair and pass into the bedchamber to mount me. But this Romeo wants to believe himself a clever sneak, and so I indulge him, promising to collect the ropes and set them where he may scale his way to her.

Taking my leave, I do not turn directly back to the Via Cappello. I need to ready myself for the quick of it — my Juliet, wedding this day. Crowded as the Piazza delle Erbe is this morning, I conjure the quiet of it on that Lammas Day fourteen years past when Pietro brought me to Ca' Cappelletti. Even in this heat, my body still shivers with that ache, that longing for babe newly born, and freshly lost. Or so I thought.

Wandering through Verona's streets, I make seven circuits around the city. First for Nunzio, my eldest. Then one after the other for Nesto, Donato, Enzo, Berto, and their littlest brother, Angelo. This is the gift and curse of memory. Though we bury our dead, we cannot ever bid a final good-bye. I circle past the places that hold especial rememberances of each of my boys, some that I've not let myself indulge since I was swallowed up within Ca' Cappelletti all those years ago. I save Pietro for last. His is the longest loop. There's not a place in this city that does not echo of him. Of us. Again and again I whisper what makes me miss him as keenly as I ever have: that from our love a new love grows, and soon Verona will bear new memories, of our Juliet and her Romeo.

The sun's climbed high by the time I return to Ca' Cappelletti. Juliet secrets herself in the arbor. Sitting in the shade of a poperin tree, she worries the ring Lord Cappelletto set upon her finger a week past. But the dazzle of his emerald'll not hold her attention once she sees me. She's on her feet asking, "Honey nurse, what news?"

Honey nurse, that sweet that gave her life. Sentimental old fool that I've become, emotions grow so thick in my throat, not a word is able to escape me.

Her color fades. "Good sweet nurse — why do you look so sad?"

"I'm aweary." I take the place she left upon the bench. "My bones ache from what a jaunce I've had."

"I would you had my bones, and I your news." She tugs at me with the same impatience as when she was three or four and thought I held some candied comfit from her. "Come, I pray you, speak."

Jesu, what haste. "Do you not see that I am out of breath?"

But Juliet was never one to be stayed. Nor have I been one to stay her. "You have breath to tell me you are out of breath," she says. "And take longer in making excuse why you delay, than the whole of the telling would take. Tell me simple, is your news good or bad?"

If it were yesterday, I'd jest with her as I often have, and tell her she knows not how to choose a man, and blazon Romeo with faults he does not have, and bid her go serve God as nunnish Rosaline does. But it's as if she's unlearned her girlish love of waggery in this little time she's known wistful Romeo.

"What a head have I," I say instead. "It beats as if it would fall in twenty pieces.

And my back, and side. Beshrew your heart, for sending me about, to catch my death."

These words are better meant for Tybalt, chiding earned by what I got when last I ventured from Ca' Cappelletti. But Juliet at least hears them with a loving and not a wrathful ear. "By all my faith, I'm sorry you're not well. Sweet, sweet, sweet nurse." She kisses my head and lays a gentle hand upon my side, which ache less under her caring touch. "Tell me, what says my love?"

How can I not answer those pleading eyes? "Your love says, like an honest gentleman, and a courteous, and a kind, and a handsome, and I warrant a virtuous —" But why do I court for Romeo? Does my love count for naught? "Where is your mother?"

"Where is my mother?" She repeats the question with such wonder — is this at last the time to tell her? Can she have already guessed the truth? But her eyes flick to the arched passage to the courtyard. "Where would she be? Why, she's within."

Is this any poultice for my sore and sorry bones? That she'll not even know me for her mother, that all I am to her is messenger?

"Lady Cappelletta is within, but my heart is without, as only you know, Nurse." She smiles, and sighs, and takes my hands in each of hers. "And without you, what comfort has my heart?" Her soft hands are still small against mine, gripping with a child's fretful need. "Come, what says Romeo?"

Those eyes flash familiar at me, and by all my years of loving her, and loving my Pietro, I know there's time enough for her to learn what I really am. That it'll better wait till she is wed, and perchance on the way to being herself made a mother. For now, there's naught she'll listen to but what she wants to hear.

"Hie you hence to Friar Lorenzo's cell, to make your shrift." I loose my hands from hers to tuck her wayward hair, straighten her sleeve, and smooth her skirts as I've ever done, although in truth such beauty needs no bettering. "There stays a husband to make you a wife."

The blood comes up in her cheeks, scarleting my pure lamb. I flush as well, the sudden fevering that's struck me half a dozen times a day during these weeks past flashing over me once more. But for all the heat, we wrap arms around each other, joy echoing with joy as we breathe air fruited by peach and poperin pear. Breathing together that sweetest of anticipation just before lips part and teeth sink in, and juice and taste explode upon the tongue.

Though I'd lieve not ever let her go, I pull away first, so I'll not feel what it is to try to hold her longer than she would be held. "Get you to San Fermo, and take care none see you till the friar's done his part. I must fetch the roping ladder by which Romeo'll climb to you once the day turns dark." I've been her age. Knowing what stirs a heart, and other parts as well, I add, "Though I'm the drudge, and toil in your delight, you shall bear the burden that'll come at night."

She laughs and blushes deeper. So new-woke with love, she twitters like a wanton's bird. Reciting some pretty poesy, she calls parting such sweet sorrow, gives me a giddy kiss, and turns away to meet her match at Friar Lorenzo's cell.

It's no easy thing to watch her leave alone. But I must think for both of us, and be ready for what comes after the marriage vows are trothed. And so I kneel next to the arbor hive, careful not to block the bees as they stream forth. Sliding a hand beneath the cut log, I draw out the box Tybalt long ago hid there.

It's no fine cassone. Not carved by a skilled hand, nor painted with some impressive scene, nor tooled in precious leather. The box he chose is simple, to attract no notice. Even the bees fly blithely by as I lift the lid and remove the sack that lies within, my fingers clumsy as I undo the knot. When the pouch opens, I rock back and pour what the hives and I have earned into my lap. Though it's not a hundredth of what Lord Cappelletto'd give to dowry Juliet, it'll buy what I'd have her have. A new drawn-thread bedsheet imported from some far-off port, to lay upon with the husband only she and I and Friar Lorenzo will know she has.

I count out enough to purchase a sheet as wide as her broad bed, slipping the coins inside my gown. Handful by handful, I work the rest into the sack. Twist and tie it, and lay it in the box, then slide the box back into place. Tybalt must not notice it's been moved. Must not question me, on this of all days. But Tybalt seems to have forgotten the bees. The clay bowl beside the hive is dry. I draw water from the courtyard well to give the honey gatherers, before making my own bizz-buzzing way from Ca' Cappelletti.

Romeo's man is little more than a boy, and for all Romeo swore he was good at keeping confidence, he's no good at keeping time, and so he keeps me waiting in the day's hottest sun. When at last he arrives with the roped ladder, my thirst's so great I'm grateful he slips out a bulging skin filled with aqua vitae, so we can drink to the marriage of his master to my mistress. A happy omen, for my first sampling of such was on the day I wed Pietro. My new husband taught me to taste the fiery liquor with his own tongue, and sang a merry rhyme to ease me to it. *The first sip is bracing, the second's a blessing, the third's your last care in the world.*

I sing the foolish verse to Romeo's Balthasar, as he tells me he is called, and he sings it back to me in a wavering contralto. Though I miss the deep resonance of Pietro's basso, I'm glad to have another voice mingle with my own, celebrating the vows Juliet and Romeo have by now already made beneath Friar Lorenzo's cross. Once we empty the skin, Balthasar bows to me and I make curtsy, and we go our ways. Mine is toward the Mercato Vecchio, where I must find among the fabric merchants a bedsheet fine enough for Juliet's parting with her maidenhead.

Just before I reach the marketplace, a flash of regal carmine catches my eye. I draw back, for the last man I want to see today is Paris.

But it's Mercutio who stumbles from the nearby passageway, his carmine robe stained with a darker crimson. A sword drops from his hand, metal clattering against street-stones as he curses Cappelletti and Montecchi.

I espy within the passageway a second sword. Wet with blood and being slid by a quaking hand back into its too-familiar scabbard. My eyes catch Tybalt's, and in that instant I read his terror at what he's done.

Mercutio lets out an animal's anguished howl. He cries, "A plague on both your houses," and crumples to the ground.

FIFTEEN

A plague on both your houses.

If Mercutio's many fornications are not enough to send him straight to hell, for this spiteful oath alone he deserves damnation. How could anyone wish such suffering as the plague brings, not just upon the Cappelletti and Montecchi but on all Verona? For the pestilence'll not stop at the boundary of one house without stealing its awful way into another. None knows that better than I do. So though I should cross myself and pray for Mercutio's departing soul, instead I spit and say, "May the devil have you."

Then I look back toward Tybalt. But he's gone.

Tybalt, my last boy. As near a son to me as I'll ever have again. And as much in danger now as mine were on that awful day they stole into our plague-dead neighbor's house.

I know what I am, and what I'm not.

Much as I ache to protect Tybalt, I turn the other way. Back to Ca' Cappelletti.

Though Cansignorio might eventually have killed his nephew himself, the Scaligeri honor'll not bear anyone else having slain him. When the prince pronounces the punishment for taking Mercutio's life, all I feel for Tybalt'll be not a pennyworth of help to him. But Lord Cappelletto — surely he'll cast every bit of favor he's ever curried with Cansignorio to save his heir.

Only when I reach Ca' Cappelletti do I realize I still carry Romeo's cords. I secret them outside the compound wall, then hurry into Lord Cappelletto's study.

When I burst in, the old man jerks up, astonished. He's been dozing among his accounting books. A happy fool, whose joy I rob by saying, "Prince Cansignorio's nephew is slain."

I need Lord Cappelletto strong, need him at his most conniving. But he shrinks, so small and weak and old. "Paris? Slain?"

"Not Paris. Mercutio. Stabbed in the street by Tybalt."

This brings him to his feet. He reaches out an unsure hand, and I offer my arm to steady him. "Where is he?"

"He vanished when Mercutio fell." The tolling of bells and blasting of trumpets drown out any more I might say.

Lord Cappelletto bolts from behind his desk, shouting for me to show him where last I saw his heir. And so we rush together through the courtyard and out of the compound, Lady Cappelletta, alarmed by how her husband cries out Tybalt's name, hastening along with us.

The street where Mercutio fell is already thick with people. Prince Cansignorio stands in the middle of the keening, kneeling crowd, far changed from the bravadoed young man who first seized Verona's throne. Looking upon his sister's slain son ages him well past his not-quite-forty years.

"Which way ran he that killed Mercutio?" he asks. "Who began this bloody fray?"

A youth steps forward. One of the ones I met at the fountain this very morning, though it seems a century ago. He bites his thumb, and points with it past the prince.

My knees buckle beneath me. They'll not support the weight of what I see. Tybalt, sprawled motionless upon the ground.

The same ground rears up at me, and something roars inside my head. My stomach twists and fills my mouth. The thundering resolves into words, shouted by that pointing youth.

"There lies quarrelsome Tybalt, who killed

brave Mercutio. And who for that crime, was slain by young Romeo."

Each sharp word stabs into my heart. Tybalt, killed. Romeo, his killer.

Lady Cappelletta rushes to where the young man points, wailing for her nephew. Dumbstruck, Lord Cappelletto follows, falling to the ground and cradling his heir in disbelief. What enfeebles him inflames her. She clamors back to the prince. Throws herself upon her knees, kissing his knuckles and kneading his fingers, pulling his hand to her heart. "Romeo slew Tybalt," she says. "Romeo must not live."

"Not Romeo." Lord Montecche erupts through the crowd, pushing his way between Lady Cappelletta and Cansignorio. "He was Mercutio's dear friend, and concluded only what the law otherwise would end — the life of Tybalt, who laid your nephew dead."

The prince swings from one to the other like a weathervane caught in an angry wind. None seem to breathe, no heart to beat, until he speaks. "Tybalt disturbed our peace, and for that paid the proper price. But Romeo took what it was my lawful right alone to take. Let him hence in haste. Banished, he may live. But if he's found again upon Verona's streets, that hour is his last."

Cansignorio calls for his guard to gather up Mercutio and carry him to the castle to be prepared for burial among the other Scaligeri in Santa Maria Antica. The crowd follows, eager to insinuate themselves into his princely grief. Only Lord Cappelletto, Lady Cappelletta, and I remain. And Tybalt, our dear Tybalt.

Creeping close, I cannot keep my eyes from the wound upon his chest. His face, his hands are already deathly pale. But that dark, wet mark — it seems the only thing alive of him.

I tear tooth into my tongue till I taste my own blood, hating myself for every harsh word I've had for Tybalt of late. I wish with all my soul that I could take them back. Why did I not keep him from this fatal fight?

Lord Cappelletto shakes his head like a dog trying to loose a porcupine's quill from its nose. "Why would Tybalt raise a sword against the count?"

"Honor." Lady Cappelletta spits the word at him. "All your talk of honor, of your precious family name. All the ancient prideful grudges of the Cappelletti. That's what laid him dead."

Lord Cappelletto touches the gold crest worked upon the hilt of Tybalt's sword. "The Cappelletti had no enemy in Mercutio. He was a relation to the Scaligeri, I'd not have wanted Tybalt to —"

"It was not for you," I say. For in this instant I realize what must have caused the quarrel: Tybalt was more like my Pietro than I've realized, dying not for some foolish male honor, but to protect precious female virtue. "Tybalt knew there was a rakehell who was trying to seduce Rosaline. He beseeched and besieged her, and would not let her be. Even came into your house to find her. Tybalt tried to tell you, but you'd not listen to him."

Lord Cappelletto loses what little color the shock of Tybalt's death had left him. I know my words have hit the mark. Know, too, it does not matter. So what if he's as sorry as I am, to not have stanched what stormed in Tybalt?

Blade, street, blood. They're Tybalt's death, just as they were Pietro's.

Lord Cappelletto pulls at Tybalt's cloak until it covers that awful wound. "I'll take him to Santa Caterina, to our family crypt." He crosses himself, plodding out each deliberate word. As though he must convince himself that Tybalt's truly gone. "Best not to make too grand a public funeral, with Cansignorio's own mourning turning him against us. I'll have Rosaline and her convent Sisters pray a month of private Masses for our Tybalt, God have mercy on his soul."

Lady Cappelletta grips one of Tybalt's lifeless hands, refusing to let go. Though it's no woman's place to travel with a body to its burial, she insists on going with him. Insists with the same wildness in her eye that haunted the years in which her womb squeezed forth one ill-formed creature after another. Her madness blazes like a fire, warming Lord Cappelletto, and me as well. Weak as this blow has made us, its her fierce strength we need.

Lord Cappelletto nods, agreeing to let her come. Turning to me, he says, "You must tell Juliet."

If all of heaven's angels sang in one great harmony, it'd not sound sweeter than what I hear as I approach Juliet's chamber: her lilting voice weaving love lines into an adoring tune. From the doorway, I watch my newly wedded girl take each of San Zeno's statued hands in one of hers, swaying as though she'd dance the saint about the room. Giddy, she twirls herself from him and catches sight of me. Taking a half-step back, she studies my grief-struck face. "Why do you wring your hands?"

I look down at my hands, as though they'd

397

speak. Wishing they might, and save my tongue the torture of answering her. "We are undone."

She stares at me, and I know those words are not enough. My eyes swim past her, searching out the window and across the arbor to what were Tybalt's rooms. "He's gone. He's killed. He's dead."

Juliet stumbles backward, catching herself against the holy icon. "Can heaven be so envious?"

"Romeo can, even if heaven cannot."

Her eyes, her mouth gape in confusion. "Romeo?"

"I saw the wound, here." I lay my hand in the tender flesh valleyed beneath my ribs, and something sharps inside me. As though the same blade that felled Tybalt gouges me as well. "Tybalt, the best friend I had. I never dreamt I'd live to see him dead."

"Romeo slaughtered, and Tybalt slain? Who lives, if those two are gone?"

I live, and she lives. Always my same awful fate. Despite this grief great enough to kill us both, through the pitiless mercy of some unseen saint we yet survive. "Tybalt's dead. Romeo killed him, and is banished."

"O God." She reaches for me, the same desperate babe who howled for me all those years ago. "Did Romeo shed Tybalt's blood?"

Such cruel relief, to still have her to comfort after all I've lost. I hold her fast against me, letting her grief curse out. "Serpent heart, hid with a flowering face. Beautiful tyrant, angelic fiend. Just opposite to what you justly seemed. Spirit bowered from hell, paradised in such sweet flesh. O, that deceit should dwell in such a palace."

"There's no trust, no faith, no honesty in men," I answer, stroking her hair and laying kisses on those precious locks. That her fond heart must learn such hate so young. "Shame come to Romeo."

Juliet yanks herself from me, so fast her emerald ring gouges my soft flesh. "Blistered be your tongue. Romeo was not born to shame."

Were her curses not for Romeo, but for Tybalt? "Will you speak well of him that killed your cousin?"

Quick as her anger came, it just as quick is gone. She knuckles her hands into her eyes, as if to blind herself to our terrible fate. "Shall I speak ill of him that is my husband? Is he a villain who killed my cousin, if that villain cousin would have killed my husband?"

I grab each of her thin wrists, pulling

those angry fists from her reddening eyes. She blinks once at me with surprise, and then a second time with the same steely resolve I watched harden Tybalt. "My husband lives — this is all comfort. But some other word you said, worse than *Tybalt's dead.*"

I shake her wrists, as if to jerk such thoughts away. What's worse than *Tybalt's dead,* so long as we both live?

Before I even force aloud the question, she answers. "Tybalt's death was woe enough. But *Romeo is banished* cuts like ten thousand *Tybalt's dead.*"

Tybalt, who loved and was loved by her for fourteen years. Who held her dear from the first day I bore her to this chamber. Whose face, and voice, and doting touch were the second she learned after mine. How does she shed tears over this living Romeo she's known but a day, and forget it's a lifetime of our dearest Tybalt that's lost to us?

"Lord and Lady Cappelletti are already at Santa Caterina," I say. Surely if she sees Tybalt lying in the Cappelletti crypt, his heart stilled by Romeo's sword, she'll share the weight of what shatters me. "Will you go to them? I'll bring you there."

She shakes her head and pulls away from

me, stumbling backward into our bed. For all the day's heat, her teeth begin to chatter. She pulls the bed curtain around her like a shroud. "Romeo, my three-hours husband, was meant to make a highway to my bed. But it's death, not Romeo, that'll take my maidenhead."

She does not speak these words to me, but to some specter only she can see. It frights me. Not because such madness is so strange, but because it's so familiar.

Have I not gazed longingly upon that same specter? Not ached to have my own life end, rather than bear the grief of living through the loss of those I loved?

Pietro's tight hold bore me through the burying of our sons. Rocking Juliet in my arms anchored me through mourning my Pietro. Loving what's in this life is the only remedy for death. If Juliet'll not let me hold her through this fresh loss, what harbor will either of us find for our grief?

I bow my head to my cockly-eyed Madonna, silently begging for her aid. All the answer I get is what Juliet whispers through her clattering teeth. "I, a maid, die maiden-widowed."

I'd not leave her for all the world. Nor look on the Montecche ever again. But hearing *I* and *die* dance together on her tongue, I know I must do something. "I'll find Romeo," I say.

I make her swear she'll stay inside our chamber while I'm gone. Whatever her despair, there's naught here with which she might undo her life. She promises, saying she'll not leave her wedding bed. She pulls the ring from her finger, pressing it into my hand to take to Romeo.

I cup the weight of it in my palm. This precious thing Lord Cappelletto gave her, which now she'll have me gift to Romeo — the one who is to her dearest loved, and by the Cappelletti and my own heart hated most.

I wit well enough where to look for Romeo: where any lovesick sinner goes to be absolved. But for once, the corridor outside the friar's cell is empty. His door, ever open to any who are in need, is instead shut fast. I knock, cracking my knuckles so hard I expect the wood to splinter beneath them. But the door'll not budge.

Leaning close, I hear voices within. I rap again with even greater might. From the other side, Friar Lorenzo asks who knocks and whence I come. Asks as though he must take care who is let in. Does this not confirm what I suspect? Surely Romeo hides here.

I might turn away, fetch some men from Cansignorio's guard, and lead them here. Why not let the prince deal Romeo a blow as fatal as the one Romeo dealt Tybalt? But uncertainty worms within me. "I come from Juliet," I say.

The door swings open. Friar Lorenzo waves me inside and latches the door after me.

The Franciscan stands alone. "Where's my lady's lord? Where's Romeo?"

He crooks a finger to a prayer niche cut within the cell. "There on the ground, with his own tears made drunk."

Romeo is huddled against the wall. Blubbering and weeping, weeping and blubbering. As though it's him, and not Juliet, who suffers for what he's done.

"Stand up." I jab my foot at him. "Stand, and be a man." Did Juliet dare compare this sniveler to my Pietro? "For Juliet's sake, rise and stand."

"Do you speak of Juliet?" He raises his head, his voice wavering like a child's. "How is it with her? Does she not think me a murderer, for having stained our joy with blood removed but little from her own?"

For all Tybalt's love, it's my blood, not his, that's little removed from Juliet's. And with all that blood's heat I answer. "She says

403

nothing, sir, but weeps and weeps." What harm is my lie, against his greater sin? I'll not use any words of hers to comfort him. "She falls on her bed, and starts, and calls *Tybalt*. Cries *Romeo,* then falls down again."

"*Cries Romeo, then falls* — as if my name slaughters her, as my cursed hand killed Tybalt." He draws his dagger. "In what vile part of this body does *Romeo* lodge? Tell me, Friar, that I may cut it from me."

With quick hand, I snatch the knife. I want to point it to his chest and drive it home. Want to feel it pierce flesh and organ and draw warm blood. To know it is my sharp thrust that drains all from Tybalt's killer.

And yet — if you've ever plunged a knife to butcher a newly slaughtered sheep, you know how hard it is to drive blade into flesh. But that is naught compared to what it takes to pull out the knife that's been so keenly driven in.

I watched Mercutio fall. I saw my Tybalt felled. Both haunt enough. Slaying Romeo would no more earn back Tybalt's life than good Tybalt's death did Mercutio's. It'd only leave my own hand guilt-stained as well.

I fling the dagger across the cell. It hits the floor and spins. Stops, pointing not at us, but at the bloodied Christ crucifixed above the Franciscan's narrow bed.

"Would you slay yourself, when happiness is yours?" Friar Lorenzo is so consumed with reprimanding Romeo, he pays no mind to me. "Juliet, to whom you vowed your love, yet lives. Tybalt, who would've killed you, you slew. The law that might punish you with death asks only exile. For each of these, you might be happy. And yet you whimper and would die miserable."

Romeo totters in shame, which pleases his confessor. "Go to Juliet, and give her comfort," Friar Lorenzo tells him. "But be mindful. Do not stay too long. Be gone before the night-watch makes its rounds so you may pass safely to Mantua, where you must stay until I've time to blaze your marriage, reconcile your families, beg pardon of the prince, and call you back to Verona. Saints be willing, we'll have more joy then than the Montecchi or the Cappelletti have known in the generations since this ancient feud began."

The marriage blazed, the families reconciled, Juliet and Romeo dwelling happily together for ever after. This is what she wants. What I, loving her, should want as well.

May Tybalt's saints forgive me — but what

death took is taken. Whatever serpent has slithered into our Eden, poisoning our joy, I'd not let the devilish creature steal Juliet as well. So when Friar Lorenzo tells me, "Go commend this to your lady," I nod my assent and force out thanks for all his counsel, before I turn to Romeo.

"My lord, I'll tell my lady you will come." My lord, I call him. For if Juliet's fate is now entwined with his, mine is as well. I slip the emerald from my finger, and hold it out to him. "Here, sir, a ring she bid me give you."

He kisses the ring, and kisses my own hand for delivering it. "How well my comfort is revived by this," he says. He cradles it as gently as Juliet did a wounded bird when she was but a girl of eight, while I tell him where to find the ropes by which he'll breach the arbor wall and reach my darling one.

I spend my night in the Cappelletti tower. Where else can I go, while Romeo takes my place beside Juliet? Tybalt's bed is empty. But I'd not lie within his darkened chamber, thinking of him already laid inside the Cappelletti tomb. Instead I climb, as he so often did. I make my way to the tower top, where I've the stars for company. Trying to forget the sight of Tybalt's lifeless body, I pray for his everlasting soul, gone from this world with all the rest I've loved.

All, save Juliet.

Juliet, who in these same hours learns what I could never teach: the pleasure of a husband's touch. Even at my age and in my widowhood, my body still quakes remembering the shivery explosions I felt when I first lay with Pietro. Love. Lust. Loss. Inseparable companions.

Lightning's bright shock and thunder's heavy grumble burst the small hours of the night, loosing heavy rain upon Verona. It's as though heaven itself weeps with me. When the first streaks of dawn lace the easterly sky, I steal my way back down to Juliet. But just as I draw near to her door, I hear above the tempest Lord Cappelletto calling Lady Cappelletta to go to Juliet.

Juliet — although she's ever a slug-a-bed, surely this once it's not the lying down but what rises up that occupies her. Romeo cannot yet be twenty, and at that age, they rise and come and rise again with such quick ease, my lamb must have passed a night well full of cock-struts. But now, it is another cock that crows, the morning lark that sings, and Lady Cappelletta that caws. And so I'll not tarry with a knock.

I cover my eyes, open the door, and call, "Madam." Madam, for my lamb is wooed, won, married, and maiden no more.

"Nurse?" she answers, and I enter. From behind my hand I peek at Romeo, half-lit by the candle that burned all night before my Blessed Virgin. He's a scrawny thing without his doublet, not broad and strong like my Pietro, nor even so well muscled as Tybalt. Still more a boy than I'd guessed him to be.

"Lady Cappelletta is coming to your chamber." I might as well be speaking in the tongue of a Far Eastern trader, dull-eared as Juliet is for me, being so full-eyed for Romeo. She gazes soft at him, and hears me not.

I turn my own uncovered gaze on him, as hard as hers is soft. "The day is broke. Be wary, look about." My warning works fast on him, and I leave young love to its fare-thee-wells.

The sala, so teeming full during the masked ball the evening before last, seems cavernous now. As I step inside, an eerie moaning echoes through the shadowed room.

A trick of the storm, perchance, the wind catching some loose shutter. But the moan sounds again, so close I let out a startled gasp. It's coming from Lord Cappelletto, who sits alone within the dark. With weak voice he calls, "Angelica?"

I've not heard my name spoke aloud in this house in all the years since Pietro's been gone. Would not have thought Lord Cappelletto even knew it, though I suppose it was writ upon the contracts Friar Lorenzo brought him so long ago. I've always been only *Nurse* to him. Though when he says, "Is that you, Angelica?" my name sounds like some delicate thing he treats with care.

I've never known Lord Cappelletto young, but now he seems more than old. Shaky, and sapped. "It's late," I say, as though sleep were any remedy to him, or me.

"Late? What hour could be so late, so dark?" He nods toward the window, which despite the summer heat is shut fast against the storm. "When sky's sun is set, the earth drizzles dew. But for the setting of my brother's son, it rains downright." Dark as the shuttered sala is, I sense more than see how deeply our newest grief etches his face. "Tybalt took so strongly after Giaccomo, it's like losing him again. Like losing both at once."

I lay my hand on his. I expect it to feel cold, an eel hooked from the fishmonger's basket. But it rests warm in mine. More comfort than I'd thought I'd get from him. "He was a good boy," I say, "and would have made a better man, had not hot temper taken him."

"We were born to die, and I'll not fault him for being quick to defend Rosaline." His eyes search out the place along the wall where Tybalt's sword once hung. "Poor broken girl. Even as she sobbed and wailed for her murdered brother, I bade her repeat to me before the Holy Abbess of Santa Caterina what she'd confided to Tybalt. How the rakehell, eyeing her at prayers within the church, pressed a secret suit. With words, and deeds, and every sort of flattery, tried to seduce her. Offered his Judas coins to buy the purity she's vowed to keep. Even masked himself and came into my house, plotting to take his lust on her."

Tybalt was always so quick to find some insult to the Cappelletti honor, I'd half-believed he'd imagined the plot to corrupt Rosaline. But I might have known Cansignorio's lascivious nephew would seek some debauched pleasure with such a pious girl. "May the saints forgive Tybalt. And may the devil take Mercutio."

Lord Cappelletto gives a fierce shake of his head, crossing himself to fend off the taint of such damnation. "Not Mercutio.

He only stepped between them. It was Romeo Montecche who ill-used my niece."

Romeo who tried to seduce Rosaline?

Romeo, who finding her already gone when he arrived here, sought another just as innocent.

Romeo who pressed his silver coin on me for offering Juliet to him, like a lamb led to a sharp-toothed wolf.

Romeo, who lies right now in our bed. Taking what he could not pry from Rosaline, from Juliet instead. Horror grips my throat, tears into my chest. How can I have been so big a fool, and let my precious Juliet be ruined?

Juliet, ruined.

Lord Cappelletto asks, "What's that you speak?"

Have I said those two most awful words aloud? But he's not heard them clear, for with watery eyes he asks, "How is my girl, my all?"

"She has much to weep for." More than she yet knows.

"Poor child, she'd wash Tybalt's corpse with tears, though by Prince Cansignorio's decree we cannot grieve publicly for him. But I've remedy for that. We'll honor Tybalt after we've won the favor of the Scaligeri once again." Resolve settles across Lord

Cappelletto's shoulders. Whatever shared sorrow shrouded us together is quick forgot as he nods a command at me. "Come, let us see how Juliet takes the gladder tidings Lady Cappelletta brought her."

What happy word can Lady Cappelletta have given Juliet? What relief could it be against this terrible truth I bear?

I follow Lord Cappelletto into the chamber. My darling lies on the bed, shaking with silent sobs while Lady Cappelletta stands turned away from her.

"How now, wife?" As Lord Cappelletto speaks, I slip past Lady Cappelletta to stroke what silent comfort I can onto Juliet's downturned head. "Have you delivered to her our decree?"

"Ay, sir." Lady Cappelletta ducks her chin, so she'll not have to meet his eye. "She gives you thanks, but will have none."

"Will have none?" In two swift strides, Lord Cappelletto's beside the bed. He hovers so close, his angry spittle hits us both. "Are you so proud? So ungrateful, when I've found a worthy gentleman to make you a bride?"

"Not proud." Juliet's voice is so small we all must strain to hear her. "And not ungrateful. But I cannot marry where I do not love."

"Cannot marry? Do not love?" He swoops his claw of a hand into her hair, yanking her from the bed. "As you are mine, I give you to my friend. I'll fettle you like a horse, and ride you out on Thursday. Then shall you be made Paris's wife."

Juliet wraps shaking arms around his boots, weeping and beseeching. But Lord Cappelletto berates my darling as he too often did poor Tybalt. "Disobedient wretch. I tell you this: you'll stand and make your vows in church on Thursday, or never after look me in the face."

He kicks her away, and reaches his hand to Lady Cappelletta. "Wife, did we ever think ourselves blessed, that God lent us but this only child? Now I see this one is one too much, and we've a curse in having her."

God lent? Not God but the friar, who borrowed and lent. Who with secret deceit took what I will ever love and gave my babe to this man who could so quick turn hate on her.

"God in heaven bless her." I curve my great body over her trembling one. "You are to blame."

Lord Cappelletto gapes as though he's forgot I'm here. "What's that, my lady wisdom? What blame is there, when day, night, work, play, alone, in company, for fourteen years all has been one care to me: to have her well matched. The more so since Tybalt's lost, and Paris is all that's left to be a son to me. A gentleman, noble, fair, and honorable."

He shoves me aside, wrenches Juliet up by her shoulder. "Whine and pule if you will, but if you'll not wed, you'll not house with me. You may beg, starve, die in the streets. I'll have naught to do with you." He crosses to the door, but turns back once more to speak to me. "Thursday is near. Look to your heart, advise her well."

Juliet raises her tear-stained face to Lady Cappelletta. But just like the hind caught by the hound, she could not even protect herself, and she cannot pity my poor girl. "Do as you will, for I am done with you," she says and follows her husband from the room.

Juliet sinks back to the floor. I cannot coax her to her feet, have no strength to carry my full-grown girl back to our bed. So I settle next to her, weighing how the very thing I wished for her just two days past now works such misery on her: for good and handsome Paris to want her for a wife.

Romeo, Romeo — over and over she whimpers his name. My darling does not know that fiend for what he is. And I'll not tell her. Not shatter more her already breaking heart by revealing how falsely he's dealt with her. Not let her know how stupidly I let it happen.

How long we sit like this, her sobbing and me scheming, I do not know. There is no bell to mark it, no clock tower to tick it off. Only the once-ferocious storm, which flashes quiet as suddenly as it started, melting Juliet's wails into urgent words. "Oh God, Nurse. By my husband on earth and my faith in heaven, what am I to do? Comfort me, counsel me. Have you no word of joy?"

Of joy, no. But of good counsel, yes. For all I want to tell her — that she is no Cappelletta, that there is naught Lord Cappelletto can take from her that values more than all I have to give — I know the fool I've been. To let myself be fooled, and let so much be nearly lost.

If Lord Cappelletto turns her out, what life is left her? Could I go begging for some household to take in the Cappelletti shame and let us live as scrub maids in their scullery? So soft a girl as Juliet would not last a week at that.

And if her secret marriage to Romeo is exposed — what then? I'd not trust her for another hour with that deceiver. I wish no less than bitter death for him. For what he did to Rosaline, to Tybalt, and worst of all to my Juliet. I'll not let the world know the only thing a lady has to trade on he's already pried from her.

Mother though I am, there's nothing I could do to save her, if it were not for Paris. Paris, who offers name, fortune, family. And even love. What more can she — can we — ask?

"Faith, here it is. Romeo is banished, has naught in all the world, and can make no challenge to you." I rush through this barest mention of him, then slow my speech to ease her to what more I have to say. "I think it best you marry with Count Paris. He is a lovely gentleman. None is so fine, so fair, and you'll grow happy in the match."

This stints her sobs. She raises eyes I'd swear can read the very depths of me, and asks, "Do you speak truly from your heart?"

"From my heart, and my soul." I make a cross over the first, to show I swear upon the second. "Or else beshrew them both."

"Amen," she answers. Adds, in yet more piety, "Go in and tell them I am going, having displeased my Lord Cappelletto, to make shrift and be absolved by Friar Lorenzo."

It does not lessen a mother's love to admit some of her babes are born obedient, while others ever struggle to assert their will. My Juliet has always been a good girl. A girl whose pleasure lies in pleasing. Whatever spell vile Romeo cast on her, it must weigh little compared to what wills her to obey me, and Friar Lorenzo, and even Lord Cappelletto.

Lord Cappelletto. Brutal as he was to her this morning — as I'm my father's daughter, I know how much a woman, a girl, will do to appease the brute who beats her. Though I'd deal more vengefully with him, I'll bide my hours and bear his presence till Thursday comes and she's wived to Paris. What is Lord Cappelletto's anger, when with my loving counsel she'll open her heart to the prince's noble nephew, and earn herself a safe and a happy future?

SIXTEEN

Juliet bade me tell Lord and Lady Cappelletti where she's gone, what she's agreed to do. And so I make my way to the kitchen. The ever-drudging cook is mashing a great mound of dates into a mass of capon livers, working knife and pestle quick as Lord Cappelletto prattles on about boar and basil salsiccetti, leek and chickpea migliacci, roasted eel minced with mint and parsley to be cooked with walnuts and almond milk into a crusted pie. Dish after dish he says the cook must make in only two days' time.

Lady Cappelletta's slim fingers finick against her mourning cloak. "Is it not too soon to throw a marriage feast?"

Lord Cappelletto swats away her question as he might a fly that's settled on the freshly slaughtered lamb. Outside the Cappelletti walls, every parish, every guild, every holy order in Verona unfurls its banners to parade in Count Mercutio's funeral procession. But he's as deaf to all of that as Tybalt, lying entombed, is. Deperate to be sure he'll marry his house to Paris, he signals a serving-man, listing out a mere dozen guests he deems it seemly to invite to the ill-timed feast.

As the serving-man departs, Lord Cappelletto catches sight of me hovering outside the doorway. His anger flashes fast again, but I step inside with a contrite curtsy. "Juliet is chastened. She's gone to make penance to Friar Lorenzo."

Lady Cappelletta glances to her husband to gauge what he will make of this before setting any emotion of her own upon her face. Lord Cappelletto only mutters, "May he chance to do some good with the peevish, self-willed child." But he piles heavy hope that Friar Lorenzo will succeed, ordering everyone within the house to the exacting preparation he deems necessary to celebrate Paris being wed to Juliet.

I'm set to picking herbs from along the edges of the arbor. Leaden-headed and swollen-eyed, I reach beneath thyme and parsley leaves to dig my hands into the warm, moist earth. I need the reassuring feel, the fecund smell of what can grow new life. Bees weave in and out of the herb beds, eager to be back at their gathering now that the rain is done. We work together, I making my green-burdened trips to the kitchen as they make their golden ones to the hive. In one of my passes through the courtyard, I catch Juliet's light step in the entryway. "See how she comes from shrift," I say to Lord and Lady Cappelletti, surprised myself by how merry she looks.

"How now, my headstrong, where have you been gadding?" Stern as Lord Cappelletto's raised eyebrow seems, lurking in his *my headstrong* I hear a fond affection, laced with the barest regret for how cruelly he's used her.

"Where I have learned to repent the sin of disobedience." She kneels and then, as though kneeling is not enough, folds prostrate on the hard stones. "Pardon, I beseech you. Henceforward I am ever ruled by you."

I might roll my eyes and urge her up, pinch her for so overladening her performance. So ill-practiced is she at deceit, she play-acts overmuch to hide her dalliance with Romeo. But Lord Cappelletto is well-fooled. Grinning like the chimpanzee paraded in the prince's menagerie, he summons the house-page, instructing him to bear this news to Paris.

Juliet pulls herself up and says she's already met the count at the friar's cell. "I gave him what love I might, within the bounds of modesty."

She plays the part so well, I clap my hands together, then must pretend I only clasp them tight in prayer, and thank aloud the saints who bless Ca' Cappelletti with this propitious match.

Lord Cappelletto nods, offering amen. "May God bless the reverend holy friar. We and all Verona are much bound to him."

Bound to him Juliet and I most certainly will be, for concealing everafter her first marriage. Bound with us, Friar Lorenzo would be, if any hint of it escaped.

"Nurse." Juliet must also feel the weight of our shared secret. "Will you help me sort such ornaments as you think fit to furnish me tomorrow?"

"No." Lady Cappelletta pecks out the word like a hen going after a worm. "Not till Thursday will you be wed. That's hardly time enough —"

"Go, Nurse," Lord Cappelletto interrupts her. "Go with her now, and ready her, and we'll all be off to church tomorrow."

He hums "Heart's Ease," a lover's ballad, while Lady Cappelletta clings as close to him as a sundial's shadow does its pointer, reminding him of how little time there is for so much preparation to be done.

Juliet sorts spiritless through her collars and hair garlands, keeping her gaze from mine. Her silence tells me how she yet yearns for Romeo, and how little she looks forward to the next day's wedding.

No mother wishes a hasty marriage upon her daughter. Nor a loveless one. But I know there are worse fates than what faces Juliet.

We were born to die. Though Lord Cappelletto spoke the truth, he said only half of it. We are born to die, but born also to live before we're dead. When I lost Pietro's kerchief and was sure I'd lost him as well, I spent desperate hours wishing my life already done. And once he was truly gone — but by then I knew what at Juliet's age none can fathom: the grief we think will drown us we'll learn somehow to bear. And the joy we'd swear is ever lost to us will seep back again.

I rub a sprig of rosemary I've snatched from the kitchen garden against the pillowcasing, to mask any lingering musk of Romeo. "Be sure to wait until Paris is well in his cups before you lead him here tomorrow night. Do not suffer a servant to bear a torch, and let the candle before the Sainted Madonna burn low before he hitches up your gown."

"Do you think me so hideous, he must be drunk and blinded to have me?"

"It matters not what I think, but what he thinks." What man does not wish to believe he lies with a virgin — and how many girls and women have lied as well to let a man believe he does? If Paris harbors any doubts within the dark, by morning light there'll be this stained sheet to dispel them. "He'd not seek you for a wife, if he did not find you pleasant to look upon. Did he not say as much, when he met you at San Fermo?"

"He said my face was his, and I'd no right to slander it." She turns that face from me, as though I've no right to it either, since telling her to let him claim it.

I step close anyway, twining the rosemary twig into her hair like it was a lover's nose-gay. "And his face, did you find it fair?"

"I tried not to think of what was fair, and unfair."

Is it her age? Or the Cappelletti wealth that she was raised in? Which leads her to believe the world is fair, when all my life and loss have taught me that it's not?

I kneel beside the grand cassone at the bottom of her bed, lifting out the lifetime of clothes stored there. Saved once for her, preserved since she's outgrown them for the children she'll soon bear. Such delicious hours we'll have when those babies come, hoarding their soft, their warmth, that milk-sweet scent between us like a miser's gold. Paris'll not begrudge such a mother as I know she'll make, with me to guide her.

I unroll the precious garments piece by piece, starting with the tiniest ones. I need only the slightest glimpse of each to recall her at the age she wore it. The striped pelisse she wriggled in just out of swaddling. The rose-robed cherub who'd shriek as I chased after her. Dark gray stripes to suit the child who pushed me off with angry fists but who, when tears welled in my eyes, spilled out her own as she clambered into my lap to kiss and be kissed comfort. Out of a quilted purple gown that carried her from her sixth year to her seventh tumbles the toy bird Tybalt gave her when she was but a babe. She long loved the little plaything, crying miserably when it was lost, until doting Tybalt said he'd got her a real bird to replace it. He led us down into the arbor, pointed to a nest within the medlar tree, and told her the warbler there was hers, which she might come watch any time. Only, she must not cry, for that would scare the timid bird away. Our dear Tybalt was clever as he was kind, and many a tear dried that year from no more than a mention of her bird.

When I hold the toy to Juliet and remind her of Tybalt's deed, a scowl pulls across her face. "Such trickery, so young. Little wonder he came to such an awful end."

Trickery. To come from her, who being deceived by Romeo has learned so fast to put on her own deceptions. Pretending the grateful daughter before Lord Cappelletto while forgetting all affection for Tybalt.

"Do you deny the love you bore Tybalt, out of some allegiance to Romeo?" I brush her cheek, as if to sweep away the speck of her resentment. "You must put such things from your heart, now that you'll marry Paris."

"There is much I must put from my heart now that you've counseled me to wed the count." She twists away from me. "What affection should I bear Tybalt, who struck down the cousin of the man I am to marry? Does not a husband's grief outweigh his wife's? Would you not have me mourn Paris's kinsman Mercutio, and curse the hand that killed him?"

Though I study her hard, I cannot tell whether she is true in this wifely submission, or still playacting at contrition. "Does Paris ask this of you?"

"Paris asks to kiss what he has yet to wed." She shudders. "That is the man he is. One who'd take advantage of maiden innocence."

Pure of heart and thick of head — is that what I've raised her to be? Kissing true-natured Paris the day before their wedding vows is far better than laying with false-tongued Romeo in an illicit marriage. But before I find a way to tell her that, she crosses herself and adds, "God save me from becoming such a harlot as could want a man who'd have her without first making her a Christian wife." She raises a hand to her mouth, going so wide-eyed that now I see for certain she is playacting. "Oh, Nurse, I have forgotten — you did as much at twelve with that Pietro."

This is too much for me. That she'd slander me a harlot, and mock the very love tales she's begged me to repeat so many times to her.

I'll not hold my tongue. I'll tell her how vile a villain her Romeo is. For what good is a willful colt, until it's broke? But not left broken: I'll bridle her to bridal be by offering a model of a proper marriage, telling how she sprung from that most wonderful love between me and Pietro. Once she knows, and there's no secret left between us, then we'll —

"Are you yet busy?"

Juliet and I both startle at Lady Cappelletta entering the bedchamber.

She shows no more joy than usual for Juliet. "My lord husband would have me offer help to you."

"I've culled what's needed for tomorrow." Juliet waves a quick hand to the trifles she's set out, before bending her knee in imploring curtsy. "If it please you, I would be left alone to pray the heavens to smile upon my state, which as you know is cross and full of sin."

This pleases Lady Cappelletta, to think Juliet so awful. I'm sure she'll leave us to ourselves.

But then Juliet straightens her leg and looks entreating into Lady Cappelletta's eyes. "Let the nurse sit up and be a help to you, for I am sure you've your hands full all, in this so sudden business."

Juliet'll not meet my gaze. Need not meet it, having grown so bold as to put me out. To put me to waiting on Lady Cappelletta, who sizes me up like I'm some dumb ox upon the trader's block, for which she'll drive a pinchfist's bargain. "Take these keys," she says, slipping a ring from her belt, "and fetch out the banqueting cloth. Scrub it to lay upon the table."

I might out-argue Lady Cappelletta, or best her into believing she does not want my labor after all. But I'll not beg Juliet to let me stay while she's caught in such a mood.

The hour's late. The too-little sleep she got last night raws her nerves. I'll leave her rest alone this once. When I steal back hours hence to tousle her awake, I'll tell all that's in my heart, for her to carry when she stands beside noble Paris and makes true marriage vows.

Just past her door, I think I hear her call me back. Does she yet long to be with me the way she did when she was a littler girl? But what can I do with her tonight but play out once more the dismal scene we've already had? I'll not chance more sore words between us. I must let her be alone long enough to be glad of me again. Just till morning. There'll be time then to tell her, first of Romeo's deception, then of my own. After which we'll never let another secret forge its way between us.

"Fetch more spices."
"Look to the baked meats."

"Find dates and quinces from the pantry."

Cocks crow, curfew bells ring. Three o'clock comes and goes, but Lord Cappelletto'll not leave off ordering me about. Ordering me, and cook, and every servant in the house. Lady Cappelletta watches over him, muttering how nothing's kept him up so late since the last of the pursemaker's daughters was married off. He says she wears a jealous hood that unbecomes her. Such an unhappy house from which to send forth any bride. But this is the last day Juliet and I must abide beside such misery. I can hide one final time behind the hedgerow of their bickering. Slinking to the woodpile that's stacked where the dovecote stood, I lie down for a doze.

I've not slept long when the serving-man seeking logs awakens me. A perfect loggerhead he is. But before I've run my tongue through half the ways of telling him what wooden fate I wish him, pipe and lute sound from the courtyard, and the house-page announces Paris is arrived.

I hurry to the courtyard, where Lord and Lady Cappelletti buzz about the count, who's dressed in the same deep mourning for his cousin that they wear for Tybalt.

Paris looks past them, lays pinky finger

beneath his eye, and nods smiling to me. He means to say my bruises are well-faded. I'd thought as much, peering at the polished plate set out in the sala, but his kind notice reassures me. Will not my Juliet do well, matched to such a man?

"Hie, Nurse, make haste," Lord Cappelletto says. "Go wake Juliet. Trim her up, tell her the bridegroom's come."

One come, one gone, and she's got the better of the bargain, the second so excels the first. It gives my tired legs strength to mount the stairs. As I cross the loggia I keep my sights on handsome Paris beaming eagerly below, as though he alone can draw joy into the Cappelletti courtyard.

"Why, lamb," I call as I enter Juliet's chamber. She's got the bed curtains pulled as tight as on the coldest winter night. "Why, lady, why, love, sweetheart. Why, bride."

My slug-a-bed's sound in her sleep. Stealing every pennyworth of rest, and well she does, for Paris'll give her none tonight. Will give her all, I mean — so oft she'll have no rest. Marry and amen to that, and may God forgive me, and her, for deceiving him.

This will be our last hour alone together, and I must make the most of it. Must find the words, the way, to tell her what she really is. What, and who, and how she came to be here, and why I've hid it all so long. This is the dowry I've got to give. Not coins or gowns or plate, but love. Love such as she's only known from me, yet love she's never known for what it truly is.

Such love surely is enough. I'll rub her in it, like a scented oil. Wrap her with it, like the finest cloth. Adorn her with it, like jewels strung in that dark, thick hair that's so like mine, and looped around her smooth young neck and dainty wrists. I'll kiss it onto those almond eyes and tell about the day I first saw it in them. The bittersweet of losing Pietro, only to find him again in her.

I'll tell it all in this precious hour. Our last hour alone. Yet not alone, for I feel Pietro with me. Feel there is in gallant Paris some echo of my own great-hearted husband. I'll make her feel it as well, so she'll know why I'm sure he's meet match for her.

"Lady." I draw back the bed curtain. "Lady, my lady."

Juliet's dressed. She must've been unnerved to wake alone. To rise so early and get herself into her clothes, only to falter and lie lonesome down again.

"What a bride you'll be, already in your bed. Should I send the count to you directly?" That ought to rouse her. But still

431

she sleeps.

I lay loving hand against her shoulder to shake her awake. Lay loving hand and feel her cold.

But no, it's me who's cold. An icy stone sunk to my stomach. A freezing through my heart. For in that touch, I know. A bitter shivering jitters my joints, rattles the teeth in my head, makes me curse the day that I was born.

Born to live to find her dead.

Dead. Dead, dead, dead. My numbed lips form the word, over and over. A whisper, a roar, I cannot tell which. Until Lady Cappelletta comes in calling, "What noise is here? What's the matter?"

What am I to say? My last child, my only life, is gone.

How can she die and leave me living?

Lady Cappelletta comes near the bed. She looks on Juliet and screams. So loud I grab my darling's hand. And find clasped there an empty pouch, its loose drawstring tied off with a cross.

The numb, the cold, heats to searing pain. I hide the pouch within my own fat fist. Use that fist, and the other, to beat my head for being such a fool. A fool, and fooled.

Lord Cappelletto rushes in, then crumbles to his knees. "Death," he says, his own face waxy as a funeral mask. "Death is my heir and steals everything from me. Tybalt stabbed, and Juliet taken with him, broken-hearted from grieving for her cousin."

The musicians are still playing in the courtyard. Thrumming out their happy tune, not knowing bliss has turned to loss. My Juliet dead, never to know the last good act Tybalt tried to do, and how untrue her beloved Romeo. Me, not knowing as I should have, the instant death took her. Not knowing when I could, I should, have saved her.

My fist's clenched fast, keeping clasped the awful truth. Between the Cappelletti's wails, I steal out of the bedchamber, through Ca' Cappelletti and off to San Fermo, to find the man who killed her.

A scaffold rises inside the upper church, and some exalted painter barks down to his assistants. Another saint is being martyred on the wall. Barbara perhaps, or maybe Dorotea. Brushes dip into garish colors to depict the virgin's torturous demise. As if those who come to pray do not have enough of death in our own lives, and need frescoed instruction in fresh grief.

I hurry past, down into the dank of the Franciscans' cloister. There is the usual dismal press of sniveling children, shame-faced husbands, wretched wives, and crag-faced crones outside Friar Lorenzo's cell. A lifetime of misery, seeking such relief as we're told only the Holy Church can give.

Pushing my way through, I heave against the door. It gives way, revealing Friar Lorenzo bending his fervid ear to a blushing maiden like a worm wriggling into ripe fruit flesh.

"Benedicte, and God give you peace." He smiles at me like I'm a child. "But you must have patience as well as penitence, Angelica, and wait your turn."

"Damn your *benedicte,* and your God. And you." I fling the empty poison-pouch at him.

Shock grays his face. But only for an instant, before he wills his features back to composed. "My dear Ginevra, you are absolved. Go forthwith to the church of San Zeno for the morning Mass." In one swift motion, he ushers the maiden out, latches the door against any other entries, and turns to hover over me. "Angelica, I did not —"

"Did not want what punishment you'd get, if it was learned you ministered an illicit marriage. So you hid the deed with poison."

"No." He snatches up the pouch and

secrets it among his cache of medicinals. "Juliet came to me in ungodly anguish. She raised a blade to her own breast. I only gave her what would still her hand, as you stilled Romeo's."

"If only I'd stilled his heart along with his hand. But he lives, while my Juliet is dead."

"Not dead, Angelica, though it's comfort that you think so."

What comfort, in seeing, touching, keening over her lifeless body? What good to him in denying she is killed?

Friar Lorenzo touches the tips of his fingers together, steepling his hands to lecture me. "What appears as death is not always death. No more than what appears as virtue always is true goodness. The remedy I dispensed has put her into a sleep so deep that she seems a corpse."

It's nearly more than my worn heart can believe. "She lives, truly?"

I make him swear to it, before Christ upon the cross. I want to trust his words, to let them melt away this tight hold of loss.

"But why?" I ask. "What could set her to such deception?"

"With her marriage to Romeo consummated, Juliet could not be married to the count, though all within Ca' Cappelletti would force her to it. To save her from such

435

sin, I deemed it best to let them think her lost. Once they've laid her within her family crypt, I'll send word to Romeo to bear her to Mantua, where they may live in secret joy."

How could he, could she, have plotted to keep such a thing secret from me? "You'd've let me believe Juliet was dead, and bid her live far-off in Mantua without me knowing?"

"Did you not tell her to wed Paris, knowing she was already bound in the eyes of God to Romeo?"

This is why he turned my girl against me? I spit out what Romeo is, what he's done. But Friar Lorenzo offers not even a flicker of surprise.

"You knew?" I'm still the fool, to need to ask. For what does he not know, sitting all day in this cold cell listening to what's most intimately told?

"Romeo is not the only man in Verona who, courting what he could not get, would come to me for counsel. Such groans, such sighs, do I hear. But no more than that, concerning Rosaline — no sin done, none confessed. Her virtue was enough to save them both. When he turned his heart instead to Juliet, and found in hers a welcoming return, I only offered holy blessing to what they'd begun. Thus was Romeo saved from sin."

"And Tybalt?"

"Romeo proclaimed a cousin's love for Tybalt, but still Tybalt raised a sword at him. As Romeo tried to beat down the bandying, Tybalt struck Mercutio. Only then did Romeo, mad with grief, lift his own blade." Friar Lorenzo pinches at his Pater Noster beads like a merchant plying abacus to calculate a profit. "God knows, I'd bring them both back if I could, and bind the families to peace as I intended. But what death takes from us we can only have again in heaven."

I've no need for him to tell me so, when everyone I've ever loved is lost to me.

Except Juliet.

If what he says is true. If my girl still lives. If for once I'm given hope instead of grief.

The deepest place within my chest aches. Just as it did when I swelled with milk, and all I sought was the sweet pain of her suck. Hope instead of grief.

But even such hope carries a sharp edge: this potion Friar Lorenzo's given her must be some semblence of what he used to convince Pietro that our infant daughter was dead. Twice, he's stolen her from me.

"Death did not take Susanna. You did."

The secret I've long kept spills from me — for what have I to lose in letting him know now all that I know? Why hide how much I loath him for all he's put me through? "Because we were poor and could make no grand gifts to the Holy Church, you stole our living baby and gave her to the wealthy Cappelletti, letting them believe that theirs survived. Deceiving us into accepting that ours was dead."

A hideous line throbs across his forehead, pulsing angry blue. "Who told you this, Angelica?"

Told. As though I must be ever told, the way a stupid beast must be shepherded. As though I'm no more than some dumb animal, and cannot figure for myself how I've been used.

"Sainted Maria." I see her before me, bare-breasted and beatific as she suckles the sacred babe. But in Friar Lorenzo's narrow cell there's no image of the Holy Mother. Only Christ, tortured upon the cross. "By the Sainted Maria, there are things only a mother knows."

He gathers himself within the thick folds of his cassock, searching out words to convince me I am wrong. But I unlatch the door and take my leave of him.

■ ■ ■ ■

Though the morning's bright by the time I return from the friary, Lady Cappelletta's gone to bed, having taken wine enough to slumber heavily. Lord Cappelletto sits alone with Juliet. Staring dull eyed, his voice so wearied I must bend close to make out what he says. "The earth has swallowed all my hopes but her. Left only this one poor thing to rejoice and solace in. But cruel death snatches even Juliet from us."

By his *us* he means the Cappelletti. I once believed his losses measured as heavy as my own, and together we took comfort as we prayed for all those death stole away. But I'll not find such fellowship with him today. He's settled the Cappelletti cap once more upon Juliet's head, and condoles himself by cataloguing how grand the funeral cortege will be. What he could not do for Tybalt, condemned as Count Mercutio's killer, he'll conjure instead for Juliet, heralded across Verona as Count Paris's betrothed. A procession led by her godfathers Cansignorio and Il Benedicto. Entire religious orders burning candles for her soul. The prince's council carrying the Cappelletti banner and shields. Finely decorated horses clad in the family colors. And Paris walking shoulder to shoulder beside Lord Cappelletto, the carved bier before them, and atop it Juliet.

"Juliet," I repeat, impatient as I am to be rid of him. "I must ready her." Immodest it'd be for a father to watch a full-grown daughter's final washing and anointing.

He leans nearer to the bed. As he brushes a fare-thee-well hand against her cheek, my heart catches, sure he'll sense whatever life pulses within her.

But grief's too constant a companion for him to disbelieve it. "Dress her in the green samite," he says. The finest gown in all the household. Lady Cappelletta'll not be pleased to learn she'll never again wear it. "It was my first Juliet's. She was married in it."

Have I ever envied wealthy Lady Cappelletta? Pietro could not have afforded even a patch of so fine a fabric. But my husband never would have dressed me in a dead woman's clothes, never made me feel there was anyone or anything he cherished more than me.

Lord Cappelletto's eyes go to Juliet's finger. Mine cannot help but follow, though I know he'll not see what he seeks there. "Where is the emerald ring?"

I tap a fingernail against one of my yel-

440

lowed teeth, as if I might chisel out the right half-truth to tell him. "She was not wearing any ring when she fell prostrate before you yesterday. Perchance it was given over in Friar Lorenzo's cell, where she made her shrift."

Every stitch I speak is true, though I sew them together in such a way that they cover over all I know. Let the scheming Franciscan, ever covetous for gems and plate and finery, explain to Lord Cappelletto what's become of the Cappelletti jewel.

I bow my head and cross myself, muttering how lucky it is to be claimed just when one has a freshly shriven soul. Lord Cappelletto murmurs amen, and sighs, and stands, and says he must go down to the family chapel to pray for Juliet, and for Tybalt.

At last my girl and I get our hour alone together. Though by my holidame, I'd not have this be our last.

I climb into our bed and turn my head over hers, hoping to feel her breath upon my cheek, as I did when she was just a babe. But I sense nothing. I lay my ear onto her chest. Something throbs between us. Heart, blood, love. I cannot separate what's hers from mine.

I let the full weight of my head sink onto

her, wrapping my warm body against her immobile one. "Dearest lamb, how you frighted me. Did you feel so despairing you thought you'd need deceive me, when all I live for is your happiness?"

Raising her too-still arm, I kiss her palm and cradle it against me. And then I tell her.

Tell how twice I did not let myself fathom what with my mother-love some deepest part of me surely must have known. The first, when I woke uncomprehending one last child had quickened in me, and in my astonishment labored two long days to bring that tenderest infant out. How Pietro's weeping told me it was lost, and how by the Virgin's grace I came here to her. How this was the second time I was so unperceiving: sure as I was that my milk, my love, my tender care was what fed her, it took years before I realized it was more than milk that bound us. How blood and bone and every bodily humor tie her to me, and to my lost Pietro. "I am your mother." The words glimmer in the golden air. "You are my daughter."

How many times have I imagined saying this, imagined what surprise and joy and deepest love she'd offer in reply? How I've wanted to have her know why what I give

442

her will always be so much more than what Lady Cappelletta offers, why what lives in her of my Pietro weighs more than every jewel and cloth and coin Lord Cappelletto ever could bestow her. I've longed to tell, and have her wrap soft arms around me, and weep with joy-filled relief to know our dearest truth, and mayhap confess to me she'd long before sensed it for herself.

But there's no joy-filled relief. Not for her, lying senseless to all I say. Or for me, who might as well've whispered into an empty cask, sealed it up, and cast it in the Adige to bob away unheard.

The brazier's been tucked away unused since winter warmed to spring, but in this full heat of summer I light a fire in it. Cool as the water is when it's drawn from the courtyard well, I wait for the fire to take the chill from it before I dip a fazzoletto cloth in, wring it out, and touch it to Juliet.

The last I looked upon my boys was when I washed each one before Pietro bore them off to be buried. Six beautiful bodies, speckled with black spots. *God's tokens.* So enchanting a name for such a horrific sight. Like insects swarming across their thighs, their arms. Those specks were worse than the plague's raised boils, which at least appeared angry, insolent. God's tokens were a more awful marring. Delicate pricks death took over and over, gently eating its way across the flesh of all my darling sons.

But not my daughter. Juliet's body is perfect. Perfectly quiet, perfectly still. Perfectly lovely.

Downstairs, Lord Cappelletto reads out some version of the liturgy Friar Lorenzo long led me in. Friar and lord can have their learned Latin prayers. I've something more holy, my hands cleansing every precious part of her.

Did I think just two nights past she was her most beautiful by moonlight? Lying here, bathed in the day's full sun, she is more pure, more beautiful, than anyone or anything I've ever seen.

From the first day I held her, I bathed and swaddled her so many awestruck times. I remember every inch of her. But I mark the difference, too. How heavy she's become. The infant I craved and cradled as though she were still a part of me is now this full-grown body I must roll carefully, dipping the soft cloth over and over into the warmed water as I slowly trace my way across her. I wash the length of her fingers and stretch of her arms, the curl of her toes and the curve of her legs. With her back to me, I part her hair, tucking it to either side to reveal the blades of her shoulders jutting like an angel's wings. The smooth rounding of that bottom I wiped when she was at her littlest. I swear, though I know all of her, my most familiar is yet a mystery to me. Could so lovely a child, a near-woman, have grown from me? Could she be so nearly lost so young?

Would she really have left me, letting me believe that she was dead while she went off to Mantua to live secretly with Romeo? I'd not have thought she could hold so much from me. But I've held all I know of who she is, and what he is, from her.

What he is. This is the one thing I've still not confided, even to these now unhearing ears. I'd not made her know it yesterday, hoping ignorance might ease her to forget him and make a loving wife to Paris. But if she'd sooner take her own life than live wedded to any but Romeo — or, living, beshrew me heart and soul just to be with him — then I must hold my motherly tongue. I'll not tell what still wears upon my heart, to keep her from shoving me away again.

With caked rose petals and rosemaried oil, I anoint my daughter. The bright floral fragrance dances with the sharp woody one. Can scents make a harmony? Yes, as surely as Juliet and I have, and always will.

In those first awful days and months without Pietro, how I craved him. My body ached to have those great paws of his upon me, the cinnamon-sweet scent of him and the tickle of his whisper in my ear. I was half-mad even just to hear the timbre of his voice again, and to use my own to say all the things I'd not realized till too late I'd never have a chance to tell him.

To not have bid good-bye to Pietro. Or to Tybalt. All I would've said and done to keep that boy from harm. Or even just to show my deepest love before I lost him.

It was no different even with my sons. When they lay infected with pestilence, we knew we'd not have them long. But Pietro and I'd not utter anything we thought might fright them, and so left unsaid what otherwise would've filled their final hours.

Always, death has robbed me of this chance to speak my fullest heart to those I love. Until Juliet.

It'll not be long before Lord Cappelletto comes to claim her. I must make for her some sign so that waking in the Cappelletti tomb, she'll know I know that she yet lives, and be comforted by my love as she shivers alone among ancient bones, beside death-struck Tybalt.

Never have I wished I could write, or she

read, until now. To have the power to close my hand around a pen and mark words upon a page that her hungry eyes could claim a whole day hence — what remedy that'd be, when I am far from her.

But I must clever out a way to make myself known without words. Did not the touch and taste of me soothe her, when she knew naught but a baby's babbling? Just as the rub of Pietro's linen shirts still succor me.

This is what I have to give our daughter. I slip one of the precious three shirts I've saved over her head, smoothing the well-worn cloth across her tender breasts. A far coarser weave than Juliet has ever donned, although she's snuggled many a night against the faded fabric, all that came between us in this bed. I work the samite gown in place, careful to hide any trace of the secret shirt beneath it. Though it's richer to the touch than the frayed-thin linen, the samite's green sallows my girl's cheeks.

I bend to give her one last kiss, and taste the friar's potion lingering on her lips. Loathe as I am to leave her when we've so little time together, I'll not have her wake to such bitterness.

I hie down the tower stair into the arbor. The air is filled with pollen-coated bees, hurrying their precious treasure into the hive. When my toddling Juliet could not abide the wormwood taste of me, I plunged a desperate hand into the waxy comb, and earned a dozen searing stings. But as I unseal the hive today, bees alight along my arm but do me no more harm than they did Tybalt, as they arced with grace around him. I dip my fingers carefully inside and lift them away honey-coated. With the other hand I replace the seal before hastening back to Juliet.

I work my broad thumb between her lips, spreading its honey on her tongue. My three middle fingers coat her pink gums and pearly teeth, the littlest one saved to trace a honey kiss upon her lips. These lips through which my suckling girl first knew me.

These lips which, with this honey, will once more drink in all my love for her.

Seventeen

All Verona believes a rich man's daughter is being laid dead within his family tomb today. Why would they not? The parish bells toll it. The holymen and noblemen who don mourning bands and accompany the gold- and fur-trimmed bier pay solemn tribute to it. The poor huddled on the benches placed to line the cortege route earn their coin by witnessing it. And Lady Cappelletta and I peer down from the sala windows, watching all of it.

Roused by Lord Cappelletto and dressed in a silk mourning gown covered by a vair and ermine mantle, a ruby necklace newly clasped to set off her garnet cross, with sapphire rings on every finger and a gold-and-sapphire garland in her hair, Lady Cappelletta dutifully rent and wept and caterwauled during the long hours of the vigil. Cursing the Montecchi and mourning the twin loss of Tybalt and the samite gown, mayhap, if not Juliet.

I let my grief for Tybalt swell to tears as well, so none would wonder why I'd not cry over my nursling's seeming corpse. But as the death knell tolls, the procession candles burn, and the cortege snakes away from Ca' Cappelletti leaving us behind, our eyes are dry, and our words are few. Insistent as she was on clinging to Tybalt, Lady Cappelletta showed no such interest in accompanying Juliet's body to the Cappelletti vault. Lord Cappelletto, ever calculating what makes best public spectacle, must be glad she's not forgotten a woman's proper mourning role now that so many Veronese are watching.

We wait side by side, each wound in her own thoughts, until it's time to leave for the Duomo. No ordinary church will do for Lord Cappelletto, nor for Count Paris, who sends the prince's own liveried carriage for Lady Cappelletta. In the thick July heat, she heaps the fur hood beside her on the bolster. I sit opposite, watching Verona's streets slip past.

When Juliet awakes, I'll not hold from her what she is to me, what I am to her. But I'll serve her better if she keeps me ever close. And so I'll feign for Romeo the very love she'd have me feel. But I'll not forget the evil that he's done. Plotting to debauch a nun. Deceiving and defiling innocent Juliet instead. Trying with his Judas coins to make me a common pander. Running his murderous blade through our beloved Tybalt. For all that, I'll show to him the same false heart by which he beguiled Juliet. If she's to travel to Mantua to make a household with him, then I must go withal, biding my time while I tend her.

Juliet need never know how cruelly Romeo's served her, so long as I secretly serve him the ruthless same. Perchance I'll find an apothecary in Mantua who'll minister an unaccustomed dram, a poison that'll do to Romeo what Friar Lorenzo's potion only pretends on Juliet.

And what then? What will become of her once he is dead?

Many a wife who's too soon widowed finds youth and beauty can win for her another, better match.

Lady Cappelletta draws back her veil, amber eyes wide as she repeats, "Another, better match?"

Her astonishment brings on my own. I'd not realized I spoke that part aloud, so fiercely did I want to convince myself it could prove true. Before I can work my tongue into some half-truth to shade my meaning, she asks, "What man would have me, when all Verona knows I cannot bear again?"

It's Lord Cappelletto's eventual demise, the only possible end she can hope for her own loveless marriage, that troubles her. Not yet thirty, but haggard-eyed as she stares out at the banners bearing the Cappelletti crest hung all along the route. "Tybalt gone, Paris lost to us." Worry curdles her words. As though the fear I first saw eddying over her when she lay in the parto bed has never ebbed. "What's left for a widow, when a husband leaves no heir?"

Rosaline and her Holy Sisters line the Duomo steps, the answer to her question. Few among them shine as Rosaline does with pious light. They stand identical in their wimples and habits, except for the youngest orphans, the ones who've no means of donning sacred cloth until some wealthy sinner buys absolution with a bit of dotal-alms charity.

Whatever dowry portion returns to Lady Cappelletta when Lord Cappelletto dies, however much beyond that he might choose to bequeath her, without nephew or son-in-law to serve as her protector, she'll end up in a convent. Just as I would've these years past, without Juliet. What else is there for a woman with neither heir nor husband?

But Juliet, still in the bloom of youth and blessed with my fertile humors — surely she'll fare better. She's barely older than I was when Pietro found me, and she'll have me to search out such a man as —

The carriage stops. Paris waits in the piazza to hand us down, his face pocked with grief. Handsome, young, and powerful. Yet so easily unmade by the despair death dances down on even the most fortunate.

Lady Cappelletta leans heavily on his arm, grateful for one final chance to hold to him. I bow my head, following in mock obedience to take my place among the mourners.

"Angelica." Friar Lorenzo winnows himself from the mass of brown-frocked Franciscans gathering to make their procession into the church. He grasps my elbow, whispering fusty breath into my ear. "The thing you spoke of in my cell, about Susanna. I cannot know what has given you such thoughts, but I must tell you —"

"You've told me already." For once, it's my eyes that bear down on his, searching out a hidden sin. "What appears as death is not always death."

He draws back as if I've slapped him. The piazza is filling with whole companies of

453

friars, nuns, and well-ranked priests, all handsomely paid by Lord Cappelletto to be here. Behind the holy orders crowd finely dressed members of Verona's most powerful families — although only the ones who bear no enmity to the Cappelletti. Or who hide such feelings today, when the family is high in Prince Cansignorio's and Count Paris's favor. Friar Lorenzo runs a lizard's tongue along his wine-stained teeth. But he'll not dare speak another word as the assemblage swells around us.

I turn from him to file into the cathedral with the rest of the women. Banners and pennants with the Cappelletti and Scaligeri coats of arms hang from every wall within the Duomo. The air is sweet with beeswax, so many candles burning along the altar and before the rood screen that the whole apse of the church seems ablaze.

What appears as death is not always death. Is this not what Christ, looking down at us from upon his cross, is meant to tell? Is this not why we pray for the everlasting life of those who've passed, and search for every trace of them in the features of their children? Why I carry such careful memories of my boys, believing that so long as love for them lives in me, they're not truly lost. Why I still wear my husband's shirt, and wrapped

454

Juliet in one as well, so his touch, his smell, might keep him close to us. How I know my own dearest lamb will rise again, as surely as Christ himself did from his tomb.

Chanting fills the cathedral, the deep voices of priests and friars surging from the chancel, joining with the harmonious swell of nuns secreted within some hidden choir. Their voices arc along the vaulted ceiling and reign back down over all who kneel to honor Juliet. The holy music hums within my very bones, as priests and deacons bless and incense and kiss sacred text, every familiar ritual meant to earn eternal life. *What appears as death is not always death.*

No more than what appears as virtue always is true goodness.

The thought pulls tight across my chest, squeezing the breath from me. *What appears as virtue.* Hundreds of Veronese kneel before me, yet my eyes cannot help but search the gilted openings within the rood screen, seeking out the back of Friar Lorenzo's tonsured head.

My holy confessor's practiced such deceptions, always cloaking them in seeming virtue. Stealing a poor woman's newborn babe, and thinking it recompense enough to contract her as servant to the rich family who unwittingly receives it. Groping so many years after a lord's wealth, only to snatch his greatest treasure, a daughter entered into marriage without her father's lawfully required consent. Counseling a mere child to play at the sin of taking her own life. Making mockery of my grief, along with Lord Cappelletto's and Paris's, by letting us believe one dead who lives.

And now, this greatest sacrilege. How can the Franciscan hide behind his own piously clasped hands praying a false Requiem Mass, and suffer me to do the same, when we both know Juliet yet lives? Unless —

Unless she does not live.

What if he's lied to me once more, and Juliet is truly dead? What if he tricked her into swallowing his poison with promise of some secret rendezvous with banished Romeo — and tricked me as well with the promise my precious girl survives?

He took the cross-tied pouch from me, the only proof of his part in this. If I speak a word against him without that, I'm nothing but a heretic and madwoman.

A heretic and madwoman. I pray to the Holy Mother and all my saints that's all I am. A heretic for bending knee and bowing head through false Requiem. A madwoman, frantic with fear until I can see my girl, my heart's delight, awakened from feigned death. Smiling and speaking and laughing once more.

All around me, people rise, turning to make their way out of the cathedral. I'm carried along by the close press of bodies, like a broken shard tossed into the Adige. Taken one last time to Ca' Cappelletti.

Fur-lined mourning robes, a quarter-mile long funeral procession, silk flags and gilt banners and a hundred blazing candles — and still there must be more to mark the mourning of ones so rich as the Cappelletti. They host a feast as well, the sala thrown open to welcome Verona's most godly and most powerful, who gorge themselves on our grief.

The Requiem Mass was enough for me. I'll not bear the banquet. So I steal my way downstairs, through the courtyard and the arched passageway into the arbor. I kneel one last time beside the beehive, drawing out the box Tybalt husbanded beneath it, grateful for the coin-heavy sack inside. Enough to keep Juliet and me in simple household. I secure the sack within my dress and replace the box, praying my thanks to Tybalt and telling myself I must do what he meant to. For his sake, and Rosaline's, and most of all for Juliet's.

But can I do it? Can I, after all, bring myself to kill even such a villain as Romeo?

Something crackles in the air behind me. Paris.

He slips into the arbor, bouquet in hand, to stare up at the window of Juliet's bedchamber. As if by the very power of his royal gaze he might conjure her there. I give a loud *amen,* so he'll think I kneel in prayer.

He whirls my way as though half-expecting her, then makes a quick half-bow to hide his disappointment at discovering only me. "You do not dine with the others?" he asks.

"Grief thieves me of my appetite."

"Grief thieves us both of more than that." He draws a pink rose from the bouquet, its petals barely opened into bloom. "So tender a heart she had, to die of mourning her beloved cousin."

So tender a heart he has, to believe that. Though I might have thought the same of Juliet, before Romeo preyed upon her.

"A too-loving nature. She had it since she was a babe." My words are true enough to satisfy us both.

I'd not've thought I'd care for company, but Paris draws me gently to the arbor bench, asking me one thing and then another about Juliet, as a babe and then a girl and lastly a young woman, and I'm as glad as ever to tell.

"You make me love her more with every word," he says. "And hate myself for hastening her death." He slides his thumb along the rose's stem, searching out a thorn. Pierces himself just for the awful pleasure of the pain. "Lord Cappelletto urged patience when first I asked for her hand. But once Tybalt was killed, he wanted no delay in trothing her to me. He told me to stop her tears with joy. But times of woe are not the time to woo."

"I urged her to it, too." For all I must hold secret, it's good at least to share as much as that. For it was my championing Paris that drove her to the Franciscan's cell. If I'd been more careful in my counsel, perhaps she'd not have turned to the conniving friar.

And yet, I see from how deep Paris's sorrow cuts that I was right in this: he is the one man worthy of her. Not just a handsome face, a full purse, a powerful uncle. He's a heart that's truly noble. If Romeo had not snuck in seeking Rosaline, what happy future might my Juliet've had with Paris?

I am a fool to indulge such thoughts. Yet what is a fool but one who hopes?

From all my life's grief, I'd forged these weeks past a single hope: that if Juliet and

Paris wed, she might make a well-loved and loving wife. It's a hope I cannot help holding, even now.

Paris knows naught of how Juliet was beguiled by Romeo. But he knows Romeo is Tybalt's killer, the sworn enemy of the Cappelletti, and by his own princely uncle's royal decree banished from Verona. Who better to rid us of Romeo? If Paris discovers Romeo's intended trespass, surely he'll take it for villainy and drive him off while Juliet yet slumbers, saving me the sin of poisoning him.

When my girl awakens among the cobwebbed bones of a hundred rotted Cappelletti, beside poor Tybalt's slowly mouldering corpse, what if, trembling with terror, she finds Romeo's abandoned her, and discovers handsome Paris guarding her instead? Seeing his grief and then his gladness, surely she'll realize for herself his worth.

Desperate I must be, to try it. But if in such desperation I can bring her a true and goodly love, then I must.

"Such pretty flowers." I nod at them as if there'd not been any bloodied pricking. "I'd take them to where she lies now, if curfew were not so near to being rung."

Paris's mourning cloak is embroidered with the Scaligeri shield, and he pulls himself tall in it. "The guards must let me pass. I'll bear her the bouquet."

And water it with tears, no doubt. So much the better, for wet lashes will show well the love that shines in his fair eyes. "Be sure to have a steady torch, so you can stay to pray the matins and the lauds for her." To linger long enough to dispense with Romeo so I'll not have to, and then find your wildest prayers come true when my lady awakes.

He bows again and takes his leave. Alone, I make one final climb up to Juliet's chamber. While the last of the feast guests stumble full-gutted from the house, I pray we'll not to Mantua after all.

Eighteen

I'm up before sun or morning lark, walking toward where dawn's first light pinks the eastern sky. I've not ever been a patient woman. I'll not keep myself from Juliet.

Last night it seemed wily to send Paris to her. To believe that when she sees the noble affection in him, it will win such corresponding love from her as it does from me. But in the restless hours since, I've worried her eyes remain too blinded by Romeo's deceit. That I alone can wipe them clear. As I did whenever some childhood malady —

"What noise?" A man steps from a darkened doorway, his blade drawn. "Who's there?"

"A mourning woman." I quaver my voice to match my morello cloak. "Making my way to Santa Caterina, to pray for one who's lost."

"Move past, or you'll be the one that'll

need praying for." With his free hand, he raises a flannel to his face. "This house is sealed up with the plague."

Plague.

The word hits like a slap. What worse omen could this eerie hour hold than the news that the pestilence's come again to ravage Verona?

The old imagined swelling throbs beneath my arms, the awful tidings driving me faster up the road to the nunnery. As though I might outrace Mercutio's last curse.

I've not got Paris's regal right to order a gate open, nor the strength to scale a convent wall. But the entry to Santa Caterina is already swinging wide, which sends me even quicker across the grounds.

I stumble in the dark beneath a yew tree. Trip across some unseen thing, heart thundering as I fall sprawled beside a lifeless body.

The seeming corpse shivers out a snore. It's pimply-necked Balthasar, moaning with some troubled dream. A new knife-slice of terror shudders up my spine. If Romeo's got to her before Paris —

I pull myself to my knees, find my uneasy way onto my feet. Head bent, I search out the winding path and hurry on.

Just as I near the entry to the catacomb,

something wraps icy around my wrist. A too-familiar voice says, "Angelica, we must make haste from here."

The only haste I mean to make is to Juliet. But Friar Lorenzo has such a hold on me that though I twist and shove, I cannot push past.

"Has Romeo already come?"

"Yes, come unbidden," Friar Lorenzo says. "The messenger who should have born my missive to Mantua was quarantined within a pestilence-ridden house."

"The plague is truly here again?" Why do I ask, as though I do not within my bones already know? Know once it's come, all that it might take.

He nods, murmuring some self-preserving Latin. "Romeo, ignorant of my scheme, believed Juliet was truly dead. And now he's gone."

Romeo, gone off again. This gives me hope enough to ask, "And Count Paris?"

"Both he and Romeo departed in a single unkind hour."

Unkind, and worse, of Paris to leave Juliet. I'd not've believed it of him. Mayhap he was afrighted by the sight of her newly woke from what he thought was death. Or worse — perchance Juliet, without me here to advise her, refused Paris with the tiding that Romeo's already wedded and bedded her.

"Where is she?" I ask. "Where is my Juliet?"

He nods toward the crypt.

"You left her alone within the tomb?"

"God forgive me, I left one who would not leave." He gropes with his free hand for his Pater Noster beads, the way Tybalt from the time he was a boy would touch unwitting fingers to where his dagger hung. "Juliet swore she'd not come away, although I begged her to."

"Well that she disobeys you, when your intent was to give my girl to live in secret exile with the false-hearted Romeo. But you're well practiced in stealing such a daughter from her parents."

He tightens his grasp on me. "I never stole, or switched, I swear it." But then his grip loosens, and he shakes his head. "And she'll not live with Romeo."

This last makes me so glad, I break free of him. I must get to my girl, must comfort and counsel her. I quicken past, worried Friar Lorenzo will follow. But some alarm sounds beyond the convent wall, and he scurries off, unmanned.

The stone steps down to the catacomb lead me into as deep a dark as swallowed

465

me during my night climbs in the Cappelletti tower. Upon the final step, I'm hit by a stench that turns my stomach. The putrefied stink of what's become of Tybalt.

Groping my way along the dismal passage, I thump my leg into a mattock. It lies beside a crowbar at the entrance to the Cappelletti crypt, along with a hundred fallen petals shaken from what was Paris's bouquet.

No. Not petals. The crimson spots are blood, slicking the marble floor.

"Juliet? My lady, my lamb?" My words sink unanswered into the dank, cold vault.

A dropped rush-and-tallow torch glows just inside the entry. I raise it up, and by its smoke and stink discover the crimson spots puddle into a carmine pool beneath Paris.

He lies motionless, his chest bearing a wound I know too well, a match to what felled my beloved Tybalt. Paris'd not had time to strike before he was struck, his sword half-drawn as the last of life slips silently from him.

God forgive me for bidding him come here. And God damn Romeo, who surely was the one who killed him.

A chill shivers over me. If Friar Lorenzo was mistaken, and Romeo is yet here after all, hidden as he waits to smite again —

Tipping the torch away from me, I call

again to Juliet. I step deeper into the tomb, and the light catches a face grimaced in bitter death. It's Romeo, his pale hand clutching an emptied apothecary's vial.

Self-poisoned, I suppose. But what comfort is dead Romeo without my living Juliet?

By the friar's mark, Paris and Romeo were both departed in the same unkind hour. But not Juliet.

"Dearest lamb. My darling girl." Why does she not answer me? How could she have voice to refuse Friar Lorenzo but not to call to her beloved nurse? "Juliet. Susanna. Juliet."

Something rasps back at me. Low and wretched, all the world's agony shuddering in it. As I turn, my torchlight glisters along the bands of gold ribboned through Juliet's green gown. And the shining silver hilt of a dagger, jutting from her chest.

The sight pierces my own heart. I drop the torch, grasp the hilt in both hands, and tug. A gurgling suck shudders up the knife as it rips free from her.

Letting the dagger fall, I cradle her to me. "My loveliest one, I bid you. I beg you. Do not leave me." Blood oozes through the thick samite, and the thin linen shirt beneath it.

I am too late.

If only I could carry her from here. Could will life back into these chilling limbs. Could breathe my breath into her, though it cost me my last gasp. I'd die willingly that she might live. But all my love cannot stanch what's already lost.

I bend my head to her breast and, baptized in the final warmth that seeps from her, beg forgiveness for not saving her.

What mother would not cling to her own child, would not hold, and hold, and hold one final time? But horse hooves thunder in the distance, along with the shouts of the night-watch coming toward the catacomb. I'll not stay here while strange men blaze torches to gape and gossip over my innocent girl, nor listen to them weave around my blameless babe some sordid tale.

I kiss Juliet. I mean to hold all my life's love within this single kiss, to bid with it one last good-bye not just to my girl, but to Pietro, and our boys, and even Tybalt. But already death has sucked the honey of her breath, leaving only the bitter truth of mortality.

With that terrible taste upon me, I turn back through the dank air of the catacomb and climb the worn stone stair. At the top, I waver. I might steal unseen into the church and offer up Ave Marias for Juliet's departing soul. But what good could my prayers do her? What good have they ever done her, or me, or any that I loved?

A brace of watchmen hastens from beneath the yew tree, bearing Friar Lorenzo and Balthasar between them. I duck around the far side of the church, shivering even as midsummer's light begins to blaze the darkness into day. It's not yet Lammastide, yet an eternity since I walked these spreading grounds between Juliet and Tybalt, all the possibility of spring binding the three of us in promised joy. What God could take them both so quick, so young?

The God who's taken all I ever loved from me. The God whose saints have always failed me.

Beshrew my soul, but this is what I think as I round the convent path and come upon the statue of Santa Caterina. I ought to bend knee, beg forgiveness, and seek comfort from her. But for all the holy icon's brilliant golds and greens, the robust pinks and red catching the rising sun, can I not see it's just dull stone that lies beneath the paint? Only hard rock, quarried and carved into the image of a woman who did naught but suffer and die, because she thought Christ wished it of her. What Christ is that?

What saint for me to bow and beg to? What model for a living, loving woman, who's never wished to be a martyr — and who never dreamt death could steal so much, and leave her alone alive to bear it?

The last time I stood before this statue, bees writhed thick upon Caterina's breast. Now every bee is gone, the relentless buzzing silenced.

I wish they were still here, clustering on me instead of her, sinking their thousand-fold stings into my breast. I crave the burn and swell and itch of those stings, a torment to match my shattered heart. But even the sweet agony of such pain is denied me.

A swarm is harmless. Pietro said as much, and so did Tybalt. What I witnessed was just bees gathering themselves to build a new hive. But what is left for me to gather, what can I build, without Juliet?

Water pools at the foot of the statue. The lingering last of the summer storm, half a dozen bees floating dead along the surface. Another awful omen. Or so I think, until I notice a single still-living bee crawling beside the water, seeking some purchase so it can drink without succumbing as the others did. Lowering my hand into the puddle, I spread my fingers, knuckles crooked to rise above the water. The bee climbs onto the thick joint of my littlest finger, holding safe on me while she bows her head and drinks her fill.

She lifts effortlessly into the air once she's done. I try to track her flight, but in the glint of sun she disappears.

Other bees must share her thirst. This is all I let my troubled mind think of, as I rise and snake my way to the convent well. Drawing up the bucket, I dip my cupped hands in. Carefully cradling the water, I cross back and forth to the pebble-filled dishes set by each hive. But I do bear a brain, and as I work it seeps into thoughts of when Tybalt, yet a boy, took over the tending of the bees. How I'd scolded him, not understanding what comfort he found in doing as Pietro'd done. Not realizing that this was how he grieved: by breathing in the raw sweetness of honey and humming along with the unwavering buzz of bees.

Not just honey — the air around the hives smells yeasty with brood, each egg tucked within the comb bearing the promise of a future bee. It sharps through me: that promise, that hope, rubbing against the cutting pain of all I've lost.

On the far side of the grounds, the convent bell is already tolling death knells for Paris. For Romeo. And for Juliet. The solemn

471

peals mark another day in which prince and lords will make their way into a church, kneeling as high priests intone the Reqiuem Mass while unseen nuns chant within their hidden choir. But I'll not go to hear the half-familiar Latin sung. Not smell the incense spicing the sweet beeswax of the candles Tybalt brought here. Not gaze upon my beloved Virgin clinging to her sacred babe. I'll not fool myself into finding comfort in such things. Not fool myself, as I've ever done.

Was I not fool enough to let Juliet deceive me? A fool to believe she'd not been capable of such a thing, even as I helped her deceive the Cappelletti. A fool to think I knew her heart, that it was ever one with mine. A fool to trust that I would always have her.

But worst — to have been fool enough to lose her. To lose her to such a violent death.

This is what, fool that I am, I've tried hardest not to know: what awful hand drove the dagger into her?

A fatal vision dances before my too-imagining eyes: Paris, discovering Juliet in Romeo's embrace and stabbing a jealous blade into her, before Romeo slashes avenging sword at him.

But surely it cannot have been so. Even horn-mad, Paris'd thrust only at Romeo.

He'd never have harmed Juliet.

That villainous Romeo might have snuck back to take some final perverse vengence on the Cappelletti, slaughtering noble Paris and stabbing my trusting Juliet — this I can believe. But why would he not skulk off again? If all Romeo wanted was to kill, and kill, and kill again, why would he stay and take some deathly draught?

Who else could have, would have, slaughtered my dear lamb?

Friar Lorenzo — once he learned his morbid plan was thwarted, he must have rushed to the catacomb. Rushed yet arrived too late, and discovered Paris already killed by inconstant Romeo, who then, with some twisted desire, drank poison in a final violation of the Cappelletti tomb. When Juliet awoke, Friar Lorenzo, afraid the night-watch would discover them, must have pleaded for her to leave with him for some other secret place. Frightened, my girl would have refused to go.

The friar must have wanted mightily to hide his part in all these dreadful dealings. Was he so desperate he plunged a dagger to silence Juliet?

The man who absolved me of my every sin. Who the Holy Church has given the power to bless and shrive and shepherd human souls. Who's hidden his own crimes from the world: the illicit marriage, the feigned suicide, the web of lies he wove that's left fresh corpses littering the Cappelletti crypt. I know them all, as he well knows. And this is how at last I know who slew Juliet.

Friar Lorenzo, having killed Juliet, could not have suffered me to live. He'd've had to lay me dead as well, to bury all I know.

Scheming and fawning and deceiving he might be. But he's no killer.

A fool I've been. A fool I am. But not fool enough not to realize that her own hands must have driven the knife that pierced her heart, stealing the life I gave her.

My precious lamb, how could you?

The answer shivers over me. Do I not know what it is to love so fiercely, to feel loss so keenly, that death seems a welcome respite? Could I not choose this very moment the metal-sharp edge of a well-honed blade, the bitterest of poison draughts, a headlong plunge into the deep, wet well? Does each not promise a final relief from love's greatest grief?

The sin of suicide. How strongly it seduces. Wherever Juliet's soul has gone, mine could follow after. What hell could there be in an eternity with her? Whatever we'd suffer, we would be together.

But I cannot forget the others. Pietro. Nunzio. Nesto. Donato. Enzo. Berto. Angelo. My first love, and our six cherished sons. They are waiting, too — in a place Juliet now will never reach.

I'd have given my life to save her. But I'll not take my life and lose them as well.

NINETEEN

I pull the edge of my widow's veil down over
my neck and tuck the corners inside my
dress. Then I pass my hands close to the
torch so they'll bear the scent of smoke.
Unsheathing my newly purchased knife, I
cut the first warm slice. It's the day before
Lammas Eve. Time to begin my harvest.

I'd not paid much heed when Pietro
taught Tybalt about the working of a hive.
Or, in the years afterward, when Tybalt
repeated what he'd learned, eager to offer
me something of my lost Pietro. But now I
gather every memory, skimming all I can.

It's the warmth that most surprises me.
The heat from countless thousand bees
clings to the sticky weight of what I take
from them, as though something lives and
breathes and beats within the golden liquid
covering the comb. My thick hands have
never been more grateful, more careful, than
cradling their warm honey-coated wax into

476

the rounded pot.

I'd not anticipated how fast the pot would fill, or how heavy the full pot would be. How I'd struggle to lift it, and how careful I must be to bear it off upright. Each step chinks the sack of hidden coins against me. Though I'll bruise purple from it before the harvesting is done, there's solace in feeling the weight of my long-saved soldi and denari, an assurance there'll be more to come. Pestilence snakes once more across Verona. No one can say for how long it will ravage, who'll be lost before it's done. In such times, the righteous will call for candles, and the wicked for bodily delights. Wax for one, honey for the other, and either way a well-earned sliver to keep me.

The harvesting takes longer than I expected. A half-day, and I'm still at the first hive, deciding how much comb to take, how much to leave. I must calculate what each family of bees will need to survive the winter, and what they can spare for me. To survive, to spare, to be spared. I'd not have thought such choices would be mine. But I labor with the same droning purpose as the bees. Relying on them as they rely on me.

While I work I imagine the weeks that'll follow. I'll skim and strain my many pots as what I've gathered slowly separates. I do not yet know who or where the chandler is that I might bargain with, how my long-past years of marketplace haggling will serve me now that I'm to sell instead of buy. Tybalt spent whole seasons clinging close to Pietro, without either of them suspecting how soon he'd be left to carry on alone. None of us ever dreamt such tasks would one day fall to me.

I suppose the hives will need me less as the days cool to autumn, frost to winter. I'll have time then to take my coins to the Piazza delle Erbe, or maybe all the way to Villafranca. I'll trade for spices and teach myself to make comfits such as Pietro sold. For this, more than linen shirts or even our cockly-eyed Madonna, is what he's left me.

I'll never again be what I've been. Not wife, or nurse, or mother. But I'll not be servant to such as the Cappelletti, nor shuttered away in a convent, either. I've my little buzzing livelihood, enough to keep me in my two rented rooms not far from the Via Zancani — and yet much further than I ever thought I'd come.

Thinking of comfits growls hunger into my stomach. I slip a slice of comb into my mouth and suck the honey off. Savoring the taste, I reach greedily for more comb. I sense too late that a bee is crawling there. In a startled flash, she sinks her only weapon in. The burn, the sting, the too-familiar pain shoots through my clumsy finger. For weeks it will ache me. But it's worse for her, for in that angry instant she is dead.

Did I ever fear bees? Was I afraid of how a sting might hurt me?

I cradle the poor bee in my palm and weep for costing with my carelessness her life. A foolish sentiment, but I'll not forgo it. What would Pietro think of me shedding tears over a bee? I imagine he might whistle, just to nettle me. But then he'd pinch the stinger out. Kiss the pain away. Rub honey where I hurt. Tell me how he adores me, how glad he is to see how I've grown to love his bees. He'd remind me of what I already know: loving what's in this life is our only remedy for death.

But I also know the more you love, the more you have to lose.

I weep for him. For her. For me. But then I press close my veil to dry my tears. I wave my swelling finger near to the smoky flame and heave myself back to my task. Whole hives still need my tending.

The days are short, the winter long. And on many of these darkened days, I hate her.

How could I not? She took everything. Everything I gave. Everything I had. Or thought I had.

Not just took. Killed. The bloodied violence of it, that is what maddens me. How she drove the dagger in. How she'd not cared who she hurt with that single stab.

Not cared for anything but Romeo. Not cared for me.

Who could love her more than I did? Who could lose more than in all my life I have?

The hate comes on quick, like the heat that's flashed over me the year past. My face goes red, my body sweats with it. But then just as quick it's gone, leaving me grief and guilt instead.

I raised six sons and then reared Tybalt. Watch boys turn to men, and you'll learn how they're drawn to danger. But I'd not known how fragile a girl can grow in the season she starts to ripen into a woman.

This is what shatters my heart, over and over again. That I'd not known, not seen, not ever sensed how fragile she was. How she could be so unlike me.

My father's beatings. The first great plague. Pietro's sudden slaying. Bit by terrible bit, every awful thing that ever happened to me taught me to survive. Not like my girl, who never suffered aught. Never suffered because I was ever near to tend and cosset her. Never suffered and so could not bear the slightest sorrow, the hint of unfilled longing, the least glimmering of loss. And so was lost herself.

Should I have let her suffer? Would it have taught her to survive?

Or was it better to keep her short life always sweet? Sweet as a taste of honey on the tongue.

You cannot live long on only honey. You cannot survive without tasting much that's bitter. Wormwood coats life's dug, and that's where we must suckle.

Slowly the days stretch and warm. Winter melts toward spring, and I wake half-thinking it's already Pentecost, though we're still in Lent. As the sun glows outside my waxed-cloth window, I rise from bed and ready myself to visit the hives.

The bees have roused themselves as well. They're already soaring out, seeking the first of the year's blooms. Pietro once said a hive was like a parish church, but to me each hive seems more like its own teeming city. The bees who guard the entryway, the others who fly far off to gather. Those that stay inside, turning collected pollen into precious nectar, and the ones deepest within who tend their brood. By some miracle each knows what it must do to keep the whole thrumming hive alive. This is the beauty Pietro found in tending bees. This is what finally comforts me.

I feel my husband's presence most here, near one of his hives. Tybalt's presence, too. My boys I feel more whenever I carry my tithe of beeswax candles through the streets where they once played, to San Fermo where they prayed. But my last — my Susanna, my lamb, my Juliet. I feel her against me, always. Carried like fragrance on a rose, like mother's milk on a baby's breath, like pollen goldened on a soaring bee.

AUTHOR'S NOTE

Juliet's Nurse isn't a book I expected to write — it feels more like the book chose me. My focus has always been on intersections of American history and literature. But after I finished *The Secrets of Mary Bowser,* a novel based on the true story of a slave who became a Union spy in the Confederate White House, the title *Juliet's Nurse* suddenly came to me. I pulled my copy of Shakespeare's play (which I'd last read in high school) off the shelf, and reread it in a single sitting.

I was amazed and intrigued. Although the events in the play take place across just five days, it hints at loyalties, rivalries, jealousies, and losses that extend far back in time. Shakespeare places the young lovers squarely at the heart of his play: Romeo has by far the greatest number of lines, followed by Juliet. But the character who speaks the next largest number of lines is not the head of either the Capulet or Montague households, nor the prince who rules Verona, nor the friar who first marries the lovers and later orchestrates Juliet's feigned death. The person to whom Shakespeare gives more lines than all of these characters is Juliet's wet-nurse — a woman whose very presence within the Capulet household seems curious, given that when the play begins Juliet has already been weaned for eleven years. What did Shakespeare see in her? What can we see only through her eyes?

Bawdy and clearly of a lower class, the nurse as Shakespeare presents her seems out of place among the cultured, wealthy Capulets. Her name, Angelica, is mentioned only once in the entire play. But in the very first scene in which she appears, the nurse reveals that she lost her virginity at age twelve, that she is the widow of "a merry man," and that her own daughter was born on the exact same day as Juliet but did not live. Writing *Juliet's Nurse* gave me a chance to explore this tantalizing, troubling backstory — while also offering a new, historically rich view onto the action at the heart of Shakespeare's tragedy.

Romeo and Juliet is the best-known play in English literature and the world's most cherished love story. Taking on such a popular literary work — a perennial high school reading assignment, a staple of theater companies around the world, and the source for powerful reimaginings from *West Side Story* to Franco Zeffirelli's classic film to the electrifying *Romeo+Juliet* starring Leonardo DiCaprio and Claire Danes — is no small task. When I traveled to Verona to conduct my research, I was astonished to learn that more than half a million people come to the city each year to visit sites associated with *Romeo and Juliet.* This deep attachment to Shakespeare's play convinced me there was an audience hungry for the story revealed in *Juliet's Nurse.*

Focusing on the nurse forces us to ask one of the most terrifying questions any person can face: What would it be like to lose a child? Delving into the history of wet-nurses, I learned that the arrangement described in the play was quite common: wealthy families in this era preferred to employ a wet-nurse whose own infant had recently died, and who thus had "fresh" milk to devote to their child. Imagine the intensity of losing your newborn, and then, that same day, being given the chance to nurture another baby — yet always knowing your relationship with her is tenuous, subject to the whims of her parents.

Now imagine experiencing those things in a world so different from our own. Violence was a regular feature of city life in fourteenth-century Italy. Divided allegiances to the ruling prince, to the Pope, and to increasing their own power and property drew wealthy families into bitter, bloody rivalries. Though most households in Verona had fewer means than the Cappelletti or the Montecchi, in the steady rhythms of daily urban life, everyone — from the poorest of the poor to the merchants and artisans we would think of as the middle class to the richest nobles — was driven by forces of honor, piety, and myriad local alliances and rivalries as they struggled to survive.

Understanding this time and place was crucial to exploring Angelica's story. Although Shakespeare tells us the season in which the play's tragic events take place — late July, just before the August 1 harvest holiday of Lammastide — the year is never mentioned. But important hints abound. The inclusion in the play of Prince Escalus (Shakespeare's version of the Scaligeri family name) places the events before 1405, when the Scaligeri lost power and Verona became subject to Venetian rule. And in the pivotal scene in Shakespeare's play in which

Mercutio is killed, he exclaims not once, not twice, but three times to Romeo and Tybalt, "A plague o' both your houses!" — perhaps the most dreadful curse for anyone alive at the time.

Plague first came to Italy in 1348, bringing unfathomable horror: in less than two years, between one third and one half of the entire population was dead. In some places, the death toll rose as high as 60 percent. Think of what your town would be like, what the nation would be like, with so much of the population suddenly gone.

Imagine the terror Mercutio's dying words would have struck in the Veronese, who knew firsthand what plague meant, for those whose bodies rotted away, and for their bereft survivors. In Shakespeare's play, Juliet has no sisters or brothers, and Lord Capulet tells Paris, "The earth hath swallow'd all my hopes but she." Even the most wealthy and powerful families were vulnerable to the loss of their children, a tragic and haunting experience that in *Juliet's Nurse* affects both the hired wet-nurse and the affluent family she serves.

What was it like to live in the wake of such devastation? How, without our modern understanding of the effects of emotional trauma, did individuals make sense of their experience and move forward with their lives, despite all they'd lost? These are some of the questions *Juliet's Nurse* answers.

Ultimately, Angelica's experience parallels one of history's great paradoxes: the horrors of the plague contributed to Europe advancing from the medieval era into the Renaissance. The death of large segments of the population created new opportunities for survivors. Peasants moved from the countryside to cities. Young men enjoyed professional prospects beyond their family's original standing. The loss of so many spouses and betrotheds caused shifts in how marriages were contracted. New markets for luxury and everyday goods emerged, as international trade flourished — bringing with it advances in transportation and the intermingling of European, African, Asian, and eventually New World cultures. As Friar Laurence reminds us in his first speech in Shakespeare's play, what's tomb is womb. The Renaissance was the rebirth following the plague's enormous death toll.

But the story also resonates in our own era. *Romeo and Juliet* ends with the suicides of the teenage lovers, following the violent deaths of other young men. Weaving Angelica's story around these incidents from the play pushed me to think deeply about violence, despondence, and suicide. What would enable Angelica to withstand the anger and grief that destroy so many of the other characters? What larger lessons can we learn from her?

This became the overarching theme of the book. *Juliet's Nurse* probes the relationship between loss and endurance, because in life, as in the novel, suffering exists not in opposition to, but as an inevitable experience of, survival.

LEARN MORE

Visit www.loisleveen.com to learn more about the medieval and Renaissance history of Verona, Italy, and to find reading group questions and resources for teaching *Juliet's Nurse* along with *Romeo and Juliet.*

ACKNOWLEDGMENTS

Novel writing can sometimes be as sweet as honey, and other times as bitter as wormwood, and I offer great thanks to many sweet people who've kept me from turning bitter.

Rosemary Weatherston is such a keen reader and dear friend, she keeps making both my life and my books better. David Garrett proved ever collegial in helping me access myriad scholarly sources. Carol Frischmann, Naseem Rakha, Kathlene Postma, and Shelley Washburn read the draftiest of first chapters and convinced me that I really had a book. The Newberry Library supported my research with an Arthur and Lila Weinberg Fellowship, and Judy Wittner opened her home to me during my time in Chicago. Dr. Michael Slater and Dr. Shoshana Waskow provided medical counsel on a variety of fictive injuries and diseases. Obscure materials on medieval beekeeping and church practices were located by Janie Rangel and translated by Armanda Balduzzi and Hanna Hofer. The far-flung participants in the Medieval-Religion, Mediev-L, and MedFem LIST-SERVs gave me insight into the period that shaped my characters. I've consulted more scholarly books and articles than I can list here, but suffice it to say that without the work of many academics, I couldn't have created this novel.

Here in Oregon, the wonderful members of Portland Urban Beekeepers not only provided a hands-on understanding of beekeeping, they taught me the power of a welcoming hive. Multnomah County Library is truly a treasure, and I am always grateful for its resources and its dedicated staff, and indebted to the voters and government officials here (and everywhere) who understand that library funding is critical to the well-being of the entire community. I continue to be sustained by readers and by the bookstore and library staffs around the country and abroad who eagerly embraced my first novel, *The Secrets of Mary Bowser,* and whose enthusiastic nagging about when I'd have another kept me from procrastinating as I wrote *Juliet's Nurse.*

William Shakespeare endowed Angelica

with just enough intriguing backstory, while also providing an inspiring model of literary appropriation. Laney Katz Becker proved once again that a sage agent benefits an author at every step of the process, and words can't say how much I appreciate all she and her colleagues at Lippincott Massie McQuilkin do to help me write the best novels I can and to connect readers around the world with them. In our very first conversation, Emily Bestler won my heart when she told me that because her name is on every book, she cares about each one as much as the author does, and she's proven it true time and again. She and Megan Reid are not only savvy readers (and re-readers), they are also so warm, supportive, and funny that it is always a pleasure to work with them, even when they make me toil much harder than I ever thought I could. Any author might feel lucky to have one such editorial team, but I am extraordinarily blessed to benefit as well from the astute input of Anne Collins. Readers often do not realize how much goes into the making of a novel, but I owe a great debt to Jeanne Lee, Hillary Tisman, Mellony Torres, Alysha Bullock, Adria Iwustiak, Amanda Betts, and many, many other people at Emily Bestler Books/Atria Books and Knopf/Random

House Canada for this beautiful book you (or your e-reader) now hold.

As ever, my deepest gratitude goes to Chuck Barnes, who has read countless drafts, engaged in spontaneous plotting sessions, put up with a too-often very moody writer, and courageously suffered through a research trip to beautiful Verona, Italy. Here's to a love story that is always a comedy, and never a tragedy.

ABOUT THE AUTHOR

Award-winning author **Lois Leveen** dwells in the spaces where literature and history meet. Her work has appeared in numerous literary and scholarly journals, as well as *The New York Times,* the *Los Angeles Review of Books,* the *Chicago Tribune, The Huffington Post, Bitch* magazine, *The Wall Street Journal,* and *The Atlantic,* and on NPR. Lois gives talks about writing and history at universities, museums, and libraries around the country. She lives in Portland, Oregon, with two cats, one Canadian, and 60,000 honeybees. Visit her online at LoisLeveen .com and Facebook.com/LoisLeveen.

The employees of Thorndike Press hope you have enjoyed this Large Print book. All our Thorndike, Wheeler, and Kennebec Large Print titles are designed for easy reading, and all our books are made to last. Other Thorndike Press Large Print books are available at your library, through selected bookstores, or directly from us.

For information about titles, please call:
    (800) 223-1244

or visit our Web site at:
    http://gale.cengage.com/thorndike

To share your comments, please write:
    Publisher
    Thorndike Press
    10 Water St., Suite 310
    Waterville, ME 04901